THE
HOOPOE

THE
HOOPOE

Christine Weston

HARPER & ROW, PUBLISHERS
New York, Evanston, and London

c 1

The lyrics on page 107, and following, are from the song "K-K-K-Katy" by Geoffrey O'Hara. Copyright 1918 by Leo Feist, Inc. Copyright renewal 1946 Leo Feist, Inc., New York, N. Y. Used by permission.

FIRST EDITION

LIBRARY OF CONGRESS CATALOG CARD NUMBER: 72-96006

for R. G.

Part One

1

"What is the very first thing you can remember?" the brother asked the sister. He had this way of asking things suddenly, trying to catch her out, so she had acquired a wariness of him, studying him from under her brown lashes, bemused and apprehensive. He was older than she by a couple of years, but thin and highly strung, with his stammer and his asthma. She greatly respected him for the tricks he played on her, her pity and protectiveness masked by an outward acceptance of his superiority.

Yet she felt she had to keep her end up. "The very first thing I remember is Mother's dress when I was three years old. A white dress with frills and a blue sash and little bunches of yellow roses."

"When you were three years old! Nobody remembers anything when they were three years old!"

The sister insisted. "I remember Mother's dress. I used to sit on her lap and look at the yellow roses. It was my favorite of Mother's dresses."

"What a liar you are," the brother declared. "You always tell lies. One of these days you are going to get caught and then you'll be sorry."

But the mother, overhearing, bore her out. "Fancy, darling, your

1

remembering that dress! You couldn't have been more than three because that was the year I had the material sent out from Harrods and dear old Mohommed Ali made it for me from a picture I showed him from *The Tatler.*"

The mother was slender, with soft brown hair and gray eyes. She smelled like a flower and had that same softness. The brother and sister adored the mother with a kind of pain, inarticulately. No one has ever explained that pitiful love which could, much later, so strangely become indifference, impatience, dislike even. But not until much later. Much, much later. At this time it was love, passionate, constant, like a bruise inside their bodies.

Did Mohommed Ali remember that dress of the mother's? He was an old man and had made hundreds of dresses on the decrepit Singer sewing machine. Dresses for the mother, dresses for Aunt Eve, dresses for the sister. Shirts for the brother, Kashmiri puttu coats for the father, very dashing coats with nipped-in waist and real leather buttons the size of chestnuts. Brother and sister could not remember a time when Mohommed Ali had not been with them. Wherever they moved, from district to district and house to house, Mohommed Ali had his appointed place of work in the inviolate shade of a back veranda far removed from wind, dust, and noise. There he squatted with his long thin legs in white pantaloons folded under him, on a sheet spread over a piece of matting, his big wooden workbox at his side and the sewing machine like a sort of idol before him. He could sit like this for hours without tiring, his thin, narrow face dark under its snowy muslin turban. He was as thin as a length of dry bamboo, and with exquisite hands and pink almond-shaped nails. He was very clean and smelled faintly of dry cracking white cotton. Mohommed Ali loved to handle the materials which arrived from England: bolts of cambric, muslin, fine flannel, and linen. He understood at once what he was expected to do when a picture cut from one of the English papers—*The Tatler, The Sphere, Queen*—was put before him. He could copy the pattern of the picture to its last detail, brooding over it for hours through steel-rimmed spectacles with concentrated, red-veined eyes.

Of all the servants in the house Mohommed Ali stood highest in the esteem of the father and the mother and Aunt Eve, and even the father's awful temper seemed never to reach out to him.

2

Had there been little windows in the mother's stomach and in Mrs. Sparks' through which the brother—and Mrs. Sparks' baby—could look out and see things? But then what about clothes? Unless the windows had curtains to match the clothes so they wouldn't show. In that case Mohommed Ali would have been the one to have made the curtains. The sister stared at Mohommed Ali, but his thin dark face remained unresponsive and she feared that the brother would have laughed if she had ventured the question. Very strange, this whole business, and to be handled gingerly. Until she was the brother's age, and that seemed a long way off. Two years! Anything could happen in two years. She might die before ever finding out. And that was another thing, another mystery. She had brought herself, one day, to put the question to the aunt when they were together, just the two of them, in the garden, on the big circular chabutra of masonry raised high above the lawn and kept swept bare and clean so that one would instantly notice a snake, or a spider or scorpion, as one might not be apt to on the grass.

On that late afternoon the sister had discovered a small dead bat lying near one of the cane chairs and had become immediately absorbed in it. It was a tiny bat, its still open eyes the size of pinheads, but no longer bright, and a regiment of ants had marshaled to drag it away. The sister dispersed the ants with a twig and asked the aunt: "Auntie Eve, what does dying mean?"

The aunt drove her embroidery needle in and out of the cobwebby creation she was forever weaving on its circular frame. Her beautiful parchment-colored face did not alter its habitual expression of resigned serenity. She was tall, with black hair coiled like a python on top of her head, broad bands of eyebrows and eyes like boiled prunes. There was a suggestion of dark down on her upper lip, and once, seeing her undress, the sister and brother had noticed what looked like birds' nests under her arms.

"Dying," the aunt now gave out, consideringly, "is simply not being alive any more. It is being with Jesus in heaven."

A paralyzing thought. "I don't want to die and be in heaven with Jesus," the sister complained. "I don't know him."

"You will understand better when you're older," the aunt affirmed in her omniscient tone. "And you must never be afraid of dying and being with dear Jesus."

7

"I'm not afraid." A trembling untruth. "But what language does Jesus speak? English?"

The aunt held the embroidery frame at arm's length and gazed at it critically. She smelled lightly of perspiration and pink face powder and she had a strong presence, with high cheekbones and a finely arched nose which stood out like a face in a photograph. She in no way resembled the father, whose sister she was. "Dear Jesus," she said at last, "speaks everybody's language. He understands everything."

The sister was silent, studying the dead bat. The ants had redeployed and were advancing on the body, antennae waving. The sister thought: They'll take it away and eat it and there won't be a thing left, not even the little eyes.

"You remember your catechism, child," the aunt said presently. "You remember what I have taught you about dear Jesus and the Holy Family."

The sister replied impersonally: "I know that Jesus was squeezed by the Holy Ghost and borned of the Virgin Mary."

"Conceived, dear, not squeezed." The aunt's black gaze rested briefly on the sister's downcast face. The child would never be pretty, though it would have been difficult to say just why not. But now, at seven years, her skin was glorious, like the sunny inside of a poppy, and her gray eyes wide apart, taking blue tones wherever she found them, her straight hair tingled with life. The aunt felt a kind of pang. What an age, seven! She could barely remember when she was seven but it had a murky sense of grayness, of black cotton stockings, cold baths, prayers, a smell of feet. That had been in Normandy, with an aristocratic background and no funds.

"Auntie Eve, are there really ghosts?"

The aunt thought in mild desperation: I'm glad I don't have children. She frequently voiced such gratitude, but without dwelling on it. She was virgin, and her fiancé, a pocket-sized Englishman, an officer in a distinguished Indian cavalry regiment, had been killed before her eyes during a polo match at Jullundur years before. The aunt would always remember him in his white silk shirt and white riding breeches and shining boots, his wrists like his pony's legs, taped to strengthen them during the game, and the mallet dangling from one wrist by a leather thong. A speeding ball had struck him in

8

the temple and he had fallen from the saddle and been dragged by one foot in a stirrup before anyone could help him, and by that time he was dead. That dear little man with his pale eyes and pale moustache and his jokes and his sweetness to her! The aunt thought now, uneasily: The child is going to ask me if Derek is in heaven with Jesus, and he wasn't even a Catholic and there had been that terrible complication with Maman and the holy fathers who wouldn't hear of marriage unless Derek accepted conversion, which he might have done had he lived. And Doey quite reasonable about the whole thing, and then the whole matter decided by the cracking sound of a polo ball and the sight of a slight figure reeling in its saddle while the other riders galloped and a great sigh rushed upward from the spectators, and beyond the crashing tempo of hope and desire in her own ears, the sound of Doey's vioice shouting orders. But Derek was dead. And now this child with her abominable questions.

Implacable. "Was the Virgin Mary married when the Holy Ghost squeezed Jesus?"

The aunt drove her needle through the hyaline pattern and turned the frame upside down on her lap and snipped a thread. It was a teacloth, one of hundreds she had made in her life. Some, the handsomest, lay devotedly folded between sheets of tissue paper in the drawers of her almirah in the house, and she rarely looked at them, afraid that she might resurrect an ancient passion from the cobwebby folds. These were to have been part of her trousseau, and they were to this day intrinsic with her unappeasement, with the itch between her legs every month, for no man had ever again asked her to marry him, and in her dreams she encountered instead the crone she would one day be.

The ants were marching now, a narrow cortege with the bat's body at the center, headed for the masonry edge of the chabutra. Somehow or other they would have to get their burden over the edge and down the sheer face of the masonry wall to the ground. What would they do? Push the corpse over the edge and then descend themselves to retrieve it? An interesting problem. The sister wondered about it. Squatting on her heels she squirmed her way in the wake of the funeral procession, thinking of several things at once. "Auntie, have you ever seen a ghost?"

The aunt laid down her embroidery frame and searched in her

little red-quilted workbox for a reel of thread. It was a magical workbox, like the inside of a cut pomegranate, each item snug in its particular sac of shining silk. The gold scissors were shaped like a bird; the pincushion was a velvety strawberry. The workbox had belonged to a grandmother and in an unwary moment the aunt had promised that at her own death it would pass to this niece. The niece was thinking of that too while she followed the bat's cortege toward the chabutra's edge. The ants had encountered an obstacle, a minute bit of loose cement, and had paused for mutual counsel, the august dead in their midst. Helpfully, the sister removed the roadblock and the procession reformed, and the aunt said: "There are no such things as ghosts and you shouldn't ask silly questions."

"Then what about the Holy One?"

And what about Derek? The aunt had seen Derek off and on since that afternoon on the polo ground at Jullundur. He had been in her bed as he had never been there in life. She had felt his slender weight pressing upon her, and the unexpected vigor of his thighs embracing hers. They had murmured together under the shrouding pallor of mosquito curtains, and had exchanged vows forbidden by Maman and Père Pierre. In the morning the aunt had awakened appeased, her smile effortless, her day tranquil from deepest sleep. But she was forty now, and Derek had been dead twenty years, and it was the crone whom she surprised more and more often in her dusty dream.

The sister, knowing very well that whatever answer she got to her last question would be no better than none, shifted on her buttocks and said conversationally: "Auntie, did you really mean it when you said that I could have your workbox when you were dead?"

The aunt smiled. It was lovely when she smiled, as Derek had often remarked. "Darling," the aunt said, "yes, but it's not very kind of you to keep talking about it, you know."

The sister said hastily: "I won't do it again. I just wondered if you remembered, that's all. Doey says there is always such a scramble for the boodle when someone pops off."

The aunt gasped. But it sounded like Doey, and these children missed nothing.

The sister turned once more to the bat's cortege, which had now reached the chabutra's edge and there paused. Confusion set in among the ranks, ants bumping into one another, feelers waving

10

impotently, conflicting commands inaudibly flung, a few officiously tugging at the body with no pertinent end in view. It was a three-foot descent to the ground. The sister redistributed her weight on her heels, leaned her elbows on her knees, and with her gaze riveted on the ants and their dilemma she fell silently to reviewing all the things she had heard and deduced about Aunt Eve. It was a pity that the young man, her fancy, had been killed playing polo, and that the aunt would never marry anyone else because she had loved him so much. That meant of course that the aunt could never have a baby. It was automatic and incontrovertible that for there to be a baby there had to be a father. The aunt had lived with the mother and father, the brother and herself, ever since memory. There had always been the embroidery frame, and furlongs of crocheted lace which Mohommed Ali, in wordless admiration, stitched on to cambric petticoats and knickers, always careful to save the finest lace for party dresses, together with bands of intricate "insertion" threaded with ribbon.

There were those teacloths which, held to the light, seemed wondrously fragile; and an enormous tablecloth which the mother kept for best, for those dinner parties when the brother and sister had to go to bed earlier than usual, and the cut glass decanters were brought out from behind locked doors in the sideboard. Then the dining room smelled divinely of crystallized ginger and almond soufflé, of sherry and crepes suzette and roasted quail no bigger than walnuts, served on adorable little squares of buttered toast. There would be sweet peas in a silver vase in the center of the table and one of these days a young man exactly like Derek would suddenly appear among the guests and fall in love with Aunt Eve and they would at last live happily ever after.

"Poof!" said the father. "Eve had her chance, and it's over."

"But she's such a dear, and so gifted. . . ."

"She's too tall and too hairy," the father said. "And she's forty. Men like Derek don't grow on trees."

And during dinner, to which no one like Derek seemed ever to be attracted, the father's sudden angry voice would be raised before all the guests: "The soup tastes like dirty dishcloths again!"

And the mother's troubled laughter: "Doey, dear."

"I'm going to shoot Junabi Ali!"

And Mr. Sparks' voice, nicer than Mrs. Sparks': "Don't shoot him.

Send him to us. He's the best cook in the station."

And sometimes there would be a smell of roast peafowl, and custards delectable with burnt sugar and whipped cream, and to the sister's twitching nostrils, and the brother's, both of them at the time sharing a big bedroom directly off the dining room, would drift the exciting, inward-stirring fragrance of the father's cigarettes. When the grown-up dinner was at an end Nizamat would come quietly into their room carrying a tray with crystallized ginger, preserved figs, little glass bowls of custard and the miniature plump legs of quail which you could eat bones and all. The mother, on her way to the drawing room to play the piano while Mrs. Sparks sang, had attended to this tray. Sometimes there were shelled pistachios, sometimes crystallized violets, sometimes squares of Turkish delight, which neither sister nor brother liked and which they let Nizamat keep for himself.

Nibbling and listening behind the curtains of their room—there were no doors—they heard the aunt rustling toward the drawing room, leaving a heavy trail of scent, quite a different scent from the mother, who, bending over them to kiss them good night before the party began, had drowned them in her softness, the flower fragrance of her hair, her love raising their love to a flood.

But the queer need to cry was forgotten at first sound of Mrs. Sparks' voice shrieking foreign lyrics in the drawing room, and of the piano's desperate efforts to bring her into key. Sometimes the songs were in English, and one—"She Is Far from the Land"—always made the brother want to go to the bathroom. No matter what Mrs. Sparks sang, it brought the sister and brother to the verge of hysteria; they would lie in their beds with a corner of their pillows stuffed in their mouths, writhing in fits of mirth.

But in which house had these things happened? For there had been so many houses. The father was a government official and transfers from place to place were frequent, often unexpected, always exciting. The brother and sister had their favorite remembrances. One the sister remembered above all was the house with the chabutra in the center of a large, formless garden. There were chabutras in most of the gardens, but this in particular seemed always to be overflowing with white petunias and a sea of perfume drifting among enormous trees, and beyond the trees the low white house with its steep thatched roof and dusky verandas with white columns. At eve-

12

and brother sat motionless sniffing the fragrance of his cigarette. *"Flattery.* Williams pisses flattery and *they* drink it."

"Enfin, Doey!" The aunt gave a little screech of laughter. She knew he liked her to laugh at his dirtiness. The mother never did.

"And all that boasting about his People at Home. The Sparkses know them. Frowsy old mother who drops her *h*'s like a goat dropping you-know-what, and the father picks his nose in public. That's Williams ancestry for you. And out here he goes about posing as county!"

The aunt's laughter was like music at a fair. "He hates you, Doey," she said. "He knows that our papa was Duc de Verriers, and because you've done things even the L.G. has been afraid to do. It was you who exposed Najib's connection with the nawabs, after all. Isn't it true, Alice, dear?" The mother was thinking: Doey knows that he should be I.G. when the time comes, and he knows that his Frenchness, his temper . . . but he won't change! Even for my sake, for the children's sake, and with no income except his pay. And with Eve to support, too. He won't change. Taking his life in his hands when he knew that Najib and the nawabs were going to try and have him knifed. Taking his honor, his future, to bring Najib to book. Najib, thief, torturer of women, murderer. All very fine and large, but it won't make Doey I.G. Passionate dedication doesn't bring promotion. Williams can get it just by making up to the I.G.'s memsahib. By leaving people like Najib alone. Najib, even in jail, has friends, and they're not going to leave Doey alone. Oh, Doey, Doey, my dearest, my bravest! You are going farther and farther away from me, your spirit is racing in a direction I can never take, and when you have vanished what shall I do? What shall I do without you, my husband, my love?

"Najib's been safe all this time largely because they have built up this thing against *his* enemies. Against men like Charan, Dulip Singh, and that crowd. Not a criminal among them, but seditionists, and government wants to bag every seditionist it can lay hands on. Government can't prove a thing against Charan and the others except a few speeches here and there, and thumbing their noses at the police, and refusing to pay bribes. But Williams and the I.G. have sedition on the brain. They're wetting their beds in a blue funk. Najib has always been their informer. Najib, mind you."

15

"Doey," the mother murmured, apprehension fluttering in her voice. "Doey, not politics."

"Don't be idiotic. Of course it's politics. You know I've told them over and over that they had better face it. It's coming. Not today, not tomorrow, probably not until long after I've kicked the bucket. But it's coming. And not only for this bloody country either. You wait and see."

"Oh, Doey, no!" It was the aunt this time, fearful, thinking: That is one thing they won't stand, his siding with the seditionists even out of fairness. This thing about fairness, and so contradictory when one thinks of how he scolds the boy, thrashes him for little things, yet always taking the side against his own superiors. Doey will not acknowledge them. His contempt, his frightful pride. And always expecting everything to be so right. Loathing clumsiness, cowardice, stupidity. Doey. Yes, winning at tennis, sitting a horse no one else would dare, going out on duty with a riding crop when any other man would carry arms. What does it prove, Doey? You'll do their dangerous job for them and they'll die in their beds in comfort, while you . . . And if anything should happen, what would I do? Become a governess? Give lessons in embroidery and music? And our papa the Duc de Verriers, and none of us girls, nor your wife, Alice, brought up to do a thing? Seditionists. You must know, Doey, you *must.* The government simply won't stand it. Anything but that, anything! For you to make excuses for men like that insolent Charan who walks into the house with his shoes on, tickles the children, and stares at me as if I were one of his own native women!

The mother said suddenly: "Just smell the petunias. Doey, shall I get the mandolin? Won't you sing?"

He loved to sing. Not always quite in key perhaps, but in a soaring, joyous boy's voice, a ringing innocence which stilled the demon in him, lightening the silence and the fear and hatred he inspired.

Nizamat, at a shout, brought the mother's mandolin and crowded past the brother and sister crouched on the steps, and pretended not to see them; but the father changed his position and saw the brother's white pajamas and his voice was hard against the first sweet, entreating notes of the mandolin in the mother's hands. "What are you doing sitting there, you two? Do you know the time? Do you want a spanking, running about in the dark without shoes, with the snakes and

16

scorpions? Do you want to be bitten?"

The mother tilted the mandolin upright on her knee and set the D string in tune. "I told them they could come out for a little while, Doey. It was stuffy indoors, and just for a little while."

She had not told them anything of the sort and the father knew it and he said coldly: "You spoil them. They think they can do anything they like."

"Doey, sing *'Quand tu ris.'* You haven't for a long time. Do, darling. We all love that song."

"Give me the key, then. No, too high." He tried again, went too high, then too low. The sister felt the brother's spasm of laughter and gritted her teeth at him in the gloom.

"There, that's better."

Huddled together on the chabutra steps, reprieved for a while, the sister and brother listened to the sound of the mandolin, heartbreaking; and then the sound of the father's voice, suddenly young, escaping in a burst of tenderness; embarrassing them, making them vaguely inclined to cry, yet making them, for a moment or two, forgetful of those frowsy enemies picking their noses in distant England.

Before the song was ended, Nizamat, standing unobtrusively beside the steps, and at some invisible signal from the mother, motioned to the brother and sister and led them noiselessly past the trees and back to the house and to bed, the father's voice and the sweet loyalty of the mandolin trailed them into sleep.

The sister had a habit of awakening at night and lying in the dim room listening for some sound that would bring the morning back faster; the sound of Peggy the terrier scratching her fleas somewhere in the house, the sound of the aunt's strangled snores, the temperamental nervous whine of the greyhounds in their distant kennel, or the first wistful summons of a dove as it sensed the dawn. In his own bed across the room from hers the brother always slept silently, intensely. On the floor between them Chota Ayah lay on her pallet sheeted from head to foot like the dead.

On these occasions the sister listened to the silence and thought: Suppose they are really all dead. All of them except me. Even the chokidar, who is supposed to stay awake all night, tramping round the premises in his heavy shoes, giving his intermittent hacking cough like a crocodile in a swamp, interspersed with an infrequent shout of menace at possible trespassers: *"Hoshiar-raho!"* But always careful to time the adjuration so as not to rouse the father, who would have rushed from the house and thrown a boot at him.

But tonight—which night?—tonight silence rose and fell like a tide around the sister, and she alone in it. They were all dead, adrift on the silence. She alone was alive, and now the darkness thinned so she could make out the shape of the brother's bed and the chair where he always hung his clothes, and on the seat his catapult with its round hard clay pellets, his penknife, a tennis ball, a paintbox, and a small dead bird. The sister could see the dressing table and the watery gleam of the mirror above it, the tall almirah, and Chota Ayah's long white body on the matting, and beyond that the paddock door which gave on the back veranda, where, during the day, Mohommed Ali sat with his sewing machine. There was no sound. No one breathed. Out on the plain beyond the garden the jackals were quiet. They too were dead.

The sister pushed aside the bedclothes and stepped out on the floor, feeling the coir matting harsh under her bare feet. Not knowing why she did it, for she was frightened by the silence, the deep night, she walked across the room to the door, slid the bolt at the bottom, and stepped out on the empty veranda. Something she did unthinkingly every day now took on utter strangeness, terror, grief, joy. How extraordinary familiar objects appear at night when one is alone and every one else is dead! The air itself was changed, secretive. Before her eyes the compound lay in pewter-colored immensity, and the trees stood absolutely motionless, the ground beneath them without pattern, incomplete.

Her heart was beating under her nightdress like something trying to run away and she put her hand on it, feeling the round seed where one day a breast would grow. It was night, but not really dark, and she could see everything. Her breath caught as her eyes picked out the huddled figure of the chokidar bunched against a column on the veranda, his turban wrapped round his head and face, his brass-tipped lathee resting beside him. She tiptoed toward him and peered closer, and he too was dead, and why not, since all trespassers were dead, all evildoers, all good people, all bad. Dead, the whole lot.

She stood on the top step of the veranda and stared toward the

18

darkest part of the garden, where wild grasses and lantana made a sort of rough barrier against the plain. She felt very daring when she thought of it, for she hated the dark. And now something was moving out there. The trees were moving, but queerly, not in wind or in rain. The trees were bending backward a little and the ground under the trees shifted, and then the ground directly before her shifted too, and the house, and everything began to tilt away from her toward the plain like a plate emptying itself in the direction of the sky, which leaned down to catch the contents of the world.

Something stirred, something enormous; an elephant perhaps, pushing, shouldering, soundless. It was the moon coming up through the branches, round and white and very close. But it wasn't coming up at all, it was falling down the sky, cutting its way through the sky as it had cut its way through the ground and through the branches which had held it back. But nothing could hold it now and she had never seen it so close, and as it sank into the ground the dust healed the place where it was buried so no one would have guessed.

Quietly she went back to the bedroom and climbed into bed and lay there a long time, her brain, her body, filled with whiteness like the sheet under which she lay.

2

$\mathcal{P}$erhaps it was in the garden of the house where
she was seven that the sister first noticed the hoopoe. There were
other birds in the garden, of course. The chatterbox Seven Sisters, the
jays, the parrots, the doves; all of which the brother stalked with his
catapult and of which he painted pictures when they were dead. But
it was the hoopoe she most admired. He was neat and elegant, with
a beak like a scimitar and a sensitive crest which rose and fell like the
curved helmets on centurions in the brother's history book.

The hoopoe had its favorite haunt under a neem tree near the rear
veranda. There it strutted or searched the dust for seeds or insects
or whatever it was it fancied to eat. The brother scoffed at her partial-
ity for the hoopoe. It was, he declared, quite a commonplace bird, but
the sister thought not. She felt a private ownership in this particular
bird and liked to imagine that the bird knew it.

While Mohommed Ali's machine whirred behind her and the
brother moved stealthily among the long grasses between the banana
trees and the custard apples, his eye missing nothing, the sister
crouched on the veranda steps and studied the hoopoe. It seemed
always to be alone, flying noiselessly down from the neem tree to land
on the dust, there to stand motionless for a second to make sure it was

20

safe. The sister admired the symmetrical spacing of the feathers, the noble crest, the alert black eye. She was convinced that he saw her and that he did not object to her presence. Every day she approached him a bit closer, hunching herself along the ground, pausing the instant he showed alarm. She felt that he was becoming accustomed to her nearness, that perhaps he was even learning to welcome it. The closer she came to him the more she admired him; he seemed not to belong in the vulgar world of shouting crows, screaming parrots, and the tedious babble of the Seven Sisters under the trees.

Fastidious, particular, solitary, he showed an odd taste, she thought, in preferring the neem tree to all the other trees in the garden. True, it threw a pretty shade on the dust, but it was evil in the sister's eyes, and for two reasons: the servants cut twigs from it to brush their teeth with, and when she had tried to do the same the taste had been so nasty that it had made her choke. Then one day, passing the tree, she noticed a deep slash in the trunk, and this was oozing a kind of blood-colored foam which smelled awful. And she had heard the mother, making a face, say to the aunt: "Like menstruation, isn't it?"

The aunt made a face. "Why on earth did anyone want to cut it, then?"

"They say it keeps away mosquitoes, or the churel, or the evil eye or something."

The sister had wanted to ask what it all meant, but she knew better. It was puzzling that the hoopoe should choose this particular tree for his haunt; on the other hand it made him even more interesting in her eyes. Holding her nose, she examined the wound in the tree, and she remembered when the milk buffalo had had its calf, and the blood and the stringy red mess, and she thought that perhaps she did understand, somewhat. The servants believed that the nasty taste of the neem twigs was good for their teeth; and out of a red foulness the buffalo calf had risen at last, blue-black, gentle-eyed, clean. Perhaps the hoopoe understood all this as he stepped dapperly among the fine shadows thrown by the leaves. The sister longed to pick him up and hold him in her hands, to make a pet of him, but although he permitted her to approach quite close there was a limit, when his crest would rise warningly and he would flit up into the branches and be lost.

21

It was in that house that she met, for the first time, the man called Charan. One afternoon she walked into the drawing room, where the mother and aunt were having tea. It was cool and shadowy and the chairs were covered in cream-colored linen with mauve roses, and beaded curtains tinkled in the doorway, and there was a scent of freshly brewed tea, and the little diamond-shaped cakes the aunt loved and which she had taught the cook to make, each cake iced in a different color, pink, yellow, white, and it took only a bite to finish one of them.

Doey was not at home and there was a kind of spaciousness and ease in the air, in the appearance of the tea table covered with one of the aunt's teacloths, the silver teapot and delicate cups and saucers, and the mother and aunt in crisp white dresses, cool and relaxed in their chairs. It was always easier without Doey, freer, you felt you could breathe a little deeper.

"You look hot, darling," the mother said as the sister made for the cake stand. "What have you been doing? Two, that's all."

The sister chose a pink cake and a white one, leaving a pink and a yellow for the brother. She sat on the arm of the mother's chair and felt the freshness from the white dress rise against her own face. The mother never smelled hot, or dirty; she never looked crumpled or tired. Fresh, clear-eyed, clear-skinned, she rose from her bed and so returned to it. Imagine her dead, imagine her old!

"I've been in the garden," the sister said. "You should just hear the hoopoe singing!"

"Hear the hoopoe!" The aunt laughed. "Who ever heard a hoopoe sing?"

"I did. It's glorious." She loved the word "glorious." "Under the neem tree where the menstruation is."

The aunt gave a sort of muffled shout. Her boiled-prune eyes turned on the mother, who said softly: "Hoopoes can't sing, darling. Don't invent."

"But this hoopoe does sing. I heard it."

"Some little people hear too much," the aunt gave out, meaningfully.

The mother murmured something in French and the sister nibbled scornfully round the edges of her second petit four. So it was a bad word. They always spoke in French when she tripped them up, but usually they resorted to it too late.

The brother came into the room, his bare knees dirty from crawling on the ground. "The neem tree's stopped bleeding," he told them importantly, swinging his catapult. "I think it must have run out. Can I have my cakes?"

"Two, darling."

He bolted them as he never would have if the father had been present, and they let him, saying nothing because of the punishment which they knew still hung over him from the day before when a pellet from the catapult had broken a window in the father's room. Perhaps the father would forget it; but he would be bound to remember it again because there was still the broken pane and the mistri had not yet come to replace it.

"I've told you and told you," Doey had said when he discovered the damage. "You won't listen so you're jolly well going to be made to after this."

It had been an accident, but the brother said nothing. He had learned that by the time he had completed an explanation, his stuttering worse than ever at such moments, he would have had his scolding or whatever other retribution was in store. His silence maddened Doey. The brother had learned this, too. He smiled inwardly at his suddenly discovered power. Yesterday, even if he could have spoken out coherently and quickly, he would not. And the defiance was in his eyes, in his compressed lips.

"It was an accident, Doey," the mother begged. "He told me it was an accident."

"This is the second accident in a week. He's got to learn sometime."

The sister had heard them going over it in their bedroom. She had listened, stiff with apprehension, remembering the sound of the razor strop on another day; remembering the brother's stubborn silence, his sudden whimpering, trying to be brave about it, then giving in, and the thin imploring scream, and the mother in the aunt's arms: "Eve! I can't bear it. Why, why can't he sometimes just see. The child. It isn't as if the child were grown up or even young. A *child!* Eve, Eve."

And the aunt's ferocious eyes. *"Doey is a brute!"*

But this afternoon Doey wasn't here and the brother lorded it, eating the last of the cakes and licking his fingers stained green from crawling about in the grass, which he was forbidden to do, and where he could have been bitten by a snake. The mother and the aunt looked at him with brooding love, thinking of the razor strop hanging in the father's bathroom, and of how little it mattered what they said or thought.

"Tea, darling," the mother said, and poured it, adding milk and three lumps. "Sit down and drink your tea nicely. You really should have washed. Look at your hands."

"It's only dirt," the brother said. There was luxury in the father's absence. The big room breathed affection, and suddenly they were laughing at the sister's reiteration that she had heard the hoopoe sing.

"I've heard it grind its teeth," the aunt contributed. "If that's what you call singing."

The brother laughed in scorn. Alone with them he felt his manhood as he never did with his father. "A hoopoe grind its teeth! Birds haven't got teeth. Nobody seems to know anything."

"This hoopoe can sing," the sister insisted. "Perhaps others can't, but this one can. I've heard it."

"You imagined you heard it," the brother retorted. "You're always imagining."

"What's imagining?"

"The same thing as lying."

"Well, I did hear it. Out there in the garden under the neem tree."

"And I suppose you think that that stuff that comes out of the neem tree is blood? Well, it isn't. It's sap, that's all it is. Sap."

"It's menstruation," the sister corrected him mincingly. She scooped the sugar from the bottom of her teacup and ate it with upturned eyes of pleasure. "Ask Aunt Eve if it isn't menstruation."

"Now that will do," the mother said in her unconvincing voice; forestalled, the brother repeated sullenly that the hoopoe couldn't sing.

He was not stammering now, and there was no asthma, and he was flushed and warm with sunlight, with happiness in the day that had passed him by, reprieved him; for the look and feel of life close to the ground where he had spent forbidden hours spying on grasshoppers, teasing a scorpion with a stick as it struck and struck again fruitlessly at his daring hand. The dense world on a level with his knees had

24

caressed him, endured him. He had no fear of it, only sometimes a kind of blind urge to lie down in it forever and let its small creatures crawl over him and make him their hiding place as they were his.

The sister was thinking: He doesn't know and he ought to say thank you to me because I've hidden the razor strop so he won't get a thrashing when Doey comes home, and he could at least say yes, the hoopoe can sing, instead of always contradicting.

Nizamat appeared in the door and murmured something to the mother and the aunt heard and burst out angrily: "Charan? No! How dare he call when he must know Doey isn't here!"

The brother and sister looked at each other excitedly. They had heard of him often enough and had seen him at a distance, the big black-bearded man always in a dark-blue turban and English-style clothes, whom the mother had repeatedly declared she simply could not allow in the house, and the father had said: "Rot! He's a damn fine chap."

"A seditionist!" the aunt had shrilled in support of the mother. "A cutthroat! Doey, are you mad? If the I.G. were to hear about it!"

"Please, Doey," the mother had besought at that earlier time. "You know you can't afford to be so casual. The way government feels about these people."

The father had shouted unnervingly: "These people! Whose bloody country do you think this is, anyhow?"

The brother and sister had felt an electric shock of terror, exquisite as when one night the aunt had admonished them against letting their legs hang down over the edge of their beds for fear of what might be lurking there in the dark.

The mother now turned to Nizamat. "Tell Charan Sahib that Sahib is not at home."

The aunt took it upon herself: "Give him *darwaza bund!*" The closed door.

But Nizamat suddenly stood aside and then the beard and turban were in the room with them, huge and brown and boisterous, tinctured with attar of roses. "I trust I am not persona non grata?"

The cheek of it, thought the aunt, flushing, her virginity congealing under the stare of his black, protuberant, amused eyes.

"Doey kindly invited me to tea. He is late, isn't he?"

25

Doey. The father's pet name, and this seditionist daring! If the I.G. were to hear of it!

The mother rose to it bravely as she did to most emergencies. "How do you do, Charan Sahib? Do sit down. A cup of tea?"

Nizamat vanished to fetch another cup and the cutthroat turned jovially to the sister and brother and exclaimed: "My goodness, how you have grown, eh?"

He picked the sister up in his arms and kissed her resoundingly, brushing her astonished cheek with his silky, perfumed beard.

"A beautiful child. Why haven't you come to play with my son Jagvir? He is your age. He is studying violin and already can play Mozart." He began to whistle.

He put the sister down and sat himself on the sofa, hugely filling half of it, then drew the brother toward him, holding him between his knees, stroking his hair. "What a handsome young son of my friend Doey! You will grow up to be like your father, I think. Brave. Brilliant. Ah, they are uncommon, men like your father."

The brother felt the man's strong arms, his strong spirit. He felt enfolded, enthralled. No man had ever held him thus, and he stood silently confused and happy, leaning back a little against the man's body.

The mother poured tea for the seditionist and the sister practiced silently how to say it. Seditionist. What did it mean? But she knew she should not ask. She would have to wait. Like that business of the neem tree. She would have to wait. But cutthroat she knew. It was in the history book, with pictures of the Mutiny, and little babies stuck like pink shrimps on bayonets, and ladies who resembled the aunt and the mother cowering against walls, hands on plumped-up breasts, eyes rolling heavenward, and men in turbans and black beards tearing about waving swords. It had been a terrible time, but exciting. She loved looking at the pictures, wondering if it had hurt the babies much.

Now the aunt had her embroidery frame and was holding it before her like a shield, but this was a mistake because Charan pounced noisily:

"What excellent workmanship! You must come to my house and teach my wife. She knits and knits, but this, no! What is it to be, may I ask?"

26

The aunt seemed speechless, and the sister volunteered: "It is a teacloth, for the tray, like that one on the table. My auntie makes hundreds and thousands of them. She was going to be married once but a polo ball killed her fancy and now she has all these teacloths all for nothing."

She came to a stop, blushing, and the brother stared at her balefully. The aunt's face had a congested expression, but the mother was laughing. Helplessly. Laughter bubbled within her, spilled over. But the sister felt ashamed, hot inside, wanting to cry.

Charan reached out and took her by the arm and turned her toward him and said sharply: "Suddenly you have lost your tongue, I think. No?"

She stuck it out at him and instantly he passed a hand over her face then opened his palm and there was a bright silver coin lying on it. A rupee.

"See what I found on your tongue," he told her gravely. Then he flipped the rupee in the air and it vanished under their astonished eyes, and while they stared he put his hand lightly inside the brother's shirt and there was the rupee again lying on his open palm.

The brother turned to him adoringly. "Do it again!"

Charan pulled a tragic face. "Ah, now where could it have gone, that naughty rupee? It is not in this hand, it is not in that hand. It is not to be seen. Where, I wonder?"

He reached down swiftly, felt in the brother's shoe, and hooked out the rupee with one finger. Magic. The sister hurled herself upon him in ecstasy. "Do it again!"

He found the rupee next in her left ear, and as she hung round his neck he lifted her in the crook of his arm and walked to the tea table, plucked the rupee from inside the teapot. Brother and sister were transported. And now Charan was all over the room, losing the rupee, finding it again improbably behind a picture on the wall, from the center of a vase of flowers, under the piano lid, from the brother's right ear, from his left, from Nizamat's grinning mouth.

Brother and sister screamed with delight. They wanted to adopt him. Imagine having him live with them forever and ever! The rupee flashed and glimmered in the subdued light of the room. It flew toward the ceiling, out a window, between the bead curtains, and popped without warning from one of the mother's streaming eyes.

"Do it again!"

This time it was the aunt's hair, and as he plucked it from the serpentine coils a great lock escaped his fingers and slid on her shoulder, giving her a madly wanton look. The mother was leaning back in her chair, helpless, when the father appeared suddenly in the door and stood watching.

"I'll be damned," he said, and Charan lunged at him and triumphantly extracted the rupee from the long brown moustache.

Afterward the aunt had been indignant and had upbraided the father.

"He walked in with his shoes on just as if he were one of us. It's no joking matter, Doey. And Alice, too. And the children. Laughing like idiots, encouraging him. Just because he played those silly tricks. And calling you *Doey*."

The father answered: "Charan is a good chap. It would be better for us if he were on our side, but of course government will never see that!"

"I should hope not!"

The aunt was thinking of the touch of that brown hand in her hair. It was the first time a man had touched her since Derek died. The touch of Charan was a kind of sacrilege, an infidelity, even though she had not invited it. She had not even felt like laughing, as Alice did. These beastly natives with their ideas about women. Seditionists, and Doey so casual about it. Even liking the man, trusting him.

"Don't be an idiot, Eve. This is his country, don't forget."

"Oh, Doey, don't start that. Please don't start that. Not politics. How would you feel if something were to happen, if they were to get out of hand. What about Alice and me and the children?"

The father's eyes were suddenly hard blue stones. "Don't be such a bloody fool."

The mother then cried out: "Doey, really!"

And the father had shouted: "I tell you I won't stand being dictated to. Charan is a friend and he has my invitation to come to this house whenever he likes, and the servants are to treat him with respect, and my family is to make him welcome." His moustache was on end. "And what has happened to my razor strop? I can't find it anywhere. It's vanished."

It silenced them. The sister, out on the veranda, heard what was

28

said and walked away into the garden out of sight of the house. Charan the magician had long since gone. It was getting dark and soon the lamps would be lighted and there would be eggplant and mashed potatoes for supper, and preserved figs, and the father would turn on the brother and demand where was the razor strop, which always hung from a hook behind the bathroom door, and the brother would say with truth that he did not know, or he would say nothing, and the father would say: "Don't dare to lie to me and don't dare to look at me like that!"

Bats were flying through the air, which smelled of petunias. The evening was another world. Gentler, smaller, kind. The sister felt herself shaping within it, felt a difference in her flesh as the light changed and the body changed with it. Certain animals, she knew, slept during the day and came to life with darkness. These had a different kind of sight, a different sense of smell, of awareness, from animals which flourished in the sanity of day. But now she felt within herself a quivering uncertainty trying to achieve a balance between the two as she stood in the shadowy garden watching the bats flip against the sky, hearing a dove moan belatedly in the distance, then turned with relief to see the lamps lighted in the house, reminding her who she was.

It became too dark to stay out and she heard the first jackal on the plain, that sound which always made her insides turn pale. And there was the thought of the churel hiding in the trees, peering down between the branches with its wrong-way-looking eyes, and these two things were worse than snakes and scorpions, which the sister and the brother did not mind at all, though the father and mother and aunt were always pointing out that the jackal rarely hurt people, it was only their noise that was frightening, and that there was no such thing as a churel, but that there *were* kraits and cobras and scorpions and it was these that could kill you.

Driven, she went back to the shining house, into the big drawing room, where now the father was sitting alone, his legs stretched on the long arms of the chair, a glass of whiskey and soda on the table beside him. The aunt and the mother were dressing for dinner and there was no sign of the brother. The sister knew that he was lingering outdoors, scheming how to get into the house without being seen. She stood looking deferentially at the father, who sipped his drink, and said presently in a quiet voice: "Perhaps you can tell me what has become of my razor strop?"

She turned one foot on its side and stared down at it, saying nothing.

"Nizamat hasn't seen it, nor has the bheesty, nor has Chota Ayah, nor anyone. It was there this morning; now it has disappeared. How am I going to shave without sharpening my razor?"

She inquired with detachment: "Is that what you want it for?"

"Naturally. What else would I want it for?"

She stood, her heart swelling.

"What's the matter?" he asked her. "Can't you speak? What is it?"

She looked at him, the pretended smile breaking on her lips. The father put his glass on the table, swung his legs off the arms of the chair, and said: "Come here."

She went to him, her feet lumps of lead, and he drew her close and put a finger under her chin, lifting it. He said slowly: "You hid my razor strop, didn't you?"

How had he found out? He found out everything. She made a slight hopeless movement, but he continued to hold her. "You hid it. Why? Tell me. I want to know."

Still she couldn't speak. Perhaps he heard her thumping heart. Suddenly he drew her into his arms and passed a hand over her hair. "You little darling," he said, and she saw his clear skin, and the faint bluish shadows under his eyes, which gave his face an unexpected delicacy. "All right," he said. "I'll let him off this time. Now go and put the strop back where you found it."

She hesitated, hating to lose the touch of his arms, her gaze sinking into the freshness, the clean look of his cheek, of his lips under the brown moustache. Their eyes were very alike. Then he kissed her and she turned away, flushing, in love for the first time in her life.

3

*T*here was a gentleman named Mr. Jensen who was quite old, or at any rate he had a completely bald head like a round pink stone, and watery eyes with red veins in them, and square false teeth like postage stamps which he liked to pop out of his mouth at odd moments to amuse people, though it was usually more frightening than funny, and not nearly as fascinating a trick as Charan's with the rupee.

Mr. Jensen called often at the house and the mother and the aunt were always jolly with him, and the aunt screamed with laughter when he popped his teeth at her, but the brother and sister were priggishly not amused, missing Charan, whom they had not seen since that day when he had come to the house for tea. This absence, they suspected, had something to do with a statement the mother had made to the aunt. "Doey is furious. He has sent off a terrible letter to the L.G., my dear! Sticking up for Charan, when it's common property that he was behind the riots last month."

The aunt had concurred morosely: "Blaming the police, when all they were doing was their duty. I quite agree with Mr. Jensen that the police should have killed off the whole boiling lot, Charan with them. Mr. Jensen thinks Doey is being very silly. What, he asked me, would Doey have done if the riots had occurred in *this* district?"

"He says it never would have happened in his district. He has his constables under strict control. He says that poor Algy Porter simply lost his head when he gave the order for the police to fire. He said Algy didn't even try to talk to the mob. He just told his men to shoot. At any rate Doey has taken Charan's word for it that *he* was not on the spot at the time, and that the whole thing was a put-up job to implicate Charan and send him to jail."

"Is that what Doey wrote to the L.G.?"

"More or less. He didn't show me the letter. He just told me."

"But what about all the witnesses who have sworn they saw Charan moving among the rioters, egging them on?"

"Doey says it is all a bloody lie, that the witnesses have all been bribed or threatened into bearing false witness."

"I think," the aunt said slowly, "sometimes, that Doey is going off his chump."

Then the aunt and the mother had fallen silent and the brother and sister left the house, glad that Mr. Jensen lived nearby with his mistress, though what a man of that age would want with a mistress had long been a mystery to the sister. Mr. Jensen, she decided, must be a very *backward* sort of person, though the brother laughed at this and looked knowing. Mr. Jensen's mistress, the brother said, was not a governess. Mistress meant something quite different, and the sister would just have to wait until she was older before she found out.

Yet Mr. Jensen owned the lockworks, and his wife lived by herself with a staff of servants in a big blue-painted bungalow next door to the English Club, and the aunt and the mother felt sorry for her because of something Mr. Jensen did or didn't do, and which was as baffling to the sister as the existence of the mistress who was at the same time not his governess.

The mother and the aunt's pity for Mrs. Jensen, and the father's also, seemed in no way to affect their parallel affection for the mistress, Miss Edna Meadows, and her mother, Mrs. Meadows. Everybody seemed to be sorry for everybody else, except for Mr. Jensen, whom they liked without apparently feeling sorry for him. It was for this reason, probably—his not liking his wife and liking Miss Meadows instead—that he had never been admitted as a member of the Club, and had been blackballed by everyone except of course by

32

Doey, who stood up for Mr. Jensen just as he did for Charan.

"Doey," the aunt remarked grievingly, "seems always to expect the impossible. After all, one can like a person without going whole hog on his account, and old Jensen really is a bit of a rip when you think of it."

"He is unconventional, of course," the mother tentatively agreed, and added with puzzling inconsequentiality: "Poor thing!"

"Who, poor thing?" the aunt demanded aggressively.

"Old Jensen. After all, he must suffer in his way."

The aunt said pooh, and that if he did suffer it served him right. "At his age, and *she* thirty years younger!"

Miss Meadows and her mother were dark-skinned, and they talked in high excitable voices and laughed a great deal, and the sister and brother enjoyed visiting them in their house, where they were permitted to do pretty much anything they wanted. Mrs. Meadows cooked sumptuous curries and pickles and jams, and had a recipe for mango fool which she would impart to no one. Some people, the sister had heard her say, just sucked up to her because they were after her recipes, otherwise they wouldn't cross the street to speak. That Mrs. Sparks, for instance, sending her masalchi—masalchi, mind you, a dirty little dishwasher, not even a proper servant—to try and chouse the recipe for mango fool out of Mrs. Meadows' own servant Abdullah. Abdullah had told Mrs. Meadows about it himself and they had had a good laugh together.

As though marriage, and being eight-annas-in-the-rupee, made such a difference. Mrs. Meadows had a way of talking to herself which entranced the sister, who followed her about the house pretending not to listen but hearing every word. Eight-annas-in-the-rupee, the aunt had elucidated, simply meant that poor Miss Meadows and her mother had *native blood in their veins.* Since there were sixteen annas in the rupee it was a matter of simple arithmetic, was it not? *Enfin,* concluded the aunt briskly, that's enough. No more questions.

But the sister was obsessed by a sense of something extraordinary. Brooding on it in silence as she followed Mrs. Meadows about the big, dim, cluttered house which smelled of China matting, spice, and incense, listening to Mrs. Meadows' sibilant chichi murmurings, the sister sometimes felt herself to be on the trail of some especially

33

deep-down complication whose origins stemmed from the wound in the neem tree and the bloody birthings of puppies and calves.

Blood. Blood in people's veins, native blood. Blood twisting in meaty tendrils from the mother buffalo; blood on the father's chin when he cut himself shaving; blood oozing from the neem tree; blood on the aunt's bed sheet and Chota Ayah's carrying it away for a secretive scrubbing. Whose bloody country is it? Don't be a bloody fool. Oh, Doey, I wish you wouldn't use such language. The children.

Once, plucking up courage, the sister had inquired of Mrs. Meadows: "What's native blood like?"

Mrs. Meadows had stared at her with large, brown, soft eyes, rather like a horse's eyes. "Now what-all!" she exclaimed in her shrill chichi voice. "Native blood is like any other blood."

Miss Meadows and her mother shared their house with Mr. Jensen, and it was different from all the other houses known to the sister and brother. The Meadowses' house was built of red brick with white marble trimmings, and it had three stories, and from the roof, which you reached by a little narrow winding staircase, very steep, you could see for miles. The bazaars, the railway station, the Club with its shady trees and its tennis courts, the fairgrounds, the mosque beyond the level crossing, and the Hindu temple with the tiger painted on its doors, across the road from the Meadowses' gate. You could see, from the roof, the river with an occasional feathery curl of smoke from a funeral pyre, fields yellow with flowering mustard or green with arrah, and in the distance and only on very clear days in winter when there was no mist from the river and no haze of village smoke, a suggestion of pale-blue mountains with the jungle at their feet.

Sometimes the brother and sister climbed on the Meadows roof with the father's binoculars and took turns studying the scene, bringing details close up before their eyes. Mostly they concentrated on the jungle, imagining that they discerned the shapes of gigantic trees and the silver explosion of elephant grass against a screen of shining cane. It was to those distant jungles that they would go—the father and mother and aunt, the sister and brother—at Christmas time, to live in tents, the father to shoot tigers from the back of an elephant loaned by some local nawab.

But now the sister and brother were preoccupied with thoughts of

34

the father's letter to the L.G. and the strange prospect of his being banished to what they had heard him frequently describe as some obscure hellhole, while the aunt gave embroidery lessons to unknown, unattractive children with stingy parents, and the mother took in paying guests. It was a frightening dimension which they apprehended dimly like something in a dream, and which they were careful not to flesh with words as they walked down the long driveway under the shisham trees, across the dusty road and the dreary gardens of the Masonic Hall, to the Meadows house.

Before the front veranda was a porte cochere with a rock garden on one side of it, and in the rock garden lived Miss Meadows' pet frog, an enormous creature with green and yellow mottles, a long pointed face, and unblinking eyes.

The sister and brother had at one time been somewhat afraid of this frog, but they had become accustomed to it and now they liked to pick it up in their arms and it allowed them to do so, its long legs dangling, its pale delicate feet trying to find a purchase on their clothes, the yellow skin of its throat nervously throbbing. When it crouched among the rocks, quite motionless, it was difficult to see, it merged so perfectly with the green and yellow coleus which grew there. But when it rained the frog stirred and gave forth penetrating croaks which carried quite a distance and which excited all the other frogs in the neighborhood, though no one had ever seen one as large as this. Miss Meadows had named it Barley because this cereal, boiled with sugar, seemed to be its favorite food aside from the insects which it caught itself. One day the sister had snared a large praying mantis which she offered to Barley, who snapped it up eagerly but then started to choke, and there was the praying mantis stuck partway down Barley's throat and only its strange triangular little face sticking out and two beseeching arms, and luckily Miss Meadows had appeared at that moment and stuck her finger into Barley's mouth and pulled out the mantis, or what was left of it.

This afternoon Miss Meadows and her mother were sitting as usual in their cane chairs on the veranda when the sister and brother appeared, and old Mrs. Meadows cried in her loving chichi voice: "Come along, children! I have some fresh jelabies for you. Abdullah just brought them from the bazaar, made specially, and they are still hot." She pronounced it "hort." Privately the sister practiced the way

Mrs. Meadows talked, and considered it funny, but outwardly she was extremely polite, for she loved Mrs. Meadows and Miss Meadows, and their house crammed with furniture, Benares brass, carved teak, peacock feathers, rotting animal skins, numdah rugs, glittering paintings of the Dal Lake in Kashmir, and of course Barley the frog, hopping, as he sometimes did, up and down the veranda and in the rooms, quite at home.

Before mounting the marble steps to the veranda the brother and sister paused to inspect Barley, asleep at the moment among his coleus, his staring eyes closed. This gave him a peculiar expression of enjoying some private joke, smiling to himself in his dreams. The brother and sister frequently wished that Miss Meadows might make them a present of Barley, but of course neither would have dreamed of asking. She was too fond of him, and besides, Peggy the terrier at home would certainly have killed him on sight. Barley frequently followed Miss Meadows up the steps in great leaps and hunted flies and mosquitoes on the veranda in a spectacular ballet of his own, or he crouched in a corner, rather incredible with his great secretively smiling mouth and sleepy eyes and his front feet, like two human hands, placed fastidiously before him.

Jelabies. The brother and sister were passionately fond of the sugary brown wheels filled with syrup, crisp outside, smelling of the bazaar, of boiling ghee, and ever so slightly of the big iron ladle with which the halwai spooned his confections into small clay pots or receptacles made of dry leaves pinned together with bits of twig. For some reason the sweets always tasted better served thus rather than on ordinary china plates.

"Now come and tell us what is going on in the great big world," suggested Miss Meadows, gazing at them fondly. She resembled her mother a little, but was taller, thinner, with a beautiful glow to her pale-brown skin. The father had once remarked to the mother: "Can't say I blame old Jensen. After all, compared to that stick of a wife Edna must seem a pretty juicy bit!"

The brother and sister seated themselves decorously on the edges of their chairs and eyed the platter of jelabies with affected detachment as the bearded servant Abdullah set the platter on a cane table before them. Unlike their own servants, the Meadowses' did not wear livery but went about in dingy pantaloons and a thin collarless shirt, a greasy astrakhan cap set cockily on his head. The Meadowses treated Abdullah as one of the family and they addressed each other with the familiar *toom*, though he never ventured this with Mr. Jensen.

When Mrs. Meadows spoke to Abdullah in Hindustani and he replied, it was sometimes difficult to distinguish between their voices because her speech then so resembled his. Native, the sister had concluded uncomfortably, because she had learned that only people who were eight-annas-in-the rupee spoke like natives. Strangely she did not include Doey in this category, in spite of his at-homeness in the language, as in French. In which category, indeed, could one have included Doey? Others, like the aunt and the mother, spoke Hindustani in a gingerly fashion as though it were somehow an exercise in indelicacy.

"Eat, eat!" besought Mrs. Meadows. "Eat while they are hort. How is your dear mummy and auntie?"

The brother and sister helped themselves daintily to the jelabies and nibbled with care. This was just the beginning. By the second helping their faces would be smeared with syrup, their eyes bemused. But manners were important, especially at the beginning. They felt that the Meadowses expected this behavior of them and that both Miss Meadows and Mrs. Meadows were somehow soothed by it, by good manners, politeness, poise. Once the sister had heard Miss Meadows remark to the father: "They are charming, those two of yours. So well brought up." And the father had later reported to the mother: "I'm glad they behave themselves with the Meadowses. Too many people don't take the trouble even to be polite, just because of the situation. Damnation! Whose business is it if Jensen prefers his greens on the other side of the paddock?"

The sister, delicately nibbling her first jelabie, parsed the details of Miss Meadows' face. Greens. Miss Meadows was Mr. Jensen's greens. Was that why her name was Meadows?

"What are you thinking, darling?" queried Miss Meadows, smiling. In her company and in Mrs. Meadows' the sister was conscious of a kind of humid, furry warmth. She could almost feel it against her skin; a limitless resignation to yearning, as if neither could ever get enough of loving, or give enough.

"Lucky," the mother once observed to the aunt, "there aren't any children on either side. Wouldn't it be too awful?"

"With that touch of the tar brush, yes," the aunt had concurred over her embroidery frame. "Though I think Edna would have made a perfect mother. They have that in them, I think. Rather animal. But pathetic, really."

The sister licked her fingers and sat formally in her chair, her sandaled feet just touching the floor, longing for another jelabie but punctiliously waiting to be asked.

"A penny," Miss Meadows enticed, smiling, showing her perfect teeth. Did she brush them with a neem twig? the sister wondered. But no, Miss Meadows wouldn't do that. Miss Meadows, the sister had long since deduced, would never permit herself to lapse into anything *native*. Which, the mother had pointed out, made the whole thing even more pathetic. Miss Meadows was a born lady actually. Good blood there somewhere, though probably not on Mama's side, the poor thing.

The sister smiled shyly back at Miss Meadows. "Nothing," she said. "I'm not thinking of anything."

"Oh, my!" cried Mrs. Meadows, heaving herself toward the platter of jelabies so that her big brown boobies popped into view at the top of her blouse. "Oh, my! Everybody is always thinking about something. I bet I know what you are thinking about, sweetheart. Another jelabie, isn't it?"

The sister squirmed and the brother giggled, and Miss Meadows said fondly: "Do. They are for you both. We bought them only for you."

"Thank you," the sister murmured, careful to pick out the smallest left on the platter so as to maintain her reputation for manners. And aside to the brother: "Say thank you, can't you?"

He turned red. "I did say thank you."

The sister glanced at Miss Meadows. She was preparing to ask her a formal question, having rehearsed it in private earlier in the day. The brother, guessing her intention to take over the conversation, eyed her with dislike. She was showing off. She would do or say something horrible, something that must demean him through their relationship, like her stupid insistence that a hoopoe could sing, that she had seen the moon crash into the ground and break into smithereens, and other faux pas. The worst thing a person could do, the aunt had instructed them, was to commit a faux pas.

The sister held the fresh jelabie fastidiously between her fingers and inclined her head toward Miss Meadows as she had seen the mother do to a guest at tea parties. Mincingly, the sister inquired: "How is Mr. Jensen feeling?"

Miss Meadows raised her fine brows slightly. "He is very well, darling, of course. Thank you for asking."

The sister licked her lips. "Not at all. I am so glad to hear it. Someone mentioned that he had been quite unconventional lately."

In the tiny silence the sister heard the brother's sharp intake of breath and knew that he would have it in for her later. Then Mrs. Meadows gave a small shriek and said: "Now what-all! Did you ever?"

Miss Meadows leaned forward and, picking up the platter, offered it to the brother, whose face was crimson. "Do," Miss Meadows urged him kindly. "They are best when they are hot." She did not say "hort." She was always very particular about such things.

Afterwards, when they were on their way home and out of sight of the Meadows house, the brother kicked the sister on the ankle and said: "Showing off again! You deserve a damn good slap."

She limped a bit but retorted: "Wait until I tell them you said damn. Just wait."

"*Unconventional!* You don't even know what it means."

"I do."

"What, then?" But he was instantly sorry he had asked. Her eyes had the sudden depthlessness he knew well. She was a fount of learning. She knew and she would not tell, or she did not know and he would never be sure that she did not know. He kicked her again and she gave a faint moan and said: "And I know what fuck means, too."

She had been saving this for some other, some greater, possibly momentous occasion, but the small inner unease following her performance at the Meadowses' had driven her farther than the indignity of his kicks. Now she trembled a little, exalted yet fearful of his expression of utter shock.

He said slowly: "If they ever heard you say *that!*"

"You say it. I've heard you."

"I'm older than you."

"But you don't know what it means and I do."

He was aghast, caught again in the coils she always managed to set for him. He stared at her in wonder. She was nothing but a girl, nothing but his sister, not even as old as he, yet at times like this he felt a real dread of her. He had learned about her hiding the father's razor strop, and he had not been punished for breaking the window, and he knew that he had her to thank for it, but the knowledge only filled him with gloom. She had no business to mystify and baffle him as she did. And now that language! That word, making her in a flash his equal. It was simply not to be borne, and as he felt his asthma coming on he kicked her again and walked ahead of her, satifaction and suffocation battling in him as he heard her fraudulent sniveling at his heels.

4

The fever struck her suddenly one afternoon when the winter light hopped along the dust and the bheesty had made his rounds of the compound, spraying water from the goatskin on his back. There was a bustle of tea being prepared in the scullery behind the dining room; anticipation of cucumber sandwiches and hot scones. But anticipation faded as the sister felt the lassitude in her limbs and the unfamiliar luxury of a headache, her lips dry, a vague desire to weep rising and ebbing in her throat.

"It's been coming on for days," the mother reflected worriedly. "It's such a business to get them to swallow quinine, although I think I got quite a bit into her."

"She spat it out," the brother enlightened them officiously. "She just held it in her mouth and when you weren't looking she spat it out in the pot."

They put the sister to bed and the mother tucked a thermometer under her armpit and the aunt came and stood nearby and said: "All day she's looked so seedy, playing in the sun and not eating."

"A hundred and two," said the mother, distractedly poring over the thermometer. "You don't think it could be cholera?"

"This time of year?" The aunt was comfortingly incredulous. "It's probably something she's eaten on the sly. We had better send for Doey."

The father was at the police courts; the thought of his annoyed return sent the sister's temperature up another notch. She complained that she was thirsty and they brought her iced soda mixed with milk for nourishment and she sipped it with a suffering air, pleasantly conscious of the brother's skeptical gaze.

Later, Doey returned from the courts and stood beside the bed and looked down at the sister. "Have you been running about in the sun without your hat?" he demanded, accusatory.

Her eyelids drooped tragically and the mother intervened: "She's got a hundred and two!"

The aunt lied soothingly. "She has worn a hat, Doey. It's probably a touch of dengue. She had it last year, remember?"

"Not the time of year for dengue," Doey reminded them impatiently. "Any diarrhea?"

"Darling," the mother interpreted for the sister, "have you had the trots much?"

"Five times today," the brother volunteered from a distance. "She said I wasn't to tell you."

The sister opened her eyes and gazed up at them glassily, reducing them to impotence. There was a kind of magic in being ill; the world was transformed; one became its center, its be all and end all. There was a sense of increase and intensity, of unlimited horizons, languid recognitions. Just as one's being was altered by the night, so was it altered by disease. One became old, old with a tingling vibrance.

They conferred, the father and mother and the aunt, while the brother kicked one foot against the other, feeling left out, deserted, fearful lest she die after all and his touchstone be no more.

Send the gardener's son running to fetch Dr. Sanyal, the dispensary babu. There was no real doctor in the station, and Sanyal was its only hope, a monster of an elderly Hindu who wore English clothes and a tiny khaki topi on his shining bald head. But he was infinitely gentle and conscientious and always prescribed cough lozenges, sweet-tasting and pungent, no matter what the diagnosis.

The sister lay in languid anticipation of the cough lozenges and possible votive offerings from the Meadowses, who, whenever one or

42

the other was ill, invariably dispatched Abdullah with a tray of delicacies. It was not the season for mango fool but there might be custard flavored with vanilla, and very thin sugar wafers, or even a lemon sherbet, which no one ever had a chance of tasting unless one happened to be really ill. The sister occasionally toyed with thoughts of what might be tendered her were she to be on the point of death. Asked, she had prepared a list: brandied prunes, sardines, petits fours with pink icing, and Delhi halwasohn.

Dr. Sanyal arrived wearing a crumpled tussah suit and the tiny topi, which he handed Nizamat on entering the house. When he lowered himself on the edge of the sister's bed it sagged almost to the floor and she rolled against his huge bottom and giggled. But her face was flushed and her eyes staringly bright, and Dr. Sanyal's plump damp fingers settled authoritatively on her pulse.

He tucked the thermometer under her arm, then drew back the bedclothes and inspected her chest and belly. "Cannot be measles," he informed the mother, and aunt, who hovered over him. "She did have measles two years ago, also chicken pox."

He probed the sister's small belly. "Does it pain you, my dear?"

The father had once explained to them that Dr. Sanyal had the makings of a first-rate doctor but that poverty had made it impossible for him to pursue his studies, so here he was stuffed off in this godforsaken hole, a government dispensary clerk with the fraudulent honorific of doctor; yet at that, Doey pointed out, a damn sight better doctor than someone could name.

It didn't pain the sister. She stared up at him, seeing his face grow immense in her developing hallucination. She felt the bed begin to sink, a foundering sensation, and beyond Dr. Sanyal's bulk the slender figures of the mother and the aunt tapering toward the ceiling. The walls of the room swayed backward; her own body burgeoned, then diminished; light became opaque.

"I can hear the hoopoe," she informed them suddenly. "Listen!"

"One hundred and three," Dr. Sanyal said, turning the thermometer in his plump fingers. "It is not the time for seasonal fevers. An infection perhaps. I would like to examine further for possible spots and purulence."

They stripped her slight, muscular body of every stitch. Her neck and face, her arms, her legs from knee to feet were the same color as Dr. Sanyal's hands: a rich caramel brown, the rest of her a vulnerable white.

Dr. Sanyal said, smiling, as he covered her up again: "You have, I think, a touch of the tar brush, my dear, isn't it? All this sunburn." "Eight-annas-in-the-rupee," the sister answered, giggling. "Like Miss Meadows, but not all over."

Dr. Sanyal's smile spread over his face in fissures. His teeth were stained with pan and he exuded the opulent odor of certain fat people, a compound of good food and sound appetite. The sister wished that he would stay. His bulk countered the peculiar formlessness of the room with its sense of a receding landscape; he shared with her a special wisdom of illness, and his imperturbable voice stilled a thin ghostly screaming in her ears.

"I think there has been administration of too great amounts of quinine," Dr. Sanyal told them at last, rising from the edge of the bed, and when it regained equilibrium the sister slid back to her place in its middle. "I think administration of quinine must be totally discontinued. I will prescribe instead one good medicament to arrest possible infection. Please dispatch your servant to the dispensary and I will send. Meanwhile." He groped in the pocket of his tussah jacket and produced a small round box, which he laid on the chair beside the bed. "Cough lozenges," he indicated gravely. "In case of tickle in throat."

The mother and the aunt hung round him, grateful, still anxious, and he said benignly: "Hallucinations can be the result of overadministration of quinine." Nizamat appeared, carrying his topi. "Not serious in this case. It will pass off. She must remain in palang and consume liquids. I will come tomorrow to examine the stools, please. I do not at the moment suspect intestinal complication but it is my unflinching principle to investigate every avenue of possibility."

The sister suddenly shot up in bed and held her arms out to him. "Listen!" she cried. "You can hear it. It's singing and singing."

"Yes, darling," the mother consoled her. "We hear it. Lie down now and try to sleep."

"Doctor Sahib," the sister importuned him. "Do you hear the hoopoe?"

He cocked his bald head on one side, half closed his eyes, and

44

listened. He looked like some strange, gigantic deity disguised in a sweat-stained tussah suit, strangling in his necktie.

"Yes yes yes," he exclaimed resoundingly. "I hear him, the hoopoe bird! Ah, how nicely he sings!"

The sister lay back on the pillow, and the brother, hanging around the door, muttered: "She knows you don't hear it. She knows you're only saying it to please her because she's supposed to be ill."

When they had gone and she was alone the sister stared at the door which opened on the veranda. Light was growing fainter, sounds becoming the sounds of evening, quite different from the sounds of the day. Mohommed Ali had gone home. He had packed his work in a neat oblong bundle and fastened it with a large brass safety pin, set the wooden cover over the sewing machine and moved it against the wall, tucked a sheet over everything to await his return the following day.

The sister heard Doey's voice bidding Dr. Sanyal good night, and she visualized the doctor mounting his frail old bicycle and pedaling away with the peculiar airiness of the obese, down the driveway under the shisham trees, his tiny hat balanced on his head. But Dr. Sanyal had heard the hoopoe sing. He was a doctor; they would not dare tell *him* that he was mistaken. She smiled, delirium taking her in its magic, luxurious fever swarming over her limbs. She felt Chota Ayah's hands massage her feet and legs. The mother and aunt had heaped blankets on her so she felt she must suffocate under the weight and the heat, but this, the mother had insisted, was to start the perspiration. Chota Ayah's fingers moved tirelessly, devotedly, over every leaden muscle; along her spine; pressed her temples as if trying to expel the fever from her eyes, led her into a kind of delicious swoon.

They had put the brother in another room until she should get well, and waking toward dawn she felt Chota Ayah's head leaning against the edge of the bed where she had collapsed in sleep.

Everything was different once more, subtly altered, subtly strange. The bed was soaked in sweat; her body felt sleek and cool; the lamp had burned low and through the half-open door she could see the milky light of the sky falling into a bottomless silence.

It was the brother's turn next. A week before they were all to leave for Christmas camp in the jungle he had asthma, and the house smelled of the aromatic powder which the mother burned under his nose to relieve him. The sister, restored from her fever, could not sleep for the sound of the brother's strained breathing and the cough which he tried to hold back for fear the father would hear it and decree that he could not go to camp with them but must stay behind in the care of the Meadowses until the camping trip was over and the father, the mother, the aunt, and the sister returned.

Whenever the brother's asthma became bad, so did his stammer. Then the sister hovered beside him, her body alert for rescue. She rushed to perform small menial tasks at his bidding, and, later, did not gallop through her prayers as she usually did but knelt like a mendicant beside her bed with eyes clenched shut and hands urgently folded as she adjured God to make the brother well so he could go with them to camp. But then she was suddenly shocked by the brother propping himself on his elbow and interrupting angrily: "Stop all that hissing and whispering! You know it doesn't do any good. We've tried it and tried it and it never does any good."

"How can you say such a thing? He'll strike you down dead, or at any rate make you much worse."

"Let Him. I hate Him."

Appalled, she crept into bed and continued to pray under the bedclothes until she wearied.

"Do-do-don't tell," the brother gasped from his pillows. "S-s-say I s-s-slept like a t-t-top."

This she faithfully did at breakfast. The brother, she informed them, had slept through the night like a top. He was really quite well again and there was no reason why he should not accompany them to Christmas camp. The father said without looking up from his poached egg on rice: "We'll see."

It was better than nothing, and the sister returned to the bedroom and in her most accomplished accents assured the brother that the father had promised they would *all* go to Christmas camp, that no one was going to be left behind for any reason whatsoever. He was darkly suspicious but it seemed to her that thereafter his asthma seemed to ease. A curious thing, she reflected. A very curious thing.

Standing beside his bed she itemized the clothes to be packed: the catapult, the Daisy air rifle, a set of dominoes which Miss Meadows had given him on his birthday and which he had never learned to

46

play. Their ponies would go along, Jack and Jill, and Peggy the terrier, and the greyhounds in charge of the sweeper Kallu, of course. Just making a list transformed hope into fact. The thought of Christmas camp on the edge of the jungles was always an intoxication. They had been taken since they were babies, an epoch lost in limbo although the sister insisted she could remember every single camping site.

It was true that there seemed always to be trees; a grove of mangoes, great fatherly trees under whose shade the tents were pitched in a semicircle, and the paraphernalia of a great bonfire stacked in readiness before them. It was not always the same camping ground though it seemed always to be the same, strangeness giving way to recognition: wildness, a sharp barking of foxes at night, the green wall of the jungle standing against the hills and a prowling presence in one's dreams as by day.

Breathing more easily in his bed, the brother listened to the sister's avid prophecies, passionately willing to take her word for it. He accepted her devotion in noncommittal silence, knowing that thus he surrendered nothing, that he could even pretend to believe in the hoopoe's song, both of them aware that neither really believed the other, but that his illness, like hers, compelled their mutual faith.

Often the aunt came and sat beside the brother's bed with her embroidery frame, and her large rustling presence was an added comfort, though normally he did not care for her. He was put off by her voice with its strong French accent, by the violent muscular way in which she unexpectedly and without invitation seized and kissed him. He disliked being touched by anyone except the mother, though he had liked it in a surprised sort of way that afternoon when the man Charan had held him in his arms. There had been a sneaking, fabulous reassurance in those arms. Reassurance, and laughter, and the sight of a silver rupee flying through the air on its magic course. He had liked Charan and had hoped to see him again, and now Charan was in jail for something the father had said he did not do.

The mother brought the brother thin slices of bread and butter with his tea, and sat on the edge of his bed and gazed at him with her gentle eyes, never able to confer enough tenderness upon him. On this unlikely son who resembled her in no detail, nor the father, but perhaps some remote ancestor, gifted, sickly, ignored, yet always unrelentingly himself in his uniqueness. The aunt had once made one of her uncharacteristically perceptive remarks to the mother: "I sometimes think he asks for it, Alice. I mean, the things he does. I mean deliberately. Just from his expression. It's as if he would rather get a thrashing or a scolding, anything rather than not being noticed by Doey."

It was too deep for the mother, all love and compassion.

"What is going to be the end of it?" she begged of the aunt. "What is going to become of him when he grows up? This dreaming, this absentmindedness, this creeping about in the grass and hiding in the garden at night, this not listening when he's told. What will he do? *Be?*"

But now, worried about the brother's not being allowed to go to Christmas camp, the sister concentrated on the father. Walking obsequiously at his side during a stroll in the garden, she discoursed sympathetically on his work and his dilemmas, the malfeasance of servants who kept pinching the sugar, of the dunderheadedness of the I.G. and of German preparations for war. She was a ragbag of remembered odds and ends and only this morning at breakfast the father had burst out: "All right, don't believe me, then. Just give the swines a few more years and Bismarck or no Bismarck, they'll be at it again."

The sister had felt a cold worm of terror in her insides as she decorously ate her porridge. They would all be killed by the Germans. Stamped to death under those swinish boots, under the triumph of those arrogant moustaches. The thought of the Germans' moustaches particularly enraged the father and he trained his own in a different style, striving at an elegant and superior *mean.*

But now, walking beside him in the garden, the sister conversed with breeding, old beyond her years; and the father, his vitals cramped with amusement, stared before him, unresponsive to the hand which, nerving herself, she presently inserted in his.

"What is she up to, I wonder?" he asked the mother afterward. "Making up to me like anything! Hope she won't go trying this on other men."

The mother smiled. "She's in love with you, Doey. After all, I am. And weren't there other women?"

He fumed, delighted. "Oh, Lord!"

"She's growing up," the mother went on craftily. "She has to begin sometime and she could hardly do better than to start with you. It will give her a—a criterion."

She brought it out unblushingly, playing the sister's game; and the father, radiant, put a hand to his moustache. "What rot! You damned women. And she's only seven."

The mother thought: She's playing up to him for the brother's sake. I don't have to worry about her, she's as strong as a horse. But my poor little boy!

Mr. Onions, the district commissioner, came to call one afternoon, driving up the avenue in his shining trap drawn by a skittish young horse which shied when it saw Peggy the terrier, and tugged at the reins when the syce tried to lead him away. There was quite a scene of neighing, rearing, and flying gravel and the father said: "You ought to have the brute gelded. He'll kick your trap to bits and you too one of these days."

"Too late now," Mr. Onions said mournfully. "He's too old and I got him for a song."

Mr. Onions was tall and very thin and pale and looked as though he wore his little brother's clothes. He smelled too, as if he had forgotten to wash under his arms, and for some reason he always made the sister feel vaguely uncomfortable. His mannerisms. He had a sudden habit of picking his front teeth with his little fingernail, and a high, girlish sort of voice. But she liked the bobbery horse and longed to see him kick the trap to bits. Perhaps it was this contrast between the horse and its owner which affected her. The horse with its flaring nostrils, its luminous eyes, its deep, quivering chest. Gelded. What did it mean? She would have to wait to find out, she suspected, because it was unquestionably One of Those Words.

"I could breed him," Mr. Onions remarked incomprehensibly while they were all having tea in the drawing room. "I thought of old Jensen's mare, but Jensen is a stickler for blood lines and as far as I can make out my brute hasn't any."

"Has Jensen?" the father inquired with a laugh, and the mother said warningly: "Doey, dear."

"I bought him from old Ghulab Hosain," Mr. Onions explained, picking his front teeth with his little finger. "Three hundred chips. I call that a song, don't you?"

"Not if you can't ride him, can't breed him, and can't geld him," the father said, passing his cup to the mother for more tea. And the mother said with her soft laugh: "You do seem to have rather a taste for odd creatures, Mr. Onions, don't you?"

"Well, I prefer them to the strictly tame," Mr. Onions replied in his frilly little voice. "I don't care for shikar, as you know, and having them about does rather keep one on one's toes!"

When he was taking his leave Mr. Onions invited them to come and take tea with him one of these days, and meet his tame panther. "I've had him since he was only a few weeks old. Spots. I call him Spots, you know."

"Original," Doey remarked, and the mother gave him another of her looks.

"Spots is about ten months old now, and very playful, if a bit rough. The servants are afraid of him, all except my sweeper, who helped me bring him up on a bottle."

"I hope you keep it chained," the aunt suggested from behind her embroidery. "At any rate when we come to tea." She was eager to see the panther, but her nerves had never been the same since Derek died, and she hoped that Mr. Onions understood this. She felt drawn to Mr. Onions, as the sister quickly discerned.

The aunt should have married someone else, people were always saying. Mr. Jensen said so frequently; so did the Meadowses and the Sparkses. It was always cropping up in conversation when the aunt was not present. Eve should really have married someone else. India was no place for a white woman to be alone in. You can't let bereavement . . . no matter how shocking . . .

And the father had said: "If Eve would do something about herself . . . Use scent, for instance. And chuck that everlasting sewing. It puts men off. And she's going to end up with a regular Kaiser Wilhelm moustache if she doesn't look out."

"Doey, your own sister!"

"Why don't you tell her, then?" the father demanded. "If she's got her eye on poor little Onions!"

"I can't hurt her feelings."

"Better her feelings than her chances, and she's getting on, you know."

"But Onions must be at least ten years younger than Eve."

50

"Well, if he knows as little about women as he does about horses . . ." the father said, with a laugh.

Later, when Mr. Onions had come for tea and gone away, whirled out of sight by his bolting horse, the aunt remarked that she felt sorry for that young man. She couldn't say exactly why, but she thought perhaps he didn't quite know how to take care of himself. And the mother said yes, life was difficult for a bachelor far from home. But he would very likely marry eventually. They all did. And a nice wife would make all the difference.

The aunt gazed absorbedly into her embroidery and the sister went quietly away to the brother's bedroom to tell him about Mr. Onions' visit, and the bobbery horse, and the tame panther named Spots. She made much of it all, as she usually did, and he listened with affected disinterest. When she used the word "gelded" he smiled. "Bet you don't know what that means," he said.

She had expected this and met it nimbly: "Too late now. The brute's too old."

Onions, the father declared, was not much to look at but he was a good chap. And no snob. Read and wrote Sanskrit, mind you, when most of them—the L.G. and the I.G., for example—couldn't even spell properly in English. If we had more chaps like Onions running these difficult up-country stations . . . But you wait and see. Onions wouldn't get very far. Too independent, too familiar with the natives, speaking their boli as well as they did themselves and even better. That always made government suspicious. Something wrong with the white man if he spoke the natives' boli too well. A kind of treason to your own kind.

The father as usual was speaking for himself, and the mother listened, saying nothing. She was glad that he should like Mr. Onions; he liked so few people; most brains were the size of buttons. The road to success in government service was to be glib. Don't speak the native boli too well and don't speak your own too well either. Don't do anything too well, and above all don't for God's sake do it better than your superiors if you want to get on.

The mother had to protest at last: "Are you being quite fair, darling?"

But he smiled, the outburst which occurred regularly every day soothing him, making life more bearable.

Glib, mused the sister. She liked the word. Slippery, like sucked toffee.

The brother could not go with them to have tea with Mr. Onions. He must not take the chance of a relapse into asthma so soon before the day they were to leave for Christmas camp. But never mind. Mr. Onions would still be here when they returned and they would all have tea together then. The brother said nothing. He lay in bed propped on his pillows, his belongings arranged on the blanket before him. He knew it would do no good to beg or to cry. When the mother was firm in this fashion she could be worse than the father; the mother's love was in some ways more overwhelming than anything the father could conjure.

The sister, dressing for tea with Mr. Onions, pushing her feet into tight white socks, was consolatory. The brother should thank his stars that the father had said yes, he could go with them to Christmas camp provided he was really well enough by that time. Think of that! After all their fears and doubts. And tea with Mr. Onions wasn't so very exciting. Just that old panther. It would still be there when they got back from camp unless it ate someone in the meantime and had to be shot.

The sister was philosophical, trying to make light of the occasion, wondering aloud whether clean socks were really necessary. The brother listened morosely. He longed to go to tea with Mr. Onions and to see the tame panther, but nothing showed in his set face. He lay in bed smelling of the aromatic powder which burned in the saucer next to his bed, and he punished the sister by remaining uncommunicative while she chattered on. She suffered, knowing that he did not want her to leave him, that he felt she should share his deprivation and halve it thereby, but this she could not do. She felt his drifting from her, as, when she had the fever, she had drifted from him. But in the heat of her own desire his outlines dimmed. She stole sly glances at his white, set face, and suddenly he seemed scarcely to be in the same room with her; he became no more solid than a lot of other people, and she sensed his awareness of this and realized that he would not forget it. Then she ran from the room, carrying with her like a remembered blow the fixed deadly stare of the betrayed.

The mother had decided that they should walk. It was a lovely cool afternoon; Mr. Onions' house was no distance, and besides, Doey had taken the trap on his own business. Nizamat would escort them, wait while they had tea, and escort them home. Outdoors there was a scent of dust and dry leaves—a winter smell. Ekkas lolloped past them, drawn by scrawny horses disguised under ornamental leather and tassels. Bullock carts creaked along laden with sugar cane and chaff for cattle, and entire families huddled amid the produce: women with glinting nose rings, bare-bellied children, men in untidy turbans riding the whiffletree and twisting the bullocks' tails to make them go faster. The sister felt stared at and inferior to be seen walking and made faces at the children in the bullock carts, who stared back at her with huge, uncomprehending eyes.

Monkeys played under the trees which bordered the road, and the aunt became nervous when one of them, an enormous male with a backside like a Turner sunset, as the father had once described it, made a threatening move toward them. The aunt, who screamed easily, seemed about to do so when the mother admonished her. "They won't hurt you. They just don't like having stones thrown at them. They're quite harmless, really."

But the big male monkey did not look harmless as he stalked on his knuckles, glaring at them out of his little red berry eyes, then turning his backside on them in deliberate insult.

"Deliberate, my dear," the aunt murmured, between fear and laughter. "He must *know* how disgusting he looks, really. Purple and crimson!"

The sister couldn't wait now to see a Turner sunset; then Nizamat picked up a stone and the monkey instantly rushed up the nearest tree and barked at them furiously from a safe branch. Seeing them stop to look at him, he immediately turned his backside toward them again and the mother said: "Don't look. He's showing off."

"So human," said the aunt, and she and the mother went off into one of their gales and the sister made a note of it to report, later, to the brother.

Nizamat left them at the steps of Mr. Onions' bungalow and went away to the servants' quarters for his own tea. The three walked up the steps together, rather timidly. Then a chuprassy in red livery appeared and led them into Mr. Onions' drawing room, which was beautiful, the sister decided at once. It was not in the least reminiscent of Mr. Onions. There were chintz curtains and a shining blue tile floor and deep squashy chairs and a cane sofa with cloth-of-gold cushions, and flowers everywhere. The room smelled like a lovely lady, and the sister sighed with pleasure. She had a taste for such things, always saving bits of silk from Mohommed Ali's collection when he wasn't looking, and sheets of plain white paper, and new pencils, and balls of soft lavender wool from which the aunt knitted sweaters, and neatly wrapped boxes of things, especially if there was gold paper on them, steeping herself in the feel of cool muslin and the black shine of new patent leather shoes.

Obedient to the mother's directing glance she went and sat primly on the edge of a large chair and folded her hands on her lap and felt her heart happily beating, thoughts of the brother at a distance; and anyway he was probably quite all right now playing with his box of Red Indians and Cowboys, the blanket a perfect battlefield of hills and hollows, and Chota Ayah would be giving him his tea with buttered chapatties and brown sugar, and I needn't worry, really, the sister assured herself, sniffing all this opulent strangeness.

The aunt strayed regally round the room examining the photographs in silver frames: photographs of ladies and gentlemen in refined dress, and vacant-faced babies, and austere houses covered in leaves. The mother, always at ease, sat on one end of the sofa with her parasol at her side and delicately tested the chintz between her fingers, knowing about such things and always very particular. Looking at her the sister thought suddenly, with a kind of pain in her throat: How beautiful she is! Light from the open door, thickened with the scent of roses, rested on the mother's face under the brim of her plain straw hat, and her eyes seemed to grow like flowers opening, and there was an undecided smile on her lips, and the hair just showing under her hat was the sort of brightest brown, and a pearl shone in each ear, pearls which the father had given her when the sister was born. My pearls, the sister thought, without avarice at that moment.

By contrast the aunt slightly embarrassed her. Tall and angular, with dust on her fancy shoes, and an astounding sort of hat. Seeing it for the first time the father had shouted with laughter and said: "If you were to put a handle on it you could use it for carrying potatoes!" Besides the overpowering hat the aunt wore a gray silk skirt with black stripes and a ruffled silk blouse buttoned to her chin, and tight

54

black kid gloves. She must, the sister decided privately, be roasting inside.

"I wonder where Mr. Onions can be?" the aunt wondered aloud, and the mother said, faintly reproving: "He's probably on the way. Do sit down, Eve, dear, and don't be so restless."

The mother felt restless too, but she would never show it; and then the sister, all eyes though discreet because if she did not behave she would not be allowed to come again, the sister suddenly saw the panther. It was lying behind a small table near a door with a blue silk curtain; its head rested on its front paws, its round eyes were fixed on the aunt, and the tip of its sinuous black tail was gently twitching.

The sister thought instantly: He is going to spring on the aunt and eat her right in front of our eyes. Her heart pounded with excitement. She wanted to get up from her chair and run across the room and examine the panther more closely, wondering if his eyes were like the eyes of an ordinary cat, like the shifting, glinting patterns in a kaleidoscope she had once owned. He looked inexpressibly handsome lying there with the shadowy light playing on his hide, turning it into a garden at night.

Slowly the sister raised her eyes and looked at the mother and knew at once that the mother too had seen the panther but that the aunt had not, and the only way to save the aunt was for her not to know that the panther was in the room with them. The sister knew what would happen if the aunt were to see the panther. She would start to scream; she would hurl cushions at it, furniture; she would cling to the mother, and perhaps faint or die of fright. She had, as the father had once annoyedly remarked, absolutely not one damned bit of self-control.

The mother said in her quiet everyday voice: "Do sit down, Eve. Aren't you tired after that walk?"

"This must be his place in Norfolk," the aunt said, peering at a photograph on the mantel a few feet from where the panther lay watching her with his ardent golden eyes. "Reminds me a little of Papa's house in Normandy, only you can tell that this isn't in France."

"Do sit down, Eve," the mother urged. "It isn't polite really to go poking about a person's belongings, is it?"

"This looks like him when he was at school. It must be. Poor little thing, so scraggy."

55

"Eve," the mother said with a little loss of breath. The panther had moved, sliding forward a tiny bit on his stomach. His black lips were slightly parted, showing a sliver of pink tongue. The aunt fascinated him. He seemed quite unconscious of the mother and the sister. The aunt sauntered, queenly, from photograph to photograph, sometimes approaching within a foot of the panther, sometimes moving away. When she moved away he would slide forward a bit farther so the sister could see almost the whole of him, silken, sinewy, his paws like brown roses. When the aunt moved toward him he lowered his head coyly and retreated backward into the shadow of the table. His tail twitched and twitched in a kind of ecstasy, and the sister fancied she heard a kind of depthless purring growl.

The mother's face was flushed and her eyes wide, petaled with her brown lashes, and her hands were trembling a little on the ivory handle of her parasol. The sister thought: She's going to do something to save the aunt if the panther springs. The sister's heart was back to normal. She was utterly absorbed, hearing and seeing nothing except the aunt's majestic figure and the enormous hat, and the panther concentrated on her every move. Then the sister saw something else. She saw the mother's hands move gently on the handle of the parasol, saw one hand slide upward to the little metal brake which kept the spokes closed, and the sister thought with intense admiration: If the panther jumps she'll open the parasol in his face!

Then like a dream he was gone and Mr. Onions came into the room from the veranda and said: "My goodness, have you been here long? I was in my office with a chap who simply wouldn't leave. He seemed to think it was a matter of life and death and here it was teatime! I am so sorry! Have you seen Spots? He should be here somewhere. Spots! *Spo-ots!* "

But the panther did not reappear and the sister and mother said nothing, and the aunt came and sat down virginly on a chair two inches from where the panther had been lying, and the mother began to laugh suddenly, witlessly, as she was given to doing for no apparent reason, and the aunt disapprovingly thought she was probably laughing at Mr. Onions, who had forgotten to brush his hair and whose necktie was twisted under his Adam's apple, giving him a strangled air. Mr. Onions laughed too, gaily, just for the sake of laughing, it seemed. "I asked the chap to come in and join us for tea, but

56

he can't speak English, and said he would have felt foolish in front of the memsahibs."

A bearer brought in a silver tray with plates of interesting sandwiches and a chocolate cake, and Mr. Onions spoke to the man in Hindustani, telling him to find Spots and bring him in to meet the ladies.

"On a chain," the aunt insisted with maidenly smile. "I'd be terrified if it were loose. My nerves."

"Nonsense," said Mr. Onions, pouring tea from a silver teapot into fragile flowered cups. "Spots is as tame as a kitten. Wouldn't hurt a fly. You should see me rolling about the floor with him when he pretends to be savage and actually takes my arm in his mouth!"

"Goodness," said the aunt, timidly shrill. "I don't think I would care for that, really."

Mr. Onions said nonsense again, and the mother went off in another small wail of laughter, and the sister thought: Imagine if the panther had jumped on Aunt Eve and rolled on the floor with her, in that hat and everything, and that was probably what the mother was laughing at, tears in her eyes, trying desperately not to. The aunt glanced at her severely, thinking: What on earth! Alice is so particular about other people behaving. Now just because this poor boy's tie is all over the place . . .

The bearer came back and said he could not find the panther anywhere and Mr. Onions said what a pity. "But never mind. You will see him next time you come. He has a way of wandering off but he always comes back."

The bearer cut the sister a piece of chocolate cake and she ate it daintily, wondering whether it would be seemly to ask Mr. Onions whether the panther had ever killed anyone, then deciding that perhaps it would be wiser to say nothing. You never knew when you might be making a mistake, because they never told you until it was too late.

5

*A*t the beginning there was the strangeness of not being in a solid house with four walls, or within the tameness of a garden, and all the stranger because of vague reminders; then these passed and the sister might never have lived elsewhere than in camp, nor did she now want to live anywhere else.

The pointed leaves of mango trees rustled above the white tents, and here it was shadowy, winter sunlight quivering with fine particles of dust and little nameless wings. Everything appeared in a fashion halved; indoors became outdoors, outdoors indoors. Danger matched safety, the near with the far, the tame with the wild. To sit athwart the braided rope threshold of the tent was to have life both ways. She became part of both and of the whole they made together.

Mornings in camp smelled different from mornings elsewhere; they smelled like something newly unwrapped, freshly gazed upon, not yet touched. And in the evening suddenly there was the barking of a fox. The sister saw him, a neat gray figure standing at the edge of a field beyond the mango grove. His sharp three-cornered face was turned toward her and his tail gave him a curious effect of being too heavy for his body. She started toward him but he was gone in a flash, leaving a new kind of silence and a slight smell like the smell in a zoo.

The hoopoe had followed her—she was sure of it. She saw him stepping ceremoniously under the trees, his curved bill searching the dust. He permitted her approach to within a very short distance before flying up into the branches, where she lost him. The brother said resignedly: "That's not the same hoopoe as the one at home. I've counted ten hoopoes since we got here. Won't you ever learn?"

"This one knows me," the sister objected firmly. "He lets me come quite close just as he did at home."

The brother walked disgustedly away to crouch in the shadow of a low mud wall from where he could study the distant jungle and the fields which stretched to its very edge. He had heard the barking of the fox but had not seen it, and this annoyed him. Had *she* really seen it? You could never be sure, with her.

The sister and brother shared a tent with the aunt whose camp cot was set between theirs. On a rickety table behind her pillow the aunt disposed her hair nets, tortoise shell hairpins, her rosary, which had been blessed by the Pope, a bottle of lavender smelling salts—elegant green glass with a crown for a stopper—and a pair of slippers. It was not safe, the aunt explained, to leave one's slippers on the floor because things might crawl into them. And again she reminded them never to let their legs hang over the edge of the bed. *Anything* could be hiding there, ready to grab, or strike, or bite. Sometimes when the aunt was not looking they did it experimentally, tense with delicious, fearful expectation.

In later years the sister tried to recall the number of tents and their order of arrangement, and it seemed to her always to have been the same, although of course the site must have changed year to year. No matter where, though, there was always a grove of trees for shade, a sense of wavering sunlight, a fox barking, and a green jungle standing in the distance. There was the remembered strangeness of knowing that it was not brick and mortar which separated one from the outdoors, only thin cloth against which living things occasionally brushed from outside, pushing the stenciled yellow lining inward.

Every day the guy ropes were tightened and the pegs driven deeper into the ground to keep the canvas taut. The father attended to this, strict about details—about guns being unloaded when not in use, about the measurement of grain for the horses, and about the dogs wearing their little green monogrammed coats when the evening chill set in. He was strict when he caught the sister and brother climbing to the ridgepole of the tent and sliding down to the ground. Tents were not playthings. "Once more and you don't go ghooming on the elephants."

A threat almost as dire as the threat of the razor strop. They adored ghooming, something they did in the late afternoon, perched in a howdah with the mother or the aunt, the mahout erect behind the elephant's neck, his knees tucked guidingly behind its great ears. One's body swayed with the slow gait of the elephant as it plodded across fields turning silver with evening, and along the border of the jungle where immense plumes of silver-tufted grass brushed the elephant's sides, and one could peer into the hearts of trees, in one of which the sister excitedly announced she had seen a python coiled.

"Where?" the brother besought her. "In which tree? Tell me. We'll go back there tomorrow."

But how could she possibly tell him which tree? There were so many, solemn jungle trees, harboring heaven knew what.

Underfoot in the tent was that sensation of straw packed between bare ground and faded blue durries, and small creatures wandered in and out through the open fly; grasshoppers and beetles, bats, moths, even birds. What was to prevent a tiger wandering in some fine day? The aunt had the possibility somewhat on her mind.

"There is nothing to prevent it," the father replied unconcernedly. "If a tiger felt like wandering into your tent, he probably would."

"We should have more chokidars," the aunt declared nervously, and the mother tried to soothe her: "Eve, dear, Doey's joking, and there are no man-eaters in these jungles. You know he would never have brought us and the children if there had been man-eaters."

But the aunt brooded, though she remained outwardly brave. It was at night that the bogeys came sidling and she battened down the tent flies, made sure that a chokidar was within earshot, and left a lantern burning in the adjoining bathroom section. This was furnished with a ramshackle washstand, a battered commode, and a towel rack. The sister and brother had a peculiar tenderness for this wallflower furniture, so out of place in a setting where tigers might appear at any moment.

But nights were magic again, with an increase of delicious dread, of heightened pulses and eyes dilated to take in the outer shadows

60

and nearer uncertainties which by day were humdrum enough—a log of wood, a chair overturned, a servant drowsing under a tree. The sister and brother could not sleep, sometimes, for thinking about the jungle where shadows shaped and melted and distant mountain peaks became a pair of pointed ears, and silence a long-drawn breath waiting to be expelled.

The father and mother's tent stood next to theirs. A little distance away was the Sparkses' tent, then Mr. Onions', who had been persuaded to join them at the last moment but to leave his tame panther at home, because, as the father pointed out, the silly brute would be sure to get shot by mistake.

There was also a local noble, His Highness Nawab Ghulab Hosain, who had lent his elephants for the occasion and who had long angled for an invitation. He had appeared with an entourage, and his tents were pitched discreetly at the farther end of the grove. This spot had instantly become chaos, a kind of midden given over to confusion, stridence, and a penetrating smell of frying ghee. The Nawab himself had arrived gloriously in a purple motorcar with his two wives and eight children, followed less gloriously by servants, baggage, and hangers-on in bullock carts.

"Why," the father fumed, "must the old devil bring his zenana with him? I invited him, not his household."

"I must say I rather like that young second wife," the mother said. "She can't be more than fifteen, poor little thing."

"Poor little thing, balls. She has a voice that will drive the game clean out of the country."

His Highness and family occupied a gigantic durbar tent comprising several rooms, which by day oozed a frayed humanity: women shrouded in burkas, children of all ages, sleazy servants. There was an endless coming and going, unceasing intake of food, and a flock of goats, udders bagged in cloth against their own voracious offspring, which the father suggested would be just the thing for tiger bait.

The Nawab was obese and bland and he exuded geniality and largesse. Possessed of huge wealth in unassessible form, he was, the father remarked, the government's own man down to his last pubic hair. The father fascinated and frightened the Nawab, and the Nawab amused the father. "Old swine. He'd like to get round me.

61

This reorganization of the district must have played hob with his little hopes and habits."

"Considering what you think of him . . ." the mother demurred ethically.

"I shouldn't have invited him? *Huk'm* . . . orders. Oh, not in so many words. Government never puts its cards on the table, you know. But play up to him, Doey, old boy. Borrow his elephants, the loan of his coolies for beaters; invite him for a drink in the evening. That's against his religious principles, but he dearly loves his whiskey peg! He's angling for a decoration—a rai bahadurship, perhaps—but there are still a few odds and ends which the government would like to have taken care of first."

To the mother and the aunt the Nawab deferred with charm. To the sister and brother he extended innocent bribes: toys, and platters of barfi, a creamy white sweet that melted in your mouth, decorated with fine silver tissue which you could eat along with the sweet.

The brother pondered: "I don't see why he should be an old swine."

"It's because he's done horrible things," the sister explained, knowingly. *"Horrible."* It was currently her favorite word and the brother was instantly on guard. "What things?"

"Tortured people."

"He hasn't! How?"

"Sticking red-hot pokers up their bottoms to make them confess."

"You're telling lies." The brother accused her angrily. "You're showing off."

She shrugged, and he burst out: "Confess *what?*"

"Where they've hidden their *diamonds.*"

"You're telling the most awful lies. I've a good mind—"

"It's true. I heard them talking about it."

"It has nothing to do with diamonds. It's about seditionists."

"Diamonds *and* seditionists." The sister yielded the point generously.

The Nawab, far from going down in their estimation, went giddily up. They bustled to accept invitations to tea in the big tent amid a welter of brats and babies and the gliding banshee figures of wives. They stuffed themselves on sweets and puris and peppered gram; they graciously accepted gifts of expensive toys imported from Eng-

62

land. The sister wondered where His Highness stored the red-hot pokers when they were not in use, and the brother speculated on whether the diamonds winking on His Highness's pudgy fingers could possibly be *the* diamonds.

Acceptance of sweets and toys was permitted by the father, but nothing else was. The aunt grieved aloud: "But, Doey, I don't see why not!" His Highness had sent her, by his second wife, an offering of pearl earrings in a ravishing little velvet-lined box but the father had ordered her to return them immediately. She must be polite about it, but firm. The gift was a blatant attempt at bribery—couldn't she see?

"But he didn't offer the earrings to you! It's Christmas and he's trying to be nice."

The father's moustache looked dangerous. "Don't argue. I won't have you or Alice taking presents from him, and that's that."

"You let the children."

"Toys and sweets don't count."

The aunt whined, but the mother was unexpectedly on the father's side. "Doey is right, Eve. One can't be too careful."

And you can't be too careful, she warned the sister and brother when they went riding their ponies. They were not to ride into the jungle without a grown-up; they were not to stay away too long out of sight of the camp. They were not to make the ponies jump hurdles, or to chase wild animals, or to do tricks on horseback.

The father scoffed at this excessive caution. He said coldly that if they did any of these things and anything happened it would be their own fault. He wanted no whining and crying afterward. "I don't," he said, "want a pair of namby-pambies. Remember that."

Sedately one early afternoon the sister and brother trotted out along a narrow path which bounded the field where young mustard was beginning to sprout. The brother took the lead on his chestnut pony, Jack, and the sister followed on the fat and rather stertorous Jill. The brother loved to ride and he had an easy, graceful seat, and could, when no one was watching, take quite difficult jumps, and do tricks, standing on the pony's rump while it cantered, riding at full gallop without a saddle, pretending to fall off then recovering his seat while the sister marveled. Riding thrilled and terrified her, and sometimes, pelting after the brother over flat ground, sensing the ponies' sudden powerful excitement, she wanted to shut her eyes, to allow herself to slip out of the saddle even at risk of hurting herself and to pretend afterward that it had been an accident, not at all her fault. But it took nerve to fall out of a saddle intentionally and she could never quite bring herself to do it.

But their chief objective on these rides was to get out of sight of the camp or house and its disapproving eyes, and to embark on The Game. The brother had invented The Game a year or two before, though opportunities for playing it were not always handy. To begin with one needed a stretch of treeless plain on the distant outskirts of a village where cattle and goats grazed untended, and where one was apt to come on the carcass of one of these which had died of some unrecognizable cause—starvation perhaps, or snakebite, or disease—lying now like a frayed bundle under the unblinking, indifferent sun.

There was almost always a vulture or two feeding on these anonymous remnants. Earlier, invisible in the spacious, white, empty sky, these creatures had circled on majestic wings, their telescopic gaze sifting the scene below. When a cow or buffalo or goat strayed away from the herd and staggered off to die alone, the pinpoint eye in the empyrean sprouted haughty pinions and floated down to earth. There, suddenly become ungainly and utterly hideous, these cannibals hopped and lurched toward their repast and fell upon it with gobblings and gurglings and obscene pecks and thrusts and worryings. Sometimes as many as a dozen vultures would pile on a carcass and then all one could see was a melee of thrashing wings, bald octogenarian heads and flaying beaks. In ten minutes nothing would be left of the dead—or as sometimes happened the not-yet-dead—except a pair of horns, four hoofs, and a cage of ribs.

Frequent interested viewings of these orgies had given the brother his idea for The Game, and at first the sister had flatly refused to play, then allowed herself to be jeered into the spirit of the thing. While the brother hid in some convenient spot with his catapult, the sister was to advance into full view on the plain, giving as convincing a performance as possible of some forlorn creature literally on its last legs. Then she was to collapse, twitch a little, and lie flat and unmoving while the vigilant observers aloft took greedy note. When, duly taken in, the Eyed Appetites circled downward, landed, and began their dreadful ballet dance toward this unexpectedly delectable *côte-*

lette, the brother was suddenly to rise up and have at them with his catapult. Whang whang! And *quelle surprise* for the filthy brutes when they saw their prospective dinner leap to her feet and speed away while a hail of pellets bounced off their horny pates.

The Game was well thought out and well rehearsed, but for some reason it never progressed beyond the preliminaries. For minutes on end the sister would lie huddled in a dehydrated posture of skin and bone, or in a more inviting attitude of recently expired succulence, while the brother lurked scarcely breathing in his hiding place, catapult at the ready. Nothing happened. Not the shadow of a wing, not the echo of a gobble, not a pinpoint gleam of an eye in the empty heavens.

The sister was always thankful when The Game came to its invariably unfruitful end. She had a nightmare dread that one of these days she would feel the harsh sweep of feathers across her face and open her eyes to find one of the creatures poised lovingly above her, and the brother inexplicably not on the job—distracted by some minor phenomenon, or retired to relieve himself somewhere, leaving her to be pecked to death.

But now when they left the mango grove behind them she saw the fields placid under the settling light, innocent of creatures alive or dead, and without a vulture in sight. Her spirit soared, and suddenly the brother laid his quirt across Jack's rump and they were heading for the jungle, dirt and grass flying under the ponies' hoofs, and in a minute the sister knew that Jill was bolting, trying to overtake her stablemate several lengths ahead.

One can't be too careful, the mother had stated meaningfully. Holes in the ground. Rocks. Slippery places. Perhaps a jackal popping out of nowhere, frightening the ponies. A bad shy, a fall; broken legs, scraped knees, tetanus—anything. And it would be the brother's fault. Defiant, proud of himself. Somehow the father would find out and there would be the razor strop and everything spoiled just before Christmas. Why wouldn't the brother learn? For it was all very well for the father to sneer at namby-pambies; he disliked them more when they did the very things no namby-pamby would think of doing.

Teeth clenched, her round white hat hanging by its strap and banging against her back, the sister sat down in the saddle and gave up trying to check her bolting steed. Jill, built like a dining table, put on a tremendous spurt and caught up with Jack. The brother turned his head. His face was shining. "Look," he said. "See them?"

For a moment, her heart sinking, the sister thought he must have spied a vulture, then she followed his pointing quirt and saw what he meant. He must have spied them from a long way off, but suddenly they were quite close; a small herd of antelope, on the alert now, then running, and gathering speed as the ponies took after them. The sister thought: How silly! Black buck are the fastest things in the world and we'll never catch up with them, and just fancy if one of the ponies fell, or if some villager spying us tearing across his fields reported back to the father....

The brother didn't care. Crouched in his saddle and lashing Jack with the quirt, he took after the flying buck, his screams of excitement blown back to the sister as once more the portly Jill lost ground, though, head down, she still bolted loyally in pursuit. The sister thought: Well, at any rate it's better than lying on the ground pretending to be a dead cow. If it isn't one thing it's another.... You can't be too careful.

Well ahead, the buck seemed as if they were entering into the spirit of the game. They slowed, then came up into a group and paused, gazing back at the two pounding ponies and their openmouthed, shouting riders. For the sister was shouting now, all qualms drowned in wild elation. The buck waited, then whirled and sped away again, silvery black and mercurial in a great arc of falling light. They were gone. The ponies halted, sides heaving, sweat like soapsuds churning on their flanks. Jill broke wind long and dolorously, and the brother laughed. "More fun than the vultures," he said, licking the sweat on his upper lip. "We almost caught up with them."

"We didn't," the sister said, always prosaic when he was not. "They're the fastest things in the whole world."

"Except cheetahs."

"And I suppose you think we could catch them!"

"We might," he said. "One day."

He was relaxed, happy. "Get down," he told the sister. "We'd better rest the ponies before going back."

They dismounted and the sister said: "We're not supposed to chase things. If they ever find out!"

66

"I don't give a damn."

"You're swearing again."

"Shit," he said. The sister's respect for him increased by leaps and bounds. "That's a bad word and if they ever heard you!"

The brother snatched a handful of weeds from the field's edge and began to rub his pony's flanks. "You, too," he commanded her. "Clean Jill. We'll walk them home partway and nobody will know."

Obediently she wiped down her drenched and trembling mount. The father had once spoken to them of horses falling dead of a heart attack, and she reminded the brother of this. He said shit again, and she felt that he was going too far, showing off. Rubbing down Jill's withers, she said without looking up: "What's the use of showing off when he's not here to see, and if he did you'd get a jolly good hiding?"

"He wouldn't touch me if I was as big as he is."

She felt the brother's hatred of Doey, and a thickness in her own throat. "You shouldn't," she said in a low voice, "talk like that. He's our father."

"Who art in heaven hallowed be thy name!" He giggled.

She was shocked, but with a renewed pride in his daring. "You better look out, because *He* can hear everything you say."

"He can't if He doesn't even exist."

She dropped the wad of weeds and stared at him in consternation. "He could strike you down dead for saying a thing like that!"

"He might if He existed."

When she was appalledly silent he said: "I don't believe in Him."

She deliberately misunderstood. "He's real, he's our father. You can't say it isn't true."

"I don't mean that one. I mean the one that's supposed to be in heaven. That's the one I mean. And I don't believe in Him."

It was terrible. The sister listened to the ponies cropping nearby, and suddenly, far away in the pale sky, a vulture wheeled on tireless wings. So near heaven, did the hideous bird know whether He existed or whether He did not? Did the tiny bright blue fly buzzing round Jill's head know whether He existed? He who had created heaven and earth, who had created tigers and fleas and the worms which she had seen creeping out of the eye sockets of dead dogs, who had created the fox and the hoopoe—did He know that *they* existed?

The brother was smiling, confident with the smell of hot horse in his nostrils, his blood still warm from that frantic gallop. The camp was invisible, the mango grove a dark blue in the distance, and from a mud-walled village half a mile away came, faintly, the sounds of humanity: voices, vibrations, things unquestioning and unquestionable.

The sister concentrated on these matters and slowly she began to feel better, safer. No harm had been done, no one had been hurt, nothing need be said. Up there in the sky the Person who had invented words understood how silly they could be, and she felt that He was not one to carry tales.

Presently they remounted and rode slowly back as they had come, and there was the mother with the aunt and Mrs. Sparks seated round the tea table under the trees, and the mother said: "Did you have a nice ride, darlings?" And the aunt said: "Goodness, they smell like a stable! Go and wash before you sit down to tea."

Mrs. Sparks said: "The boy's growing up. He seems much older than nine, especially when he smiles."

And the mother, pouring tea, thought: They've been up to something. Hot. Racing, probably, when they know they shouldn't. It seemed to her that they turned to danger naturally as most people turn away from it. The thought made her catch her breath as she watched them emerge from their tent, wearing expressions of impenetrable innocence. How can I protect them? she asked herself desperately. How can I protect them?

The father had a small office tent pitched in a remote corner of the grove, and here he spent most of the day when he was not afield. A police orderly was continuously on duty outside the tent, running errands or shooing away intruders. The orderly was young and his name was Ram Lal, and the brother and sister had been told that a man had once tried to kill Doey, and that Ram Lal had felled the assailant with a blow from his heavy shoe. This made Ram Lal something of an enigma to the brother and sister; he seemed such a weedy youth, afraid of wasps.

A table was set up under the canvas eaves of the tent and here Doey worked on his papers and interviewed callers. His khaki topi rested on the ground beside his chair, smoke from his cigar tinctured the air, and Ram Lal made regular pilgrimages to and from the

68

kitchen, bringing him cups of tea. Villagers from the countryside came in little groups to pay their respects, to bring petitions or complaints. It pleased Doey that they seemed to turn naturally to him rather than to Mr. Onions, who, as district commissioner, was largely responsible for such affairs. The villagers were for the most part tall men dressed in rough white cotton shirts and dhotis; they wore clumsy country shoes with curled up toes and carried massive lathees, and some carried spears. Doey was always happy to see them, greeting them familiarly as father, brother, or son, according to their ages. His entire manner changed when he was with them; he became gentle, jocular, enthusiastic, and the aunt murmured wonderingly to the mother: "Just as if he were one of them."

"These people are the real thing," he informed the aunt and the mother explicitly. "I'd like to see the country go back to them, not to the babus and the contractors, as of course it will."

"But, Doey, these people can't even read or write!"

"They are men," the father said clinchingly. "They are the real thing."

From where he sat in his office tent Doey could see the entire camp spread in a semicircle: the smaller tents of the servants, the cookhouse tent, the makeshift stabling for elephants and horses, and the lean-to shelters where grooms and mahouts slept and cooked their meals. From this spot he could see the mother and the aunt seated under the trees with Mr. Onions and the Sparkses, and the smaller figures of the children. This was Doey's world in microcosm. Beyond it stretched the cloudy generalities upon which his personality could make no impact. The knowledge troubled him, turning him in on himself without humility and without hope. Knowing himself to be exceptional, superior, he still had to defer to lesser men; a skeptic, he was expected to act as a believer. He lacked his wife's naïve trust, his sister's desperate faith, and there were moments when he felt the burden of his own intellect as a kind of curse. Better to be bookish like Onions or an all-round good chap like Sparks, each in his way knuckling under to the imperfection of things—to the hypocrisies, the stupidities.

He sometimes felt that he was being appraised by the infantine minds of his children. And what had he to pass on to them, looking at this moment like mushrooms under their big hats? He frowned, watching them from a distance. Here in this primal setting life was deceptively simple, but what, in the longer, complicated run, could he give them? Certainly not money. He couldn't even earn it in any quantity—just his official pay and a meager pension at the end. Distinction, yes, while the job lasted, while he lasted. But a new world was brewing, in which the children would be obliged to compete in a fashion beyond his present guessing.

They will grow up, he thought. The boy ineffectual, stubborn, self-centered, already prefiguring the lifelong invalid. Probably end up becoming some kind of a piddling Proust or a struggling painter or something of the sort, taking himself seriously, petted by women and amounting to nothing. But the girl, what about her? She had a high spirit and he could not see her long overruled by ordinary events. She would marry, of course. He hoped some upstanding, strong chap, with sufficient cash. The father thought: I would not want her ever to be needy, in straits. He violently would not want her to share his sister's lot, with that bloody awful needlework and wallowing in dreams of an unfructified bed.

Odd how little a man could do for his own children! Plan, of course. Try to set aside a little money. Nurture ambition, illusion. Give them as much education as he could afford. Next year the boy would go to school in England, and they would have to think of something for the girl. The mother and aunt favored a convent school in the hills where at least she would be in a healthy climate for part of the year, and perhaps absorb a few essentials—history, geography, math. Neither of them, he knew, was endued with aptitudes that came naturally to him. And they would leave a hole when they were gone. The mother lived in dread of the coming separation, but that doting was bad for them, and for her.

There remained, for the moment, the simple present. If they are lucky, the father had told the sister and brother, they might hear a tiger roaring as it roamed the jungle. It was not given to many to hear a tiger roar in its natural habitat. Think of all the poor dowdy children all over the world, with their unimaginative ready-made playthings, who never had a chance to hear a tiger roar, much less see one.

The sister and brother tried to think of distant unknown children for some reason wearing clothes too big for them or too small, with runny noses, and clutching matted-looking teddy bears. There were

70

those cousins in London with whom they had once spent a dismal summer in the house of an old lady, their grandmother. The cousins were girls—shy, pale, and timid—and the sister and brother had lorded it over them, boasting. The cousins had never set eyes on a real tent or a real gun, and they were appalled when the brother lay on his stomach on the drawing room floor with his air rifle and took potshots at the little bird which intermittently popped out of a cuckoo clock on the wall.

Now in the camp nights passed, and they yearned for the sound of a tiger roaring. It was, the father had warned them, rather a rare occurrence; the tiger had to be angry or be trying to drive off a rival or intruder. Usually it made quite untigerlike noises, sometimes even imitating the call of the sambar deer. "But you wait," the father adjured them. "You'll hear it roar, all right, and no mistake about it."

He himself was waiting for khabbar—news—of a tiger; then he would go out and hunt it, and suddenly he turned to the brother and said casually: "Would you care to come along?"

The brother choked with happiness, and suddenly there was Christmas pouring into their veins, a dazzlement, a prospect like no other the year round. There were the unopened packages discovered hidden in the father and mother's tent; some in brown paper and string with English stamps, just as they had arrived from England. Others were loosely wrapped, awaiting a more careful disguise in labels and ribbons. The hoard had been privily investigated by the brother and sister, bumps and angles speculatively fingered, commented on. The sister suffered from an unconfessed sense of uncertainty, not sure whether she wanted the things to be unwrapped or not. They were deliciously exciting in their mystery.

The brother said offhandedly: "Guess what? I've made a book."

It was constructed of small squares of notepaper cut and trimmed, ingeniously bound, and filled with drawings copied from his history book. There were smaller versions of the Mutiny pictures and the babies impaled on bayonets.

The sister sighed in admiration. "I wish I could draw like you!"

"Everyone can't, of course. But you haven't noticed, have you? Look again."

She pored over the drawings and gave a shriek of discovery. He had provided the babies with sex, unlike the originals in the history

71

book, and the recognition brought on fits of laughter, tears streaming.

In his office tent the father covered sheets of foolscap in his small intricate handwriting. He smiled faintly as he worked and occasionally paused to stroke his moustache, his glance lingering with a kind of secondary alertness on the small occurrences around him. Then he leaned back in his chair, feet planted on the table, ankles crossed, and in a leisurely fashion read what he had written. He picked up his pen and drew a line through the word "respectfully" and tossed the paper on the table. It would do. And tomorrow was Christmas Eve and the villagers had promised him khabbar by tonight. He would take the boy; it was time he was introduced to the manly sport, to the companionship of men, and the proximity of risk. Something for him to remember, at any rate. Who dared bet that fifty years from now these jungles would still stand and tigers roam at will?

The sister made her way deviously toward the elephant lines. There were three elephants chained by their hind legs to trees, amid a litter of straw and dung. Proximity to the elephants always made her breathless. They seemed never to be still but swayed from side to side as if to some unheard rhythm. Their trunks stretched, reaching and inquisitive, with that sensitive finial from which they derived their native name, *hath*—hand. The sister had been told that these lofty beings disliked small creatures—children, puppies, mice—and she had heard the mother tell the aunt that they did not care for the smell of pregnant women. To the sister the elephants seemed altogether impressive, knowledgeable, and complex, as her gaze traversed the panorama of humped backs ridged like mountains. It struck her as somehow pathetic that they should have real eyelashes, and the female her boobies up in front and only two, like the mother's and the aunt's.

The elephants blew through their trunks and mumbled in their throats, and when excited they squealed like girls. In moods of affection they caressed one another with their trunks or leaned battering-ram foreheads against each other, fatuously benign.

The sister never tired of them. Whenever she visited them she went alone, unwilling to be distracted by silly commentaries, or to hear them being in any way belittled or ridiculed. It was a personal relationship and one she did not care to share even with the brother. Carefully lowering herself to the ground, she lay flat on her back and tilted her head so she saw them over her own forehead. This for some reason made them more interesting; their gaze seemed to sink directly into hers; she felt a tentative, rubbery touch on her hair, and had a vivid glimpse of two pinkish-black cavities which were, astonishingly, thumb and nostril in one. She drew the sour exhalation into her body as the tip of a trunk caressed her hair, flipped across her face, and blew into her ear. Then it discovered a morsel of sugarcane and transported this languidly to a soft, silly, fetal mouth. They made no move to hurt her; they seemed not at all to mind her presence so close to them, and once, reaching out her hand, she touched a great half moon of a toenail and made a wish.

At night the servants lighted the bonfire already laid in the semicircle of tents, and the flames made a ceiling of light against the leaves. The sister and brother, lying on their beds, faces cupped in their hands, studied the group seated around the fire. After dinner Nizamat threw more wood on the fire; His Highness the Nawab emerged from his tent, formal in a tightly wound cloth-of-gold turban, black jacket, and snow-white pantaloons, making everyone else look drab as sparrows. He took a seat between the mother and father, and accepted a glass which Nizamat tendered on a silver tray. Firelight illumined hands and faces; it seemed to fix the moment, as in a charade.

Nizamat brought the mother her mandolin, and Mr. Onions and Mr. Sparks sang Christmas carols in which everyone joined except the Nawab, though not all were sure of the words. Then Mr. Onions sang "Good King Wenceslaus" all by himself in a sudden, surprisingly deep voice which brought tears to the aunt's big black eyes. The father said: "Let's have something cheerful for a change."

He sang, and Mrs. Sparks attempted what she called "seconds," whereupon the father broke off abruptly in the middle of a verse and said: "You might at least let me finish, I should think!"

"I was only singing seconds!"

"Well, it puts me off," the father snapped while the mother plucked tactfully on the strings and Mr. Sparks and Mr. Onions lighted their pipes and the Nawab experimentally sipped his drink.

The father was cajoled into resuming his song:

"I sang to myself and my old black mare,
As I rode through the woodland shady,
'Hurry on, hurry on, the day will be gone,
I ride to the feet of my lady.' "

It presently became unavoidably Mrs. Sparks' turn to sing. The father folded his arms and stared ungraciously into the fire, and the sister and brother writhed in anticipation. Mrs. Sparks' voice always induced a diuretic effect upon them, but they would not have missed it for the world. She now burst ringingly into her favorite:

"Down in de canefield, hear dat mournful sound!
All dem darkies am a-weepin',
Massa's in de cold, cold ground."

The Indian evening came to an end with these lunatic incongruities mounting to the stars; then everyone went to bed. Was it at this Christmas camp or another that the brother and sister first heard the tiger roar? Memory is never still; it strives and pauses, in light and darkness, recreating itself on its own ruins. But there was always a mango grove, fields quivering in winter light. There was always the jungle, inviting and withholding, the restless change of feet, snorts, unaccountable animal frivolities in the night-smelling dark, always the hoopoe leaving its delicate imprint in the dust.

The embers of the fire had fallen in, and the chokidars, assured that their masters slept, wrapped their heads in their dirty scarves and slept likewise.

The aunt awakened to hear the tiger's roaring. The sound filled her ears, her chest, her veins, her brain. It crashed against the sky and cracked open the earth. It brought her stiffly upright in bed, her lips turned to stones. The lantern in the bathroom had burned low and the big tent seemed to be softly afire in a diminished glow. The children's beds were empty and the loosened fly of the tent fluttered in a suggestion of air. The roaring was quite close, just beyond the frail membrane of canvas, in a predawn blackness. And the children were gone.

As every dog in the encampment, every elephant and every horse now unleashed a concerted din, the aunt, aerated by fear, leaped from her bed and, scarcely touching the ground with her bare feet, floated into the father and mother's tent and cast herself upon them

74

in suffocating incoherence and streaming hair.

"For the love of God!" cried the father. He hurled the aunt aside and he and the mother rushed out into the pandemonium where smoky lanterns bobbed in the darkness.

The tiger's roaring died away as if exhausted by its own fearful energies, and from the edge of the grove the sister and brother, wraiths in their white nightclothes, crept stealthily toward their tent. Doey barred their way. He stared down at their two pallid faces, and the thought crossed his mind that this was how they were compelled to view the universe—only by craning upward, always upward, toward omniscience.

"Perhaps," he said slowly, "you will be good enough to tell us just exactly what you think you're doing?"

The brother began: "We. I. We."

Had the tiger really passed them so close that the sister could have touched it? She swore it had, but he knew that he would never be sure. Now she addressed herself to the father in the pedantic tone she reserved for such emergencies:

"You see, you told us we might hear the tiger, and then we did hear it, and it seemed so close we thought that if we went out very quietly we might get a chance to see it."

She listened to the delirium still raging among elephants, horses, dogs, with an obbligato from the Nawab's quarters. It was impressive and it quite enthralled her. She felt it to be entirely proper and fitting to this Christmas Eve when she was seven years old, and the brother nine.

6

The Harper family lived in a great anthill of a house a short distance from the Meadowses. The Harper boys were dark-skinned and noisy, and given to riding furiously everywhere on their bicycles, bells shrilling, shouting swear words at the bullock cart drivers and at people walking harmlessly along the road. The brother and sister found them quite fascinating, but only at a rather timid distance.

The father had said to the mother: "I would rather the Harper boys didn't come over here to play with ours."

The mother replied soothingly that there was not much chance of it since the Harper boys were all so much older. "Although, if they should want to, I don't see we—"

"I don't like them," the father interrupted decisively. "Especially that oldest boy, What's-His-Name."

Afterward the mother murmured uneasily to the aunt: "One can't go hurting people's feelings."

The aunt backed up the father. "My dear, we can't be too careful, with a little girl growing up. And that oldest Harper boy has rape written all over him."

Rape. The sister pondered the word and decided to put off making inquiries of the brother. He was becoming daily more overbearing because next year he was going to school in England, and she merely to the hills, to a convent for girls. It was a prospect from which she shrank as she shrank from few things. That, and the thought of the brother leaving them for what he described as "years on end."

"I will not," proclaimed Doey, "have any sniveling!"

The sister felt better during the daytime, thinking that perhaps none of these things would come to pass after all. Things such as those German swine threatening France, the father being transferred to some hellhole, and the aunt being reduced to earning her bread by the sweat of her brow. These were in the category of bad dreams. Words were never really made flesh. The brother would still be with them next year, and something was bound to happen to prevent her being banished to the convent for girls, where the climate was Himalayan and she would learn prayers and needlework from the kindly nuns, and how to be a little lady.

"It's about time," the aunt declared, with enthusiasm. "All this romping about scratching your knees and being rowdy. People have to grow up, you know."

People had to grow up. They could not be too careful, especially of huge noisy boys with rape written all over them.

One morning Miss Meadows came bicycling up the drive in tears of grief to inquire whether anyone had seen Barley, the frog. "He was safely in the rockery last night when we went to bed. We heard him croaking. Now we can't find him anywhere."

She had already called on the Harpers. Vociferous and unanimous, they had not seen Barley. Abdullah had not seen him, nor had the gardener, nor anyone of whom Miss Meadows tearfully inquired. It was terrible. Barley was only a frog and who would be apt to guess that he belonged to anyone in particular? Miss Meadows wept aloud, remembering her pet's unwinking, innocent gaze, and his pale, delicate hands and feet. How quick he was to catch flies, how sweet the way he hopped about the veranda after her, or crouched among the coleus!

The aunt attempted comfort: "One thing, he was too big to have been swallowed by a bird."

"There are snakes," the brother tactlessly suggested. "A cobra could have bitten him and he could have gone off somewhere and died."

The aunt and Miss Meadows screamed in unison and the sister whispered fiercely: "Do you have to make it worse?"

Miss Meadows pedaled disconsolately away, and later word reached them that Barley had been found. Flattened, brittle, dry, a mere diagram of his former self. He was discovered by What's-His-Name Harper in the Harpers' driveway, where he must have hopped on some mysterious errand of his own, and it seemed as if he must have been run over by a succession of bicycles and rendered so unrecognizable that no one noticed.

The Harpers were very sorry and Mrs. Harper shed real tears. She was a kindly lady, bullied by her husband and sons, and spent most of her time in the kitchen cooking, or in a broken-down rocking chair on the veranda, fanning herself with a little palm leaf fan. Doey had once remarked that the poor bitch knew more about her sons than she dared let on. She was afraid of them, and no doubt they would drive her into an early grave.

Mr. Harper was much younger than his wife, fair while she was dark, and he always dressed dashingly in riding breeches and jodhpurs, and a sombrero which he had sent for from America. He greatly admired Buffalo Bill Cody and even rode his bicycle as though it were a bucking bronco. This greatly amused Doey, who remarked to the mother: "I bet Buffalo Bill never swindled his government the way Harper does!"

"We don't really know, do we?" the mother objected, hating injustice.

"No one ever really knows anything," the father said. "But one can suspect. All those expensive bicycles, the house in the Hills, the fancy clothes. And he's talking about buying a motorcar. On a railway contractor's income?"

In addition to everything else, the Harpers owned a flock of prize-winning geese of ferocious disposition, and What's-His-Name Harper let it be noised abroad that it could just possibly have been the geese which killed poor Barley. Only for God's sake, said What's-His-Name, don't tell the Meadowses. Edna'd have a fit.

But Miss Meadows heard the story somehow, and after that the

Meadowses and the Harpers were never again on what the aunt called "speaking terms."

The father had his doubts about the geese killing Barley the frog. He wouldn't, he said, take What's-His-Name Harper's word for anything. What's-His-Name was a bad lot. They were all bad lots in that family except for poor doormat Mrs. H. "And I saw What's-His-Name throwing stones at Peggy. He denied it to my face, the dirty little liar."

The brother and sister always felt somewhat wistful about the Harpers and would secretly have liked to know them better. They lived in a state of fabulous disorder, amid an uproar of geese, hens, guinea fowl, unidentifiable dogs, pregnant cats, bicycle bells, and ferocious interfamily rows. They were given to shooting off firearms at any time of day or night, and it was as much as one's life was worth, the father declared, to wander into the Harper compound unannounced.

It was shortly after the death of poor Barley the frog that the sister set forth on one of her favorite excursions, a walk to the ruined temple beyond the farther boundary of the compound, a spot where she could see a great sweep of uninhabited plain and the tiled roofs of a village in the distance. Fearful lest the brother decide that this was an ideal setting for The Game, she had kept these excursions to herself and ventured forth only when she was sure he was otherwise occupied.

First, she took the father's binoculars from their place in his bedroom. This was forbidden and she did it tremblingly, yet elated by her own daring. The next move was to leave the house without being observed. Always those questions: Where was she going? What was she doing? Why?

With the binoculars dangling heavily round her neck, a pistol at her belt (no pistol actually, merely an invented one), she crept out of the house into the long yellow light of the afternoon. It must, she was to decide later, have been toward the end of February. There was a scent of fading flowers, a breath of future heat, and the brain-fever bird had begun its preliminary tonk-tonk high up in the trees. Soon, she knew, it would be burning summer and the world turned white hot and inert. Then life withdrew from the glare, and suddenly four walls spelled a fresh intimacy. The sister felt this impending change and it excited her and made her restless.

Conscious of her solitariness, always half fearful of it and half enchanted, she sidled past the lantanas and the banana trees, past the
well where the gardener's bullocks were drawing water for the
lawns, and on to the mango grove at the bottom of the garden. At
once it reminded her of Christmas camp—when? Last year? The year
before? Time didn't matter. Only the event remained, stirred a sleeping ecstasy. Anything could happen, any hidden presence spring into
life. A tiger come prowling, an elephant charge squealing out of
nowhere, trees shake with enormous suggestion.

What, she asked herself years afterward, was it that made such
moments always familiar yet with this aura of discovery? There was
nothing especially arresting in the scene with its flat green fields and
the brown plain beyond, a sky the color of egg white, and a narrow
cart track winding dustily toward the Meadowses' house and beyond
that to the Harpers', both invisible behind identical thickets of shrubs
and trees.

Perhaps it was due to the density of the trees at her back, cutting
her off from disciplined realities; perhaps it was a heightening of her
sense of isolation, the boundaries of her own flesh, such as she never
felt when the brother was with her or the father or the mother or the
aunt, which now brought her to a halt with a catching of breath, a
tingling in her palms and the soles of her feet.

Beside the cart track stood the ruined temple. Little remained
except two broken walls forming an angle, an arched entrance, standing free. The walls threw a shadow—all that they had to offer against
the void. Large, handsome grasshoppers fed on the milkwood bushes,
and she had seen a scorpion sunning itself on the warm stones. Bits
of fallen plaster still held traces of faded color and even a touch of
gilt. The sister liked to stand on the inner side of the arch and gaze
through it at the vista beyond, seeing it thus framed. Long afterward,
grown, the brother and the father dead, the aunt vanished, the
mother old and groping, the sister would without warning find herself once more within this moment, gazing through the arch at fields
and plain lidded with strands of blue smoke from the distant village,
the whirring sound of grasshopper wings in her ears and a smell of
sunlit dust rising from the ground.

With dismay now she heard the ting of a bicycle bell and there was

What's-His-Name Harper riding down the cart track toward her. His khaki shorts were smartly starched and flaring, his stockings turned neatly down below the knees, and his bare head glistening like patent leather in the sloping light. Reaching the arch where she stood, he flung one muscular leg in a lordly sweep over the rear wheel as he dismounted and propped the bicycle against the arch. He smiled at the sister, his teeth very white and even.

"Hullo," he said. "What are you doing here?"

She replied with hauteur: "Nothing. I often come here."

"I know. I've seen you."

It made her nervous, but she turned her plain little face toward him and her eyes were hard. "It belongs to my father," she said. "This place."

"Rot!" He laughed. "Your father's only stationed here. All this"—he waved a hand—"belongs to my dad. He bought it."

She captured, to perfection, Doey's raised brows. "On what—his contractor's income?"

What's-His-Name's smile vanished. He seemed immensely tall, broad-shouldered, cruel. A full brown throat showed in the opening of his khaki shirt, the black hair grew low on his forehead, and his lips were red and rather puffy, reminding her of Nizamat's. Ten-annas-in-the-rupee, the aunt had once said of the Harpers. And the mother had said: "It's not their fault, after all."

The sister stood her ground as What's-His-Name towered over her.

"What did you just say?" he asked, dangerous.

"Nothing."

"Well, you better not say it again." He reached over and attempted to take the binoculars from her neck. She pulled away, clutching the strap, her eyes never leaving his face. "You can't," she told him. "They belong to my father."

"Oh, all right. Just wanted to have a dekko, that's all. What strength are they, do you know?"

She replied loftily: "Oh, they're very strong. You could drop them and they wouldn't break."

He giggled. "Little idiot. You don't even know what I mean."

He planted himself before her, staring down at her from his superior height. She thought suddenly, agonizedly, of the brother, of his pallor, his wiry refinement. He was fearless but this great boy could

81

have knocked him silly with one slap of that shapely brown hand.

He glanced disdainfully round him, at the rubble. "My dad's going to pull this thing down. It's an eyesore, he says."

"Why? It's not doing any harm."

He giggled again, looking down at her. "Rum kid you are. Where's little Spindly?"

"I don't know what you mean." But she did and her cheeks burned.

"Your brother. I thought he might be here. I was going to give him a damn good hiding."

"What for?" Her heart blazed protectively, in terror.

"Going about telling lies. Telling old Edna Meadows that I killed that silly frog of hers."

"He didn't."

"I happen to know he did because Edna told me so herself. Bloody little sneak."

Breathlessly she said what she truly believed: "He'd have told me first!"

"I'm going to bloody well break his neck."

Afraid yet not afraid, she stared at him. "You're nothing but a coward. You'd run like lightning from anyone as big as yourself."

The color rose in his brown cheeks. "Little bugger's gone round telling everyone I ran over the silly frog on purpose, he has."

Rage ignited her. "Wait till my father hears what you said."

"I'm not afraid of your father."

She saw this at once, saw with bleak clarity the degree of her own defenselessness. "You're a coward," she repeated. "A born coward. I'm going home now. Good-bye."

"Oh, no you don't!"

He held her, his strong hand on her wrist. "Running away, eh? Insulting my father, insulting me, then running away?"

She tried to pull free but it was as if she were harnessed to a mountain. She had never wept from fear; now she did, slow tears welling, sliding down her cheeks.

"Crybaby," he jeered. "What's the matter?"

She managed a kind of steadiness. "If my father knew, he'd kill you."

"Knew what?" He seemed less boy now than man, more than man,

82

for no man had frightened her like this. He said: "This happens to be my dad's property, and you're trespassing. You could be fined for it and thrown in jail."

She believed him and the tears fell faster, silently. After a moment she said that if he would let her go now she would never come back. She would not tell anyone she had even seen him. He laughed. "Think I mind whether you do or not?" He pulled her toward him. "You're pretty in a way, like a little rabbit. Are you like that all over? Undressed?"

Where did it come from, this overwhelming shame, this terror she had not dreamed existed? His grip was hurting her as she kept up the strain of trying to pull away. Suddenly he let her go and she staggered, then as she regained her balance and started away from him he again barred her path. His face was strange. Everything about him was strange. He had unbuttoned his shorts and his flesh stood erect before her. But he did not try to detain her. She ran, the binoculars swinging like lead from their strap round her neck. Then she was in the mango grove. Swift on her sandaled feet she sped across the garden and reached the house. No one saw her. She was dimly aware of voices, of familiar endearing sounds from the aunt's room, and from the veranda the whirring noise of Mohommed Ali's machine. She was safe, but she did not pause until she reached the father and mother's bedroom. It was empty, and it smelled of their clean, eternal bodies.

The sister returned the binoculars carefully to their hook behind a door, then seated herself on the edge of the big bed and folded her hands on her lap in an attitude she had copied faithfully from the mother, and which at this moment she found extraordinarily soothing. As fear subsided she regained her breath and steadied her shaking heart. That awful boy. And how peculiar that thing. Could it be that What's-His-Name Harper was *deformed?*

She heard the father whistling as he crossed the drawing room. Then he pushed aside the curtains in the door and came into the bedroom, looking hot from a bicycle ride from wherever he had been, and the sister suffered a momentary relapse into terror. Suppose he somehow found out about her being with What's-His-Name Harper out there in the old temple. She had no doubt whatever that Doey would rush immediately to the Harpers' house and kill What's-His-

Name. Then he would be sent to jail and hanged. It would be the end.

He glanced at her suspiciously. "What are you doing frowsting in here?"

She explained in her most formal voice that she was merely taking a little rest.

"Well, run along."

The brother was waiting for her on the veranda steps. "I've been looking for you everywhere!" He had a worried, intense expression. "That oldest Harper chap has been riding his bike up and down the road outside the gate. Nizamat says that he—What's-His-Name—thinks I told Miss Meadows that he killed Barley."

The sister eyed him bitterly. "Did you tell Miss Meadows?"

"Nizamat told me he'd seen What's-His-Name run over Barley, but he was afraid to go and tell the Meadowses himself, so when Miss Meadows asked me ... Now What's-His-Name says that if he catches me he's going to break every bone in my body." The brother finished in a shuddering whisper: "He's bigger than me. I couldn't do anything."

They stood in a trance of apprehension. It never occurred to either that they might turn for succor to the father or the mother or the aunt. Out on the dusty road beyond the gates at the far end of the lawn a bicycle bell tinkled. Most mundane of sounds, one they heard every day of their lives, indispensable and trite. But now full of menace. And the formidable image of the rider, afraid of no one. He loomed in their lives, dwarfing other terrors, other dreams.

The father went frequently to call on Mr. Onions to discuss official affairs and to drink a whiskey peg with him afterward in the pleasant drawing room which had always the gentle, old-fashioned smell of England. The sister was occasionally invited to accompany the father. They usually forgot about her as she sat modestly sipping the lemonade which Mr. Onions ordered for her.

She rarely saw Spots the panther, because he had become what Mr. Onions described regretfully as "unpredictable," so had to be chained up most of the time. He had frightened the bobbery horse, which had bolted, fallen into a ditch, and broken a leg, and so had to be shot. That was bad enough, but Spots had also clawed the gardener's son and had taken to stalking the other servants, completely unnerving them. It was a serious problem and the father had promised to try to think of some solution. "I won't," Mr. Onions had declared forcefully, "allow Spots to be shot, Doey, so there's no use your suggesting it."

They had turned to other matters, less interesting to the sister, though she listened with polite and pointed detachment. The father, leaning back in a long cane chair with his legs stretched on the arms, said one day: "I realize that it is not my business nor yours, Onions, but the fact remains that old Harper is not honest. You can't, you know, on a contractor's income, live on the scale he does. He's just bought a hotel in Naini. Must have cost thousands."

Mr. Onions replied, shrugging. "Not in my department."

"But government should ask a few questions. He's taking it out of government, don't forget. Mind you, I don't think he's a bad chap otherwise, and I like the missus, though I can't stand the brats. And it must cost something to support that tribe."

"You've got enough to worry about in your own job, Doey, old boy," Mr. Onions reminded him. And then: "I'm going to miss you, you know. Not many people here I feel I can talk to."

"Well, it's promotion, of course," the father said without elation. "More pay, and with the boy going Home to school and the girl to the Hills . . . expensive."

Mr. Onions nodded, perhaps thinking how strange it must be not to have private means. Energy, pluck, *verve*—yes. But what happens to one's wife and children, not to mention penniless sisters, if dysentery or enteric, or a dacoit's bullet, carries one off? And such a stickler for honesty as Doey was, morbid really.

"I hate to leave this district," the father said suddenly. "Alice and Eve love it. So do the children. And I feel there is so much more I could do."

"You've done all you can, and they won't let you do any more." Mr. Onions laughed. "They're afraid you'd go too far. You never do seem to know when to stop once you start, you know!"

The father smiled, pleased. "But look here, Onions." He swung his legs off the chair arms and rested his elbows on his knees. The sister was always to remember that posture—the total engagement, the intensity. "Why can't they see what's coming? I can, you can. Do they imagine that men like Charan and the rest are going to wait forever?

85

Even if such men were resigned, their sons wouldn't be!"

Mr. Onions looked thoughtful. "To be honest, I don't look forward to what's coming. I love the damned country. Hate to see it go downhill."

"Downhill or uphill, it isn't ours," the father stated, coming back as he always did doggedly to the crux.

Mr. Onions shook his head. "Perhaps not. But how can you be so sure that it is theirs—the Charans, the Gandhis? It's like trying to assign ownership to all the bits and pieces in a patchwork quilt."

"My dear chap, you've been out here too long!" The father was on the verge of a quarrel, but Mr. Onions was not having any. He smiled a rare, affectionate sort of smile.

"My dear old boy, so have you. Even longer than I. But it is not a question of *divide et impera* as your pals try to make out. Division exists. Always has. We'd be blind fools if we didn't try to exploit it."

"Clichés," the father snapped incomprehensibly, while the sister gazed earnestly into her glass at the caked sugar at the bottom.

"The trouble with clichés, Doey, old chap, is that they are usually based on truth. As for Charan and company, their own numbers will defeat them in the end."

"Numbers?"

"The simple fact of fornication, dear boy. Two and two making four ad infinitum." Mr. Onions glanced at the sister. "Dear me. I keep forgetting little pitchers."

The sister felt a jarring of the ground under her feet. The foreverness tilted, shaking her as when she had watched the moon fall into the earth. Holding her empty glass and trying not to look too long-eared, she struggled to recapture the sense of wholeness. The brother would not after all go away to school in England nor she to that convent in the Hills; Miss Meadows' frog was not really dead but hopping about happily somewhere, catching flies; What's-His-Name Harper had intended no harm. The moon would rise again, and next Christmas they would all go to camp as usual and there would be that smell of sunlight on canvas, and a fox barking, and the jungle standing imperishably in the distance, and the voice of a tiger would celebrate the arrival of the infant Jesus, who in no way resembled the babies skewered in the Mutiny nor Mrs. Sparks' flatulent little James.

The father and Mr. Onions were talking about Spots the panther, for the father had arrived, at last, at a satisfactory solution to the problem. Spots would be shipped away to the Calcutta zoo. "I know the chap in charge," Doey assured Mr. Onions. "They'll be good to the beast. Lucky to get him actually. He seems in fine condition."

Later, the problem shifted on how to cage Spots. Chained by the neck to a post in a shady part of Mr. Onions' garden, the panther seemed to divine that something unpleasant was in store, and would permit no one to approach. Even Mr. Onions hesitated. "Funny, all of a sudden. He's always been perfectly friendly with me, though of course the poor brute doesn't realize his own strength. Latest thing, he bit the sweeper in fun and the blighter's still in hospital."

Unquestionably, the time had come. "A net," the father advised. "Good one-inch hemp he can't bite through. Small mesh on account of his damned claws. Then ask Sanyal to give him a dose of some narcotic by hypodermic, and there you are."

It was to be an occasion, and Mr. Onions invited people for tea. The father and mother, the aunt, the brother and sister, with Mr. and Mrs. Sparks and Dr. Sanyal.

"Cheer me up to have a tea party," Mr. Onions said sorrowfully. "I've become so fond of him. A lovely pet really, until recently."

"You can't make pets out of wild things," the father laid down. "Least of all with the big cats. They're bound to turn on you sooner or later."

Shudderingly, the aunt remembered the tame bear which had turned on a distant cousin and had taken off an entire leg. And there was that story of Kipling's, "Bertran and Bimi," where the orangutan killed the lovely young wife out of jealousy. And another story which His Highness the Nawab had told them at Christmas camp, of a friend of his who had been partially ingested by a python. It had been quite a job to extricate the friend even after the python had been cut in half to facilitate rescue. No, it was best that Spots be shipped off in a cage to the Calcutta zoo, where he would be well taken care of.

On the appointed afternoon Dr. Sanyal arrived at Mr. Onions' house by bicycle, his medical satchel strapped to the carrier behind him. Spots, already secured in the net, lay helpless and glowering under the trees. There was an air of jubilation, expectation, tension.

Tea in Mr. Onions' drawing room, with the silver teapot and the delicate cups brought from England; hot scones and sponge cake, and the mother's tranquil gaze. The aunt all sympathy for Mr. Onions at the impending loss of his pet, her own relief shining in her black eyes. "You must get something to take his place, dear Mr. Onions. A young antelope. A baby monkey perhaps."

"A young wife," the father suggested, faintly ironic. "Something that can be depended on not to bite the servants, at any rate!"

Dr. Sanyal, flattered to be entrusted with so onerous a task, but nervous, drank four cups of tea heavily sugared, and perspired freely. He and the father and Mr. Onions had computed the amount of narcotic to be administered the panther: roughly three times the dose normally given a man weighing, say, two hundred pounds. But was Mr. Onions perfectly sure that the animal was securely bagged? No danger of a reaching paw, rending tooth? Mr. Onions was quite sure. Dr. Sanyal could see for himself. The poor beast was helpless in a cocoon of heavy netting; only his eyes moved, and the pink cavern of his mouth opened in a frightful snarl.

"Oh, my good God," exlaimed Dr. Sanyal. "You are indubitably certain, sir, he cannot escape?"

"My dear Sanyal," said Mr. Onions crossly, "how could he possibly?"

"Yes yes yes," Dr. Sanyal assented. "Now let me see. In the buttock, I think. But where is the animal's buttock? Tail is in the way."

Mr. and Mrs. Sparks were late arriving, and Mr. Onions was anxious to get the operation finished. The aunt preferred to remain quietly in the drawing room, leafing through a photograph album. Nothing would have induced her to witness the operation outdoors.

"Where *are* the Sparkses?" Doey wanted to know. He feared that Dr. Sanyal might quail at the last moment. "Come on, Onions. No point in waiting. Let's get it finished."

Mr. Onions' servants gathered in an excited bunch on the veranda steps, and the mother held the sister and brother at a little distance, whence they had a fairly good view of the proceedings.

Dr. Sanyal, bathed in perspiration, handed his topi to a servant and, hypodermic in hand, advanced upon the motionless bundle of sleekly mottled fur and stout hempen rope.

"Give him the entire dose," Doey advised. "No sense in half measures."

"Yes yes yes, isn't it," groaned Dr. Sanyal.

Mr. Onions knelt beside his pet and murmured apologetic endearments. The creature spat at him, then emitted a roar which brought the aunt agitatedly to her feet. The mother was beginning to founder in her habitual witless mirth, and Dr. Sanyal gazed beseechingly at the father.

"Please direct me to the correct buttock, sir. It is most difficult to discern."

The father crouched beside Dr. Sanyal. "There, that looks like the right place. Hope your needle's sharp, Doctor Sahib. There's a lot of muscle in that backside."

Dr. Sanyal sighted along the hypodermic as though it were a harquebus, and jabbed the needle unerringly into the panther's left testicle.

Mr. and Mrs. Sparks, pedaling their bicycles in leisurely fashion up the driveway toward the house, suddenly spied, rolling rapidly toward them, a spitting, screaming bundle from which only a long black tail escaped, convulsive as a serpent. Springing from their bicycles, the Sparkses made for the trees as the object careened past them and fetched up at last in a drainage ditch beside the gate.

7

*P*atrice Verrier. She had never given her name any particular thought, nor that of the brother, who was called Clement. It had always been sister and brother, father, mother, and aunt. Part of one another, part of the whole. Even when they addressed one another, as of course they did continuously, it was the relationship that counted. Names separated people; being with them, thinking about them, one forgot the name. There was no apartness then, there was the whole.

But now the whole had collapsed and here she was encased in her name, between these cold school walls with mountain mist hanging like dirty rags among black, alien trees. No mangoes here, no hoopoes. Mountain sounds to which she would have to become accustomed. The singsong of Pahari voices on the winding road behind the classroom. Mule bells; a lonely bird which cried somewhere, at regular intervals: "Come!" A bird she had never heard before, which she could never trace. "Come!" it invited her, forbiddingly. Come where? Go where? The bird did not explain.

Bells. Bells to waken you in the early morning in the long dormitory with three rows of beds down its length; a row of cubicles at the end, for the senior girls, and behind the cubicles the ghastly washrooms and w.c.s smelling of urine and disinfectant. Bells. After waking up and washing in a brown tin washbasin in cold water, trying numbly to hold the hard lump of yellow soap, more bells warning that it was time to pray. Our Father and Hail Mary, but thinking about breakfast instead.

"Patrice Verrier, are you praying?"

"Yes, Sister."

Sister Teresa, with small blue eyes in a long narrow face, and shreds of red hair peeping from under the starched white headdress. And a special technique with the ruler when one misbehaved in class.

"Did no one teach you the Hail Mary?"

"Yes, Sister."

But strangely, no one ever had. Doey she was sure never said prayers; the mother had taught her and the brother the Lord's Prayer. The aunt had been more ambitious but no more successful. "It goes in one ear and out the other," she complained, and more or less gave up.

"What sort of a family?" Sister Teresa wondered. "You are a pucka little jungli, child!"

The other girls laughed sycophantically, but had any of them heard a tiger roar, or slept in a tent, or chased antelope on horseback?

Bells for early morning breakfast in the refectory at a table with five other girls, most of them like herself newcomers and homesick to the point where they could scarcely eat. It buoyed her up a bit, set her teeth. Anything rather than snivel!

For breakfast there were thick cups of lukewarm tea and slabs of bread and butter. Unless you were taking Holy Communion, and then you did not even take a sip of water. Patrice had not yet made her First Communion nor even begun preparation for it. She had only the vaguest notion of what it was all about, and determined to fend off discovery of her abysmal ignorance at any cost. But the idea of Communion hung over her like an uneasy dream. To take the Body and Blood of Our Lord into your mouth, though not really, of course. Just one of those little round cake things which Father Francis pressed on people's tongues. What did it taste like? she inquired conversationally, casually, so as not to appear more of a jungli than she was. Like nothing, she was told. The wafer did not taste like anything because it was not supposed to. That was the whole point. Then, sneering:

"Fancy not knowing!" And the word passing round like lightning: "She doesn't know anything!"

The strangeness, the gnawing ache. Trying to shape emptiness into beloved form, to create a voice out of the void. Closing her eyes, there was the white house with pillars, and the garden with the round chabutra, and every evening the aunt straight-backed in her chair with her embroidery frame, the mother coming down the veranda steps, smiling her private smile, and the father whistling for Peggy the terrier; and always the brother preoccupied and intent, and the day eternal, and the eternal night. But the brother had disappeared into England and was not easily visualized, and the father and mother and aunt transplanted from that dear house to one unknown, unseen. Uprooting, a sense of desperation which kept her awake and scheming at night when her classmates slept in the shadowy gloom of the dormitory, snoring, breaking wind, sniveling into their pillows, and her misery turned to hate. Hate of these aloof, arrogant walls, of the imprisoned creatures within them, of the implacable beings who ruled them.

Bells again for early Mass, and the scent of incense in the little stone church modeled after one in some far off place; and then the mysterious goings-on at the altar with the little brown-bearded priest, his stomach like a football, and white active hands. Father Francis. And that was confusing, too. *Father*. And there was Mother Superior, Mother Imelda. And the Sisters. Sister Teresa, Sister Florian, Sister Frances de Sales, none of whom were sisters to one another, and none, she was sure, mother to anyone else, just as Father Francis was not a father at all since priests are not allowed to marry. Of so much at least Patrice was sure, all ears as usual to such affairs.

And in Saint Stephen's College for Boys up on the hill beyond the little stone church were *Brothers*. Brother John and Brother Joseph and Brother Matthew and uncounted more. Irish and jovial, clattering down the stony road in their big black boots and black gowns, to call on the Sisters on Feast Days, and to joke with the seniors. Scandalous rumors swept through the w.c.s between classes and after lights out. Brother John, the tall, handsome one with curly fair hair, was in love with Sister Florian. Father Francis was in love with Mother Superior. Illicit love was rife among these sainted persons, and Patrice thought vengefully: Wait until I go home and tell them

92

about it! Meantime she brooded, wondering whether Sister Teresa removed her extraordinary headgear with its veil when one of the Brothers kissed her—if he ever did. What did the Sisters wear when they went to bed? What did they look like in their baths? Did they menstruate? It was a word, she was happy to discover, unknown to her classmates, although they had their own versions of it, unfamiliar to her.

The senior girls had their loves also, among the senior boys at Saint Stephen's. Notes flew to and fro by mysterious channels; there were perilous trysts beyond the convent walls. Minnie McCann and Cecil Somebody, Naomi Stokes and Dicky Somebody Else. Big handsome glamorous girls with their hair braided in door knockers, privileged to wear huge butterfly bows and to attend the Lieutenant Governor's ball once a year if they behaved themselves. The ball was of hysterical importance, and the most severe punishment imaginable a denial to attend. To be caught clandestinely in company with a Saint Stephen's boy was to invite this punishment, from which there was no appeal. Morning dawned, night fell in an aura of wrongdoing, of sex, of hopeless longing for home, from which the youngest were not exempt, giggling or whimpering in corners, in w.c.s, in bed.

The silver bell at Benediction and a sudden warning silence as Father Francis raised the beautiful golden object above his head. Once, furtively glancing upward, Patrice was overwhelmed by the sight of the Figure impaled on its cross. How beautiful He was, and how sad, His naked feet somehow indecent in their bleeding pathos. She had an impulse to leave the pew and walk up to the altar and climb up it and try to free Him, to have Him slide down into her loving arms like a great doll.

The girl next to her nudged her savagely. "Put your head down, jungli!"

You are not supposed to look. To listen. To speak. To ask why they had done that horrible thing to Him and why they seemed to have become so used to the sight. You were not supposed to read your own letters from home until some stranger had opened them and read them first. Letters from the mother written on dark gray-flecked paper so Patrice could spy it across the length of the refectory table when letters were handed out. Always the envelopes neatly slit across the top. Better be careful what you write home, the others had warned her. Better say nice things about the Sisters and the grub, and how happy you are, or you'll get what-for. Your eyes were read, your lips, your thoughts. Like being turned inside out like a stocking, Patrice thought; turned inside out and given a good shake to dislodge the least shrinking particle of yourself.

Dissolution in an ocean of strangeness. Dressing and undressing, not even allowed to choose your own clothes. Every Saturday the Lay Sister—in gray robe and unfrilled bib whereas the other Sisters wore elegant black robes and frilled bibs—the Lay Sister placed a complete change of clothing on every girl's pillow.

"My blouse doesn't match my skirt," Patrice pointed out to the Lay Sister, who looked astonished, then laughed. "So the blouse doesn't match the skirt? Ah, get along with yez!"

Once a week a bath in a brown tin tub between wooden partitions. Always the anxious thought that someone was watching you from between the cracks. Stifled giggles, and swift reprimands from the Sister on duty. Here the water did not smell of delicious woodsmoke and lavender soap as it did at home. Here the towels were small and damp, the soap had grit in it. There was no Chota Ayah to scrub your back and to remind you that you couldn't stay there forever, it was the brother's turn.

And with all these girls— a hundred or more of her own age—no one was ever seen naked. When you undressed for bed you pulled your nightgown over your head and used it as a kind of tent under which you somehow sloughed your clothes. In the morning you reversed the process. The body was an evil thing, Patrice learned. Wondering. This firm, round, muscular flesh, the tiny pink buttons on your chest, all were evil. Did one ever get used to the smell of sweaty clothes, urine, unwashed crotches? It stuck in one's nostrils, evoking, at night, peculiar dreams.

Once the girl in the bed next to Patrice's tried to get into her bed. She was skinny and unattractive and cried herself to sleep every night, or thrashed about, keeping others awake. On this night Patrice wakened to find Mavis Robbins in bed with her, Mavis' clawlike hand fumbling between her legs.

Patrice got out of bed on the near side. "I'm going to call Sister!"

"Please!" whimpered Mavis. "Please don't. It's just that I'm so lonely. Please!"

Patrice had a wild impulse to stamp on Mavis Robbins, to crush her.

94

"I'm going to call Sister and tell her."

"Please!"

But Mavis returned to her own bed, and next morning they avoided each other's eyes. Patrice knew that she would not have called the Sister on duty, that she could never have given poor Mavis Robbins away, but she suffered from a kind of sick loathing of the girl, and sometime during the year Mavis was expelled from school. No one seemed to know why, though for days afterward the giggling and whispering burgeoned into a kind of hysteria, quelled at last by the sheer burden of thousands of "lines" dealt out during classes: "I must not whisper during lessons." "I must not giggle." "I am a very silly girl."

The fourth standard classroom glittered with yellow varnished woodwork, and above Sister Teresa's desk on its dais hung an immense glossy picture of Our Lord pointing to His exposed and bloody heart. This picture did not affect Patrice like the figure on the cross in church. She disliked the picture with its vacant blue eyes, its girlish white hand pointing to a fat red heart which reminded her of the aunt's pincushion at home, stuck full of pretty colored pins—blue, yellow, pink. Practically all the pictures in school looked more or less like the one in her classroom. There were half-naked people being stabbed, beaten, scorned; some were tied to posts and their bodies stuck full of arrows. Martyrs, she was told. It looked like a gigantic shikar with people instead of animals for game.

To distract her gaze from the picture Patrice gazed out of the big windows at the playground, where immense horse chestnut trees soared into the mists. Sometimes a family of big gray monkeys called langurs frolicked in the chestnut trees or sat in a solemn row, tails hanging, their black faces illumined by bright boot-button eyes. Watching them Patrice forgot everything else. She tried to signal them and fancied they saw her and that they responded.

Sister Teresa rapped on her desk with the ruler. "Patrice Verrier, what are you staring at?"

"The langurs, Sister. In the chestnut trees."

"Well, if you would like to join members of your family in the chestnut trees, you may do so."

It brought down the house, and Sister Teresa smiled a gratified smile.

But I love the langurs, Patrice thought. I would like to live with them, to be one myself. She daydreamed through arithmetic class, seeing herself stealing into the church and rescuing the Figure from its torment and fleeing with Him into the chestnut trees to live among the langurs. This thought of escape became an obsession. It became a kind of armor, too. Secretly plotting her flight, she found she could endure the endless oppressive days, the black desert of night, the ceaseless yearning for her own bed in the big bedroom which gave out on a garden which smelled of petunias, where the moon soared and sank through a friendly sky. Even the jackals. Even the churel with its backward-looking eyes.

She would never get used to this other place. She would never like these girls, these strange women in their black dresses and shut-in faces. She would never learn to pray properly, to feel anything but a chivalrous urge to rescue the slight, white, suffering Figure pinned to its cross.

"Please, Sister, may I be excused?"

"This is the second time in an hour. Aren't you feeling well, Patrice?"

"I would like to go to the bathroom, please, Sister."

"It's just an excuse. You may not be excused."

Patrice's neighbor at the adjoining desk was an undersized Hindu boy with an unpronounceable name that sounded like Cucumber. The convent accepted boys, some Indian, as day scholars, provided they were no more than ten years old. Sons of rajas or rich merchants from Delhi. It was all part of the confusion. They did not attend Mass, and their food was brought them by their own servants, in shiny brass containers which exuded mouth-watering smells of curry and pickles and rich sticky sweets. Memories of His Highness Nawab Ghulam Hosain, of Mrs. and Miss Meadows, of the brother fastidiously licking his fingers after gorging on jelabies on the Meadowses' veranda, and Barley the frog croaking among his rocks.

Cucumber was very dark, with an anteater profile, watery eyes, and thick black hair which smelled of coconut oil. He wore European style clothes much too large for him, and was the butt of the class. They called him "chokra" and "lounda" and jeered when they saw him crouched in a corner of the playground eating his lunch with his fingers while his Hindu servant squatted nearby. Cucumber ignored them. He was by far the cleverest member of the class, always first

96

in every subject, held up as an example by Sister Teresa.

"A native, and he even speaks your own language more correctly than you do! Not one of you others can parse a sentence properly. I am ashamed of you!"

In the beginning Patrice disliked Cucumber and resented being seated next to him in class. Why did it have to be her, just because she was a newcomer! But Cucumber ignored her as he ignored the others. He never asked to be excused to go to the bathroom, and he scarcely moved during class, sitting like some fledgling bird with his big nose drooped over his book. But one hundred percent in everything, including English. His voice when reading aloud flung them into convulsions, but he never faltered. "The Burial of Sir John Moore at Corunna" was his favorite poem and he knew it by heart, recited it without expression at lightning speed, and accepted, with the barest glimmer of a smile, Sister Teresa's unstinted praise. "There is not one of you who could do as well. One more giggle and you will stay in after class and learn that poem by heart!"

Patrice, hopelessly bogged down in algebra, felt, one day, a moth-like movement at her elbow and a small piece of paper slid across the desk under her eyes. It was the solution to a problem which had stumped her for days. "A dunce." Sister Teresa shrugged, resignedly. "The biggest dunce in the class. Patrice Verrier, I will give you one more chance, then you go to the very bottom of the class and stay there."

Now here was the answer supplied by Cucumber. He did not raise his eyes or in any way acknowledge her presence beside him. Patrice completed her assignment with the solution provided by Cucumber, and handed in her paper. Sister Teresa studied it and observed in a chilling voice: "Better late than never!"

Thereafter Cucumber did all Patrice's mathematical assignments for her and her marks shot up. "Application," Sister Teresa deduced with grudging approval. "You see for yourself nothing is impossible if you *try.*"

Cucumber scarcely exchanged a word with Patrice, or with anyone else. Between classes they went their separate ways, but sometimes she felt his watery gaze upon her and felt an impulse to make some gesture in response, but she never did. Aloof and condescending, she permitted him to do most of her lessons for her, and miraculously both escaped detection. But she had a curious feeling about Cucumber, recognizing his devotion, despising him for it, accepting his services without scruple and without thanks. He did not appear to expect thanks. Silent, smelling of the bazaar, scarcely seeming to breathe, he labored over her lessons and his own.

Many years later Patrice was to learn that, his brilliant promise fulfilled, Cucumber went to America as a design engineer for an important automotive firm. He returned to India on his first home leave and died of poisoning at the hands of a kinsman jealous of his luck.

Once a week there were singing lessons with Sister Cecilia. Massive and deaf, a tin ear trumpet suspended from her neck by a black cord, Sister Cecilia taught music and nothing else. Her domain was the Music Room with its five grand pianos like dinosaurs, draped in blankets when not in use, with little charcoal stoves burning beside each to keep out the damp.

The class, in two rows, feet together and hands dangling. Sister Cecilia waving her trumpet with one hand and striking a note with the other. "Ve vill now zing 'Liddle Red Ving.'"

Excruciating. A sudden agonizing impulse to laugh, and then the old diuretic effect of Mrs. Sparks' voice, of the father's voice, the first unbearably sweet notes from the mother's mandolin. Oh, where were they all at this very moment . . . where? Where?

"Vod is der madder mit you, Badrice?"

"Nothing, Sister."

"Zen vy you are grying?"

"I'm not crying, Sister."

"Id is silly to give in to *heimweh.*"

"Yes, Sister."

Three months, four months, an eon. And in June the mother wrote: "It is terribly hot here, darling. You wouldn't like it. But when you come home the weather will be nice. Lovely at Christmas. You will love this new house and will have your own room with all your things. And I have news for you. Mrs. Meadows and Edna have taken a cottage not far from your school. Darling, I am writing Mother Superior, asking her to let you visit the Meadowses on a weekend. Darling, we miss you but it won't be for very long now."

Not for very long. Six more months. *Six months!* That squeezing of the heart, next thing to dying. I simply can't, thought Patrice, bear it. Then the miracle, the ecstasy. A note brought by a coolie, with the present of a tin of guava jelly from the Meadowses.

"Mummy and I are staying at Briarwood Cottage just behind Valerio's Hotel. Do come for tea this Saturday, darling Patrice. Ask Mother Superior, and I will send Abdullah to fetch you and to take you back."

Mother Superior's gray eyes, not unkind but not exactly kind, either. "I have not heard from your mother, Patrice. I cannot let you go and visit these friends until I hear from your mother."

"But she has said she was writing you. You've seen her letter to me."

"I have not yet received her letter to me."

"But you know!"

"It is not sufficient for me to take the responsibility."

"But Miss Meadows is our friend. We have known her for years and years." Years and years. The past one's sole possession, now suddenly snatched from one. What had happened? How had it happened?

"We will not argue, Patrice. When I hear from your mother we shall see."

"But—"

"No buts. Run along."

A sudden scorching behind the eyes. "It's not fair, Mother!"

"What?" Metal in the voice, steel.

"I said it's not fair not to let me go and have tea with my friends."

"Are you trying to instruct me on what is fair and what is not, my child?"

"I'm not your child." A kind of meaning to it, insidious, derisive, and a stain of color in Mother Superior's cheek.

"I do not want to have to punish you, Patrice. You will do as you are told, do you understand?"

I don't understand. But one didn't say it. What was the use? That towering presence in its dense black skirts, the big, pale face framed in starched white, the adamant gaze. This stranger exercising jurisdiction over one's life! *Mother* Imelda . . . Had she ever played a mandolin, called someone Doey, felt herself enwrapped in his arms in that big sweet-smelling bedroom at home? Had her voice murmured with laughter: "Doey, darling, not now! The children might come in. . . ."

Outside Mother Superior's office ginger lilies were growing in the flower border and the school mali squatted on his haunches, weeding. Strong black trees pushed through the mist, then there were the monkeys. Leaping from branch to branch in lunatic joy. One of them paused to stare at Patrice, its pointed black face wreathed in silver fur, its long gray tail demurely hanging. Divine creatures! Her heart rushed toward them, followed them as they crashed away through the trees, nothing to stop them, no one to tell them no.

In the Music Room someone was playing the piano, masterfully, beautifully. It would be Sister Cecilia, a Prussian noblewoman before she had taken the veil. "Id is silly to give in to *heimweh.*" German for homesickness, and Sister Cecilia seemed to understand it well enough as she played. It was more than Patrice could bear.

The path to the gate passed by the statutes of the Virgin Mary with the Infant Jesus in her arms, and one of Saint Joseph, each under their protective canopies. The Virgin wore a kind of blue sari, and the light touched her hair and the Child's sausagy curls. The mali's back was toward Patrice, and not another thing moved on the friendless scene.

Her decision was instantaneous. A quick genuflection—just to be on the safe side—one to the Holy Virgin, the other to Saint Joseph. Then the gate shut quietly behind her. A shady road where branches arched over her head, and two cheerful Pahari carrying conical baskets of charcoal on their backs greeted her with smiles. It seemed as if no one had smiled at her for a long time. And then the monkeys suddenly appeared in the trees, applauding her. The world opened before her, natural, at ease, welcoming.

In a few minutes she had reached the bazaar and was haggling with the one-eyed ghora wallah for hire of a bony chestnut horse which she had observed on a certain dreary Sunday perambulation of the class under Sister Teresa's watchful eyes. The man wanted to be paid in advance, and she thought: Not even to have a few annas of one's own pocket money! They read our letters, spy on us in the w.c., and take over our pocket money, doling it out at intervals to spend on Holy Pictures or to put on the plate on Sundays, or to fritter it away on silly things in the school shop—lace doilies and writing paper and little plaster statues of the Holy Family. Even your very own money which the mother sent faithfully every month!

But Miss Meadows would pay for the horse's hire, and the mother would pay her back later. The ghora wallah gave in. His son would accompany her, loping along on foot far in the rear, and would bring the horse back afterward. The saddle was too big and the stirrups too long but she could have done without either. Her heart raced.

She plied the quirt and the horse bounded under it, almost unseating her. Joy pounded in her veins as the beast settled into a resigned canter along the edge of the Mall with its border of willows trailing in the water. An English gentleman was fishing for mahseer. Two ladies in big hats were carried past in dandies, the carriers wearing handsome scarlet livery. Government House, Patrice thought, savoring it with elation. Her entire body seemed to have regained its numbed senses. People on foot scattered, then turned to stare after the charmed face, the flying brown hair of a very young Val kyrie.

How funny, how easy! Months of doing nothing, of just being obedient, miserable; crying herself to sleep at night, half existing through the day. Now free! Now free, free, free! The canter broke into full gallop and air whipped past her ears. Christmas camp and the antelope fleeing before her, and the brother hunched in his saddle, and the exultation which drowned all calculation. The camp ground would still be there, far away on the brown plain; the dust perhaps still hold the imprint of her feet, and the brother's and the father's and the mother's and the aunt's. The great elephant turds would have powdered away but the holes made by the tent pegs might remain, and the hoopoe stepping delicately under the mango trees, and the fox barking in the distance. It would be lonely there now, haunted by lost voices, forgotten thoughts, remembered dreams.

Halfway round the Mall the road to Valerio's Hotel branches upward into a tunnel of firs and her mount slowed to a panting walk. A celebrant streak of sunlight reached between the branches to touch her head, and there before her was Briarwood Cottage, mildewed, its roof slightly askew, and doubtless the home of scorpions and of small sidling things, but sanctuary just the same; home, heaven.

Mrs. Meadows gave a small shriek of welcome: "Darling! You have come! Edna, Edna, she is here!"

Dark, familiar, loving faces; embraces, endearments. "How you have grown, darling! All legs. And those rosy cheeks."

Yes, of course they would pay for the horse. Or they would give her the money and she could pay the ghora wallah when she returned to school later, after tea.

"I'm not going back."

"What, sweet?"

"I am not going back to that damn place ever again."

Glances, swift, worried. "Tea!" Mrs. Meadows cried, practically. "And your dear mother sent an order to Valerio's, so we have a chocolate cake. But if we had only known you were coming today I would have ordered fresh jelabies from the bazaar."

It was a tiny veranda crowded with potted geraniums. Hydrangeas of an electric blue swarmed beside the dilapidated steps. Everything a bit shabby and down-at-heel, the feeling of a place once deeply loved, a creation of limitless nostalgia, wrenchingly abandoned.

"It is all we could afford," Mrs. Meadows explained happily. "Drafty, and a bit lonely until we get to know people. But so nice really, don't you think so, darling? And furnished. All we had to bring were our clothes and a few little things to remind us . . . and of course Abdullah. You remember Abdullah?"

He appeared grinning, carrying a loaded tea tray. The same greasy, untidy look, dirty cap, familiar manners. But glad to see her. And now it was as if she had never left them nor they her. Mrs. Meadows chattering excitedly, Miss Meadows smiling her gentle smile. There is something, but I mustn't ask.

Miss Meadows had had such a nice letter from the mother just the other day. Wasn't it lovely about the brother? So happy in his English school and getting such good marks. Only Patrice knew that he was not happy and that his marks were anything but good. He was clever at drawing and math, but that was all. And he talked little because of his stuttering, which made the other boys laugh. They made him sing "K-K-K-Katy, Bub-bub-bub-beautiful K-K-Katy!" And they thought him stupid, not guessing at his true cleverness.

The Harpers? Mrs. Meadows, pouring tea into a cup, spilled some in the saucer. Oh, the Harpers were still there; that is, Mr. and Mrs. Harper were, but the boys were at school in Lucknow. If they hadn't been expelled. Miss Meadows gave a faint laugh. "Now, Mummee!"

102

"Now what-all? Dirty pigs. Liars. They killed our poor Barley frog, and—and—"

A tear rolled down Mrs. Meadows' cheek. Then the horse boy arrived at the veranda steps and began to whine and she screamed at him to go to Jehannum, but Miss Meadows got up from her chair and paid him and he went away. Returning to her chair, her eyes met Mrs. Meadows' and Patrice sensed their communion over her head. She said: "I can always sleep on the floor, you know."

"Darling, we have a bed, of course. But do have some more tea. Another slice of cake?"

Miss Meadows said: "You know your dear father has given us this house for the summer?"

"Given?"

Well, she might as well know. The mother had apparently not mentioned it in her letters. It was all very sad.

"Edna," Mrs. Meadows murmured, and another tear slid down her cheek.

"Why not," said Miss Meadows. She laid her slim brown hand on Patrice's knee. "Darling, you will hear it sometime so we might as well. Our dear, dear Mr. Jensen died very suddenly six weeks ago. He came back from dinner somewhere late at night on his bicycle and missed the gate to our house and rode instead into the Harpers' compound, and those awful geese attacked him and he fell off his bicycle and died of a heart attack there on the spot."

Miss Meadows began to cry in a gentle hopeless sort of way. It had been so sudden and they had no time . . . and Mr. Jensen had always been so kind and thoughtful. They had hoped, even expected . . . not having anything themselves, not even the house which he had shared with them for almost fifteen years. But when his will was read it was found that he had left everything to his wife. Everything. *Their* house, though of course it was not really theirs and never had been. *Their* furniture, only of course . . . And not a penny, Absolutely nothing. Such a shock and nowhere to turn.

"And this is not a country to be stranded in," murmured Mrs. Meadows, not even trying now to hide her weeping.

"What country is?" asked Miss Meadows, controlling herself. She patted Patrice's knee. "There, darling. Now you know. And your dear, dear parents . . . not having a great deal themselves . . . so

103

unselfish, so kind. A check for two thousand rupees to tide us over, and the rent paid on this place for six months."

"And after that, what-all?" demanded Mrs. Meadows in a thick voice.

"Something will turn up, Mummee, dear." Miss Meadows was certain of it.

"Already you have made application for positions to teach and three refusals without explanation! Just because."

"Now, Mummee."

"Just because people are narrow-minded. Even one's private life."

"There is no such thing," said Miss Meadows, then quickly: "What will Patrice think? Darling, never mind. More cake? Lovely. I love to see you eat. How I wish the brother were here with us."

Patrice felt the thickening in her own throat. Not daring, yet, to speak, for fear of her voice coming out funny. Not looking at them but out into the tangled garden where once some homesick old colonel had labored to plant his English roses and put copper nails at the roots of the hydrangeas to turn them that ferocious blue, and turned his shrapnel accents on some quaking, long-dead mali: "No bloody marigolds, damn your eyes! Bloody native minds never get beyond marigolds!"

Whence, now, came the recollection? Patrice had never known that old colonel, that mali. A story of the father's about old So-and-So, old Barbed-Wire Brisket . . . and the mother's laughter, and the aunt coming into it: "They have to plant marigolds, what with their endless weddings and funerals."

"We think we might start a little boarding house," Miss Meadows said brightly. She was very proud and it hurt her to cry. She had been Mr. Jensen's mistress and there must have been uncounted snubs and slights to swallow besides being eight-annas-in-the-rupee. And he had left every penny to his wife. What did he think was going to happen to them, to her and to Mummee? No country to be stranded in. Nowhere to turn.

"Paying guests," Miss Meadows said, visibly cheering. It suddenly seemed quite feasible, something to look forward to. Self-respecting. Friendly amusing people, company. And Abdullah such an excellent cook and Mummee splendid about kitchen arrangements and accounts. It would be a success. A small but steady income. They would

104

be able to pay back the two thousand dibs to the father in no time. But of course the father and mother wouldn't hear of taking it back. It was not a loan, it was a gift. "I don't want any nonsense about this," the father had warned. "Not a damned word, do you understand, Edna? *Not a word.*"

"But suppose nobody wants to come to our boardinghouse?" Mrs. Meadows brutally raised the obstacle. She must have waited a long time before bringing herself to say it. A third presence made it somehow easier, and after all it might as well be said.

"Why shouldn't they want to come?" demanded Miss Meadows.

"For the same reason you can't get a position teaching." Mrs. Meadows was weeping again. "Everybody knows what has happened to us. About you and Giles."

Giles. That must have been Mr. Jensen's name. Funny. Patrice had never thought of him except as Mr. Jensen. Thick in the middle, with an untidy moustache and a smell of brandy. He used to bring her and the brother toys, odd things that pleased them. Once it was a matchbox containing a little rubber snake which jumped out when you opened the box. And once it was a ring with a naked lady on it, in gold, and a rubber bulb attached which you held in the palm and squeezed when someone asked to see it, and out squirted a jet of water from the lady's you-know-what. Then there was a tiny dictionary no bigger than a pillbox, which you had to read with a magnifying glass, only unfortunately it was in German. A pretty little bottle of perfume marked Violets, which when you put some on your handkerchief had the most frightful smell. But Mr. Jensen had a loud hearty voice and laughed a great deal and it was difficult to think of him as being dead. Fancy falling off your bicycle among a lot of hissing geese and dying of a heart attack then and there!

"Mummee, please." Miss Meadows held out her cup and her hand trembled. "Not as strong as last time, please, dear. Thank you."

"People are dirty snobs," Mrs. Meadows whimpered. She shouldn't, Patrice thought, snivel. Doey would not have liked it.

"All these pukka types. Any excuse to look down on us. Those memsahibs with their tennis rackets. No breasts, just like their husbands. Even the Harpers imitating them! We'd probably get keranies like ourselves or bad native types. Fat contractors looking for their greens and preferring white women, or almost white."

105

"Mummee." Miss Meadows had flushed.

"Don't keep saying Mummee! It was you who gave up everything for Jensen and now see what-all! Hated his wife and never went near her and lived with you fifteen years and then goes and dies and where are we, I'd like to know?" Mrs. Meadows' voice suddenly making one feel ashamed. "I'll tell you then! You will become a prostitute, that's all. A common pro."

Miss Meadows rose and held out her hand to Patrice. "Wouldn't you like to see the garden, darling? It's a bit of a jungle because we haven't been able to find a mali, but it must have been a lovely place once."

Once upon a time when the birds shit lime and the monkeys chewed tobacco. The brother repeating it to her, laughing. He had learned it somewhere, from one of the Harpers perhaps. Or perhaps from Mr. Jensen.

"Luvlee," said Miss Meadows, a little breathless.

The father saying: "If I ever hear you imitating the Meadowses! They are human beings. Ladies. Don't let me ever hear you. . . ."

Out of sight of the veranda Miss Meadows said: "Poor old Mummee. She is so homesick. You mustn't mind."

Patrice thought: They can't help me. They are frightened and poor and they can't even help themselves. Blinding thought that this should happen to grown people. Tears, terror. And now even home was not there. The white house with its slender columns, the garden with the chabutra, the trees at night with the moon elbowing through the branches. Even the jackals. And in total darkness, even, finding one's way because one knew it so well. And now nothing. What was the use of thinking about it, of dreaming?

Miss Meadows was talking in a bright voice, forgetful for some reason of her accent, about which she had always been so particular not to sound like the Harpers, like Abdullah, even like her own mother.

"Such a luvlee new house, darling, and they say a very gay station. So luvlee for your dear mother and auntie. They will wear their prettiest dresses from Home."

Home was England. Home to Mrs. and Miss Meadows and to the Harpers, none of whom had ever seen England. But Home because it was that half of themselves which they had chosen to be, not the murky other half, the remaining eight-annas-in-the-rupee.

106

"And promotion," Miss Meadows went on, warming. "Your dear father. So brilliant. He is bound to end up as I.G. Just think of it, perhaps even a Sir!"

They were picking their way through wild raspberry canes which tore at Patrice's legs through her stockings. She felt the struggle in Miss Meadows' voice and glanced at her furtively. Miss Meadows looked flushed, different from other times. "Edna," the mother had once remarked, "has a profile like a true cameo, don't you think so?"

And the father had said: "Better for her if she were ugly as sin."

"Oh, Doey, no!"

"What in God's name is going to become of them? Kept women or starvation."

And the aunt, judicious: "Edna asked for it, after all. She didn't have to give up her governess position to go and live with someone else's husband."

"She thought she was getting security," the father said in an angry voice. "She did what a lot of other women do and have always done for the sake of a roof over their heads."

"But, Doey!"

"Money. The bottom of everything. Or every woman's bottom." His short hard laugh, not funny. "Nobody would give a damn who Edna Meadows slept with if she had money of her own."

"If she had money of her own she probably wouldn't have picked old Jensen," the mother ruminated while the aunt primly sewed.

"Old swine . . . the kind who always thinks he can have his cake and eat it, too."

"Well, I only hope he leaves them something. He's got enough, heaven knows."

Miss Meadows stooped to free Patrice's stockings from the brambles. "You are looking so fit, darling. Much better than on the plains, where it is so hot this time of year. Luvlee for you to be here!"

Patrice said: "Is it very far away from here?"

Miss Meadows straightened up and looked at her finger, bleeding a little from the brambles. She sucked the wound and her brown eyes met Patrice's. "Very far away, darling. A whole day and a whole night by rail."

"Then I could just stay here with you and you could teach me lessons and I wouldn't have to go back to that place."

"Darling, I couldn't. I would be taking advantage of your dear father and mother, who have been so kind when everybody else..."

Miss Meadows' whole face seemed to be trembling. "Your education," she managed, speaking very carefully. "So important. You must study hard and master some profession so you will never... Your dear father told me he wanted you to do that, so you will always be independent."

"What's independent?"

"It means that you never have to ask anybody for anything."

And it means that you can always sleep in your own bed, Patrice thought, knowing now that she could not say it aloud. You can always sleep in your own bed and not have to sleep with someone else. And a roof over your head. And knowing where the next meal was coming from. But, she thought silently, she would choose a tent and listen to the rustle of leaves against the canvas and feel the outdoors leaning against the frail walls, and closing her eyes see the hoopoe asleep on its branch, and the fox watching on the edge of the field. And the tiger calling, the hot sound filling her chest. Going out into the darkness with the brother, walking toward the Voice, terror and delight making your feet soundless as moths.

"Your education," Miss Meadows said tenderly. "So necessary, darling; and the dear Sisters, such an example. They will be so proud of you, your dear father and mother and auntie, when you go home for Christmas after learning so much, and such good books."

Miss Meadows broke down. Putting her thin arms round Patrice, she leaned her cheek on Patrice's head and her whole body shook from head to foot. Patrice tasted the salt tears from Miss Meadows' eyes raining down her own face and she silently held Miss Meadows, and thought: How awful, really. One shouldn't. One should never.

And the lonely garden smelling of strange weeds and knowing that she would after all have to go back to the convent and that Mother Superior would punish her. So many whacks with the ruler on both hands, so many hundred lines: "I am a wicked ungrateful girl." So many prayers, and no more holidays because she had taken this one against the rules.

I don't care, thought Patrice. I don't care and they can't make me care. And I'll never ask for anything. And they'll never see me cry like this—this awful sound like a dog that's been kicked. One shouldn't. One should never.

108

8

*T*he brother did not come back. Gradually he be-
gan to fade in the sister's consciousness, and his personality to take
on, imperceptibly, the unsubstantial form of his letters, and those
were few and far between. Only the father's face, the mother's, the
aunt's, remained burnished by her longing. There were moments
when she thought she felt their clothing brush against hers, caught
the special tones of their voices, their separate fragrance. Such moments stilled her paroxysms of expectation, but only for a little while.
They were nearer to her in space than the brother in England, yet
they did not come to her when her misery was at its height.

"I don't understand that child," Sister Teresa complained to
Mother Superior. "She simply will not adjust."

Mother Superior was firm and experienced. "It sometimes takes
longer with one than with others. The Verrier child has a stubborn
streak. But this ignorance of religion I cannot understand!"

"A real jungli," Sister Teresa offered. "The father a bit of a free
thinker, I rather imagine. And the mother inclined to be casual about
such things."

"The mother was Protestant before she married him," Mother
Superior recalled, frowning. "But the father and the aunt always

Catholic. A very good Norman family." She smirked in a reflected glow. "I'm afraid, though, that you are right, and that in respect to Mr. Verrier's faith . . . So tragic for the child! But she will have to learn like everyone else. Too quick to take advantage. And insolent. One has to be firm."

There had been swift retribution following that stolen afternoon with the Meadowses. Ten cracks on each hand from Mother Superior's ruler; an extra hour of study every evening, alone, after classes; a thousand lines to be written over and over again: "I am an untrustworthy girl." And in addition she was forbidden to leave the school premises for the rest of the month.

Sister Teresa rubbed it in. "What do you expect, after running away and causing such anxiety? Then calmly coming back as if nothing had happened, as if you had the *right* to do just as you pleased. But you'll find you've got to learn like other people!"

A membrane of defiance enclosed Patrice, an opacity through which she silently appraised the outer world. The father had been strict, but he was her father, shield and buckler against the shrieking jackals and the churel in the garden; fearless, a touchstone against all doubt. But the memory of those blows from Mother Superior's ruler sank into the sister like a cicatrice. She had been worse hurt falling off her pony, Jill, or climbing trees; this other left a kind of stain, making her flush whenever she thought of it.

Here and there among her classmates she encountered friendly, even admiring eyes. Unable to help her with her lines, Cucumber slid half a sticky jelabie to her across their desks, and in total silence completed her entire algebra lessons for her with results that won a mystified acclaim from Sister Teresa: "You see, a little punishment doesn't hurt after all!"

But there was a revived interest in studying the pictures. Saint Stephen bristling with arrows. Saint John the Baptist lolling on a velvet couch, his head unaccountably reposing on a tea tray at his feet. Lions placidly eating Christians. Handsomely muscled men beating people with iron hooks. And everywhere Our Lord bleeding, bleeding. Patrice thought often of how the mother buffalo at home had looked with blood streaming from her backside when the calf was born. Blood on the aunt's bed sheet, blood oozing from the neem tree in the garden, native blood in Miss Meadows' brown veins. And

110

here in this improbable place which smelled of carbolic and incense, blood dripping in every picture. Blood congealed on that Figure nailed to His cross. And the women! The Holy Virgin and Saint Mary Magdalen, faces contorted in grief. Nobody, it seemed, ever smiled, not even the Holy Infant, toyless, joyless, and overfed.

Constrained by wrongdoing to her own company, Patrice sometimes thought about Nizamat, the young servant at home. She remembered his trim figure in its white tunic, carrying a prayer mat out under the trees, kicking off his shoes, and prostrating himself before God. Usually old Mohommed Ali the tailor joined him on a separate prayer mat. Both men washed their hands and mouths carefully with water from a silver urn and before kneeling down they stood side by side with their arms folded on their breasts, eyes closed, lips tenderly moving.

Patrice and the brother occasionally prayed with them, standing a little to the rear; inventing the words, following every move. Neither Nizamat nor Mohommed Ali paid any attention to them, except that the old tailor always made sure that they had washed their mouths and hands at the start of these devotions.

The father and Mr. Onions had come upon them one day and Mr. Onions had said: "It looks as if you were going to have a pair of little Ishmaelites on your hands, Doey, my boy!"

The father replied unconcernedly: "No harm in that as far as I can see."

"What?"

"Do you ever stop to wonder whether perhaps Christianity may have had its day?"

"My dear chap!" Shocked, Mr. Onions—High Church Anglican— lighted his pipe while under the trees near the cookhouse Patrice and the brother bowed their foreheads to the dust and mumbled their own version of the prayer at their servants' side.

All that school year Cucumber sat at the desk next to Patrice, his marks always the highest in the class, his accent regularly driving them into convulsions when he recited one of his favorite poems:

> "On Linden when thee sun was *loh*
> Bloodless lay thee untrodden *snoh*
> And dak as winter was the *floh*
> Of Yser *rohling* rapidlee!"

As days lost their outlines so did weeks, months. Patrice began to keep a diary, using an exercise book given her by Cucumber. It had a purple marbled cover and glossy white paper ruled in blue. Cucumber must have bought it in the bazaar, and he handed it to her without a word or glance. Patrice inscribed her name in full on the first page, and then it happened: a surge of excitement, a voluptuous delight in putting words down on a white page. From that moment she began to take great pains with her handwriting; she copied entire pages from other books and took to consulting a dictionary. There followed a rich increase in self-consciousness, and days of respite from malaise.

Sister Teresa took her aside after class one day and said: "Why do you dislike us, Patrice?"

"I don't, Sister."

"But you won't make friends. Why not?"

Well, why not? Silently, Patrice kicked the back of one shoe with the toe of the other. Sister Teresa's ice-blue gaze studied the top of a dusty head. A faint scent of kerosene rose from it. There had been an epidemic of lice and the younger girls had had their heads well scrubbed with kerosene by the school ayahs.

Sister Teresa continued helplessly: "You would be so much happier if you made friends, if you learned to pray properly, and behaved like other people."

"Yes, Sister."

"It's not healthy to moon about by yourself with your nose in a book."

"No, Sister."

How explain that she didn't need friends, that she felt a disloyalty in trying to fill the blanks left by the brother's absence and by the father's and the mother's and the aunt's? How explain that her heart, her parts, her guts, her being were knotted with theirs and not to be picked apart?

Sister Teresa experimented with flattery. "You are quite intelligent but you won't try. When you do apply yourself you do very well. Look at your algebra! No one ever gets very far without trying, not even the cleverest."

"Try what, Sister?" One had to be reasonably polite.

"Try to be more like other people."

"But I am."

112

Sister Teresa chewed a dry lip. "Well, there really doesn't seem to be much use in talking to you."

"No, Sister."

Sister Teresa gave up, confused perhaps. I must pray for that child. She must not be lost to the Lord, the poor little thing. Brought up in a casual household; nothing but those homemade prayers, not even the Credo, not even the Rosary. It was all very strange.

Watching Sister Teresa walk away, tall and thin, her rosary with its heavy silver crucifix clanking at her waist, Patrice thought: I wonder what she'd say if I was to tell her about What's-His-Name Harper's thing, his deformity? Recollections of it still returned to puzzle her and she would have liked to discuss it with someone but could never quite bring herself to do so. One might of course broach the subject by being judiciously conversational, as when inquiring about the cause of a leper's cratered face she had once observed on the Mall during a Sunday walk. Sister Teresa had explained at length. A terrible disease, leprosy, but fortunately confined mostly to beggars. Incurable, catching.

But there had been nothing diseaselike about What's-His-Name Harper. Tall and strong and healthy, and frightening to younger boys with his threats. He had not tried to frighten her, not really. There had just been something different as he purposely opened his fly and revealed himself. It was most peculiar and the more she thought about it the more convinced Patrice had become that it would be safer not to mention the subject to Sister Teresa. Like that question about Thou Shalt Not Commit Adultery. There had been a forced mildness in Sister Teresa's response: "Never mind now, Patrice. Some things we understand better when we are older."

But now there was December and the cheerless days became suddenly interesting because there were so few left before the end of school. Glossy horse chestnuts strewed the ground under the trees. A throat-catching scent of balsam fires filled the air. One collected the horse chestnuts simply because it was inevitable that one collect things. A leaf turned delicately crimson. A magpie's feather, blue and debonair. And always the feel of that exercise book in one's hand, a thick, rich sensation, a few of its pages covered in a meticulous writing in bright blue ink. Not a mistake, not a blot:

"Courage!" he said, and pointed toward the land,
"This mounting wave will roll us shoreward soon."
In the afternoon they came unto the land
In which it seemed always afternoon.

And this, a figment of her own: "Desirée was beautiful and good but her lover was a sot and he used up all his money drinking and gambling and never kept his promise to amend."

Occasionally, when no one was there to see, Patrice went to her desk in the empty classroom and lifted the lid to gaze at the contents. The purple-covered exercise book; four bronzely shining chestnuts, the magpie's feather, the mother's and the brother's letters neatly tied together with string. All her wealth.

The Christmas holidays started on the fifteenth of December and the knowledge took her by the throat. The past nine months had been a weird dream from which she would shortly awaken. The drabness, the sadness, the bewilderment; everything disliked and abhorred became suddenly quite bearable. How could she have minded it all so much? Suddenly, now, noticing three wiry hairs growing out of Sister Teresa's chin, and the hem of Mother Superior's black habit a bit threadbare, and their boots with broken patches showing on the soles when they walked. They were poor. They had no money, no home, nothing. Not even their own names. Suddenly, too, noticing that the statues of the Holy Virgin and Saint Joseph were not as tall as grown people but nearer one's own height, and they needed repairs. The Infant Child had lost one of His sausagy curls, Saint Joseph a little finger, the Holy Virgin part of her left foot.

And after these discoveries that surging happiness, the cold smell of the mountains, and the lake a dark green now and the willows turning yellow. She was leaving them. A passionate moment of pity, flooding her. Pity, but not sorrow, not regret.

Then the day of departure and the hills fading behind her; holly berries in the dusty hedgerows beside the tonga road, mistletoe like great birds' nests in the tops of the dwindling deodars; mountain voices and mule bells fainting on the transformed air. She smelled the steam from the train waiting in the shabby little railway station, the long, dark red train waiting to carry her home.

Home. Knowing that it was not the place she had left almost a year ago, and yet now expecting to find it—the low white house with

114

pillars supporting the steep roof of the veranda, shadowy rooms where light picked up a silver cup won by the father at tennis, deep chairs holding the contours of familiar bodies, the door with the green bead curtains which made music when Nizamat pushed through them carrying the tea tray, and where the seditionist Charan had made merry with his magical rupee. And her own room, which forever she would remember she had shared with the brother, the sensation of coir matting under her feet and the smell of woodsmoke in the bath water, and an old remembered ache of fevers long past.

Instead, here she was now in this new house in this new place, her mind a ferment. An unfriendly, yellow-painted house and a stiff garden with neat hedges and prim trees. The coarse shapes of other houses intruded on either side of the garden; there was no chabutra, no wilderness of custard apple and banana tree, no mango grove with fields of yellow mustard beyond, no ruined temple where the big mottled grasshoppers whirred like machines.

And there were electric lights. She violently missed the smell of kerosene lamps, the deep glow of their topaz light seen through the darkness of that other garden. What had happened to the special scissors which Nizamat used to trim the wicks? What happened to the lamps, silver-plated bowls with shining chimneys and gay reflectors about which Doey was always so particular?

True, there was a hoopoe strutting on the alien grass, but he flew away the moment she appeared, and did not return. True, too, there was her own remembered bed, but it seemed forlorn in a strange room with nothing that belonged to the brother, not even the smell of his pockets with their trove of dead beetles and catapult rubber and half-sucked throat lozenges furred with lint. Better, the aunt advised, that the sister not be reminded too much. The dear Sisters at the convent had written that the child seemed unable to adjust. And after all she simply had to get used to his not being here. No point in moping.

But it seemed just as if he were dead in his bed in that distant house where the door opened on a veranda and where, in daytime, Mohommed Ali sat whirling the silver wheel of his sewing machine, one end of a seam clutched between his toes, and a scent of white petunias drifted under the trees.

Something had happened. Something awful, about which they

115

were determined to keep her in ignorance. On the second day of her return from school Patrice nerved herself to ask the question of the aunt. At any rate the embroidery frame had not been left behind; something fresh and gossamer was materializing in the aunt's beautiful nervous hands.

"Is he dead?" Patrice shot the question as she balanced on the arm of a chair in a square room which totally lacked enchantment.

"What?" The aunt, startled, raised her black eyes. "What did you say, darling?"

"I said is he dead."

"What are you talking about?" Old Jensen, the aunt thought frantically, and now those awful questions. Did Mr. Jensen's moustache droop when he was dead? And being unconventional could he possibly have gone to heaven? You would think the dear Sisters might have explained . . .

"You know who I mean," Patrice, unrelenting. Why don't they tell instead of hiding all his things and talking about him in those silly bright voices.

"But I don't know, darling. Nobody is dead. I mean . . ."

"Mr. Jensen is dead. Miss Meadows told me."

"Yes, darling, of course. So sad. But nobody else."

"I haven't had a letter for a long time. Where is he?"

The aunt understood perfectly and she put down her embroidery frame and gazed into eyes that were very like Doey's eyes, gray and accusing.

"Darling, how can you think such a thing? He's in school in Sussex, and doing so well at his lessons. And he has *grown!*"

A relief so intense, it flushed Patrice from her center to her brow. "Then why doesn't he come home for the holidays?"

"England is too far away, and very, very expensive. You will see him next year when we all go Home on leave."

Next year! They talked of time as though it were a single minute. Next year. Formless, like that feeling when she had fever and the walls receded and stood away from her and the floor swayed under her feet. And between this year and next, what? The end of Christmas; return to that dormitory with its dreary rows of beds, the dank washrooms with dented tin basins and yellow soap smelling of disinfectant, and the air smelling of drains and homesick flesh. The echo-

116

ing classroom, and notes of a piano in the distance, and outside in the chestnut trees the gay monkeys beckoning her imprisoned spirit, and beside her Cucumber and his black oiled hair. And always the bells . . . the bells. "The bells of hell go tingaling-aling for you but not for me!"

"Wherever did you learn that?" Sister Teresa rapping on her desk with the ruler. "Don't ever let me hear you again. . . ."

Patrice stared past the aunt's persuasive smile. "I don't want to go back."

"Darling, you must. Your education."

And even the mother conniving: "One must be brave. And it won't be for long."

"I don't want to be brave."

They simply could not understand. "And I hate this new place, too." Alone with her, the aunt was businesslike and brisk. "What on earth has happened to you, darling? You don't like anything. And this is such a lovely place, much nicer than that shabby old house and that jungly garden with snakes. Don't you like the electric lights? There are only three houses in the whole station that have electricity, and this is one."

"I hate it."

"One must be sensible, darling. And hating isn't sensible."

The aunt's embroidery a giant cobweb, her hands pale spiders spinning. And above her heavy brows the hair black and luxuriant in the latest coiffure copied from a Parisian magazine of fashion at least a year out of date. They had changed everything including the way they did their hair. Their dresses were different, too. Mohommed Ali had not come here with them because he did not want to leave his home and his family and he was getting too old to travel. Chota Ayah had become simpering and conceited on the father's promotion, and even Nizamat seemed somehow remote.

Estrangement, despair, a slow hardening into rebellion. "I'll run away, I'll keep running away until they expel me, and then you'll have to let me come home."

"One mustn't," the aunt reproved after a long silence, "talk nonsense. One doesn't run away."

"I ran away to the Meadowses' for tea and all that Mother Superior could do was punish. She couldn't kill me!"

117

The aunt's troubled eyes. "Darling, one gets used to things. One gets used to everything."

"I don't want to get used."

"But don't you understand? Running away doesn't help. One has to go back." Her voice was suddenly shaky. "This place or another. What difference does it make? One is always stuck."

"I won't be, ever."

"That's silly, as you will soon find out." Then the lecture, long drawn out. All the drab things: giving in, being good, being obedient, being sensible. Growing up. Understanding. The bravery of it all, the unheroic stance underneath; your ribs stuck full of arrows, your head cut off, lions waiting to pounce, everlasting snivel.

"It's hard for you to understand just now but you will when you are older."

Condescension. Suddenly from nowhere the remembered barb flung at the brother: "I know something you don't know!" Even when she hadn't known, it had worked.

Swiftly, a little out of breath, Patrice informed the aunt about What's-His-Name Harper's deformity, revealed to her that afternoon long ago in the ruined temple behind the garden of that other house.

This time the aunt did not put down her embroidery frame to lend emphasis to whatever it was she had to say. Instead she lifted the frame to the light and stared through it at Patrice. Behind that flimsy screen Patrice interestedly watched a wave of color dye the aunt's face and throat. "Deformity, darling?"

"He showed it to me himself."

"What else did he do?"

"Nothing."

The aunt's lips were trembling. "What did you do, darling?"

"I just went home."

"Frightened?"

Patrice rose from the arm of the chair and stood contemptuously before the aunt. "Of course not frightened. He couldn't help it if he was deformed, could he? There's nothing to be frightened of just because a person is deformed. And it wasn't even catching, like leprosy or anything."

The aunt thought: She's not even nine years old and what can I tell her? If Doey were ever to hear . . . he'd go back and shoot that boy.

118

But later, Alice—unpredictable Alice! The aunt listened to that reprehensible breakdown into laughter, a girl's laughter, wildly innocent despite marriage and two thumping children: "Oh, Eve, my dear! How *killing . . . deformed!*"

But now the aunt put on a maternal role. "Patrice, darling, listen to me. I don't think that this is a nice thing to talk about. I think it would be better if you just didn't talk about it to anybody else. Not to anybody. Try to think about something else, something nice and lovely. About next year when we will all go Home together and see Clem. About your birthday and what you would like for a present. Promise me, darling, that you won't ever mention that subject of poor young Harper to *anybody*. Later, when you are grown up, you will understand."

Patrice heard a sound from the garden beyond the open door where Nizamat, carried away by a new sense of splendor, had spread a rug on the grass under the tea table. The sound was faint and musical, rather like a run-down music box. Patrice went to the door and looked out. A hoopoe was walking on the grass beside the rug, and it did not fly away when she approached. She watched it for a moment, then said over her shoulder to the aunt: "Did you hear?"

"Hear what, darling?"

"The hoopoe. Out there on the lawn. Singing."

"Darling, hoopoes don't."

"They do." She felt a tingle of authority, of confidence, not bothering to ask herself where it came from. But she knew that she would not go back to the convent, that she would not learn to love this new abode, that she would promise nothing. "Hoopoes do sing. I just heard one."

9

There was a year in England, when the brother joined them for the summer holidays. Another kind of strangeness, intoxicating, a little sad. Now Patrice was certain that nothing stayed, therefore everything had a special value. She would never go back to the old house and to the feelings experienced there. She would never be seven years old again. From now on there would, instead, be memory. Names and words would take the place of real things; names and words would become daily more important, odd, like the look of a broken arm clumsily set and always, now, separate from the whole.

People whom one knows well, when encountered in strange places, become part of the strangeness, and so it happened with the brother seen again after two years' separation. She could scarcely bear to look at him for shyness. He had grown; his hair seemed to have changed color, become darker, his features more pronounced, his voice alien. And he was condescending, ignoring her or talking over her head. How could she expect to cope with this lordliness?

He basked in the mother's gaze, and in the aunt's. They raved over his sketchbooks, prophesying fame and splendor, and attended with diffidence to his boasts of exploits in school. Still thin and stooped at

120

the shoulders, his asthma and stammering worse than before, he excited a flooding tenderness in the women, but the father disliked him perhaps more than ever. It showed in small ways: in silence and indifference, toward which the brother reacted daringly with a practiced, mocking smile. His strength seemed phenomenal, like a weed springing out of a rock.

Early summer in London and the house in Kensington, and the grandmother tiny, pink and white, dressed always in a high-collared black moiré dress, with pince-nez, and a little enameled watch fastened with a gold fleur-de-lis on her bust. Very gentle, very refined. The mother and the grandmother were quite alike, sharing the same gentleness, the sudden soft laughter, love. Love for each other grown out of the love of woman and child to a kind of sister thing, forgiving and compassionate.

When, at the beginning of that summer, the grandmother fell sick and died, the mother was with her. All day and through the nights the mother nursed the grandmother, sitting beside her bed and holding the small soft hand no bigger than the sister's hand but with delicate transparent nails each showing its half moon, and on the left hand the broad wedding ring of bright Indian gold and a big round diamond which glowed in the subdued English light.

The mother never left the grandmother except to go to the bathroom. "You simply must get some rest," Doey protested, but the mother was adamant. On the night table beside the immaculately tended bed stood a bottle of Sanatogen, a heart tonic; there was also the grandmother's Church of England prayerbook with a purple silk marker, and the enameled watch, which the sister, allowed briefly into the room, coveted more each day. There was always the musty smell of an old person dying, and the imperishable scent of the mother, trying to hold her back.

"Alice'll wear herself out," the aunt said somberly. "Why on earth won't she get a nurse?"

"Her ideas," Doey murmured, his headlong spirit daunted a little by this other, this transcendent older love. "Her mother brought her into life, and must not be left alone when the time comes."

They were in awe of this flawless passion, and the grandmother died contentedly and the two stayed like that for a long time, hand in hand. Out on the street newsboys were shouting news of a great

121

ship gone down among icebergs, and the aunt, meeting the father on the stairs, said in disbelief: "The *Titanic?* It can't be true!"

In the white-paneled drawing room of the grandmother's house there was a portrait of the grandfather in epaulets and scarlet sash and dashing clothes, one hand resting on a sword hilt. A kindly face and straightforward eyes. A soldier with ribbons on his breast, he had died not in battle but of a fall down some steps, and was buried in Nice, France, of all places, where he and the grandmother had been spending that last year of his life.

The cuckoo clock of a previous visit had vanished, but there was an enormous rocking horse which belonged to the two spectral cousins, Vera and Veronica, which the brother rode with such violence winning the Derby that he broke the rockers. The cousins' mother, who had been the grandmother's second child, had died when these twins were born, and their father had quickly married the pretty governess and had gone to live with her in Italy, from where he regularly sent money to the grandmother, and presents for the girls, but never came back himself. What, now, would become of the twins? To Patrice it was all quite awesome in a secretly rather thrilling way. There is something exotically baffling about relatives and their affairs, people mysteriously bound to oneself yet somehow remote.

And then there was the grandmother's funeral. In all funerals, Patrice was to reflect later, there is this distinction, something honorable, noble, fine. And for the modest, dignified little grandmother it was no less imposing: the black hearse with glass all round and the coffin elegant in black velvet with a sheaf of roses, and the two stately horses with black plumes in their headbands and the coachmen with black bands round their tall hats, and the mother's face white under her black veil, the grandeur meaningless for her, her heart bruised beyond mending by this superlative loss.

After the funeral the aunt went to stay with friends in France. The father insisted that he must take Alice away for a little change to the Isle of Wight, and the brother and sister were to stay in Kensington with the cousins and a nursery governess called Miss Bipper. She had excellent references, the father tried to console the mother. Nothing to worry about. Experienced with children, and she had worked only in good families. And it will only be for a week or two, darling, while you get a little rest.

Bipper's face was yellow and her eyes streaked with little red veins. She wore an impressive uniform of gray serge with white starched collar and cuffs, and when she went outdoors, a gray fedora with black satin streamers down her back. Her smile was infrequent and unlovely. The day after the departure of the father and mother for the Isle of Wight Bipper threw a breadboard at the brother and cut a gash in his left eyebrow, the scar of which he carried for the rest of his life.

When Bipper bathed the twins she jabbed spongefuls of soap in their eyes and said that would teach them, though what it was they were supposed to learn remained a mystery. She found the father's brandy supply and went to it with a will, and ferreted about until she discovered his store of Turkish cigarettes, and smoked them with the air of a confirmed boulevardier.

She scrabbled about in every drawer and desk, read every letter she found, and transferred various small objects, including the grandmother's enameled watch, to her own trunk in her bedroom. She instructed the brother and sister that if they didn't keep their dirty little mouths shut they'd get what-for. The twins, catatonic with terror, vomited up their food at meals, and Patrice and the brother conspired together how they might escape from the house and find their way to the Isle of Wight, or even across the Channel to France, where the aunt had gone. The brother thought they might chop up a lot of glass very fine and put it in Bipper's tea, and Patrice wondered whether, between them, they might somehow lure Bipper to an upstairs window and push her out.

They existed in this conspiratory condition of premeditated murder while Bipper served them revolting meals of weak tea and Grape-Nuts and a kind of watery stew which the brother whispered to Patrice and the twins reminded him of diarrhea. This brought on a fit of hysterical giggling and Bipper boxed their ears until they reeled, and told them that if they did not appreciate good wholesome food they could bloody well go without.

Suppose, Patrice thought, in desolation, that the father and mother should not come back after all? Suppose they were to drown in a

123

boating accident, or the father take it into his head to run away with some pretty nursemaid as unlike Bipper as one could conceivably imagine, and the mother to die of grief. What then would be left except Nurse Bipper. . . .

Bipper battened on these unvoiced but visible terrors. She told them ghost stories which she more than half believed herself. The grandmother's room, left open by the mother, and sunny with flowers on the table beside the bed with its gay counterpane, was now meaningfully closed by Bipper. Not, she pointed out, that that made any difference, since ghosts could walk through closed doors. She had, she whispered sibilantly to her quaking audience, seen the grandmother's ghost with her own eyes, walking about outside *their* bedrooms, and even in the drawing room late at night. They had loved the grandmother; now they dreaded her worse than they ever had the churel in those far-off, never to be forgotten, beloved trees.

And what, Bipper wanted to know, made them so bloody sure that the father and mother would return from the Isle of Wight? Parents who selfishly went off to have a good time, abandoning their children . . . And the money left her to buy food was running out. Where the bloody hell was more to come from was what she would like to know, not to mention her *wyges.* Having reduced them to paralysis, Bipper betook herself to the last of the father's brandy and his Turkish cigarettes. Cruelty became her, and within two weeks she looked ten years younger. She smelled younger too, with a glorious tincture of Courvoisier and the best Turkish leaf.

When at last the father and mother came home Bipper was all smiles, her molars clicking welcome. The father said nothing at first, but he sniffed the air with interest. The mother read the truth instantly in the children's faces and her heart ignited with fury. Next day was Bipper's promised day off and the father and mother questioned first the brother, then Patrice, then the twins. With memories of Bipper baleful in their minds, they knew nothing. Nothing about the brandy and cigarettes, the ashtray with a silver lizard for a handle, the grandmother's enameled watch.

"I'm going to have a damned good dekko for myself," the father announced, and fell ravening on Bipper's belongings in her room. Lucky, Patrice reflected, that I didn't take the watch myself. He would have found out, all right. But now . . . sheer joy at the prospect of Bipper's imminent undoing. The father was courteous enough at first, in his deadly way; then he escorted Bipper from the storied architecture of empty bottles and cigarette tins in the cellar to the cache in her black trunk at the foot of her bed. She was immediately highly indignant and denied the evidence of all eyes. The father called her a stupid vicious bitch and gave her the sack. She spat accurately into his face and stood by her rights, vociferously demanding her *wyges* and threatening him with the *lor.* They went at it hammer and tongs while the brother squirmed with excitement and the others held their breath. Then Bipper proceeded to have some kind of a fit and the father and mother put her to bed, where she sank into a sinister calm, and the father said: "By God, you could light a match with her breath!"

They sent for a doctor but before he arrived Bipper revived somewhat. Catching Patrice loitering interestedly in the passage, she dragged her into the room and bent her backward over the black trunk. Her hands round Patrice's throat were steel claws. Patrice thought: If she forces my eyes out of their sockets and they drop on the carpet will they still go on seeing? She bit Bipper's arm and kicked her, but Bipper's fingers had found the windpipe and Patrice was being strangled to death when the father and doctor burst into the room.

"She'll be all right," the doctor said when five minutes later Patrice came gaspingly to life in the mother's arms. "A narrow squeak, though!"

They had forgotten Bipper but she reminded them soon enough. Raging naked down the staircase, she reached the front door and the front steps before she tripped and fell. Her flat gray breasts like stale pancakes hung on each side of her, and the father, looking away while he helped the doctor, thought: This was once a woman. Then the mother arrived with a blanket, and the police came, and they carried Bipper away in a kind of hearse affair, and the quiet after that was dim and velvety, with a bit of a sore throat and a great sense of languor and little glass plates of ice cream to make up for it all.

"One must," the mother declared later that summer, echoing the Holy Sisters, "learn to adjust."

She sounded tired, the sparkle dimmed a little with the grandmother's death and the recurring nightmare of what Bipper might

125

have done. "We shall not," she said, "be going back to India for a while, and when we do everything will probably be different. Perhaps we'll have Nizamat with us again, and Chota Ayah, and Mohommed Ali if he isn't too old and blind. We shall have to find a new house, a new place."

Patrice thought bleakly: Why should things be different? Why this continuous changing, the loss of landmarks, the disappearance of friends? Like gypsies, the brother suggested, rather pleased with the idea. Away from school he affected a fondness for it and for his chums, praising everything he really feared and hated. But his marks were poor and the father was bitter. "Here I am giving up the service to sit for bar exams at Gray's Inn. Starting over again at my age, and you won't even try to do better than B's and C's in anything except those damned silly drawings!"

To give up the service and sit for bar examinations at Gray's Inn. To live like gypsies. To, as the aunt said gloomily on her return from France, "Pass up the bone for the shadow." Did it mean that they would live in tents as they did for fun during Christmas camp? Did it mean they would simply be poor, too poor to afford a house? Poor like the Meadowses, desperate, weeping? What was poor?

"It's not having any money," the brother explained, unconcerned. "If you don't have money you're poor. You can't buy food or clothes or anything. People don't like you. Then they get sick of helping you and you die of starvation."

Patrice felt a draining away inside of her, a brand-new kind of fear. Finding the mother's purse, she opened it and examined the coins for the first time with deep interest. There was a gold sovereign with a picture of a man spearing a dragon. Saint George. The king's head on the other side. Some silver shillings and big brown pennies and one very thin threepenny bit like the kind people put in Christmas pudding. How beautiful money was really, round and shining, taking warmth from your hand, each piece separate, distinct, each meaning something different. Without enough of these a person would starve and go without clothes. Be naked like Bipper when she fell down the front steps with her bobbies flapping while the father said angrily: "Stop staring and go away, all of you!"

The aunt said disapprovingly: "I think Doey is making a great mistake to give up government service. After all, it is something

126

certain, to be depended on. He has already done so brilliantly. If only now he'd be patient, tactful . . . he could easily be I.G. when he's sixty, and Mr. Onions told me a long time ago perhaps even a knighthood!"

The father fumed. Why must women harp so on security? As if there was such a thing! As for him, he would no longer prostitute himself to any bloody government. He had had enough. He knew too bloody much. Government was hypocrisy, its puling about the good of the governed poor rot.

"But one must," the mother protested, "have *some* sort of government. What is the alternative?"

Doey didn't give a damn. A man must learn to sort things out for himself. And the writing was on the wall. More and more, men were turning into cowards. Making excuses like love and responsibility and duty to one's family and law and order, just to dodge the truth. He was tired of being a blasted policeman, lording it over other men. A mercenary, when you came down to it.

The mother was upset. What *was* the alternative? There had to be policemen, magistrates, district commissioners, inspectors general, lieutenant governors, viceroys. There had to be certain people to protect other people. There had to be soldiers. And why should Doey find it preferable to be a barrister than a government official? Why should the understanding and application of law be superior to the law itself, and to order, and a decent peaceful existence, not rich perhaps, but with honor and distinction and a pension at the end of it? After all, there were the children and one did not oneself stay young forever. . . .

"There you go!" Doey cried in exasperation. Couldn't she see that it was a question of how much of a man one could hope to be? How much nerve and integrity . . . how long avoid the rigor mortis of hypocrisy and habit?

Men, the father went on excitedly, never really try themselves out, never really exert their might and main. Look at Onions. A fine chap, but satisfied with his own and other men's limitations. Look at Sparks. A menial at heart. Even a race horse puts more into life! There was, the father suddenly began to shout, something obscene in being a government servant. "It makes a bugger out of you."

"Doey, the children."

"They might as well hear it. They'll grow up in a generation of *voyeurs.*"

The brother twitted Patrice later: "I bet you don't know what that means—bugger."

She countered recklessly: "And I bet you don't know what voy-yer means."

"I can always find it in my French dictionary at school."

She said no more, letting him win.

10

*I*n the early morning the river had a silvery unreal appearance and Patrice could not be sure where the water's edge merged with the shore. Then the birds appeared, dropping out of a sky colored like the water itself. Stints and avocets and lapwings and sandpipers with delicate shining legs like the black stems of maiden-hair fern scurried along the water's edge in search of food, and when they flew their voices filled the air in silvery particles of sound.

There was always a precarious minute or two when Patrice got out of bed and stood on the veranda overlooking an unkempt garden where night still lingered, shadowy and cool. She was sixteen, brown-haired, thin, surprise subsisting in her eyes. Her body had matured early but her mind retained its mixture of innocence and guile, as it would for some years to come.

She set great store by these moments of solitude and privacy, spying unobserved upon the world. Seen thus every detail sank into her consciousness so that long afterward she had only to recall one detail and have the rest crowd upon her. This habit of posting herself at odd moments at a distance from people and events had grown on her with the established absence of the brother, who had disappeared into an Australian wilderness from which they rarely heard an echo.

The father, dying of tubercular meningitis in one of the rooms behind her, sometimes murmured bitterly about his son, about filial ingratitude and serpents' teeth. The mother, secretly mourning the lost son and preparing for further grief, thought: You never loved him. But she did not say it. She said little as she moved, now, warily between the present and the prowling future.

There was a little money saved, some insurance, and her jewels, and the aunt had returned to France, whence she wrote cheerfully that they were not to worry about *her*—she would manage. Dear friends had kindly taken her into their home as companion to a decrepit relative, and anyhow her needs were modest. Of course, the war made an enormous difference in everything, and to everyone. Dear Papa's estates in Vernon had been blown away by the German guns and she had heard there was nothing left, my dear, nothing. India seemed very remote from all this, but safe!

Doey and Alice must think of themselves and of the girl, Patrice, since the boy, Clem, who might have fitted himself to be of some help, had taken himself off. The aunt wrote nostalgically of Doey's great promise in everything that he had ever undertaken. Of course, leaving the service had been a mistake, but the new venture as barrister had opened brilliantly and the rewards, while they lasted, had been worthwhile. Who was to say that it might not eventually have led to a judgeship in the High Court, if it had not been for the accident of this sudden dreadful illness? But who could have foreseen that Doey, that fine mechanism of a man, would be laid low by disease, and in the very prime of his life?

Doey said: "When it's over I want you and Patrice to go Home. This is not a country for women to be stranded in."

The mother held back her tears. She had had ample practice. "Don't talk nonsense, Doey. You are going to get well."

"Marry again if you find the right chap. You are still young and lovely and there's no reason—"

"I never," the mother interrupted unsteadily, "heard such nonsense!"

"Alice, listen to me. Things are going to pot out here for our jat. It would have happened war or no war. When the change comes these

130

people are not going to want us. They'll have barely enough to go round for themselves. You have seen the fate of women out here—of Indian women, of people like Edna Meadows and her mother, of poor whites. I don't much believe in the hereafter but I want to feel sure, now, that you and Patrice will go Home. At any rate there you'll have a sporting chance."

She tried raillery. "What at? The right chap?"

"I'm not joking. And there's the girl. No place, this, for her to grow up in without protection, without money. I don't want her marrying some kuchnai Englishman or university-bred raja simply because she may have an eye on his horse!"

Doey had a little time left in which to meditate on matters which had often troubled the mother and the aunt. He had taken life full tilt and had been thrown, and now it rankled that he should find himself at last stuck with the same puerile misgivings as women—insecurity, ineptness, dread. Fighting his way sometimes out of a smothering dark, he looked at Patrice seated beside his bed with her nose in some damned book. When he indicated to her that he would like her to take his hand she did so without glancing up, but with a faint compliant smile.

She read indiscriminately or spent hours scribbling in her room when she should have been in the fresh air. Both his children had these absurd notions of their destiny: the boy to be an artist, this one to be a writer. Where had it come from? Not from him, not from Alice. *Her* antecedents a long line of distinguished nincompoops, his own hard-headed, cold-blooded rentiers glorified by Eve into aristocrats. And now here this brother and sister without education to speak of, both incandescent with imagination, restive, vaulting. Where had it come from? Where would it take them?

Where had life taken *him?* Impatient, scorning the pedestrian approach of better-trained, even-tempered men, where had his headlong passage taken him? Into this dank tunnel of illness, dimly lit by realizations and perceptions arrived at too late.

Doey's thoughts, when he had any that were coherent, turned on the sound of Patrice's voice, and her laugh rather too loud for a girl, bursting out of her like a rocket. He liked to feel that he might have passed something of his intrepid spirit on to her. Occasionally when the morphine wore off a bit he had a strange idea that he might like

131

to marry her. Certainly between them they would never produce such a son as he had with Alice—a son selfish, puling, sickly. But oh, Patrice, my darling, stay with me, stay with me forever after in the hereafter with your strong hand on mine and your voice ringing through these borrowed rooms and your bright gaze holding me . . . holding me.

For Patrice the best time of day was the early morning. Leaving the house before anyone was awake, except for Nizamat scraping burned toast in the kitchen, she took her daily walk down the weedy path toward the road and the sand flats, mother-of-pearl at this hour. Sand and water mother-of-pearl and silver, and everything fragile, glorying in its brevity.

Reaching the dusty, deserted road, she looked back at the house half hidden behind a frieze of palms. Disliking it at first, she had become fond of it, of its ornate gardens gone to the dogs because no mali could cope with its European complexities. She had become accustomed to odd-shaped rooms crammed with moldering furniture, and casement windows which came off their hinges when you tried to open them.

A borrowed house, offered them by a distant eccentric cousin in a spasm of generosity when Doey fell ill. At least, the cousin had pointed out, it will be a roof over your heads until . . . And I am never there, what with my engagements in Calcutta and Bombay, not to mention London and Paris and New York. Princess Sita Devi, this distant cousin of Alice's called herself, dumpily and totally English, duping foreign audiences with her fraudulent Indian dances performed with the aid of an aging and torpid python.

Born Kitty Braithwaite, only child of a wealthy indigo planter in Bihar, this cousin had an adventurous spirit from the beginning, with a taste for the gaudy and bizarre. What she lacked in beauty she made up in a sense of fun, a flair for sex, and a lot of luck. A sense of rhythm totally unrelated to talent completed the picture, but she was, while she lasted, something of a sensation if not wholly a success. And she could be kind. When it reached her ears that Doey's illness would be fatal she had written to Alice offering this house as a haven free of charge.

It had seemed like a good idea. It was in fact the only idea available, and whatever was to come afterward . . . But Alice's thoughts

132

shied from such prospects. She marveled a bit at Patrice, serenely unconcerned as she read *Anna Karenina* under the palm trees in the crazy garden, or sat with Doey in his big, quiet, airy bedroom, or simply daydreamed about her first, her new and absorbing, love, the young Roland.

Thinking about it the mother drew her breath. Roland! Twenty years old with a piddling job in the office of a sugar factory nearby, and what prospects? And Patrice obsessed. I must talk to her, Alice admonished herself sternly. I simply must. Only sixteen, and he twenty! Even if she were older and he better situated . . . The first time one falls in love! And God knows few enough opportunities in this country . . . And without the father's strength . . .

One early morning Patrice walked quickly down to the river. Here the sand was scribbled with patterns of birds' feet, human feet, jackals', the broad trail of a crocodile which had heaved itself out of the water to sprawl on the sand before scrambling back to its lair. The light was changing fast, losing its polish. The air smelled damp, with a hint of cold smoke from the burned-out funeral pyres which lay scattered on the sand. A long low boat shaped like a gigantic eyelash, with a brown lateen sail, drifted down the river and a man crouched in it played a reed flute, three or four minor notes, intimate and troubling. The sail turned to rose, then was gone, and there were only the water birds shining like toys along the river's edge, and the ruined pyres where already kites and crows were delving for an eye, a wrinkled intestine, a tongue still caught between blackened teeth.

She thought of The Game she and the brother played years ago at Christmas camp. Would she ever see him again? And what did he look like now, a young man with a moustache and dark hair and eyes strangely unlike her own or the father's or the mother's or the aunt's?

Patrice stirred a burned-out pyre with a stick and the white bones of a human foot bloomed intricately in the ashes. She found herself drawn to the fact of this death, this translation, to the thought of a vulture feeding on a pair of eyes then soaring into the empyrean. What visions did it liberate up there? What memories? What news? The stilled rhythm of this dead person, his passion and gaiety and hunger and hope, his heartbeat—here it was, all of it, tinctured with the night and the first rotting of the sun.

How silly to be revolted or sad! And how mistaken Roland to

exclaim in disgust that she was morbid. And he had immediately held the country to blame for it—these bloody natives and their barbarous ways. Patrice suffered in his esteem for having been born among them, and of such feckless parents as she had. Not to be raised a seemly English miss with a smug little maidenhead and breath sweetened with Lyle's Golden Syrup amid the amenities of Wimbledon or Saint Ives . . . what rotten luck!

Roland was handsome in his way, with thick tennis-playing hands and a strong sense of sahibhood. He was afflicted with an almost continuous sexual urge and schemed to seduce Patrice. But how was it to be achieved under the circs? The father dying by inches in that weird old house, and the mother's sibylline watchfulness. And everywhere the blasted natives—house servants, gardeners, ayahs, coolies! Ubiquitous genies popping up from nowhere, from behind every bush and tree. They didn't know the meaning of privacy themselves. The whole damned country a race of peeping toms, making the girl nervous.

Well, he had a two-year contract with the sugar company and then by God he'd look for a job with some maharaja or other, or perhaps as assistant on one of the big plantations across the river. Polo and tennis and shikar. He must learn to ride a horse, brush up on his imaginary ancestors, sandpaper his Lancashire accent. Better chance then to meet some pukka English girl with a complexion of roses and cream and a bank account. That, or he would go back home and forget about aspiring to be a sahib with a big S.

Meantime there was this kid Patrice. He would naturally try not to get her in a fix . . . after all, a mere kid! But still just about the only thing available. Unless one counted those dried-up old mems flapping about the tennis court uttering hoarse cries, like storks, and giving you the glad eye over crème de menthe of an evening.

If only Patrice . . . She confused him. He sensed her ardor, her newly awakened desire. She was artlessly and recklessly in love with him and his dark blue eyes and his hair smelling of Eau de Quinine, his fine teeth, his kisses, his urgency which he could easily pass off as responsive love. Patrice, a mere kid whom he felt sure he could have for the asking, or for that matter without asking. But those baffling eyes which looked straight through you to some distant zone, and that obstinacy. Loving him though she did, unmistakably, she

134

was still proof against his trying to educate her. "I'm not morbid. It's just interesting, that's all. And in a way poetic."

"Poetic!" They were walking along the edge of a field above the river where it flowed under the ramparts of an ancient Mogul fort. "Poetic! Dead nigger guts in a funeral pyre poetic! Well, I must say."

It was, he decided, due in part to all that reading she did. She was a strange mixture. Bookish, yet she could ride anything on four legs and shoot rings round him with rifle or gun. The poor damn sick father responsible for that side of her, no doubt. But what an upbringing! That ease among the natives which they'd take advantage of one of these days. And fluent in their boli, even daring to correct *him:* "You don't use the feminine when you want to speak in the informal. . . ."

"I don't want to damn well use any of it!"

"But why not try to speak it properly?"

Roland had assumed his compatriots' curious notions about learning to speak a foreign tongue so it could be understood. An apt pupil of the Ow-Jow school, with a few foul swear words thrown in, he spoke Hindustani with a strong Lancashire accent which convulsed Patrice. He was not amused, and once warned her darkly that her own proficiency might do her no good in the long run. The more one talked like *them* the more one became like *them.* One ended by going native. Had she considered that dire possibility?

Patrice frowned. "What is there to consider, really?"

"Marrying," he explained. "If you expect to marry a decent white chap you better not go about jabbering like the sweeper's wife."

Patrice laughed. He never could make her wince or weep. He was her first and only love and nothing would change that fact. It transcended all things; it was her initial exercise of that charity which is most exacting: forgiveness by the intelligent of the stupid. She did not understand this at the time, thinking no more than that he was a bit of an ass but that she craved him beyond words English, French, Hindi, or any other.

Roland wondered why he bothered with her. She was not his type and never would be. She had no money and her family was not the sort that could be expected to give a chap a leg up in the world. Besides, he had lusher ambitions. Yet given half a chance he could have the clothes off her and the whole thing neatly over and done

135

with. Well, why not? The father was helpless, and what could the mother do or say in face of the fait accompli? It did not necessarily mean a baby. She was very young and the first time ... perhaps even the second time ... It almost never happens except in books.

Almost every afternoon after work Roland bicycled across the fields from the factory to the old house above the river, and the mother invited him to stay for tea. She was courteous, gentle. Through her exquisite breeding she implied a trust in him which he knew damned well she didn't feel. In a mysterious and maddening fashion she put him in his place and he hated her for it.

Now as Patrice walked along the river's edge in the first gleam of morning she was on her way to meet Roland at the Mogul fort. It was Sunday, and he was free for the day. He had begged her the day before. He had something particular to say to her, to ask of her. He was tender, protective, solemn, and the mother's anxiety, timidly voiced, was uncalled for, even base.

Patrice felt her pulses sing and nothing could have prevented her going to meet him. Although innocent she was not ignorant; her body recognized its urgency, and it was none of the mother's business. "Don't try to tell me, Alice. I'll ask you if I ever want to know anything. But I don't, not now."

Intimidated, the mother recalled in silence a day four years ago when Patrice had come rushing to her to announce that she was bleeding to death. She was twelve years old and the physiological inevitable had come upon her rather sooner than anticipated. It had been a frightful occasion, a kind of delirium of fear. Babble about neem trees in the garden, of Our Lord hemorrhaging on His cross, of clotted martyrs, and a mother buffalo dropping her bloodied calf.

The father had demanded in consternation: "Why didn't you warn her that it might happen?"

The mother, distracted: "I didn't think. Darling, darling, it's all right. You are not dying. It's nothing. It's natural. You'll be perfectly well again in a few days, I promise you!"

But now the mother wakened to hear Patrice leave the house and start toward the river. The mother thought: I'm alone. Doey unconscious. And she's gone off to meet that beastly boy. And he means business. The way he stares at her. And she's dotty over him. Oh, God.

The mother ran into the garden, where the first birds were begin-

136

ning to stir. Patrice had vanished. The mother thought: I'll send Nizamat after her. But where would she have gone? How find her? They had undoubtedly arranged it so no one would know where to look for them. The mother thought: She'll let him do anything he wants. And it will be too late. I should have said something long before this but she has held me off with those eyes, hostile, warning. Anyhow, she would never have listened. Carried away on this first tidal wave, she'll hand herself over to him with zest. And I can do nothing, nothing!

Then the father called to her from his sickroom and she went to him, ironing out her anguish. If it had been Doey I would have done the same and after all didn't I? But that was Doey . . . Doey my perfect man, not this clod of a boy with his smirk and his blackheads. God protect her. Protect her, God, dear God.

Roland was waiting under the wall of the old fort where a small path ran beneath it just above the river. He had long ago selected the ideal spot, a kind of hollow shaped by age among the ancient sand-stone curtains. He had brought along an ulster and had anointed himself with cologne and brushed his teeth until the gums bled, all in preparation for this pathetic debut. It would not be the first time he had lain with a girl; the last had been several months before, with his servant's sister, and there had followed a week or two of acute mental anguish when he thought he might have contracted syphilis from her. It turned out to be a bad case of prickly heat but it had frightened him and he had decided on a regimen of stern self-control until such time as Miss Right came along . . . and by God here she was as she had promised she would be! Flushed with walking, the brown hair damp on her temples, her eyes shining like the moon-colored river below.

Roland wasted no time. He dared not trust his own excitement too far, and she might take fright or some stupid bastard of a coolie come meandering round the corner and spoil things.

"Darling!" he said, and took her in his arms. Her body felt light, vibrant, timid. He crushed her against his chest and kissed her raven-ously with an ungainly violence such as he had not dared until now for fear of putting her off. "Darling, dearest, sweetheart," etc., etc., etc. He mouthed the endearments between her teeth and felt her trembling. It intoxicated him. He felt omnipotent.

Patrice, fresh from reading *Anna Karenina* and vaguely expecting something different, she could not have said just what, found herself suddenly borne down on the ulster already carefully spread on the ground. He pulled her skirt up round her waist and stripped down her drawers.

"Why on earth did you wear those things today of all days?"

"Don't tear them . . . they're brand new!"

He was kissing her wildly, biting her, and she felt the great racket of his hand between her legs. Then he lay on top of her and suddenly she thought of What's-His-Name Harper years ago in the broken temple below the garden of that house which remained forever the single home of memory. What's-His-Name Harper and his peculiar deformity. So this was what it had meant all the time. This.

The mother had sent Nizamat in pursuit after all, and he, having missed little all these months, had no difficulty in tracing Patrice's footprints along the shore to where a path branched up the bank to the great wall of the fort. Nizamat was now a man of fifty years, dedicated to the father and mother, to their house. Bent on his dual mission he walked fast, running part of the way. Now he climbed the path until he was alongside the sandstone curtain and could see a corner of the hollow where Patrice lay suffocating under her lout. Nizamat coughed loudly, cleared his throat, coughed again.

He was none too soon. Roland raised his head and bellowed: *"Jow, bhainchut!"*

Nizamat coughed again and explained in a matter-of-fact voice that the Memsahib wished Patrice Miss Sahib to return immediately to the house. It was most urgent. He would wait to escort her.

Roland scrambled to his feet and dragged on his trousers. He rushed out of the little cavern and saw the servant standing discreetly against the wall. Nizamat was dressed in his customary livery of dark-green jacket buttoned to the chin, white pantaloons, and white turban with Doey's monogram. He was a dignified figure and no one had raised a hand against him until this moment. Roland struck him in the face, making him reel. "Dirty sneaking spying swine! Let that teach you."

Patrice, rumpled but intact, walked past Roland to her servant. Blood slipped down his cheek and he mopped it with the end of his turban and said quietly: "The Memsahib wishes you to come to her

138

immediately." And then he said with that strange little sound which in France buglers call the *sanglot:* "My child, your father is dead."

Patrice took his arm. Turning their backs on Roland they walked down the path and then back along the river's edge where the water birds flew shining in the brilliance, uttering their small, questing cries.

II

From France the aunt wrote long letters in her beautiful upright hand on gray marbled paper with a deep black border for mourning. And between repeated expressions of devotion and grief was her concern that *this* should have happened to Alice *of all people.* Why of all people, Patrice wondered. Well, because Doey would not have had it so, that Alice be obliged to work for a living. Doey, the aunt hinted, would turn in his grave if he knew that Alice had accepted a *position* to teach French in the convent. French, in which dear Alice herself was anything but proficient. French to a ragtag crew of piebald urchins who couldn't speak their own boli any too well! But how else keep the wolf from the door? How else enable Patrice to complete her "education"?

Cucumber, turned an imperceptible twelve years, had been summarily transferred to Saint Stephen's up the hill. Concupiscence might rear its ugly head at any moment and the Sisters were taking no chances. Deprived of his loyal collaboration, Patrice's marks slithered to the bottom and there they stayed. Sister Teresa was at a loss. "You were doing so well. Now why all of a sudden . . ."

Mother Superior judged, pityingly: "Perhaps her father's death. Perhaps when she begins to get over it she'll do better."

They promoted Patrice just the same, on the strength of a marked superiority in English composition and a providentially discovered aptitude for history and something called natural science—the last consisting of drawing butterflies and dead leaves "from life."

And every year those stories taking shape in exercise book after exercise book. The mother, furtively and guiltily turning the pages, was by turns horrified and hilarious. Where in the world could the child have got it all? These characters, these events and places she could not possibly have experienced, and all put down with obviously a minimum of plagiarization except where *Anna Karenina* had made a hit, or *The Count of Monte Cristo,* or Ouida.

The exercise books went far to explain those determined forays into musty little club libraries, and pocket money squandered at railway station bookstalls. Patrice craved books as some children crave sweets. The mother, herself the product of nursery governess schooling and a youth innocent of intellectual necessities, now found herself confronted, in her own child, by that most unsettling of apparitions: the human imagination.

After Doey's death they lived at the convent and Patrice went back to the old habit of counting the days for the Christmas holidays, when they must return to their own place, wherever that might be. Perhaps the aunt would come back from France, perhaps the brother from Australia. Perhaps. She waited in vain for the mother's joyful concurrence in these hopes, for a lighting up of anticipation, an excited unfolding of plans.

The mother's smile remained indulgent but noncommittal. And yet her delicacy had suddenly become a thing of steel. It was Patrice's turn to ask herself: Where did *that* come from? Unskilled, untutored in almost everything except the niceties of a febrile existence gone forever, Alice rose to the occasion like a bird to the air.

One had after all to go on living, to wear clothes and pay bills. There was for instance the bania Shapurji threatening to sue simply because one just didn't happen to have money with which to pay his bill. So first the emerald brooch was sold. Then Mr. Onions, now Collector in an important district, getting wind of the situation and freshly engaged to a lovely girl from Home, wrote with infinite tact to ask whether the mother could bring herself to part with those pearl earrings he had always admired in the old days, and which Doey had

had made for her when the sister was born.

The mother hesitated a long time over parting with the earrings. But then Shapurji called in person—that bania with ocher caste mark between his gimlet eyes, smelling richly of attar of roses and ghee. Wasn't he after all himself a poor man? Did he not also have to live? And this bill had run its ninth month. Like a fetus, the mother reflected wanly. But how could it have added up to so much? What an insidious thing, money! Just quietly piling up on the wrong side of the ledger. All that imported wool for knitting sweaters for herself and Patrice. Tins of guava jelly, of tea, of condensed milk; Huntley and Palmer's biscuits, Buncombe's sweets, sardines, tapioca; a tweed jacket for Nizamat, a sari for Chota Ayah; tussah silk shirts for the brother in Australia, presents for the poor dear Meadowses, fancy notepaper on which to write long letters to the brother and the aunt.

Shapurji carried everything in his shop in Burra Bazaar. His bills were written in iridescent ink on sheets of foolscap without a single mistake. He performed complicated feats of addition, with very little subtraction, on the digits of his fingers and toes, and the total was always frightful, an abortion of a thing rounding out its time and landing on your doorstep. When Doey was alive he had handled all the household accounts and had made her an allowance for her own and the children's clothes. There had never seemed to be any problems, any debts. They had lived "within their means"; but then, there had been means!

Sighing, the mother parted with her pearl earrings to Mr. Onions, and Shapurji, paid off in full, squirmingly extended further credit. People like the mother always paid up in the end. It was one of the wonderful things about them. He never hesitated to extend credit to the mother and to let the bills run six months, nine, a year. And without charging interest, whereas with the truly needy and therefore unreliable he tacked on fifteen to twenty percent or more.

Secretly Shapurji admired the mother, recognizing her jat, and even more secretly he coveted the girl. When the bill was paid he dispatched his servant with an offering of fruit and freshly made sweets and a garland of jasmine. A pretty touch which Doey would have seen through at once. But then if Doey had been there, there would have been no such bill. Shapurji knew this well. He appreciated the impregnability of these people, their élan. And let him so much as cast a single meaningful glance at that leggy high-spirited wench, and some male friend would pop up from nowhere and shoot him on the spot.

Not so with the Meadowses. For two years Shapurji had kept Edna Meadows and her mother, sleeping with the daughter, indulgently providing for both. So it had come to that and everyone knew it although Edna Meadows held her head high as though everything that was the case was not, and anyhow they could all go to hell.

But for *Alice* to be forced to sell her jewels, to take a position teaching . . . The Sisters, it was true, had made it as easy as possible for her. They were understaffed and needed a French teacher, and felt themselves lucky to get a *lady* in the bargain. The mother and Patrice were allocated rooms in Mother Superior's own house next to the little stone church, and Nizamat and Chota Ayah godowns with the school servants. Rent was deducted from the mother's salary. A salary! Her own earnings. Struggling at night with a French grammar, the mother, married twenty years to a Frenchman to whom nothing had ever seemed difficult, paused occasionally to marvel at herself, at fate, and at the asininity of her kind. Brought up to be leeches on their men, and later on their children. Not seeing it in that light, of course—how could she? But reluctantly aware, now, of fresh values tainted by daydreams, by a stubborn conviction that this state of things could not last. It was no more than a passing aberration of fate. Something was bound to turn up, life to return to the charmed norm she had always known. Hers was no more than a gallant gesture deserving of the warmest praise.

One had to be impervious to the fact that in the entire country were millions of women selling body and soul for a handful of rice, hedged in by a degradation which didn't count because they did not happen to be white. Yet the mother was racked by pity for those she encountered, and cursed in her fluent Hindustani and her broken French the brutes who made such a world possible . . . though what else could one expect? And she was recklessly generous, piling up that bill at Shapurji's so that she might send Edna Meadows a basket of imported groceries, English wool for a dress, fine lisle stockings and Yardley's cologne. Pounds of flesh, these, on which Shapurji could hardly, on the face of it, exact his fifteen or twenty percent.

One must never, the mother admonished herself, echoing Doey, give in. When all was said and done there could be no such thing as *stooping* to something *beneath* one.

"Claptrap!" The brother wrote scathingly to the sister from Australia, where he was now married and working on a farm near Perth:

> What's wrong with work? If people can't afford their delusions they better chuck them overboard. I tell you, a few months in this country cures one of a lot of soggy ideas. Here they simply loathe the Sahib. I used to think the chaps in school in Sussex were a rough lot, but you should see these people. The entrance to this place has a sign nailed to it saying: "Shut this fucking gate, you!" Their idea of humor is to slit your saddle girth so you can take a damn good toss and if you break your silly neck it merely adds to the joke. They piss themselves laughing at my stammer. For weeks, although I had signed on as assistant in the office of the manager, my only job was to clean out the stables and to wash the horses' arseholes with my bare hands—forty horses, mind you.
>
> Next they promoted me to something else. Because of the unusual formation of my teeth I was ordained Chief Castrator to the sheep department, and this meant that I was expected to put a gunnysack over my head with holes for my eyes and mouth, and bite off the budding testicles of baby sheep. That's what I did for six months. I've been here two years and have done every damned thing they threw at me and done it without whining. According to the happily-ever-after bilge they taught us at school I should have won over these hearts of oak, but don't you believe it. The truth is that the more I endure, the surer they are that I must somehow be reduced to whimpering pax so that *their* judgment can be proved correct.
>
> You know, there is something frightful about white people. You have to see them in one piece really to understand this. When I first came here I was convinced that I was somehow superior, more sensitive, more intelligent, certainly better bred, and gifted. Well, it's all balls. We are all the same because we're all whites and my guts are no different from *their* guts. If mine had been really superior I'd have thrown in the sponge and let them win, and I would have won, too. It takes white men to compete in this kind of shit and I'm nothing if not white.

The brother never wrote in such vein to the mother, and Patrice kept his letters to herself. Occasionally she had a return to the old awe of him, of that skinny little boy with his hoard of forbidden words and his wizened wisdom. Why had he left them—left the mother and herself? Deserted them, when you came down to it. It was the way friends saw it, contemptuous and angry. But the mother was always quick to defend him.

After all, what opportunity was there in this country for a young man unfitted by training, temperament, health, for the kind of job his father would have wanted for him? Nowadays the best he could have expected was some subordinate post in the railway or the police. . . . Doey' s son, bred to better things! "And what about you?" friends demanded of the mother. "What about a memsahib's job for you?" It was a poser. There simply was no such thing as a memsahib's job—it didn't exist. One had to be invented, as the Sisters in the convent had invented it, out of pity, out of snobbery, out of unerring self-interest.

But for a white man to work with his hands as a laborer in a society where every stratum has been preempted for a thousand years! Hopeless outlook. Better that the brother migrate to a white man's country and take his chances there. Patrice reflected: The mother is trying to persuade herself, to console herself for her own bewilderment. The mother must know that the brother had run away from more than "this country" and its lack of suitable opportunity. He had run away from her, and from the sister. He had run away from the dead father, and even from the aunt. From memory. From himself.

Reading his letters, Patrice fumbled toward some sort of understanding. Occasionally he struck a judicious, philosophical note, and soared once again in her wistful estimation:

> There have been four generations of us in India, and that's enough. Our grandparents probably got the best to be had out of the country. They were a simpler lot, and they lived in simpler times. In those days you had to love India in a very special sort of way because once you were in it there were damned few chances of your ever leaving it until they buried you at the bottom of your own garden beside your dogs, or in one of those godforsaken little cemeteries where jackals dug you up every so often until there was nothing left but your skull smiling benignly under an oleander bush. In our grandfather's day there were scarcely any books to be had, or newspapers. Letters from abroad arrived once every two or three months. There were no libraries, no theater, no music, no really interesting company. There was precious little mixing with the better-class Indians simply because better-class Indians were not inclined to mix, thank you.
>
> You might say there was precious little of all this in our parents' time and in ours, but at least we had some sense of communication with our

own world, whereas our forefathers had none. No wonder that some of them went native, married low-class Indian women or slept with them, and produced a society of half-castes like the Harpers and the Meadowses. And the Harpers and the Meadowses would not have been so badly off if they hadn't been shoved into an inferior social pigeon-hole by subsequent generations of whites and Indians!

In another letter the brother continued:

Doey was a far more complicated product. In the first place there was his French ancestry and his French temperament which set him off from the stick-in-the-mud blokes he had to deal with. He was, actually, always bollixed up about life. Its contradictions. He felt himself to be on sufferance with his English colleagues, and it was this feeling, I believe, that made him sympathetic with a certain kind of Indian. The discontented, the intellectual, the rebellious. Do you remember a man called Charan who used to come to the old house when you were seven and I was nine? I remember once hearing Doey telling Charan something about the hopeless paradox of trying to practice what one preaches when one's premises are wrong to start with. For instance, you can't, said Doey, be a believing Christian and a burra sahib at the same time. And I remember Charan replying that you couldn't be a believing anything and a burra sahib at the same time. Doey's tragedy was that he was always logical, or trying to be. It was part of his dislike of me. In producing me he'd reproduced a bit of himself and he was forced to look upon the little freak every day, with its stuffy nose and its stutter. There I was, flesh of his flesh, and nothing he could do about it. He might have tried talking to me. After all, I was not a fool, and he knew it.

Patrice brooded over these letters in yet another strange room where windows gave out on a blue lake glistening between branches where the gray langurs sat sedately gazing back at her.

Between farther hills the snowline flashed against the sky. Barbets called interminably from the valley floor and she could hear their voices, sweet and melancholy, between the intermittent clangor of bells. But it was better now that the mother was with her, and Niza-mat to wait on them at table, and Chota Ayah to prepare their baths and make their beds. Nothing in the servants' manners reflected their recognition of a change in the family fortunes. Doey was gone, but loyalty to him and to his house remained unflawed. So for Patrice the sense of strangeness lessened somewhat except at night, when, waking, she became aware of the mother lying sleepless in the next bed, in the dark.

146

"Are you all right, Alice?"

"I'm all right, darling. And you?"

"I'm all right."

The brother sent Patrice a drawing of a hoopoe:

> Remember how you used to like this silly little bird? You always insisted that it could sing! This is the only bit of drawing I've done for a long time. I work like a dog all day and at night I'm so fagged out I fall dead asleep. Poor Melissa, too. She works in the farm kitchen, cooking for the hands. They pinch her bottom and mimic her English accent, but she takes it like the good sport that she is. I gave up all thought of trying to paint or draw after some of the chaps saw a nude I'd done of Melissa. To them nudity is a dirty joke.
>
> It now seems that we are going to have a baby, in which case we'll probably clear out of this place and go to the city, where I'll try to get a job doing cartoons for a newspaper. It'll give us both a bit of civilization and I think we've earned it! . . . You ask if I'm ever homesick. I suppose I am, sometimes. Waking in the early morning and smelling woodsmoke from the kitchen fires, or hearing a crow shouting somewhere in the distance. After all, we are not far from the Indian Ocean. I think that India does something very special to one's imagination, and that a lot of us who were born and lived there when we were kids will never be entirely happy, or entirely unhappy, anywhere else.

Patrice thought: If he had written letters like this to Doey would it have made any difference between them? But it was too late now. The brother had not even been present when Doey was buried in that godforsaken little cemetery behind the Mogul fort above the river where the young man Roland had tried to seduce her.

Doey was buried among moldering English graves, alongside a row of six little stones marking the places of children of a single family, the last of these stones bearing an incised despairing plea: "Father, spare Thy hand!" Nearby was the splendid tomb of Master Algernon Fitzherbert Featherstone Finch, born June 6, 1854. *Lived one hour.*

No, the brother had not come back from Australia to take his stand beside Alice and Patrice at the graveside. Doey was battened ignominiously down in a monstrous black cloth-covered box with brass nails. And the grave was too short to take the coffin, and there was a flurry of embarrassment as coolies were sent for to make the grave larger. Overhead a pale-blue winter sky shone like those skies above the camping ground long ago. There was a shrill cry of wheeling kites, a hoopoe stepping nervously among the graves, and a Reverend Father Somebody-or-Other in a brown cassock, and with a square

147

brown beard, waiting disapprovingly for everything to be ready so that he might intone the committal prayers in Latin and sprinkle holy water on the black box. The aunt had written desperately from France that this be done. Even though Doey had always been so casual about his devotions, and had foiled everyone by dying abruptly before he could receive the Last Rites. After all, reasoned the mother, if poor Eve wants it so badly . . . and Doey wouldn't have cared one way or another.

Doey would certainly have cared about the grave being improperly prepared. It was the sort of sloppiness which always drove him frantic. Patrice, her arm in the mother's, feeling the pent, incredulous protest, thought: I wonder if Doey knows what's going on. He had never cared for priests—Christian, Brahman, or any other. And at this most inopportune moment as she stood beside his grave she remembered a ride she had taken with him years before. Trotting their horses into a village, they had noticed a Brahman priest in saffron robe, his bald head glistening like a chestnut, squatting within a large circle drawn in white chalk on the earth. The Brahman was eating fastidiously with his right hand from a brass bowl, and his left hand was extended at right angles from his body and beyond the circle of white chalks.

Doey reined his horse and greeted the Brahman respectfully, addressing him as Maharaj, and then inquired why he held his left hand thus. The Brahman explained that the left hand was one with which he washed his private parts, and that therefore it was not proper that that hand should be in proximity with the hand with which he ate his thrice-blessed food.

Doey pondered a moment, then with the utmost politeness inquired: "But, Maharaj-ji, is there not a contradiction, since your private parts are themselves within the prescribed circle?"

The Brahman had turned haughtily aside. And now, while she listened to Father Somebody-or-Other commending Doey's unregenerate soul to everlasting peace, Patrice had an impulse to laugh, recalling how he had laughed on that distant morning when he and she trotted away, leaving the Brahman squatting in his magic circle thoughtfully eating his thrice-blessed food.

A few friends had come to Doey's burial and they stepped forward and cast bits of earth into the grave, but the mother turned away and

148

rested her head on Patrice's shoulder, and Patrice held her quietly. Alice's surrender was, she supposed, in the nature of an accolade, a recognition not so much of her maturity—she was little more than sixteen—as of her precocious strength. Strength of body, strength of will, strength of mind. All three would be called upon often enough in the years to come by the weak and the importunate, who unfailingly recognize such strength when they see it.

Money now became a problem, but miraculously in the year when she was eighteen there came a windfall in the shape of a bank draft from the father of those spectral cousins in Kensington. It seemed princely enough, translated from pounds into rupees, and the mother headily decided that they should spend that winter on the lower hills, where the weather was less biting than in the cold convent buildings at seven thousand feet above sea level.

Doey had wanted us to go Home, the mother reminded herself. But what on earth . . . and she reflected shrinkingly on England without him, without the little grandmother, without the brother or Eve. She thought of the desolation of cheap rented rooms, of neat streets and little wrought iron gates giving on pavements where noisy brats played hopscotch, and inquisitive eyes peered from behind complacent shrouds of lace.

"I would rather," Patrice voted without hesitation, "damn well rather die where we are!"

But your future, the mother demurred to herself. Eighteen now. Sex in your rough sunburned hands, sex in your eyes, in your laugh, in your supple and altogether too feminine body. What about *you*, my only child, my girl? What about some fine decent man to marry you, to give you a home, happiness, a daughter, perhaps a son? An assured husband to give you pearls for your ears and "just a song at twilight, when the lamps are low" in that joyous voice slightly off key . . . To give you all the things Doey gave me and which have drained away like the monsoon rain. Some strange man to love you and take you away from me. Take you away, and then what will I do?

It must have been with the prophetic sense of the trapped that the mother guessed, at that moment, that he was already on the way, the tall handsome stranger of every woman's dreams.

12

There seemed to have been always that sense of never staying in one place among the same people, and for that reason perhaps the places and the people making a mark on one so one could not forget them even if one had known them a very short time. Liking them or not, there was that certainty that one must surely be going to see them again. Even when one knew this was not so. Even when one knew that those places were far distant, the people dead. The father and the grandmother suddenly disappearing and not in the least like ghosts, but so vivid that one might have reached out and touched them. Even hearing their voices! Even the way they laughed. The way they frowned. Other people seemed to take it all for granted: the changes, the differences, parting, loss, dreams and nightmares come true, facts. Odd, thought Patrice, that I can never get entirely accustomed to anything. There is always that catch of the breath, always that surprise.

The strangeness, for instance, of the brother having gone to Australia. Then dragging his wife and the baby to Spain, from where he wrote unconcernedly that they were living "from hand to mouth." Painting pictures no one wanted to buy or even to look at. Drawing cartoons, at which he seemed to be more successful. Washing dishes

150

in sleazy restaurants in order to make a little extra cash. But adoring Spain because of what the Moors had given it. The dark muscular touch of the Moorish hand everywhere.

Every country, Clem asserted with exuberance, ought to be raped just once, and perhaps every woman. Violence in love knocks the nonsense out of you. For himself, he was trying to slough off everything he had been born with, peeling himself down to the absolute, no less. And poor plain Melissa trailing after him, besottedly adoring. Ten years older than he and with little except her tiny patrimony for bait, she probably never would have found another man and had had to go to India to find Clem. Squandering her passion from the very start. Loyal, generous, recognizing his fathomless need, she gave him everything. And nine months later almost to the day the miracle of their little golden-haired son. The strangeness, Patrice mused, of *their* lives!

Alice demurred. "But, darling, everyone's life is strange, when you think about it. Look at my dear parents, and their lives. Leaving home, breaking away, running off to Timbuctoo. Pillar to post. All of us. My family, Doey's family. Never satisfied to stay where they were or with what they had."

She had, with time, become reflective, and her bewilderment more than ever marked. "I don't understand why, exactly. People who end up with money, houses, acres, things, usually do it by staying in one place, accumulating, salting away." She sighed. "It would be nice to be settled somewhere, all together. Loving each other. Safe. Forever after. Or at any rate for years and years."

But how silly to brood. Doey was dead and the aunt living in France, and the brother drifting from the Antipodes to Spain on Melissa's few remaining pounds. Fatefully drifting toward a morning on a tropical island, when, with another woman and another small son, the ramshackle bus on which they traveled with thirty Negro laborers flew off the winding highway into a grove of palms. The bus fell apart like a rusty can, spilling its freight among the coconuts and the hibiscus. Thirty blacks and three nondescript whites sprawled among their bundles, these in turn spilling shirts and shoes and patent medicines and nameless shabby precious things, for all on board were poor. And the only dead among them was Clem, cut in half by a jagged edge of metal, his last thought: Jesus Christ, why don't they

151

learn to *drive?* But that moment was still a long way off, and now he was in Granada, walking among the lovely fountains, caught like them between the future and the past.

It would be so nice, Alice mused in her increasing bewilderment, to be settled somewhere, all together. Loving each other forever and ever. And what had she and poor Melissa ever done except love? As if for a woman there was any other way!

Patrice had just turned eighteen the winter they spent in yet another borrowed house overlooking a small lake on the lower hills, twenty miles distant from the convent where Alice, for nine months of the year, had obtained what the Meadowses would have described as "a position," striving, with grim incredulity, to teach French to forty or so equally incredulous minds.

The house was small, and backed against a hillside where, at night, they could hear a muntjac give its short startled bark when the local leopard was on the prowl. The place smelled of mold; its floors were uneven, and there was a leak in the roof. The furniture looked as if it might have wandered into the house by mistake. The stuffed heads of three deer stared dejectedly from the dining room walls. There were scorpions in the bathroom, and a family of scrawny spiders which skittered across the bedroom floor, scaring Alice.

The drawing room, however, had a kind of sere and yellowed elegance. There was a bookcase filled with ancient novels which fell apart at a touch, and over the smoky fireplace hung a large reproduction of a painting titled "Wedded." Patrice brooded occasionally on this fatuous masterpiece, on the young bridegroom's improbably handsome legs and the dairymaid charms of the bride. But it was a decided change for the better from the necrophilia of the convent, especially since a previous tenant had adorned the bride's face with a luxuriant black moustache.

Their unknown benefactor—a suitor for the hand of that remotest of cousins the Princess Sita Devi—had left his spoor everywhere, a kind of seedy masculinity. Three tarnished brass regimental buttons in a cracked saucer. A package of obscene postcards tucked away in a drawer. Some old rancid pipes. An album of snapshots, among them groups of young men in uniform against a shattered background, inscribed: "Somewhere in France, December 1915."

And in that bookcase in the drawing room Patrice came on a

152

volume which bore the title *The Hound of Heaven,* with a sentence scrawled in ink across the title page: "I bought this damn thing thinking it was a handbook on training dogs!"

Everywhere a kind of decay. Mediocrity really. But Patrice took it all to her still unravished heart, illumining the neglect and the drabness, enduing it with personality. She thought she might write a story about this unknown Englishman, about these abandoned possessions, about all the people she knew, however slightly. For by now her exuberant imagination was beginning to seek out the disciplined ways of creativity: there was no detail too slight for her interest as she found herself quite often inexplicably moved to tears, to mirth, to passion. A coolie's smile could do this to her; the sound of a reed flute, wild and fleeting in the late night; a gust of rain against the walls of the old house; the look of Alice as she sat at times silent and motionless, thinking of Doey.

Nothing commonplace had ventured into the garden which flowed round the house, green and luxuriant even in this winter season. Crape myrtle leaves patterned the blue sky, heliotrope in a sunny nook swarmed over a broken wall. There were citron trees, and a gnarled oak where the girgitan lizard preyed on butterflies and moths.

At night, alone in her bedroom with the moon turning everything outdoors the color of milk, Patrice listened to the leopard making its rounds. Crouched at her window she occasionally spied it, hearing first the slight jarring of the gate below the garden path as the leopard took it in a bound, its heavy tail brushing the topmost rail. One night the beast passed directly under the window where she watched. Shadowy, heavy square head lowered, tail curled at the end, it appeared and vanished, leaving a memory of its terrestrial kinsman, Mr. Onions' pet, and the scent of tea from delicate English cups, and of Aunt Eve in elegant black hat and tight shoes unsuspecting of a brooding topaz gaze.

But this, now, was no tame spirit gliding past her vision and melting into the heliotrope. Patrice's eyes lost him there but she fancied she caught the silken rustle of his progress into the night. Thrilled, she kept his nightly visits a secret, fearful lest someone get wind of this beauty and from a safe distance blast out its fiery life.

One warm, windless afternoon Patrice sat curled up in a dilapidated chair in a corner of the veranda, a book open on her knees. She had begun to read at random and had become instantly absorbed, forgetful of Alice seated near her, knitting.

> I sought no more that after which I strayed
> In face of man or maid;
> But still within the little children's eyes
> Seems something, something that replies,
> *They* at least are for me, surely for me!
> I turned me to them very wistfully;
> But just as their young eyes grew sudden fair
> With dawning answers there,
> Their angel plucked them from me by the hair.

"What are you reading, darling?" Alice asked, but Patrice glanced up unseeingly, then turned back to her book.

> I fled Him, down the nights and down the days;
> I fled Him, down the arches of the years;
> I fled Him, down the labyrinthine ways
> Of my own mind; and in the mist of tears
> I hid from Him, and under running laughter. . . .

The cadence swept through her, stirring unknown, dormant things, and Alice repeated jealously: "What is it, Patrice?"

Well, what was it? Patrice could not have said, and especially not, now, to Alice. This was the discovery, this the first secret parting of their minds. A shock of brightness blinded her, dividing her forever from the old habit of love.

"Nothing," she said, answering Alice's question. "Nothing."

Alice caught the unfamiliar note, and thought: This growing-up business. It was very marked, she thought—the woman pushing through the child. But still those absurd, round, strong legs, the childish skin roughened by weather, the precocious eyes. Still wearing her own habit of love, the mother thought: Eighteen! And finding everything she wants through those silly books, and no longer coming to me with questions. Shrinkingly, the mother faced the truth: It will be different between her and me. It will never be as it always was between me and my dear little pink and white Mama. Mama and I understood each other without talk and twaddle. The big important things, the small unconfessed things, the sorrow, the joy. Adoring our men, putting up with them, their rages, their condescending mas-

154

culinity, their everlasting demands in bed even when they knew you were sick to death of it. Yes, my little Mama and I were alike, more sisters than parent and child. And our men were alike—pigheaded, chivalrous, strong. But this moody creature curled like a pretzel in her chair . . . already I have begun not to understand her.

It would have been better had Alice left it at that, but not. Obstinate, sidling, like a child rebuffed, she begged for more. "Darling, it looks like poetry. Won't you read to me? I love poetry."

I love poetry. "The boy stood on the burning deck . . ." "This is the forest primeval . . ." "Tell me not in mournful numbers . . ."

Patrice had a moment of desperation. It wouldn't kill me, she adjured herself fiercely. After all this time it wouldn't kill me . . . my own mother whom I love . . . yes, whom I love, damn it! Whom I love.

She rose, dropping the book on the chair seat. "I think I'll go for a bit of a walk in the garden."

"Yes, darling, do. It's bad for your eyes to read so much."

Down on the lower terrace in the flashing afternoon light among the scented weeds Patrice listened to the sounds coming up from the little bazaar below the hill, and to the nearer cry of a black partridge somewhere on the slope behind her. *"Shir dharam ke shakrak!"* I have milk and honey!

The light, all lambent, rose about her knees. She was torn apart by that strange poetry of Francis Thompson, by the wounded look in the mother's eyes, by the glory of this burdened, golden moment.

Then she heard the gate click and turned, half expecting to see the leopard come strolling across the terrace toward her. It would have completed the incongruity of everything. It was not a leopard but a man, tall and slender, a pipe in the corner of his mouth, a gun on his shoulder, his surprised eyes filled with the sight of her standing there afire with light from the sky.

"You are," Patrice informed him coldly, "trespassing."

"Am I? I didn't know. There's no sign."

"There's the gate."

"It was open."

"One usually asks," she told him, "before roaming all over somebody else's property!"

"I'll go," he said urbanely, "if you tell me to."

She thought: And gentlemen usually take their pipes out of their mouths when they address ladies. But she did not say it. She said nothing, and so for that moment they faced each other, illumined in each other's gaze.

Up on the veranda the mother put down her knitting and stared down at them. Her heart turned over. It was pure storybook, and after all she was herself not much more than forty and had not yet succeeded in schooling herself to deprivation. From missing Doey she had passed on to dreaming of him, and the dream differed not too subtly from the husband and the man. Nights of lonely darkness had changed her from the unquestioning wife to a woman more on fire than she had ever been. And here at last was a man, not much more than ten years younger than herself, but with eyes only for the girl —for the girl down there on the terrace, with her turbulent hair and tanned brows and inquiring gaze.

Swiftly the mother strangled the treason in her blood. For even at this distance she had grasped it, grasped what was happening down there in the shimmering afternoon. Grasping what had already happened. Doey's iron strain in Patrice had given way to an older impulse of submission, hero worship, devotion until death should them part.

"I heard the partridge," the man said conversationally. "Thought I might get a shot." He smiled. "Or is the partridge private property, too?"

"Naturally it is."

"Lucky you saw me in time, isn't it? May I introduce myself? Adam Bannister. I've just come up from Calcutta and I'm staying at the dak bungalow."

"I'm Patrice Verrier. My mother and I are spending the winter here."

"Rather a godforsaken spot, isn't it?"

"Oh, we always stay in godforsaken spots. We like them."

"So do I."

He could not look away, and did not try. There was about him none of the male coquetry she was to find, later, in other men.

He went on: "I heard from the dak bungalow servants that there has been a leopard prowling around the neighborhood. I rather think I saw its tracks back there on your road."

Obviously not an Englishman. Her heart bounded. "Are you Australian by any chance?" Perhaps from Perth? Perhaps he would have met the brother and would bring news!

His reaction was forceful. "An Australian? Good God, no!"

"What's the matter with being an Australian? My brother spent many years there. He owned"—she expanded regally—"extensive property near the city of Perth. He is at present in Spain. Painting very fine pictures. People think very highly of my brother in—in Granada."

"Well, I happen to be an American from Massachusetts."

It might as well have been Mogadiscio or Murmansk, for all she knew. But she still could not account for his accent, which was quite unlike that of the only other American she had ever met, a missionary lady who had rolled her *r*'s as though she had a mouthful of oats.

She studied him thoughtfully. "How do you pronounce 'barley'?" she asked.

" 'Barley'? Why, *barley*, of course."

"That doesn't sound American to me."

"You probably mean because I don't talk through my nose. Most of us don't."

"I didn't mean to be rude."

"You weren't. I'm often taken for an Englishman. Probably because I'm from New England."

"Where's that?"

He said abruptly: "Look, what about that leopard? Have you heard of one around?"

She hesitated. "Well, there is one. I've seen him once or twice."

"Perhaps you'll let me sit up for it one night?" All his attention had shifted to this objective and she felt herself become on the instant secondary. He was a hunter, the intelligent killer in love with death, but how was she to know?

She hedged. "You'll have to ask my mother. She's up there, in the house." And with a grande dame air which became her about as well as a grande dame's hat, she said: "Would you like a cup of tea?"

"Thank you, I would."

They turned and walked side by side through the fragrant weeds; Alice, watching from the veranda, summoned Nizamat and bade him set the tea tray for three. Nizamat, catching sight of the pair as they climbed the sunlit slope toward the house, went away to get the tea, and congratulated himself on the fitness of this occasion as compared to one from which he had rescued the girl two years before.

Alice took the visitor in with no more than a single glance of her guileless eyes. He was plainly outside all her categories but she recognized a kind of distinction, and instinct told her that Doey would have approved. Instinct also told her that despite a directness of manner and an unmistakable refinement, this was not a man she could ever hope to understand or charm. Instinct! It was what she had lived by, and after five minutes she discerned the same touchstone in him. They disliked each other at sight.

But, of course, she assured Adam Bannister, he was welcome to sit up at a window of the house and shoot the leopard, tonight if he wished. The gardener was worried for the life of his goats, and Chota Ayah scared to set foot outside the house after dark. Mr. Bannister would be doing everyone a favor if he would rid them of the prowling beast.

Patrice said little. The turmoil which had engulfed her earlier on reading Thompson's poem had been further complicated by the arrival of this most appropriately named of men. Something had happened to her that had never happened before. No stranger to strangeness, she knew herself to be changed. It was an almost physical sensation, as though she had swallowed some potent substance which acted on all her nerves at once. And all in the space of a single afternoon! It was like having a whole brand-new world thrust under your nose. It was like becoming, without warning, a brand-new person. And yet even while she wrestled with this sense of strangeness, and with the sound of Adam's voice in her ears and his image growing into her brain like an intaglio, she was scheming how to save the leopard.

That evening Adam reappeared carrying a high-powered American rifle and invited Patrice to share his perch at the window. In the waning moonlight they listened to the muntjac's telltale bark, and heard the ruffle of moths' wings in the heliotrope below. The dark was charged with unspoken, unspent force, and Patrice felt her own trembling communicate itself to Adam as they stared into the unresponsive night. The leopard did not appear. On the third night Adam reached out and took her hand and carried it to his lips.

On the fourth night the moon had set and in the total silence

Patrice heard the flick of a furred tail against the gate and fancied she saw a liquid shape move in the gloom below the window. Adam's hunter's ear had picked up the infinitesimal sound. He raised the rifle delicately to his shoulder and to Patrice there seemed something feline in the movement, something which matched the beast in the darkness below. Her nerves braced for the shock of the explosion, for the rush of death on the white stones.

She sneezed.

Adam lowered the rifle. He said softly: "God damn." He said the brute would never come back. Couldn't she have held out just another moment?

She caught a note of petulance and said apologetically: "I'm sorry. You see, I have this infirmity."

"This what?"

"In my nose. I'm awfully sorry, really."

"It didn't sound to me like a real sneeze." He had put aside the rifle and was filling his pipe. "Why if you didn't want me to kill it you had to . . ."

His temper ignited hers. "The leopard probably knew we were up here all the time. He'd never have given you a proper shot."

Adam rose from the cramped seat beside her and unloaded the rifle. "If you think it's a joke, let me say at once that I don't see it."

She had risen too and they stood staring out into the moonless garden. The sneeze, she informed him, had not been intended as a joke. "Then what the hell?"

"Anyhow, I'm glad he escaped!"

"I might as well run along," Adam said in a hard voice. "Good night. And thanks."

"Good night," she said. "And good-bye."

Adam propped the rifle against the wall and took her in his arms. He had not, he told her roughly, come ten thousand miles to find her only to lose her. Perhaps he had no right to kiss her, to be with her at all. For all he knew she might be engaged to someone else . . . and as far as he was concerned most women simply did not exist.

Resting against him, Patrice had the thought that his heart was beating like a frightened beast's, and this unexpected notion steadied and restored her own.

13

*I*t was a strange love affair, both of them coming to it green, and more than once the thought occurred to Patrice that for Adam it was more than strange, that his heart beat too often like that of a frightened animal. He was by turns passionate and grudging, eager for them to be married and as abruptly equivocal. He seemed truly happy only when he and she were alone together, tramping the hills in quest of game—pheasants, partridges, muntjac, mountain goat. He loaned her a light shotgun and praised her skill, her endurance, her flawless sight. She was like a boy, he declared with admiring approval. Like a younger brother. It was not what Patrice would have wished to be considered by him, but he had cast a net of emotion upon her, enmeshed her heart, her mind, her generosity.

So she strove to please him though her soul revolted against the murder of birds and deer. That she was a naturally good shot and blessed with exuberant health and vigor were things she had always taken for granted. That Adam should value her for these commonplace attributes struck her as odd, but in her new humility she made the most of them. Anything to please him, to amuse him, to hold him. For she had quickly sensed his duality—his inclination toward her, and his holding her off. In her obsession with him Patrice lost sight

160

of herself, of that newly discovered self which had sprung to life on an amber afternoon when she sat reading Francis Thompson, and later walking in the garden had turned to see Adam striding toward her through the gleaming weeds.

During their daily exploration of the countryside Adam revealed something of himself and his affairs. He was thirty, and his parents and a married sister lived "at home," in that place in New England with the unpronounceable name. He was employed by an American export company in Calcutta, a job he liked because it made no great demands on his time and afforded ample opportunity for shikar. There were snipe and duck in the great marshes outside the city and big game not much farther afield.

Adam felt it incumbent upon him to explain to Patrice that aside from his salary he had no income whatsoever, and with a desire to make him feel that he was not alone in this deprivation Patrice confided that she too had no income of her own, that in fact she and Alice were chronically hard up. But they got along somehow. It all depended, she exhorted Adam robustly, on how one looked at things. And Doey had always been a stickler about whining and sniveling.

Her cheerful dismissal of penury as something beneath one's notice occasionally brought a frown to Adam's brow, raising doubts in Patrice's mind as to whether she had, after all, said the right thing. She reflected that he lived in a far from exigent style, traveling with a personal servant, with an assortment of expensive guns, and well-tailored clothes.

He had come to the hills to recuperate after a bout of dysentery, and was due to go home on extended leave before the hot weather set in on the plains. In all likelihood he would have to find another job, in America probably, since the doctors had warned him that his constitution was not equal to the hazards of the Indian climate. It was different, of course, up here in this mountain air, but unfortunately there were no jobs to be had in the hills. He hated the thought of leaving India; he loved the untrammeled life, the comfort of servants, the limitless opportunities for sport. And he plainly disliked the prospect of returning to his family. "They are kind and decent, but we have never seen eye to eye about too many things."

Patrice listened, possessively enthralled. It struck her that Adam must in one way and another be a fortunate being. It was a life, a condition of society entirely foreign to her experience and she was by turns dazzled and confused.

Covertly, she set about observing the outward trappings of what seemed to her innocent eyes a costly elegance which had been noticeably absent in Doey and his friends. And as the mellow Himalayan winter slipped toward spring and she plunged deeper and deeper into love, she divined, in Adam, the hint of an insecure spirit at odds with itself. There were moods of hesitation and indecision when he seemed to drift away from her, when he became cool, even brusque. He loved her, yes. It had, he told her, come upon him like a storm. He believed that their meeting in this most unlikely of spots was in the nature of a miracle. He wanted to marry her. But.

One morning when they paused on a grassy slope after hunting pheasants, Adam suddenly turned to her and said abruptly: "You will have to hold me to it, Patrice!"

"I don't think I understand," Patrice said. She picked up a pebble and skimmed it down the slope.

"Darling, hold me to our engagement. Make me marry you!"

"How can I, if you don't want to?"

"I do want to. I want to more than anything in the world. It's just this . . . Hell, it's this business of commitment, I suppose. Of responsibility . . . things like that."

She turned then and smiled at him. "I will hold you to it," she told him calmly. "I will make you marry me, Adam, whether you want to or not!"

He gave a queer laugh and caught her hand. "Darling!"

An extraordinary lightness of heart seemed to break upon him. "We'll be married right away. We'll go back home together. We'll be happy together, ever after. Oh, Patrice, I need you!"

It was easier said than done. The Sisters at the convent disapproved because Adam was not a Catholic and it was not possible for them to be married in the Church. It would therefore have to be a civil wedding, and then it was Alice's turn to disapprove. She craved a proper wedding, with a bridal gown and veil, bridesmaids and a wedding cake and champagne; but alas, there were no funds.

"I'll borrow from old Shapurji," she declared recklessly. "What are a few thousand rupees on an occasion like this?"

"You won't borrow from Shapurji." Patrice opposed her roughly. "I

162

don't want a fancy wedding. I only want Adam."

It was Mr. Onions, that friend of the past now District Commissioner of the area, who came to the rescue. He provided Adam with a special license and married them himself. "For auld lang syne," he explained as he kissed Patrice and shook hands with Adam, thinking privately: "Looks like a good chap." And then comfortingly to Alice: "You must come and spend this Christmas with my wife and me. The Sparkses are coming and I've invited old Ghulab Hosain. . . . Remember him at Doey's Christmas camp years ago?"

Clem wrote jubilant congratulations from Spain: "Hurray! America is a great big Christmas tree! I wonder what you will make of it. I wonder what it will make of you. . . ."

Alice, with Nizamat in attendance, had traveled down to Calcutta to see them off on their ship to London. Alice, her despair in tight rein, kissed Patrice swiftly and said in a firm voice: "Au revoir, my darling. Come back, won't you?"

"Of course we'll come back. Wild horses . . . wild horses . . ."

"And don't worry about me. I shall spend Christmas with the Onionses and the Sparkses. Time will pass."

Adam had sauntered away down the dock to let them take their farewells in private. But there was nothing left to say, and it was painful to meet each other's eyes.

"Don't, darling,"the mother implored her. "Darling, don't cry."

"No, I won't. And I'll write every week, and we'll be back next year!"

Next year. And above the hideous city clouds heaped themselves in majestic indifference. Patrice and the mother thought in desperation: Better get it over with. Better anything rather than this hopeless lingering, with everything said except the unsayable.

Then the ship gathered itself together and bellowed like a cow. Adam had turned and was walking toward them, hoping it would all be over before he reached them. The mother murmured quickly: "It's going to be wonderful, Patrice. It all seems so sudden just now, but I'll have time to think about it when you are gone. To think and to be happy for you and for Adam."

Her heart was in it, her entrails, her soul. Love, Patrice decided bitterly, was not much fun.

Then Adam's arm was round her shoulders, his voice gentle in their

163

ears: "Au revoir!" He turned her gently toward the gangway. "Au revoir, au revoir!"

Nizamat came forward and salaamed, and Patrice took him by the hand. "Ah baba!" he murmured, unashamedly in tears as he had been when he found her beside the old fort above that other river, and broke it to her that Doey was dead. "Ah baba, baba!"

As evening fell the ship dropped down the muddy reaches of the Hooghly and the shores glittered with little lights. The eyes of India, watching her depart. Figures moved across luminous doorways or sat contentedly on their thresholds. There was that scent of dung-and-charcoal fires; a voice singing to the beat of a drum. *These* eyes would open, tomorrow, on the familiar sun-flushed vistas of home, hers on the empty sea. Adam was standing beside her at the rail and he drew her strongly against him. "We've got each other," he reminded her in a voice from which every doubt seemed to have fled. "Darling, we've got each other!"

In the Red Sea a ferocious sun scorched the decks and burned the soles of their shoes. A mysterious sickness came on Patrice and she found it difficult to eat. It was unlike any malaise she had ever felt, and the cockney stewardess was all knowing sympathy.

"Wot a shime, you so young and newly wed, 'ardly more than a biby yourself!"

Shades of Nurse Bipper, but kindly. "If you'd rather not 'ave it I can give you the haddress of a friend of mine in London, dearie, wot would tike care of it. You know wot I mean?"

"But it can't be *that* already!"

How could it be *that?* On the other hand had she not encountered something in the amused and friendly eyes of their fellow passengers, to find it, now, reflected in Adam's dismayed face when he came into their cabin and found her gingerly sipping a wineglass of Worcestershire sauce on the stewardess's recommendation?

"She says it will stop the sickness. She thinks it's a baby."

"Oh, God, no!" said Adam.

Patrice felt like lifting her nose to heaven and howling like a dog.

"I won't have it if you'd rather I didn't, Adam."

"But are you sure?"

"I don't know. Perhaps I should ask the ship's doctor. I feel awful, and the sea's as calm as a pond."

164

"But how in hell? We've been so careful!"

They had indeed been careful. Coitus interruptus, and the fearful expectation every month of the three before they took ship. And their increasing desires making things more risky.

"We can't, Patrice. We simply mustn't. I haven't got a job and I'm broke and a baby at this stage . . ."

They had been lucky until now, and now all Adam's blitheness vanished. Patrice had hoped that he would take her in his arms and comfort her; that he might even rejoice in the thought of a baby. Instead he sat down heavily on the edge of his bunk across from her, and began slowly to fill his pipe. He had large, beautiful, sensitive hands, and she watched them in hypnotic fascination. She wanted to warn him that the first whiff of tobacco would raise her gorge again, but she kept silent. Don't snivel. Don't, on any account, whine.

Adam said constrainedly: "I suppose things will work out somehow. I just wish it could have been later instead of right now."

"What difference would that make?"

"I've already told you. I have to find another job and we are going to be more or less on my family until I do."

She had known this when she married him, and so had he. He had begged her to hold him to their engagement, to *make* him marry her, but she had not had to do so: he had been all eagerness and tenderness and desire. What were jobs and money compared to this love, this imperative need of one another? When she thought about the future at all it was to remind herself that America was a rich country of endless opportunity, and that his parents had written affectionate letters welcoming her "home," offering hospitality and promising help.

But now here was this swamping anxiety, making her feel that the whole thing was somehow her fault, and hers alone.

"The stewardess says she'll give me the address of someone in London, a sort of doctor, who'd do an operation and take the baby. She says it's quite simple, really, and doesn't cost much. Then I'd be all right and we'd be just the same as before."

Adam tamped the tobacco into the bowl of his pipe and reached for matches. There was in every move a kind of hesitation, as though his thoughts fumbled like blind creatures, searching for they knew not what. Perhaps he hoped that she might make her own decision and leave him out of it. For a long time they sat in silence in the little white-painted cabin, with its whirring electric fan and portholes open to the molten sea. Adam lighted his pipe. He began slowly: "I don't know . . . perhaps when we get to London . . ."

The smell of tobacco mingled with the smell of painted metal. The sun leaped off the sea and glared into Patrice's eyes. She took a gulp of the Worcestershire sauce and made a beeline for the bathroom, and when she returned to the cabin, Adam had gone.

The stewardess found her lying face down on the berth. "There, there, dearie," she said kindly. "There's 'ardly one of them likes the idea of a biby right off, so to speak. Your 'ubby wants you for hisself, that's why he behives unsympathetic like. 'Ere, you keep this haddress, just in cise."

That night, holding Patrice in his arms, Adam said: "It's not that I don't want a baby, Patrice. It's just—as I once told you, remember? Up there on that hillside months ago!—I have never had to take responsibility for another person, and it scares me." He went on quickly: "I've never had much love, myself. Not even my parents' love. And kids . . . well, they are bound to get in the way. I remember that I seemed always to be getting in my parents' way. Perhaps I imagined it. My father is a sentimental egotist, and my mother has never been able to show emotion, or to feel much, I daresay."

He might have been talking Swahili for all that it meant to Patrice. She cried passionately: "The baby and I wouldn't get in your way, I promise!"

"Oh, darling!" Shaken, ashamed, he kissed her. Everything, he now tried to assure her, would be all right. His family were bound to love her. She was not to worry. They would live in the States until the baby was born, then perhaps go back to India. "I'll try to get back my job in Calcutta, or perhaps another, better one farther up-country, in a textile mill or something."

It was what she wanted to hear, but now it somehow fell rather flat. "But do you know anything about textile mills? And what about your health?"

"Don't worry, darling. We'll fix things up somehow."

Six weeks later Patrice watched a placid Connecticut landscape slide past the train windows. She told herself that she found it all a trifle disappointing. These tidy green fields, painted wooden houses,

166

the occasional mild, pointing finger of a country church. Her eye, her ear, craved some strong, jarring note, something in keeping with the excitement and upheaval of her life during the past few months.

Adam had talked to her casually about his country, and had been frankly taken aback by her abysmal ignorance. While they were in London before taking another ship for New York they had gone shopping for books, and she had buried herself in Whitman and Thoreau with the passion of an addict.

It was a new kind of reading, out of which she fashioned her own image of the country from which he had sprung. It was an exciting image, an improbable palimpsest stitched by her incorrigible imagination. The insipid realities of this early summer day on the train taking them to Boston now struck her as a letdown, and she was inclined to sulk—a condition foreign to her temper and one to which, as she knew, Doey would have given short shrift.

"What did you expect?" demanded Adam, annoyed. "Cowboys and Red Indians?"

> "The place where a great city stands is not the place
> of stretched wharves, docks, manufactures,
> deposits of produce merely . . ."

Patrice quoted Whitman aloud, and Adam said shortly: "That's a poet's view, not reality."

They were in the dining car, waiting to be served lunch, and he picked up the menu. Patrice derived a familiar comfort in the cadence of Whitman's verse. She had a parrot memory; words tasted like food in her mouth and there were moments when she gave Adam the impression that she was engaged in an endless dialogue with herself. Now she said abruptly: "I wish we could have stayed longer in New York. Was that the city Whitman was writing about?"

Adam said he didn't know. He wished he had not given her the Whitman. She had this way of immersing herself and coming up like a sleepwalker, startling him. He found himself wishing, in a queer way, that she was older, steadier, calmer. The approaching reunion with his family had thrown him into a mood of rebellion. What he most desired at this moment was a stable, prosaic companion to reassure him and lend him strength.

He said brusquely: "What would you like to eat, Patrice?"

"Steak."

"It's expensive. Wouldn't you prefer spaghetti?"

"All right. I don't care."

Adam turned to the waiter and she thought: How was I to know that steak is expensive? A few weeks ago in London it had been strawberries. Pregnant, nauseated, she craved strawberries, and her insistence had got on Adam's nerves. It got on his nerves when she suddenly decided to augment this diet with kippered herring and soda water for breakfast. They were staying at a small hotel on Wigmore Street, a cheerless place even in summer, and the moth-eaten old waiter, a friendly soul, had taken her order with a straight face.

Adam had protested: "You can't, Patrice! Who ever heard of soda water for breakfast?"

"I don't feel like eating anything else."

"Why not cereal and a soft-boiled egg?"

"Would you like me to vomit all over this table?"

"You're acting like a spoiled child."

"The spoiled child's inside me. If it was inside you, perhaps you'd understand!"

The old waiter went discreeetly away and returned with her kipper and a siphon of soda water, but by that time she had again lost all interest in food. This too got on Adam's nerves. It got on his nerves that she did not feel like walking in the park or going to the zoo. It got on his nerves to see her sitting rigid on the edge of her bed, white-faced, her teeth clenched against the spasms which beset her.

Patrice registered Adam's frustration, his apparent disillusionment with her, and she brooded. Was this the inevitable concomitant of their love—this gagging and hawking, this hanging dizzily over the w.c. or lying in bed too exhausted even to weep.

The mother had warned her that she might on occasion feel "a little unwell," but that it was nothing. It was perfectly natural and would soon pass. To Patrice everything *natural* now became accursed. Blood, vomit, a swimming head, the heaven of fresh sweet fruit corrupted in one's mouth. Why had she allowed herself to get bunged up with this damned silly business? None of it had been fun really. The hysteria of desire, the reckless orgasm, the terror of being caught in pregnancy. And she had been caught! Love wasn't fun. Love was rending and pain and embarrassment. And what the aunt

168

had lyrically written from France as being "one of the sacred mysteries of life" was neither sacred nor a mystery. No wonder *once* had been enough for the Virgin Mary!

But now here she was gazing out of a train window at a red-brick factory and a mountain of coal on which children were playing. "Here I am. Married. In another country. The mother, all reality, all make-believe, left far behind me." But were they? She suffered a disembodied sensation, a blurring of the edges of things, then Adam laid his hand over hers on the table. "Darling, you could have had the steak. I just thought . . ."

"It doesn't matter. What's that building with the deer's horns over the door?"

"Elks Club, probably. Are you feeling all right? Does the motion of the train bother you?"

He was trying to match her mood, but again her mind veered. She thought of a group of young girls on the dock at New York come to welcome friends off the boat. Dressed in cloche hats and tweed knickerbockers, singing in chorus "Yes, we have no bananas!" they had seemed to Patrice to be enviably gay and carefree, and turning to Adam, who leaned on the ship's rail beside her, she had said: "Let's spend a little time in New York! Let's go to the theater, to the pictures! Let's have some . . . some *fun!*" Laugh together, be gay together.

> Two together!
> Winds blow south, winds blow north,
> Day come white, or night come black,
> Home, or rivers and mountains from home,
> Singing all time, minding no time,
> If we two but keep together!

But theaters and "pictures" were expensive, and they had taken the train for Boston next day. Now Patrice stared at Adam across the narrow dining table. His voice pulled her thoughts back from their wandering. He was telling her that they were passing through one of the oldest regions of New England. Those stone walls had been raised two hundred years ago at least. That house was called a saltbox because of its shape. Those trees were known as wineglass elms for the same reason.

169

Patrice turned to the window again and watched a procession of automobiles on an asphalt road. Billboards. Somebody's Fish Cakes, Somebody's Baked Beans. Feen-a-Mint. But it all meant home to the people who lived here. In her present mood of equivocation she thought she detected a kind of confusion under the pleasant veneer: drabness and wealth, care and neglect, orchards and dumps, each existing by and for itself.

She mused on the children playing in back yards, on women hanging washing, on men driving the sleek automobiles. But were these, too, fragmentary, cut off from the wholeness of things? And she reflected with a pang on the life which she had left. It had had its drawbacks, but there one could never escape the sense of *wholeness* in its dusty, relentless embrace. She could feel it even now, even here in this unfamiliar land. The exile, Doey had once observed, is always prisoner to the past.

She tried to recall more Whitman, but all that came to mind was her recent glimpse of dirty tenements when the train passed 125th Street. Incomprehensible, those sooty caverns compared to the glitter and elegance of the city beyond! If only Adam would explain things a bit . . .

The colored waiter brought their lunch and she gave him a smile. "I'd like some Worcestershire sauce, please."

When he had gone Adam said: "I thought you were over that stage."

"This rocking brings it back, a little." And she added: "I almost spoke to him in Hindustani! The dark skin, I suppose."

When Adam remained silent she went on: "It must give one a queer feeling to belong to a race and not have one's own language or even one's own costume."

Adam shrugged. There were moments when she really irritated him. It was rather like being in the company of an intelligent but wayward child and he had never liked children.

Patrice continued meditatively: "Fancy, in a country as rich as this, having to live all huddled up in those frightful places with bedding hanging out of the windows and dead plants in pots!"

"What about Calcutta?" he shot at her. "The City of Dreadful Night! You won't see anything here to equal *that.*"

"It's not the same thing."

170

Adam sprinkled grated cheese on his spaghetti. "A lot of white people don't live much better than the Negroes do. It's largely a matter of choice. And the Negroes are a darned sight better off here than they would be in some other places I could name, including your beloved adoptive India!"

"I don't call it being better off when you're forced to live huddled up in places that look—and probably smell—like a prison. I don't believe that they like it. I don't believe it's a matter of choice. I believe that it's what Doey would have called 'keeping people in their place.' If I were a Negro I'd mutiny."

"Why don't the Indians mutiny?"

"They did once. Doey said that they would again."

He began to eat with a bored air, but she gazed dubiously at her overloaded plate. "Goodness, I've never seen so much food all at once!"

"You ordered it."

She glanced up from her plate to find Adam's gaze fixed on her. Suddenly he smiled his rare, sweet smile. "You silly little thing! What did you expect to find in this country, right off the bat like this?"

"I don't know. Something terrific, I suppose. Something that would bowl me over." She relaxed, and laughed apologetically. "I wanted the first sight, the first feeling, to be quite unlike anything I had ever known in my whole life, in my dreams even."

"Well?"

"When one dreams about a person or a place one in a way invents them, I suppose."

"Don't tell me you're disillusioned . . . already!"

"Oh, no, not that. How could I be?"

"I have an idea you could be a lot of unexpected things."

The train rocked along the roadbed. Bridgeport. Adam turned to his sporting magazine, open on the table beside him, and Patrice repeated Whitman's lines under her breath: " 'Two together! Winds blow south, winds blow north . . .' "

Very soon now she would be meeting his family: his parents, his sister, Caroline, and her husband, Barto Williams, and their young son. Their numerous cousins, their friends.

She would, on the instant, become one of them—Adam's wife carrying Adam's child. No more gypsying, no more uncertainties

171

sought or unsought. Something would be expected of her: she would be a dynastic cog. . . .

She became aware of Adam's gaze once more fixed upon her from across the dining car table. "Penny," he offered, smiling.

"Adam, what time is it in India now, this minute?"

"All of twelve hours' difference, I'd say at a guess."

You mean it's still yesterday there?"

"Yes. Patrice, why did you order spaghetti if you knew you wouldn't be able to finish it?"

One o'clock in the morning! The gray monkeys would be asleep on their branch, the leopard moving soundlessly on his rounds. Every being she knew would be asleep, unconcerned with her wakefulness! Five hours must elapse before the hoopoe left its twig and fluttered down to the ground to feed, before the sky opened to receive the light.

Adam put aside his magazine. "We'd better get back to our seats. Providence is the next stop. After that, Boston."

Part Two

14

A long summer evening fell across the garden and the sea and a flock of little sailboats drifted toward their moorings under the benevolent eyebrows of the shore, to which the sea played up like an indulgent, well-to-do aunt. She could change in a flash and become the bitch she truly was, but at this moment she smiled like a sweet bosomy thing, keeping her dirty thoughts to herself.

Presently the sailboats, expertly moored and tidied up by their owners, rested demurely on the water, and the owners appeared moving through the shrubbery toward big, comfortable houses barely visible amid the urbane wilderness. There were young men in white duck trousers, and fathers looking like older brothers. Capable children dodged among them, wearing life jackets, teeth encased in corrective devices, eyes behind corrective lenses. Their voices rang with assurance, for they were as at home on land as they were at sea, and as they would probably at some later date in history be at home under the sea and in the skies.

Adam stood before a mirror in the guest room of his parents' house, and adjusted his tie. "They might," he said, "have waited a bit."

Patrice emerged from the adjoining bathroom. "Who might have waited for what?"

"The family. Throwing a party the very evening we arrive."

"I think it's lovely!"

"Aren't you tired after the train and everything?"

"I was, but I'm not now."

Excited, like a kid. He turned to see her draped in a bath towel, bending over a suitcase. "I can't find the pink sash to go with this dress."

The dress, a gray silk, lay on one of the twin beds. The material had come from Shapurji's emporium in the Burra Bazaar, and Mrs. Meadows had "run it up" on her sewing machine. It looked it, Adam thought. Ill fitting, fussy, in bad taste, but one of her treasures, and after all, as he reminded himself guiltily, she didn't have many.

"They might at least have waited until tomorrow before throwing a party." He picked his jacket off the back of a chair and slid his arm into a sleeve. "Given us a chance to rest a bit and get our bearings after all that traveling."

"Who wants to rest? And I'm just beginning not to feel sick all the time."

Upended like a terrier, she pawed through the suitcase. The bath towel slipped, revealing a rosy bottom. Adam had looked forward to that too, on this still, warm evening behind their locked bedroom door. Now that the initial stage of her pregnancy was past she had regained the old buoyancy and he was conscious, for the first time, of a possessiveness toward her, a disinclination to share her company with others.

"Just like the family—always dragging in friends and relatives on the slightest excuse!"

"I don't call this the slightest excuse! They haven't seen you for four years and they've never set eyes on me until this afternoon. Oh, Adam, do cheer up!"

"We won't have a minute to ourselves—you'll see."

Patrice carefully arranged the pink sash across the waist of the dress and stood back to admire the effect while Adam sat on a chair and watched her. Flushed from her bath, young shoulders bare above the tightly wound bath towel. And still that fresh, virginal look. Didn't she understand, yet, what had happened to her? Didn't a lost virginity betray itself in the eyes? He said abruptly: "Too bad you couldn't go down to dinner just as you are! You look wonderful."

176

He said these things too seldom, and she spun toward him. "I will if you like, Adam!"

He laughed. "Not on your life. Not with my brother-in-law present, not to mention various and sundry dirty old men."

He should, Patrice reflected, have been happy and excited to be home after this long absence, but he obviously was not. Puzzled, wary, she went to him and sat on his knee. "It's all beginning to be the way I imagined. I mean, this place; your family, everything! They are wonderfully kind, Adam. Driving all that distance to meet our train, and the flowers and chocolates, and telling me over and over how glad they are to see me, when they haven't the faintest idea, really, what I'm like."

Adam kissed a damp shoulder. "What are you really like? Damned if I know myself."

"Your father is an old duck. On the drive back from the station he told me a lot about my family. He'd looked it up somewhere. Their history. I didn't even know we had a history. I didn't know that Alice had an ancestor who fought in one of the Crusades."

"The old man is nuts on the subject of family history. Barto Williams thinks he's a godawful snob."

"Your brother-in-law thinks that about your father?" She was shocked.

"Well, they don't get along too well. Barto is a law unto himself."

"Even with those crutches?"

"Even with those crutches."

"Is that why he didn't come to the station to meet us?"

"He rarely does anything en famille if he can help it. One of his little peculiarities."

Adam rose, pulling her up with him and turning her so they confronted their images in the long mirror on the bathroom door. "Aren't we a handsome pair? You in your sarong and I in my nineteen twelve tuxedo. Do you realize I've had this thing since I was in college?"

"Your mother," Patrice said softly, "treating me right off as if I were her own daughter!"

"Well, I don't believe Ma was putting it on, at that."

"And your sister Caroline making me feel ... making me feel as if she and I had known each other all our lives. You never told me they would be like this."

"Didn't I? I suppose I sort of took it all for granted."

"You never told me about Barto's crutches."

"I must have mentioned that he was lame." After a slight hesitation Adam went on: "If you want to know something else, I've never been particularly fond of my sister Caroline."

"She seems very fond of you. They all do."

"Oh, well! They were probably congratulating themselves on having me off their hands at last. Emotionally at any rate." He laughed shortly. "I've always been a pain in the neck to them one way or another."

"Adam, can't you . . . I mean, after four years . . ."

He loosened the towel and let it fall. Breasts like apples. Long, fine legs, a belly still flat. It would be some time, yet, before she surrendered these to her condition; and he murmured against her neck: "Let's go to bed."

"Heavens! They're waiting for us downstairs."

She wriggled free and returned to the bathroom, and Adam turned to the window. The sun had gone, leaving a pinkness on the sea. There was a green smell of freshly mown grass. A complicity of discretion everywhere, Adam reflected. A place for everything and everything in its place. Even sex, though in a nice way.

He tried to control his restlessness. Patrice was right; he ought to be glad to be home. Four years in the tropics—*quel* glamour! By going away and staying away, then by bringing home a bride they could accept without reservations—all this had repaired his standing in his family's eyes. And yet, how had that standing been questioned in the first place? Just by his never having been able to feel at home with them, by this lifelong resentment of small, petty things?

Away from home he had not missed home, but now he found himself missing something else. That big dark office in the strangest, foulest city on earth. The swarming babus. Those agile brown fingers clicking typewriters. A swishing of dhotis, flash of brown legs in colored socks and suspenders; clumping shoes. The mingled odors of hair oil and attar of roses. Tiers of glossy black heads, discreet intelligent faces. And outdoors, on this famous international throughfare of Clive Street, sacred bullshit on the pavement, and the stench of money, or the lack of it.

Searing contrasts, if you dared look. The homesick Yanks and their prosaic, capable wives, filled with the milk of American kindness, determinedly making silk purses out of sows' tits. He had hit it off with his compatriots, more or less, and more or less with his British colleagues, who couldn't make him out and were boredly not disposed to try.

Yet he had grown to like the life, and to embrace the exile he had chosen. It had, curiously, dulled the edge of alienation as he felt himself afloat on a tide of brown humanity that peopled the city of dreadful night, and equally dreadful day. In a barely understandable, inarticulate fashion Adam had reached out to that sense of humanity, to its limitless resignation, its indestructible will to live.

And on his days off from work there was always that brown watery landscape with its slowly moving cattle, and sheaves of birds' wings turning in silver light. The deep satisfaction in his own skill as a hunter. And the cooling damp of his own sweat darkening his shirt and running down his bare strong knees. But it was more than all these things put together. More than his pride in his own litheness and unerring eye. It was the sudden look of the Indian sky, nacreous at dawn; of the first sunlight shivering in the waters of a jheel as the women came out from their villages with their water pots balanced on their heads and sent the disturbed plover wheeling and crying above the reeds.

The congested, stifling, murderous city eternally preoccupied with itself, and the artless landscape which surrounded it! There were moments when Adam heard himself saying breathlessly, aloud: "If I only belonged! If I only belonged!"

Now, standing by the window of his parents' summer home, and smelling the sharp scent of mown grass, Adam reached for his pipe and began to fill it. Here he was in truth, home again home again jiggity jig. He should rejoice. Instead he felt that he had been in some sort of a collision, everything jolted out of place.

Three figures crossed the lawn below him, headed toward the front door. His cousin Thomas Edwards, and Thomas's wife, Edith, and their son, Damon. Thomas scarcely changed in four years, big and ungainly, growing bald, and with that remembered air of peering to right and left like an old turkey. And Edith marching at his side, tall, flat-chested, her hair dyed the color of manure above a hawk-nosed, sexless face. How in the world had they managed, between them, to produce that Greek god of a son? Damon must be sixteen now, Adam mused, watching the boy walk a little to the rear of his parents, his head radiant in the fading light.

All three vanished round the corner. Another figure detached itself from the shrubbery and started toward the house. Daisy Prentice! Adam drew back from the window. Daisy! Willowy as ever, with that faintly old-fahioned air about her that some people found so charming. Old-fashioned my arse, Adam thought, smiling sardonically. Those letters she'd written him to India, reeking of poetry and hot pants. Caroline's dearest friend. They had gone to Miss Sampson's School together, had become inseparable, graduated together, traveled to Paris and Rome together. And together they had conspired to net Adam. . . .

Daisy, Caroline had informed him once, years ago, was bats about him. Absolutely *bats*.

"She's bats, all right," Adam had agreed nastily. It was his last year at Harvard. He'd had little to do with girls and had not missed it particularly, being fastidious and hard to please, and, possibly, scared. He had meditated, on occasion, going to a brothel, but fear of the clap or other involvements had put him off.

Caroline had been affronted by his reaction to Daisy. Daisy was a beautiful person. Hers was a pure and lovely spirit. She was highly intelligent without being intellectual, and what was more, she stood to inherit money someday. Adam, Caroline said, could do a darn sight worse than fall in love with Daisy Prentice.

And now there she was, sauntering gracefully toward his parents' front door, unaware of his sardonic presence at the window above, and scarcely changed from the day when he had first set eyes on her more than twenty years before.

Patrice, in the gray silk dress and pink sash, her hair plastered to her skull, came and stood beside Adam at the window as Daisy, Junoesque, disappeared in the Edwardses' wake. "Who is the pretty girl?"

"Caroline's pal Daisy Prentice."

"Was that the girl you told me about, who wanted to sleep with you?"

He had been a fool to tell her about it, but she had pestered him, a few nights after their marriage, to admit whether he had ever slept

180

with another woman. The inevitable query. He did not have to ask *her* whether she had ever slept with anyone else—not with that maidenhead, tough as vellum! Adam had tried to temporize: Nice men, he pointed out primly, did not, before marriage, sleep with nice women. Nice men, if they slept with anyone, slept with whores.

But Patrice was not to be put off. What about Daisy Prentice? Well, yes, he had had something of a session with Daisy in his parents' house in Cambridge one hot deserted afternoon when his family and hers were away for the summer. What ensued had been in the nature of a fiasco on the parlor sofa. Both of them had been too nervous, too nice, and too inept. Recounting the incident to Patrice at her insistence, Adam had made a funny story of it, sorry that he had mentioned Daisy's name and hoping to God that Patrice would forget all about it.

But now, standing beside him at the window, she asked determinedly: "Was that the girl?"

"Oh, lord—if you must know, yes!"

Patrice was jealous, and he wanted to laugh. Imagine . . . Daisy Prentice! She had worn white tennis shoes and thick stockings that afternoon; a white wool skirt and high-necked blouse, and her underclothes had put him in mind of lace curtains.

"What's so amusing?" Patrice asked him, now, but with an artless relief in her tone.

"Darling, it was ages ago, and neither of us really gave a damn. Forget it, won't you, please?"

Caroline's voice resounded from the hall downstairs: "Adam! Patrice! *Cocktails!*"

Patrice clutched his arm. "Adam, do I look all right?"

He stared at her. Brown hair sticking uncurled to her head, a face innocent of makeup, timid, defiant eyes. The silk dress had a homemade look and the pink sash was all wrong. Adam had a feeling for style, and hers upset him. She took it in at once and turned away, shaming him. "Patrice, darling!" He seized her hand. "Oh, darling, why in hell did we ever come home?"

"I don't understand you," she said slowly. "Why shouldn't you come home? They love you. I don't understand. . . ."

How should she be expected to understand what he himself did not, quite. How understand this revulsion in him, the revival of old

181

resentments, old suspicions, old dislikes. He had been free of them for four years. For four years he had been his own man; mature, independent, going his own way. The prospect of marriage had shaken him temporarily, but he had regained his balance, turned with love, with passion, to this young wife.

Then there had come that first glimpse of his parents as they waited for the train at South Station. There was his sister Caroline. *His* family, his flesh, his blood. His father's broad, stocky figure with its fine head and weak features; his towering, reserved, sensitive mother. And Caroline, red-faced, overweight, out of breath, her beady black eyes devouring first his face, then Patrice's. Adam had had to fight off a crazy impulse to climb back into the train, to run away, to disappear.

Patrice's fingers had clung to his. Excited, loving voices had showered upon him: "My dear children! Adam, Patrice! Welcome home . . . welcome home!"

"We had better go down," Patrice said. As they had earlier at the station, her fingers curled round his, and as she had murmured earlier at the station, she murmured now: "Adam, your hand is like ice!"

Side by side they started down the stairs. A minor tornado raged in the big parlor with its French windows, which Patrice had seen briefly on her arrival. Now she recognized her mother-in-law's voice: "It was such a strange dream! I suppose the what-you-callum doctors would say it was symbolic or something, but *I* say it was prophetic! Anyway, there I was in my dream and very excited because I'd just had a letter from my son, telling me that he was married. Of course, that part of the dream was not really prophetic because it had already happened. Well, the dream went on and this part of it gave me quite a turn. I was sitting in this very room waiting to receive my new daughter-in-law and sure enough, she appeared. Coming through that door. And she was dressed in a long white robe thing, her face hidden in a kind of veil so I couldn't see what she looked like, although I seemed to be quite sure that it was Adam's wife."

A voice which Patrice recognized as that of Adam's father broke in on the recital: "Just imagine poor Dorothea's feelings had our new daughter-in-law walked in shrouded in mystery, only to turn out to be coal black!"

There was laughter, then Mrs. Bannister's sharp protest: "Wilbur!

182

That isn't funny. You know Adam would never look at a black woman." "I wouldn't bet on it," declared a third voice, gay, bantering, unfamiliar to Patrice.

"That's Barto Williams, Caroline's husband," Adam murmured to Patrice. "What fun they're having with us, aren't they?"

"For the comfort and assurance of those of us who have not yet had the pleasure of meeting Patrice, here she is!"

Mr. Bannister made the announcement in a trumpeting voice as Adam followed Patrice into the room. She had a fleeting, vagrant thought: Suppose Adam had married someone like Edna Meadows; what would they have said, done?

The question was rhetorical and instantly forgotten. Although Patrice had already met several of the most important members of the family, she now suffered a moment of panic. She was not accustomed to crowds, and the room seemed to be literally jammed with people. Some stood in groups of two and three, others sat. Every chair and sofa seemed occupied, every inch of space. The air was close, heavy with a smell of people, of alcohol, of cigarettes. She felt herself become, on an instant, the target of innumerable pairs of strange eyes. . . . Strangers, she thought, with a queer sense of inner desolation. Strangers . . . all of them strangers!

Then a stout jolly woman with black hair and berry eyes took her arm. Caroline Williams, Adam's sister. "You look scarcely older than my Timmy! Come, let me show you off."

Caroline Williams seemed designed, like a chair, for size and comfort, and Patrice turned to her with gratitude.

"Patrice, let me introduce our cousins Thomas and Edith Edwards, and their son, Damon."

Patrice felt at once the boy Damon's glance, measuring life from some indefinable advantage. He barely touched her hand, looked quickly away, yet she knew that she had been intently observed.

"Doctor and Mrs. Redditch. Old, dear friends of the family, as Adam must have told you."

Adam may have told her, but she had long since forgotten. There followed warm handclasps. A blur of faces; curious, kindly, welcoming. All had known Adam since he was born, and now how delightful to see him happily married. Lucky Adam, lucky Patrice!

On and on, round the big room. Faces, hands, voices. Patrice began

183

to feel giddy and was glad of Caroline's firm clasp of her arm. "Ma and Pop felt we should invite them right away to meet you—cousins, old friends. You will be seeing much of them from now on. All part of the family, actually."

Then the damned pink sash coming undone. "Let me fix it for you, dear. There. You look darling!"

I don't. Patrice saw it suddenly, bleakly. I look like the little jungli that I am. But these people . . . knowing each other so well. At home. Self-assured. They know everything, they have everything. I might as well be swinging by my tail from a tree in the Himalayas, but they are too kind to let me see they think so! For the first time in her life she felt completely out of things and at a loss. Cowardly tears rose in her throat and she longed to be back with Alice and Nizamat and Chota Ayah, or alone with Adam on a ship headed toward some never-to-be-attained destination. "Two together! Winds blow south, winds blow north . . ."

"And here," said Caroline, savoring the lollipop moment, "here is Daisy Prentice. My oldest and dearest friend. Daisy, this is Adam's wife."

Milky skin, eyes a blue bar across the oval face, faery hair, long lissome body. A goddess body. Patrice sensed the venom that flowed through the marble fingers which, fleetingly, touched hers.

"How glad I am to meet you," Daisy murmured. She turned at once to Adam, who had materialized out of the crush. "Adam, dear! You haven't changed one teeny-weeny bit!"

"Nice to see you, Daisy." He sounded breezy, out of character. "You haven't changed either. Beautiful as ever."

Patrice thought wonderingly: He manages to make it sound like a slap!

"Do let's find a place to sit down," Daisy implored him. "I want to talk to you, after all this time." Husky. A bedroom voice, structured by practice. Patrice thought in desperation: I must learn. From the back of the throat, partially through the nose, seductive. And that blue quartz gaze melting into cream and petals, swamping the dead fly of another woman's image. Adam had spoken of her as though she were a joke, but she was no joke.

Then another pair of eyes sought hers. Round eyes, agate-colored like a cat's. Barto Williams, supporting himself on his crutches, held

184

a glass toward her. "Would the child bride like a drink?"

"Thank you."

Caroline laughed. "Shucks! I forgot you hadn't yet met Barto. He'll look out for you while I go and help Nora with the canapés. And you look out for him if you know what's good for you, Patrice!"

Patrice took a swallow from the glass which Barto had handed her. It tasted like a lighted cigarette and epsom salts. She gasped.

Barto said: "You don't have to drink it. I told the old man he'd made it too strong."

Patrice felt that she might explode, become a cinder. "It's just that I'm not—you know—used to—to—"

"Homemade gin. No, obviously not."

Strange, inquisitive eyes, boring into her like slow bullets. And the painful stance, suspended between his crutches. She suggested hesitantly: "Perhaps we could sit down somewhere."

"I don't mind standing."

"I was just thinking . . ."

"Of my comfort. Thank you."

It was disconcerting. Adam had told her that Barto Williams was touchy about his lameness, but he had not elaborated. He had, actually, told her little about his family, provided her with no warnings, no pointers, leaving it up to her to find her way alone. But she knew that Barto's had been a ridiculous accident: a fall from a bicycle when he was a child, and injury to the spine. A succession of experimental operations had achieved little, and he was helpless without his crutches. He had been as brave as hell about the whole business, Adam had told her. Hating to be pitied. Hating to be fussed over. The family and friends had become accustomed to his often brusque reactions, but it was embarrassing to strangers.

Now his brown eyes seemed about to unravel her. He said, rather shortly: "You'll have to get over trying so hard, Patrice, my dear."

"Trying?" Daisy and Adam had moved away together. She lost them in the crowd.

"Trying to please, to do the right thing, to make everybody happy and at their ease."

"But shouldn't one? I mean, be considerate to people?"

"Depends. Overdo it at the start and you'll be expected to keep it up. Becomes a strain after a while."

185

"Well, what *does* one do, then?"

There was a gleam of laughter in his eyes. "My, you're an earnest little piece! You know, I find it rather amusing to watch people trying to cope with an unfamiliar or an embarrassing situation. For instance, take me. All wishing I'd sit down, or stand up, or do whatever else they deem necessary to their own peace of mind!"

Puzzled, Patrice said nothing. He went on confidentially: "You see, I have to create my little diversions. I can't be a sportsman like Adam, or play tennis like Cousin Edith Edwards, or even swim like my wife. But you'd be surprised to know how facile one can become. Oh, it's small potatoes, of course, compared to being a hero in the war, like old Redditch, for instance."

Patrice listened awkwardly, thinking: He seems to have to talk. But why won't he sit down? How uncomfortable, those crutches . . .

"Or take my wife, Caroline. Even for a woman she's just about everything I can't be, and she'd have loved to be a man." The smile deepened in his eyes. "One of my favorite diversions is the study of my own wife."

He drank unconcernedly from the lethal potion in his glass, and inquired in a casual voice: "Think I'm being disloyal?"

Patrice thought that he was being pretty loquacious for a first encounter, and she replied coolly: "Aren't you, just a bit?"

"Not at all. I'd die for Caroline if I could be sure she'd miss me."

Patrice could think of nothing to say. She watched her sister-in-law in the offing, dispensing canapés. Pudgy, eyes too small, bottom too big, clothes too tight, but exuding a kind of effervescent good nature.

"I see," said Barto after a pause, "that you have met Caro's friend Daisy Prentice. How'd you like her?"

"Beautiful."

"She's that, all right. Poor Caro uses her as a kind of trick mirror. They couldn't be less alike, she and Daisy, but whenever Caroline looks at her she fancies she sees herself."

Patrice played along, gropingly: "And Daisy? Does she see some-one else?"

"If she does, it isn't Caroline!"

Barto laughed as he spoke. He had magnificent teeth. The thought occurred to Patrice that he might have been a magnificent man had it not been for that fall off a bicycle. "Daisy," Barto went on casually,

186

"has the supreme advantage of being a single-minded woman. She has one aim and desire in life, and one only."

When, again, Patrice remained silent, he said: "I often wonder how she'd react if she were ever really to be laid."

"Laid?" As though she were an egg?

He peered solemnly into his glass. "In our national idiom to be laid is to experience sexual intercourse."

"Gee whiz," said Patrice, and laughed. He gave her a pleased, somewhat surprised glance. "Well, you're no prude, I'm relieved to see. I suppose you realize that you have been unreservedly taken to the tribal bosom?"

"If you mean everybody has been very kind, and that they haven't minded showing it . . ."

"Not like your reserved English, you mean? Oh, we can be reserved toward the undeserving, don't think we can't."

Wilbur Bannister appeared suddenly and put an arm round Patrice's waist. She turned to him with relief. She had, from the moment of their meeting at the railroad station, felt drawn toward him.

"My dear child!" He peered into her still unemptied glass. "Not drinking, and this a celebration in your honor?" He continued without waiting for her embarrassed reply: "I don't know whether you are aware of the noble experiment at present being conducted in our poor country, whereby freeborn Americans are deprived of their right to drink what they please, where and when they please? Prohibition! A blanket term—or more accurately, a wet blanket term!" He giggled, and Patrice wondered whether he might not be just a little bit drunk.

"I wish, dear child, that we had something better to offer you than this concoction of orange juice and what is described in the local vernacular as bathtub gin, though I assure you it has nothing whatsoever to do with bathrooms."

"It's delicious," Patrice lied bravely. "I don't happen to be accustomed to—to strong spirits, that's all."

He gazed at her fondly through his pince-nez. "A well-brought-up young thing, as I told Dorothea the moment I set eyes on you. Now finish what you have in your glass and I'll replenish it."

Mr. Thomas Edwards loomed beside them and dropped a heavy hand on Wilbur's shoulder. "Darn good cocktail, Willy! Wish you'd give me the exact proportions. Edith insists that when I make it, it tastes like paint remover!"

"Let us first ascertain how the prescription affects what I would take to be a totally unspoiled palate," replied Mr. Bannister. He smiled at Patrice. "What would you say, dear? A touch more orange or, for the sake of dryness, a dash more gin?"

There was no escape. Patrice raised the lukewarm glass to her lips, swallowed. All her clothes caught fire, her hair, her throat. It took all her self-control not to cough the liquid up in his face.

With a little parting pat of his hand Wilbur Bannister moved away with Thomas Edwards. "I would say that perhaps the correct proportions would be one part gin to two parts orange. *Absolutely no sugar.* A dash of bitters perhaps, though Dorothea doesn't agree. . . ."

Barto said quietly: "Let's sit down."

He hobbled to a corner of the room and they sat on a small sofa. He was expert with his crutches as he set them to one side and stretched his legs. His trousers were beautifully cut and pressed, his shoes gleamed. He waited until she had recovered from her spasm of choking, then reached out and took the glass from her hand. "It's what I meant a little while ago when I told you you'd have to get over trying so hard."

She stared at him, stupefied. "What else could I have done? I couldn't hurt his feelings."

For a moment Barto looked as though he were about to make some devastating remark, then he shrugged. "As the old man said, you've had a proper upbringing. All to the good. You may find you'll need it."

He reached in a pocket for a cigar and she watched resignedly. After all, the smell couldn't begin to match the taste of that drink.

Barto looked at her, brows raised. "May I?"

"Of course."

He replaced the cigar in his breast pocket. "A *very* proper upbringing!"

Silence fell between them and her mind raced. He had, a moment ago, been on the verge of telling her something. What could it have been? And why—oh, why—had Mr. Bannister insisted that she finish that dreadful cocktail? She was haunted by the memory of the faint smile on his face as he turned away with Thomas Edwards. It was all a mistake, an accident. He was the kindest of men. How would she ever forget that meeting this afternoon at the South Station? That warm embrace, the huge box of sweets, the flowers, and holding her hand in his during the drive back to Berry's Landing. "My dear child, if you knew how my wife and I have counted the days for this moment!"

Barto said presently: "I hope you'll come round to the house tomorrow and see my shop."

"Your shop?"

"My workshop. Oh, not professional. I work with gems and semiprecious stones, just for the fun of it."

"You mean you don't have a real job?"

"Not the kind you probably mean; no."

The party was well under way. Voices seemed to bounce against the ceiling, to an accompanying tidal undertow of noise. Patrice was aware of glances directed toward her and Barto—indulgent glances, amused. It was rude, she thought, for her to be sitting here with him when she should be mixing with the others. But the cocktail had brought on a return of nausea. She felt as if her legs were stuffed with cotton; her pupils seemed to swell, blurring her vision. Only Barto's voice at her side came through the haze: "They are telling each other that I have made a conquest. I always know, when Caroline laughs on that special note. . . ."

"Tell me," Patrice began carefully, "more about your shop."

"It's a room above my garage. I spend all day there working on my rocks, or just sitting alone and smoking. King of my castle."

After a moment he went on: "I like being my own boss, working on something as hard and as positive as stone."

"And do you sell them, afterward?"

"Oh, no. As I said, I do it for fun."

He rearranged the crutches at his side. He had, she noticed, well-shaped, fastidious hands. She said painstakingly: "But what about a profession, earning a living? One usually has to, doesn't one?"

He smiled, and it changed his face. "I don't make money. Didn't Adam tell you that I was stinking rich?"

Adam, she replied, had in fact told her practically nothing about his family. "He's a funny sort of person. You know . . . detached."

189

She added apologetically: "It isn't that he isn't *interested* in his family. . . ."

Barto laughed. Then cheerfully, as if he felt that between them they had broken some barrier, he said: "You see, I inherited something of a fortune from two sources—from my father and from an aunt. It bothers Caroline and her parents. Oh, not my being rich, but my not working. I am totally lacking in what old Wilbur calls 'noblesse oblige.' My ancestors, if you can call them that, made their money in coal, and it took me all of five years, after marrying Caroline, to learn to say 'noblesse oblige' and not 'oblesse noblige.'"

It was Patrice's turn to laugh, and she saw Caroline turn in their direction, and Daisy too, from a distant corner of the room. Two pairs of eyes trained full upon Barto and herself, women's eyes, seeking them out despite the crowd.

A maid passed carrying a tray of cocktails and Barto reached out and helped himself deftly. Catching Patrice's eye, he said lightly: "I'm used to this stuff. Learned to depend on it, actually." After a moment he went on: "You and I are in the same boat in a way. Me married to Caroline and you to her brother."

"You make it sound as though you thought it might be a life-boat!"

She felt she really should get up and join the rest of the party, but her legs felt weak. It occurred to her that people seemed to accept the situation, that they took it for granted Barto should monopolize her. The noise had increased in a well-bred sort of way. Faces had taken on a puce tinge. The room seemed to be twice as crowded as it had been, as the occupants formed and reformed in little knots and groups.

Daisy Prentice and Adam had created a small island for themselves near one of the French windows. Her fair beauty seemed a perfect foil for his dark good looks. The pale-blue hand-knitted dress Daisy was wearing cased her body like a second skin. Daisy Prentice and Adam, Patrice thought wanly. Made for each other!

"I suppose," Barto was saying, "you've been briefed about me? About my accident, my peculiar disposition?"

Conceit. He couldn't get away from himself. Sensing something sardonic in her silence, Barto said in a careful voice: "It may be some time before you and I are given another chance to talk together,

Patrice. Not that there's a hell of a lot to say, but I'd rather like to get in the first lick!"

Adam was filling his pipe and Daisy seemed to be staring at him with a peculiar fixity. Indifferent to the company, perhaps even unaware of it; absorbed, Patrice decided, in each other. Imagine them in bed together! And here she was with the bulge just beginning, that mound of strangeness. She had heard, or had read somewhere, that many a man was unfaithful to his wife during her pregnancy, and now, looking at Daisy, who would blame Adam?

She had no desire to go on talking with Barto Williams, nor did she know how to escape. She thought: I bet people generally try to avoid being stuck with him! That's it. He embarrasses them by his directness when they try to be tactful. But what does he expect? A cripple, out of things. All his life since he was five years old. In spite of everything he had still succeeded in producing a child, the boy Timothy, whom Caroline had brought to the station this afternoon. Slim and perfect, Caroline made beautiful in his childish flesh, Barto restored to litheness in the same flesh. It must be some consolation.

Barto set the second cocktail glass, empty, beside the first. Or was this only his second? There was a stain of red on his cheekbones, his eyes seemed unnaturally brilliant, yet he gave no recognizable hint of being drunk. He was staring at her. "You met my son Timmy this afternoon." It was eerie the way he plucked things out of one's mind! "A fine kid if I do say so. Best thing that ever happened to me, or to Caroline."

"It must be a comfort," Patrice murmured, feeling horribly trite.

"I tried to have another child, but after Timmy nothing."

Patrice touched his knee gently. "Couldn't a doctor have helped?"

"I tried 'em all. Turned out it wasn't my fault. I could have had fifty kids."

Patrice gazed at him helplessly. "Well, then?"

"Caroline didn't want any more children. She was sure they'd turn out defective because of my condition. She had decided that Timmy was just a bit of good luck and that it wouldn't last. She had been taking the necessary precautions right along and I didn't know it."

Across the room Caroline was laughing with the Edwardses and another couple. Her dark head was thrown back, revealing her short, thick throat. Her breasts sagged under her green silk dress. She

191

looked respectable and unimaginative, a woman who probably went to bed wearing a flannelette nightgown and her hair in curlers. And yet, Patrice mused, she had a fullness, a ripeness, an excitability. And she had had the power to attract this queer magnetic man.

Barto went on as though, now, he talked more than half to himself: "I want something very special for Timmy. A good pair of legs to begin with. Perfect health. I can give him all the material where- withal—more than he'll ever need, probably. And that could be a mistake. I was an only child and after I was hurt my parents settled everything on me in a nice fat trust fund. My father's sister, who had no children of her own, did the same for me. Having left me un- supervised for the first five years of my life, so I was free to fall off a bicycle too big for me, they couldn't do enough to make up for it! Forty grand a year, and when I was twenty-four all three of them died and I came into the capital. In my turn I've fixed things so no one can get their hands on it. Caroline would like to; so would her father, who fancies himself as a financial wizard. I think Caroline would know enough to manage the dough; she has conjugal respon- sibilities toward it, feels herself practically married to Electric Bond and Share, Westinghouse, and a few others, but not allowed to go to bed with them! She feels bitterly that I ought to do something about it . . . but I'm thinking of Timmy. I want him . . . I would like—"

He broke off, then said abruptly: "Stupid, isn't it? I should be grateful if he just grew up healthy and normal. After all, money can only give one a relative freedom of choice. In the long run it's all I can do for him."

Years later Patrice was to recall this first strange conversation with Caroline's husband. Timmy Williams grew up healthy and normal enough. At thirty he was a tubby little mediocrity making his way in the stock market, married to the right girl; devoted to his mother, long ago divorced and married to another, even richer man. Barto's son, Timothy, bald at thirty, disliking his father, avoiding him . . .

I really should, Patrice adjured herself once more, get up and join the others. But wouldn't it look rather pointed, deserting Barto? Why didn't Adam pay some attention . . . ? It appeared a conspiracy, this leaving her alone so long with Barto.

He said abruptly: "Don't want to pry, but has Adam any ideas about finding a job?"

192

The change of subject startled her. "I don't know."

"He may not find it altogether easy, you know, to adjust, after this long time away from home. I have a suggestion you can pass on to him, if you care to. I happen to have an interest in a boatyard in Berry's Landing. They build everything from fishing dories to sailboats. If, within the next few weeks, Adam doesn't find something he likes, I could fix it so he could take on some of the clerical stuff at the boatyard. It won't pay a hell of a lot but it should be enough for the two of you to live on for a while. You'd be independent of the family, at any rate. And there's an apartment near us which I know you could get for a small rent. Berry's Landing isn't too bad a place in the winter, and Caroline and I would love to have you living near us."

She thanked him. Overwhelmed, but wariness persisting. He went on, offhandedly: "I know Adam loathes living in a city. Sure, he lived four years in Calcutta, but that was different. Just another version of the jungle, and he likes jungles!"

"You're very kind, Barto. But of course it's up to Adam, isn't it? We had not planned to live in America. We want to go back to India. I mean, after the baby."

"A baby? You would consider taking a baby back to—to India?"

"Why not?"

He hesitated. "Well, what about Adam himself? Do you believe that in spite of his restlessness—and I grant you he is restless; always has been—do you believe he'd be content to leave his home and his country permanently?"

"I don't know." What, really, did she know about Adam? Love was not understanding. Going to bed together was not understanding. Having his baby planted inside her was not understanding.

She temporized: "We could, I suppose, always come back for visits."

"Ten thousand miles. A month's journey, more or less, each way. Takes money."

Everything took money, as who should know better than he, heir to two fortunes. Yet millions of people somehow lived without money, or with very little. Patrice felt ignorant, defiant.

Barto went on calmly: "Adam has always considered himself a misfit at home, and in many ways he is a misfit. But don't forget that he is a New Englander, too."

193

She felt a sense of opposition rising within her. "What exactly does it mean to be a New Englander?"

"It means, among other things, that they don't transplant very successfully."

She thought of Doey, transplanted from his native France, and of Aunt Eve likewise. She thought of Alice, transplanted from Kensington. Of Mr. Onions and the Sparkses, of the Sisters at the convent; of Clem, transplanted first to Australia, then to Spain. And what about herself? She knew very well that if it came to the pinch she would readily transplant. She had that resilience, and after all, what was *home?* A broken arch through which one saw a field of yellow mustard dancing in the sun? A grove of trees where a hoopoe sang? A tent at the jungle's edge?

Again Barto seemed uncannily to read her thoughts. "Very much overdone, this whole business, I agree. Homesickness is an animal trait. Dogs, cats, wild things suffer from it. Perhaps savages. But for civilized people . . ."

He left the sentence in the air. Then he said: "There is one point on which you need have no doubts. Everyone is tickled to death that you married Adam. Everyone, that is, except perhaps poor old Daisy!"

Patrice said with an attempt at lightness: "Should I be concerned on that score?"

"As far as Adam's feelings are concerned I'd say not by a long shot." He went on quickly: "Women never have been what you might call Adam's major interest. He has always preferred nature in its simpler forms—that is, until he met you!" Again that hard brown gaze. "I bet Daisy'd give a good deal to know how you did it, Patrice."

"Did what?"

"Nailed Adam. Probably one of those old jungle tricks she never found in the book."

"I just happen to share his tastes, I suppose."

"Don't think Daisy didn't try to share them! She spent months boning up on the private life of the mollusk, and related subjects. She even bought herself a gun in the hope that Adam would give her lessons in marksmanship, but I guess he decided it would be too risky an undertaking in one way if not another." Barto laughed. "Now that

194

she has definitely lost Adam to you, it wouldn't surprise me if she went after Lawrence Redditch. You haven't met Lawrence yet. He's in the Merchant Marine, son of that couple over there—the doc and his wife. You'd never guess the relationship, though. Lawrence is a diamond in the rough even if he was born in Louisburg Square!"

"There seem to be so many diamonds in the rough and misfits about," Patrice remarked. She had a sudden sense of relief from tension, a lightness of heart. "You imply that Adam is one, in a way. And that boy over there—the handsome one. What's his name? Damon Edwards. I'm sure there must be something the matter with him, too."

Barto caught her lighthearted mood. "How right you are! That lad's a prodigy. He goes to Harvard this fall, at sixteen!"

As though he had overheard their conversation or the utterance of his name, the boy, standing alone in a far corner of the room, turned his head toward Barto and Patrice. The late twilight from the windows framed him, giving him the luster of something golden and archaic. His gaze seemed to seek out Patrice, to dwell on her from this safe distance.

Then Barto, equipping himself deftly with his crutches, rose as the boy's mother and her husband approached. "Barto has monopolized you for long enough!" declared Mrs. Edwards, in a soft, rather monotonous voice. Her smile, Patrice noticed, seemed to turn itself off and on like a defective light bulb. In no single feature did these pleasant, conventional parents resemble their extraordinary son. "Thomas and I have been dying to tell you how happy we are to have you in the family. I'm Dorothea's cousin, you know. Several times removed, whatever that means!" The smile turned itself on once more. "You must always call us Cousin Edith and Cousin Tom, just as Adam does. And now do tell us about your trip from India. Wasn't it dreadfully hot?"

15

Yes, Patrice agreed, it had been very hot, especially in the Red Sea. But heat was one of the many things one had
to become accustomed to, living in India.

Thomas Edwards jerked his head nervously, like a turkey. "Yes,
yes! We have always heard that Englishmen and mad dogs prefer the
noonday heat!"

"I cannot imagine living in such a climate," declared Mrs. Edwards. "So enervating. What *do* people do for exercise?"

"They ride," Patrice said vaguely. "Play tennis. That sort of thing."

"It can't," insisted Mrs. Edwards. "be very pleasant, living in the
tropics."

"India is not in the tropics," her husband corrected her. It was
amazing how much he resembled a turkey. Then, plaintively:
"Women never get these things right. Like centuries. Edith always
insists that fourteen ninety-two was the fourteenth century!"

"Well, wasn't it?" demanded Mrs. Edwards.

"Gobble gobble!" said Mr. Edwards, dismissingly.

"Now tell me, Patrice," implored Mrs. Edwards, "—you don't
mind my calling you Patrice? I've known Adam since he was born.

196

I could hardly call you Mrs. Bannister, could I?" She gave a small deprecating laugh.

Mrs. Turkey. Perhaps that accounted for it. Some beautiful rare bird had laid a snow-white egg in the Edwardses' nest and they had between them unwittingly hatched that beautiful son.

"Tell me," Mrs. Edwards went on earnestly, "do they play a lot of tennis in—what is the name of the place where you lived, dear?"

"We lived in so many places."

"But your own home, dear?"

There had not been one that was not, somehow, home, with the dear shabbiness, the affectionate climate of home. They unreeled before Patrice's eyes like old snapshots, faded and distant, yet somehow indestructible.

"And now do tell us about your stay in England. We love England. Gobble gobble."

"Oh, to be in England," chanted Mrs. Edwards, lyrical on orange juice and gin, "now that April's there!"

I could tell them about the strawberries, Patrice thought in some desperation. Of the taste of fresh strawberries eaten from their hulls, and hoping that Adam would not come back too soon from his walk and catch her. For strawberries had been expensive, but the old waiter at the hotel on Wigmore Street had been very understanding. If she were just to pay for the strawberries in cash they would not appear on the bill and so nobody would be any the wiser. But she didn't have the cash. Or at any rate she dared not part with a penny because of that operation. Alice had scraped together a hundred English pounds in Indian rupees and Adam had had the money changed at the bank in London. It seemed like a lot to Patrice, but she had no idea of what the operation might cost. The stewardess on the ship out from Calcutta had not been sure. "Not much, dearie— that is, considerin' . . ."

But Adam had come back from his walk and waylaid her as she was setting out for the abortionist. "Darling, darling! No no no !" As if his heart would crack open with shame. "Thank God I came back in time. You damn silly little fool . . . I love you . . . I might have lost you!" Picturing her pallidly dead perhaps, or maimed, crippled at the hands of some filthy quack. "Patrice, promise me, promise me that you will never . . ."

197

Passion and terror, and the drumming of his heart against hers. She had thought that she might drown in the full flood of her responding love, drown herself and him. And there had been that moment of happiness, matchless, complete.

Patrice stared now at these kindly faces, at Barto's dark mystery. There was something dreamlike to her in the utter irrelevance of this conversation. Long afterward she was to wonder whether this first evening at the Bannisters' was to set the tone for most future communications between herself and them and their friends. A tone of affection definitely devoid of almost any other content. A tone of implied understanding and acceptance on her part of all the factors which comprised their relationships with one another. She had a distinct feeling that on this first experimental assay it was definitely up to her to follow all cues set for her: to try to become as much like them as humanly possible, and so to preserve the harmony in which they honestly believed they existed. She could not guess, nor could they, that she would herself change as they had made it their business not to change, not in one iota, from that harmonious concept of themselves.

Mrs. Edwards raved on: They simply adored England. "We are English by heritage, you know." Most of the really good families in New England . . . though things were changing. The Irish swarming, and the Italians. Unfortunately she and Thomas had not been able to visit England since their own honeymoon there more than twenty years ago. But they were sending their son to Oxford to round out his education.

"Of course, he will finish Harvard," Mr. Edwards interpolated. "Then a summer in Europe if we find we can afford it. He is in love with the Greek idea, has been since he was a little boy. . . ."

Pride in their eyes, in their voices, and why not? The future was theirs, a fine fat plum cake. "We don't want to push the boy too hard. By all accounts he is rather exceptional."

"Don't boast, Tom!" Mrs. Edwards reproved him complacently. "We just happen to be very lucky parents. Of course, Damon's grandfather—my father—was the youngest chief justice on the State Supreme Court, and Thomas's grandfather wrote the first history of the founding of the Massachusetts Bay Colony, so it is safe to say that our son comes by his talents honestly enough!"

Caroline barged in upon them. Her cheeks blazed, she had a top-heavy look. "If you two are talking about your son and heir," she screamed, "*everyone* knows he's a genius. Don't be so darned coy about it!"

"Pipe down, Caro," Barto warned her. "How many drinks have you had?"

"What's it to you?" She could scarcely stand. "Goddam crape-hanger you are, Barto Williams!"

"My darling child!" It came as a curious bleating sound from Mr. Bannister. "Whatever is your wretched husband saying to you *now?*"

"I'm telling her she's had too much to drink," Barto said dispassionately. "She's as drunk as a skunk, to be exact."

Mr. Bannister flushed. "Nonsense. In my own house to tell me that my own daughter . . ."

"Plastered," Barto said. "As usual."

Caroline swayed toward Patrice. "And what about our little bride here? Sober as sober on a night like this!"

"She's not used to drinking dynamite," Barto elucidated. "She happens to be a well-brought-up, innocent young person."

Caroline laughed raucously. *"Innocent?"*

"Cut it out, Caroline."

"Oh, dear, there they go." Mrs. Bannister had joined the little group. She glanced anxiously at her daughter. "Caroline, dearest . . ."

"Barto's trying to teash me the difference between innocence and *viginity,* aren't you, Barto, honey?"

"I said to cut it out."

"You're funny as a crutch," Caroline said. She caught herself. "Oh, Barto, honey, I didn't mean that!"

"You mean I'm funny as two crutches," he corrected her, equally. "Well, so I am, so I am."

The Edwardses looked distractedly at Patrice. They had lost their cue, and it was, again, left up to Barto to supply one. Smiling at Patrice, he said in judicial voice: "You'll find that there are two sides to every question, my dear—the sober side, and the drunk."

"In vino veritas!" Caroline proclaimed with a thick laugh. "I've heard you say so yourself, Barto. . . . Jesus Christ alone knows how often I've heard you. . . ."

199

A maid appeared and announced that dinner was served, and Mr. Bannister offered his arm to Patrice. Possibly because his wife was glaring at him, he had decided not to take up the cudgels in his daughter's defense against her husband. Instead he began to whistle, tunelessly, the opening bars of the *Lohengrin* Wedding March, and Patrice thought in wonder: "How queer that they should all get so drunk so suddenly!"

Mr. Bannister led her into the dining room and held her chair and she sat between him and Dr. Redditch. They tended on her flatteringly, two elder gentlemen, and she the diffident young bride. But what was the difference between innocence and what Caroline had called *viginity*? She thought: I'll have to write this to Clem. It will remind him of the days when he and I pretended each to know better than the other.... "What's imagination?" "Same thing as lying." Well, but was it?

The crescendo from the parlor had invaded the dining room. It was, like the room she had just left, pleasantly proportioned, with many windows, fumed oak paneling, paintings of sailing ships, and silver candlesticks which gleamed the length of a long table set with a linen tablecloth and petunias in a big silver bowl. I'll get used to things, Patrice thought. Get used to knowing everyone, always living in the same place among the same possessions. Wouldn't it be nice, Alice had suggested, wistfully, if we could all be together somewhere, forever . . . together! But Alice had been left behind in the convent with the Sisters, eating her meals in that dreary refectory, her thoughts always with the son in Spain, with the daughter.... A person halved was Alice now—no, quartered, by love.

Dr. Redditch passed her the olives. What, he wanted to know, were her views of the Hindu caste system? And did she believe that British rule in India was threatened by growing nationalist sentiment, and wouldn't it be a great pity?

Doey used to say that caste was tommyrot. Patrice tried to recall his exact words. Tommyrot . . . tommyrot. And in the midst of tears . . . and under running laughter.

"Probably a good thing, caste," Dr. Redditch mused. "Makes for a stable society if nothing else. We have something of the sort ourselves. You must have heard of the Boston Brahmins?"

She had not heard of them, and Mr. Bannister smiled paternally.

200

"Well, you will. As a matter of fact, there is one sitting next to you at this moment. Doctor Redditch is a member of one of the highest castes. Aren't you, Dick?"

Dr. Redditch, in his early sixties, was darkly handsome in a conventional style. He smiled at Patrice. "Do I look to you like a Brahmin?"

It struck her rather surprisingly that he did, certainly more so than anyone else in the room, for he had that air of *caste* which Doey had always dismissed as tommyrot but for whose members Nizamat was expected to fetch a chair and before whom even more imposing but uninitiated beings unhesitatingly gave way. What, Patrice wondered, would Doey have made of this group—Doey the individualist, perennially at odds with groups of any kind? She decided that he would probably have taken to Dr. Redditch, but not to her father-in-law. The thought seemed to occur to her of itself, startling her, and she glanced covertly at Mr. Bannister as he arranged food on the back of his fork in the English fashion before transferring it to his mouth.

Dr. Redditch did not press her for an answer to his question, but went on to speak of Indian agitation for independence. Patrice dredged up an opinion she had not, until this moment, realized she possessed. "I think that independence must be a very precious thing, especially if you haven't got it, and the Indians haven't—yet."

Mr. Bannister frowned. "The Indians don't know when they're well off. I'm all for the British."

Dr. Redditch laughed. "There speaks the incorrigible Anglophile!"

"Patrice cannot be any less a one than I," Mr. Bannister gave out, as though that clinched it. Then he gave her a sidewise, challenging glance: "Am I not right, my dear?"

Patrice thought it over. Again, her answer seemed to be waiting for her to utter it: "Doey always hated the idea of some people bossing other people. I think I hate it, too."

"Doey?" Both men uttered the name simultaneously. How alien it sounded on their lips!

"My father."

"Ah, yes," said Dr. Redditch. He carefully trimmed the fat off a slice of ham. "But there are, don't you agree, graver issues than a shallow nationalism. There is the destiny of millions as yet unfit to govern themselves. And there is the destiny of one of the most honor-

201

able, the most spectacularly successful governments the world has ever seen."

"Hear hear, Reddy, old boy!" cried Mr. Bannister. "A good point, a darn good point!"

Patrice watched him take a piece of meat from his plate and drop it into the slavering jaws of an ancient spaniel which lay beside his chair. She felt vaguely on the defensive, though she could not quite have explained why.

Wilbur Bannister went on to declare that in his opinion it was never more vital than today for people to stick to a consciousness of their heritage, and with Dr. Redditch he held the English to be by far the most significant race in the world since the early Romans. He for one was proud—darn proud—to belong to that race.

"But," Patrice objected, "you aren't really English any more, are you? I mean, it's all right, of course, to be proud of one's heritage, but when one has broken away from it as you have it can't mean the same thing, can it?"

A small dewdrop of moisture quivered at the end of Mr. Bannister's nose. "My dear"—he was gentle but firm—"one does not break away from one's heritage when it is as fine as yours and mine." Then, leaning toward her confidingly, he murmured: "If you don't want that little bit of ham might poor Koko have it?"

Daisy Prentice was seated directly across the table from Patrice, between Barto Williams and Adam. Daisy's eyes were a field of for-get-me-nots, her breasts a pair of fists pushing through the silk of her dress. How could any man be indifferent to her? Barto was eyeing her in a curious unashamed way, and Adam was laughing at something she had just said. All three shared something Patrice did not share, could not share. And that's it, she told herself. That's what I've been missing ever since I arrived—that sense of sharing. My life has been full of doors and windows through which people, things, events have rushed away. But here invisible walls house these people. Daisy, Barto, Adam—the Bannisters and their companions. The years they have shared are still with them; the time through which they have moved, words they have spoken, events they have observed through each other's eyes—none of this is lost or ever could be lost since all have their part. Yes, even Barto has a part; he shares this world as if —as if—what were the words? As if to the manner born. They did indeed belong to a caste, all of them; and just as in that other, that Oriental, arcane society, to enter it one must first die and then be reborn.

Daisy had turned wholly toward Adam and was speaking to him in a low voice, her head close to his. And again Adam laughed. It was gay, unforced, and at the sound color flooded Daisy's sumptuous throat. Her eyes were no longer forget-me-nots pleading to be remembered: they were two blue-black sponges soaking up Adam's face.

Dr. Redditch, following Patrice's glance, said abruptly: "Charming, isn't she, Daisy? I've known her since she was born, as I've known your Adam. Daisy is a great friend of my boy Lawrence. He is in Australia at the moment but we expect him home very soon."

Patrice thought viciously: "By the time she's forty she'll have thick jellied legs like a sick person. But in the meantime . . ."

Her father-in-law was peering at her. "You are not eating, Patrice. Don't you feel well, my dear?"

She reassured him. She was feeling quite well. Just a little tired. But the food did in fact taste heavy and overly rich. I've simply, she warned herself, got to stop carping so! If Clem had been near he would have kicked her under the table and hissed: "Do you want to eat curry *all* your silly life?"

Mr. Bannister begged her to tell him what she thought of Rudyard Kipling. "I personally regard the *Just So Stories* as bully. My children were brought up on them. But Doctor Redditch holds out in favor of *Kim*. What is your choice, Patrice?"

Patrice settled for *Kim*. Lucky, she thought, that I happen to know it! "But the Indians," she went on, trying to sound learned, "don't like Kipling a bit. They think his attitude toward them is insulting and that anyhow he doesn't know anything about India. And the English regard him as vulgar. They think it's infra dig to read his books."

"Infra dig?" Dr. Redditch sounded startled. "But why infra dig?"

"Well, they think there must be something wrong with a white man who takes so much trouble to write about the natives."

"My goodness! But you just said that the natives . . ."

"I know. It does all sound rather silly, doesn't it?"

"I am sure," observed Mr. Bannister after a slight pause, "no one could feel that way about Kipling if they were to hear old Copey read

'The Bell Buoy.' Could they, Reddy?"

Dr. Redditch explained: "Copey is Professor Copeland of Harvard. But of course, 'the Bell Buoy' is hardly what one would call Kipling's genre. I gather your English friends took exception merely to the Indian tales?"

"Such nonsense!" proclaimed Mr. Bannister before Patrice could think of an answer. He peered with suspicion into the dish which the maid was proffering at his shoulder. "What is this, Nora?"

"Applesauce."

From the farther end of the table Mrs. Bannister addressed him in a sharp voice: "You asked Ella to cook it especially for you, Wilbur. Now eat it."

Mr. Bannister winked at Patrice. "Orders is orders," he murmured resignedly. Then, to the dog at his side: "No, Koko, dear. You wouldn't like applesauce. Bad for bow-wows, especially at your age."

At a loss, Patrice let her gaze wander toward Barto. He appeared to have lost interest in Daisy and was staring morosely at a wedge of watermelon which had just been placed before him by the maid.

Dr. Redditch had reverted to Kipling. "Could you perhaps enlighten us uninitiates as to why the Indians should feel about Kipling as you say they do?"

"They just think he's making fun of them."

"Gracious!" exclaimed Dr. Redditch. She might have propounded some shattering theory of relativity. "But tell me, don't literary considerations enter into the Indians' judgment? Kipling after all is a master craftsman, as even his American detractors—and there are some—are forced to concede."

"We must," Mr. Bannister interrupted fervently, "arrange for Patrice to hear Copey read 'The Bell Buoy.' As a matter of fact, I might be persuaded to read it aloud myself, after dinner." He waited expectantly for the proposal to be carried by acclaim, but no one seemed to have heard it.

Patrice thought: Why won't Adam look at me? Why do his eyes keep sliding down between those two balloons of hers? She certainly doesn't *look* as if she had never been—what did Barto call it? Laid. Soft, submissive, scented; pink like watermelon, glistening.

Did Patrice, Mr. Bannister suddenly inquired, like poetry?

She pulled herself together. Oh, yes, she liked poetry. Whitman for instance. Adam had given her a beautifully bound little volume when they married. She had never, until then, even heard of Whitman. Reading him had made her want to see everything in America that he described. The huge unfolding plains of the west. Lilacs in New England doorways. Live oaks in Louisiana. Bridges and rivers and mountains. Leaves of grass.

She was carried away, her voice rising. But still Adam did not look at her. He had forgotten all about her. He was back at the beginning of things with Daisy Prentice. "A Woman Waits for Me . . ." Daisy was the woman who had waited for him and nothing would make any difference, not even marriage to someone entirely different thousands of miles away or even three feet away. Patrice felt her youth and inadequacy as something hopeless and despicable, something of which Adam must surely already have tired past endurance.

Then, quite disconcertingly, from the farther end of the table, Mrs. Bannister's voice soared above all the other voices:

"O Captain! my Captain! our fearful trip is done!
The ship has weathered every rack, the prize we sought is won,
The port is near, the bells I hear, the people all exulting . . ."

The voice quivered, faltered. Mrs. Bannister turned to Damon Edwards, seated beside her. "Finish it for me, Damon, dear. You are still in school—you must remember it!"

The boy shook his head, mumbled something.

Mrs. Bannister raised her voice again, imposing silence on the surprised company:

"O the bleeding drops of red
Where on the deck my Captain lies,
Fallen cold and dead."

She finished in a normal tone: "I have always admired that poem of Whitman's. He must simply have *loved* Abraham Lincoln."

Barto leaned forward suddenly and addressed his son down the length of the table. "Timmy, run down to the drugstore and buy a quart of ice cream. Tell Gregg's to charge it to me. Chocolate. And hurry."

Caroline lifted a drooping head. "Barto, for heaven's sake! It'll take him half an hour to go to Gregg's and back. Why don't you have the applesauce if you don't like watermelon?"

"You know Daddy hates applesauce *and* watermelon!" the boy Timothy piped, pushing back his chair. "Granny, you know Daddy never eats anything for dessert except ice cream!"

"Run along, Timmy," Barto directed in a bored voice. "If they haven't got chocolate, get vanilla."

The boy ran out of the room. There was a small, uncomfortable silence. Beside Patrice, Mr. Bannister breathed into his plate: "Honestly, such manners."

Mrs. Bannister had flushed. "Barto, I did think that perhaps just for once watermelon instead of ice cream ... and there are other people."

Barto was smiling genially. "It's all right, Mrs. B. Don't mind me!"

"But I do mind you. I rather think that it is up to you to mind . . . to mind . . ."

"Don't give it a thought, Mrs. B. Timmy'll be back with the ice cream."

Patrice stared at him in disbelief. Could he really be so trivial, so inane? He met her eyes and smiled. He had a pleased, almost rhapsodic look. She looked away and was immediately conscious of the magnet of another pair of eyes. Damon Edwards' eyes, sending a tiny electric shock through her nerves. Damon's eyes were glittering with tears and she caught her breath as she realized that he was in the throes of a paroxysm of laughter which he was silently, desperately, trying to suppress.

206

16

A yellow moon hung above the sea. Along the North Shore electric lights seemed to founder in the overall brilliance, except where an advertising sign blazed like a Christmas bauble at odds with the insinuating heat of the summer night.

Standing at the window of their bedroom where she and Adam had stood earlier that evening, Patrice had a sense of weariness, of surfeit. The party downstairs had gone on for what had seemed to her a long time and she had felt a creeping ennui like a malaise. Barto had taken Timmy home early and had not returned, and the boy Damon Edwards had seemed to evaporate, leaving no trace. Patrice had had a last glimpse of him walking across the darkened lawn in the direction of his parents' house beyond the distant trees, and it had seemed to her that with his disappearance something mysterious and charming, of which she had become increasingly conscious as the evening wore on, had vanished too, leaving a kind of blankness, like regret. She heard Mrs. Edwards explaining to Mrs. Bannister: "You were busy and Damon didn't want to interrupt. He has some studying to do before he goes to bed. He said to tell you . . . to say good night . . . he had such a good time. . . ."

A strange, shy lad, Patrice thought at the time, shrugging. He had

207

not even thought it necessary to bid her, or Adam, good night. He had had, as he walked quickly away into the shadowy night, an *overcome* look, as though something had been too much for him. Bored, probably. He was young, precocious, full of himself.

And later Daisy had driven Caroline home before returning, herself, to Cambridge with the Redditches. For the half dozen guests who lingered past midnight Mr. Bannister had produced a bottle of contraband rye whiskey and had persuaded Patrice to take what he called a sip, which had speedily put the finishing touch to a condition bordering on coma. Seated beside Adam in a corner of the sofa, she had battled her fatigue while Mr. Bannister read "The Bell Buoy" with éclat, and Mrs. Bannister, smiling the fixed smile of long habit, fell into a doze in her chair.

Now, naked beside the open window, Patrice felt the warm breath of the sea and the garden play on her skin. Adam lay on his bed, watching her. It was past two o'clock and in the adjoining room his parents' snores mingled with the snores of the old spaniel, which shared their bed.

"It's terribly late. Come to bed, Patrice."

"There's a moon. It's just about to set."

"Don't tell me it reminds you of something! I'm too damned sleepy."

"Adam, do you believe that some people transplant better than others?"

He yawned with luxury and abandon.

"Heliotrope," she murmured maddeningly. "It's always some one thing."

There had been heliotrope in that garden in the hills where the leopard prowled at night. And there was the chabutra on the lawn of that house which she remembered best of all, where the aunt would sit doing her embroidery, and the churel lurked in its tree, scratching a scaly armpit. And the Christmas camp, where she had studied the elephants upside down. Whiskers like black wires growing out of their chins. Big fringy eyes. The rough tip of a trunk exploring her hair; the smell of dust, of dry fodder, of beasts.

Adam thought resignedly: Not a peep out of her all evening, and now she'll talk to daylight. "I wonder," he said aloud, "whether the moon and the stars will ever remind you of me?"

208

"Why should they have to? We'll always be together, won't we?"

"Did you have a good time tonight?"

"Except for the drinks. I nearly got sick again."

"I warned the old man not to give you that stuff, but he's so damned conceited about his special brew ... determined that everyone should try it."

"Barto was very kind. They were all very kind. I suppose I'll understand them all better eventually."

He caught the note of uncertainty. "They are not so difficult to understand. Except Barto, perhaps."

"And Daisy Prentice."

"What did you think of Daisy?"

"She is in love with you, I think."

He sat up abruptly. "Did somebody hand you that stuff?"

"She doesn't try to hide it."

"Well, you're on the wrong tack. It's not me she's after—it's Lawrence Redditch."

"It wouldn't do her much good to be after you, would it?" She turned her head to look at him. "I mean, you married to me and everything."

Adam said slowly: "She had some kind of a crush on me years ago, but she soon got over it. Now it's friendliness, that's all."

"Barto doesn't seem to think so."

"Oh, so it was Barto!"

"He wasn't trying to make mischief. Just trying to keep me amused, I suppose." She turned wholly from the window, facing him. "Barto said he could get you a job here in Berry's Landing, if you wanted it. I think he is going to speak to you about it himself."

Adam was suddenly wide awake. "What?"

"He wants to help us."

"So they've started already! I bet Caroline put him up to it."

"But wouldn't it be natural for them to want to help you?"

"Goddam officiousness!" He held his voice low, with an effort. "I scarcely set foot in the place after four years, and there they go with their meddling."

"But he thought you might be happier living in Berry's Landing than in Boston or New York."

"Because he happens to like living in Berry's Landing! And because it would give my sister a chance to stick her nose in our affairs!"

Patrice stared at him through the gloom. "I don't believe Barto would do anything at Caroline's dictation. He is a kind person. I don't understand your attitude, Adam. Really I don't."

The curious strain which Adam had been under all evening lifted, releasing old, suppressed resentments and frustrations. He started to speak in a queer, muffled voice: "Years ago when I was a kid I wanted to be a biologist. Even at that age! But it was something that stayed with me all my life. Through school. Through college. I wanted to make biology my career. But the family had other ideas. They were paying the freight and I was not allowed to forget it. My father and my grandfather had been lawyers so I was to be one, too. It was an expensive education, but it was something they had set their hearts on. They had this horror, you see, of a man going all out for something no one in the family had ever done before. Something that guaranteed neither money nor fame. Perhaps they had Lawrence Redditch in mind as a dreadful example. You met old Redditch this evening. Nice guy. They are all nice guys. Too nice, I guess, for Lawrence. So when they tried to shove him into a proper school to follow in his father's and forefathers' footsteps, he thumbed his nose at them and went off to sea!"

Adam lowered himself on his elbow. His voice had a harsh sound in the quiet room, and Patrice thought: All evening while I thought he was so happy to be with Daisy, he was going over this old ground, building new ruins on old ruins. She felt a great relief and tenderness toward him, but restrained herself, sensing his need to talk it out of his system.

"The old story. A cliché in every country, in every age. My father . . . well, you've had a chance to see him, to hear him. Amusing, intelligent, kind. Devoted to his family and his friends. And a 'character' besides. Do you know what it means when we describe a person as a 'character' in this crowd? It means that by keeping people amused and impressed you might get through your entire life without being found out!"

In the next room the snores reached a crescendo. There was a sound of heavily turning bodies, a muffled yelp from the dog; then the snores resumed.

"So I became a lawyer. I was taken into the office of one of my

210

father's oldest friends. They had been in the same class at college. They were members of the same select college club, which, by the way, I never made, and don't think that that didn't rankle with the old man! But anyway old Charlie Winslow took me into his firm although it was pretty evident that I was no more cut out to be a lawyer than I was to be a trapeze artist. Then we went to war, and my father pulled the necessary strings and I got a commission. I had to be an officer, don't you see, because he couldn't stomach the indignity of his son being a common private! But I liked the army. I had a fairly cushy post, aide to an old fart of a general, who, in his turn, had wangled himself a cushy post well behind the lines. What fighting I ever saw was at a safe distance. I honestly did try to get up to the front. I wanted to see action. Perhaps in a dumb sort of way I wanted to impress the family, prove to them that I was a man after all, even if it meant getting myself bumped off in the process. But the war was over before I could make it, and I realized that I was about to get back where I started. A year in France had liberated me, in a way. I felt I was beginning to get a grip on myself. War does that for most men, I suspect . . . a vicarious kind of pseudo responsibility. I kept running into fellows I'd been in school with, and in college, and some from the law offices on State and Milk Streets at home. A few had gotten themselves little French mistresses and a heady sophistication which wouldn't survive their return to Dedham or Newton or Brookline. But all in all the war didn't take much of a toll among the people I knew. Then here I was back home again and I knew better than I had before, even, that I could no more fit into a lawyer's office than I could in a straitjacket."

It was as though he had been reading aloud from a book. Patrice said gently: "Adam, why, after all this time, does it still matter so much?"

"Because I've been remembering—all evening—that day in February nineteen nineteen when I got back from France. The family had a party to welcome me home and it was exactly like tonight except that we were all in the house in Cambridge, and you were not around. No . . . you and Caroline's kid Timmy and young Damon Edwards, but all the rest were there. Cousin Thomas Edwards and Cousin Edith; the Redditches; Daisy. The others."

A warm breeze blew into the room. Patrice raised the sash higher and saw that most of the lights along the North Shore were out but that the big advertising sign still blazed, seeming brighter than ever.

"The family," Adam went on, "were all excited because Caroline had just become engaged to Barto. Now if only I would get myself settled in some decent job and perhaps marry Daisy Prentice . . . They didn't say so, of course, or anyway not that evening, but I was made to feel very much aware of what was going on in their minds. And so on that very first evening, back from the wars, I realized that nothing had changed. Any decision I made would not be my decision —it would be theirs. They believed that all they really wanted for me was that I stand on my own two feet, exert my independence, play the man. But only if it was along the lines they laid down for me."

Patrice said: "Daisy is beautiful. Weren't you attracted at all?"

"Maybe I was, a little. But mostly because so far as I could see she was just about the only human being around who really liked me as I was and not for what I was expected to be. Actually, though, she bored me."

He sank back on the pillow, drawing the sheet up to his chin, staring at her where she stood beside the open window with the curtains floating behind her, like wings. "So back I went to old Winslow's law office and slogged along for a few more years. I was in a state of apathy which I couldn't seem to shake off. I wasn't making a hell of a lot of money, so I lived with the family—at their insistence. They had—they have—this horror of spending money unless you are absolutely forced to, and there was the house in Cambridge with plenty of room now that Caroline had married and gone away. I'm not saying that my parents didn't like having me around. I am not saying that they were not—that they are not now—fond of me. But it seemed to them to be a good working arrangement, and so it was after a fashion. Every weekend and vacation I cleared out—into the country. I went to Ipswich to shoot shore birds in the fall, or just to walk along the dunes. I used to go for endless walks, and of course there was always the sea. I bought myself a small sailboat, an expensive little number, and I was supposed to be saving money. The parents disapproved, exactly as if I'd been an irresponsible brat of fifteen instead of a grown man."

He was silent and Patrice asked the question inaudibly: Were you a grown man?

212

Adam said: "Just the same, that sailboat saved my life, or my reason anyway. I had dreams of sailing away in it and never coming back. But of course I never did. Queer, the things that can happen to you. Without shock, without a wound, injury, anything. Just something inside you, like a growth, sucking up all your vitality, your will to live. I knew there was something wrong with me, that I was a leech, a spineless good-for-nothing. I couldn't seem to make friends, or get interested in women, or anything. I despised myself. And I did nothing about it. Just went on working for Charlie Winslow and scheming how I could stay away from home."

And here you are, she reminded him inaudibly. Bringing me with you, and the baby. Landing on the parents again. Hating them, blaming *them* . . .

Adam lay on his back, staring at the ceiling. "I shouldn't get mad at Barto, and I'm not. It's just the thought of Caroline always in the picture somehow, meddling, interfering. . . . But Barto has always been nice to me in his peculiar way. I never really found out for sure but I have a pretty good idea that it was Barto who got me my job in India. He has a lot of important connections in the business world and he is as hard as nails when it comes to practical matters, in spite of the fact that the family like to think of him as a poor little rich boy! Anyhow, once in India I was on my own again as I had been in France during the war. I loved the life, even in Calcutta. I loved the jungles, the great flat jheels with their water birds, and the trips into the hills. And out there I even made a few friends, English and American, who shared my taste for the outdoors." He laughed softly. "It had never occurred to me how little it takes for a supposedly complicated person like myself to be happy! If it hadn't been for that damned dysentery and the doctors' ordering me out of the country for a long spell, I would never have come home."

He had seemed to be talking to himself. Now he turned his head and looked at her. "I just wanted you to see the picture . . . my bit of it anyway! Not very exciting, is it?"

She crossed the room and stood beside his bed and stared down at him. "Adam, why, when you were young and so sure of what you wanted to do, didn't you go ahead and do it?"

He replied without hesitation: "Because I didn't have the guts."

He reached out and took her hand, drawing her down so she

213

perched on the edge of the bed. "I had guts enough to make a nuisance of myself, to be a problem to my family, but not the kind of guts to make my own decisions. After all, I had it easy at home. Everything taken care of, paid for. There was a certain—what shall I call it?—a certain way of life that I had been born into and which I couldn't imagine doing without. In other words, I'd rough it for the fun of the thing, but not if I had to."

"Do you think your father would have cut you off if you had insisted on doing what you wanted—studying to be a biologist, for instance?"

He smiled at her old-fashioned literalness. "I don't believe so. That would have taken guts on his part, and he's not too strong on guts himself. After all, don't forget that most of his income comes from a patrimony. And when you get down to it, decisions, really tough, intellectual, moral decisions, had never been part of his experience. He'd had it easy, as I had. We could both take lofty attitudes and nurse our grievances, but there really hasn't been a hell of a lot to choose between us."

She was thinking, gropingly: You see things clearly enough; you can talk about them clearly enough. Then why . . . ?

The moon had set and the window was dark behind her. "So it never came to a real showdown between you and your father, did it?"

He shrugged. "No. We both hate scenes. Eventually I lost interest in my hobbies except as mere hobbies. Nothing seemed to me to be very serious after all. I didn't crave a lot of money, and I certainly didn't crave success. I wasn't cheating anybody out of anything."

Suddenly all over the house on the identical second and in their varying voices, clocks struck the half hour. It was already another day.

Patrice left him and went into the bathroom. Turning on the light, she stood bathed in its radiance, in the reflected glow from the mirror. She suffered a guilty relief in escaping, for a moment, from Adam, from his futility. Yes, his futility. A shiver ran down her thighs. My husband. My love. My dear one. *Futile.* And all that gaiety downstairs this evening, and all the welcome and fondness. Rich food. Silver. Sheen of damask. A high tide of friendly voices, smiles. "Winds blow south, winds blow north,/Day come white, or night come black . . ./If we two but keep together." And he had crossed oceans and continents to find her in that unkempt garden among alien hills. Surely that was something!

She took her time, brushing her teeth, combing her hair. She loved this bathroom, its elegant spaciousness, its inviolability. The enormous white bathtub, the shining washbasin with its silvery fixtures, the glass shelves with pretty bottles lettered in gold: TALCUM, COLOGNE, BATH SALTS. Towels soft and heavy like the pelts of rare creatures. Even the w.c. had distinction—an immaculte sleighlike throne.

How different from the bathrooms at home, with their rickety commodes and great enamel chamberpots the size of a top hat. In those remembered bathrooms it was necessary to make sure that some peeping tom had not scratched an open space in the protective paint on the window. One then propped a towel rack against the door because there never seemed to be a key or a bolt. Before undressing one investigated dark areas behind the earthen jar which held cold water, just make sure there were no snakes, and one scrutinized walls and corners for scorpions. The tub was made of zinc, just large enough to hold one's body upright. And the water always smelled of woodsmoke, and the soap was usually out of reach in its dish on the floor, and Chota Ayah would have forgotten to put out towels, and just as one was stepping into the bath or out of it the sweeper would give his interrogatory cough outside the door as he arrived with his wicker basket to remove the pot. He always managed to be there at the wrong moment. When his services were really needed one or the other of the servants could be heard bellowing: "Jemadar!" to apprise him and the world of the blessed event.

Emerging from the bathroom she tiptoed across the darkened room and crept into Adam's bed. He had fallen asleep and she lay quietly beside him, thinking: Here I am, at the beginning of something . . . my existence intertwined with another's, and ours with the corm I can just begin to feel under my heart.

17

"*I* must say it does seem a bit peculiar. Brides usually have a trousseau, but Patrice seems to have nothing!"

Mrs. Bannister brought it out casually, though the subject had been on her mind for some days. She sat now, imposingly, in a chair beside the big double bed in Caroline's bedroom, sipping a cup of coffee after putting Mr. Bannister and his green law bag on the eight-forty train to Boston. Caroline seldom rose before ten o'clock, and mother and daughter enjoyed these seances, with Mr. Bannister safely on the train, Timmy out of the house, and Barto immured in his workshop above the garage.

Caroline followed up her mother's remark. "Not so strange when you remember that her family hasn't a dime."

"I can't," Mrs. Bannister objected with an uneasy laugh, "imagine a really fine family like the Verriers not having a dime!"

"Your own son hasn't much more!" Caroline spoke with studied detachment, and Mrs. Bannister stirred her coffee in silence. She hated criticism, implied or otherwise, by any member of her family against anyone within it.

"My back," Caroline complained, yawning. "Ugh!"

"Dear!" said Mrs. Bannister. "I'm so sorry. I'm afraid you worked too hard for the party the other night."

"It was a swell party," Caroline declared with enthusiasm. "Worth a twinge or two. Everyone had a good time."

"Do you really think so?" They had covered the ground on several occasions since the party, but both were given to these recapitulations, which lost nothing in the process.

"I thought Daisy looked adorable," Caroline mused, watching smoke from her cigarette curl overhead. "Would anyone believe she was going on thirty?"

"It's her coloring," Mrs. Bannister said. "Blondes don't show their age as quickly as brunettes." She smiled disarmingly. "Dear, I don't mean that you . . ."

"Forget it, Ma. I know only too well."

"Nonsense. There isn't a gray hair in your head and there won't be for ages. And I thought your dress was every bit as pretty as Daisy's. More becoming, in fact."

"Should have been," Caroline murmured with a laugh. "Cost enough!" There was a brief pause, then she murmured reflectively: "Poor little Patrice."

Mrs. Bannister poured herself another cup of coffee from the silver pot on the bedside table. They had reached the point, and she waited, rather nervously, for further development.

"Throw me the cigarettes, will you, Ma? There, on your side of the tray."

Mrs. Bannister handed her the almost empty package. "You smoke too much, dear." She reproached her daughter with a light touch.

"Ugh," Caroline repeated, leaving the subject of Patrice dangling just within reach. "It must be the curse. Always hits me in the back."

"My poor child! But I wonder if all this smoking—"

"Ever since Timmy," Caroline interrupted her, warningly. "You know I never had an ache or a pain until after Timmy was born."

"That's true. You really should try to spare yourself more. I should think that Barto . . ."

She broke off and shrugged, leaving the criticism tacit, for after all, Barto could scarcely be considered actually *of* the family. She and Caroline were more or less in agreement about Barto, although both were glad enough to leave the understanding tacit. Mrs. Bannister brooded in private on her son-in-law's insensitivity toward his wife's well-being. His own infirmity, Mrs. Bannister had once decided, had made him callous toward other people, not excepting his own wife. Still, it was going a little far for him to declare in public, as he often did, that there was nothing the matter with Caroline a little healthy exercise and abstention from liquor and cigarettes wouldn't cure. She smoked too much, drank too much, ate too much, and lay around too much for her own good. These truths were self-evident, but Barto's airing of them inspired, in both women, a kind of helpless, incandescent rage.

Mrs. Bannister frequently asked herself what poor Caroline would do without a mother to minister to her. Thank goodness marriage had not placed too great a physical barrier between them. Berry's Landing, where Barto had elected to live, was no more than thirty miles by automobile from Cambridge, and in summer when the Bannisters moved to Berry's themselves it was a mere twenty-minutes drive by car from door to door.

Although Barto made no pretense of being fond of his wife's parents, he never interfered with them, and even welcomed his mother-in-law's morning visits during which she enjoyed endless cups of coffee with Caroline in the bedroom which he himself left punctually at six every morning, to eat his breakfast alone in the kitchen, before the Negro butler and his wife were awake. His own breakfast finished, Barto roused his son and fed him and sent him off to school or to play before repairing, himself, to his workshop, where he remained ferociously undisturbable until lunch.

He had long since given up trying to stir Caroline out of an indolence which she had successfully concealed from him until after their marriage. In the beginning he had asked himself, in frustration, what in hell she would have done had he been a fisherman or a day laborer, but the question was purely rhetorical: she would never have thought of marrying him! Or even if she had it would have made little difference, for nothing could have deflected her for long from her enjoyment of those morning hours after he had left her side. The endless cups of coffee, the endless cigarettes in the big, handsome room swathed in tobacco smoke and whiffs of expensive perfume.

The windows gave out on a view of the sea, and were hung with imported chintz curtains in the Tree of Life design. An Aubusson carpet graced the floor; there were hand-picked items of antique furniture, several authentic Frank Benson etchings on the walls. Low bookcases flanked the fireplace, and held finely bound editions of Trollope and Jane Austen, their pages still uncut. Caroline was breezy about such matters. "You don't," she had once pronounced, "have to be an intellectual snob about reading books to enjoy them. Just looking at those bindings does something for me, as fountains are intended to do for outdoor decor!"

It sounded authoritative, and no one ever challenged Caroline on such matters. Barto was indifferent when he was not sarcastic, and no one else cared enough.

Well, thank God—Mrs. Bannister frequently apostrophized that hazy but beneficent Presence—that Caroline had had the chance to marry a rich man. It was all very well for Wilbur to aver, as he occasionally did in a facetious vein, that he would have preferred blue blood to greenbacks; it was unquestionably an enormous comfort to know that one's precious daughter had "everything." True, Barto Williams was not the easiest person to get along with and could be unpardonably crude and rude, as he had been that evening over the business of watermelon for dessert.

And what if his family, unlike her own and Wilbur's, had their unexplored roots deep in the Pittsburgh coal mines? Someone had had the brains and the energy to make a success of it, and more power to him! Mrs. Bannister was an honest woman and she believed in the invincibility of her Yankee principles of integrity, modesty, charity, and hard work; or she honestly thought she believed in them, which probably amounted to the same thing.

Wilbur on the other hand was a snob of the old school and gloried in it. He was convinced that wealth and education were, or should be, the perquisites of aristocracy, and it annoyed him more than he was prepared to admit even facetiously that his son-in-law should not only not be aristocratic by birth or background, but that he should go out of his way to summarize this entire concept as a lot of goddam crap.

Just the same, as Mrs. Bannister frequently pointed out to her husband, you had to hand it to Barto that he was good-natured where money was concerned. He usually managed to be humorous about his wife's extravagance. And no matter how deeply one might love one's only daughter, there could be no denying that extravagance, which, on occasion, bordered on the outrageous. It sometimes quite took Mrs. Bannister's breath away, as on the day when the Aubusson carpet arrived with the price tag still sewn on the bottom of one corner: six thousand dollars.

Caroline had brushed aside her mother's visible shock with the sexy laugh that often accompanied her buying sprees: "That's nothing. You should have seen the one that got away!"

Oddly enough, generosity was not the word one would naturally have applied to Barto's indulgence of his wife. Caroline was still obliged to ask him for what she wanted, and all bills and charges were referred to him. It appeared sometimes as though in his sardonic fashion he relished forcing Caroline to come to him with her requirements.

"Well, shit," Caroline was fond of observing to her most intimate friends. "Let Barto pay. He's got it. I put up with enough. Not even a normal life, when you get right down to it, and God knows I'm a normal enough woman! If I can't blow myself to a good antique once in a while, or a decent dress, or a night in town with a show and dinner at the Ritz . . ."

This was a side of Caroline which her parents never saw, for while Wilbur enjoyed an occasional off-color story—especially if he was the raconteur—four-letter words were taboo, and if Mrs. Bannister understood what they meant she very blandly gave the impression that she did not. Both parents adored Caroline. They adored her physical family likeness, her bounding vitality, which in no way diminished —in their eyes—the contradictory role of a languishing Camille. They adored her because she was *theirs* in a way, and to a degree, that their son was not and never had been. Caroline was a passion Mr. and Mrs. Bannister could share as they had not shared one for a very long time. Caroline was in truth flesh of their flesh. And Caroline adored *them,* or at any rate they were unalterably persuaded that she did, which made it all perfect.

If on occasion Mrs. Bannister detected a certain deviousness in Caroline, she was careful to look the other way. She was herself neither devious nor calculating. More often puzzled by life than troubled by it, she had never gone on her knees at the altar of emotion. One could, she believed, love people without becoming soupy about it, although this did not necessarily apply to young children and to

220

dogs, before whom one was free to make a fool of oneself without fear of complication.

It was only very recently that something had happened to disturb, a little, the equable pattern of Mrs. Bannister's life, and she was finding it strangely difficult, this morning, to bring up the subject with her daughter. She did not want to be considered *soupy,* but she had, this morning, wakened feeling mystified by a sense of delicate agitation, a luminous something which refused wholly to reveal itself. What bothered her about this feeling, if it could be called a feeling, was that it seemed vaguely familiar, something—a thought, a dream, a kind of impact—which had happened to her a very long time ago. She was not given to psychic imaginings, but this odd state of mind in which she found herself came close to being psychic, if anything. She was dying to speak of it to someone and would have brought it up with Wilbur except that she dreaded his facetious response.

Now she felt that she and Caroline had beaten about the bush long enough. Putting her empty cup on the tray, she looked at her daughter. "That dream of mine," she said abruptly. "About Patrice. Did you think it was a silly thing to mention at the party the other night?"

"What dream?" Just when, Caroline asked herself uneasily, did I begin to get really corned that night? This was one of the unpleasant things about getting corned—this forgetfulness.

"Darling," protested Mrs. Bannister. "You heard me tell about it. My dream about Patrice coming into our house wearing a sort of veil over her head . . ."

"Oh, that." Caroline stubbed out a cigarette and fumbled on the bedcovers for the package. "What about it?"

"Well, I've been thinking that it was a silly, romantic sort of thing to bring up at a party. Tom Edwards joked about it, so did your father. But it wasn't a joke at all. It was a very strange dream, Caroline. And beautiful."

What, Caroline wondered, has come over Ma? She never talks about her dreams. I doubt that she ever has any. And her face . . . flushed, youthful.

Mrs. Bannister went on hesitantly: "It has left me with this feeling about Patrice. I've never had it before, about anyone."

Caroline lighted another cigarette with nicotine-stained fingers. When she put the cigarette between her lips she did so with a curious

221

grimace that gave her face an animal-like expression, rather forbidding.

"It is her being so young, I suppose," Mrs. Bannister mused. "And her innocence. Not—you know—in experience or anything like that. I'm not sure just what I do mean. It's just this queer feeling, ever since I had that dream, as if I were myself at the beginning of something. Or as if I had gone back, just for a little while, into some past moment of—of happiness!"

She was silent, smiling in an embarrassed, defiant sort of way. "Do let me try to describe it, Caroline, dear! It's silly, I know. But I can't seem to forget it, to get it out of my system. It bothers me. Let me see if I can put it into some sort of concrete form. If Patrice had been *different* in a way I could really grasp—if she were some little foreigner trying to adapt to *our* ways, *our* language; trying to conform to *our* way of life, selflessly giving up or losing her own identity, as happens every day in our society . . . as for instance Susan Sampson marrying her Italian doctor, or Margot Means that Jew—if, as I say, I could see Patrice in that light . . . but somehow I can't. There is more to her than just someone who has married my son. There is something mysterious, as though that veil would always be there between us, as though I shall always be expecting an unknown person to emerge from behind it. . . ."

She broke off and gazed appealingly at her daughter. Caroline blew smoke. "If it hadn't been Patrice it would have been someone else," she remarked in a practical voice, but with narrowed eyes. She was not often surprised by her mother, and now in addition to surprise she felt faintly disturbed.

Mrs. Bannister shook her head. "No. It had to be Patrice!"

"Stuff," said Caroline, shrugging her shoulders in a welter of pink marabou. "And what about Patrice? Do you feel that for her it just had to be Adam?"

Mrs. Bannister hesitated. "For the first time, for her . . . yes, I do think so! Most people aren't made for each other, as we are too much in the habit of believing. But in Adam's case, in Patrice's . . ." She broke off again and Caroline thought: I've never known her to use this exaggerated language. Now what in the world!

Mrs. Bannister went on as though fearful of losing the thread of what she was trying to say, and perhaps to discover. "You know how peculiar Adam is. How in a way *difficult.* Those dreadful psychological books have a word for it: introverted. How I hate words like that!" She laughed nervously. "But the fact remains he is difficult and always has been. I've seen it and have never known quite what to do about it. And your father hasn't been able to help, much. You know how he detests anything even vaguely unhealthy."

"Pop is right," Caroline replied decisively. "Pop's always been right about Adam. A darn good kick in the pants is what he's always needed."

"No," said Mrs. Bannister firmly. "I don't think so. I'm not saying that I have always understood my own son. I've always gone along with your father in this matter of bringing up our children as I have gone along with him in most things, but now I wonder about Adam."

Caroline blew a trumpet of smoke. "Bunk," she said.

Mrs. Bannister seemed not to hear. "I want them to be happy!" It came from her in a kind of sigh. "I have never wanted anything so much in my life. Not even for myself." She looked strangely at her daughter. "I never worried about you, Caroline. Somehow I never doubted that you would always fall on your feet."

"Thanks," Caroline said dryly. Again Mrs. Bannister seemed not to hear. "Perhaps the reason I want their happiness so much—in such a peculiarly intense way—is that I feel they have the capacity for it. That they—both of them—have the capacity for so much."

It was as though she were intoning a hymn, and Caroline murmured impatiently: "Oh, well!"

The glow dimmed in Mrs. Bannister's eyes, and Caroline registered the dimming with relief. "Talking about Patrice," she said briskly, "she's been quite frank about this trousseau business. Told me that her mother simply could not afford to buy her one."

Back to the mundane, Mrs. Bannister shook her head. "Poor child. We'll have to see what we can do about it."

"I didn't," Caroline continued, relaxed, "like to ask too many questions. Not that I had to. She has a way of coming out with things quite naturally. The way she did to Barto about the baby."

"The baby!"

"The night of your party. Barto said she just sort of mentioned in passing that she was expecting a baby."

"Oh, dear," said Mrs. Bannister, frowning. She had confused feelings about babies. Their imminence disrupted her sense of decorum, and Caroline, looking at her, thought wonderingly: Who would have thought that only a minute ago she was getting off all that psychic stuff!

"I must say I didn't expect . . . that so soon. Oh, it's natural enough, of course. But still, Adam with no job. Your father won't be too pleased. I do wish they had waited."

Caroline said after a pause: "You know, I think someone ought to talk to Adam."

Mrs. Bannister visibly shrank. "Talk to him about what?"

"About his responsibilities as a husband and prospective father."

"You know how Adam feels about what he calls 'meddling'!" Then, with a return to her earlier mood: "I do so love to see them together! Patrice follows him around like a puppy, have you noticed?"

"I have. A puppy or a little brother. But she happens to be his wife, and pregnant at that. I think it's about time that my brother woke up to the facts of life, don't you really, Ma?"

Mrs. Bannister's face became suddenly expressionless. Caroline, she decided unhappily, was trying to start something. After four years of separation from her brother she could still feel it in her heart to resent him. And I had so hoped . . . Mrs. Bannister sighed resignedly. Could they not, she now suggested to her daughter, put their heads together, she and Caroline, in the selection of a wedding present for bride and groom?

"A present?" Caroline echoed. "You've already given them a nice fat check for a thousand dollars!"

"But that was such a practical sort of present. Just something to tide them over until Adam finds something to do. What I mean is something for Patrice, say. Something personal, intimate. You know what I mean. After all," Mrs. Bannister went on quickly, recognizing a mulish mood developing in her daughter, "after all, Patrice is one of us now."

Patrice was indissolubly a member of the family, and the gift, whatever it was, should be in keeping with the truth that she was here to stay.

"And you always," Mrs. Bannister concluded with a fond smile, "have such good ideas about these things, dear. What do you think Patrice would like?"

Caroline pondered. Possessions—the giving of them, the acquiring —were her passion. Now she touched the heavy linen sheet under which she lay, tracing the ornate monogram with her finger. She had insisted on pure linen at her marriage, and Mrs. Bannister had had the sheets woven in Ireland, awed by the expense but comforting herself with the practical reflection that after all they would be inde- structible and that Caroline's children would inherit them eventually.

The substance of riches surrounded Caroline in one form or an- other, whether she wore them or merely lived in their midst. She liked things to be dense and weighty. And genuine. There was not a reproduction or a fake among all the objects under her roof. She had the glutton's taste too, so that everything she owned seemed to run to fat.

"Let's see," she mused aloud. "What about that little pine bureau in the attic in Cambridge? The one Cousin Sarah Osgood left you."

"I'd like to make the gift more personal. Patrice doesn't seem to own any jewelry. I was wondering about that sapphire ring which used to belong to your Aunt Millie. I never wear it."

"Didn't you," Caroline recalled creamily, "tell me once that you were saving that ring for Timmy's wife—when he gets one?"

"Did I? Well, then, perhaps Patrice would like the little pearl-and- ruby pin I inherited from my Aunt Caroline."

"A little old-fashioned for Patrice, I'd say. But she might like it. She doesn't seem to have the least idea of what's what, actually. Did you ever have that pin appraised?"

"When I last renewed my insurance, yes. Shreve's valued it at roughly three hundred dollars, if I remember right. It's not the money value I'm thinking about," Mrs. Bannister added, meaning it. "It's just . . . something that would be part of the family. And Barto told me that he considered that ruby to be especially beautiful."

Caroline's eyes seemed to settle in her head, giving her an inward expression. Desire—any kind of desire—added years to her age; once satisfied, she could look merely constipated.

"Did Barto tell you that? He's probably right. He knows about gems. I tell you what, Ma. Let's drive up to Cambridge this afternoon and look over what you have in the house. We'll take Patrice and show her a bit of Cambridge. Adam can have lunch here with Barto and Timmy."

It was a warm, overcast afternoon, and the Charles River a placid pewter color. There was a tincture of coal gas and sewage in the air, with a hint of mown grass and flowers wilting in the heat.

Mrs. Bannister drove her big black Packard with aplomb. She loved to drive and was secretly delighted that Wilbur should steadfastly have refused to learn, just as he stubbornly refused to carve the meat at meals or to perform any small chores around the house; he seemed content to leave such normally masculine duties to his wife. It had never occurred to this devoted woman that her husband had brought many of the mores of a sultanate into his home, but since these in a sense served to emancipate her, she would not have had it otherwise for the world.

On this afternoon Patrice, squeezed between her mother-in-law and Caroline on the front seat, watched the golden dome of the State House rise above the muted tones of the old city, giving the scene an ornate and exotic touch. Somnolence lay on everything. She felt that she was suspended between two worlds. Alice had written her, recently, from that house in the hills: "I am doing very well and you must not worry about me. Dear Edna Meadows and her mother are staying with me before moving into the little guest house which they hope to open up for business later this year. I am afraid that it must be that old budmash Shapurji who has set them up. Where else would they get the money? But they never mention the subject and of course I wouldn't dream of asking. The weather is very warm even here in the hills, darling. The garden is full of heliotrope and all day I can hear the barbets calling in the trees, and sometimes the black partridge on the lower terrace. Everything reminds me of you and Clem. I wonder if I shall ever get used to the surprises of life. It is, I know, wrong to live as I do, dreaming of things that are finished or of things that might be. Perhaps someday I shall have saved enough money to join you in America. Who knows? I am writing this letter as I sit in the balcony looking over the lake and the garden where you first met Adam, where I first saw you together. Now the pumpkins are getting fat in the mali's garden and I can see him and his wife cutting grass for their cow, and Nizamat is squatting under the trees with the Meadowses' servant Abdullah. I wish that man would occasionally change his clothes. He goes about looking like a villain. I have mentioned this to Edna and she says she'll speak to him about it, but so far she has not. One simply has to keep one's servants up to the mark, as one has to keep oneself. . . ."

But now the bright spires of the university thrust above the elms and Caroline said: "That's Apthorp House, where Adam used to room when he was in college."

Patrice gazed round her with jealous curiosity. Like his friendship with Daisy Prentice, this scene was something she herself had not shared with Adam, and the thought evoked a familiar pang.

She said abruptly: "I wish I had grown up with Adam. I wish I had known him when he was a boy."

Caroline laughed. "Perhaps it's just as well you didn't!"

Mrs. Bannister, her strong hands on the wheel, said placatingly: "Adam could be a bit of a problem at times." Quickly she added: "I do want to tell you again, Patrice, dear, how wonderful I think it is that you share Adam's interests as you do."

Caroline's smile was a trifle set. "Does he share your tastes, Patrice?"

"I don't have many. Just writing."

"Writing?" Una voce, politely taken aback.

"Well, I've thought sometimes that I would like to be a writer."

How presumptuous it sounded! How absurd! Patrice felt herself blushing. But the words had sprung from a sudden passionate need to have something of her own, to be something herself, when *they* seemed to have so much, to be so assured, so much in possession of themselves.

Mrs. Bannister smiled indulgently. "I suspect that you are going to have plenty to keep yourself busy without your trying to *write,* my dear."

Caroline added: "Yes. Somehow I don't feel that the artistic muse, if that's what you mean, and the patter of little feet would make for the most harmonious duet, do you, Ma?"

"I'm afraid I do not," Mrs. Bannister agreed. In both voices that note—what was it? Warning? Skepticism? Derision? I was a fool to have said it, Patrice thought, and felt her cheeks burn. Alien, she was. An uneducated jungli, and she had asked for this. . . .

Mrs. Bannister glanced at her sidewise. "Are you feeling all right, dear? Does the driving bother you?"

No, it was not the driving, nor was it the baby. It was the face of

Sister Teresa, years ago. Sister Teresa's thin smile, her thin voice: "Does this exercise book belong to you, Patrice?"

That exercise book with the marbled covers, given her by Cucumber. And her name in beautiful lettering: *Patrice Verrier, Her Life.*

Sister Teresa's investigative hands had unearthed it from Patrice's desk, from under a collection of horse chestnuts, old letters, magpie feathers, snapshots, and holy pictures.

"Do you," Sister Teresa had demanded menacingly, "call this *writing?*" There would come a day when Sister Teresa would be dead, laid out in her coffin with those bony white hands clasped on her flat chest, her blue eyes forever closed, her dry gray tongue forever still. She would have died without ever finding out where babies came from and whether it hurt; whether the Holy Ghost was deformed in the same manner as What's-His-Name Harper. Sister Teresa would ascend unto heaven never having seen a neem tree bleed in the garden, nor ever having heard the hoopoe's song.

But on that far-off day Sister Teresa was very much alive. She was exuding her special angry smell of black serge and virginal sweat. "And all this is supposed to be *your* life?"

Silence.

"Answer me, Patrice Verrier. Is this supposed to be your life?"

"It's only a story, Sister."

"A story about you?"

"Just a story."

"And this person—this Eurasian boy. Who was he?"

"Nobody. I invented him."

"Where did you learn such things? Who told you?"

"I may have read about them in books."

"Where did you find such books, if I might ask? In your parents' house?"

Sister Teresa would write to Doey. The world would come crashing.

"No, Sister."

"Then where? I insist . . . where?"

"I don't remember."

Sister Teresa's eyes cut you open; they stared straight into your whirling heart. "Filth," said Sister Teresa. "Utter filth—and at your age!"

And Sister Teresa's powerful fingers had torn the book into shreds, cover and all. She must have been terribly strong.

Terror, hatred, shame. Afterward, the tonic rage which had made Patrice whole again, though it could not restore the book and all the thoughts and feelings, the bits of dreams, the questing which had gone into the First and Last Life of Patrice Verrier.

"Here we are," Mrs. Bannister announced cheerfully, and stopped the car against the curb before a square gray-painted house set back from the street in a formal garden shaded by trees. There was a small marble fountain on the lawn. The fountain was dry, full of dead leaves, and the place had a pleasant, expectant air. It was firmly planted in its proper place, shaped and molded by the people who had always lived here. Mrs. Bannister got out of the car and turned smilingly to Patrice. "Here, my dear, is the house where your Adam was born."

"And there," said Caroline, pointing, "is the Prentice house, where Daisy was born."

The houses had a staid and comfortable air, the trees were stately, and presently down the middle of Brattle Street came a procession of dogs led by a small, panting, bedraggled terrier bitch.

"Can that be the Prentices' Judy?" said Caroline as the procession gaily approached. "Hadn't we better catch her? Here, Judy, Judy, Judy!"

"Judy!" shouted Mrs. Bannister. Then, indignantly: "Really, Charles Prentice doesn't deserve to own a dog! He keeps breeding Judy to registered males and nothing happens, but she's always getting into trouble with mongrels. *Judy!*"

In the Prentices' house across the street a window flew open and a small brown-bearded face appeared, its spectacles glittering. "That you, Dorothea? And Caroline? What in the world are you doing in town?"

"Mr. Prentice!" screamed Caroline. "Don't you know that Judy is in heat? Daisy told me she'd warned you."

"I don't mind the heat," Mr. Prentice called back cheerfully. "In fact I rather enjoy it. Daisy's at Berry's Landing with the Redditches. They're expecting their boy Lawrence, you know, so I guess I won't be seeing my daughter for some time." He gave a high, piping laugh. "I don't mind. One can get through a lot of work when one is alone.

But can't I offer you something? A cold drink? Cup of tea?"

"Deaf as a post," Mrs. Bannister said bitterly. "But you'd think the least he could do would be to watch out for poor Daisy's dog. She left Judy home purposely because of the Redditches' poodle."

Caroline screamed again: "Mr. Prentice! Judy's going to get in trouble if you don't come down at once and catch her!"

"No trouble at all," the bearded face cried gallantly. "I'm batching it here these days. Let the cook go on her vacation. But I think there are some digestive biscuits in the pantry. Do come in. Door's on the latch."

"Judy!" wailed Mrs. Bannister. "Judy, come here at once!" The delinquent paid not the slightest heed. Tails wagging, tongues hanging, the procession vanished merrily down Brattle Street in the direction of Harvard Square.

"Just give me five minutes," chirped Mr. Prentice gaily. "I'll run down and put the kettle on." He disappeared like a jack-in-the-box and Caroline said angrily: "Wait until Daisy hears about this. Really, what that girl has to put up with." She glanced at Patrice. "We are all devoted to Daisy Prentice. She has had such a wretched life. Her mother ran away years ago and poor Daisy has never known anything but neglect."

"What she would have done without your friendship I just don't know," declared Mrs. Bannister fondly. "I doubt that Charles Prentice has a thought in his head aside from that stupid treatise he's writing on the Arawak Indians, whoever they were. But come, let's go in."

She opened the front door of her house. Patrice thought that the accumulated odors coalesced to build a personality of its own, compounded of the owners, their preoccupations, their past. The rugs had been put in storage for the summer, but curtains still hung in the windows, filtering a dusty light, and there were pictures on the walls. At Berry's Landing the summer house was furnished in rustic simplicity; here everything aimed at permanence and formality. There were touches of gilt in the old-fashioned wallpaper, in the bindings of the books, the knickknacks.

Patrice was afflicted by a sense of crowding, an absence of color, space, light. Her eye sought some note of austerity, a plain surface, some unadorned detail. In the houses she had lived in at home there

230

had always seemed to be some crevice through which the wilderness crept in: a sparrow chirping on a curtain rod, a frog hopping experimentally across the floor.

The master switch had not been turned off, and now Mrs. Bannister put on the lights. "This is the parlor. It's just the way it used to be when the children were growing up, except that we had to change the wallpaper. That"—she nodded to an oil portrait above the mantel —"is a painting of my husband done by our good friend Margot Means a few years ago. A splendid likeness, don't you think so?"

Patrice agreed dutifully that it was indeed a splendid likeness, although privately she was rather intimidated by the fixed expression of the small, cold eyes behind their pince-nez.

"That is the very last portrait Margot ever painted," Mrs. Bannister explained. "Poor Margot!"

"What happened to her?" Patrice inquired politely. "Did she die?"

"She married," Caroline explained, "a Jew."

"Now let's show Patrice the dining room, then we'll go upstairs."

The purpose of this pilgrimage had already been explained to Patrice, and she was partly exhilarated by the thought of acquiring new possessions, and partly embarrassed. The simplicity and sparseness of her own background seemed abject by comparison with what she could not help but see as opulence. Brought up in a climate which gave short shrift to material things, she had had little chance to develop her acquisitive instincts. Now she was beginning to wonder whether there may not have been something wrong with that background, something that Adam and his relatives might, in the end, hold against her.

Nor was she able to understand their occasional oblique reactions against Jews, Irishmen, Negroes, and foreigners generally. Doey and Alice and Aunt Eve had not been without prejudice but those prejudices had been on the silly side, concerned almost entirely with questions of food, dress, manners, and a style of doing one's hair; and there had certainly been nothing oblique about them! Now Patrice suffered from a distinct and uneasy feeling that Doey would not have approved of Mrs. Bannister's tone when she used the word "Jew," just as he had always condemned certain persons for slighting the Meadowses because they were Eurasians, and poor. She thought, resignedly: I have a hell of a lot to learn . . . a hell of a lot!

231

"This," Mrs. Bannister explained with a wave of her hand, "is the dining room. The sideboard is Hepplewhite, and the chairs Hitchcock. The table, as you can see, is Sheraton. When things are really good it doesn't make a bit of difference which period they belong to. They *go* together."

Patrice was being instructed, and she listened with respect. Over the Hepplewhite sideboard was a painting of what appeared to be a bald-headed lady smelling a rose. "My grandmother," Mrs. Bannister indicated. "No great beauty, but an interesting face, don't you think?"

Caroline was peering earnestly at the dining table. "This could do with a bit of oil, Ma. And you'll have to speak to Nora. She's getting very careless. Look at those glass rings!"

"I declare! Get a cloth from the pantry, will you, dear? We might as well fix it as long as we're here."

While they set to work to burnish the dining table Patrice reflected on the dining rooms she had known at home. Molting tiger skins hanging from the walls, the stuffed heads of antelope and bear. Elegant furniture usually fell apart in the monsoon damp or from the ravages of termites. Small articles were stolen, or they just disappeared. And now she found herself, for the first time, regretting the mother's few jewels, sold to pay for everyday needs. There had been a kind of recklessness with which the mother, Aunt Eve, Doey himself dealt with emergencies. No point in crying over spilled milk. If one had to do without, then one did without, and let's have no sniveling about it. But still, perhaps with a little forethought, a little planning, a little care . . .

The Sheraton table restored to its pristine brilliance, Mrs. Bannister announced that they would show Patrice the room where Adam was born. It was on the second floor, a large square room with windows giving on the street. A massive four-poster bed jutted from one wall, like a stage, and it was in that bed, Mrs. Bannister informed Patrice, that Adam was brought forth. A big baby. Huge, actually.

"Poor Ma!" Caroline condoled. "Almost killed you, having him, didn't it?"

Mrs. Bannister laughed. "It was no picnic!"

Patrice was flooded with tenderness. She wished suddenly that Caroline were not present. She longed to come close to Adam's mother, and she made a slight diffident gesture toward her, which Mrs. Bannister failed to notice. Patrice withdrew her hand, and Caroline said brightly: "Now for the attic! Watch your head—the ceiling slopes rather suddenly."

The attic was a gigantic warehouse stuffed to the rafters with furniture, trunks, bundles, books; everything was arranged with meticulous neatness, a sort of shopkeeper attention to detail which amazed Patrice. In time to come she was to recognize many of these household gods, when, retrieved from this limbo, they served the purpose for which they had been preserved, and appeared in the guise of presents at Christmas or birthdays, to fill a void which otherwise would have necessitated spending money for something new.

Caroline switched on an overhead light and in its dusty glow Patrice's eye met the steady gaze of a large stuffed owl atop an ancient bookcase. Instinct told her that the owl must have belonged to Adam once, as a family of dejected-looking dolls on another shelf must have belonged to Caroline.

Mrs. Bannister and her daughter began their excavations with the dedicated air of archaeologists. "But, Ma! I thought you kept your jewel case in your safe deposit box at the bank!" Caroline exclaimed after several minutes of concentrated rummaging.

"I do, of course, except for a few little things which I think I may need in a hurry." Mrs. Bannister was on her hands and knees, delving. "Mercy! How these mothballs do smell. It's not here, Caroline. I must have hidden it behind the pictures."

"It isn't behind 'The Dreamer' or 'The Colosseum,' " Caroline said, a trifle shortly. "I thought you made a note of where you hid it each time."

"I mean to, but sometimes I forget." Mrs. Bannister rose and dusted off her knees. "Now let me think. Last time I was here I was looking for that little lacquer box I wanted to give Daisy for her birthday, and I remember seeing the jewel case behind that card table in the corner. I make a point of hiding it somewhere different each time so there'll be no chance of some snooper finding it."

"You seem to have done a good job this time," Caroline said, with an impatient laugh. "How about looking in that old hair trunk?"

"Here it is!" exclaimed Mrs. Bannister, in triumph. "Under the cushions of that old rocker. Goodness, I was beginning to be afraid someone might have helped themselves."

Caroline swept three chairs clear of their impedimenta, and she and Patrice sat down with Mrs. Bannister between them. "I was going to give you something very special, Patrice, but Caroline reminded me that I had already promised it to Timmy when he gets married. But I know we can find something nice for you."

Patrice, affected by the airless atmosphere of the attic, murmured that it really did not matter. She seldom wore jewelry anyway. It sounded grand—almost as grand as her earlier statement that she wished to be a writer—and again she felt herself blushing.

"What do you think of this?" Mrs. Bannister held up a gold chain with a small gold locket dangling from it. "It used to be mine when I was a little girl."

Before Patrice could speak Caroline said: "It's a bit childish for Patrice, isn't it, Ma? And very old-fashioned."

"Perhaps you're right," said Mrs. Bannister, and dropped the chain back into the jewel case. "Let me see if I can find that pin. I hope I didn't give it to someone else. There have been so many marriages and birthdays in the family, I might easily—"

"There's that sapphire ring, Ma. Don't you think I might as well take it now? Not very safe, leaving it lying around like this."

"I guess so," Mrs. Bannister agreed, with a shade of reluctance. "Better put it in your safe deposit box, Caroline, until the time when Timmy becomes engaged!"

She poked among the tangle of chains, pendants, brooches, rings. "There! This is the ruby pin I want you to have. Isn't it pretty?"

It was pretty, a heart-shaped ruby encircled with pearls, and Patrice felt a thrill of pleasure in the thought of owning it.

"May I see it?" asked Caroline. "I'd forgotten how lovely it was!"

She took it from her mother's hand and held it to the light. "Barto was right to tell you that it is a beautiful stone. It has something engraved on the back. . . . I never noticed before."

Mrs. Bannister fumbled for her spectacle case. "I never noticed that it was engraved. What does it say, Caroline?"

It says 'Caroline.' " She gave a slight laugh. "Of course; it used to belong to your Aunt Caroline, didn't it?"

"Of course," said Mrs. Bannister. There was a brief pause. From its perch on the bookcase the stuffed owl gazed fixedly at Patrice, who thought: It's eyes are like jewels; eyes invented by men, copies of real eyes, but without sight.

Caroline looked up from the ruby pin in her hand. "Would you like it, Patrice? Ma said you could have it. Perhaps we can get the name changed from mine to yours. It's a lovely thing and probably worth quite a bit."

"I don't really want it very much, Caroline."

"I'd hate for you not to have it if you've set your heart on it, darling!"

"If you want to know what I think," Mrs. Bannister broke in with an air of discovery, "it is that Patrice would like that little bureau down in the guest room. It's true Colonial, and I'll send it in to Harvey's in the Square, and have them refinish the top. Don't you think you could use the bureau, Patrice?"

Patrice said that she would like the bureau very much.

Mrs. Bannister closed the jewel case and Caroline added the ruby pin to the sapphire which she had already deposited in her pocket-book. Her eyes glowed; there was a moist, happy look to her mouth, as if she had just been passionately kissed.

Mrs. Bannister laid her hand affectionately on Patrice's. "Is there anything you see here that you would like, my dear? Do tell me."

Patrice hesitated. "Well, I'd rather like that owl. It used to belong to Adam, didn't it?"

Caroline rose and put her arm round Patrice's shoulders. "You funny creature! What a thing to want!"

Noticing Patrice's pallor, she said quickly: "Come, let's get out of here before you faint."

Outdoors on the garden path, with the owl clasped to her breast, Patrice reminded them that they were expected to go across the street for tea with Mr. Prentice, but Caroline laughed. "Heavens, no! The old coot's forgotten all about us. Ma, dear, would you like to drive home, or shall I?"

18

*A*dam was spearing fish, and Patrice, leaning on her oars, watched him. He had shown her how to row in reverse, pushing the dory stern first over the water at low tide off the rocks below his parents' house, while he knelt in the stern with fish spear poised.

A month had passed since their arrival at Berry's Landing. The warm, aimless days had slipped past like things observed from the window of a train, and Patrice realized that she was bored. She was not accustomed to apathy, to the monotony of a cut and dried existence no matter how pleasant, well-ordered, and, at times, even gay. One day exactly resembled the next, and taken together they added up to a kind of surfeit.

Certainly in India her life had not always been eventful in the sense that it offered exotic distractions, but there she had been on her own; she had developed an inner dialogue with herself and had learned to depend on that sense of *strain* on which the spirit thrives.

There were moments when the past and everything contained within it took on a wonderful freshness and strength, when she felt that she was seeing it at last stripped of all pathos, nostalgia, and romance. The past had really happened; and she caught her breath

236

in the blinding impact of remembered happiness.

Well, she asked herself now as she watched Adam craning over the gunwale, peering into the shallows, am I not happy this minute? Am I not grateful to Adam and his family for everything they have done for me—for their affection, their hospitality, their patience, their generosity? This self-searching evoked pangs of guilt and shame that she should ever for a moment have lapsed from a sense of gratitude. But nothing could alter the fact that she was bored, and that boredom brought restlessness. Perhaps this was why she feared the child growing within her. *It* could not share the past. It was a stranger, occupying her body, a stranger she would never know, who would never know her. It would call her "mother," and she would call it "child," but neither would be a person one to the other.

There were moments when she wanted to cry out at this thought, at the suspicion that she was forever lost not only to the joy of being what she had been, but to the anguish also. From now on all joy, all anguish, would have a different nature. She could not accept her body's independence of her spirit. It was her body which had loved Adam and which had accepted his child, but her spirit remained untouched.

Alice had written ecstatically: "Darling! How wonderful that you are going to have a baby! It is what we are created for . . . and it will bring you and Adam closer together."

But Patrice thought: It didn't bring you and Doey closer together to have Clem and me. Doey never really wanted to be as close as all that to anyone. You and Aunt Eve are the kind of women who will always be half-people, having given away the other half of yourselves —you and Doey, Eve to that ghostly Englishman who had died before her eyes on a polo ground!

Patrice's reflections shied violently. Did she love Adam with as whole a heart as the mother had loved the father?

Love is the only true happiness, crooned Alice, writing long letters despairingly under the pitying eyes of the half-women at the convent. Don't, darling, try to *understand* love. Don't try to understand the big important things. They are like earthquakes, like war. Don't be always analyzing and failing as Doey did and as Clem is doing now. You are a woman, Alice insisted with a catch in her throat as she scribbled away, and perhaps the gray monkeys making love on their

237

airy branches on the hillside paused to watch her as, still exquisite, impulsive, insatiate, she poured forth her adoration on a writing pad in a sunny window, far away. "You are a woman and it is always *different* to be a woman. We can never be independent or strong the way men can be. We should never try."

Patrice steadied the dory on the dark-green water, guiding it with gently dripping oars over the ground where the fish lay on patches of sand or on the pebbled floor of the sea. On windless days the sea had a marvelous clarity. Rocks and pebbles made elegant designs with an occasional glitter of something blue or beryl green or purest white. Great tendrils of kelp reached languidly toward the surface and finer weeds shot up on end like frightened hair. Half concealed in these arboreal shadows hung the formal shapes of fish, wonderfully serene.

Patrice felt the sea rise under her like a monster drawing its breath. Dipping the oars she held the dory steady so it scarcely moved above the luminous depths. She thought: When I am an old woman I shall remember this morning: myself rowing, and Adam kneeling in the stern, tall and graceful, his spear in his hand, his hunter's eyes probing the depths. I shall remember the look of the shore sweeping toward the water's edge, the hot brown rocks with little trees growing in the crevices, the oval shapes of clamshells dropped by gulls, and higher up, beyond the shore, I shall remember the white birches, the lawns, the big comfortable houses of people who have lived here for so long. Perhaps when all these things are in the past I shall see them more clearly, understand them, perhaps even love them!

Behind her and out of sight round a bend in the shore she could hear faint sounds from the boatyard in which Barto Williams had offered Adam a job. There was a throbbing noise of lobster boats returning from their fishing grounds farther out to sea; the occasional hoot of an automobile horn, children's voices, a chatter of lawn mowers, and closest of all the dripping of water from the oar blades as she lifted them, dipped them again. Live in the moment, something told her. Live in the moment because there is nothing more.

Adam spoke abruptly: "Hold it, Patrice! I see a grubby over there. Hold it!"

She laid her weight on the oars, braking the drift of the dory. Adam raised his spear, then thrust it downward in a single savage lunge and lifted out his prize, a hideous struggling object whose blood ran down the shaft of the spear onto his hands.

Patrice's dreary mood gave way to revulsion. "I don't like those things!" she said as he dashed the still living fish off the spear into the bottom of the boat. "We don't eat them. Why kill them?"

Adam jabbed the spear point through the fish's head but it continued to struggle in its own blood together with a dead flounder and two rock cod. The grubby hardly looked like a fish—a deformed mottled thing covered with spines and furnished with a ludicrous tail. It had been lying harmlessly on the sea floor, secure in its protective coloring, until an omniscient human eye spied it and brought it impaled into the lethal air.

Adam washed his spear in the sea and Patrice tried to ignore the dying grubby, whose astonished eye seemed to be trying to meet hers. Blood. Again blood. Blood from the mother buffalo dropping her calf. Blood from the neem tree in a summer garden. Blood in people's veins. Menstrual blood screaming in terror: "I'm wounded! I'm bleeding to death!"

"Darling, it's nothing. It's perfectly natural. . . ."

Patrice bit hard on her lip and immediately tasted the salt of drawn blood on her tongue. Could one ever get away from it? The old stupid argument: One killed to eat. But Adam killed for no reason at all that she could see. Well, hadn't Doey done the same? Those Christmas camps, the pheasants and partridges; the antelope; the tiger roaring in the night, next day lying humbly dead in the golden grass, and Doey unconcernedly ejecting the empty cartridge from his rifle and pushing back his khaki sun hat, showing the brown hair sticking to his forehead with sweat; and the smell of the tiger's fresh blood where already the iridescent blowflies were swarming. Yes, but then there had been lightheartedness, a tingling expectancy of danger, the not really giving much of a damn whether one killed or not. Not *this* cold fanatical murder!

Patrice's mind heaved like the sea but could not vomit up its uncertainties. In the beginning she had enjoyed these outings with Adam. She loved the strength and movement of the sea, the look of little dark islands floating like rootless things, though she knew that they were the peaks of oceanic mountains, their hidden regions the haunt of porpoises and seals. In the beginning it had been a joy to escape with Adam, escape from the parents and the hordes of friends and neighbors who converged upon the house at all hours of the day. To escape from the faces, the voices, the gestures which crowded upon her, when she felt her identity foundering.

She had written to Clem, living in Granada now, among those fountains and mosaics; painting, doing the things he had always wanted to do.

Life here is a bit like living in a mela. A perpetual fair. The Bannisters never seem to be by themselves for long, nor do they want to be. It must be a bit like life in a joint family system, which has something of the character of a mela. I have a hard time trying to keep them all sorted out in my mind because except for one or two they all more or less resemble one another and have the same tastes and ideas. In fact they are so much alike that they seem to know it and are anxious to prove that they are not, and so continuously point out each other's little eccentricities, describing him or her as a "character." To be a "character" you must wear a small beard perhaps, or odd-looking clothes, preferably on the dirty side. You must be rude to your wife in a humorous way, like Armenian cooking, and talk baby talk to your dog. It helps if you have spent a little time in Paris and look knowing about it, or can play the accordion or tell funny stories. The stories are always the same ones; nobody ever seems to have learned a new tune on the accordion, and after a while you begin to wonder whether a person's craze for yogurt or his rudeness to his wife isn't something reserved for social occasions only.

I must say I am quite bowled over by their kindness. Or do I mean their generosity? I sometimes ask myself whether they are truly kind at heart, and this seems a terrible thing to say, except that lately I find that I think a lot about things I never used to bother about. What I mean is, I wonder whether they would try to share your sorrow, or really try to understand what makes you happy. These people seem always to be trying to make up for something by giving presents—something that costs *money.*

When I first read Walt Whitman's poetry I thought it would give me a true idea about America. It did in a way, but not about Boston. I expected to find Whitman but I find Jane Austen instead. When I mentioned something of the sort to Adam's mother she seemed quite pleased. They like to be reminded of their English origins and to be told that they resemble the English in appearance and way of life. Actually as I get to know them I feel that it is not the *English* they want to resemble, but a certain class of English. Clem, isn't it funny that I don't seem to remember any of us behaving or feeling like this at home? Of course, Aunt Eve used to brag a bit about her and Doey's

240

aristocratic forebears, but it always irritated Doey—remember? And somehow I can't imagine Doey saying about Paris or London what Adam's father said the other night about Boston: "This used to be *our* city, but the Micks and the Wops have taken it over." It's all very interesting, but I wish you were nearer so that we could talk about it instead of having to depend on letters, which take such a long time to come and go.

The dory drifted slowly over the water. Something moved among the bayberry bushes on the shore, and Patrice came out of her reverie to see young Damon Edwards sitting among the rocks with a book open on his knees. The sun shone on him, green shadows played on his golden head. He did not look up as the dory glided past, nor did he make any sign of recognition, yet she felt sure that he had seen them. She felt a stab of envy, a sudden desire to climb up on the sun-warmed rock and sit beside him, and ask him what he was reading. But the dory passed on without the exchange of a word.

They floated into a tiny cove. Here the beach rose sharply, and everything had a wild, lost look. A rubber boot like a dismembered foot lay on the stones; a piece of driftwood raised its skeletal arms toward a sky where presently a gull hovered a moment, and was gone. There was a scent of wild roses, of drying kelp, of sea and summer air. It was a spot created for make-believe, where anything could happen.

The dory lurched under her as Adam thrust his spear into the water and brought up another impaled grubby. Patrice watched him scrape the writhing body off the barbs and her mood ended on a surge of hostility. "Adam! Must you?"

"Hold it, Patrice! There, to your right. A big one."

"I won't hold it!"

He turned his head to stare at her. "What's the matter with you? There's a big flounder over there by that rock."

"I don't care. I hate the way you do things."

Adam flung the spear into the boat and sat down in the stern seat.

"All right," he said coldly. "Pull in to shore and we'll change places. I'll take you home."

"I haven't got any home and I hate this place."

"And you hate me too, I don't doubt. All this pretense of liking the outdoors, of enjoying sport!"

241

"Sport! You call spearing innocent fish *sport?*"

They glared at each other. Under her fury she felt incredulity. Could he and she really be yelling at each other like this, they who loved each other so much?

Anger made Adam look as if he had TB. He said slowly: "I don't understand you these days. I thought you enjoyed being with me. You didn't have to come today."

"It's the way you do things—cruel, useless things. Spearing grubbies. And when you were a boy you used to shoot owls!"

"I'll take you home," Adam repeated in a flat voice. He picked up the spear and punted the dory into shore. Patrice sat frozenly and watched him jump out and haul the dory a little way up the shingle.

"All right," he said. "Get in the stern and I'll row."

"I'd rather walk."

"In that case you can take the path up there and it will bring you to the Edwardses' back fence."

"You don't have to tell me."

"Give me your hand," he said unemotionally. "Watch out you don't trip."

He helped her out of the dory and for a moment they stood staring into each other's faces. Adam said: "Ever since we came home things have been going wrong between us. You don't want to share things with me as you did in India. You'd rather fool around with Caroline and Ma."

"And you'd rather have me clambering over rocks and having a miscarriage!"

"Clambering over rocks is a damned sight better for you than frowsting in an attic!"

"That was only once. And they have been very kind to me."

"And you let Caroline get away with that pin when Ma had promised it to you. Caroline gets away with everything. She always has."

"You're jealous, that's what's the trouble with you, Adam!"

He said bleakly: "Perhaps I am. One usually is when one loves a person."

"I wonder that you can speak of love. I wonder whether you know the least thing about it."

She thought: This thing that has been happening to me all these weeks, under all the gaiety, the excitement, and now the boredom

242

. . . this has been happening to him, too. The piling up of feelings we never expected, that we never even guessed could exist. Otherwise why did he throw down his spear so suddenly and turn on me just as though he'd been expecting all along that I'd lose my temper? Why did he stick that grubby, unless it was to provoke me?

She said slowly: "Your sister at least understands about the baby."

"You think I don't understand about the baby? It's just as much mine as it is yours."

"You don't really want me to have it. You haven't, from the beginning."

She was horrified by what she was saying, yet she went on: "I thought for a little while—when we first arrived—that everything was going to be all right. But now I don't know. Your family think it's fine for me to be having a baby, and I'd think so too, only you won't let me."

"That's not true."

"You know it's true." Oh, let him deny it again, cried her heart. Let him deny it, keep on denying it.

But Adam said no more, and unable to bear the look in his eyes, Patrice seized his hand. "Adam, I'm sorry! I didn't mean to talk like this, to feel like this. Let's go away together before it is too late. Let's go back to India!"

"What with? I haven't got any money and I've still got to find a job."

"Then find a job. Any job—I don't give a damn what. Let's just be on our own. There must be *something*. . . ."

"It's so easy for you to talk."

"But you've had jobs before!"

"Everything seems to get less and less easy for me. And now you have to rub it in."

Turning from her, he began to coil the dory's painter and said in a muffled voice: "There are times when I find myself wondering, too. You talk about love. What about your love for me? Even at night, now . . ."

She flushed. "I can't help it. It upsets me and I can't sleep afterward."

"You didn't use to be that way."

"It's just that—"

"It's just that you don't respond any more, that's all."

"You don't wait. You never think of *me!*"

He said coldly: "Jesus."

He walked away to the dory and tossed the coiled rope into the bow. Paralyzed by misery, she watched him in silence as he climbed into the dory and pulled away from the shore, and she thought dimly how well he did the things he liked to do—rowing, hunting, shooting, fishing. It must be what people meant when they talked about a person being in his element. Nature was Adam's element. Nature, wilderness, physical exertion, oblivion. And to the exclusion of almost every other element. That was the point. That, most unfortunately for her, was the point.

He rowed without once looking back in her direction and she watched him disappear round a bend of the shore, and listened to the click of rowlocks die in the distance.

Patrice started up the slope in the direction of a little path which was visible just above the beach. The fragrance of bayberry rose against her face. The path was no more than a rabbit run and in the sudden silence, in the downbeat of the sun, she might have been in a jungle.

A voice hailed her suddenly from beside the almost invisible track where she walked: "Why don't you sit down and rest a bit? It's nice here."

Something golden flashed in the sun as Damon Edwards' head showed among the leaves. He smiled, his expression completely changed from the secretive face she remembered from half an hour earlier, and before that at the Bannisters' party the day of her arrival. The path had curved back from the little cove to pass close beside the eyrie where she had spied him with his book on his knees.

"Cousin Patrice," he said, faintly mocking. "You look all hot and bothered."

Patrice made her way through knee-high bushes to where he sat, and now she was in the open again, facing the sea where she and Adam had passed in the dory. The sun blazed on the water. The stones on the shore had a molten look and her head swam in the rich perfume of bay and pine. Overhead a gull wheeled in the gossamer sky; the only living thing, it seemed, besides herself and the boy. He sat where she had seen him earlier, his back against the overhang of the shore. When she appeared he moved slightly and patted the ground beside her. "Lots of room for two," he said, tilting his face up toward hers.

Patrice stared at him. He was certainly changed from the shy being she had met before. He seemed older, and there was nothing childish in his smile or in his gaze. And how beautiful he was! Handsome wouldn't do at all. Beautiful, gracile . . . and she thought regretfully: I wish I knew more about Greece and the ancient gods. He reminds me . . . the turn of his head, the strong, young neck, the delicate lips . . . a picture, a photograph of sculpture she must have come across in some book.

Patrice was unaffectedly staring at him, and he stared back, no doubt accustomed to such bemused scrutiny. He said genially: "Cousin Adam go away in a huff?"

"How did you know?"

"Voices carry on a day like this, and the wind was in my favor."

"You mean you eavesdropped."

He smiled. "You were both yelling your heads off. Won't you sit down?" Drawn, Patrice lowered herself on the space beside him. A cool earthy smell rose from the bank at her back. The boy was so close to her that she could see the down glistening on his upper lip and bare arms. He smelled like some fine young animal. The proximity disturbed her and she shifted to one side but he immediately moved closer, so that their shoulders touched. He said: "Would you like a cigar?"

"I don't smoke."

"Mind if I do?"

"Of course not."

He produced and lighted, of all things, a very large expensive-looking cigar. It wore an ornate gold-and-crimson band which he removed and placed carefully on a stone beside him. Suddenly he looked up, directly, deeply into her eyes. Not even Adam had ever looked at her with such intensity. The look sank down into her body, sending a shudder through her nerves.

They sat in silence. He smoked in a leisurely fashion, and out here in this ardent air Patrice felt no revulsion to the smell of tobacco. Something weird was happening to her; something compounded of her fury against Adam and the proximity of this boy. Elation poured

245

through her as she sat staring fixedly out to sea.

Damon took the cigar from his lips and said without looking at her: "Better?"

Patrice drew a deep breath. No need, now, to pretend. "Yes, rather."

"Good. I hated to see you so sad. And so mad."

"It was my fault. Why does one have to fight over such silly things?"

"Married people usually do."

She was amused. "What do you know about it?"

"Plenty. You don't have to be married to know these things."

"Well, how much do you know? Not much, I bet." Elation merged into a blitheness she had not felt for a long time.

Damon puffed meditatively. He said: "I watch them. It's quite an education. A matter of bed or bread, as a rule. I sit at table with couples. Relatives, friends. One has cooked something special *she* knows about. Some concoction. Or the other has spent most of the day mucking up the kitchen preparing a bouillabaisse or quiche Lorraine. It's generally some foreign exotic mess. And all this done grimly, without love . . . enough to poison you! Competition, that's what. That, in one form or another, is marriage."

"Wrong," Patrice said, with authority. "It may not be a bed of roses but it's not what you make it out to be. There's a lot more to it. Fun. Laughing. Sharing."

"Or they try to be pals," Damon continued as though he had not heard the interruption. "*Chums.* Sharing healthy interests like spearing fish."

"What's wrong with sharing healthy interests?"

"Nothing—until they get married. I mean, that's what I've noticed."

"Then you can't have noticed much. Besides, you're not—"

She broke off, laughing.

"Go on. You were about to say that I'm not old enough." He put the cigar back in his mouth. His profile was like sun-tinted marble. Adonis with a cigar.

"Well," Patrice said judiciously, "you're only sixteen, after all."

"True, but I attained the age of puberty three years ago."

"I attained it at twelve."

He twisted round to look at her. "Did you now? I suppose that in

246

the torrid clime where you grew up—" He broke off, then said abruptly: "Know something? Remember that evening at the Bannisters, when we came to meet you at dinner?"

"What about it?"

"You came walking into the parlor with Adam. It was the first time I had seen you. I'd heard all about you, of course. The whole family was agog at the idea of Adam getting married. It was all they could talk about, for weeks before you arrived. Your being English, and from such an unlikely place as India. Shades of Kipling and the sahib-log! Perhaps that had something to do with it—I mean, what all the talk and excitement and anticipation did to me." He gazed out to sea, his smile sly and amused. "For weeks before I saw you I dreamed about you. Not really seeing you, of course—how could I? I hadn't even seen a photograph of you. I don't think anyone had because Adam was rather remiss about sending one. But my dreams weren't a bit like the one Cousin Dorothea said she had about you —veiled and mysterious and all that!"

Patrice felt suddenly that she did not want to hear any more. She started to speak, but he went on quickly: "I put myself in Adam's place when I went to bed. I dreamed about you at night. And during the day I daydreamed." He smiled at the reaching, glittering sea as though he were addressing himself to it. "Then, that evening, you came walking into the Bannisters' living room and you were wearing that silly dress with the pink sash like a rather dowdy kid at her first party, and I wanted to laugh. You were not at all the girl I had dreamed about, that I had invented!"

He paused, and Patrice thought: I better damn well get up and go. But her body seemed weighted, anchored by the sound of his voice.

"I had expected to see the usual type of girl, not really the individual of my dreams. Someone like that sap Daisy Prentice. Nearer the type I've always known. Then suddenly there *you* were, sunburned, your hair all over the place, your eyes wide open like a rabbit's."

His shoulder shifted, pressed against hers. He blew a plume of smoke into her hair, and laughed. "You came marching into the room trying like mad to look like what I suppose you imagined was a woman of the world. And then a most embarrassing thing happened to me."

Patrice said faintly: "I don't remember anything embarrassing."

247

"It was embarrassing for me. But nice."

Patrice rose. Damon had risen too, and now he faced her, the cigar between the fingers of the hand which hung at his side. He was debonair. They stood in a shower of pine and bay, with the sea at their feet. He said: "Don't look so scared."

She burst out: "This sort of thing . . . long ago . . . with What's-His-Name Harper . . . then Roland . . . I don't . . ."

"Oh, so there were others besides my cousin Adam?"

"No, there were not others besides your cousin Adam!" she blazed at him. "There never has been, never will be!"

He seemed quite unimpressed. "I must tell you something else," he said conversationally. "I guess maybe I'm quite precocious in some ways. I know I'm supposed to be, intellectually. Maybe the other thing goes with it. I dreamed about girls long before I was thirteen. And since then I've had chances, you know. Older fellows often try to get me to go down to Scollay Square with them, or to places in Cambridge. I've wanted to. I just don't happen to have."

Patrice said with scorn: "A virgin at sixteen!"

"Patrice." He uttered the name softly. "Know something? It was wonderful, that night, seeing you for the first time. And I know that every time I see you the same thing will happen to me. Even if you get to be an old woman and I not quite as old, maybe . . . when I see you it will happen to me!"

Patrice said: "I think you must be cracked. Don't you know that I'm going to have a baby? Adam's baby?"

He put his hands on her shoulders. The smoke from the cigar floated against her face. His face came closer to hers and she gazed into sunlit, perfect skin, into the clearest of eyes. "Patrice! Wonderful Patrice."

"I love Adam. I'm married to him. You are absolutely cracked."

"I'm absolutely sane. Do you know Faust's plea to the flying moment? 'Stay, for thou art fair!' It never does stay, of course. That's one of the troubles with marriage."

"You little ass! Talking as if you knew everything."

"Listen, Patrice. I'm leaving for England tomorrow and I'm going to be away a long time. You can forget all about this if you want to, but for now . . ."

His arms were round her. His mouth closed on hers. His breath

tasted of lemon flowers and cigars and bay. It was a tremendous kiss.
It was a discovery.

Then he let her go and blind instinct carried her back to the world
of lawns and lawn mowers and wicker furniture and the urbane
sound of a tennis game going on somewhere out of sight behind her
mother-in-law's house.

19

The house was empty when she reached it. She stood in the hall and felt the emptiness well around her, and she remembered a day when she had come running from the ruined temple behind the mango grove after her encounter with What's-His-Name Harper, and had taken refuge in her parents' bedroom. Well, it was a different kind of fear which assailed her now, one from which not even Doey could have saved her.

The elation of the past half-hour down there on the shore with Damon Edwards soured into a sense of guilt and self-disgust. His kiss seemed glued to her lips. Here she was, newly married to a man she loved, pregnant by him—and this thing had happened to her! And she had let it happen. How pretend that she had not welcomed Damon's invitation to sit beside him on the sun-warmed rock; that she had not experienced sheer physical pleasure in being with him?

Confusion eroded her. Oh, Adam, Adam, where are you? Why had Adam rowed away alone—God knows where? How could he have deserted her so? She would never desert him—this she knew. "Two together . . . winds blow south . . . winds blow north . . ."

Slowly her heart regained its normal rhythm, but she continued to stand in the silent hall, trying to draw comfort from its already famil-

250

iar appearance. An Oriental rug stained by generations of incontinent household pets. A time-darkened engraving of the Battle at La Hogue. On the hall table the stuffed owl which she had brought back from Cambridge.

Vaguely Patrice remembered that this was the maids' day off and that Mrs. Bannister had mentioned going to tea at the Redditches. Great emphasis was laid on the maids' day off, and the ceremonial of a "light" supper to be prepared by Mrs. Bannister, or a chowder by Mr. Bannister, served with pomp and circumstance. During the light supper the conversation would bear heavily and almost exclusively on the topic of food, and although Patrice was well over the period of easy nausea she found it difficult to face the combination of milk, fish, and onions. Now as she stood in the hall the unmistakable aroma of this concoction drifted toward her from the kitchen. Mr. Bannister must have taken the morning off from his office to prepare his spécialité. Patrice thought shrinkingly: I will simply have to make an effort to keep it down this time. On the last occasion she had had to leave the table in a hurry, and Mr. Bannister's feelings had been visibly wounded. "Competition, that's what. That, in one form or another, is marriage."

That little brute of a boy . . . a member of this proper family, but if they only knew! Remembrance of that bright head, those mocking eyes, that imperious embrace made Patrice's legs tremble. She walked to the foot of the staircase and sat down on the bottom step. Perhaps Adam would come walking in through the door and find her here, contritely waiting for him. How quiet the house seemed without his presence. Not a fly buzzed against the windows; there was no sign, even, of the rachitic Koko.

Patrice called experimentally: "Adam!"

Her voice crept through the empty house and died. Adam was not home. He was still rowing angrily out to sea. Into black, rising waves. There would be a storm, one of those sudden unheralded squalls. The dory would be dashed upon the rocks of one of those small islands and Adam drowned, the last thought in his mind a bitter memory of her.

There was a sound of tires on the gravel outside and an automobile horn insinuatingly blown. The front door was open and she heard Barto's voice: "Anyone home? Patrice?"

He had had an automobile especially equipped for his crippled condition. It was a handsome low-slung roadster which the Negro handyman kept in shining splendor. Patrice went to the door and saw Barto sitting behind the wheel, bareheaded, alone. He smiled as she appeared.

"Adam home yet?"

"No. Oh, Barto, have you seen him?"

"Half an hour ago. He left the dory below my shop and said he was going for a walk."

Barto stared at her. Her face was puffed from tears, her shoes wet from salt water, her stockings torn from walking through the underbrush. He said abruptly: "I'm going to Salem on an errand. Like a ride?" He leaned over and opened the door on her side. "Come on. Keep me company."

Patrice slammed the front door and got into the seat beside him. She murmured: "Where did he go?"

"Just walking it off, I guess."

Walking it off. So Barto knew or guessed that there had been a row. She sat silently while he slipped the clutch and they glided away from the house. It was late afternoon and the Bannisters safely at tea with their neighbors. By the time she saw them again she would be back to normal, and the die which she now suddenly and perversely determined on would have been cast. She felt a jolt of excitement, of defiance.

Barto stared ahead, driving deftly, easily. His feet rested in quite normal fashion on the floorboards, his crutches were propped against the seat at his side. An ingenious adaptation of brakes and clutch were attached to the steering wheel, and Patrice had heard that this piece of made-to-order engineering had cost what Caroline described as "a mint."

How nice, she thought, to be able to afford it. To afford anything one wanted. What then, given a choice, would *she* have chosen? A fancy car, a house of her own, Adam always at her side, a first-class ticket on a ship bound for—where? Fat chance!

Barto said gently: "Don't worry about Adam. He's all right."

She said: "I wonder if you'd do something for me, Barto."

"Name it."

"I'd like to stop at a telegraph office."

252

"Salem office do?"

It was an impulse born of reaction. The moment she learned that Adam was not dead, drowned, vanished, resentment poured through her like wine. She would telegraph Alice to send her money for her return to India. It was as simple as that. Her marriage and everything connected with it had been a mistake. She couldn't carry on with it, spend the rest of her life in this self-sufficient, self-satisfied household where one day was exactly like another, and the maids' day off equal in importance only to the day the laundry truck called to collect the week's dirty linen.

True, she did not have much to offer herself, but whatever it was it was preferable to this perpetual boredom. She would never fit. She would never be one of them. There would always be patronage, no matter how kindly and well meant. Adam would never achieve independence and he and she would spend their lives sponging on others.

Barto drove up a narrow street between crooked old houses set among old-fashioned gardens where hollyhocks seemed to sprout from every crevice. Like the cobbles over which Barto drove, these houses had been here a long time and the same families had lived in them. Houses and owners had grown curiously to resemble one another: weathered, mellowed, permanent. And when they died they would move unobtrusively up the hill to the old graveyard with its slate headstones carved in skulls and angels, overlooking a sea no less permanent than they.

Barto began: "You and Adam seem to have set a matrimonial example to the neighbors." When she remained silent he went on: "The expected has happened. Lawrence Redditch is home from sea and he and Daisy have announced their engagement."

"They're fools," Patrice said coldly.

He ignored this. "Wouldn't you know that Daisy would wait until the last minute before making up her mind? It was only after seeing you that she really gave up all hope of netting Adam."

"She can still have him," said Patrice.

"So the fishing expedition was not a success? I rather gathered as much from my brief glimpse of Adam. What happened?"

"He kept sticking grubbies." She stared at the sunlit street. "And it's nothing to laugh at, either."

"I'm not laughing. Was that what you quarreled about?"

253

"All that blood, those awful staring eyes!"

"Come on. I don't believe that was it."

They left the town and turned on the main highway. Old-world charm gave way to ugly brown shingled houses, battered-looking factories, and weed-grown lots advertised FOR SALE OR LEASE.

Barto said: "When Caro and I have a fight we usually pretend it is because of some piddling thing like bills, or whether or not Timmy should be made to brush his teeth after every meal, whereas it is almost always because of something neither of us is willing to admit."

"You and Caroline have your house, your child, your interests. All of you—the Bannisters, the Redditches, the Edwardses, and now Daisy and her young man—you are all proper and secure and bubbling over with happiness!"

"Envious?" Barto asked lightly.

Patrice was silent.

"And you've been crying," he said. "If you keep this up you'll spoil everything. It will be all over town that you and Adam are breaking up."

"It might not be so wide of the mark at that."

"So soon?"

She turned to him. "You might as well know that this telegram I'm going to send is to my mother. I'm going to ask her to send me some money so I can go home."

"Will your mother be able to afford it?"

"She'll raise it somehow."

As she spoke another thought struck her. She had forgotten to bring her purse and so would have no cash with which to pay for the telegram.

Barto said presently: "By the way, have you taken up smoking cigars?"

"*What?*"

"I seem to smell panatelas, and it comes from your hair."

Patrice flushed. "Adam's pipe, probably."

"I smoke panatelas myself so I ought to know."

"You know everything."

He laughed. "Now tell me. What about the baby? I mean if you decide to walk out on Adam. It's as much his baby as yours, don't forget."

254

"That's what he tried to tell me, but he doesn't really want me to have it." She went on headlong: "He doesn't want me to have a child. I've known it from the beginning. And that's not all. He doesn't want me, either. Oh, I know. He's been free all his life, done what he wanted to do. But he has never taken on another person. Now he's stuck with me, and presently there'll be the baby."

Barto said thoughtfully: "None of this makes Adam very different from most men. He just doesn't bother to hide what a lot of us never even admit to ourselves. The truth is men don't always look on marriage the way most women do."

"Do they look on love the way women do?"

"I can't say that I know much about love, except where Timmy is concerned." And after a moment he went on: "Mind if I talk about myself for a bit? It might take your mind off yourself."

She was grudgingly amused. "You've done it before. At the Bannisters', that very first evening, when you'd had too much to drink, I expect."

"Well, you were a fresh audience!"

"And you seemed very cold-blooded."

"I never said that I was running out on Caroline, though, did I? I wasn't planning to send a telegram to Mama asking for money so I could leave my wife."

"You would not have had to send such a telegram. You told me yourself that same evening that you were stinking rich."

"Coarse of me. I must have had one too many of the old man's cocktails. But listen, Patrice. I'd like to have you understand things a bit in relation to Caroline and me. Because if by chance you should change your mind about sending that telegram you'll be seeing quite a bit of us."

"I don't think that either you or Adam are fair about Caroline."

"As far as Adam is concerned he and Caroline have never got along. She's always put it over on him, ever since they were kids. And the parents were always on her side. They petted and spoiled her. She was cast in their mold, whereas Adam was not. She's always been grasping, even with people." He gave her a sidewise glance. "For instance, this bare-faced trick she has of swiping one's friends."

"But isn't it possible to share one's friends?"

"Caroline has never been a sharer. She's swiped quite a few of my

255

friends. It's usually the men. In my condition I can't hope to have many women friends. I'm always afraid they might be pitying me, and I couldn't take that."

"I must make a note of it," Patrice murmured, and he said quickly: "What I just said doesn't apply to you. You can feel as sorry for me as you please and I shan't object!"

Patrice touched him lightly on the knee. "I don't feel sorry for you, Barto. If I feel sorry for anyone it's for Caroline."

"You probably wonder why, talking about her as I do, I never married her. We are not the most ideally suited pair in the world! But I was drawn to Caroline from the first day I met her. It was during my junior year at college, and she was being beaued around by a classmate of mine named Hugh Cameron. But he was a poor boy from the wrong neighborhood of New York City, and old Wilbur would have none of it. He'd gone to some trouble to find out that the Cameron part of Hugh had nothing to do with kilts and clans and coats of arms, and he made it crystal clear that no daughter of his was going to throw in her lot—or her little—with someone whose father was nothing more distinguished than a foreman in an electroplating plant, who'd saved every cent he could to give his son an education and a good start in life."

"Anyway, one afternoon after the Harvard-Yale football game Hugh took me over to the Bannisters' house in Cambridge for tea. You know they've always been strong on that afternoon tea business. Part of the English heritage! I knew that Hugh was keen on Caroline, but it didn't take more than a cup of Lapsang souchong and a crumpet for me to see that he didn't have a prayer. Caroline herself didn't care enough about Hugh to take a stand against her father. There's nothing trivial about the old man's snobbery—it's the real thing. He carries it to the damnedest lengths." Barto gave a short laugh. "Did Adam ever tell you the story about the Bannister nomenclature? No? I can see why he'd hesitate. He has nothing of the old man's snottiness and I always felt that that little incident stuck in his craw. Well, anyway. Bannister isn't really Wilbur's name at all—that is, it was his mother's maiden name. His father's name was Brown. Well! Along about the time Wilbur decided on getting married himself he changed his name legally from plain Brown to Bannister-Brown. Hy-

256

phenated it. Then right after Adam was born he quietly dropped the Brown altogether."

They were approaching the city. Factory chimneys stuck up above the dusty elms. The traffic increased and Barto slowed down. "But to go back to Caroline and Hugh Cameron. He got his walking papers from Wilbur long before he'd had a chance to propose to Caroline, and that was that. I took his place. I wasn't such a close friend of Hugh's as to suffer from any mawkish qualms on the question. And I was given every encouragement by Caroline and her parents. I could no more rustle up a coat of arms than poor Hugh, but I had two advantages over him: I was always sure of myself, and I had plenty of cash."

Patrice asked anxiously: "But you loved Caroline, didn't you?"

"I was drawn to her. She interested me. She amused me. She was so damned healthy, and that appealed to me too, cripple that I was. But chiefly she amused me. She had this idea of herself as being a woman of devastating brilliance, charm, and sophistication!"

Skillfully, smoothly, Barto bypassed a truck. "Her parents had seen to it that she got the right kind of education for a young lady of her superior social standing. Miss Barstow's Boarding School for Girls, followed by a year in Europe, where she picked up a smattering of French and a veneer of Continental vivacity. She became an authority on matters European, and although I knew she couldn't boil an egg it did not mean she wasn't a connoisseur of French cuisine!" Barton laughed without venom. "She fascinated me. She couldn't parse a sentence in English, but she could hum the better known arias from Italian opera *almost* in tune. And she could talk the handle off a chamberpot. She held the family spellbound. Not Adam, of course. With her he was either bored, or downright rude. I tell you, tea at the Bannisters' with Caroline in good voice was worth all Broadway to me. Yes, I know what you're thinking—that I was nothing more than a low-down, cold-blooded *cad*. Well, perhaps I was. Except for one thing. Even while I was laughing at Caroline I was becoming fond of her. There was something so frenzied in all that self-delusion! I used to want to just take her in my arms and tell her to relax. The whole atmosphere—the half-arse intellectualism without a single idea, the old man's brutal snobbery, Mrs. B.'s complacence—would strike me

257

suddenly as being utterly pitiful. If pity is akin to love then, yes, I must have loved Caroline. And it hadn't taken me long to realize that it was me she wanted, and that she was using all her expensively acquired wiles to get me. It was as simple as that. The poor kid. I've no doubt that she had convinced herself, as she did her parents, that hers was a chaste and simple devotion compounded of democratic respect for my intellect and compassion for my crippled condition. A cool, calculating eye on a million and a half bucks' inheritance did not, of course, enter the picture at all."

Patrice said coldly: "Why, then, if that's what you believed—"

"I've already told you. I was not without compassion myself. Also, I was a fairly normal guy, and lonely. I had a pretty good idea that no woman was going to fall for me just for *me*. And in a way I couldn't help admiring Caroline's single-minded devotion to her own interests. It was the most genuine thing about her. She was—she is now —a far more sincere person than either of her parents. I had even hoped that I might have made her a happy one. But I had neglected to take something else into account." He hesitated a moment. "Caroline's inordinate appetite. For everything. Including sex."

Patrice stared at the handsome avenue opening before them. She thought: I wonder what he would say if I told him about Damon Edwards . . . this morning.

Barto continued: "Sex can let you down, after all. It let me down, and I let Caroline down. But money is a different story—that is, if you're smart, and I was always smart! And so I was able to comfort myself with the knowledge that if I couldn't give her all the physical satisfaction she craved I could at least give her money. Fair enough?"

"If that's what you call being fair," said Patrice.

"Perhaps if I'd had a chance to go to bed with her before marriage . . . but nice girls don't do that sort of thing. And I was not settling for anyone else. I felt pretty sure that I'd never have a chance to know another girl as I had learned to know Caroline. I did not go into marriage blindly. I have never trusted Caroline. I have never let her in on my financial affairs and I have never let her handle my dough."

Patrice said slowly: "What a peculiar life!"

Barto smiled. "Not really. A bit on the Oriental side, maybe. Isn't that the way marriages are arranged in your native India? With a strictly practical eye to the main chance? And as far as Caro and I

258

are concerned it has worked pretty well. I give her all the cash she wants, and she gave me Timmy."

They were in the center of town and he pulled up in a dingy side street.

"Here we are. I hope they've got the damned thing fixed."

Patrice watched him ease himself out from behind the wheel and adjust his crutches. He met her eyes and smiled. "Mind waiting a bit?"

In a few minutes he was beside her again, the crutches placed carefully between them. "Now I've got my polisher back—I broke it last week—I can finish the little present I've been working on for you."

He started the car and they slid away from the sidewalk. "I feel badly that you didn't get that ruby pin from Mrs. B. So I've made something for you. It just needs a bit of polishing and I can do that when we get home, if you won't mind coming into the shop and waiting a few minutes."

Presently they were driving along a wide street flanked by handsome old houses and towering elms. Patrice said in an uncertain voice: "The telegraph office?"

Barto stopped the car in the heavy shade of the elms and twisted round to look at her. "You really intend to send that telegram?"

She was silent and he gazed at her impassively for a moment. "So you're fed up with marriage after three months of it. You're not even willing to give it a chance to work."

"If you're starting to pitch into me . . ."

"It's time someone pitched into you. I'm sick of pretense. I've had to live with it all my life and I'm sick of it. You know damn well you don't want to send that telegram. You don't really want to leave Adam."

Patrice sat chewing her lower lip and he went on dispassionately: "Trouble with you is that you don't know what you want. So you pretend. No, listen to me. You yap about marriage . . . well, O.K., so do I! But I don't pretend, God damn it! A woman has everything to gain from marriage, but has a man? See what it does to men. Takes away our irresponsibility, our freedom of action. Some of us become like women because we are forced to take on the characteristics of our wives. Some of us turn into hermaphrodites—and they probably

259

make the best husbands of all. Others live like Siamese twins, both partners trying desperately to ignore each other's existence. But it's always the man who takes the rap."

Patrice said wanly: "Is it? Well, I'm frightened. I'm frightened of having this baby. I'm frightened of the pain, and perhaps something going wrong. And afterward of its growing up. Living with it."

Barto said after a moment's silence: "I had not expected anything quite so despicable from you."

Tears, held in abeyance, now rose blindingly to her eyes. "All right," said Barto in a flat voice, "I'll turn round and take you to the telegraph office."

"Oh, Barto!"

"Now what?"

"I haven't any money. I left my purse at home."

"I'll be happy to lend you some."

"Oh, Barto, please don't look so—so angry!"

Suddenly he laughed, reached over the crutches, and pulled her head toward him, kissing her hair. "Phew! Panatelas, I'd swear!" Then: "Look. I'll make a deal with you. Forget that telegram for now. In a day or two if you still feel you want to send it come and tell me and I'll give you the price of a first-class ticket by ship for home. O.K.?"

Her head on his shoulder, Patrice stared up at the deeply cleft chin. "O.K.," she said. He kissed her again, lightly. Neither saw a small light-blue roadster with its top down, Daisy Prentice at the wheel and a dark young man beside her, come toward them down the street, slow down, then pass on.

Barto's workshop was a small room above his garage. A carefully contrived staircase led from his garage to the shop and on the first occasion when she had seen him ascend his staircase Patrice had been embarrassed. It seemed an acutely painful proceeding. Now as he drove into the garage and shut off the motor he said: "Nobody home, I guess."

She asked how he knew.

"I can usually tell. Something in the air."

Like a blind person, she thought, as she followed him out of the car. A sixth sense. His crutches tucked under his arms, Barto paused at the garage doors and looked out over the little harbor above which his

260

house was built. The harbor was gay with yachts at anchor. The music from an accordion reached them from a large black sloop anchored within hailing distance; the sound of voices issued from the cabin, and a woman's laugh. Caroline's.

Barto turned. "Hal Johnson throwing a party. Wish he'd learn something besides 'Madelon.' Mind if I go up first?"

She turned aside, hating to watch what appeared to her to be an ordeal. With his crutches gripped under one arm, Barto grasped the stair rail with his free hand and mounted with a squirming, thrusting action like a wounded man. When he reached the top Patrice followed. It was pleasant and airy, lighted by windows giving out on the water. Between the windows and at intervals along the walls were narrow apertures resembling loopholes in a fortress, each furnished with casement-type panes, and, as Patrice noticed for the first time, each affording a separate and distinct view of the surrounding terrain.

Barto made his way to the window overlooking the harbor. The smell of the sea and the strains of the accordion drifted into the room as he turned and smiled at her. "Squattez-vous. Like a drink?"

He poured her a glass of ginger ale, and something for himself out of a silver flask which he took from a shelf above his worktable. Everything was neat, orderly, clean. More, Patrice decided, like a doctor's office than a workshop. Attached to the long deal table were vises of different sizes, and several electrically operated machines for cutting and polishing stones. On the wall hung a large geologic map, flanked by an assortment of stonemasons' tools carefully arranged to give an impression of decoration rather than of use. Two large chairs stood one on each side of a window, with a low bookcase between them, filled with books on mineralogy and gems.

Patrice sank into one of the chairs and raised her glass of ginger ale. "Cheers!"

Barto tossed off the contents of his glass, then crossed to a small safe under the worktable, fiddled with the combination, and returned to Patrice's chair. "Here," he said. "It needs a bit of buffing, but it's a nice thing anyway."

He dropped it into her hand, a round odd-colored stone with a green tinge. "Beryl," Barto explained. "I found it when I was digging in Maine last summer. It will make up into something nice

261

for you, I think. A ring perhaps. Or a pendant. It needs just a touch more. . . ."

He took the stone from her and hobbled over to his workbench, where he worked busily for several minutes. Then he came back and stood before the window, holding the stone to the light. For a moment it seemed to Patrice that his eyes and the stone were of an identical color and polish.

"Golden beryl," he murmured. "A good specimen." He leaned against the wall, supporting himself lightly on his crutches. "You pick out a setting you'd like for a ring or whatever, and I'll have it made up for you. Gold, I think. Or maybe platinum would show the stone off better."

Patrice began diffidently: "Barto, you're sweet, but I don't think . . ."

"I know. You don't think you can afford it. Never mind that. Just pick out the setting and I'll take care of it."

He wrapped the beryl in a piece of tissue and dropped it into her lap. "Caroline has ordered some Swedish glass for you for a wedding present, but this is from me with my—what do you call it in your native India? My salaams."

He reached into his breast pocket and produced a cigar. "Mind if I smoke?"

Patrice wanted to laugh, thinking of the boy Damon. And now here was this man, this considerate, brotherly spirit, making her feel at home. Barto lighted the cigar and carefully blew the smoke away from her face. "What's so funny?" he asked, gazing down at her.

"Just that you're so sly, taking me into town, bringing me back, giving me this lovely present—all so that I should forget about sending that telegram!"

The music of the accordion seemed suddenly louder as it carried across the water. The air was turning faintly blue; there was a blue pallor in the sky, a blue silk look to the water. And Caroline's laughter sounded sweet and innocent, mingling with the strains of the old war song, "Madelon."

Patrice felt as at ease as she had, more unaccountably, with Damon Edwards earlier that day. The old apathy seemed to have left her and a fresh kind of happiness to have taken its place. In a little while she

262

would leave Barto and walk back to the Bannisters' house, to Adam. He would be waiting for her in their bedroom and would take her in his arms, and both would laugh shamefacedly at the memory of their silly quarrel. Another barrier would have been crossed—another of those trip wires which beset the path of intimacy. And she had Barto to thank for it.

Then she saw him suddenly hobble with extraordinary speed to one of the odd-shaped little windows, crouch, and peer through it. He shouted: "Timmy! Get out of that boat. You know you're not supposed to go out on the water alone!"

The boy's voice reached Patrice: "I was just going out to the *Blue Heron* to say hello to Mumma and Mr. Johnson!"

"You heard me! Get out of that boat and stay out."

Barto turned back to Patrice. "A kid was drowned in this harbor last year, fooling around in a skiff with no one to watch him."

"But Timmy can swim, can't he?"

"So could the kid that drowned."

Patrice said slowly: "Those funny little windows . . ."

"My spy holes. It's how I keep tabs on Timmy. I had them set so there's scarcely a yard of the area I can't command from this one room."

"But you can't command everything from this one room! I mean, what about when you're not home or when Timmy's somewhere else?"

"When I'm not around someone else is. I pay for the service. See that telephone in the corner? It's a direct line to police headquarters."

Patrice gave him a troubled glance. "What is it you are afraid of, Barto?"

He took the cigar from his lips and consulted the ash. "Lots of things. A kid of Timmy's age has no judgment. Besides, I'm known to be a rich man, and there are kidnappers."

Patrice had a sense of shock. "Does Timmy know that you keep tabs on him like this?"

"He knows about these windows, of course. Though he sometimes forgets, as he did just now. But he doesn't know about the private detective arrangement. It's always a different person, so he has never caught on."

"Does Caroline know?"

"She knows about this direct line to the police, but not about the detective. No one knows about *that* except myself, and now you. And I trust you not to mention it."

"Of course I won't. But tell me, does Caroline worry the way you do?"

Barto shrugged. "Hell, no! She thinks I'm nuts. She thinks it's an unhealthy way to bring up a kid—unfair to him. In a way she's right. But try to see it as I do. With these damned legs of mine, what could I do in an emergency? And what does Caroline do about it? Spends her mornings swilling coffee with her ma. Rest of the time she's fooling around with Daisy Prentice, or else she's out on the boat with that cheapskate Hal Johnson."

Patrice had met Hal Johnson, a tall, genial, red-faced man in his early forties; something of a hero in the last war and before that something famous on the Yale football team. He exuded health, wealth, and happiness, and Patrice murmured, more to herself than to Barto: "You don't like Hal Johnson."

"No," Barto replied calmly. "I don't. But Caroline does."

Patrice was to recall this occasion years afterward. She was to recall this pleasant, airy room with its workmanlike atmosphere and the sound of an accordion drifting in through the window. She was to remember Barto propped on his crutches, smoking his cigar, the still, contained look in his eyes. Years later, when on impulse she went to call on him in his dingy hotel room in New York, he was alone. He had lost most of his money, and he was slowly dying of cancer.

"I never see Timmy these days," Barto was to tell her then in a quiet, resigned voice. "He never comes near me, never calls me up. But I understand he's doing very well."

But on this late summer afternoon Caroline's laughter floated into the little workshop to the strains of Hal Johnson's accordion, and Caroline sounded happy. Some years were to pass before she left Barto to marry Johnson and to sail away with him on his fine steam yacht for a honeymoon among the Caribbean isles.

20

$\mathcal{F}$rom Granada, Spain, Clem had written:

Your letters make me realize that you and I and Alice live in a three-cornered world. I am thankful that you, for one, are safe and happy in Christmas Tree Land, but for myself I don't think I could stand living there. From what I gather by your letters there is a deadly sameness and people have to wear false noses or become neurotics in order to preserve any kind of individuality! Of course, it must be nice to be the richest country in the world, even if the greatest common denominator is the commonplace. To be rich, after all, is what most people want, even when they pretend they don't. To be poor and keep your nobility I think you would have to be an Arab and be born in a tent. Even rich Arabs managed to hang on to their nobility, at any rate here in Spain. I see the hand of Islam everywhere, and sometimes I think I hear it in the language.

When I walk among the fountains and the cypresses in the Alhambra and look out over the bone-white city and listen to the Gypsy voices I feel a kind of happiness I've never known before. Not doing anything, not trying to "put it down" in paint or paper! Just existing for the sake of existing. Of course, this would never go down with your Yanks, who have to be busy every minute of their lives. I've run into quite a few here—travelers, students, some artists. Nice, decent people, most of them, but always on the go. Perhaps this is a more constructive philosophy than the Arab resignation, but not for me.

And in another letter he wrote:

> Things seem to be getting pretty much out of hand in India and I
> wish we could get Alice away somehow. I wrote to her once suggesting
> that she come and stay with Melissa and me. We could manage. I sell
> the occasional odd picture and I've got a job guiding tourists, since I
> now speak the boli quite well, and it gives me a bilingual advantage.
> The job is a Christly bore, but with the pay and the tips we eat and
> pay the rent. Alice wrote back to say she couldn't bring herself to leave
> what she calls "home," and that anyhow, if she left India it would be
> to go to you since she believes that a mother's place is with her daugh-
> ter! Frankly, selfishly, I'm quite relieved. I feel as if an age had come
> between Alice and me. I can swallow the sentimentality, the cannibal-
> istic mother love, in her letters, but could I live with it? Once you've
> outgrown your parents you can never honestly go back to them. And
> Alice will never slough off her memsahibness. I suspect that she some-
> times sees herself in the role of another heroic English martyr, as the
> cutthroats close in with their scimitars!
>
> But I do worry, rather. Wish you could get her over to America,
> where at any rate the language would not be a problem. I'd be glad to
> contribute whatever I can. Think it over, Patrice, and let me know.
>
> As for India, it's going to blow up. Perhaps not right away, but
> eventually. I often wonder what Doey would have thought about it. He
> was a liberal, even a radical, for his time, but aren't such liberals as a
> rule people who can afford to have their cake and eat it, too? And if
> Doey had suddenly realized that his own and his family's cake was
> being eyed by the underdogs—millions of them—would his liberal
> convictions have survived? Well, as far as I'm concerned, the sooner
> the underdogs take over the better. I'm sick to death of the burra sahibs
> and the pukka types and their second-rate values. Doey escaped being
> second-rate because he was essentially an intellectual. And he was
> wholly an aristocrat in a sense that poor old Aunt Eve was not. He died
> with his values intact, but I know that I never could have stayed on in
> India. I'm no Goya, and the disasters of everyday life out there deaden
> one's sensibilities. I know that you were never a victim of that deaden-
> ing process. You were always mentally and physically healthier than I.
> In other countries—even in middle-class Blighty—a man like me could
> find another—a painter, a writer, a poet—in whose company he could
> make some sort of a world, but not in India. I don't know what sickens
> me most at this distance: the run-of-the-mill Indian who blames every-
> thing on the white man, or the white man himself.

Patrice put Clem's letter with the steadily increasing bundle of
letters, from him and from Alice, which she kept in her bureau
drawer in the bedroom of the Bannisters' house. As that first summer

266

in Berry's Landing progressed in a succession of warm, sunny days, these letters took on a character of their own, strangely divorced from the personalities of their authors. Perhaps distance and separation had something to do with it, but she found herself brooding over these personalities with a detachment she had not felt when she was with them.

Alice, she knew, would never change, never "slough off," as Clem had put it, her "memsahibness," nor her fanatical sense of motherhood. She was doomed to an old age of bewilderment and yearning for the past. But it was different with Clem, and inevitably Patrice fell to drawing comparisons between his restless, fugitive nature and the natures of the people who now surrounded her and who had become part of her life.

It was not in Clem but in men like Adam and Barto, women like Mrs. Bannister and Daisy Prentice and perhaps Caroline too, that Patrice was conscious of a sense of waste, of, in a deeper sense, failure. Not failure in politics, not failure in the making of money and the acquisition of *things*. Not really any failure except the failure to change, to become, to find out. The tragic failure to take life in your two hands and feel its wildly beating heart.

Now, having read Clem's last letter and added it to the collection in her bureau drawer, Patrice turned to the typewriter which Adam had given her a few days after he had gone to work, at last, in the office of the boatyard at Berry's Landing. To Patrice the typewriter had an air of seductive mystery as it sat on a bridge table beside the window. How easy it had been to write when she had had nothing to say! Those airy inventions, echoes from the last novel she might have been reading at the time—Baroness Orczy, Maud Diver, A. E. W. Mason, Rider Haggard! And of course Tolstoy, simply because a set of the novels seemed to accompany Doey wherever he went. Ponderous volumes they were, bound in black with gold lettering, their deckled edges nibbled away by generations of white ants.

Now Patrice sat bemusedly before the new typewriter, a fresh sheet of paper in the roller, waiting for the magical moment. She had, for some weeks, played with the idea for a short story and the plot had seemed clear and succinct in her mind. Now paralysis descended upon her, and all that came to utterance was a song Clem used to sing:

K-K-K-Katy, beautiful Katy,
You're the only g-g-g-girl that I adore,
When the m-m-m-moon shines over the c-c-c-cowshed
I'll be waiting at the k-k-k-kitchen door.

She heard Mrs. Bannister's voice behind her: "Ready, Patrice, dear?"

Patrice lowered the cover on the typewriter and rose. "Just my hair," she said.

Mrs. Bannister watched her draw the comb through her hair. "Pregnancy becomes you," she said. "You look so well!"

"I feel like a lump!" said Patrice. She had tried to enliven the sackcloth and ashes style of a maternity dress by wearing the beryl which Barto had given her. It hung from her neck on a fine gold chain and Mrs. Bannister's expression changed slightly as she noticed it.

"That was nice of Barto," she remarked. "He must like you. He's not in the habit of making presents!" She added kindly: "You'll get over feeling that you are a lump! One does, as I learned myself."

Patrice tried to visualize this disciplined figure caught in the trap of parturition, but it was always impossible for her to picture Adam's mother in any but the most conventional of situations, as she was at this moment, hatted and gloved, on her way to Daisy Prentice's wedding reception.

"Two brides in almost as many months! You and Daisy. But how I wish you both could have had a regular church service instead of that registry office affair. But of course since Lawrence's ship sails so soon he and Daisy are lucky to have these few days together. Oh, dear, I do hope that girl will be happy!"

There had, during the past few weeks, been a succession of parties in honor of Daisy and her fiancé, a continuation, it seemed to Patrice, of almost identical parties given for Adam and herself. It had appeared to Patrice that Lawrence Redditch was distinctly a fish out of water in this milieu, but she now observed to her mother-in-law that he had impressed her as being a good sort.

"Oh, Lawrence is good enough, I guess," Mrs. Bannister conceded. "After all, he is a Redditch in spite of his gangsterish looks. It's just that Lawrence has never really been one of us, as, for instance, you are!" She smiled affectionately at Patrice. "He has never fitted. In fact, he's always rather acted as if he didn't want to fit. And then he has weird friends."

"Weird?"

"Common. Not at all the type one would care to invite to one's house, if you know what I mean."

"In that case," said Patrice, "how does it happen that Daisy . . ."

Mrs. Bannister shrugged. "They've known each other, off and on, since they were children. Wilbur puts it down to the attraction of opposites, which is mild, coming from Wilbur, because he detests Lawrence. You see, Lawrence never even made college. He left school when he was fifteen and went off to sea." Mrs. Bannister frowned. "I must say I have never been drawn to the boy. But as long as our sweet Daisy loves him, why, we'll make the best of it."

Mr. Bannister's voice floated testily up the staircase: "For heaven's sake, you two! It's getting late."

"Coming, dear!" cried Mrs. Bannister.

As she followed her mother-in-law's elegant back down the stairs Patrice thought briefly of Lawrence Redditch. Powerfully built, swarthy, pitilessly silent, he jutted from this urbane background like a forbidding, half-submerged rock. Daisy alone seemed unawed by the man she had so abruptly made up her mind to love, honor, and obey. What did she see in him? Aside from that tenuous bond of childhood . . . And Lawrence, what did he see in her? That she was beautiful, yes. Yet somehow he did not, in Patrice's budding judgment, give the impression of a man easily pleased. Then at a recent party she fancied she caught a hint of the mystery. His brilliant black eyes had sought Daisy out of the effusive throng which surrounded her and there had been an instant's transformation of his brooding face. Patrice had caught her breath. "He adores her," she told herself. "Lawrence Redditch simply adores Daisy Prentice!"

The automobile was waiting to take the Bannisters to Caroline's house. Because Mr. Charles Prentice was considered far too rattle-brained to be trusted with the complicated arrangements for his daughter's wedding reception, it had been Caroline's idea that she and Barto should give the couple a farewell party, after which they were to take a train for New York for a twenty-four-hour honeymoon before Lawrence's ship sailed again for foreign ports.

269

As Mrs. Bannister prepared to install herself in her customary role in the driver's seat Mr. Bannister suddenly raised his voice: "Koko!" Mrs. Bannister turned to him. "No, Wilbur. We are not taking Koko." His green law bag clutched in his hand—he never moved without it —Mr. Bannister ignored her. "Here, Koko, Koko, Koko!"

Patrice wanted to laugh. Adam took her arm. "We might as well get in," he said.

They got into the back seat and Mrs. Bannister started the motor. Mr. Bannister continued to stand in the driveway, yodeling.

"All right, Wilbur," Mrs. Bannister spoke with heavy composure. "You can stay here. We are going."

Patrice whispered to Adam: "Do they really mean it?"

Adam's face wore the look of sardonic amusement which she sometimes surprised there, and which, curiously and rather disturbingly, brought out his resemblance to his father.

Mr. Bannister delivered his ultimatum with passion: "If Koko doesn't go I don't go!"

Mrs. Bannister experimented with the choke and her voice rose above the shattering eructations of the engine: "I am not going to allow Caroline's party to be spoiled just because of Koko. You know how Barto feels about him."

"I don't give a dman how Barto feels!" Mr. Bannister shouted. "I don't see why I should be expected to kowtow to my own son-in-law."

He screamed once more into the unresponsive ether: "Koko!"

"It won't do any good for you to shout, Wilbur," declared Mrs. Bannister. "He can't hear you."

Mr. Bannister whirled in her direction. "Koko can't hear me? What in the devil do you mean?"

"I arranged for Nora to take him for a little walk." She glanced at her watch. "We have five minutes. Are you coming?"

Silently Mr. Bannister climbed into the seat beside her. Glancing up, Patrice had a glimpse of Mrs. Bannister's face in the rear-view mirror. It was expressionless, but as the car rolled down the driveway Patrice thought that her mother-in-law wore her funny little straw hat as though it were a crown.

Caroline's parties were invariably large and noisy and they had a way of starting a good half hour ahead of schedule, so that when Mrs.

270

Bannister drove into the yard there were already a dozen automobiles parked on the gravel, and Timmy, cherubic in a new sailor suit, was directing traffic.

"Here you are, Grandma," he piped. "I've saved a space for you."

As they got out of the car Patrice glanced round, half expecting to see some shadowy figure in surveillance over the boy, but she found herself instead caught up in a stream of new arrivals advancing gaily toward the front door. Timmy sidled up to his grandmother. "That will be ten cents," he informed her in a businesslike voice. "I've been holding that space specially for you!"

Patrice liked this house and she would have liked it better if she were not incessantly called upon to admire some detail over again: the view from the south window, a Chinese rug before the fireplace, the Stuart portrait of an ancestor above the Queen Anne sofa, the Tang horses, the antique needlepoint. It seemed as if Caroline could never have enough praise of her possessions, as if she gleaned a fresh satisfaction from each reiteration.

Although Barto employed servants—a colored couple and a gardener—Caroline seldom bothered to prepare meals in the house when the company numbered more than half a dozen. Food was ordered from a firm of caterers in Boston, and it was always superlative. Today, with upward of fifty guests, waiters and a bartender were likewise in attendance. There were flowers from Carbone, and champagne—the real thing, as Caroline whispered to her mother. The real thing bootlegged by Hal Johnson, who had made a special trip beyond the three-mile limit in his yacht, and had brought back *cases*.

"Darling," Mrs. Bannister murmured with a rather dubious smile, "you certainly do things in style."

"It's for Daisy, and little enough on this day of days!" Caroline turned to Patrice. "Sweetheart, you look exactly fifteen years old!"

She bustled away into a gale of voices and Patrice retreated to the uncertain seclusion of potted ferns and orange trees in a corner of the big room. She had not yet conquered her shyness of crowds and of these people who knew each other so well, where first names and pet names filled the air like shrapnel. Some of the faces she now saw were already familiar: the Redditches, the Edwardses, the Lucan Bannisters, the Pitmans, the Parsonses, the Pitts; cousins, distant cousins, neighbors, and friends of Adam's family. With one or two exceptions

271

they bore a sort of family likeness, and though there were many whom she had not yet met, she felt that she might have met them but could not for her life remember their names, not to mention their diminutives—the Fatty Freemans, Pinky Pitmans, Bunny Barstows, and the rest. She on the other hand remained unmistakably and gauchely the newcomer to be accepted as one of them and put at her ease.

Patrice sensed their warmheartedness under a cascade of Pats, Patsys, Pattys—the truncation of her name into the diminutive, a sure accolade. Yet she could not rid herself of a feeling that this show of acceptance was strictly conditional. Much was expected of her in return; everything, in fact, was expected of her. Compliance and surrender—not ostentatious nor even obvious, certainly not abject, but surrender nevertheless.

Mrs. Bannister's remark earlier this afternoon—that she, Patrice, *fitted,* whereas Lawrence Redditch did not—was intended as a compliment, no doubt, possibly as reassurance. But it was unmistakably a warning: Fit or be rejected or at best taken on sufferance. And now as she lurked amidst the hired greenery in Caroline's handsome parlor with the din of the party rising round her, she thought: My child will fit. He will have been born into it. Afterward it doesn't really matter whether you rob a bank, become a drunk, or never take a bath: you are One of Them.

The party got under way fast. Patrice had already learned to gauge the tempo by a certain leveling of the general orchestration, and by the rising tide of puce in people's complexions. She wished that she dared risk drinking the liquor handed round by the waiters and downed so unconcernedly even by her mother-in-law.

Several of the guests approached and were jolly and attentive, as if they had known her all their lives. They assured her admiringly that she looked just about fifteen years old and she let the compliment pass without demur, thinking ruefully: I'm twenty and pregnant and this damn thing inside me has started to kick!

Scraps of conversation drifted to her ears: "I was in New York last week. Stayed out at Glen Cove with the Marshalls. You remember Manny Marshall? Thought he was in your class—twelve? Manny thinks we're headed for trouble. Advised me to start getting out of stocks and into government bonds. Of course, Manny has always been scared of his own shadow. On the other hand, he knows his stuff."

"Julie comes out next year. I can hardly believe it. Seems only yesterday we gave her a fifteenth-birthday party and it poured with rain, remember? All those lovely Chinese lanterns in the garden! And your Damon crawled into the goldfish pond and Lawrence fished him out!"

"Damon lands in Southampton the end of this week. He has been traveling in Europe. We made him promise to cable, but he's so casual. Tom and I are thankful that he will be going straight down to Tom's aunt in Devonshire. They've taken a house there for the year round, did you know? The rent is frightful . . . but a lovely place."

"Sixteen, did you say? A prodigy, of course. And so disgustingly good-looking!"

"*Everything* marked down at Hollander's in Magnolia. All week. Don't miss it."

"Listen, Barto, that son of yours will go far. He's collected five bucks this afternoon, to my certain knowledge!"

Patrice thought: What is the matter with me that after ten minutes of this I have this terrible sense of ennui? It never happened when she was alone, or with Adam, or with just the family. It took a group like this one to bring it on—a feeling of lostness, of exhaustion bordering on despair.

Barto spied her from a distance and immediately started in her direction. Somehow he managed to carry an ordinary water tumbler in one hand and a cocktail glass in the other.

"Greetings, little wallflower!" He stood before her, smiling. "Take your choice of beverages. Extreme Unction, which means gin and orange, or plain ginger ale."

Patrice chose the ginger ale. His glance picked up the beryl she was wearing, and he raised his cocktail glass in salute. "To your health, my dear." And in a lower voice: "Tell me, is Adam happy at the boatyard?"

"Quite happy, I think, Barto." He looked at her speculatively for a moment. "It's not the answer, you know," he said. "Just a stopgap. He will have to look for something better."

273

Suddenly Daisy's voice soared above the others: "Caroline has given us the most divine Chinese Medallion tea set! I adore Chinese Medallion!"

Patrice saw her for the first time this afternoon, dressed in a pale silk which exactly matched her eyes. She was standing before the fireplace, arm in arm with Lawrence Redditch. She had a luminous, excited look, and instinctively Patrice glanced round in search of Adam and saw him making his unhurried way toward Daisy.

Barto, following Patrice's gaze, said gently: "You look lovely yourself, kid. You should always wear dark green, and beryls."

"Should I? Isn't green supposed to be the color of jealousy?"

"It's a nice dress anyway. New?"

"Adam bought it for me. And he bought me a typewriter. Thanks to the job you gave him!"

"Don't say I gave it to him. He applied for it and got it as anyone might have. And now that you have a typewriter to play with perhaps you won't feel at such loose ends."

Patrice glanced at him suspiciously. "Did you put Adam up to giving me the typewriter?"

"My dear girl!" Barto's laugh was almost convincing.

"Well," said Patrice, "it's not like him to give me presents. Of course, he hasn't been able to afford to, until now."

Caroline joined them. A new dress in her favorite color, red, added to her ebullient appearance. She addressed herself to Patrice:

"Happy, dear?"

"Very, thank you."

"Me, too. Here I am, losing my very best friend in all the world, but I've gained a sister-in-law. I can't complain."

She put out a pretty, plump, connoisseur's hand and touched the beryl pendant. "It's lovely. And do you know something? Barto never even thought of giving Daisy a present, though she's an old, old friend."

"Your age exactly if I remember correctly," Barto murmured.

"You remember everything correctly when you want to," said Caroline. She turned to Patrice. "Know what? I thought he'd give them a check. Daisy hasn't much ready cash of her own and she won't have until that old fart of a father of hers kicks off."

"You're so refined." Barto complimented her over the top of his

274

glass. "So elegant in your language. Where do you get it? I mean from which side of the family, the Bannisters or the Browns?"

Caroline gave a small shriek of laughter, masking her rage. She must, Patrice thought in dismay, have been spoiling for this moment for some time. "Here's Daisy, my oldest and best friend, getting married, and you'd think the least we could do would be to give her something really worthwhile. I mean practical. And what could be more practical than money?"

Barto agreed cheerfully: "There *is* nothing more practical than money. But vulgar, don't you think? Commonplace, actually."

He signaled a passing waiter, placed his empty glass on the tray and helped himself to a full one. He said in a conversational tone: "It was because I did not want to appear vulgar in your eyes, or in Daisy's, that I decided on something more delicate than a mere gift of filthy lucre. I decided on giving them this party—the whole works, including the limousine which I've hired to drive them to Boston afterward."

Caroline looked murderous. She said slowly: "The party was my idea; so was the limousine . . . as soon as I realized that you had no intention of doing anything about a proper wedding present."

"What about that Chinese Medallion? I call that proper enough. I saw the price tag."

"You dare to talk about vulgarity!" She controlled herself with difficulty. "What about the champagne? After all the trouble and risk Hal Johnson has gone to to get it, are you going to pony up or aren't you?"

Barto smiled genially. "I aren't."

The crimson deepened in Caroline's cheeks. She gasped: "Barto! You can't renege on the champagne. Not after Hal—"

"Who's reneging? *I* didn't ask Hal Johnson to get the stuff."

"All right, so I did. But it was Hal who took all the trouble, who risked getting pinched and losing his boat and everything. Barto, please!"

Barto took a long deliberate sip from his glass. Then he looked at his wife. "Tell me, has Hal Johnson given Daisy and Lawrence a wedding present?"

"Barto! You're not suggesting . . ."

"Why not? I'd say that three hundred bucks of good fizz would make an eminently suitable present, under the circumstances. And that's not taking account of the gas for his engine and the wear and tear on his nerves. And he probably had to dish out something to the cops, too. But then, Hal Johnson can afford it. He can probably afford it a damn sight better than I can."

Caroline's lips froze in a small, catlike smile. "So you're determined to humiliate me? You are going to force me to go to Hal and tell him that we are not going to pay for the champagne after all? When I asked him specially—"

"He did it for you," Barto interposed calmly. "To please and oblige you. I'm sure he'd be delighted to round out the picture by paying for it."

Caroline turned away and flashed a brilliant smile round the room. Watching her, no one would have suspected the passion which shook her from head to foot. She said in a flat, soft voice: "I see it all now. You're jealous. You're rotten with jealousy all the way through."

She walked away and Patrice met Barto's gaze. He smiled. "Don't look so tragic, Patrice!"

"But it is tragic. You're so kind to me, to Adam ... why not be kind to Caroline?"

More guests had arrived and the big room seemed crushingly filled. Barto adjusted his crutches and moved closer to Patrice. "Listen," he said quietly. "Let me tell you something so you won't take these little scenes so much to heart. They are a substitute merely. A substitute."

She asked reluctantly: "A substitute?"

"For everything a husband and wife normally share."

A young woman whom Patrice vaguely recalled as having a talent for whistling the latest musical tunes now moved through the crowd and greeted Patrice: "Patty Bannister! Isn't this wonderful—*two* brides!"

Her glance skidded observantly over Patrice's figure. "Must be catching! Who's to be next, I wonder?"

She melted away and Barto watched Patrice frantically searching her memory for a name to attach to the speaker. "That's Betty Newhouse, Pinky Pitman's latest girl. She's pinning her hopes on Pinky's making her our next bride, but not if his parents have anything to say about it."

Daisy's voice again: "Do look at what Uncle Wilbur has brought us!

276

These lovely silver ashtrays, and engraved with the Prentice and Redditch coats of arms! Darling Uncle Wilbur, how did you *know* we needed ashtrays?"

"Kiss me!" commanded Mr. Bannister. "I resent parting with you, my dear child. It's like losing my Caroline over again."

Lawrence Redditch's black glance flitted from face to face as he stood, smiling nervously, arm in arm with his wife. For a second, across the crowded room, Daisy's eyes sought Patrice's in a glance like a steel dart. Then Patrice saw Adam appear at Daisy's side, saw her clasp two pale arms round his neck and draw his dark head down to her blond one as she kissed him. For the first time? For the last?

Hal Johnson's accordion began to bleat the first nostalgic strains of a Strauss waltz and the couples nearest Patrice swayed as best they could to the rhythm. Adam took Daisy in his arms and their bodies moved together beautifully in that constricted area. Patrice had a glimpse of Mr. Bannister clasping the senior Mrs. Redditch to his breast, and of Mrs. Bannister gyrating sedately in the embrace of the older Mr. Redditch.

Barto looked at Patrice. "How I wish I could ask you to dance!"

Before Patrice could speak a voice inquired suddenly at her elbow: "May I have the pleasure?" and she stared into a small bearded face and a pair of gleaming spectacles. She recognized Daisy's father, Mr. Charles Prentice.

"You are Adam's wife," he murmured as he put an arm round her waist and grasped her wrist, an empty tumbler still clutched in her hand. "I've been so busy that I have missed you at all these parties. But people have been telling me how charming you are. No one, of course, has bothered to introduce us. This casualness in social behavior is typically Hyperborean, and we are nothing if not Hyperboreans, taking as we do everything for granted! Are you familiar with the legend of the Hyperboreans?"

Patrice shouted abjectly that she was not.

"A mythical race, worshipers of Apollo. We should have stuck to Apollo instead of taking up with all this Episcopal cant, or Unitarian bathos. Imagine passing up a golden and gracious way of life for a front pew at funerals, or dreary arguments on the singularity of an equally dreary god!"

"But," objected Patrice, into his good ear, "you just said that the

277

Hyper—the Hypers were a mythical race!"

"So they were, so they were. And so are we, so are we, or we shall be, a thousand years from now!"

Was he joking? He seemed serious enough. "So you are charming, I'm told. It is the correct thing to say about brides—that they are charming. Dear me, this is rather impossible, isn't it?"

They circled a foot or two of space, and Patrice, holding her glass on high—there seemed nothing else she could do with it—fancied that she must look rather like the Statue of Liberty being towed from her foundations by a very small tug.

"You know my daughter, of course," Mr. Prentice went on, as Patrice, her face close to his, counted the crumbs of several digestive biscuits in his beard. "And my son-in-law Lawrence? Great relief to me to have my child married. Lawrence is just what the doctor ordered."

"You think perhaps he is a Hyper—Hyper, too?"

Mr. Prentice laughed. He had finely pointed teeth, like a fox. "Wouldn't surprise me if he was Apollo himself, under that awful suit he's wearing. So kind of Caroline and Barto to give them this party. I'm no good at these things. Quite an effort for me to leave my work and get down here. But I had to, of course. One's only child!"

Patrice inquired politely what had happened to Judy.

"Judy?" echoed Mr. Prentice, blinking.

"Your dog Judy."

"She's going to have puppies. There is an old collie up the street ... but as I keep telling Daisy, Judy is *her* responsibility, not mine."

He backed masterfully into another couple and all exchanged genial apologies. "Tell me," said Mr. Prentice, "do you miss India?"

Patrice replied noncommittally. He held her close to his breast, in order to hear better, and she felt horribly uncomfortable. It seemed indecent for her, in her condition, to be in the arms of this musty little man who had obviously taken her on at the dictate of some vestigial sense of tribal duty.

She longed to tell him that she was tired and would like to sit down, but his birdlike agility kept her helplessly whirling in a press of bodies, and feet which trod on hers, amid faces which smiled identical smiles in a steady gale of identical laughter.

"Of course," continued Mr. Prentice relentlessly, "you have read the Abbé Dubois's great book on Hindu manners and customs. A classic on the life of the Orient. I have been told that conditions are not very much changed from the Abbé's time. What would be your opinion?"

Patrice, who had never heard of the Abbé Dubois, improvised heroically, hoping that her words might be drowned in the babel. Mr. Prentice, she realized, was doing his best to be courtly and entertaining, trying to make her feel that he considered her a well-educated, sober young woman who must surely have had some access, however slight, to his own boundless erudition.

"Why," he murmured presently in a plaintive voice, "they feel they must dance at this stage of the game . . . even before the champagne . . . but I suppose that when in Rome . . ."

He took a firmer grip of her waist and in a sudden access of protectiveness crushed her against his breast so that his beard went into her eyes, blinding her. Where was Adam? Why didn't he come and rescue her? Giddy and half-suffocated, she heard the voice of Mr. Edwards, Damon's father: "Harding is dead. Had you heard?"

"Harding?" repeated another, unknown voice.

"The President."

"Really?"

"No great loss. Have another drink?"

The President of the United States was dead. Patrice waited for some signal that would bring the festivities to a fitting pause, for an authoritative voice to impose silence, a respectful gravity. But the man who had spoken of the President's death drifted away in search of another drink. More guests arrived, and Daisy's voice trilled above the noise: "How heavenly! How *did* you know that I've always pined for Italian lace doilies?"

Clutched against Mr. Prentice's breast, Patrice gasped that perhaps they had better stop dancing. "The President is dead!"

"Oh, well," said Mr. Prentice as, waltzing in the German fashion with his hand holding hers high in the air, he whirled her round and round.

Patrice heard her father-in-law say: "Old Warren? Are you sure?"

"Heard it on the train coming down. Where is Barto with that gin?"

Why don't they stop, wondered Patrice in desperation. The President of their country is dead. Why don't they do something, say something solemn and fitting to so portentous an event? If it had been the King of England who had died, or the Viceroy of India!

The waltz had petered out and Hal Johnson was shouting hoarsely: "Barto! The orchestra craves refreshment. Bring on the cupbearers, damn it!"

Mr. Prentice released Patrice with a formal little bow which almost threw him on his face as someone backed into him. "Charming! So happy for you and Adam... known him all his life. Must get Caroline and Dorothea to bring you up for a cup of tea one of these days. Show you my rare edition of the Bhagavad-Gita and an autographed copy of Tagore...."

Patrice thanked him and escaped upstairs to Caroline's bedroom. The windows were open and she breathed the cool salt air. Sounds from downstairs beat against the floor, but she felt blissfully apart from it all. She felt the child stir within her, and she pictured it curled up like an anchovy, its sex already determined, its fists clenched, as someone had once told her the hands of the unborn are always clenched, on its individual fate.

She felt a wave of tenderness for this being compounded of herself and Adam, and for the first time in her life she thought she understood the significance of family continuity. No matter what happened to Barto and Caroline they would have had Timmy. No matter what happened to Adam and herself their love would have brought forth this separate, living, mysterious creature.

Downstairs the accordion burst into one strain which she had no difficulty recognizing: "Tipperary." Then she heard quick, light footsteps on the stairs and turned from the window to find herself facing Daisy. As their eyes met Patrice went toward her, holding out her hand. "Daisy, I haven't had a decent chance to wish you happiness. I do, with all my heart!"

She had not intended to sound effusive, but the mood of tenderness was still with her, seeking expression.

"Do you now?" said Daisy. She walked to the big bed and stared at Patrice. Her eyes were cool, almost leeched of their color, like flowers in the sun. Between her lips, so pink that they never needed painting, her teeth showed white and slightly pointed—the only detail in which she in the least resembled her father.

280

"Do you really wish me happiness?" she asked, ignoring the hand Patrice held toward her.

"Of course. Why shouldn't I?"

Downstairs, "Tipperary" flowed inevitably into the strains of "Madelon." Patrice could not tear her gaze from Daisy's face with its little vulpine smile. It must, Patrice reflected, have been from her mother that she inherited that flawless skin, those upstanding, shameless breasts. No wonder Lawrence Redditch came home again and again. Simple, strong, intense, despising the others, he returned because of Daisy. Daisy, always there in that house on Brattle Street—like a lantern set in a dark window to light her sailor home.

Now Daisy seated herself at the foot of the bed and wrapped her arms round one of the posters, leaning her head against the wood.

"Why did you come here?" She shot the question at Patrice. "Why, with the whole world to choose from, did you come here?"

"You mean, why did I come here today, to this house?"

"I don't mean to this house. I mean *here,* into our lives. You could just as easily have stayed away."

"I don't know what you are driving at," Patrice told her, though she had a pretty good idea.

"Why did you marry Adam? That's what I would really like to know. Yes, I really would!"

Patrice thought swiftly: She hates me. And a further thought occurred to her: That hatred of the first water, as this obviously was, might well have something in common with first love, with all the vulnerability of first love, and all its ruthlessness.

She felt curiously elated as she stood facing Daisy, with her back to the window. "I married Adam for the same reason you probably married Lawrence today. Is there something so very strange about that?"

"I think there might be something strange. After all, Lawrence has always loved me, whereas Adam ..." She caught her lower lip in her teeth and her face had a sudden distorted look. She went on with a rush: "Adam has never loved anybody. He is not the kind that loves. But he always liked *me.* I was closer to him than to anyone else in the world, and he to me. We could have become closer. Then you had to come and spoil it all."

Patrice stared at her. "If I felt the way you feel I don't think I'd go around telling people about it. At any rate not after I'd gone and married someone else!"

"Oh, you wouldn't? You'd be too proud, I suppose. Well, what about Barto? He seemed to be pretty deeply in your confidence, to judge by what I saw of the pair of you in Salem the other day!"

Without waiting for Patrice to speak, Daisy flashed out: "In broad daylight on a public street! In his arms! What do you suppose poor Adam would have thought of that?"

Patrice reflected: If she could have overheard young Damon that morning on the beach! But Barto of all people . . . She said coolly: "You're talking rot. I went to Salem because Barto had an errand there, and wanted company."

"I'm sure of that," Daisy said, with a laugh. "And easy pickings for both of you, I'd say, crutches or no crutches!"

Patrice seethed with sudden anger. "Adam told me you were a fool. He couldn't begin to guess how right he was."

"You can't make mischief between Adam and me," Daisy assured her, rising abruptly to her feet. "He and I know each other too well. We've known each other all our lives, better than you will ever know him, or he you. We are the same kind of people, whereas you . . . who knows anything about you, anyway?"

"You must be drunk," Patrice said slowly. "Drunk, or mad."

"I don't drink, and I'm not mad. I am not answering for your peculiarities, but I must say I wouldn't have expected such behavior from Barto. At any rate not when you were carrying another man's child."

Patrice's fury had spent itself; so, it seemed, had her sense of humor. Now she felt that she might be sick. Wind from the sea blew the curtains, and downstairs Hal Johnson had embarked daringly on the Marseillaise.

"The queer thing about you," said Daisy as she moved in a leisurely way toward the door, "is that you look so damned innocent."

"I am innocent," said Patrice.

"Poor Adam," Daisy said softly. "Poor old Adam! Too decent, too clean, too wrapped up in his birds and his bees. And poor Caroline, too."

"Hadn't we better go downstairs?" Patrice suggested. "They'll be wondering."

282

"I'm going. But since you're here you might as well wait for Barto. It would be a pity to disappoint him."

Wait for Barto. So she thinks I came up here for a tryst?

Adam's voice reached them from the foot of the stairs: "Patrice!"

Daisy smiled at Patrice. "Don't worry," she said. "I am not going to wreck Adam's peace of mind by warning him about something he will no doubt find out for himself sooner or later."

She left the room and Patrice went to the bed and sank upon it. thankful for the breeze from the window, and hoping that Adam would come up the stairs and sit beside her and take her hand. Take her in his arms, hold her, tell her that all was well, that he loved her. But he did not come, and she lay for some time watching through half-closed eyes the Tree of Life curtains billowing gaily into the room.

21

*F*or a long time after Caroline's party, Patrice lay wide awake in her bed, unable to sleep, her mind whirling. Following the little scene with Daisy she had come downstairs and recklessly consumed two glasses of Hal Johnson's champagne. It had gone straight to her head, and the last she remembered was a vision of Daisy and Lawrence Redditch waving good-bye from the limousine that was to take them to Boston. Timmy was gleefully throwing rice and confetti, and Hal Johnson's accordion was giving forth the opening bar of *Lohengrin's* Wedding March in tireless repetition.

There had been a drumming in Patrice's ears, then she felt Adam's hand on her elbow, and heard his voice: "Darling, you look ghastly!"

Hours later she had awakened in the friendly gloom of their own bedroom, and now she lay listening to Adam's quiet breathing in the bed next to hers. Her head began to clear and she picked bits of confetti out of her hair. The room was not really in darkness, for Adam had fallen asleep with the bed light burning, a book lying open on his chest. Patrice experienced a sense of stolen luxury, of being alone and unobserved, something that happened to her rarely in this familial household. Turning on her elbow, she studied Adam's unconscious profile, seeking some clue to his dreams, to a nature which after

284

nearly four months of marriage continued to elude her.

He had taken the job at the boatyard and every morning at eight-thirty he left the house and walked down to the harbor, returning late in the afternoon. He seemed contented enough with his work though he said little about it, and there were days when it seemed to Patrice as if he moved in a world entirely his own, only partly aware of her existence. It occurred to her that he seemed to be waiting, with an air of fixed detachment, for something to happen. But what? She was often tempted to shoot the question at him without warning, to jar him into awareness; but his mood began subtly to infect her, adding to her ennui. If his parents and Caroline noticed anything they were careful not to allude to it in her hearing, and she was too shy and too loyal to Adam to ask them for advice and enlightenment.

He was earning very little money, but that did not appear to trouble him, nor did his beholden state. Casting back in her memory to that evening when he had unburdened himself to her on the subject of his youthful frustrations, Patrice wondered now at this torpid acceptance of his parents' bounty and the day-to-day contiguity of this existence. She was beginning to feel her own position as a dependent, to feel it keenly and with increasing embarrassment.

The Bannisters and Caroline were generosity itself, showering her with gifts of clothing and the nameless odds and ends in which she was herself woefully deficient. And exuberant preparations were under way to provide a layette for the baby. Generous they were—as the books say—to a fault; tactful in their fashion. Yet they lacked that sixth sense which makes the giving of gifts a delight and not a duty.

Patrice's gratitude, her growing realization of obligations she could never expect to repay, induced a kind of paralysis, rendering her inarticulate. Intercepting an occasional injured glance between the donors—what! didn't she care for what they had just gone out of their way to procure for her, and at some expense?—she began to feel like Lear's tongue-tied daughter, and even imagined that she read in their eyes Lear's own myopic query: "So young, and so untender?"

When Adam was not at the boatyard he took long walks, in which she sometimes joined him, or spent his spare time reading in the bedroom, coming downstairs only when there were visitors and then only when his mother begged him to.

His air of withdrawal was becoming more and more marked. A few days before Caroline's party for Daisy, when the family jabber of anticipation was at its height, Adam had remarked offhandedly that he had decided not to go. "I loathe Caroline's mobs, and anyway there'll be so many that my presence or absence wouldn't make the slightest difference."

Mrs. Bannister had been openly distressed and Mr. Bannister openly angry. "Daisy and Lawrence are our lifelong friends. Daisy particularly. Her feelings would be terribly hurt."

"Nonsense," said Adam. Opposed, he could look mutinous, like a small boy.

Mr. Bannister interrupted in a voice edged with temper: "You are going to Caroline's party. I won't take no, do you understand, Adam?"

Patrice was appalled as she glanced from one suddenly, incomprehensibly childish face to the other. Adam had said no more but had retired upstairs to the bedroom and slammed the door.

But he had gone to Caroline's party nevertheless, and had even appeared to enjoy himself in his casual fashion. Now Patrice thought: I wonder whether Daisy found a moment to spill the beans to him? *Spill the beans.* What beans? There had been no beans to spill. Just that silly incident in which she and Barto had apparently been observed by Daisy when they had parked for a moment on the street in Salem. But if Daisy had spoken of it to Adam he would surely have taxed me with it, Patrice mused. And surely he would not be sleeping as soundly as he was at this moment, his face relaxed and youthful as it rarely was awake. Absurd as the whole thing is, I should tell him about it myself, she thought. I should explain that I had gone to Salem with Barto to send a telegram because I was upset and angry after that ridiculous quarrel over his spearing grubbies. But here Patrice pulled herself up short. Was it not something else that had driven her to running away that day? Was it not because of her encounter with young Damon Edwards on the beach after Adam had left her? Wasn't it the truth that she had been strangely frightened, as if by some portent in a dream?

I should make a clean breast of all this nonsense, for nonsense it is. We love each other, we are not children, and Adam would be the first to laugh at Daisy's exhibition of jealous spite. But would he? Patrice

286

stirred restlessly under the bedcovers, remembering the little tableau vivant between Adam and his parents when he announced that he would not attend Caroline's party for the happy pair. Patrice's mind shied from the implications of the scene as it was followed, almost immediately, by a recollection of another scene, years ago in the garden of that house in the hills, where she had ridden on a bazaar hack to visit Edna Meadows and her mother. They were grown-up people and she had gone to them for help and comfort and they had not been able to give it. How grown up did one have to be? Patrice asked herself now in the silent, lamplit room with Adam asleep in the next bed. How grown up did one have to be not to behave like a child?

She heard clocks striking all over the house: the big clock with its gold eagle in the hall downstairs, the French clock in the parlor, the ormolu clock in the dining room, the ugly wooden clock in the kitchen, and lastly the pretty silver clock in a pigskin case—a wedding present from Daisy—on the mantel of this room.

The clocks struck the hour in their individual voices with a single stroke: One. Daisy would be in bed with Lawrence and, happy at last, she would have recovered from her malaise about Adam. And with this thought of Daisy in her mind Patrice at last fell asleep.

The morning's routine took its customary possession of the staid household. It was Saturday and Adam had gone to Ipswich with Timmy Williams to look at birds. Mr. Bannister received a telephone call which necessitated his immediate presence in his office in Boston, and Mrs. Bannister drove him to the station to take his train, after which she proceeded to Caroline's house for that indispensable hour of gossip during which both retraced, in luxurious detail and tireless repetition, the events of the day before.

Alone in the house, Patrice turned to her new acquisition, the typewriter, to compose her weekly letter to Clem.

> Already I feel that I have been here most of my life. I suppose it's due to the feeling of habit. Day after day the same things happen. We go through the same motions, say the same things, plan to do tomorrow what we did yesterday or the day before. Even when something important happens, like the death of the President of the United States, no one here seemed to be especially moved. Of course, they were excited about a wedding in the family and so there wasn't much emotion left

287

over for anything else. I had thought, this morning, that there might be something new in the wind, that something had really *happened,* when Mr. Bannister suddenly announced in a peculiar voice that he had to leave for his office at once, though most offices close on Saturday and his secretary would not be there. Mrs. Bannister kept asking him if it was something serious, whether anyone had died or become ill. You see, Mr. B. is a lawyer and takes care of a number of his friends' affairs, their wills and so on. But Mr. B. was quite snappish with Mrs. B.'s questioning him and muttered something about "ethics" and "confidence" as he bustled out of the house. So I suppose we never will know what it is all about. What a pity!

Today is one of those pewter-colored days which for some reason make me homesick. There's not a breath of wind, and looking out of my window I can see a few flags hanging at half mast on some of the moored yachts. Even the flags look as if they didn't care!

Caroline, coming into her mother's house later that afternoon, shouted up the staircase: "Hi, stay-at-home! Where are you?"

Patrice's heaven-sent solitude was over. She went downstairs to the hall, where Caroline waited. "Ma has gone to call on the Edwardses, then she's meeting Pop's train. What do you say you and I have a quick drink on the porch before they all get home?"

The maid brought them a tray on the porch and as Caroline mixed herself a cocktail she said with revived enthusiasm: "Lovely party yesterday, wasn't it?"

"Lovely," Patrice agreed, politely determined not to betray her surfeit with a subject which had already been discussed ad nauseam. Caroline went on cheerfully: Hadn't Daisy looked just too beautiful for words? And even Lawrence had seemed rather more civilized than usual. What had Patrice thought of the refreshments? It was the first time she—Caroline—had served coquilles Saint Jacques at a party, and if she did say who perhaps should not, it had been a great success. "I shudder to think of Benson and Robbins' bill for the catering, but what the hell! Of course, I'm still in a horrible fix about that champagne. Barto simply won't come across, insists that it is up to Hal Johnson."

She glanced at Patrice. "Don't you think it's mean of Barto? It isn't as if he couldn't afford it. Honestly, I could murder him at times!"

Patrice stayed uncomfortably silent. When Caroline offered her a cocktail she asked for ginger ale instead. Caroline shrugged. "Of course. Nora will bring you a bottle. But don't tell me you intend to

288

drink that nasty stuff for the rest of your life! You've simply got to get used to our booze, you know."

"Perhaps after I've had the baby," Patrice said apologetically. Caroline's brusqueness made her uneasy. "It's just, you see, that I'm not used to booze. We never had it at home. I mean, the men did, of course, but not the ladies."

"Really?" Caroline could not have cared less. "You poor mite! What did you do for fun, I wonder?" She went on breathlessly: "The truth is Barto's green with jealousy over Hal Johnson. I realize that Hal isn't the most refined type in the world. But he did go to Yale if not to Harvard, and he's been very successful in business." She gave her tough little laugh. "You'd think from the way Barto acts that it was *he* that'd had all the social advantages. I know Ma and Pop don't care for Hal either. Snobs, all of them." She drank thirstily and Patrice thought: A bit early to get started.

Caroline exploded anew: "And I could really have killed Charles Prentice! Did you know that when he was dancing with Ma he backed into a Tang horse on the bookcase and smashed it to bits? Didn't offer to pay for it, even! I called Yamanaka in Boston this morning, and they told me it would cost all outdoors to have the horse repaired even if it could be done, which they doubted." Her face took on a hard, strained expression. "How I detest careless, clumsy people! When I think of what Daisy has had to put up with all these years!"

During a pause which followed, Caroline finished her cocktail and poured herself another. She said abruptly: "I'm going to ask you to do me a great favor. Will you, Patrice?"

Patrice took refuge in banter. "Depends!"

Caroline stared at her. "You know of course that Barto is very fond of you, don't you?"

When Patrice hesitated she went on impatiently: "Come on! He's crazy about you. Oh, don't get me wrong, I'm not suggesting anything. He just admires you. He's told me so. Anyway, I'm pretty darn sure he would do just about anything for you if you were to ask him."

"Barto has been very kind," Patrice murmured. "So have you, Caroline."

"Shucks! Look. What I want to ask of you is this. Go to Barto; make it appear to be of your own accord. . . . You shouldn't have any difficulty because he trusts you. Anyway, when you get a chance—next time you see him—sort of manage to bring up the subject of Hal Johnson and the champagne. Try to explain what a hell of a fix I'm in. . . ."

Her voice took on a note of urgency: "Listen, Pat. You have no idea what an embarrassing position this silly business puts me in. I *asked* Hal to get the fizz. You know about our stupid prohibition laws. It's a felony to bootleg liquor. I had no right even to suggest such a thing to Hal. He's a good friend, generous and endlessly obliging. And of course he wouldn't dream of suggesting that I reimburse him. It's true, he could have got the stuff through the usual channels, through his bootlegger, or I could have. But I would have had to pay cash and I just didn't have the money handy. And then very foolishly, because I wanted to do something unusual for Daisy, I took Hal up on it when he half jokingly suggested that he'd take his yacht and sail out to where the rumrunners wait for people to come to them.

"It meant all kinds of preliminary spy work to make sure that the *Heron* wouldn't be spotted by revenue men. And although Hal hasn't mentioned this I know damned well he had to bribe people heavily, right and left, to make the trip a success. I had every intention of paying him back. In fact I swore to him that we wouldn't accept it unless he let us pay."

Caroline was running out of steam, her eyes moist with emotion. "Hal just waved it all aside. He has that manner, you know, but he means it. If Barto and I were hard up it would be a different matter. But Hal knows Barto has scads, and now he probably thinks we're trying to put something over. It makes me sick."

"Have you," Patrice inquired diffidently, "mentioned this to your mother?"

"God, no! If there's one feeling she shares with Barto it's this dislike of Hal Johnson. She'd have a fit if she thought I'd obligated myself to him in any way. Oh, she'd come across, I know. But I'd rather die than have to live with a double cloud of disapproval hanging over me—Ma's and Barto's. And she'd be sure to tell Pop, and that'd make three!"

Patrice wondered unhappily how she should be expected to cope with this tempest in a teapot. She had an instinctive revulsion against doing what Caroline asked, but before she could think of something to say Caroline suddenly put her cards on the table.

"You know why Barto is doing this? Because he wants to cheapen me in Hal Johnson's eyes. Hal is easygoing and naïve in many ways, but like many rich men he lives in constant fear that people are going to try and take advantage of him. If anyone understands this Barto does, and he knows that if Hal were to believe that *I* had tried to use him, it might be the end of our friendship."

Caroline leaned back in her chair and stared at Patrice with tragic eyes. When at last Patrice spoke it was in a meditative voice, almost as though she were talking to herself: "Do you love Barto, Caroline?"

Caroline reddened. "What the hell has that got to do with it?"

Koko's sudden barking broke an uncomfortable spell as Adam and Barto appeared round a corner of the house below the porch. Caroline gulped down her second cocktail and bestowed her dainty, cat-like smile on Patrice. "Let's skip it for now," she murmured, and stretched her plump arms negligently behind her head. The distraught manner had vanished; she was the old Caroline, indolent, sexy.

Adam came up the stairs and kissed Patrice. "I stopped by Barto's to drop Timmy, and Barto drove me over."

Sun and exercise had brought a glow to his face. He looked strong, confident, and Patrice felt a rush of love and desire toward him. Perhaps sensing it, he smiled into her eyes, then went to the table and poured himself a drink. Barto limped to a chair and propped his crutches beside him. "Adam's got his young nephew all enthused about bird life," he observed. "Seems that a pair of binoculars now goes on the birthday list." His extraordinary eyes rested fleetingly on Patrice. "Why so solemn, little one?"

"It's that nasty pop she drinks," Caroline said. "I've just been telling her she's got to learn to like honest booze if she expects to enjoy life in these United States."

Patrice, obsessed with thoughts of Hal Johnson and the champagne and of her expected role in the imbroglio, smiled feebly, and at that moment Mr. and Mrs. Bannister emerged from the parlor door and Mrs. Bannister sank with a kind of deflated majesty into the nearest chair while her husband, gathering the old spaniel in his arms, sank into another. Both wore the startled, incredulous expressions of people who have just escaped annihilation under the wheels of a train.

291

Both, as though uttering an incantation, brought forth the single word "Daisy!"

Caroline stared at her parents. "What about Daisy?"

Mrs. Bannister removed a hatpin from her hat and jabbed it savagely into the ancient straw. "Day-sie," she repeated with deliberation, "*Daysie* has left Lawrence Redditch!"

"Ma!" Caroline cried. "You're crazy!"

"Your mother is telling the truth," pronounced Mr. Bannister in sepulchral tones. "The poor child, after twenty-four hours of marriage! But we should have guessed. What can you expect of a man like Lawrence Redditch?"

Adam turned on his father. "Do stop beating about the bush and tell us what happened, Pop!"

Mr. Bannister, pursuing an errant tick through Koko's matted curls, assumed an air of impenetrable reserve.

"Oh, for God's sake, Pop!" wailed Caroline.

Mrs. Bannister spoke up in a weary voice: "There's no use asking your father for details. He won't even tell *me*. All he has said on the way home from the train just now is that Daisy called him first thing this morning from New York and begged him to meet her at his office at the earliest possible moment. She arrived on the two o'clock from New York and came to your father's office in a state of collapse. It seems she couldn't even bring herself to go to her own father. Oh, Wilbur, for heaven's sake surely you can tell us *something!*"

"Either you do," Caroline declared menacingly, "or I'll go straight to the telephone and call Charles Prentice's house myself."

"She went there only because she had nowhere else to hide her head," Mrs. Bannister explained, tears in her eyes. "The poor child! *Wilbur,* you simply must tell us *something.*"

Thus beset, and after a further minute or two of portentous silence, Wilbur Bannister began: "Daisy is going to file suit for divorce against Lawrence. As her own and her father's friend, one who has known her since she was born and whom she knows she can trust, she has begged me to act as her legal counsel. Beyond that I am not at liberty to disclose anything."

"But how can you act as her legal counsel?" demanded Adam. "You're a friend of the Redditches too, aren't you? How will they take this?"

292

Mr. Bannister glanced sharply at him and snapped: "Are you presuming to tell me what I should do and what I should not?"

Mrs. Bannister interposed: "Don't be silly, Wilbur. Adam is only saying what we are all thinking. What *do* you intend to do about the Redditches? They are just as close to us as Daisy and her father. I'm afraid this will kill poor old Reddy."

"If Reddy was aware of his son's nature and did nothing to prevent his ruining the life of a lovely innocent girl, he deserves to suffer. If he was not aware, then he's a fool and deserves what he gets. That's all I have to say on the matter."

But Caroline was far from done. "You can at least," she declared, "give us some hint of Daisy's state of mind now. Didn't she say she would like to see me? Surely she'd want me to call her up!"

"As I told you, she's with her father at the moment, but how long she proposes to stay with him I don't know. I have advised her to go into seclusion for a few weeks, or until she has recovered somewhat from the shock."

"What shock?" stormed Caroline. "What did Lawrence Redditch *do* to her? What could he have done in such a short time? Pop, for the love of Pete!"

Patrice glanced at Barto, who wore the expression of a man whose thoughts are far away. Caroline, near tears, went on: "And why didn't Daisy send for *me?* Aren't I the best friend she's got?"

"My dear child!" Mr. Bannister admonished her sternly. "You must understand that this situation demands something more than a mere exchange of girlish confidences."

"But you might at least," Mrs. Bannister implored him, "give us some idea of the grounds she intends to get her divorce on. It's bound to get into the papers, so we'll know anyway, eventually."

"I shall use every means to ensure that the case is heard in judge's chambers," Mr. Bannister replied, and then: "Now I repeat: I can tell you nothing."

He had once more reckoned without Caroline, who now brought the wiles of childhood to bear upon him. She crossed the floor to his chair and leaned her head against his. "Pop, darling," she whimpered, "did Lawrence . . . could he have beaten, abused Daisy?"

Mr. Bannister heaved a long, quivering sigh. "If you must know, he abused her. Shamefully."

Barto gave a sudden, uncontrollable laugh, at which Mr. Bannister turned on him and, pale with anger, declared that he would not permit so grave a matter to be treated with levity under his roof.

Barto reached for his crutches and maneuvered himself to his feet. "Come on, Caroline. Time for Timmy's supper, isn't it?"

Mrs. Bannister rose to accompany them to the door, and Patrice escaped upstairs to change for dinner. So, she mused, it had all been wasted, the party yesterday. The Tang horse broken to no purpose, Caroline's involvement over the champagne made nonsense; the music, the dancing—all the anticipation, the joyous propulsion into the future—all gone for nothing.

Presently Adam came into the room, closing the door behind him. Meeting her questioning eyes, he shrugged. "They should never have been married, I suppose. Lawrence has always been a rough character, and she was always a fool about sex."

"How can you be a fool about sex? Either you love someone or you don't."

Adam sat on the edge of his bed and began to unlace his boots. "Pop told me something after you and the others had left the porch. He didn't say much, but he mentioned that he had never seen anyone in such an emotional state as Daisy when she appeared in his office. He couldn't trust her to take the trolley out to Cambridge so took her to her father's house in a taxi."

"But can't your father do something to help? Can't Mr. Prentice, or Lawrence's parents, do something?"

"You mean to bring Daisy and Lawrence together again? No. None of them are the kind that would know what to do. Too constipated emotionally."

He looked at her. "I'm going to let you in on something. Barto said I might. The telephone rang in his workshop just after Timmy and I got back from our walk. Someone wanted to talk to Barto particularly. It was Lawrence, calling from New York. He was upset, and begged Barto to do whatever he could to help Daisy, since obviously, Lawrence said, he himself could not. Seems she staged some sort of hysterics on their wedding night. Last night, to be exact! Called Lawrence a filthy pervert and accused him of trying to perpetrate unnatural acts upon her fair white body." Adam's laugh was much like Barto's earlier that afternoon. "I didn't hear the conversation because Lawrence was talking directly to Barto, but I could gather from the tone of his voice at the other end of the wire, and from what Barto answered, that poor Lawrence was shot to pieces by whatever had happened. Anyway, it's all over between him and Daisy. She can have her divorce any time she wants it." Adam pulled off a boot and tossed it on the floor. "According to Barto Lawrence said something else. Daisy is still a virgin, and so far as Lawrence is concerned she'll damn well stay that way!"

Patrice said thoughtfully: "I suppose there are two ways of looking at this: as something funny, or as something sad."

"Or perhaps both," Adam said indifferently. Patrice gazed at him. His skin was bronzed by a fresh tan over the old, his body had the faint sweet smell that was peculiarly his. He never smelled unpleasant no matter how hot the weather or how long he went without a bath. There was always in his skin the freshness of sunlight on new leaves, on new grass. The instinct of possession was strong in Patrice at that moment. She crossed the room and stood beside him where he sat on the bed, and he put his arms around her and laid his head against the rounding globe of her body.

"Adam," she murmured, and pressed his head closer against her. "Adam, don't let's ever get like Daisy and Lawrence. And when I'm really huge and ugly, don't stay away from me, will you?"

He laughed and pulled her down on the bed and as the evening colored the windows Patrice heard the sea endlessly clasping the shore, endlessly letting it go.

22

*T*hanks to Mr. Bannister's legal talents on the scene and possibly behind them, Daisy was granted her divorce with a minimum of publicity and immediately departed for Bermuda, accompanied by Caroline, since it was generally agreed that poor Daisy should not be left to her own devices at such a time. *"Anything,"* Caroline had suggested with sinister emphasis, *"anything* could happen."

"Such as what?" Barto wanted to know.

"She's in a highly nervous state and could do something reckless."

Barto was skeptical. "She's not the type do anything reckless, as I should say she has proved beyond the shadow of a doubt."

Caroline, who had learned of that telephone conversation between Lawrence Redditch and Barto, held her tongue, and Barto smiled. Then with one of his unforeseeable gestures of generosity he dropped a check for two thousand dollars in Caroline's lap. "Run along and have fun in Bermuda. Buy yourself some of those expensive English sweaters and treat Daisy to half a dozen, too."

Caroline stared at the check for a moment, then said in a low voice: "I just wish I had the guts to tear this damn thing up!"

"I wish you had, too," Barto replied lightly. "But it would be out of character. Take care of Daisy. See she doesn't sprain an ankle or get herself engaged again. One good guy punished for nothing is enough."

"Good guy! You still persist in thinking of Lawrence Redditch as a good guy!"

"I do. He just happened to have spent too many years among the kangaroos and it spoiled him for life on Brattle Street, that's all."

Lawrence Redditch had sailed for Australia two days after his disastrous wedding night, and if his parents heard from him they were reserved about it. Both looked thoroughly wilted from the shock, and although Mrs. Bannister made gallant efforts to behave as though nothing had happened, it was grimly evident that something had.

Dr. Redditch made no secret of his belief that Wilbur Bannister had acted with almost as great a recklessness as Daisy herself, and that had he given her the right kind of counsel and urged her to think things over for a week or two, the marriage might have been saved.

For his part Wilbur Bannister expressed himself as amazed and grieved at this distortion of his avuncular role, when all he had tried to do was to meet his moral obligations, in proof of which he could state with truth that he had refused all pecuniary reimbursement for his legal services.

Adam, who shared Barto's feelings toward the affair, remarked privately to Patrice that this altruism on his father's part reminded him of the story of the old lady who offered a small boy twenty-five cents if he would undertake to drown a litter of unwanted kittens. The urchin had responded with enthusiasm: "Do it for nothin', ma'am. Do it for fun!"

"I do hope, dear," Mrs. Bannister appealed to Patrice, some time after the divorce, "I do hope you won't run away with the idea that this sort of thing is a common occurrence with us!" She managed a deprecating little smile. "As a matter of fact, I know of not one single case of divorce among my own old friends." Then, thinking it over: "Of course, there was Adela Prentice, but she was never a friend. One of those weird bookish women, and a suffragette into the bargain. Wilbur simply loathed her."

Patrice said cautiously: "Barto seems to feel that there might be something to be said on Lawrence's side, too."

Mrs. Bannister frowned. "I wouldn't attach too much importance to Barto's opinions, if I were you. He is Caroline's husband, and I am fond of him in spite of his rather noncomformist pretensions. But the fact of the matter is Barto does not have the same values we do. You know his family were all coal miners? Humble, respectable people, I am sure, but . . . Please don't think I'm being snobbish; I'm not! I am merely sticking to facts. I sometimes wonder whether it is not his own background that makes Barto feel he has to take sides with the underdog." She finished in haste: "Or someone he imagines to be the underdog!"

Patrice knew Adam's mother to be essentially sensitive and kind. She was rather better read than most of her friends, and with a nice little sense of humor. Remarks of this nature, such as she had just made in regard to Barto, threw Patrice into a state of confusion and vague hostility. Her own nature was developing along lines of which she was not yet entirely conscious, and her reactions were still apt to be impulsive as when, now, she came to Barto's defense: "I think he would always be fair, and as a matter of fact, Adam shares his feelings in this business of Daisy and Lawrence Redditch."

Mrs. Bannister's frown deepened. "Adam," she said abruptly, "knows no more than Barto about what happened between Daisy and Lawrence."

Patrice stood her ground. "Do any of us know?" she asked.

Mrs. Bannister replied magisterially: "Your father-in-law knows, and that is all *we* need to know!"

Later that day Patrice settled down to her typewriter to write to Clem:

> I sometimes get the feeling that I am living among people who see themselves as "characters," but who very likely wouldn't speak to the author if they were to meet him! I keep missing something, but I can't put my finger on it. They laugh a good deal, but they don't strike me as being truly gay. And they never cry. It is as if they were always a little afraid of something . . . you know? Like children in the dark. I am sure they would be brave if the necessity arose. I can't see any of them flinching in face of physical danger; and I feel that they are quite like Doey in their dislike of *sniveling*. Then why do I have this feeling deep inside me that there is something missing. . . . And when I keep saying "they" I mean it, because they resemble each other so much in the big things that the little things, the little differences, don't really count.

It was August and there were still, hot days when the sea took on a glaze of sunlight and little sailboats stood motionless against the sky. Every afternoon the thud of tennis balls came in through open windows; Mrs. Redditch's little electric coupé crunched on the gravel drive as she drove Dr. Redditch to the station to take his train to Boston, and once in a while she stopped to call on Mrs. Bannister or to take her for a drive. Appearances were being kept up. Lawrence's name was never mentioned, and it was always possible to laugh together good-naturedly at Mr. Prentice, whose treatise on the Arawaks went on and on.

On weekends Adam took Patrice for walks in the countryside or they borrowed Mrs. Bannister's automobile and drove to Ipswich to look at shore birds. But she suffered from a growing disinclination for long walks, and he went without her, leaving her with hours for reading or writing letters on her typewriter. She felt bulky and middle-aged and hated to look at herself in the mirror. All her life she had been lithe, agile, and active, and now she longed for the baby to be born, to return to her original state.

The doctor whom the Bannisters had chosen for her and to whom she reported every two weeks assured her that all was well and that she was "doing fine." He was efficient, matter-of-fact, and impersonal, and Patrice loathed her visits to his office. She loathed the physical examinations, the smell of antiseptic, the brisk manner of the nurse in her cementlike uniform with her puppet smile. As time passed Patrice grew lax in these visits to the doctor and found excuses for missing her appointments or canceling them. No one insisted that she go. Adam was frankly relieved and happy that she should feel so well as to be independent of continuous medical advice and attention, and Mr. and Mrs. Bannister, having provided Patrice with the normal facilities, were content to leave it up to her thereafter.

Caroline and Daisy lingered in Bermuda, whence Caroline wrote lyrically to her mother, describing the charm of the island—so English—and the vast improvement in Daisy's health and state of mind. Another week or two in this enchanted setting and the poor darling would be completely restored to normal and ready to come home.

President Harding had been buried and Mr. Coolidge had taken his place. Things happened, but mostly in the newspapers. Life at Berry's Landing went its urbane way and Patrice began to have difficulty in distinguishing, in retrospect, one day from another. Every morning, except on weekends, Mr. Bannister kissed his wife and his dog au revoir before boarding the eight-forty for Boston. Nothing would induce him to accept a lift in Mrs. Redditch's electric coupé. "What in God's name," he demanded of Mrs. Bannister, "would Isabel and I have to talk about?" "What have you talked about all these years?" snapped Mrs. Bannister, rather testily for her. She was beginning, herself, to feel the strain of trying to keep up these particular appearances, for she missed the unquestioning rapport of her earlier association with the Redditches, both of whom, for all they tried hard, could never quite pretend that nothing had happened.

Temporarily deprived of those early-morning séances at Caroline's bedside, Mrs. Bannister distracted herself by reading aloud to Patrice —she had an odd predilection for Shelley and Keats—and in teaching her how to knit, and giving her lessons in Mah-Jongg. But Patrice, bored and growing heavier by the day, felt increasingly out of sorts. She began to resent Adam's prolonged absences, and she was also beginning seriously to worry about their future.

Although the subject was never mentioned by Mr. and Mrs. Bannister, or by Adam, she thought she detected a developing tension. Who, she asked herself, was going to pay the hospital bills for the baby and herself? When this house was closed at the end of the summer and the Bannisters had returned to Cambridge, what was to become of Adam and herself and the child? She made tentative attempts to tackle Adam, but he was always evasive. "Quit worrying, darling. Things will work out."

Letters from Alice and Clem did not help much, for she could read between the lines: Alice's loneliness, Clem's chronic pecuniary condition.

"I am taking extra pupils for French," Alice wrote. "At night. Two of them are the children of His Highness Nawab Ghulab Hosain. Do you remember him at our Christmas camp, with the Sparkses and Mr. Onions, long ago? These are the children of H.H.'s youngest wife— naughty old man that he is! But it brings in a little extra paisa, which I am putting away in the bank in case I should ever fall ill or have an accident. And teaching helps pass the time. I have never given much thought to time until now, when I find myself without you and Clem. Now time seems endless."

300

And Clem wrote from Spain:

Yesterday I got the sack from the rotten little restaurant where I have been working. I took the job in addition to the guiding because Melissa is pregnant again. Well, I had been building up quite a philosophy on the art of washing dishes in a third-rate hole like the Parnassus, as it is pleased to call itself. You've no idea what this dishwashing job entails. Not only plates and cups and saucers but serving dishes of all shapes and sizes, glasses, cutlery, cookpots. Amazing the number of utensils these bastards feel they've got to dirty in order to enjoy their food! When I think of that farm in Australia where one tin plate had to do for everything! Here the management doesn't give us much to work with in the way of tools. You use your 2ngernails to scrape the grease o1, then slop the muck into buckets which are usually over3owing from the last meal. There were two other chaps besides me—a Frenchman and a young German, named, as you might guess, Pierre and Franz. God knows what they are doing in Spain—we don't ask each other personal questions in this milieu! Neither Pierre nor Franz speaks English. Franz can't speak French and Pierre can't speak German but both have a smattering of Spanish, and I am better at that than they are. I taught them the password to international understanding and goodwill among peoples. Pierre pronounces the word "sheet," and Franz "shid," and it forms—or formed—the basis of friendship between us. But to go back to the job ... when you've scraped the damned plates clean of their *merde* you plunk them into an enormous trough of lukewarm water (they don't know the meaning of hot water in this dive), then plunge up to your elbows with a bit of foul yellow soap and a rag, and scrub and scrub and scrub. When the rag wears out, as it does fast, we improvise.

Franz found that a broken china cup was useful for scraping burnt fat, and Pierre that by letting one of his fingernails grow long like a Tibetan's he could pry into corners. Presently an interesting chemical metamorphosis takes place: what was originally a fairly opaque surface gradually changes. A gray scum rises, embellished with a few peas, a bit of potato peel, orange rinds, a cigar butt. Using the edge of your hand as if it were a saber you slice off this scum into the bucket, or if that is full, as it usually is, onto the floor. Then you go back to scrubbing, scratching, prying, and soon what had appeared to be soap and water churns into a sumptuous brown gravy out of which you dredge the plates one by one and wipe them dry—or try to—on sodden rags the same color as the gravy. Because water is scarce in these parts you are not supposed to throw away this delectable *roux* but to strain and reserve it for next time.

I see I've been writing in the present tense, which, as of yesterday, has for me become the past. Three days ago after the customary gorging which passes for a Spanish luncheon, or *almuerzo,* the three of us were taking a breather in the pantry, and I amused myself and my pals by doing a few sketches with a pencil on the back of an old menu card. I made one sketch of our most important patron and his giraffe of a wife, both in the nude, taking a connubial bath in our dishpan. You know I've always been rather good at caricature, and this was a speaking likeness, if I do say so. It helped lighten the tedium for the three of us before we returned to the stern business of life.

Next day I found myself on the mat before my boss. Seems that that menu had turned up at a table and the person who examined it recognized the subjects, and hilariously passed it around. Inevitably, it came out that I was the gifted artist, and I got the boot. But this means that Melissa doesn't get the extra grub which the doctor insists she must have if she is going to survive this pregnancy, because it seems she's anemic. Patrice, old girl, I hate to ask you . . . and of course I can't ask Alice. But could you possibly spare a bit of cash which I'll pay back when the tourist season gets under way again?

Could she possibly spare a bit of cash! Patrice had not a penny of her own. When she needed postage stamps she was obliged to go to Adam for the change. She now meditated selling or pawning her engagement ring, but gave up the idea, fearing that Adam would be sure to notice its disappearance. She might of course ask her mother-in-law for a small loan—but from this possibility she shrank at once. She and Adam were already under the greatest obligation to his parents. To ask for more was out of the question. There remained Barto. For days Patrice brooded on her dilemma, torn with anxiety for Clem, mortified by her own helplessness.

One afternoon, finding herself alone in the house, she walked through the pleasant little town to Barto's workshop. Barto was busy at his worktable. In dungarees and blue work shirt, his hair rumpled and his face flushed with exertion, he had a relaxed, happy look. She had come frequently to this simple room above the garage, with its windows overlooking the harbor, and, beyond, half a dozen small islands furred with trees. She liked the atmosphere of the workshop, its economy, its space and light. Here was nothing superfluous, no trivia. And she enjoyed watching Barto at work, admiring his nimbleness despite the crutches, the concentration in his eyes and hands. It was because of these visits that she had learned to banish pity and sentimentality and to accept him as a whole person, just as Adam,

302

tramping through the countryside, became in his own fashion a whole person.

Sometimes while Patrice sat in the old chair by the windows, loafing or reading, Barto would hobble across the room and stare out on the pebbled beach and the area, his eyes seeking his son. Occasionally Timmy came up to the workshop and played with the odds and ends of material and tools which Barto gave him. Oddly enough, during these weeks of Caroline's absence in Bermuda her name was scarcely mentioned; her household seemed complete enough without her.

On this warm August afternoon Patrice found Barto alone. "Make yourself comfortable, chick." Barto spoke without looking up from his worktable. "Ginger pop in the icebox, and I believe there's a bit of Dundee cake bought in your honor a week or so ago. Probably still edible."

"If you remember, I don't like Dundee cake."

"Thought all Limeys lived on it."

Patrice stretched luxuriously in the chair, wishing she could just sit here and relax and forget the embarrassing errand which had brought her today. Barto always put her at ease. She was more at home with him than with any other member of the family, at times even more so than with Adam. It was an unwelcome thought and she frowned at herself. She felt Barto's eyes upon her. "Feeling all right?" he asked. "You look a bit peaked these days. Brat raising hell?"

"I'm all right," Patrice assured him. But Barto, sensitive as an animal to currents often missed by other people, gave her another quick glance, then put aside his tools and pulled a bandanna handkerchief from his pocket and mopped his face. "Bloody hot day, mate," he murmured. It amused him to mimic what he liked to think was the cockney accent.

"Your accent," Patrice told him, "leaves much to be desired, and I'm not your mate."

He tucked the handkerchief in his pocket. "I wish you were," he said simply. "I sure wish you were my mate."

He often made love to her in this casual fashion, as though it were the most natural thing in the world, and it neither startled nor embar-

303

rassed her, as the boy Damon Edwards' declaration had done months before.

Now as she sat in the shabby chair which Caroline had long ago consigned to the dump and which Barto had retrieved, he suddenly tucked his crutches under his arms and crossed the room to her side. Propping the crutches against her chair he let himself slide to the floor at her feet, then laid his open hand on her knee, and she stared at the beautiful stone which lay on his palm.

"Amethyst," he said. "The purest I've been able to find. I'm trying to shape it so it will do for a ring, sometime, for Timmy's bride."

"Timmy's bride! He's got a long way to go, hasn't he?"

"I'm going to have it mounted in yellow gold, with seed pearls. A bit on the rococo side maybe, but I have a fondness for the rococo, and it will be something for him to remember me by."

When, years later, Timmy became engaged, his girl chose emeralds, and no one ever knew what became of this amethyst, lovingly cut and polished by the crippled man who crouched, now, on the dusty floor, his head bathed in the summer light.

Barto dropped the stone in his pocket, then took one of Patrice's ankles in his hand. "I'd like to make you a pair of anklets. Gold, with jade and alabaster, or perhaps lapis lazuli from Afghanistan and moonstones from Siam. Which would you prefer?"

"Both. One pair for ordinary wear with my tweeds, the other for formal occasions."

"You shall have both pairs, also rings on your fingers and bells on your toes, and music wherever you goes."

Patrice gazed down at his head with its luxuriant hair, its fine brows, and the memory of Mrs. Bannister's patronizing remarks on his ancestry and background returned to trouble her. She felt a recurrence of her own confusion, of hostility toward her mother-in-law, as she laid a hand on Barto's hair.

"I wish I could see twenty years ahead," she said. "I can feel the baby growing, and I feel myself changing—mentally, I mean. Or perhaps it's just that I'm growing up, too. Ideas, I mean. Things I'd like to do. Writing mostly. But when I sit down to write everything melts away. And when I read books about America—Henry James, Walt Whitman—I feel hopelessly at sea."

Barto said after a pause: "Perhaps you are not ready. Perhaps you just need to give yourself more time, live some more."

This too was part of his charm for her. He never tried to cut her down to size, he never condescended as Adam sometimes did, as his parents did, and Caroline. She felt a rush of gratitude and affection toward him and he must have sensed it, for he put up a hand and took hers, and, kissing it lightly, let it go.

"I wish I could do something to make you happy, Patrice. People ought to help each other, but they don't much, do they?"

He twisted round and stared up at her face. "Yes," he said meditatively. "I think I see it now. You will never be one of them, nor one of anything in particular."

"But to be happy one must be part of something!" Patrice protested. "Adam's mother tells me that I *fit,* and I do try to. After all, I love Adam, and I am fond of his family."

"Do you remember something I said to you that first evening after your arrival at the Bannisters'?" Barto asked her. "I warned you not to try too hard."

"But shouldn't one try? I want to be happy. I want to do the right thing by the people who trust me. To be faithful, loyal, never to hesitate or to doubt. Then I remember Doey and how he went down to his dusty grave still questioning, still doubting."

Barto squeezed her ankle. "Well, don't let it get you down, kid. And don't let yourself be carried away by your uncertainties. They aren't so important. The reality is your being married to Adam and having his child and making a go of things without knocking yourself out in the process."

Patrice felt the tough edges of Clem's letter in her pocket, but she still could not bring herself to broach that particular reality to Barto. She said, after a pause: "You told me once that the only person you really loved was Timmy. Timmy is your reality. How are you going to cope with that?"

"Simply by trying to keep him alive and healthy and helping him all I can. I want him to be as normal and happy as a mortal can expect to be, provided he doesn't fall off some goddam bicycle or drown in ten feet of water tangled up in an old anchor chain while people go on playing their accordions and telling dirty stories so they can't hear a child gasping to death within a few yards of them."

Patrice hardened her heart. "Yes, I know. But if Timmy grows up

305

as you want him to—cared for, protected, everything—after that what? What do you want for him when he becomes a man?"

Barto shrugged. "It will be up to him, I guess. I am seeing to it that he'll have plenty of money so he can make his own choice, his own decisions once I feel he is really on his own feet." He laughed shortly. "And I mean on his feet!"

Muted sounds from the harbor drifted through the windows and Patrice thought of Adam at his desk in the boatyard office, occupied and at peace with himself. In a little while she would walk over to the boatyard, and they would saunter arm in arm down the cobbled street of the little town toward his parents' house.

When Barto spoke again it was in a matter-of-fact voice: "Anything bothering you, child bride? Another telegram to the mother, maybe?"

Again this uncanny ability to pick thoughts out of her mind! Impulsively, Patrice dove into her pocket and produced Clem's letter. Barto read it unsmilingly, then he said in that same matter-of-fact voice: "Would a couple of hundred dollars help?" He went on quickly: "Just let me take his address and I'll have the bank translate dollars into—what's the currency in Spain? Pesetas?"

"It might," Patrice told him after a moment, "make all the difference between their eating and not eating."

Barto jotted down Clem's address and handed the letter back to Patrice. He said lightly: "Just to sidetrack possible complications, what do you say we keep this little transaction to ourselves, O.K.?"

"O.K." She bent and kissed the top of his head. "I shan't try to thank you. What would be the use?"

The telephone rang in a corner of the room and Barto scrambled to his knees, reaching for the crutches. Swiftly he hobbled across the floor and lifted the receiver. After a few moments he replaced it and turned to Patrice. "Nothing. Just the watchdog to report all is well with my son, aside from six frankfurters at the picnic—three more than he's normally allowed."

Patrice rose and went to him. "Barto."

"Nuts. Just come and see me whenever you feel like it. That's thanks enough."

They stood side by side facing the windows, where light enriched the sea and sky. Unthinkingly Patrice remarked: "I don't see Hal Johnson's boat."

"You haven't seen her for some time. She left three weeks ago—for Hamilton, Bermuda, I wouldn't be surprised." He smiled at Patrice. "I had a telegram this morning, from Caroline. She and Daisy sail tomorrow on the *Monarch* and arrive in New York Sunday."

Patrice said warmly: "It will be fun to have her home again!"

Barto plucked a cigar from his breast pocket. "Yes," he said absently. "Yes, I suppose it will."

Walking home in the fading light with Adam, Patrice said hesitatingly: "You've been working for four weeks now. Don't you think we ought to offer to pay your parents something toward our keep? I mean, with two of us it must add up."

"They wouldn't hear of it. Besides, I'm trying to save for next month's hospital bills."

The cheer which Patrice had enjoyed with Barto ebbed as she walked beside Adam in the lovely late afternoon. He felt her withdrawal and his face darkened. With an effort at being casual he said: "I saw you had a letter from Clem in yesterday's mail. Any special news?"

"Just the usual."

He was not really interested. She had once let him read a letter from Clem and he had returned it without comment. He never asked to see Alice's letters nor did he ever inquire about her, and Patrice had long since given up trying to interest him in her personal concerns.

Two evenings later, after dinner, when the family returned to the parlor, Mrs. Bannister suddenly excused herself and went upstairs, leaving Adam and Patrice with Mr. Bannister. A light rain was falling, and the big, comfortable room had a cosy air in the lamplight. In the dining room the maid cleared the table and withdrew. Adam seated himself in a corner of the sofa with his book on birds open on his knee, and Patrice sat beside him, waiting a cue from her father-in-law. Would he want to read aloud to them this evening—in which case she would kick Adam on the ankle as a hint for him to close his own book—or would Mr. Bannister retire to his bedroom, where he occasionally read aloud to his wife long after she had fallen asleep?

Throughout dinner—there had been no guests this evening—Patrice had become conscious of an increasing tension between her parents-in-law and had felt a responsive nervousness in herself. If Adam felt it he gave no sign. Everyone was all politeness and the conversation normal enough: a résumé of Mr. Bannister's activities in town, where he had lunched with a friend at the Union Club and the lamb chops had been on the tough side; an account of Mrs. Bannister's afternoon with her sewing circle, from which poor Isabel Redditch had excused herself because of a migraine headache.

Adam volunteered the information that Dr. Redditch, who earlier this summer had ordered a small sailboat to be built at the boatyard, had called up to cancel the order. "He said he had intended it as a wedding present, but had changed his mind."

"Poor Isabel," sighed Mrs. Bannister. "It's not like her to complain of a headache."

"Reddy will barely speak to me on the train nowadays," Mr. Bannister stated aggrievedly. "One would think that he and Isabel would have gotten over their peeve by now!"

Mrs. Bannister said hastily: "Isn't it lovely that our dear girls will be home again next week? I can't wait."

"Sunday, isn't it?" Patrice inquired conversationally. She was more and more conscious of something being amiss. The tones of voice . . . the glances . . . and now a certain grimness in Adam's expression, a sure sign that he was at last beginning to register the tension.

Mrs. Bannister stared across the table at Patrice. "Sunday, yes. But how did you know, dear? Barto only rang me up this afternoon to tell me, while you were out."

"Barto told me. He said Caroline and Daisy were sailing Friday from Bermuda."

"Barto told you? You've seen him, then?"

"This afternoon. I dropped in at his workshop to say hello."

Mr. Bannister spread a piece of bread thickly with butter and dropped it into the expectant jaws of Koko, crouched, as usual, beside his chair.

"Did Adam," Mr. Bannister inquired lightly, "know that you were calling on Barto?"

Adam interposed sharply: "Of course I knew. And what difference would it make if I didn't?"

308

Mrs. Bannister moved swiftly to change the subject. "I do hope Caroline was able to get me one of those nice English cardigans. I've always wanted one but could never find my size in just the shade I like."

Half an hour later, with Mrs. Bannister in retreat in her bedroom, Patrice studied a drop of moisture which seemed to quiver with unusual agitation at the end of Mr. Bannister's nose. He had ensconced himself with his customary ceremony in his particular chair and had gathered the spaniel on his knees. Without preliminary he addressed himself to Adam: "I don't wish—as you would say—to butt in on your affairs, my dear boy. But there are one or two matters I feel it is time we discussed."

Adam put down his book and lighted his pipe. He said nothing and Mr. Bannister stroked the dog's curls with loving fingers. His eyes behind their pince-nez seemed oddly to have shrunk in his head.

"In the first place," he began, "I must register your mother's and my mild—and I mean mild—disapproval of Patrice's running over to visit Barto, as she has apparently been in the habit of doing almost every day since Caroline has been away from home."

Patrice started upright in her seat. "What?" she exclaimed angrily, but he continued as though he had not heard. "There has been one scandal in our circle. I do not, and neither does your mother, relish the thought that there should be even the faintest suggestion of another. Nor even of gossip. I am sure you understand what it is I am trying to say?"

Patrice turned to Adam. His profile was rigid, but he put out a hand and took hers. She waited tensely for him to speak, but he said nothing. His fingers closed on hers, so she fancied, with a kind of urgency, seeking what? Support? Courage? Help?

She drew a sharp breath and turned to Mr. Bannister. "You mean you think there is something wrong about my going to see Barto? Why?"

"Because, my dear child, people talk. That's why." His voice was kindly, even indulgent.

"Talk about what?" Patrice demanded. She was trembling.

"Talk about you and Barto," Mr. Bannister replied dispassionately. "You must know that the world is full of people who have nothing better to do than talk about other people!"

309

Patrice laughed. "Isn't that just what we are doing?"

Mr. Bannister raised his head slightly and peered at her across the room. "Are you raising your voice to me, my dear? To your husband's father?"

Patrice's heart was pounding. Why didn't Adam say something, do something? Was he deaf, blind? Didn't he grasp what his father was driving at?

She addressed herself directly to Mr. Bannister. "I don't mean to raise my voice, to be rude. But I'm trying to understand what you are saying. Or perhaps I do understand. Perhaps what you are trying to say is that there is something *bad* in my going to see Barto. Is that what you're trying to say?"

Mr. Bannister had evidently not expected to be taken up on it. The color mounted to his face as he played nervously with the dog's collar.

"I am not *trying* to say anything. I am voicing an opinion, as I have every right to do in my own house. And it is my opinion—and Adam's mother's—that it is not proper for you, under the circumstances, to be seen visiting my son-in-law in his house as frequently as you have been doing while his wife is absent and there are no third parties present."

Patrice gasped. "You talk about circumstances. What circumstances?"

"Among others, these: the local bank called up here yesterday— that is, one of the officers did—and asked to speak to you. Since you were not home your mother-in-law inquired whether she might take a message. The man explained that he had a foreign draft made out to your brother in . . . is it Spain? but that there was some question about his address. He had, the man explained, called Mr. Barto Williams to check with him, since apparently Mr. Williams was the sender of the draft, but it seemed that Mr. Williams was himself unsure of the address so had suggested that the officer call you at this number." Mr. Bannister paused, removed his pince-nez, and polished them on his handkerchief. It was a classic gesture and Patrice watched him in fascination. He replaced the pince-nez and went on: "Your mother-in-law assured the officer that she would deliver his message to you. A few minutes later he called again apologetically to say that the matter had been take care of by Mr. Williams, who had discovered the mistake and rectified it. Your mother-in-law was, needless to say, taken aback. The amount involved was not negligible, at least by our modest standards. Two hundred dollars. Naturally she wondered where you had managed to procure such a sum, and on taking everything into consideration it was not difficult to arrive at the conclusion that Barto must have provided it."

Mr. Bannister gazed steadily at Patrice. "Your mother-in-law would have taken this matter up with you herself but after she and I had debated we decided it would be better for me to do so, and"—he paused dramatically—"and, my dear child, to ask you for an explanation which, I am sure, will clear up the whole situation without equivocation."

Ignoring the pressure of Adam's hand, Patrice said sharply: "There's no question of equivocation. My brother happens to be hard up at the moment, and I asked Barto if he would help me. I showed him my brother's letter, and he offered, without my asking him, to help Clem. That's all there is to it."

"And was Adam informed of this . . . transaction?"

Patrice answered coldly: "No."

"May I ask why not?" inquired Mr. Bannister with an appropriate lifting of brows.

"Because I felt that it was something entirely between Barto and me."

"I see," said Mr. Bannister, and went back to stroking Koko's curls.

Patrice was thinking: It has only been these few weeks and I started by liking him, certainly by respecting him. But why have I never been able to forget that very first evening in this room, when he pressed that horrible drink on me and turned away smiling when I choked on it? She felt a sudden numbness and her hand turned to ice in Adam's.

Mr. Bannister said slowly: "Unfortunately that is not all. Your mother-in-law and I also have dealings with this particular bank, where we are old and valued clients. Our good name is as much involved in this affair as yours. One does not, if one has any real breeding, approach other people for gifts of money no matter how altruistic the reason, unless it is for some public enterprise or charity. I must ask you, Patrice, so long as you are a guest in my house, never again to commit what, out of consideration for your youth and inexperience, I am willing to let pass as an unfortunate . . . shall we say solecism?"

311

Adam, who up to now had remained stonily silent, suddenly burst out: "Oh, for God's sake, Pop!"

The mask of restraint dropped from Mr. Bannister as he turned on his son: "Don't dare to address me in such a tone! You seem to forget, my boy, your position in this house. And since we are being frank with each other at long last, I would suggest that you exert yourself to find employment which will enable you to meet your financial responsibilities toward your wife and child, and that you devote rather more of your time to Patrice's welfare and less to your own selfish pursuits."

It was a notable performance and, as Patrice felt sure, a sincere one. Mr. Bannister wriggled out of the deep chair and marched to the door, his dog at his heels, the exit marred only slightly by the anticlimax of his parting shot: "Please see that all lights are turned off before you go to bed. The electricity bills have been nothing less than horrendous these past few weeks."

When he had gone Adam rose and walked to the tall French windows overlooking the patio and the sea. Fireflies danced in the shrubbery, their brilliance matching the distant glitter of lights on the farther shore.

Patrice said in a flat voice: "Why didn't you stand up to him?"

"He happens to be my father, don't forget."

"He happened to have said some rather rotten things."

"He has the right. This is his house."

Patrice's heart turned black within her as she rose from the sofa. "We are not children. What the hell are we doing in this house?"

"Living in it," Adam said. "Off him."

She caught the scream before it left her lips: *Coward!*

Adam remained standing with his back to her and she crossed the room and locked her arms round him, leaning her head against his coat. He made no move and they stood thus for some time, neither of them aware of the absurdity of their predicament as they listened to the striking of Mr. Bannister's carefully regulated clocks all over the house.

23

$\mathcal{T}$he bed was hard and narrow and the coverlet felt like white pasteboard, and everything had a shining immaculate whiteness. There were no pictures on the white walls, no decoration except for a play of light and shadow from the window during the day. Patrice luxuriated in the bareness, the spareness—like a sheet of paper, she told herself, on which, so far, nothing had been written. You might cover the purity of the paper with your insect writing, but beyond the edges of all your careful thought, your contriving, disorder reigned.

The baby, a girl, had been born dead, and Patrice had insisted on seeing it before they took it away on its little enamel tray. Adam had protested violently. "Patrice, darling, must you?" And even Caroline had sided with him on this, and had tried to persuade the doctor and the nurses not to let Patrice see the child. But she was fierce about it: "I can't just let her go like that, without even a look!"

"Morbid," Mrs. Bannister had murmured, shaking her head. And she had added later, speaking to Adam and Caroline when she thought Patrice was asleep: "I must say she's taking it very well. I don't think I could have borne it if she'd broken down."

And Mr. Bannister sent flowers and an affectionate little note, telling Patrice not to worry. Everything would be taken care of, all would be well. She was a brave girl, and when she had recovered from this tragedy, which was no one's fault, there would be other babies, and she and Adam would begin a new life together in Maine, where there was a position waiting for him in a firm of forestry experts . . . just the kind of work Adam would like. And all would be fine, just fine.

Barto had not come to the hospital to see her, but he too had written her a note, in which he said: "I think of you as young and strong and lively and that's how I always want to think of you, and that's how you will be when I see you again, before long." He kept her room filled with flowers, and ordered books to be sent to her from Lauriat's in Boston.

Everyone had been very kind. Patrice lay in bed thinking about how kind they were. . . . Mr. and Mrs. Bannister and Caroline and Barto. The Edwardses, the Redditches, Daisy.

And Adam came to see her almost every afternoon and sat beside her bed and held her hand and gazed at her with troubled eyes. There was about him, these days, a kind of desperation Patrice found hard to account for. "Adam," she said, trying to console him, "it couldn't be helped. The doctor told me that this sort of thing sometimes happens with a first baby. It was nobody's fault."

He looked away from her face and said with an effort: "No, it was nobody's fault."

But alone, Patrice drew the coverlet over her lips and stared steadily at the white ceiling, her heart shaken with its unuttered confession: "We didn't really want her and she knew it."

Then one afternoon a few days before she was to be released from the hospital Adam brought Daisy to see her. Daisy bent over the bed and kissed Patrice delicately on the forehead, and for hours afterward Patrice breathed the lovely fragrance of Daisy's clothes and her eyes swam in reflected blue of Daisy's eyes. "Dear Patrice! We have missed you so!"

And when Adam stepped out of the room for a moment to speak to the nurse, Daisy said quickly: "You must take care of yourself for his sake. This has been a terrible shock to him, you know." And she added with a sigh: "I think these things are always harder on the men than on the women, don't you?"

314

Daisy did not take the chair which the nurse had brought for her, but continued to stand, as though poised for flight, beside the bed. She was slender and exquisite in her favorite shade of blue that matched her eyes; under a tiny silk beret her spun-gold hair gleamed round her ears, and to Patrice she seemed vibrant, pent up, barely troubling to conceal the desire which filled her.

"I am going to take Adam out to dinner tonight, just to give him a little change from the family!" Daisy smiled down at Patrice. "You don't mind, do you, dear?"

Patrice gazed back at her steadily. I do mind, but what can I do about it? Her lips did not shape the words, but her eyes did, and Daisy turned, dimpling, as Adam came back to the room. "I'll wait for you out in the car, Adam. Don't be too late; our reservation is for eight o'clock sharp, and it's a bit of a drive."

When the door had closed on Daisy's lovely back Adam murmured: "She's been wonderful to me all the time you've been sick. We owe her something after all, Patrice."

"Yes," said Patrice. "I suppose we do."

She felt the strain in him as she always felt it when he came into this room. He had a horror of sick people; suffering made him uncomfortable, as though he were in the presence of something indecent. It was a characteristic he shared with his parents, and from which Caroline was entirely free. It was Caroline who had taken charge of the situation when Patrice's labor pains set in four weeks ahead of schedule. It was Caroline who had telephoned the doctor and alerted the hospital and who had driven Patrice and Adam there in the small hours of the morning, and who had stayed beside her throughout the ordeal, and who, at the end, had taken her hand and told her gently that the child had been born dead. It was Caroline at her best: strong, sensible, kind, without what she herself would have described as slop.

Now Adam moved restlessly in his chair, glanced at his wristwatch, and said: "Caroline is coming to see you first thing in the morning."

"And you?" Patrice asked, looking at him.

"Daisy insists on driving me over tomorrow afternoon. She's at loose ends, rather, and it would save my having to borrow Ma's automobile, or paying for a cab."

Suddenly unable to endure the strain of his impatience, Patrice said: "Why don't you go along now, Adam? The nurse will be coming with bedpans and things ... and Daisy expects you."

He hesitated, then rose to his feet, kissed her, and left the room. Patrice heard the sound of an automobile starting up in the parking lot under her window, and her mind vividly pictured them driving away together ... where? To some pleasant, dimly lighted restaurant with candles on the table in a corner, seats side by side against the wall, discreet waiters, music. And afterward to that empty house in Cambridge where he had met Daisy once, long ago?

In the farthest green disorder beyond the white coverlet and the oblong of white paper someone had set a great bouquet of roses. Dark red roses drooping now in the heat. Roses in a golden jungle where the tigers roamed, walking stiff-legged, their whiskers well combed and formal, their black lips glistening above clean pink gums and scimitar teeth. Peacocks flew into the trees, their tails hanging like splendid curtains, Tree of Life curtains in the heavy stillness of the jungle.

Clem moved through the greeny shadows with his catapult at the ready, hunting the tigers. Nothing frightened Clem. Doey didn't really frighten him. Nor life. He would walk into starvation humming: "K-K-K-Katy, Beautiful Katy!" He had learned that when you sing you don't stutter. Did he sing to the tourists as he guided them among the fountains and mosaics in that distant Spanish city under a Moorish sky?

The tiger's whiskers were white as the walls of this room; then they were suddenly crimson like the roses growing on the jungle's edge. Crimson like the blood of the mother buffalo dropping her calf, like the blood in people's veins, or blood from dying fish.

And yes, blood from one's own body. The pain had been quite frightful and she had felt that they were turning her inside out like an old sock. And then she had heard the hoopoe quite clearly singing somewhere in the room, though she could not see it. The song formed in the darkness of her skull in little golden notes and streamed through her in pure delight, and it went on singing when they brought the baby to her and she gazed down at it and she thought how complete it was, how separate from all known things, and unlike anyone she knew, and it was how she herself had looked, and how Clem had looked when they were inside the mother when she wore the white dress with the yellow roses. And if this baby could have

316

spoken she would have said: "I bet I know something you don't know!"

But now the hoopoe's song must have reached the nurse's ears because she came into the room and bent over the bed and said gently: "Yes?"

"Listen," said Patrice, lifting a warning hand. "Listen!"

Part Three

24

It had snowed since early morning and fields beyond the old red brick house were transformed. A wheelbarrow forgotten and left outdoors was no longer a wheelbarrow, nor the hydrangea beside the well a hydrangea. The outline of the driveway had disappeared, and in this overcast light there were no shadows to give a semblance of life to the wrought iron forms of trees. For Patrice, standing at the window of her living room, winter seemed a continuous bal masqué in a world of transvestites.

Every year for almost ten years she had watched the Maine landscape move from the explosion of spring to the humdrum of summer, from the lion hues of fall to this pale oblivion. Her eyes had built up a sense of ownership; she was no longer indifferent to the vulnerability of things. There had been a time when the wheelbarrow was a thing of beauty, painted red and with an iron-shod wheel. Now it was an old wreck used for lugging potatoes from the vegetable garden to the cellar door. But for the moment it wore its ermine with a regal air.

As for the hydrangea, Patrice's neighbor Rosanna Burden had dug it out from her own garden and brought it as an Easter offering. "I hope," Rosanna said deprecatingly, "I hope it turns out to be one of

321

them pretty pink ones. They don't always run true. You'll just have to wait and see."

It had turned out to be a pretty pink one, and it was beautiful enough now, its leafless twigs heavy with white blooms that swelled and blew away under Patrice's eyes.

Rosanna had come trudging across the fields that Easter morning when Adam and Patrice had lived just one year in the house. "We better," Rosanna said, "get this thing into the ground right away."

They chose a spot near the old well and Patrice dug a hole and Rosanna settled down on her knees like a circus horse. She was splendidly large, with untidy brown hair and smooth round arms like poplar boles. She had set the plant carefully in the earth and watched Patrice shovel back the soil and tread it firmly round the single spindly stem.

"Funny thing about you," Rosanna remarked. "You don't look like you had the strength of a flea. There, that'll do, honey. Don't go killing yourself."

She rose ponderously to her feet and wiped her muddy hands on the faded apron she habitually wore over a faded print dress. No matter what the season Rosanna never wore wool. "Gives me the itch," she explained. And she rarely wore stockings. "Takes too much time to put them on, then take them off again."

That spring morning she had gazed round her at the early green of the lawn and the first wistful signs of life in Patrice's tulip bed. "Looks real nice," said Rosanna. "You done wonders since you been here. But you don't want to overdo, Patrice, honey. Why not let Adam take a crack at some of these chores once in a while?"

"He does," Patrice had replied hurriedly. "When he's home long enough."

Rosanna's quick black eye had singled out the clothesline beside the woodshed. "You'd ought to send them sheets and towels out to the laundry. There's some of us," she added, "like me, can take it. But you want to carry through with a baby sometime you better watch out."

That had been almost ten years ago and the hydrangea had prospered. Rosanna, a fanatical gardener, was always bringing Patrice odds and ends from her own flower beds. "There's no room in the

322

cemetery," she explained once. "And I just can't bear to throw them away."

Patrice had observed that at this rate the garden would end being more Rosanna's than hers, and Rosanna replied: "Well, I can't help taking an interest in it, you know. It was my grandfather planted them sugar maples along your drive." She smiled her sudden, rare, sentimental smile. "Wonder what he'd of thought of a girl all the way from India coming to live in his house?"

It was from Rosanna and Ralph Burden that Mr. and Mrs. Bannister had bought the house as a gift to Adam and Patrice when they moved to Maine from Berry's Landing.

"We can't," Patrice had objected helplessly. "Adam, we simply can't let them give us a *house!*"

But something strange had happened to Mrs. Bannister at the time of the baby's death. Herself a neophyte to tragedy, she could not accustom herself to Patrice's stoical digestion of it. There was a kind of gratitude too—gratitude in reverse!—for Patrice's self-restraint in shock. "I couldn't have borne it," Mrs. Bannister had declared to Mr. Bannister and to Caroline. "I couldn't have borne it if she had broken down."

And in that first spring after Rosanna had sold her grandfather's house she walked often across the fields from the little house where she now lived, bringing the hydrangea to celebrate that Easter, and in the following summers honeysuckle vines and hollyhocks flourished against the sunny brick walls, and a lilac by the front door. In such small ways Rosanna Burden tried to communicate her instant "taking to" Patrice, and, with time, her concern.

"Land sake, dear, ain't you never going to become pregnant? It don't do to wait too long. I don't understand. Ten years married, one child dead, and the rest miscarried."

On her knees, planting a clutch of tulips, Rosanna had stared up at Patrice, who stood leaning on a shovel at her side. "It ain't natural," Rosanna said, shaking her huge shoulders. "Both of you young and healthy. And this house was made for kids. When my grandfather owned it there was anywhere from five to fifteen children runnin' around in them rooms and in the yard. I was one of 'em. And when your folks come here and asked would I sell it and you and Adam

323

standing quiet and dutiful, I thought: There now. It's going to be like old times again."

And not so much of a move for Rosanna and her husband, at that. Just a few hundred yards across the fields and the little cemetery to Aunt Jinny's house, which they had inherited at her death the year before.

It couldn't, Mrs. Bannister had declared with an enthusiasm she rarely felt about anything, have worked out better. And Wilbur Bannister had conceded that it was a good investment. With a change of scene, work he seemed disposed to enjoy at last, and a home of his own, Adam would be a different man, and Patrice a different woman.

One day when they had been in the house five years Rosanna had returned like a boomerang to her obsessive concern: "Who'm I to be givin' all this advice? Me with my one. Not that I'm complainin'. My Monty's all the good Lord chose to give me and he's all I want."

On this later winter afternoon as Patrice stood by her living room window she stared at the falling snow and saw it gradually filling in the depressions made by Monty Burden's rubber-booted feet. She had not heard him nor seen him approach across the cemetery and circle the house, his opaque gaze taking in the windows, the firmly locked doors.

"There's some folk," Rosanna had told her once, "got it in for my Monty. Oh, they know better'n to come to Ralph or me with their shitty talk. That sister of Ralph's, that Lucy Burden lives over by Tom's Corner. Never lifts her finger to do a lick of work, just sets on her arse readin' *norvils.*" Rosanna's thick neck flushed. " 'There ain't nobody,' says Lucy to me, if you please, 'there ain't nobody goin' to give your Monty a job.' And she makes them eyes and purses up her mouth, like as if there's things she could say only she's too kind. Shitty talk about her own nephew, and I told her as much!"

There had been, on that distant occasion, something tragic about Rosanna. Her big round face, her huge breasts, her Percheron limbs had sagged; tears had glittered briefly in her sharp black eyes.

"Just because someone's different. Just because he maybe ain't built like everybody else and don't always act like everybody else and because God Almighty made him like he is, every stinkfinger in the neighborhood's got somethin' to say about it."

Rosanna had put her hand in the pocket of her apron and brought

324

out a small object which she handed Patrice. "This belonged to my grandaunt Susie Perkins," she explained, suddenly shy. "I don't never have cause to wear such things so I'd like for you to have it, Patrice."

It was an old-fashioned gold brooch shaped like a fleur-de-lis. Patrice met Rosanna's entreating eyes. "Rosanna, dear! It's sweet of you, but I can't accept it."

"Please! Please take it, honey. It'd make me happy. You been so good to Monty. So understandin'. You, a stranger from a foreign land, when his own father's sister . . ."

Patrice dropped the proffered bribe back into Rosanna's apron pocket. She said gently: "Rosanna, dear, I do understand, but I can't accept a valuable present like this. Save it." She smiled down at Rosanna's flushed, miserable face. "Save it for when Monty gets married!"

Rosanna's gaze clung to Patrice. "You don't mind takin' flowers. And I ain't askin' nothin' of you, you know that, don't you, honey?"

"I know it," Patrice replied, and laid her hand for a moment on the great, quivering shoulder of her friend. "I know it, Rosanna, dear."

Busybodies on the telephone called Patrice to say: "If I were you I don't think I'd encourage that character Monty Burden to hang around the house the way you do!"

And: "He's getting over being a kid. If he can't finish school he ought to go find himself a regular job, not spend his time peeking in neighbors' windows and masturbating behind the barn."

When she reported these communications to Adam, he had shrugged. "Use your judgment, darling. Someone's got to mow the lawn when I'm not home! And Monty can weed the garden at least, can't he?"

Over the years Patrice had developed a habit of talking to herself, of keeping up her side of a dialogue in silence. On the morning of her reporting the neighbors' telephone conversations to Adam, and on his characteristic shrugging it off, she had cleared the breakfast dishes from the table and carried them to the kitchen sink, and she had answered Adam in her own fashion, without words: Why don't you tell Monty Burden you don't want him hanging round the house when you're not here?

Adam never would, as she knew well enough. For him to take such

325

a step would mean involvement, a stepping outside the ramparts he had created for himself. Had he caught Monty Burden stealing or ill-treating a dog he would in all likelihood have felled the boy to the ground, but this other, this was a different matter entirely. This made complex demands, and Adam hated complexity. It undoubtedly meant looking into Monty's queer opaque eyes. Listening to Monty's stumbling: Why. Why don't you all of a sudden want me to wash the car and mow the grass once in a while or do a bit of painting or carry a load of firewood? Why not? What have I done?

"If you don't want Monty around tell him so," said Adam to Patrice. "Or tell Rosanna."

"I can't," said Patrice, knowing that she couldn't, but that her reasons were not Adam's reasons. For him such problems as Monty Burden fell in the category of household bills, support for Alice, fear of pregnancy. All these matters, he had long ago decided, could well be left in Patrice's capable hands. And capable they had become in the past ten years; more so than Adam realized; more so than Patrice would have had them become.

During their second summer in this house there had been a second miscarriage. She had been alone, as she was most of the time, since Adam's work took him away from home for weeks on end. He worked for two dollars and a half a day when on the job, and his parents still contributed the essential balance to the till. Patrice no longer raised shamed objections to this state of affairs, for she had learned to accept the fact that so far as responsibility was concerned Adam had reached the point of no return.

But Adam had given her the baby which, that summer, she was abruptly to lose as she climbed the staircase from the lower hall to the upper, carrying a pail of water and a mop. Outdoors, Monty Burden, now fourteen years old, with runny nose and staring eyes, was supposed to be weeding the tomatoes. It would, Patrice knew, have to be done over again when he was through, but Rosanna had sent him with instructions to do what he was told and he would not, now, take no.

Halfway up the stairs Patrice had felt something give way inside her, but she climbed to the upper hall, sunlit from an open window which overlooked the garden, the vegetable patch, and the open fields. It was June and the wind flowing over the grass gave it a look

326

of molten steel. The scent of summer filled the house as Patrice set the pail and mop on the floor and sank down beside them.

"Damn," she said aloud. "Damn, damn, damn, damn."

Pain stampeded her. She crawled to the window and shouted to Monty where he crouched among the tomatoes: "Go get your mother. Tell her I need her."

Then she subsided on the floor and tried to hold on to whatever it was that was trying to leave her body, but it responded with a gushing spasm, and she thought: Three months' accumulation, and it feels like calf's liver.

When she opened her eyes Monty was standing beside her. "You sick?" he asked. His gaze wandered over her where she crouched against the wall under the window.

"Go get your mother. Please, Monty. And hurry."

He continued to stand, staring down at her. "You cut yourself or somethin'?" he asked. "You runnin' blood all over."

Patrice suffered from an overpowering sense of loneliness, and an impulse to burst into tears. Monty squatted on his heels beside her, his eyes flickering with interest. "I don't hear it cryin' nor nothin'. Looks like you cut yourself." He hitched himself closer and put out a hand to touch her skirt. Patrice stared into the lusterless disks of his eyes. "Will you," she said between clenched teeth, "get the hell out of here and go tell your mother I'm sick?"

His face quivered. "You lemme see the baby and I'll go. You lemme!"

Patrice thought: The telephone is in our bedroom down the hall and I'd probably faint before I got there. She was alone with Monty Burden, an overgrown lump with the strength of two. She was alone with him in this big, cool, friendly house. Adam's dogs were outside, slumbering in the long grass under the trees. She could hear a car pass on the highway below the house, and all the faint, familiar crepitations of everyday life: ice melting and running down the drainpipe of the icebox in the kitchen, the clock in the living room striking the quarter, the nervous cluck of a robin on the lawn.

"You lemme see the baby," Monty insisted urgently. She could smell his clothes, the mud on his hands. "You lemme," he whispered. "You goddam well lemme."

Patrice slapped him across the face and as he keeled over on his

327

buttocks she said: "You go and get Rosanna or I'll see that your father beats the living shit out of you!"

He went then, and presently there was Rosanna bending over her; Rosanna smelling of freshly ironed linen. Smelling of heaven. "Honey," Rosanna said. "I told you you'd ought to take better care of yourself."

She put her strong arms around Patrice and lifted her from the floor. Over her shoulder she snapped at Monty: "Go in their room and turn down the covers and hurry!"

With Patrice in bed, Rosanna had telephoned the doctor, then fetched water, soap, and towels. She washed Patrice and rolled the bloody mess in a towel. Her huge body seemed to fill the room with comfort, with love. Monty had disappeared and in the midst of her weakness and between stilettos of pain Patrice thought: I hope he didn't tell her about that slap. The mark of her hand on his cheek had shown like a scar, but Rosanna had said nothing. While they waited for the doctor she sat on the edge of Patrice's bed and held Patrice's hand and Patrice thought of Dr. Sanyal in that far-off time in that far-off house where the churel lived in the trees and the hoopoe sang in the sunlight. Illness had been a kind of luxury then, a kind of adventure. What had become of that earlier magic?

Now in this other far-off time and far-off house Rosanna Burden stroked Patrice's hand and said: "There ain't nothin' worse. For a woman there ain't nothin' worse than to lose 'em. All the love of a man that goes into it, all the answerin' love of a woman. All the hope. All the plannin' for a crib, for them little soft blankets. All the dreamin' and gettin' over the fear, and maybe when you're young and ain't quite made up your mind . . . maybe the notion that things ain't goin' to be the same as they was when it was only you and him. And then bein' sure at last, and the feel of a third person growin' inside; and choosin' the name." Rosanna pressed Patrice's hand. "All endin'," she said heavily, "all endin' in red flannel hash."

Adam had been summoned and had come home from his job, distraught. A temblor had rocked his fortress, not for the first time, but in a week Patrice was on her feet, coping with his need for reassurance, with Alice's impassioned pleas that she be allowed to move into the house and take charge while Patrice stayed in bed. "When you needed help it was not me you sent for!" Alice's eyes accused her. "I who would die for you, go sleepless for you, starve for you."

Yes, Alice was nearby, lodged in her two rented rooms with kitchen and bath in a house across the river from where Adam and Patrice lived.

The miracle had been achieved; the money for her passage saved, borrowed, earned, for Patrice had sold a story at last and five hundred dollars had seemed a fortune set aside to bring Alice "home."

It was a changed Alice, grown a little heavier, nearsighted, her faery laughter a thing of the past. She did not like America and she was desolate alone in her rented rooms, and Wilbur Bannister stated in one of his asides to Adam: "She is going to be an Old Woman of the Sea on your and Patrice's back!"

And Mrs. Bannister had asked of Caroline: "How are they going to support her when they have so little themselves?"

And in one of her interior dialogues Patrice had asked herself: What does one do about one's mother?

And when Patrice miscarried for the second time in that red brick house on the hill, between the river and the fields, Alice's gaze, her voice, filled Patrice's exhausted mind: "When you needed help it was not me you sent for ... I who would die for you, go sleepless for you, starve for you!"

Patrice thought: How can I explain? How can I tell her that her love stifles me, that the child I was is as dead as the child I have just lost, that the old love is dead ... dead ... dead?

But it was another day and long afterward that Patrice stood by her living room window and appraised the snow-covered hydrangea, and the wheelbarrow which Monty Burden had left outdoors. She heard the wind move into the northeast and shake the maples which Rosanna's grandfather had planted a hundred years ago. A little shiver of delight touched her nerves as she listened to the wind shaking the snow blossoms from the hydrangea bush.

She was alone, and solitude always brought her this sense of increase as her submerged other self stirred and came to life. She became at once two persons in one, possessor of two separate worlds.

Behind her Adam's dogs whined and scratched the doors to be let out. Once out they hated the cold, hated to lift their legs against the frozen statuary of an earlier snowfall.

Patrice turned away from the window and opened the kitchen door to let the dogs go out. They stood shivering, tails between their legs, gazing at her reproachfully with eyes that were suddenly Alice's eyes again, filled with insatiable discontent. Monty Burden's footprints had vanished in the fresh, uncorrupted snow.

Patrice closed the door on the dogs and heard the telephone ringing in the room known as Adam's den, next the living room. The den was furnished with Adam's gun cabinet, racks of fishing gear, bookcases filled with sporting books, books on flora and fauna, and the walls were covered with stuffed animal trophies and framed photographs of Adam in hunting garb. Adam in India, his foot on a dead tiger. Adam with windrows of dead ducks lying at his feet. Adam holding a twenty-pound salmon killed in the river a year or two before. Adam fishing for trout. Adam, gun to shoulder, bringing down a partridge on the wing. Adam with dead deer, with dead woodcock, with dead rabbits, with the monstrous spread antlers of a bull moose.

The room smelled of formaldehyde, desiccated fur, dogs, and tobacco. A leopard skin, perhaps the same golden presence, which had haunted the garden in the Indian hills, now sprawled before the hearth, snarling at a faded tiger skin that faced it. And in the midst of this Madame Tussaud menagerie the telephone was stridently ringing.

Patrice hesitated as she listened to the sound. It went on and on. Something in its obstinacy made her sure it would be Alice calling her from the unbearable vacuum of that apartment at the other side of town.

"Darling, I hope I am not disturbing you!"

"That's all right, Alice."

"I just wanted to find out how you were all alone in that house and in this dreadful weather."

"I'm fine, thanks."

"Snow is pretty if one doesn't have to be out in it, and if one is not alone."

Pause. What was there for Patrice to say that had not been said over the years?

"Have you heard from dear Adam?"

"I expect him home sometime tonight."

"He's been away a long time."

330

"Three weeks."

"I don't like the thought of your being left alone in that house."

"I have neighbors, Alice."

She thought of Monty's footprints hidden in the snow. In summer too he left traces of his prowlings in the telltale grass.

"Yes, your neighbors, darling. But the best of neighbors are not the same as one's own family, are they? And I can't help worrying about you. I see so little of you."

On and on. As the telephone continued its stubborn ringing Patrice continued her imaginary exchange with Alice. She had it down pat.

"I have been listening to the radio, darling. Such dreadful things happening in Spain. I am so relieved that dear Clem and his family have left the place. But I wish I knew where they were. I wish Clem would write. Almost a year, and not a word!"

"He may have written and the letter gone astray."

"You always say that. But one's only son. You would think . . ."

On and on. An excuse to talk, to fill the void. Patrice could imagine that rented room crammed with photographs. Photographs on the walls, on tables, on the bureau; everywhere. Snapshots. Ornate posed portraits. Velvet and ribbons, parasols and gloves; helmets, moustaches, epaulets. There they were, Doey and Alice and Aunt Eve. There were Clem and herself and the servants. Chota Ayah, Mohommed Ali the old tailor, Nizamat. There were Mr. Sparks and Mr. Onions, the Meadowses; Mother Superior at the convent, Sister Teresa; other faces, other gestures unknown to Patrice, or forgotten. Faces and figures snared in time against a background of shadows. Which house was this? Which Christmas encampment? Here a pair of eyes gazing directly into one's own. A smile . . . what had been the joke? A hand holding a letter . . . from whom? From where?

"They are all I have got left," Alice stated, sighing. "They are all I ever had, all I ever wanted."

"You can't," said Patrice, "spend the rest of your life in the past."

"Then where," Alice asked, with those accusing eyes, "where should I spend it?"

With Alice's voice ringing implacably in her ears Patrice stared with equal obstinacy at the dead leopard and the lusterless tapestry of the tiger, both snarling into space. Vitality strained through formaldehyde. Alice, perhaps, had had no choice, but this had been Adam's.

With the receiver in her hand Patrice turned her face once more to the window. Snow danced in the air, but the storm was blowing itself out. She had a glimpse of the river beyond the highway, the water leaden between snowy shores. Blocks and cubes of buildings loomed among a starkness of trees, and she fancied she could hear the distant hum and stir of traffic under the quilted sky.

"Patrice, darling, are you still there?"

"I'm still here."

"And you are not lonely?" Oh, if only Patrice were lonely!

"I'm not a bit lonely, Alice."

"No, I suppose not." The faintest of sighs. "I don't know where you get this self-sufficiency. You must be very strong."

"Well, one learns to be strong, doesn't one?"

"Does one? You must teach me how, my darling child."

She was finished at last and Patrice hung up the receiver. I'll go and see her tomorrow, she thought. First thing after the snowplow has gone through and the roads are clear I'll go and see Alice and stay an hour or so with her. We'll look at all those old photographs and talk about the old times, and wonder how poor Eve is making out in a Paris suburb, giving lessons in embroidery and music and living on tea and toast while she, in her turn, glories and drinks deep of the past. We'll talk of Clem, seeing him always as that slender child with his old-young eyes, his stutter, his asthma, his defiance; not as the unresolved man with a disillusioned wife and three puzzled children, and the grass always greener on the farther side of the fence.

After all, thought Patrice as she stooped to straighten the tiger's puppy-chewed tail, I am not lonely. I am not growing old, and I am, as Alice never tires of pointing out in that faintly accusing voice, *self-sufficient.* Though Alice cannot guess, as no one can guess, that I am not too self-sufficient for love. I have this thought of Damon burning in my brain, in my pelvis, in my fingers, in my feet. Because of Damon the future is a birthday present, it is Christmas and Easter and Thanksgiving. Feast day and celebration. Love is a plum cake, half for him and half for me.

In Clem's last letter to Patrice he had written:

I am selfishly relieved, of course, that Alice is with you. Things seem to be going to pot in India, and she could not have stayed there alone and without funds. Think of the poor Meadowses! The Indians are not going to give a damn about all these derelicts of the British raj. Can you see Alice as another Edna Meadows, going to bed with a banian so she can eat? Can you see her as a subservient governess to the spoiled brats of some potbellied nawab, or earning her bread in a shop? Oh, I know there's no stigma attached to honest labor, and why in hell shouldn't a healthy normal woman work for her keep? Not in India. There are just not the jobs for people like Alice. And in any case one has to be a rather special type of person to overcome one's ingrained sense of belonging to an elite, a sense in which Alice was born and brought up.

Perhaps in America it will be different. Perhaps Alice is still young enough to try to make some sort of a new life for herself there. And what could I have offered her? I can't even take proper care of Melissa and the kids. Poor Melissa! The truth is the bloom is off our marriage and only the diapers remain. Oh, Patrice, how inexcusable this is! I know I'm a rotter. Yet having got it off my chest to you I feel better.

It was not a letter for Alice's eyes, and Patrice had kept it to herself. It was the last she was to hear of Clem for some time.

Patrice returned to the door, where the dogs were scratching to be let in. They greeted her boisterously, as they never did when Adam was home. They were very definitely his dogs, not hers, and no mistake about it. Now she herded them into the kitchen and dried them on towels, smelling their wet hair, warding off their slobbering caresses. The telephone rang, and she waited, kneeling on the kitchen floor with the dogs. Alice again? On the other hand, it could be Damon calling her from New York.

Dropping the towel, she returned to the telephone. It was Adam, his voice blurred by storm and distance. "I'll be late getting home. Hell of a storm and we're having trouble with the car."

There was an interruption and Patrice visualized the blizzard sweeping down a white channel of highway from the north. Adam had been gone three weeks and now she hung on his voice, surprised as she always was by the depth of her relief on hearing it. "You all right, Patrice? Dogs all right?"

"We are all fine," Patrice assured him. *We.* She had fallen into his custom of using the inclusive pronoun when speaking of the dogs, for to Adam his dogs were his children, a sentiment to her bordering on obsession and fatuousness.

When he had rung off Patrice turned once more to the window and felt the luxury of solitude begin to ebb. Part of her always missed Adam during his prolonged absences; part of her wanted him home, yet on his reappearance she was conscious of an instant shrinking of her personality, a withdrawal of her total self as a reflexive action quite independent of her will.

Staring out of the window at the sailing flakes of snow, she brooded awhile on the manuscript which lay on the table upstairs, in the room which she had taken for her study. It was furnished in Spartan fashion, with an old table she had picked up for two dollars; a chair, a bookcase, and a still life in oils painted by her friend Jonas Brayne. There was also a small reproduction of a Persian miniature which Damon Edwards had given her the year that they became lovers, the year of her twenty-seventh birthday. Aside from the two pictures the room had an ascetic atmosphere forbidding to all intruders, including Damon himself.

But once here and with the door closed, it exercised its peculiar magic. Fantasies here took on a created substance with the emergence of that secret self which could share nothing with those closest to her, not even with Damon.

On this day of the snowstorm Patrice had planned to spend the afternoon in that room, working on the manuscript, but she had delayed too long and now the mood was gone. She was only now, in her thirtieth year, beginning to understand and to dread that implacable second self who, once in command, took entire command. It was this unconfessed dread that lay at the bottom of most of her procrastination. How much simpler to dream and put off than to shut the door and get down to the job!

And there was always the reality that was Damon. Damon at twenty-six, author of poems which had won literary acclaim and a Bollingen award. Puffing a cigar and with his elegant feet propped on a chair, Damon had one day out of the blue taken sides with Adam, with the Bannisters, with her own familiar procrastinating self: "Darling Patrice! You don't know the fuckiest about writing! To begin with you have no roots, no point of departure, nothing to write *about*. If you had been brought up in a civilized environment—Europe, say—instead of a half-arse colonial one, it might have been different."

334

Rootless, with nothing to write about! It seemed that unless one was a genius and could vault from the springboard of all the proper advantages as Damon had done in his gracile, effortless way, one might as well make up one's silly mind that one did not have a prayer.

And as that enigmatic other self shrank under the caustic, procrastination took on a seduction of its own. What the hell are you going to write *about?* You don't draw inspiration out of your belly as a spider draws its silk. Perhaps there was something in what Damon had said, after all. So far as you knew there was not a single writer or painter or musician in your family, and no point of intellectual reference. True, they had had their drawing room accomplishments: those naïve little watercolor sketches, the embroidery, the sickly songs. The best that could be said for these practitioners was that they did not take themselves seriously. It had been left to Clem, and to you, so to take yourselves.

Yet the self which shrank under one man's indifference and another's spite reasserted itself with growing resilience. How could Adam and the Bannisters and Damon be so sure that they were right? Adam had never expressed the faintest interest in anything she had written, and Damon, on reading the one story which she had nervously shown him, had waved it aside with the pronouncement that she had not the fuckiest knowledge about writing.

Thus the habit of secrecy had grown upon Patrice as she tapped out stories and poems and sent them, surreptitiously, to magazines, burying each in an old tin trunk as it was returned, and burning the rejection slips in the kitchen stove.

In the day-to-day life she shared with Adam events showed up like rocks above the surface calm. Caroline divorced Barto and married Hal Johnson. Barto left Berry's Landing and went to live in New York. Daisy Redditch married Pinky Pitman and bore him twins. Mr. Charles Prentice married his housekeeper. Dr. Redditch died of a heart attack and Mrs. Redditch moved to Australia to live with her son, Lawrence, now married to an Australian woman and with a hefty family of boys and girls.

Mrs. Bannister was philosophical in the face of what she called These Musical Chairs: "Thank God," she observed, wholeheartedly, "for you and Adam. Don't let me down!"

And perhaps, later, Adam would make some kind of a success in this new job. He enjoyed working outdoors, the responsibilities were few, and he was at ease with his colleagues, men less complex than himself. True, he still earned very little money and Mrs. Bannister probably realized that he would never be entirely independent of her financial assistance. But she would do anything, she insisted to Mr. Bannister, *anything* to keep Adam and Patrice together.

Wind shook the windows and the dogs came into the room and pressed against Patrice's legs. They were troubled by the storm, by their master's absence, and by her own prolonged immobility. Patrice spoke to them soothingly. "All right, let's go and call on Rosanna."

Following the dogs to the empty garage, she lifted a pair of snowshoes from their hook on the wall and strapped them on her feet. Outdoors the snow brushed like feathers against her face and her spirits lifted as she left the house behind her. Procrastination again. She knew she was not running away merely from thoughts of Adam and his family, of Alice, of Damon. She was turning her back on that sardonic presence which lay in wait for her in the room where she had left her unfinished manuscript, that presence which did not give a damn whether she went or whether she stayed.

The elm trees stood defiant against a slowly clearing sky as she headed toward the old cemetery. Most of the stones were buried in snow and she picked her way with care, the dogs trying to get a foothold on her heels. Beyond the cemetery the land dipped and she had a glimpse of the Burdens' chimneys and caught a fragrance of birch bark burning in the kitchen stove.

A gust of wind struck her between the shoulders and the toe of her snowshoe caught in something. She kicked free and bared a wreath of imitation flowers, garish against the prevailing white. This was Jinny Burden's grave. They had got Aunt Jinny into the ground before it froze hard, because Rosanna hated to think of the dead biding their time in the mausoleum for what she called the spring planting.

"Always better in the ground," said Rosanna. "I don't mind the ground. Something you can understand. You walk on it, dig in it. Grass and violets grow out of it. But cree-mation now! That I couldn't take. Nasty heathen invention, like your Hindus. I've made Ralph swear on his mother's Bible he won't have me cree-mated, and if I kick off the

336

wrong time of year he's got to see the ground's thawed out and me put in it, else I'll come back from wherever I am and sit on his feet every night until he's done something about it."

"Don't see why you make such a fuss about cree-mation," Ralph Burden complained. "Place you're goin' will be hot enough so you might's well be cree-mated here as there!"

They shared these simple jokes and Rosanna's laughter made every dog within earshot wag its tail. Well, Rosanna had seen to it that Ralph's Aunt Jinny was put in the ground, and the wreath of wax flowers lovingly arranged above her.

Patrice had a special, private feeling about Aunt Jinny because she had written a story about her and it was the first and only story she had managed to get published in a magazine. It was the money she received for this story which had gone to help bring Alice "home" to those rented rooms across the river, and she was convinced that Aunt Jinny would have been pleased to know about it.

Aunt Jinny was ninety years old when she died. She had been a sea captain's daughter, and never allowed the neighbors to forget it. A tiny shriveled old thing, half blind and almost entirely deaf, she lived for many years alone in her little white clapboarded house half a mile up the road from Ralph and Rosanna. She could have made her home with them, but she was, as Rosanna remarked, proud and indipindent as an old sea lion.

The neighbors' children had enjoyed tormenting her by calling her on the telephone: "This Miss Jinny Burden? The sea captain's daughter?"

"Speakin'!" trilled Aunt Jinny excitedly.

"Davy Jones callin'!"

Aunt Jinny had often been to sea with her father, a widower, and she remembered strange ports of call—Capetown and Mozambique, Amirante and Bombay, and she loved to rattle off the names to whoever cared to listen. There were usually a few irreverent ones who urged her to tell of her adventures on her father's four-master, named *Jinny Lou* after his dead wife.

The neighborhood kids thought Aunt Jinny as funny as hell. For as long as they could remember she had worn the same old-fashioned black dress with trailing hem, felt slippers, an ancient embroidered shawl over her skinny shoulders. Summer and winter, the same

337

clothes. She probably never bathed but she never looked dirty, and when you got close enough to her she smelled rather pleasantly of old tarred rope.

Aunt Jinny "minded" her own house and her own business and she never asked for help. She read the daily paper page by page, taking all day to do it because of her poor sight; she enjoyed listening to the radio which Ralph Burden had fixed up for her, and she spent much time polishing her father's brass compass case, his telescope, and a pair of ship's lanterns, keeping these mementos in what she called spittin' clean order. Her sole concession to Ralph and Rosanna's concern for her welfare was to agree to a telephone beside her bed. She slept in a room next to the kitchen because she was now too feeble to climb the stairs.

Aunt Jinny must secretly have adored that telephone. She crocheted a pink wool dust cover for it and it stood on the table beside her pillow so she couldn't miss it even in the dark, an icon to which she turned when she felt like communing with the world beyond her four walls. She would dial the operator and ask for her party by name, and the operator, familiar with Jinny's ways, always gravely obliged.

Perched like a little black cricket on the edge of her bed, Aunt Jinny would converse with animation and at length. When the operator rang her number she would hurry to the telephone, radiant with expectation. "Miss Jinny Burden? Hold the line for Mozambique!"

Aunt Jinny occasionally caught on to the game, but she more often than not fell for it and lived on the glory of these far-flung communings for weeks afterward.

Then had come that blizzard and the world beyond Aunt Jinny's windows churned like surf on an invisible shore. The radio reported an exceptionally severe storm, then went dead. So did the telephone. Power lines were down everywhere and the highway below Aunt Jinny's house was submerged in five-foot drifts. Aunt Jinny lighted her ship's lanterns and sat down to watch the weather make, as she called it, and to await the plodding arrival of some worried neighbor from down the road. Rosanna trudged through the snow to make sure that she was all right, and later sent Monty on the same errand. When they had gone, Aunt Jinny watched darkness fall and felt the surge and lift of the wind and heard it lash the panes.

Staring out the window, she saw a great ship plunging through the flying murk. The masthead light blazed in the darkness, spray beat against the tautly spread sails. As it drew near she could see the great white wings of the ocean sweep on either side of the bow and she realized that it was a matter of minutes before the vessel struck on the shoals below her house.

Aunt Jinny never hesitated a moment. Grabbing one of her father's lanterns and not bothering to pull on her overshoes, she let herself out the back door and plunged into the vortex, waving her lantern frantically to warn the watch in his crow's nest above the heaving smother of the waves.

Ralph Burden and his companion in the cab of the snowplow never saw Aunt Jinny. The great searchlight on top of the cab bored a yellow tunnel down the clogged highway, missing the turnoff into her obliterated driveway in all that whirling confusion. Aunt Jinny, a snow-covered speck in the drift, fell, losing her lantern. She pulled herself up and struggled down the slope into the path of the oncoming plow.

Afterward, Ralph said to Rosanna: "I was wonderin' could we get the plow into her driveway, when I thought I heard her voice quite close. But it seemed crazy to think of it in that goddam storm and the racket of the plow and everything. But still I thought I heard Aunt Jinny's voice cryin' out somethin'—God knows what. Didn't even know when we went over her in the dark. Didn't even feel it."

Later they traced her passage, down from her door blown off its hinges in the wind, and the channel her body had forged through the snow. They found the ship's lantern still alight, glowing like a yellow rose in its caul of ice. But they couldn't for the life of them imagine what could have brought Aunt Jinny out in that storm, to die under the great vanes of the snowplow, nor could they quite believe it when Patrice, who had known Aunt Jinny slightly, reconstructed the truth for them.

And then there was the developing story of Rosanna herself, a woman of passionate loyalties, worshiping her husband and her son —that opaque character who drifted through life smoking cigarettes and morosely consulting his acne in the kitchen mirror. Monty, that pimpled, pallid boy who, years before, had found Patrice huddled in anguish at the head of her own stairs. Monty had simply elongated in space and time. He had no friends, and his orbit was his parents' house and Patrice's, both of which he haunted like some pale, uneasy dream. He was inarticulate and ubiquitous, neither daft nor really half-witted—merely Claremont Burden, Rosanna's beloved son, and sometimes when Patrice awoke alone in the house toward dawn she heard the soft crunch of his feet on the gravel outdoors and the responsive thumping of the dogs' tails as they recognized his presence, and she assured herself that she would not let another day go by without complaining to Rosanna. . . .

"He just makes me nervous, Rosanna, that's all. Prowling around at all hours as he does, never announcing himself . . . it just makes me nervous!"

Patrice would rehearse her piece and, word perfect, tramp purposefully across the cemetery and down to Rosanna's door to deliver her protest. But she never did. There was Rosanna, always rosy and huge, smelling of freshly laundered sheets. There were Rosanna's eyes begging her, begging. . . .

Years later Patrice was to be thankful for her self-restraint. Monty Burden joined the Navy and in 1944 he was to die of wounds on his ship in the Atlantic, and Rosanna, weeping in Patrice's arms, railed against the fate which prevented his being buried in his native soil among four generations of Burdens, laid in rows under their little silken flags and their wreaths of waxen flowers.

"Buried at sea!" Rosanna moaned, tears sluicing down her ruddy cheeks. "All his folks up there in the cemetery, and Monty lyin' at the bottom of the sea!"

Monty with his pimples and his marble eyes. Monty, whom no one had wanted to have around. Monty batting to and fro in his human frame now become a ghost in fact. How desperately they had sought to give him flesh, to make him real, to make him whole—poor Ralph, poor Rosanna. What strange caper of love had created him to begin with?

Monty had come home on leave before being sent overseas. The spots were still there, and the evasive eyes, but he looked something of a man at last and he died a manly death. One day when Ralph was not home Rosanna and Patrice talked about the dead boy and Rosanna burst out: "They're givin' him a medal. A post—post—what-you-call-it. And I guess this makes me a Gold Star Mother. Gold star my big fat ass! *I want Monty back.* I want to see him sittin' there

340

where he's always sat, squeezin' his pimples and frettin' about the girls. I want for things to go on like they always done. Ralph comin' home from work every evenin', Monty forgettin' to wipe his shoes on the mat before steppin' on my clean floor. I want the three of us together round that table like we always been. I don't want to spend the rest of my life thinkin' and dreamin' about Monty lyin' by himself at the bottom of the sea."

Patrice held the defrauded mother in her arms. "Rosanna. Dear Rosanna."

"There's them that didn't like Monty," Rosanna said, trembling. "There's them said he hadn't ought to have been born. That he had queer ways. That he wouldn't never have amounted to anything. And them that didn't say it looked it." She stared at Patrice. "You *didn't*. You knew well as I did that Monty was real, that he was human like the rest of us." She drove her knuckles into her eyes. "They got all the answers! Your country this, your country that! Your duty, your flag. All of it. But they got no answer to this one: What'd I have him for?"

But this afternoon as Patrice trudged through the snow toward the Burdens' house Monty Burden was still living and his parents still sure that he would marry, have children, and be the pride and staff of their old age.

They were never to learn of that morning when Monty had planned to kill Patrice. Alone in the house, she had gone into the garage and surprised him standing there with a freshly sharpened sickle in his hand. He was supposed to be trimming the long grass under the trees, but as she stepped from the kitchen door into the garage she knew at once that he had been waiting for her. The dogs were used to him; they would be no help. She was alone with Monty but he was no longer the child whose face she had slapped, once, a long time ago.

Now they stared at each other and her eyes told him she knew what was in his mind. Killing her was all that he could do to her and as the seconds slipped by in their measured fashion her thoughts ran with them: Voyeur . . . stuff of spies . . . peeping tom of espionage . . . keyhole perfectionist . . . pervert of impotence . . . To kill was all he had in his power to do to her.

The kitchen door had snapped locked at her back and she watched him cross the garage floor toward her, his knuckles white against the short wooden handle of the sickle. She stared into his eyes and saw the sickle rise and hang above his head like a slivered moon. He spoke in a hoarse whisper: "I knows all about you. There ain't nothin' I don't know about you."

"You're dead," Patrice said slowly. "You're dead, Monty, and you don't even know it."

The words seemed to utter themselves, and Monty stood so close she could see faint blond hairs on his chin. Their eyes seemed locked together, then he lowered his uplifted arm and went away, and she heard him chopping at the rich grass under the trees, while out in the fields a meadowlark sang and sang.

Patrice kept the incident to herself, but now a queer test of strength developed between them: murder in him, in her the determination not to show her fear. And round and about Monty and herself she felt Rosanna's wordless gratitude, her hapless, quenchless love.

25

"*C*hrist, but you're difficult to paint!" complained Jonas Brayne. He stepped back from the easel, squinting. "Like trying to paint a chameleon." He shuffled back to the canvas, added a touch to the portrait, then laid his palette and brushes on a table. "Time out for coffee, little Patrice."

Patrice rose from the chair where she had been posing, and stretched. Walking to the easel, she studied the portrait, a head and shoulders now almost completed. Jonas's style was impressionistic, and this was not a portrait Adam cared for; certainly his parents would have disliked it, as they disliked Jonas and all his works.

Patrice had agreed to pose for him partly for the fun of it, and because she welcomed any excuse to be with Jonas and his wife, Netta. They had, over the years, become her escape hatch from the diurnal round of her household existence and the increasing restlessness of her spirit. The Braynes' house was unlike any other in this staid New England town; it was a messy house, chaotic, smelling of paint and children, of exotic food, and vibrating to the sound of Netta Brayne's piano or of an ancient phonograph which gave forth, at all hours of the day or night, creaky renditions of Mozart from the Braynes' rather spotty collection of records.

To Patrice, a neophyte still in what she considered the world of art, Jonas and Netta offered more than friendship; they were her introduction to a kind of existence in which, for the first time since her marriage to Adam, she felt completely at home. They were, besides, an exhilarating pair, misfits and birds of passage in a community into which Jonas had been born forty-odd years before.

Heir to a fortune left him by his grandfather, and early orphaned, Jonas had, in his own words, fiddled and diddled his way through college and therefter exiled himself to Europe and to the spasmodic study of art, to become self-consciously and determinedly a Bohemian, with a wardrobe of indescribable clothes. Gifted and undisciplined, possessed of enormous physical vigor and the magnetism of wit and money, he had become something of an international figure long before Adam and Patrice caught up with him. The First World War found Jonas in France, where he served with an ambulance outfit for the duration. Pugnacity was not in him. He detested what he saw of the war. He could paint it and parody it, recount hilarious scatological stories about it, but in the end it left him sickened and sobered.

When she first met Jonas and his wife, Patrice was still a long way from a critical insight into people and affairs, still groping toward some understanding of her own needs and nature, green enough to stand enthralled at the sight of Jonas painting at his easel and Netta thumping on her baby grand. But it was in Jonas's house that she was first to hear a Mozart symphony and to gaze on a landscape by Cézanne, and that she was to discover Stendhal and Flaubert. The Braynes were her introduction to sophistication and irreverence, as they were to be her bridge toward a self-realization for which, eventually, Jonas was not especially eager to accept the onus. The most serious thing about him was his creative ardor, and there was, as Patrice had sensed from the beginning, honey in the man somewhere.

Jonas was forty when he undertook the great adventure which he apostrophized as Holy Bedlock with Netta Stevens ... Netta, twenty years younger than he; impoverished, Jewish, dark-eyed, beautiful, and impressionable.

Jonas adored young, small, impressionable women, in whom, as in many men, he evoked a kind of hero worship. He had fallen in love with Netta the day they met—or so he declared. Four years and three babies later Netta wearily confided to her friends that Jonas had fallen in love for the first time and all time with himself. But by the time she had made this discovery she was too devitalized to resent it much. In any event Jonas would have been difficult to resent for long. He was too big, too exuberant, too full of himself ever to submit to harness, or to the exigencies of day-to-day life. But there was no question about his affection for his children, a trio of blue-eyed hellions who made bedlam of the house. They set mousetraps among his memorabilia so he caught his fingers and howled in rage. They ignited wastebaskets, and spent happy hours squeezing his paint tubes dry. They posted his mail in the water closet and remained obstinately unhousebroken themselves. At meals they flipped spinach at each other in innocent fun, and embarked on inexplicable hunger strikes which made Jonas mad with worry.

Anarchy reigned in the house, which he complained smelled like an orphanage in Hong Kong. Netta moved through this frenetic existence like a somnambulist, or sought surcease in her piano. Jonas had built a music room for her where—ideally—she might practice undisturbed. He was by turns generous, uxorious, tolerant, and suspicious. In his heart he may have feared that she might suddenly take wing, for this big man—six feet six in his socks—seemed prey to every imaginable terror. Many of these probably had their roots in vanity. He was a conqueror of women, but the possibility of being deserted by one gnawed him like a canker. The children being flesh of his flesh, a mishap to one posed a threat to him. Profligate with money, he was chronically short of funds and suffered seizures of apprehension lest his grandfather's trustees commit a malfeasance with his inheritance. When not absorbed in painting he fretted and fumed through life, exhausting his household's natural supply of oxygen so that Netta and the children wore a curious pallor, rather like turnips.

Possibly as a counterirritant to Jonas's appearance—shaggy beard and hair, accentuated by a sort of street peddler's garb—Netta decked herself similarly. She designed her own hats, when she wore any, and her clothes gave an impression of being worn inside out and back to front.

Somehow this pair survived, somehow their children throve. But one could forget the chaos in an atmosphere of books and music and

345

unregenerate mirth. That there were contradictions, inconsistencies, hypocrisies behind the mask of bohemianism Patrice was not to discover for a long time. And when finally she made this discovery about her friends she was older, and—to a great extent thanks to them—wiser.

In the years that she and Adam had lived in Maine they had grown to share, more or less, what Jonas disdainfully described as the house-and-lot existence of many of their friends. Adam seemed content. He was doing what he wanted to do. If the earlier, more ambitious dreams of his youth had come to nothing, present realities seemed to serve him well enough. That he earned very little, that he and Patrice were still largely dependent on his parents' bounty, did not trouble him overmuch, and somehow five hundred miles of physical distance between himself and them made the situation less of a strain. Adam had faced, and had made them face, and Patrice face, something he must always have known: Responsibility was not for him. And fate had connived, for after the birth and death of their first child there had been no more.

But Patrice's own exuberance would not be denied. Despite all the divergences between them, their fundamental differences of temperament, they still loved each other, and as the woman outgrew the child Patrice had too long remained, she turned the full force of her femininity upon Adam, only to learn for the second time that he was no more prepared to accept that challenge than he had been prepared to accept the first.

Exuberance assumed more complex forms and discovered other outlets. She began to write in earnest and felt the creative impulse grow under discipline and strain. Writing became an inner necessity, a compulsion she could not deny except through procrastination, so her struggle became threefold: against Adam's indifference, against her own insecurity, and now against Damon Edwards. Ironically these three subtle enemies were to provide her with that prerequisite for a growth of spirit: a private inviolability.

Jonas and Netta Brayne, standing outside the circumspect facade established by Adam's family and background, set Patrice an example of irreverence for shibboleths, and a corresponding seriousness toward intellect and work. They revealed to her the indestructible barrier between art and hobby, between the frivolity of the amateur

346

and the gaiety of the professional. It was a lesson she had always craved, and that she should now turn to the solution—a double life —was as inevitable as day following night.

Jonas laid down his palette and lighted a cigarette. He raised his voice: "Netta!"

A shapeless bundle on a sofa in a far corner of the studio stirred, and a voice said apathetically: "What?"

"Coffee. And why the hell aren't you practicing?"

"The piano's out of tune."

"I thought you just had the damned thing tuned!"

"I did, but the kids have been at it."

"Why the hell don't you keep the door locked so they can't get in?"

Netta yawned. "I did, but they got in just the same."

She emerged from her blankets and sneezed. "I thought I'd be quiet in here," she told them reproachfully. "I think I'm coming down with something."

Jonas eyed her with disfavor. He despised debility, and believed that Netta was inclined to pamper herself. All those heavy clothes, all that aspirin, those nose drops, when a little exercise and fresh air would have done the trick.

"Well," he growled, "get us some coffee before you fade away completely."

Netta sneezed again. "Why don't you go to the head of the stairs and wind your wreathèd horn?" she demanded, with a show of spirit. "Just when I was getting a little hard-earned rest!"

"It's goddam unhealthy the way you lie around. You'll get bed-sores."

Netta staggered yawning to the door. "It's not bedsores I'm afraid of," she said darkly, over her shoulder. "It's something a damned sight worse."

"God! Pregnant again?"

"I'm not sure." She put her knuckles in her teeth, staving off another yawn. "Time alone will tell."

She left the room and Jonas turned to Patrice. "Another kid! I love 'em, of course, but enough is enough."

He squinted at the portrait. "It'd be fun to have a baby around the place again, but the trouble is the little bastards don't stay babies."

He shuffled back to the easel and began to paint and Patrice

347

watched him, thinking: Time and compression, and dissonance too, like that Prokofiev thing Netta plays. It excited her to watch Jonas at work and to hear Netta play. These were moments when, clowning put aside, they became themselves, and their singleness of purpose stirred her own unrest so that it seemed as if the strain of effort became an end in itself.

"Hell, little Patrice," he had exclaimed once, with a Continental shrug of his shoulders. "The artist has to crack the whip over his own arse. He is his own slave and his own slavedriver. Who cares whether you write or whether I paint? Who's to say what is and what isn't?"

It was, he continued, the *perceived* detail, modest, even prosaic, which often lit the fire in one's brain. The curl of a cup handle in a still life by Cézanne, or those little true facts which so concerned Stendhal. "And for Christ's sweet sake avoid the solemn as you would the clap!"

Now as they smoked their cigarettes and waited for coffee to appear, Jonas turned to her abruptly: "How's the opus coming along?"

"I seem to be stuck."

He nodded. "Remember, this is your first major attempt, little Patrice." With Jonas as with many big men, in moments of tenderness all women became "little." "Bound to be difficult. Like one's first picture. One's first girl." He laughed. "It'll be easier once you've lost your literary virginity."

He had said it more than once, and Patrice felt comforted and reassured. She was unable entirely to forget or to dismiss Damon's comments on her writing—that she was rootless, an alien; how could she expect an audience to *identify* with any theme suited to her limited powers? The word "identification" had come to join the words "artistic" and "intellectual" in Jonas Brayne's index of culpable terms. When Patrice had on one occasion repeated Damon's strictures to Jonas he had flung his palette and brushes on the table with a roar. "*Identify?* Identify with what, with whom? Your pal sounds like just another literary boob. He probably uses the word 'intercourse' for making love!"

Well, Damon was no boob, and Patrice had changed the subject. She was aware that Damon tried to bludgeon her with weapons he felt would hurt her the worst, and, recognizing his intent, she re-

348

sponded in the fashion of most women at the hands of a passionate and jealous lover. She wiped her eyes, blew her nose, and came back for more.

As they waited for Netta to appear with a tray, Jonas studied Patrice. He had small, bright, yellowish eyes under shaggy brows. "Finish whatever it is you're doing, little Patrice. Don't let anyone try to stop you. Never mind even if you sometimes feel it isn't any good. *Finish it.*"

He could be candid about himself in this as in other matters. "Not completing a job has been my curse. Laziness. Cowardice too, in a way. Reaching an impasse and deciding to call it done. And no one can help you, really."

"You have helped me, Jonas. You and Netta."

His gaze rested on her with sudden tenderness. "It's good having you around, little Patrice."

He shambled to the door with his polar bear gait and bellowed down the stairs: "Goddammit, where's that coffee?"

Returning to the easel, he squeezed a bird turd of paint on his palette. "I repeat, you go ahead, Madame B. Ovary. And when you've completed the opus we'll go to New York and tackle my old pal Hart Barrow."

He had promised this before. Jonas knew everybody, and Hart Barrow was everybody in the publishing world. Patrice said uneasily: "Barrow wouldn't look at my stuff."

"There isn't a manuscript comes into Barrow's office he doesn't look at," Jonas assured her. "Listen, you and I have gone over this before, so quit being so coy. Think of some of the people Hart has put on the map after they'd been turned down by practically every publisher in the country!" Jonas twisted the hairs in his beard, glancing from the portrait to the model. "Hart has some kind of insight into the people who bring him their stuff. It amounts to genius, in a way." He hesitated. "Trouble with you, little Patrice, is you're a solitary sandpiper. Won't let other people see what you're doing, shy away from what you're afraid might be hostile criticism, mistrust praise!" He smiled at her. "Can't say I blame you. I could do with a bit more solitude in my life. I see too many people, write too many letters, talk too much. I let the kids distract me, and Netta . . . Well, we all carry our own cross. You for instance don't get much encouragement round the home, do you? I like old Adam, but I can see that he doesn't give much of a damn for anything aside from *le sport* and worming his dogs." He glanced away from her and muttered as if to himself: "Don't see how he can hold it against you if you feel like turning to fresh fields and pastures new. . . ."

Patrice had no doubt that the Braynes must for some time have suspected her relation with Damon though she had never confided the truth to them. But now she wondered whether, by his last remark, Jonas might not be inviting just such a confidence. Partly from a spirit of mischief—to keep him guessing—and partly from some saving sense of discretion, she said nothing, and waited while he busied himself with turpentine and rags.

He went on in his discursive fashion: "People like the Bannisters are the enemies of promise. They can't help themselves and it's a waste of time to blame them. They look on you and me as infidels, and so we are. Oh, they'll tolerate the artist—damn it, there I go again! —so long as he acts the clown and makes them laugh. They'll even tolerate his telling them to go to hell. But they won't stand for an infidel in the family. It's too risky."

Patrice had heard it all before. Conversation with Jonas was invariably a *continuo* of all previous conversations with him: there were occasions when she felt that he was talking for posterity, that he was in fact shaping his thought as he went along, using her as a sounding board. But he had a strong intuitive sense and she guessed that much of what he said was intended to liberate her from her own doubts and uncertainties and from her bouts of guilt and frustration in respect to Alice, to Adam, and to the Bannisters.

Jonas somehow made her see the strangeness of her own childhood and upbringing as no more than the essential strangeness of an individual life. She would, he implied, always be something of a stranger among people who mistrusted the strange. Once before, a long time ago, another man had said something of the sort to her—Barto Williams in that sunlit workshop above the garage in Berry's Landing: "I can see it now. You will never be one of them . . ."

Well, she had even grown away from Alice; she would go on growing and changing until the day she died. There was to be no surcease, no satiety. And she was beginning to wonder whether the quest for peace of mind was no more than a longing for death. Jonas had

350

warned her against solemnity, by which he perhaps meant too great
an exercise into introspection. He was not, himself, given to introspection. There was a large measure of bluff and bluster in his pro-
nunciamentos, and this too was a tonic for Patrice. He was after all
a rich man, and like others that she had encountered, he could afford
his eccentricities. He was not a person one needed to be sorry for,
and that was tonic, too.

She was indeed grateful to Jonas, who taught her much. He put
books her way and he could talk about them with perceptiveness and
ardor, firing her to enthusiasm. He taught her a measure of discrimi-
nation, and above all he came into her life at a point when she was
most susceptible to any new, galvanizing force. Long afterward the
Bannisters were bitterly to hold Jonas Brayne's early influence responsible for everything that went awry with Patrice, and how
should they have been expected to see it otherwise? Whatever went
awry was not with Patrice, but with the pattern, or the mold, in
which she could no longer sit still.

"Boobs," Jonas reiterated, tying knots in his beard. "Refined boobs
if you like, but boobs just the same. Scared of new ideas. Jew haters.
In their more neurotic versions one of them might go so far as to
marry even a Negro, but he'd never be friends with one." And: "Hell,
little Patrice. Every one of us has to make a choice sooner or later.
People like the Bannisters have had their choices made for them; so
in a way has Adam. It's going to be up to you to make yours—
eventually."

A figure appeared in the doorway, carrying a tray. It was Charlene,
the Braynes' much put-upon maid of all work. "Cawfee," she said as
she set the tray on a table next to the easel. "Yestiddy's. We're fresh
out and Mrs. Brayne she keeps forgettin'."

Charlene stood a moment staring at the portrait, and when Jonas
asked her genially what she thought of it she said, succinctly: "Nothin'."

On her way out the door she paused. "You better come downstairs
and do somethin' about your kids, Mr. Brayne. Lorelei's gone
and locked herself in the downstairs privy with an egg beater,
and the others has crawled under the back porch with a box of
matches."

She left the room and Jonas turned somberly to Patrice. "Two

351

women in the house and they don't know enough to hide the matches."

He gulped his coffee and set half a dozen brushes in a can of turpentine. "Guess we'd better call it a day. Come down and help me, will you, little Patrice? I'm too big to crawl under the porch and the little bastards know it."

Half an hour later, Lorelei liberated from the privy and the others flushed from under the porch with the aid of a garden hose, Jonas accompanied Patrice to the street. It was a pleasant street on the outskirts of the town, and the sound of traffic was muted by distance. An oriole sang in the branches over their heads, and Jonas said: "If you'd stay for lunch I'd drive you home."

"I'd like the walk."

"Adam home?"

"For a few days, yes."

Jonas twisted his beard thoughtfully. "Don't you ever get lonely, little Patrice?"

It was an obsession with many of her friends, and with Alice. Patrice shrugged. "Not really; no."

Jonas said abruptly: "Why don't you come to France with Netta and me this fall? It won't cost you much. You could stay with us."

It was not the first time he had proffered the invitation, nor the first time that she had explained: "I wish I could, but as you see I'm tied here."

"By Adam?"

"And by Alice. And the house, and everything else." She made it sound light, but he frowned. "You need a change of scene, little Patrice. Netta thinks so, too."

"One of these days, perhaps, Jonas!"

He shook his shaggy head. "You'll leave it until too late then do something silly. I sometimes wonder whether you really know which side your bed is buttered, little Patrice."

Patrice laughed and left him, turning once to see his towering figure disappear into the house. The oriole's song followed her down the street, then she lost it.

The town of Garside stood on a height overlooking the river Gar. It was a compact town of white-painted houses, church spires, brick business buildings, and an air of discreet prosperity. A generation of

352

people older than Adam and herself had weathered the bad times of 1929, and these still lived in the more pretentious houses on Otis Street, a tree-shaded avenue north of the town proper. Fortunes made in shipping and lumber a hundred years ago, and bolstered by canny management ever since, supported these pleasant mansions built of stucco and red brick. Professional gardeners tended the grounds, Filipino butlers waited at table, and there was a comfortable sense of there being more of everything where this came from.

There were not many such families in Garside, but enough to give the town panache. The sons went to Harvard or Yale, the daughters married well. There were trips abroad—to Europe in summer, in winter to Bermuda, Florida, or the Isle of Pines. The airplane era had not arrived and people traveled by train and ship. There were as yet no monstrous arterial highways scissoring the beautiful landscape; beside the new limousine waiting at the curb there might be a horse or two in the unconverted barn, a buggy, and an open sleigh. Men walked or bicycled to their offices, and on the edge of town farmers still used oxen to plow their fields. The more prominent families were still close enough to their ancestors' way of life to enjoy such simple, even Spartan pursuits as hunting and fishing, mountain climbing and canoeing. In winter they cut holes in the ice on the river and fished for perch or smelt, or they skated, or snowshoed through the woods. Something of a rugged past still clung to these people, to the women as well as to the men. They had a sense of style which set them apart from such innocents as Patrice's neighbors Ralph and Rosanna Burden.

The children of Garside's best families spoke French or German after a fashion; there was excitement about books, even a fling or two in the realm of "the arts." It was a generation which came closer than its predecessors or its descendants to evolving an aristocracy based on money and education. Forty years later it would revert again to the ideal of a single society, but with a difference. Patrice would live to see the handsome old houses knocked down to make room for supermarkets and gas stations, the great trees die from gas fumes or be felled to create space for parking lots. She would live to see the disappearance of passenger trains, and the sight of people walking for pleasure or riding horseback would be a thing of the past.

In the years that she and Adam had lived here Patrice had grown fond of the place. While it could not have been said to bear any true resemblance to her own lost background, there was something in the tempo of life, in its simplicities, and in the sense of an open country-side which evoked unexpected pangs of nostalgia and surprise. There were days in early spring and again in fall when a certain quality of light, a fragrance in the air, a sound, would immobilize her and fix her eye, her ear in a trance of expectancy. She felt that she should have been happy in this unpretentious, friendly town among unpreten-tious, friendly people, but something invariably came between her and a total surrender to this amiable existence which had been chosen for her.

Perhaps it was Netta Brayne, herself an exile from serenity, who put her finger on it: "In this kind of society the only adventure left for people like you and me is to have a nervous breakdown. In simpler souls it might be a rousing good murder, or something grotesque like a ten-year-old boy raping his grandmother."

But Patrice was not yet ready for her nervous breakdown. She had Damon, and when he was not with her she held the thought of him in her brain, in her body, drawing on its secret elixir like an addict.

When she had left the Braynes and started down the main street the air was full of summer and she longed suddenly to be back in her own house, preparing a meal for herself and Adam. Toward evening the air would turn cool enough for a fire in the living room, and Adam would settle himself in his chair with his pipe and a book, his dogs at his feet. "Home ... rivers and mountains from home .../If we two but keep together."

Patrice could not for her life feel guilt in this balancing act of the secret mistress and the dutiful wife. Adam she loved in one fashion, Damon in another. Physical love was as essential to her as food—physical love and the flattery that goes with it and perhaps the perils too, for she had never quite outgrown the inquisitive child who walked out to find the tiger which roared in the night.

She came to the end of the street and smelled the river, rank and brown, out of sight behind the railroad yard. Light shone on the faces of pedestrians coming toward her. One detached itself from the others and she heard Alice's voice: "Patrice, darling!"

"Alice. I'm on my way home from the Braynes'."

"It seems ages since I've seen you, darling."

354

"Two days."

"It has seemed like two months."

They stood together on the sidewalk, making a little island of their bodies. Alice chatted with a kind of desperation—trivialities, extending the moment, unashamedly clinging. Since she had come to live in Garside she had put on weight, but her skin was a girl's skin and her hair still bright. Only her eyes were haunted. In them Patrice found the past. The past of old snapshots and old letters and locks of childish hair. Stronger things had perished. Doey would be brittle now in that dusty graveyard above the Indian river, but Alice had kept every letter he had ever written her. What had become of the houses they had lived in, the gardens they had walked in? Where were the servants who had waited on them? Where the friends? Where the son whom she had cherished?

Alice might have remarried. She might have found an occupation, made a new beginning, become a bustling energetic matron like so many of those among whom she now lived. She might have acted on the sensible advice they gave her ... but she had done none of these things. Her gaze was fixed on the past and in its reflection Patrice too often found herself drowning.

Alice waited beside her on the sidewalk. Take me into your home, she begged inaudibly. Take me into your home, let me be part of your life as I used to be, as you have always been, and are, wholly my life. All I ask is everything as you once asked it of me and I always unhesitatingly gave.

"How are dear Jonas and Netta?" Alice inquired now, frantically making conversation. "They are always so kind when I call them up to ask for you."

Patrice thought: I should ask her to walk home with me, to have a cup of tea, spend the evening. It would be the normal, the decent thing to do. But she gets on Adam's nerves, and every day things become more strained, the warmth more artificial, words hard to find.

She felt sometimes that she must suffocate in this tidal love. True starvelings are quickly sated, but not Alice. Doey had died too soon, leaving her unspent.

"I was wondering," she said with spurious lightness, "I was wondering, darling, if you had heard. . . ."

"From Clem? Not a word."

Alice made a slight, futile motion of her gloved hands. "So strange," she murmured bleakly. "A whole year and not a word!"

"He did write once last year, you remember."

"To you, not to me, and you never showed me the letter."

They had been over this ground a hundred times. "If I just knew what to do," Alice murmured, her eyes filling. "If there was some way of finding out where he is, how he is."

"Perhaps he just doesn't want to be bothered with us."

It was cruel and Alice's face quivered. "But just a few lines! He must know we can't help being worried."

Patrice said: "I'll come round tomorrow and take you for a drive. Adam won't be using the car."

The sop, the consolation prize, and Alice became instantly radiant. "Will you, darling? I'll count the minutes."

She would count the seconds. Patrice kissed her and walked away toward the bridge, her heart knotted. We are beset by other people's loneliness, other people's deprivation. We feel like screaming: For God's sake! And that's where the Christian spirit should come in, and the Ten Commandments . . . a scab covering the wound of hate, or denying the death of love. What had happened to her love for Alice? When had Alice's love become a hippogriff?

Patrice knew that were she to look back Alice would be standing where she'd left her, waiting for that backward glance. Her patience was inexhaustible, like a dog's.

Oh, damn it, damn it, thought Patrice, walking faster, trying to outstrip the memory of that forlorn figure standing, staring after her.

If I were Rosanna Burden I'd take Alice into my house and cherish her without stint just as in her time Alice had cherished the little grandmother in that house in London and had held the small dying hand in hers until the last. If I were Rosanna Burden I'd be a better person. Rosanna understands love. She understands it as I do not, as Alice cannot. It is not something you think about, something to which you add or from which you subtract, or drool over, or batten on. Love is Rosanna's universe and she is at home within it. But as for Alice, as for me . . .

Patrice was almost running when she reached the entrance to her own driveway. She was flushed, her heart hammering in mockery: Running away! Running away!

She paused to get her breath and saw the late sunlight strike the windows of the house, drawing fire. Dandelions flared in the tall grass under the trees and at sight of them she stood quite still, a different cadence in her veins. She did not need to see him to know that he was there as he had been on that first day when she had come home to find him sprawled among the dandelions beside the empty house, in which, before that afternoon was over, he had taken her in his arms.

And just as on that other day, so now Damon Edwards rose from the grass and came toward her, his head burnished in the fading light. Patrice felt the leaden guilt fall from her shoulders as her gaze reached toward his.

"Careful," he murmured as he approached. "We are not alone."

He made a drama of it, low-voiced, and Patrice saw two cars parked under the farther trees, Adam's tubby black sedan and a glistening red roadster she had not seen before.

"Daisy Pitman," said Damon. "I was at Berry's Landing yesterday visiting Pa and Ma and ran into Daisy, who said she was driving down to Northeast Harbor and would I like a ride as far as this. Of course I jumped at it, taking a chance I'd find you home."

Patrice glanced at the house and had a glimpse of Adam and Daisy. They waved and Damon murmured: "I asked for my vacation in two installments so the summer wouldn't seem like eternity without you. Oh, Patrice, my darling!"

Patrice felt the four winds of heaven beat through her. Alice was forgotten; the Braynes; her book—everything. Nothing had any meaning for her except this resplendent young man.

She said slowly: "I don't know how I'm going to get through the evening."

"I don't know how I am, either, but at least I can look at you, hear you, perhaps touch your dress."

More often than not their encounters were no more than that: a glance, a word, a touch. Like athletes they had learned to subsist on little, and continence gave them both a roseate health which had not been lost, for one, on Jonas Brayne. Nor perhaps on someone else, and now Patrice was very much aware of Daisy Pitman's porcelain gaze trained on her from the window.

Damon said: "Hadn't we better go in?"

Side by side they walked across the lawn, the current running so strongly between them that it acted, strangely, like a barrier. Both felt that if they should brush against each other, however lightly, their bodies must explode. Neither word nor touch was necessary, for it seemed they existed in some third dimension, in an iridescence which colored the meanest object on which their dazzled eyes came to rest—the russet beam of the setting sun on a tree trunk, the stir of wind across the grass.

When they walked into the room where Adam and Daisy waited the sky behind the windows took the last shock of sunset, and to the lovers it seemed that all four people must burn to death in the holocaust.

Daisy's slightly nasal voice sent the sun on its way: "Surprise!" she said. "Surprise, surprise, surprise!"

Patrice floated lightly to earth. "Sorry I was out when you came. I've been modeling all afternoon, for Jonas."

"Not in the nude, I hope." Daisy laughed her little-girl laughter. Patrice decided that she was if possible lovelier than ever. Time, marriage, the bearing of children seemed only to have enhanced her looks. And Patrice thought: This is how it will be until she is quite an old woman. To stay beautiful, to stay young, will become the single overriding compulsion of her life, and twenty years from now her friends will say: "Isn't Daisy extraordinary? Would you ever guess her age?"

Daisy had turned, smiling, to Adam. "Do you allow your wife to pose in the nude, Adam?"

Nowadays on the rare occasions when they met, Daisy had a peculiar effect on Adam. He became distant, sometimes even curt. Now he seemed not to have heard her question as he moved closer to Patrice and slipped his hand under her arm. "How'd it go?" he asked lightly.

"About as usual. It's almost finished. Jonas says he'd rather paint a lizard than paint me."

"A lizard?"

"A chameleon is what he said." She felt lighthearted and in command of the situation, to which Daisy's presence lent a kind of zest.

"Wasn't it nice," said Daisy, "that Damon could drive down with me today? Such a boring trip alone."

She, too, was all verve, with no more than a hint of some private amusement in her brilliant glance. "So lovely," she went on, arranging herself tastefully in a chair with her back to the fading sky. "So nice to find Adam home with the bow-wows when we arrived. I'd have telephoned along the way but I didn't want to upset any plans you may have had. Patrice is always so busy, and you are so seldom home, Adam, dear."

She prattled on, quite at her ease. Patrice said politely: "You'll spend the night, I hope?"

"Thanks, no. I'm due at Northeast to meet Pinky and the boys. They're sailing down from Boothbay on the *Pegasus*. Of course, it's early to be sailing, but the boys couldn't wait!"

Patrice turned to Damon. "You'll stay, Damon?"

"If I may."

"Nice to have you," said Adam, and sounded as if he meant it.

Daisy fitted a cigarette into an ivory holder and looked brightly at Patrice. "I have news for you," she said. "I've already told Adam. Caroline is coming to visit us at Northeast. She and Hal are sailing all the way from Jamaica. They've already been *weeks* at sea. So sporting of them, don't you think?"

"Why," demanded Adam, "aren't they going to stay with my parents at Berry's Landing?"

Daisy shrugged. "My dear, you know your darling old papa isn't exactly head over ears with poor Hal! Caroline and I decided the best thing would be for Hal and herself to come to us. Pinky and I are planning a party at our place one day next week, and of course we've invited your dear pa and ma. They could drive down with Damon's family, with Timmy. Everyone meeting like that, on neutral ground so to speak, ought to make things easier." She was the soul of kindly practicality. "It goes without saying that we expect you and Patrice. You too, of course, Damon, if we wouldn't be too lowbrow for your taste!" She smiled upon him dazzlingly, and Damon smiled in response. "I'd love to go to your party, Daisy. That is if Patrice and Adam are going."

Adam said brusquely: "What's this about Timmy? I thought he was supposed to spend weekends with Barto at the Cape."

Daisy sighed. "I'm afraid Timmy has other ideas. He put on quite an act when he heard that his mother and Hal were to be at

Northeast. Insisted that he join them."

"I call it a dirty trick," Adam said coldly. "The agreement was that Timmy should spend his weekends with Barto. That was the deal—or part of it, aside from what my sister got away with when she left him."

Daisy sighed again. "My dear, we all know that. But what is to be done in a situation where the child himself—and Timmy's no baby now, you know—when the cruel truth is he seems to prefer being with Caroline and Hal?"

"Barto has as much legal right over Timmy as Caroline has. Morally I'd say Barto's right was even stronger than Caroline's!"

He had never conquered his dislike of his sister, but it occurred to Patrice that he seemed to have it in for Daisy, too.

"But Timmy adores his mother!" cried Daisy tearfully. "And he's crazy about his stepfather!"

"And it's thanks to them that he's the spoiled little bastard he seems to be," Adam retorted, and began angrily to fill his pipe.

Daisy's blue gaze dwelt on him with deliberate, unveiled tenderness. "Adam, dear!"

It was caressing, even sensuous, and Patrice caught Damon's faint, satiric smile as he turned away to examine a magazine on a nearby table.

Patrice said quickly: "Couldn't Caroline do something? I mean, as you say, Timmy's still only a kid. Couldn't Caroline make him see that he owes his father *something?*"

Daisy shrugged her graceful shoulders. "Doesn't it occur to you that Caroline too might have strong feelings on the subject? Let's forget the legal and moral aspects for a moment. Caroline is a mother, with a mother's feelings. As a mother myself I have some insights. . . . How do you suppose poor Caroline feels when the boy weeps, goes off his food, throws tantrums whenever it comes time for him to visit Barto?"

Adam tossed a spent match into the fireplace. "Barto happens to be his father, and even Caroline can't change that—now."

Daisy flushed her particular, entrancing flush. "You're right, of course, my dear. No one can alter the facts of the case. But you know as well as anyone that Timmy has never got along with Barto. All those years at Berry's Landing, ever since he was a baby . . . Private detectives spying on him, and later, not being allowed to lead a normal child's life, with Barto hysterical whenever he wanted to go swimming or sailing or even riding a bicycle! Just because Barto had been crippled by an accident when *he* was a child, his own was to be deprived of every normal risk or pleasure."

She was gentle, compassionate, understanding. Glancing at Adam Patrice surprised something like fear in his eyes. He said nothing, and Daisy, smoothing her well-cut skirt over her knees, went on: "There's something else. Terrible as it may seem, cruel as it may seem, unjust ... there is the comparison." She hesitated. "I mean the comparison between Barto and Hal. Hal so healthy, so hearty, so outgoing. The kind of man a young boy is bound to be attracted by, whereas poor Barto!"

She left it in the air, her myosotis gaze fixed on Adam. Patrice thought of Barto. After the divorce he had moved to New York and busied himself with his few hobbies, an occasional trip abroad, a diminishing circle of friends. He had taken to speculating on the stock market and was said to be losing a lot of money. On the few occasions that Adam and Patrice saw him he had seemed withdrawn, indifferent to people and events. His whole life now appeared centered to the point of obsession on the son whom he saw at decreasing intervals as the bond between them slackened, and it had never, as Daisy had said, been particularly strong.

She rose from her chair and carefully extinguished her cigarette in an ashtray. "I must be off!"

She turned directly to Adam. "What about next week? Pinky and I thought Saturday would be just right. Gives everyone enough time to make arrangements for getting down to Northeast. Lunch, we thought. Let's pray for a nice day. June can be so *tricky!*"

Adam spoke without hesitation: "Sorry. I'll be away on a job."

She made a tragic gesture of dismay. *"Can't* you arrange it somehow? We see so little of you nowadays ... you've become so *elusive.*"

"Sorry. I couldn't possibly."

"I'd put it off to another time," Daisy murmured distractedly, "except that that's the only week Caroline and Hal can be with us. They plan to visit just about all their old friends, and then they're going back to Jamaica." She turned with a sort of overflowing motion to Patrice. "You'll come next Saturday, won't you, Patrice? You know

Caro would love to see you . . . and Mr. and Mrs. Bannister coming too, and everything. It should be just like old times—except for you, Adam. I don't think I can forgive you."

"Sorry," Adam said for the third time, and Daisy whirled on Damon. "I can depend on you, can't I? Promise?"

"There's a little problem of transportation," Damon began, when Adam said quickly: "I shan't be using the car. You and Patrice can have it Saturday, of course."

Daisy laughed. "There! The complaisant husband if I ever saw one."

Adam gave her a queer look but said nothing, and Damon smiled his most disarming smile. "Thanks for the ride down, Daisy. It was fun."

As she passed him Daisy put out her hand and touched his cheek. "You get more seductive every time I see you, Damon Edwards. I feel sorry for the girls—not to mention us crones!"

26

The water was cold as it closed over her head and, half paralyzed, Patrice felt herself sinking in the lambent depths of the pool. Then Damon's strong arm was under her shoulders and she came up into the keen blue air with the sun hot through crowding leaves. The pool had a color of strong tea from the woodland debris of years. Where the stream poured into the pool off a great rock sunlight struck pale gleams and the sound of the waterfall drowned all other sound.

Patrice turned on her back and paddled to where the stream gushed from the rock, and ducked under it. Flagellation, fury. She rushed away and collided with Damon and they sank again, locked in each other's arms, sending the frightened trout dashing downstream. Again Patrice surfaced and, with ice forming round her spine, she made for the bank and scrambled out of the water.

They had left their clothes and towls arranged on a sunny rock, and she dried herself while Damon, his face sunk in the tawny water, swam lazily round the pool. His body had the tapered lines of a great fish, coppery in that light.

Since that day when she and Damon had become lovers for the first time—Patrice could not have said when—she had felt herself pos-

363

sessed by the great commonplace of life, which inexorably takes precedence over all others, in her case over her bondage to Adam and to Alice, and the self-imposed tyranny of her work. Alone with Damon, the commonplace of their love became self-sufficing, for her at any rate, if not always for him. For Damon took love in his stride. He gave himself as naturally to love as to the pool, master of both.

Crouched on her rock, Patrice stared down at his misty form in the water and at the trout which nosed timidly back to their lair under the bank. She could see the rose-moles on their sides, the delicate motions of their fins. She could see Damon's hair move on his head like seaweed, and the dark triangle between his thighs compact against his white skin.

Suddenly behind her a whitethroat sang above the noise of the stream and she shivered under the pelting notes, sure in her love-besotted soul that the song was intended for Damon and for her.

Wrapping herself in the towel, she shifted to a larger patch of sun, where, presently, he joined her, and arranged himself fastidiously on his towel before lighting a cigar. They had made love earlier and now a companionable languor enfolded them. They could meet each other's eyes without constraint, talk lightly of matters which had little to do with their love.

Patrice, teeth chattering, rummaged among her clothes and produced an envelope. "Mind if I read Clem's letter again? It's been so long."

Damon bundled his clothes under his head and blew smoke into hovering squadrons of mosquitoes. He had a sleek, subtly muscled, almost hairless body in which he took enormous pride, as he did in most things that belonged to him. Before lighting the cigar he had removed the gilt-and-crimson band and placed it ceremoniously round Patrice's toe. "With this ring," he intoned solemnly, "I thee bed."

Clem wrote:

> I didn't want to leave Spain but Melissa had the wind up because of the war. Of course she was right. We had to think of the kids, besides which we were using up other people's space, other people's food. We had managed to save a bit of cash and a dear old English widow bought one of my paintings. So we decided to get out of Spain while the going

364

was good. We crossed into France before the glut of refugees and miraculously there were no complications. How easy it is for people who are not committed! The talkers, the shiners in reflected glory! For the first time in my life I began to realize the fundamental tyranny of family ties and all its insidious lures. It's not conscience that makes cowards of most of us—it's the thought of missing bacon and eggs for breakfast. When we were quitting Spain I really wished the hell I was someone else. I saw men grabbing scythes, sickles—anything they could lay hands on—and heading for the fight, most of them knowing damn well they hadn't a chance. My old pals distinguished for nothing except that they are Spaniards, and what a distinction, that! You know I've always held war to be the ultimate shit, but civil war is the most exciting shit of all, to be in this one. Both sides have the same fanaticism and ferocity. I'm afraid that the Long Live Death wallas are going to get away with this round and that I should have sent Melissa and the kids away and stayed myself and heaved my little rock. But because of Melissa and the kids I didn't. Can't you hear Doey's groan of disgust? I can.

Patrice laid the letter on her bare knees and stared down at the brown water. Damon had put aside his unfinished cigar and his eyes were closed. He was snoring softly. Light traveled the length of his body and encircled his head. Sleep made him seem strangely unreal.

When you get down to it [wrote Clem] we are all in the clutches of the urbane assassins who arrange these things. Maybe one day there will be a great vomit of boredom against them, and then all the young men of killable age will to the woods to gather May. . . .

Damon opened his eyes. "Read me your brother's letter," he said lazily. Patrice read it aloud and when she had finished Damon said: "Silly to muck around with great big undigestible ideas." And after a moment he added: "Clem's never been sure of anything, has he? Sounds as if he never would be."

"Are you so sure of anything?" she asked bluntly.

"Of great big indigestible ideas—yes, I am. I leave them alone."

He retrieved his cigar, sniffed it, and tossed it into the pool. "Damn. That was my last. Why did you let me fall asleep?"

He went on: "I'm sure of a few other things besides. I'm sure some

365

people are improvable if they can be taught to keep their tempers. I'm sure 'improvable' is a lousy word. I'm sure that reading poetry and trying to write it is essential to my life. I don't try to answer for other people, as Clem does. I'm sure that John Donne was wrong, and that every man *is* an island, and better for the archipelago that he stay an island."

Patrice said ponderingly: "Clem is an artist. I know it's a much abused word; Jonas Brayne says it gives him gooseflesh. But perhaps being an artist, or trying to be one, is what makes Clem what you call unsure about the big undigestible ideas."

"He's not artist enough, that's his trouble. It's your friend Jonas Brayne's trouble too, and yours, if you don't mind my saying so."

"You've said it before."

He went on imperturbably: "I don't believe there will ever be a time when killable young men will to the woods to gather May instead of to the woods to gather bullets. I don't believe in the brotherhood of man. A lot of brothers hate each other, as we learned in Genesis. Safer to be an island."

Safer to be Damon Edwards, Patrice reflected, studying the sunlight as it painted his eyelids gold. Fortune was indelible in him, or so it seemed. After a moment he said: "I'm glad I don't have your dilemmas, or Clem's. As for my parents, I like them very much. They are sensible and unimaginative. They were thoughtful enough not to upset my life by providing me with brothers and sisters. They admire me and they don't drive themselves or me nuts trying to understand me. A very fine arrangement all around."

Behind them the whitethroat had fallen silent. In the pool the trout hung motionless in the current, and the noise of the waterfall filled the air with a drowsy cadence. The cold had left her limbs and she let the towel slip from her shoulders, feeling the sun slide on her bare skin. In a little while they would dress and walk back to the house and prepare for the long drive to Northeast Harbor and Daisy Pitman's party. They would rejoin that world of relatives, parents, friends, shared preoccupations—a world which remained irrevocably part of themselves even at the moment of their farthest distance from it. Patrice knew that Damon was very much part of that world from which, with every year, she felt herself increasingly an alien. Her love for him was no part of that world, any more than Adam's love for her was part of it. Sufficient for the day and for the countless days ahead was the make-believe thereof.

Now Damon rose and drew her to her feet. They stood motionless, clasped. The whitethroat sang for them again, the stream flowed for them, the trout swam for them, and over Damon's naked shoulder Patrice saw a movement among the trees, and the opaque gaze of Rosanna Burden's son closed upon hers. With a swift movement she leaned to one side and plunged into the pool, taking Damon with her.

The Pitman house dated from the year 1900 and was built of assorted local stone with a green trim. There were turrets, oriel windows, balconies, and buttresses, all of which combined to give it a vaguely reptilian air as it crouched rather than stood in what was described by the admiring and envious as extensive grounds.

"It's so wonderfully hideous!" Damon remarked enthusiastically to Patrice as they drove along a narrow dirt road between somber ranks of spruce. "It cost a fortune to build and it would probably cost a fortune to pull down, even if anyone should want to pull it down, and certainly Pinky wouldn't dream of doing that—thank God!"

Damon's parents had been close friends of the elder Pitmans, who were now dead, and Damon had often visited here as a child. Patrice attributed his fondness for the place as a hangover from his undiscriminating infancy, though it seemed to her, occasionally, that he rather went out of his way to admire the ugly and to express a kind of patronizing affection for it, in the fashion of medieval royalty, which kept dwarfs and hirsute grotesques for their private amusement. More and more frequently now, when she had been alone with Damon and they had exhausted themselves making love, she found this carping spirit in herself and strove, not always with success, to curb it.

"They built for keeps, those old boys," Damon went on discursively. "They were convinced that their world was never going to end. I love to think of the days when the nouveau riche gloried and drank deep. And they really did, you know. The Pitmans ate fried chicken and apple pie for breakfast, and they had servants—mammies and nannies and Uncle Toms, and later Japanese gardeners and Filipino houseboys. An era of extroverts—lovely era!"

Patrice eased the car over a bump in the road and murmured plaintively that she wished the owners would employ a scraper on the surface. "I've been in second gear all the way from the gate!"

Damon said reflectively: "Poor Pinky! He inherited everything except that primordial lust for life, and now he's scared stiff someone may come along and take everything away from him."

Patrice replied cooperatively that she thought Pinky's fears natural enough, and Damon nodded solemnly. "After all," he said, "you don't miss what you've never had, but to lose it when you've grown to love it, take it for granted!"

Patrice slowed almost to stopping for another bump. "Just the same," she said crossly, "I wish Pinky'd blow himself to a decent job on this damned road of his."

"He likes it this way," Damon told her loftily. "He's quite a simple sort of guy really, in spite of all his dough."

Patrice said nothing, but she was conscious of a vague depression, a letdown from the élan of the past two days. The air smelled of sunlit spruce, of the nearby invisible sea, and it stirred a sudden nostalgia in her for she knew not what. Damon glanced at her profile. He said quickly: "A penny!"

"I love you," she told him. "I wish there were some other way to say it, and even wishing it seems trite."

She took his hand and held it against her heart and he said: "It beats like one of your Indian tomtoms, all through the day, all through the night." His voice took on a new, a deeper note. "I love you," he told her. "I don't give a damn how trite it sounds. Sometimes I feel that there must be a surfeit, but there isn't. It just goes on and on, more and more."

Magically the depression left her, life and color rushed to her face, and Damon lifted her hand to his lips. "That's better," he murmured. "That's the real you, the real Patrice!"

Voices reached them from beyond the trees, sunlight flashed on windows and on the metal of parked automobiles. "We're late," Patrice said. "They'll wonder what the hell."

Dogs barked the shrill effete barking of pampered creatures. Daisy specialized in small ragged-looking animals of obscure but impeccable breed, with watery eyes and sore behinds. She exhibited these specimens in dog shows, and her photograph, soignée and beautiful,

368

appeared regularly in the rotogravure section of the Sunday paper with Pitman's Sunny Boy III or Pitman's Moon Baby IV crouched on her lap.

A lawn of green velvet bordered by ornamental urns spilling geraniums unfolded in the sunlight, and Damon said: "They'll be on their first cocktail. You know, I do believe that the Volstead Act gave your father-in-law and his friends their first and possibly only taste of vice, the only opportunity for civic defiance they ever dared. Remember those scofflaw buttons? Remember those righteously indignant letters to the press?"

"I remember the cocktails," said Patrice. "Ground glass and epsom salts."

"And I remember you. I must have been about fifteen, and I'd been dreaming about you without having set eyes on you. Lascivious dreams. Then there you were with your flat shining hair and your dowdy dress."

"And I remember meeting you on the beach one morning when Adam and I had had a row and he'd left me to walk home by myself. Suddenly you popped up out of the bushes and made indecent advances to me."

"And I've been making them ever since, and I shall go on making them until death do us part."

"I won't," she said angrily, "I won't let it us part!"

"Nor will I if I can help it."

Patrice parked the car among a dozen others, and they turned to see Daisy and her husband and Caroline descending the balustraded front steps. It was more than a year since Patrice had seen her sister-in-law; Caroline appeared stouter, ruddier, exuding a sexual vitality reflected even in her clothes—a pink sweater and yellow slacks too tight for her, her dark hair with an orange streak that had not been there a year ago. Under her clothes her body bobbled and bounced like a hutch of rabbits, and Patrice had an immediate amused pleasure in seeing her.

"Darling!" she greeted Patrice. "Still unpregnant? Lucky you!" She turned to Damon. "And fancy seeing you! I'd have thought you'd be spending the summer on Mount Olympus."

"They don't feed us on Mount Olympus. Ambrosia isn't my idea of an adequate diet."

369

He was quite at home, assured of his place in this paddock of relatives and friends.

"Daisy tells me that stick of a brother of mine couldn't be bothered to come to the party!"

"Adam had to leave on another job," Patrice explained, and Caroline smiled dryly. "The hell with Adam!"

Daisy was looking on benignly, one of her dreadful little dogs tucked under her arm. "You're late," she remarked to Patrice. "What kept you?"

Patrice looked her in the eye. She had long since given up caring what Daisy might think of her. "We went swimming and forgot the time."

Daisy laughed. "Well, well! I can just see Pinky leaving me alone with a handsome young man for weeks on end!"

Pinky Pitman—his real name was Kinkham—murmured something about perfect love casting out all fear, and it occurred to Patrice that the exorcism did not appear to have been effective in his case; he had the peculiar half-arrogant, half-diffident manner of a man perpetually afraid of something. Although he had in the past held a distinguished record in the army, the exigencies of peace left him insecure, afraid of housebreakers, trespassers, and the possible ill will of neighbors. He disliked any deviation from the strictly conventional, and now, recalling certain hints dropped by Daisy, he gazed on Patrice and young Damon Edwards with the latent hostility of a man who instinctively espouses the lost cause of all cuckolds. Pinky's first thought on seeing Damon this afternoon was a morosely disapproving one: "At his age I was in the front lines at Belleau Wood."

They turned back to the steps and Caroline took Patrice's arm. "I am so happy to see you, Patrice, dear. I see so little of you and I miss you." She added in a lowered voice: "Do make up to Pop. Whenever he and Pinky get together Pop starts venting his anti-Roosevelt spleen on the nearest scapegoat. Nowadays it happens to be poor Hal. Who the hell could I have married that would have satisfied my father, will you tell me?"

"You could have married Pinky before Daisy got him," Patrice suggested gravely. "Your father's crazy about Pinky."

Caroline laughed. "Not my type. I love him, of course, but he's better off with Daisy, as I am with Hal."

Patrice glanced at her. "You look happy, Caroline. Are you?"

"Very. I've never been happier. If there is such a thing as being ideally suited, then Hal and I are so. After those dreadful years with Barto!"

They fell into step behind the Pitmans and Damon, and Caroline went on earnestly: "If it were not for Timmy I wouldn't have a care in the world. He's here today, you know. So lovely to have him. He's *grown.*"

Patrice was silent and Caroline went on: "He adores Hal, and you can imagine what that means to me. But there's always Barto in the background, if he'd only stay in the background."

Arm in arm in the wake of their hosts and Damon, Caroline and Patrice passed through the big airy rooms toward the veranda at the rear. Doors and windows stood open to the breeze, which carried a fragrance of sea and roses, and everywhere the pale sea light of this part of the world dealt gently with things—with worn, old rugs, with human faces, human gestures—and Patrice reflected: It takes generations of the same kind of people to achieve this synthesis. There must be something to be said for keeping one's thorny inner self buried under layers of circumspection until the hard outlines of individuality powder away and only urbanity remains.

A dozen people were seated in the chintz-covered rattan chairs on the veranda, which overlooked the harbor, not yet crammed with yachts, as it would be later in the season. An enormous wisteria, gnarled and knotted like a rusty hawser, made a living, scented frame for the scene without and the stage within, and Patrice had a shock of memory, of Daisy and her first bridegroom, that strong uncouth figure of Lawrence Redditch standing before the hearth in Caroline's house at Berry's Landing a long time ago; of herself in love with Adam, carrying Adam's child.

She thought, now, of time as something sly, ubiquitous, a presence you would not care to run into in the dark, always up to something, and leaving its spoor for your speculative, daylight eyes.

Her glance went at once to her mother-in-law, in a light summer dress which made her appear younger than her sixty years. Mr. Bannister, his back to the company, was studying the harbor through binoculars, and Damon's parents were seated so as to catch an uninterrupted view of their son as he approached. Sunlight glinted on bottles and glasses arranged on a large tole tray. Beyond the veranda and out of sight behind a towering hedge of white roses, a game of tennis was in progress to the accompaniment of children's voices and the melancholy strains of an accordion playing "Smoke Gets in Your Eyes."

Mrs. Bannister held out her hand to Patrice. "My dear child!"

Patrice stooped to kiss her, and Mrs. Bannister asked: "And Adam?"

"Off on another job." She met Mrs. Bannister's affectionate gaze. "He loves it, you know."

"I was thinking of you, my dear. Alone so much." She hesitated. "Patrice, I don't want to—you know—talk out of turn. I suppose it's not my business, yet in a way it is. After all, you are Adam's wife...." She had flushed. "Before the others hear us ... My dear, it is not true, is it, that you pose for that artist person—Jonas Brayne —that you pose for him in the nude?"

Patrice controlled a wild desire to laugh. "It doesn't happen to be true," she replied soberly. "But if it were wouldn't it be my business?"

"There! I've annoyed you and I didn't mean to. I just felt that I should speak of it to you ... and that you would understand."

She took Patrice's hand and held it in a close, imploring clasp.

"Patrice, dear, we live in a small world and people *talk.*"

"So it seems."

Mrs. Bannister said in agitation: "Of course, I know you would never do anything to hurt Adam and our good name!"

For an instant Patrice felt herself trembling on the verge of a devastating revelation that would free her, and Mrs. Bannister also, forever from all further pretense. But perhaps sensing the imminence of danger, Mrs. Bannister suddenly released Patrice's hand, and raising her voice with a false sprightliness she cried: "Wilbur! Here is our Patrice!"

Wilbur Bannister turned, the binoculars hanging from his neck by their thong, which for some reason gave him an absurdly rakish air. Patrice went through the motions of another filial greeting and Mr. Bannister brushed her cheek with his moustache. "You are late, my dear. And what's this about Adam not accompanying you?" He peered at her through his pince-nez. "Think of my being the parent

372

of two children and enjoying so little of their company! Why, I see more of my dear Daisy and her husband than I do my own son and daughter."

"Wilbur," Mrs. Bannister said firmly, "I thought you were going to help Pinky with that second drink."

"You were indeed, sir." Pinky Pitman seconded her dutifully. "I await your instructions." Pinky was like that with his older friends, and it charmed them.

Mr. Bannister declared with a simpering air: "Pinky mixes as good a martini as anyone I know."

"And who," Pinky demanded gallantly, "should be a better judge than you, sir?"

They walked away toward the tole tray and Patrice found a chair beside Mrs. Bannister and felt herself subside in a familiar drone of voices and a drone of bees in the wisteria. Her moment of recklessness had passed. It might never have been.

"Just like old times," Mrs. Bannister exclaimed happily. "So nice to be together again." Patrice thought: There will be no more references to posing in the nude or, from her at any rate, any more risky overtures. Mrs. Bannister was flushed, smiling, grateful for the moment, asking nothing more.

Damon had gone at once to his parents and now he stood bending over their chairs. They gazed up at him humbly, glowing in his presence like embers blown into new life. Just so did Rosanna Burden gaze on her son. Without their children these parents were shells stranded on desert reaches, and Patrice thought of Alice seated by the window of that rented room overlooking a prosaic street, reading and rereading the last letter from Clem, pausing to glance hungrily out of the window for the sight of a car stopping at the curb, listening for the sound of a known step coming up the stairs.

Caroline sank into a chair beside her mother and laid a hand affectionately on her knee. "I'd like to kidnap you, Ma. I'd like to carry you off with us to Jamaica."

"Perhaps this winter," Mrs. Bannister replied ardently. "If I can get your father to leave Cambridge. He ought to get away. He's terribly worried just now, as you know. The way the country is going with Roosevelt and everything."

Caroline said robustly: "Blah!"

"That's all very well, dear, but you know your father. His convictions."

"Hal thinks Roosevelt may have saved our shirts for us," Caroline stated after a pause. "He has no more use for the bastard than Pop has, but he still believes that under all the half-baked utopianism Franklin's saved the country from going completely to the bow-wows."

"Mercy! Hal thinks that? For goodness' sake, don't let your father hear you say it."

Caroline laughed. "I must say Hal's come out of the shambles pretty well," she confided. "We've had to take in sail here and there. Sold the place in Carolina, as you know. And I've cut down on the staff at Montego. Hal says we've done ever so much better than lots of our friends. He's got stock in chemicals and electronics, so that even if there should be a war we wouldn't do so badly." She took a reviving drink from her glass. "Thank God Timmy'd be too young for the draft."

Mrs. Bannister gazed at her wistfully. Since Caroline's remarriage they saw one another seldom, largely because Wilbur Bannister made as little attempt to conceal his dislike for his current son-in-law as he had for his first. Daisy Pitman had come subtly to take Caroline's place in Wilbur's affections. Daisy could do no wrong. After her single tragic mistake in marrying Lawrence Redditch she had retrieved herself by marrying Pinky Pitman, who shared in every respect Wilbur Bannister's views of the world in general and politics in particular. How different were Daisy and Pinky from his own children! From a son who, provided with the best possible education and the amenities of a refined and cultivated background, chose to work in the wilderness on a day laborer's pittance. And a daughter who exchanged one socially unacceptable husband for another equally unacceptable. It was all very well for Dorothea to keep reminding him that Adam and Caroline were in their separate ways every bit as individualistic as he, their father. Wilbur Bannister would frankly have preferred Daisy and her husband and their pleasant, well-managed, uncomplicated way of life to Adam's eccentricities and Caroline's inexplicable vulgarity.

More guests appeared on the veranda, neighbors of the Pitmans from Philadelphia who also owned houses and sailboats at Northeast

Harbor. As often in the past, Patrice became instantly conscious of a kind of family resemblance between them. Everyone knew everyone else, and intimately. It was all first names and nicknames—Pinky and Patsy and Dimples and Doodles. Everyone talked at once in loud, self-assured voices. It could not by any stretch of imagination be called conversation, and as the third round of cocktails was passed the veranda seemed to expand with the crowd. The scent of the wisteria was drowned in an aura of gin and cigarettes, and the bleating notes of the accordion intruded forlornly upon the heedless throng.

Mrs. Bannister turned impulsively to her daughter. "Poor Hal! Why doesn't he join us?"

"You know why," Caroline replied shortly. "He's scared of Pop."

"My dear, don't. You must make allowances for your father. Roosevelt has got him so *down.*"

Caroline muttered "Blah" again, then rose and, leaning on the veranda rail, raised her voice resonantly: "Hal! Come on up here and join the party."

She turned, laughing. "He's trying to learn the 'Jewel Song' from Gounod's *Faust.* Listen!"

They listened, and a big tweedy man standing beside her said with a grin: "Sounds suspiciously like 'Madelon' to me."

A woman with huge knuckles addressed the tweedy man in tragic accents: "Bill says we are going to have to sell *Vagabond.* With things going the way they are we shan't be able to put her in the water another year."

"Sell *Vagabond!* Annie Masterson, I just can't see you and Bill without *Vagabond.*"

"I can't see us either. It's just like dying. That's what I said when Bill told me. 'It's like dying,' I told him. 'If we have to give up *Vagabond* it'll be like dying.'"

"But ..." began the tweedy man in an overwrought voice, and she shook her head. "We've never managed to make a comeback," she explained. "Up to our ears in General Electric and American Can and you know what that means."

"Jesus. Bad as that?"

"And with Bill Junior at Groton and Bitsy getting ready for Bryn Mawr, you can see we really haven't much choice." She held out her glass to the tweedy man. "Get me another of the same, will you, Fatsy, dear?"

Wilbur Bannister was stirring his cocktail by twirling the stem of his glass in his fingers. He spoke with passion: "Promise the hoi polloi something they've never had and don't deserve and they'll vote for the man in the moon. This country was founded and has grown to grandeur on the brains and sinews of the Anglo-Saxon race, but to hear that son of a bitch in the White House, you'd think we owed everything to the riffraff who put him in office. Bribery, chicanery, chauvinism . . . plain downright cheating, if you ask me."

Caroline directed another blast in the direction of the tennis court: "Hal! We're all up here on the veranda, for God's sake!"

Mrs. Bannister winced. Mr. Bannister savored his drink and his face cleared a shade from its gloom. "Just right. Perfect, in fact. Of course, the brand of gin makes all the difference." He beamed on Pinky, who smiled modestly. "Better make the most of it, sir," he said. "Who knows what we'll all be drinking this time next year?"

Caroline addressed them over her shoulder in an acid voice: "It was that son of a bitch in the White House who gave us back our likker, wasn't it? Might as well give him credit for something."

Mr. Bannister stared at her. "Am I to understand that you are in favor of our distinguished incumbent?"

Caroline shrugged her plump shoulders. "Oh, for Christ sake, Pop!" She turned to Daisy. "Hal's pretending he doesn't hear me, and I don't believe he's even had a drink yet."

Daisy said soothingly: "I'll run down and bring him up here myself."

The "Jewel Song" quavered irresolutely but inevitably into "Madelon," and Patrice saw Daisy's graceful figure, trailed by an assortment of small dogs, stride across the lawn toward the tennis court. Then she saw something else. Another car had driven into the parking area, just visible from the veranda, and emerging from behind the wheel, hatless, crutches gripped in his hands, was Barto Williams.

Mrs. Bannister had seen him, too. Her face flushed deeply as she turned to Patrice. "What in the world," she whispered, "can Barto be doing here?"

Although the question had been directed to Patrice in an almost inaudible voice, the group on the veranda reacted as if it must have

376

heard. The high range of voices sank to a diminuendo and all eyes turned on the garden below. Barto had his crutches under his arms and was hobbling toward the house.

It was at that moment that his son, Timmy, in white shorts and shirt, swinging a tennis racket, appeared from behind the rose hedge. The three figures—Daisy, Barto, and the boy—converged, it seemed helplessly, like three vessels drifting on an invisible tide, to an inevitable collision on the lawn under the bemused gaze of twenty pairs of eyes.

Mr. Bannister swung toward his daughter. "What is the meaning of this intrusion, Caroline?"

Caroline made no reply. Her face was crimson, her plump hands, covered by too many rings, clutched the veranda rail. "The bastard!" she muttered. "The dirty double-crossing bastard!"

Mrs. Bannister murmured entreatingly: "Caroline, dear. Please not that!"

Mr. Bannister turned with a kind of wilted desperation to Pinky. "I can stand anything," he declared hoarsely. "*Anything* except vulgarity. Pinky, my dear boy, how can I apologize to you and Daisy for this unpardonable invasion?"

Pinky patted his arm. "It's all right, sir, it's perfectly all right. Don't let it disturb you. Daisy will take care of the situation, I know."

Barto's deep voice carried easily to the attentive throng above: "Timmy! You know you were supposed to spend this weekend with me at the Cape."

The boy stood at Daisy's side, his back to the house. Every line of his slim young figure expressed defiance. He said nothing. Barto went on: "You didn't show up last week, nor the week before. You never let me know and I had no idea where you were and had to telephone all over the place to find out."

Daisy spoke up brightly: "Now, Barto! Pinky and I are having a party and this is a rather special occasion. Why shouldn't Timmy spend the weekend with us?"

Barto ignored her. His attention was riveted on his son. Patrice thought: How old he looks! Barto's fine rich hair was thin and dingy, his once mobile features attenuated, his clothes had a second-hand look.

"I've come to fetch you, Timmy," he said after a pause. He seemed

377

quite oblivious of his audience. "Go get in the car. Never mind your things. We're going to the Cape."

Timmy's muttered reply was inaudible to the listeners, but Barto's had a ring of metal: "You heard me. Go get in the car."

Again Daisy intervened with unimpaired sweetness: "Barto, dear Barto! Don't spoil his fun. Just this weekend!"

Barto turned his gaze slowly on her. "Just this weekend? He's been sailing with you and your husband and no one had the decency to let me know."

"We tried to get you on the phone," Daisy told him smoothly. "It was not our fault that no one answered. And I sent you a postcard just the other day."

Barto interrupted brusquely. "Don't hand me that guff, Daisy. I've had too much of it."

Pinky Pitman set his glass on the veranda rail and said in a trembling voice: "There's an old-fashioned word that just fits him, and that's 'cad.' If he wasn't crippled, and if I wasn't sure that Daisy knows how to deal with him, I'd go down and knock his block off."

"Please," Mrs. Bannister begged. "Please, Pinky, no! Please."

Barto was saying: "You know that Caroline has withdrawn Timmy from school and plans to take him back to Jamaica with her?"

Daisy hesitated. "Barto, try to think of Timmy's feelings."

Caroline's voice broke in like smashing glass: "Timmy! Come in the house right away."

The boy half turned. He was flushed, sullen. Patrice heard him speak to his father without looking at him: "I don't want to go with you, Dad. I want to stay with Mum and Hal."

"You'll do what I tell you," Barto replied, with precision. "You'll do what *I* tell you, understand?"

"How did you know I was here?" the boy demanded, and added bitterly: "You've been spying on me again. That's not part of the deal and you know it!"

"There are going to be no more deals. If I have to fight this rotten business to my dying day, there are going to be no more deals."

"I'm not going with you," Timmy said doggedly. "You can't make me."

As Barto hung there, crucified on his crutches, Caroline screamed:

378

"Timmy, goddammit! Don't stand there arguing with him. Come on in the house at once."

Mrs. Bannister raised her fine, sunburned hands to her face. Her eyes were full of tears. When Patrice glanced back at the group on the lawn it had broken up. Timmy was running toward the house, Daisy was continuing on her way to the tennis court with her dogs, and Barto was making his painful journey back to his car.

Mrs. Bannister raised her eyes to Patrice. "Run down and speak to Barto, dear. Tell him that we—that I—that I am terribly, terribly sorry, that I wish . . ." She broke off, and Patrice said softly: "Why don't you come down with me and tell him yourself?"

Wilbur Bannister broke in sharply: "My wife will do no such thing. What is finished is finished, and Barto had better accept it once and for all."

Patrice left the veranda and ran out of the house to the parking area. Barto saw her and waited and she ran to him and kissed him. "Barto, dear."

He said quietly: "Hullo, Patrice. I didn't know you were around."

Wildly she tried to think of something to say to comfort him. "Barto, Mrs. Bannister asked me to give you a message . . . she said to tell you she was terribly sorry about this business."

He laughed shortly. "Big of her."

"Barto, do you remember this stone you gave me a long time ago? A golden beryl you said it was. I always wear it. We love you, Barto. You must believe it, dear, dear Barto!"

His face looked dreadful, but his eyes gazed steadily into hers. "She's won," he said slowly. "Caroline has won, as usual. She got what she wanted out of me, then she got herself a richer guy, and now she's got Timmy." Gently he freed himself from Patrice's embrace. "They've all won," he said in a ruminative voice. "They stick together, don't they?"

After a moment's silence he said: "No doubt they sometimes tell one another with that bighearted impartiality of theirs: 'I always rather liked Barto. Always felt he had *something.*' But they'll never tell you what it was they thought he had. Well, Barto could tell them: two screwed-up legs and a screwed-up life. Everything screwed up except his prick."

He nodded to Patrice in a casual fashion, wormed his way behind the wheel, then backed the car in a half circle and drove away. Patrice turned back to the house. She had a vague impression of Damon and Pinky Pitman standing at the head of the flight of steps, gazing down at her, but she walked past them on the lawn to the hedge, where the roses, wilting in the sun, dropped their petals like fat white eyelids on the grass.

She had a sense of loss, of having mislaid something. Her friendship with Barto might have deepened into one of those close relationships rare between men and women. Sex would have had no part in it. There would have been trust, an amused and tolerant affection such as she had been denied with Clem and had never achieved with Adam and which their passionate relationship made impossible between Damon and herself. The germ of this friendship had always been there, in herself and in Barto, and both had been conscious of it under the misdirection and triviality which had so far ruled their lives.

The sound of his car had died away in the distance. Hal Johnson and Daisy were crossing the lawn on their way to the house, and Daisy, spying Patrice standing alone beside the rose hedge, said gaily: "All's well that ends well. *Déjeuner est servi!*"

27

One day in the late summer of 1940 Patrice gathered up the last sheets of her manuscript and stacked them beside her typewriter. Methodically she tidied up the old table which she had bought years ago for two dollars, and closed a dictionary which for the past month had lain open at the letter H. What, she wondered idly, had been the word she was seeking? She could not remember, and now it did not matter.

These minor chores completed, she sat for some minutes in the big, airy room, coping with sensations of elation and disbelief. The book was finished. An hour ago and almost two years from the day when she had begun to write it, the story was told, the fable completed.

She brooded now on the life of Rosanna Burden as she had fashioned it . . . out of what? Out of the real Rosanna? Out of herself? She had intended to portray a certain aspect of love which, in her eyes, had seemed out of the common, and had promptly fallen afoul of the trap which presumption sets for its practitioners. For Rosanna, under another name and another guise, had taken the bit in her teeth and obstinately refused to budge from her original self, nor would she surrender her own aspect of love for another.

Throughout these six hundred-odd pages Rosanna had moved with inexorable logic, her simple gaze trained on her would-be creator, missing nothing of the creator's private bafflement. Life, Rosanna had let it be known—speaking without a cue—life is two parts heartache, one part headache, and one part pain in the arse. In this view of universality she seemed rather to share that of Jonas Brayne, who had consistently adjured Patrice to shun solemnity as she would the pox.

As for Patrice, she had no qualms about her utilization of Rosanna as protagonist for what she wanted to say, for after all, the ethical dilemma was minuscule in its relation to a wider horizon and a deeper involvement. Never mind if Rosanna, in whatever guise, should loom heroic against that background and emerge triumphant from the involvement; even if she had been a villain she would have had her place there, whether she turned the tables or whether she didn't.

For two years Patrice herself had lived on several different planes of existence at one and the same time. She had been one person and many; she had murdered and brought forth, she had been faithful and faithless, pitying and pitiless, traitorous and staunch. There had been moments when she had wondered whether she might be going a little mad. Where did these visions come from, these landscapes, oceans, houses, streets? Where had she encountered these faces and heard these themes?

Then, her day's work done, she would surface to the sane and sunny world, hear a meadowlark winding itself up on a fence post and the mailman stuffing the daily newspaper in the mailbox, and would catch, from a corner of her eye, a glimpse of Monty Burden dodging among the trees. Adam would call to her from somewhere in the house, Alice on the telephone, and Damon would write: "Sincerity and intensity are not enough, don't you see? And what else have you got to offer, darling?"

But never mind now. She had completed the job she had set herself. She had written a book.

She rose from the table and went downstairs to find Adam. He was in his den, cleaning a rifle, the dogs at his feet, and he spoke without glancing up from his task. "Alice just called. I told her you were busy."

Patrice said: "Adam, it's done."

"What?"

"I've just finished it."

He lifted the rifle to his shoulder and sighted along the polished barrel. "Good," he said. Was it congratulation or merely a comment on the condition of the rifle? Patrice felt a touch of the old letdown, then the telephone began to ring and she let it ring for several seconds. It would be Alice, breathless and apologetic: "Darling, I don't want to bother you . . . ."

Shrinking in anticipation, Patrice picked up the receiver. It was Jonas Brayne. "Little Patrice? I've just had a letter from Hart Barrow. Says he'll be happy to see you and to take a look at your opus any time you are ready."

Fate. Patrice stammered into the receiver: "Jonas, it's done. It's finished . . . the book."

There was a second's pause, then Jonas's warm, bearded voice: "Good for you, little Patrice! Old Hart must be clairvoyant. Let's go down to New York and see him, then celebrate. Think Adam would care to come?"

Patrice turned to Adam. "Jonas wants to know if you'll come to New York with us when I go to see Hart Barrow."

Adam set the rifle back in its cabinet and picked up another. An astringent smell of nitro solvent tinctured the air. He said without looking at her: "You know I hate that goddam city." He had been in New York perhaps twice in his life.

Patrice returned to the telephone. "Jonas? Adam doesn't think he can make it."

"What the hell's the matter with him?" Jonas growled. "I suppose if you'd just gone and blown the daylights out of some unoffending jackrabbit he'd be proud as punch of you!"

Patrice put her hand over the receiver, but she need not have bothered. Adam was not listening. He went on cleaning his gun, watched by the dogs. His world was complete. Patrice thought: Living together, sleeping in the same bed, sharing the humid air of marriage, they had lost each other.

She hung up the receiver and Adam said in a detached voice: "I'm glad you've finished the book, but that isn't all there is to it, after all. You've still got to get it published, and you still can't really count on that, can you?"

"No, I can't count on it. I'm trying not to count on it."

It was the truth. She had disciplined herself to run ahead of events, to wait for them to catch up with her. She felt that she had lived through many varieties of experience while working on the book, and now it seemed to her that this very moment was familiar, that she had been here before. She might write fifty books but she could never compel Adam to recognize her capacities. He was like Damon in this, and probably for the same reason. Neither wanted to exchange the known woman for the unknown; it was as simple as that. But did it really matter? In the incandescence of her present mood Patrice decided that it did not matter. Something had happened, something partly of her own doing, partly of her stars—and perhaps of Adam's stars also.

She said after a moment: "I'll be going to New York with Jonas and Netta, probably at the end of this week."

"Fine." He hesitated. "There's just one thing, though. How do you propose to manage for money?"

It was a recurring dilemma. Patrice had learned the difficult art of living on a shoestring and of stretching it to include Alice, but that was as far as her financial ingenuity had taken her. Where Alice was concerned Adam asked no questions, and if he had any suspicion as to how she met her few meager expenses, it betrayed itself only in a certain coldness of manner toward her on the infrequent occasions that they were together. It offended his sense of the fastidious that Alice's teeth were in obvious need of dental attention, that her eyesight was bad and her glasses inadequate, but these after all were none of his business; nor, in the circumstances, did he see how they could very well be Patrice's business.

In her more lighthearted moments Patrice rather enjoyed the game of making-do without involving him in the problem, but the question he had just asked still had power to disconcert her. She said slowly: "Jonas and Netta will stake me to this trip and I'll pay them back somehow."

Adam stroked the gunstock lovingly with an oily rag. "You mean when you strike gold?" He looked at her. "I'd hate to have you set your heart on it, Patrice, and then have nothing come of it."

"I don't know what you mean by striking gold, but I'd be a hypocrite if I were to say I didn't hope Hart Barrow will take the book. Anyone who *does* anything . . ."

His face darkened. "Oh, I know! You have these grand ideas."

384

She shrugged. "Let's say it's like shooting at a bird. One occasionally misses, doesn't one?"

"Well, if you want to know, I don't especially like the thought of your being indebted to the Braynes—or to anyone for that matter. I just don't see how we'd ever manage to pay them back."

Patrice replied coldly: "You and I are indebted up to our ears to your parents, but you've never let that get you down."

"Do we have to go over that ground again?"

Patrice intoned in a flat voice: "They have plenty of money, and they must surely have become resigned to the prospect of having us on their necks for the rest of their lives."

Adam drew the oily rag through the gun barrels and said nothing. These exchanges between himself and Patrice had long since lost the character of a quarrel; they were passionless, led nowhere. She said in a changed, practical voice: "Of course, I don't want to involve you in any expense. As I said, I'll pay it back to the Braynes somehow."

"It's what you say, but I still don't see how you intend to do it. And it wouldn't look so good to my parents, either, if they were to know."

Patrice felt the return of an old fury. "Why the hell should they know?" Why shouldn't Adam, just for once, be generous about things? Why couldn't he say: Hell, yes, go ahead. We'll manage somehow. But he never did. He left it up to her.

Patrice waited until she had got her temper in hand, then she said: "I'll try to get some sort of job. I haven't any training for anything, but there might be something in a store, or perhaps in the public library."

Adam flushed. "You have all you can do taking care of this place, and anything you earned wouldn't make that much difference." He waited a moment, then finished: "I know we are hard up, that we have always been hard up, but what the hell! I don't want a lot of dough. We have this house, enough to eat, an occasional bottle, friends, leisure. I can't see . . ."

But couldn't he, really, see? Couldn't he see that should one or the other of them fall ill his parents would foot the bill, as they regularly did when the coal bill came due, the real estate tax bill, the bill for insurance—for just about everything over and beyond their everyday needs?

By any standard he and Patrice lived a good life and she should

385

have been satisfied. She reflected now: As far as that goes, I am satisfied. I don't want a lot of money. I don't want luxury. Adam knows it. He can't accuse me of being spendthrift or of loafing on the job of keeping his house even if I do give part of my time to the typewriter! But he doesn't understand about Alice, about there being more to it than just providing her with three meals a day and a roof. He doesn't understand and he will never accept responsibility for another person's self-respect. And besides all that there is this guilt I have about his parents, a sense of unfairness toward them. They don't care for Alice any more than he does, and probably for the same reasons. They have us on their necks; why should they, however obliquely, be made suspicious that perhaps they have *her*, too? If only he and I could talk this thing over between us, let the air in! "Winds blow south, winds blow north . . ./If we two but keep together."

The telephone rang. "Darling, I don't want to bother you. I was just wondering . . ."

That conversation finished, Patrice turned to find that Adam had gone, taking his dogs. She saw him pass the window but he did not glance up. She watched his tall figure stride across the fields toward the woods, the dogs racing ahead of him. At such moments he had a special grace, an air of purpose, a self-contained strength. The feral being.

It was raining in New York the day Patrice and Jonas Brayne were to meet Hart Barrow in the Ladies' Bar at the Ritz on Madison Avenue. Jonas had taken rooms at the Lafayette Hotel downtown, and Netta had lost no time disappearing in the general direction of Greenwich Village, haunt of her younger days. The city was always Netta's sanctuary from Jonas's overpowering presence and from the bedlam of her house. She could lose herself in the anonymous crowds with the happy abandon of a swimmer in the sea. What would have dazed one less sophisticated was, to Netta, the breath of life. No sooner had they registered at the hotel than she bade Jonas and Patrice a precipitate farewell, promising to meet them for dinner that evening.

Scowling, Jonas watched her vanish through the doors into the rainy street. "All she'll do is moon about the Village inhaling monoxide and pawing over junk shops," he complained to Patrice. "Her idea of what she calls 'escape.' Escape from what? She doesn't know when she's well off, with me and the kids at Garside. Country air gives her bronchitis and bird song drives her nuts. Goddammit, you take a person like Netta away from her bagels and coffee three times a day in some long-haired dive and expose her to the amenities of life and she begins yapping about escape. . . ."

In the taxi driving uptown Jonas brooded on Netta's iniquities. "Doesn't have the decency to tell me where she's going or what she plans to do all day, or where I could reach her in an emergency. One of the kids could get sick. She could get knocked down by a taxi, or raped, or arrested for smoking hashish—she looks the type! And there'd I be, left alone to bring up my kids. Jesus."

It was his recurrent nightmare, this giant of a man, as fearful of his fantasies as an elephant of mice. Patrice patted his knee. "Dear old Jonas," she murmured. She was, herself, in the throes of a bad case of stage fright. "Jonas, promise you won't leave me alone with Mr. Barrow, will you?"

He peered at her absentmindedly, then laughed. "You're not scared of old Hart, little Patrice!"

"I am."

Jonas shook his head and returned to his obsessive rage at Netta's desertion. "Bitch. It wouldn't have killed her to come along with us. All that Greta Garbo 'I want to be alone' crap. I don't even know whether she has the price of a subway fare on her. She's so goddam rattle-brained. Last time we were in town she had to borrow a nickel from a complete stranger to telephone me she'd had her purse stolen from the women's room at Penn Station. And what was she doing at Penn Station? She'd walked three blocks to get a free pee!" He clawed his beard. "Hell of a lot she cares if I worry myself into the grave wondering whether she's all right."

Rain painted the city in ocher shades, and his uneasiness found another channel. "War," he growled. "As if the last one wasn't enough. Well, they won't get me this time. It was different in nineteen fourteen–eighteen. We were young. There had been a long stretch without war and we all had that special feeling about France and the Frogs. For a lot of us it meant Paris and the exalted sense of mission, and the little *poules,* and a respite from our stupid middle-class lives. Never mind the poor devils who never made it home. Now here we go again."

Long ago, Adam had said something of the same sort to her in that bedroom in Berry's Landing overlooking the sea. Now a little worm of ice stirred against her heart. "I don't see why we in this country . . ."

"Thank Christ my kids are too young," Jonas muttered. "And you haven't got any kids, and Adam is past the age. So we're not so badly off." He gave her a sidelong glance. "No, Adam won't be called up. But there are all the others."

There were all the others, and there was Damon. Patrice's mind recoiled from the rattlesnake thought. Damon! Although she had been twenty-four hours in New York she had not telephoned him. She had not written him that she had finished her novel and that she was coming to New York to see Hart Barrow. She was superstitious about the whole business. She would wait until she had met Barrow. It would all be easier then. She would have crossed the Rubicon.

She became conscious of Jonas's speculative gaze. "Perhaps," he said abruptly, "perhaps young Damon won't have to go. Perhaps this country'll manage to steer clear of the bloody show after all. Let the Frogs and the Limeys take care of their own hides."

Patrice listened with divided attention. The huge events in Europe had been remote enough from her life in Maine, from the house overlooking the river and the fields, from her own self-contained existence. Now something fierce, obdurate, grasping awoke in her. She would not surrender that existence, she would not surrender Damon. The stubborn spirit which had brought her so far would carry her farther; a will that had imposed itself on her spirit would reach out to affect larger events. There would be more strenuous efforts, an unfolding of fresher landscapes. War in Europe would never reach America, and there would always be Damon and their private life together.

Incorrigibly resilient, she felt her mood clear as the taxi carried Jonas and herself up the avenue in the rain. She loved New York. The city made her feel youthful, it ignited her. She thought of that day eons past when she and and Adam had landed in New York after their voyage from England. Nauseated by her pregnancy, exhilarated and fearful she'd been then, and totally in love, on the threshold of

388

a new life. She could smile at the cliché now, but it had been real enough at the time.

"Here we are," Jonas said, squirming to reach the wallet in his hind pocket. Rain glittered in his beard. He was hatless as usual. His necktie was ancient and he smelled of paint. But he radiated confidence and as he took her arm and guided her across the sidewalk, through the handsome doors into the crimson-carpeted lobby, he murmured: "Hart'll be in the bar. Down those stairs to your right, little Patrice."

A man seated alone at a table against the wall rose, and Jonas greeted him jovially: "Hello there, Hart! Netta couldn't make it. Had a date with her palmist, or something."

He introduced Patrice, and they shook hands. She had expected an ogre, thin-lipped, with Cyclopean stare. She gazed instead into a rather narrow face with a high forehead, pale steady eyes, a nervous mouth. Everything about Hart Barrow seemed neutral, sand-colored, diffident. He extended a shy courtesy which, she was to learn, concealed a shrewd and perceptive mind. At this moment she had a feeling that he had instantly divined her panic, and to give her time he addressed himself with an air of amused affection to his old friend Jonas, in whose large assurance shyer men could relax.

They had been classmates at Harvard and had not then had much in common. It was not until years later that they had become friends in the casual fashion of preoccupied men. Totally unlike in appearance, character, outlook, they were probably drawn together by the mere accident of oppositeness. More than most people Jonas lived up to his appearance—the shaggy Bohemian of a past era, familiar to the survivors of that era and to its literature. Barrow was attracted to the big, the burly, the extroverted. To such men, not wholly mature in spirit, he could respond as mentor and guide. Reticent himself, Puritan, he seemed acutely self-conscious with women, and sometimes with men who, however slightly, resembled him.

Jonas had always recognized his own role as a catalyst, and now he took it up with gusto. When they had ordered their drinks—Barrow explained that he was one martini ahead of them—Jonas launched into an angry denunciation of the war, of the Germans, the goddam Italians, the kiss-arse French. "For Christ sake, Hart! I fought alongside the Frogs in nineteen seventeen. I drove their bloody ambulances for them. What's come over them?"

Barrow lighted one cigarette from the stub of another. He was a chain smoker. He said after a slight hesitation that he was himself temperamentally incapable of understanding the Latin spirit. He did not believe that the French were cowards. It was simply that they were skeptics—pliant and devious in the bargain. He did not approve of skeptics. He preferred the Anglo-Saxon doggedness. He did not for a moment believe that the British would be defeated in this war, and he felt equally strongly that the United States should not involve itself, though he mistrusted Roosevelt's emotionalism and his political guile.

Barrow's voice was gentle, husky, hesitant; out of character with the force of his opinions. Patrice sensed the obstinacy in him, like a hidden rock.

The drinks arrived and she watched with curiosity as he produced an old-fashioned gold watch from his vest pocket and laid it on the table beside his glass. Catching her eye, he smiled faintly. "My train," he murmured by way of explanation. "I hate to miss trains."

Jonas now embarked on a succession of more or less scatological anecdotes of his experiences in the First World War, and Barrow listened with lowered eyes and a faint smile. He never indulged in profanity, yet seemed not to object to it in his friends and certainly not in his authors. Once or twice as Jonas talked Barrow glanced fleetingly at Patrice, perhaps to see how she was taking it. She had heard it all before, and now she maintained an amused detachment, sensing Jonas's motive in loosing this flood of irrelevance: it was intended to give her time, to give Barrow time in which to assess one another before they got down to business.

While he rambled on Jonas drank absentmindedly without appearing to notice what he drank. Alcohol had the effect, merely, of making him more exuberantly expressive than usual, and often a good deal less intelligible, but his reputation for funniness was such that it was almost as often honored in the breach as in the performance, or as he himself had been heard to say: more often in the performance in his breeches.

He could be shocking, but it was part of his extraordinary perceptiveness that at his most reckless he was careful not to outrage those whom he felt could not take it, for as he had once remarked to

Patrice, it was more often the word and not the deed that people feared.

After the second round of double martinis he seemed temporarily to run out of steam, and Patrice thought with a return of panic: Barrow is going to bring up the subject of my book. I'm going to have to make intelligent comments. I can't think of a single intelligent thing to say, so what the hell am I doing here anyway? She felt her color rise, her palms turn damp. But Barrow made no move to take up the subject. He showed no effect of the three martinis he had drunk, except that his glance turned rather more frequently to the watch beside his glass.

To bridge a silence which threatened to become a strain, Barrow suddenly inquired whether either of his guests had read W. H. Hudson's *The Purple Land.* It was, he said, one of his favorite novels and he read it on an average of at least once every two years. This obviously was a pet topic, one which could be depended upon when the conversational going became tough. Barrow in his turn recounted an anecdote or two—far from scatological—about Hudson's early literary struggles, his meditated suicide, his discovery and rescue by the distinguished English publisher Gollancz, and his eventual rise to fame and success.

Barrow obviously enjoyed telling the story to a new audience. It seemed to touch some romantic chord in him. His cheeks flushed, his eyes took on warmth, and Patrice thought: There's something besides ink in those veins, after all.

Jonas recovered his garrulity and inquired about a mutual friend, a novelist whom Barrow had "discovered" several years before and who had become an enormous literary success. Barrow abandoned *The Purple Land* with evident reluctance. "Manfred," he replied to Jonas's query, "is on his way to getting his third divorce." He glanced at Patrice. "I'm old-fashioned," he confessed mildly. "I've always held that marriage was a—a sacrament." He turned again to Jonas. "You know I like and admire Manfred. In my opinion he's just about the best novelist writing today. But I must say he puzzles me. In regard to his personal affairs, I mean." He sighed. "All this marrying and divorcing . . . it doesn't make any sense."

"Perhaps," suggested Patrice, "perhaps it's like tearing up an old manuscript and starting a new one."

Barrow gave her a long, direct glance, and the nearest approach to a laugh she had heard from him. "That's an idea," he said. "I never quite thought of it in that light." He looked pleased. "Yes, I wouldn't be surprised if that didn't go far to explaining Manfred Evans."

The conversation continued erratically. Jonas told a few more stories. He waxed philosophical about art and life. He drank down his third martini and became maudlin about the lost joys of the unmarried artist in Paris twenty years ago. The little girls who gave their all and asked nothing in return. The simple meals at the little restaurant on the Rue du Bac, and the simple wine and the simple you know what afterwards. The greatest painting in the world had its impulse in that kind of simplicity, before Freud set the world to picking nits out of its goddam subconscious. . . .

Once more he began to run out of steam and cast anxious glances at Patrice, raised his brows, looked as if he were preparing to take the bull by the horns in regard to Patrice's book, thought better of it, and lapsed into an aggrieved mumble on the inexplicable contrariness of his wife. "Give her everything . . . house-and-lot . . . dough . . . travel . . . kids . . . piano . . . And all she talks about is *escape!*"

Hart Barrow signaled a waiter, paid the bill, and turned apologetically to Patrice. "You'll forgive me if I leave you? I have to catch my train."

He had never been known to miss the six-twenty to Westchester, where he lived with his wife, his eight daughters, and his old dog.

Jonas and Patrice accompanied him to the lobby, where he retrieved his hat. For certain men their hats are as symbolic of mysterious quirks of nature as women's hats are openly revealing of theirs. No one would have mistaken Barrow's hat for anyone else's hat, for the reason that it seemed so out of character with the owner. The hat was a modified sombrero type, a nondescript gray with a discolored band and a shapeless crown. It was too big for him, but he had never been known to wear another. By itself the hat had a kind of panache; on Barrow's head it somewhat resembled a candle snuffer, and therein, perhaps, lay the symbolism, if there could have been said to be one.

This hat in hand as he waved his guests toward the big glass doors, Barrow suddenly turned to Patrice. Surely, she thought, appalled, he's going to mention the book. She waited, tense. He came close to her and spoke in an undertone: "See that man sitting there in the corner across from the checkroom?"

Patrice had noticed the figure as they emerged from the bar. Barrow said in the same conspiratorial voice: "That's Somerset Maugham. I know him slightly. I would have introduced him to you, but I don't approve of him." He paused. "I greatly admire his work, but I don't approve of him."

The rain had stopped and the street glistened in silvery light. Jonas, a trifle unsure on his feet, paused to comb his numerous pockets for cigarettes. A taxi drew up at the curb and Hart Barrow opened the door, waving Patrice in. "I always walk to Grand Central," he explained gravely. He waited, hat in hand, while Jonas struggled to light a cigarette without setting fire to his beard. During the past two hours nothing had been said about the purpose of this meeting in the Ladies' Bar of the Ritz Hotel. Not a word. Patrice, alcohol coursing in her veins, grappled with confused emotions of disappointment and relief.

Hart Barrow, his hat at last on his head, stooped and peered at her where she sat in a corner of the back seat, waiting for Jonas. "Send the manuscript to my office," Hart told her, unsmiling. "Tomorrow. My secretary will see that I get it right away."

On the drive back to University Place Jonas looked at Patrice. "Not as bad as you expected, was it, little Patrice? I heard what Hart said to you just now. Good guy, old Hart." He added with a laugh: "I was afraid he never would get down to brass tacks. But that's Hart all over."

"What a strange person. I wonder whether one ever gets to know a man like Hart Barrow."

"What the hell do you care? Your opus'll be read and you'll get a straight answer from a straight guy. That's something." He puffed at his cigarette, which had gone out. Cursing, he tossed it out the window.

Patrice said after a moment: "Anyway, I've taken the great step. Do you know, Jonas, I never really believed I would? Even when I was working hardest, something inside me kept saying that it was all unreal. I never would finish the thing, I never would meet a publisher —let alone publish anything. I still don't believe it."

Jonas had curious stubby hands, small for his great size. The nails were encrusted with paint. The smell of paint, of old musty tweed, filled the cab. He took her hand and squeezed it in both his. "You are hedging your bets, little Patrice, and maybe you should. But tell me something. Suppose this book is published; what'd you do then?"

"Start another."

"And if that's turned down?"

"Start another."

He gave her hand another squeeze and released it. "That's what I told Hart. Glad I was right."

She said abruptly: "I owe you a lot, Jonas. More than I think you realize."

He beamed. "Hell, little Patrice. I had a look at the size of that opus when you took it out of your suitcase. Hart likes to see thumping big wads of manuscript. He has a theory that bulky wads of the stuff are the marks of promise."

Patrice said after a moment: "Would you drop me off at the corner of Thirty-fourth Street?"

It took him by surprise and his geniality ebbed perceptibly. "Drop you off? Aren't you going to dine with Netta and me?"

She explained composedly: "I shall be going home tomorrow, and this is my only chance to see a friend."

Jonas shrugged his huge shoulders. "If that's what you want, little Patrice." He stared at the driver's prosaic back. "I don't intend to horn in on—on whatever it is you have on your mind, you know. But remember I do feel a kind of responsibility for you while you are, so to speak, in my custody." He tried to make light of it, but Patrice sensed his sudden change of mood. She patted his knee. "I'm not going to get lost, stolen, or strayed. I'm just going to say hello to Damon Edwards."

It did not occur to her to try to deceive Jonas, but nothing would prevent her from trying to see Damon tonight. She was aware of Jonas's suspicious scrutiny as he asked: "Hadn't you better call him up first and make sure he's home?"

"He has an apartment on Lexington. If he's not home I'll take a bus downtown to the hotel."

Jonas hesitated, nervously tying little knots in his beard. Patrice could guess at the conflicting emotions which assailed him through his genuine fondness for her: his dependence on her reassuring com-

394

pany in the event that Netta failed to show up for dinner as she had promised; his unconscious masculine solidarity with Adam; his natural jealousy of a younger man; and his anxiety not to appear a prig. It was all there in his brooding silence, in the agitated tying of those little knots in his beard. She wanted to laugh, to chaff him out of his gloom, but before she could speak he said brusquely: "I'll drop you off at Damon's apartment, then. It might start raining again."

It was not a note on which Patrice would have chosen to part company with Jonas for however brief an interlude. She suffered a guilty pang in the thought that he would consider her unappreciative and ungrateful for what he had just done for her, and he made it plain enough that he expected the least she could do in return was to stick by him through the uncertain and perhaps uneasy hours of this evening in case Netta, the bitch, did not show up and his nervous tic got the better of him. But the thought of Damon's proximity was too strong for her. They had not seen each other for several months, and now there was this news of her meeting with Hart Barrow, and a singing, surging excitement which could find release only in Damon's arms.

Impulsively, as the taxi stopped outside an ugly brownstone apartment house on Lexington Avenue, Patrice leaned over and kissed Jonas on the cheek. "Don't worry," she whispered. "I won't be late, I promise."

He gave her a rather piteous, envying look, then smiled. "Take care, little Patrice!"

Then the taxi bore him away and she ran up the steps and pressed the bell under Damon's name in its brass slot. There was no answer and she rang again, then again. Still no answer. He was not home... or perhaps he was not receiving callers. Patrice made a move to press the bell again, then hesitated. She had long schooled herself against jealousy, warning herself that she might very well have cause for it. Damon was not given to candor, nor she to prying, but he was after all attractive, sensual, susceptible. Hints and rumors had reached her off and on during the long course of their love affair, and she fancied herself to be armored against possible anguish and despair. This after all was one of the perils of love: the peril of betrayal, if one could call it that.

Unable to control herself, she pressed the bell again, and Damon's voice—a parody of it—grated against her ear: "Who is it?"

She laughed into the speaking tube: "Patrice! Hope I'm not intruding?"

"Patrice? Good lord."

The buzzer sounded and she pushed open the door and stepped into one of those dreadful varnished interiors which for some reason invariably smell like stale meat pie. A self-service elevator carried her creakingly up three flights, and Damon was waiting for her when it stopped on his floor.

They stared at each other in the mortuary light, then swift unfailing desire made both as light as air. Arms locked, they walked in silence to his apartment and Damon locked the door behind them. "Patrice!"

He was wearing old gray flannels and a faded shirt; he was barefoot, his hair unbrushed. Over his shoulder Patrice glimpsed the big old-fashioned, high ceilinged room, and—to her—its endearing disorder. There were makeshift bookcases halfway up the dingy walls, books stacked on a table between two windows which opened on the avenue, and on the same table were several issues of the monthly magazine for which he performed an unidentified editorial service, aside from contributing to its departments of poetry and literary review.

Under one window stood a pot of geraniums sent him by his mother, who, he had once told Patrice, "kept" him in flowers. There were photographs of his parents, both wearing somewhat uneasy expressions in this alien setting; group photographs of friends at Oxford and at Harvard, framed college diplomas, and a small bronze Nataraja which Patrice had given him on his last birthday and which he had since regarded as his most cherished possession because it typified, he said, his most cherished ambition: to go to bed with someone who possessed two pairs of arms.

For several minutes now they stood embraced, with pounding hearts. It was always like this. Before quarrels, after quarrels, meeting, parting, and at any random moment when they found themselves together. It was a seizure, a kind of fit, making them unrecognizable while it lasted. They did not even kiss; they just clung, their skulls pressed together, the sound of their heartbeats like drums in their ears.

Damon let her go. "In a minute I'm going to take you to bed, but first, what the hell brings you to New York?"

She told him, the words bubbling out of her with happiness. And as she spoke she registered for the first time a change in the order of the room from the order—or rather the disorder—in which she had always, unfailingly, seen it; in its furnishings, its arrangements. She broke off, staring at him, the tendril of ice curling round her heart. "Damon, what goes on?"

He hooked an arm round her neck and led her to the window, where lamplight shone on the geraniums. "I was going to risk calling you up at Garside," he began, after a moment. "Then I decided it would be better if I just sent a telegram, or wrote you a letter. I wanted to break it in the best way, without being too hard on you, Patrice, my darling."

He had found another girl. He was going to be married. It was bound to happen sooner or later. Patrice waited, feeling his arm heavy on her shoulders, smelling the faintly acrid scent of his skin.

"I've enlisted in the Marines," Damon said with a slight catch in his breath. "Yesterday. I've got a few days to put things in order, then they're sending me off somewhere for training. South, I imagine. I was packing when you rang the bell."

Patrice turned slowly in the arc of his embrace. The sun of last summer lingered in his skin; his eyes had that extraordinary health, his head that gold she remembered from the first day she had set eyes on him in Berry's Landing when she had come, a bride, into Adam's parents' house.

"The Marines?" she repeated. "You've enlisted?"

"Listen." He rocked her slightly to and fro. "The French are licked. It's the British next, then us. We'll be in this thing next year. I know. So I decided to take Pinky Pitman's advice: enlist and not wait to be shoved."

She was silent and he went on: "Remember that lunch party at the Pitmans' last summer? Pinky talked to me then, a little. And since then I've had letters from him. I know you don't think much of him, but he's a good guy. No ball of fire, but straight and brave and decent. He was in the last war and he felt that there were things that I should know. His family and mine have always been friends. It was the reason, he said, why he felt it was his duty to give me a bit of advice."

"Pinky Pitman?" Patrice stared at him. "What does Pinky have to do with your decisions?"

"Well, he's convinced that the United States is going to get into this war, and he says he'd advise any young friend to go ahead and enlist and try for a commission. Be more useful to the country as an officer, and all that stuff." Damon hesitated. "I'd end up being drafted anyway, and this seemed a better bet."

Patrice flushed. "Pinky Pitman!"

"He's going to see what he can do about recommending me for a commission. He knows a lot of the big brass."

Revulsion rushed upward, it seemed, from her viscera. Rage shook her to the soles of her feet. "No! I won't have it. I won't let you go. We're not going to be in it. We're not, we're not."

She had forgotten her book, she had forgotten Hart Barrow, the genial afternoon at the Ritz. And Damon, staring at her, had forgotten, too.

"Patrice."

"No!"

He pressed his lips to hers, stilling them. The storm took them, shook them, lifted them, bore them across the big quiet room to the divan which served him for bed. They made love as they had not made love in all their lives. The steel went out of Patrice. She was remorseless, exigent, while darkness filled the windows and the telephone rang unheeded beside them. At the end of it they lay side by side, their skins shining in each other's sweat, their nostrils breathing the seminal air.

Damon got up and handed her cigarettes and lighted a cigar for himself. He went to the tiny kitchen and brewed a pot of tea and rummaged in the refrigerator for bread and cheese. Returning to the room, he set the food on the table beside the geraniums and the Nataraja and stood back to admire the effect. "Will you tell me," he asked conversationally, "why screwing should make one so damned hungry? I could eat a horse."

Patrice lay watching him. She thought of that day when they had gone swimming in the brook behind Rosanna Burden's house. She thought of that pair of eyes which had watched them from the summer leaves. Those eyes had seen what she now saw: a young man contrived for eternal life, or dying, if he had to die, with nothing of his life left undone. Dying by some ordinary kind of accident—of drowning, perhaps, in middle age; or of a heart attack at seventy; of a broken pelvis at ninety. But living out his youth, leaving it to shimmer on some summer bough, or like one of those hyaline skins which serpents shed, blowing among flaming cactus flowers.

But she knew it was not going to happen in that fashion. She watched him as, naked, silvery in the lamplight, he poured tea from the brown teapot and cut the bread for their meal. He was not going to be asked how he chose to die, or how his parents would have him die, or how Pinky Pitman would think fittest, or how his love might arrange it. He was simply going to be butchered, and they both knew it.

Lifting the teapot, he turned to look at her. "Strong or weak?"

She said nothing. Her eyes were two fiery pools of salt, and putting down the teapot, Damon came back to the bed and laid his body on hers and his forehead on her forehead, and slowly drank her tears.

Part Four

28

The engines had stopped, and Patrice, unpacking a suitcase in her stateroom, peered out a porthole and saw the ship's searchlight playing on a heavy gray sea. They were preparing to drop the pilot. There had been a long wait for the tide at Astoria, and she and Adam had lingered at the rail watching lights flicker along the Oregon coast.

Earlier, there had been the usual fatuity of a dockside scene: idle forklifts, stranded bits of cargo, a few stragglers going through the ultimate little gestures of farewell. Patrice had longed for the ship to get under way. There was a drumbeat in her blood, a recurrence she could not have named, resembling one of those unheralded thoughts or dreams when one is startled by a sense of recognition of something which dissolves instantly before one's eyes.

No one had come to the dock to wave good-bye to her and Adam, for they knew no one in the area, and Patrice had been quite content to have it so. Not so, perhaps, Adam. Always at home in the wilderness, he had a New Englander's peculiar timidity in unfamiliar situations and among strange people, a timidity which had grown on him through the years. He had not really wanted to leave Garside, to leave his house and his dogs and the settled sequence of his days, and he

403

had been frank about it to Patrice: "I've become a stick-in-the-mud, and I'm afraid I rather like it."

He had come round to the idea at last, perhaps lured by the thought of big game hunting in a region which in all probability had not changed greatly in the past twenty-five years. Shipping was still scarce since the war's end, but Hart Barrow had pulled strings and got them passage on this Dutch passenger-freighter sailing from Astoria in Oregon to Calcutta, across the Pacific, via Java and Singapore.

Now, as Adam had watched the last-minute activities on the dock, he said with lingering wistfulness: "It would have been nice if someone had showed up to wave good-bye to us, wouldn't it?"

Patrice had said lightly: "I see a rather attractive dame down there who might wave to you if you gave her the sign!"

A tall young woman in a fur coat and Russian-style fur hat was standing near the gangway, and as she lifted her face toward the few passengers lined up against the rail, Patrice had a sudden crazy notion that it might be Daisy Pitman, for there was the same roses-and-cream complexion, and a hint of golden hair under the dashing fur hat. Did the same thought strike Adam as he impulsively took off his hat and waved to her? But Daisy was some three thousand miles away, and a telegram from her lay among others in their stateroom below. The telegram had been addressed, with particular exclusiveness, to Adam: "What are we going to do without you? Come back soon."

Two sailors had moved to haul in the gangway and the young woman in the fur coat ran nimbly up its length and disappeared on the lower desk. Adam turned in consternation to Patrice. "She must be one of the passengers. What in hell will she think?"

Patrice laughed. "What would you?"

They had gone down to their stateroom and Adam said abruptly: "You know, I'm glad now that you dreamed up this trip. It's like our getting married all over again.

Patrice put her arms round him, unable to give coherence to her own emotion. They were no longer young, and there had been more than one moment since their leaving Garside when the drumbeat of excitement in her had faltered, when her unspoken hope for a new beginning had seemed the stupidest kind of cliché.

Adam kissed her, then went back on deck, and she tried to exorcise

404

a queer onset of nerves by busying herself with the flowers that had been sent to the boat and by unpacking and hanging up her own and Adam's clothes. The stateroom was spacious and well fitted out, for the *Cornelis* was a brand-new ship—this was in fact her maiden voyage.

The analogy of a maiden voyage with marriage amused Patrice. I must remember to tell Barto, she thought as she set the freesias he had sent her in a vase on the bureau. It would, she felt, delight Barto to think of the ship's maiden voyage as a happy augury for Adam and herself.

A year ago Barto had driven down from New York to spend a weekend with them at Garside. He had been told by his doctors that he had an incurable cancer, and he looked a great deal older than his fifty-odd years. But he had recaptured something of his original sardonic spirit and seemed to have resigned himself to an almost total estrangement from his son.

He had also lost most of his fortune and was in fact quite poor, though the fact did not seem to depress him greatly. The doctors had assured him that he might live two or three years provided he took good care of himself, a stipulation which he appeared to find amusing.

"A quiet life," he remarked to Patrice when they were alone. It was spring, and Adam had gone trout fishing. "A quiet life for the dying, Patrice, my girl. Nothing in excess. A little booze, a little tobacco, simple food. Books, movies, my stone-cutting, one or two friends. That's about it."

Seated in Adam's chair across from her, a small fire in the grate throwing its glow on his drawn features, Barto had raised his glass to Patrice. "Here's looking at you. And you look good. Like the best Scotch, you age well, Patrice, dear."

She smiled at him with affection. "So do you, Barto."

He laughed. "You've even become a bit of a social liar, which I must say I never expected of you. I don't age well and you goddam well know it."

He went on to speak casually of Caroline, of his son, Timmy, of past days at Berry's Landing. "Dreams! Did any of it really happen? Did I ever own a beautiful house by the sea? Did I have a wife, a son? Was I ever rich, with lots of friends?"

405

"You have friends now," Patrice reminded him. Barto arranged his crutches on either side of the chair and smiled. "No," he said. "Aside from you and Adam, practically none. Most of them have dropped me. My condition embarrasses them and they're deathly afraid I might try to touch them for a loan."

"Barto!" She thought of his past generosity. There were, she suspected, many of those friends who had touched him for a loan in their time and not gone away empty-handed.

He nodded without rancor. "Don't think I don't see it and understand. Possibly in their shoes I'd feel the same way." He glanced at his feet. "I need a new pair, I see. But the crutches are holding up well, don't you think? They are the identical pair you saw the first time we met."

"You shocked me, rather, that first time we met," Patrice said reminiscently. "You were so outspoken. I didn't know what to make of you."

"And I remember wondering just what to make of you. The jungle maiden standing tiptoe on the threshold of a new world." He leaned forward suddenly and said in a changed voice: "Now tell me what's eating you, kid."

She made no attempt to dodge. "Does it show so much?"

"Some." He hesitated. "There have been rumors, you know. They all go back in one way or another to our friend Daisy Pitman. She feels so sorry for poor Adam."

Patrice shrugged. "So do I, at times."

"You had a phase of hitting the bottle, a near squeak in some accident." He leaned back in his chair and delved in a pocket for a cigar. "Not like you, Patrice. I've known you to sail close to the wind —but not that close."

She said nothing and he went on: "I'm not going to ask you whether you are happy. You know I've never subscribed to our fabulous American ideal of obligatory joy—a loaded gut, unlimited booze, all the screwing one can take, dough in the bank, swarms of friends, loving kids, adoring mate . . . shit." He got his cigar going and for an instant Patrice felt an overpowering sorrow and nostalgia. The fragrance of good tobacco, unequivocally masculine and assured, brought back in a flash the image of Damon. Insubstantial, turned to leaf mold himself on that Pacific atoll where he had died, Damon was

406

beside her. She met Barto's eyes. "The wrong guy?" he asked gently.

She shook her head. "No guy at all."

Barto sighed. "That's not what I've been led to believe, but I'll take your word for it." He blew a trumpet of smoke in the air. It hung there a moment, then spread in a thin veil through which the little French clock on the mantel ticked busily. Barto said after a moment: "I'd guess that if anyone had it made, you did."

"I'm not complaining," said Patrice. One of the dogs came in and slumped at her feet and she put down a hand to stroke its head. Barto watched her. "I've often thought," he murmured, "how nice it would be to sit at some woman's feet and have her stroke my hair, as you are doing with Fido."

"His name happens to be Rip."

"Short and succinct when required in the bosky glen. Whatever happened to that ghastly pup of old Wilbur's?"

"If you mean the one I think you mean, it died of old age, but he got another. And another and another."

Barto leaned forward again, his face grave. "You know something, kid? I admire you more than anyone I know. I'm not being sappy either. When I said that if anyone had it made, you did, I meant no double entendre. It's just that, having it made . . ." He broke off, shrugging.

"You feel that I am not in the seventh heaven as I should be, is that it?"

He shook his head. "I just told you that I didn't believe in seventh heavens or their equivalent here, there, or anywhere. But people don't undergo such drastic changes in personality as you seem to have done in late years without there being some pretty damned serious reason."

"But so long as one goes on functioning, doing one's stuff, I can't see that it signifies a hell of a lot."

"Maybe not. But if the American obsession with happiness is what the Limeys call cock, then I believe that indulgence in misery is a vice. It's also shockingly unintelligent. You happen to be more than usually intelligent, and therein lies the anomaly which bothers me." When she remained silent Barto went on: "I think I can see the picture, or part of it. Everything has happened to you all of a heap. After running uphill most of your life you've suddenly arrived at the top, and now you find there's nowhere for you to go—except off the deep end." He smiled disarmingly. "All that boozing you've been doing, that running around with Tom, Dick, and Harry, that crazy driving. You were lucky to get off with a broken collarbone."

Patrice flushed. "Daisy's been pretty busy with her snooping, hasn't she? I wonder why she cares so damn much what I do."

"She doesn't except where it affects Adam, and where doesn't it affect Adam?"

"If it does, I've taken darn good care to see he doesn't know it," said Patrice with sudden grimness.

Barto looked at her strangely. "He's probably been at some pains not to know it himself."

A birch log in the fire spurted flame and they watched it in silence, then Patrice said: "Anyway, it's all water over the dam, isn't it? After the first headiness of success and sudden wealth, I've reformed. Once again life is real, life is earnest—and if that's any comfort to Daisy she's welcome to it."

Barto blew another trumpet of smoke. "The hell with Daisy Pitman. Listen, Patrice. There's something I've got to get off my chest. I'm fond of Adam, and I love you. I have taken a whole lot of comfort in the thought of you and your marriage. When I knew that mine was going on the rocks I used to turn to the thought of you and Adam."

"Well?" she asked defiantly.

"It's not well and you know it. Just keeping the legal tie isn't the answer. There's a different answer, I guess, for different people. But I can't bear to see what's happening between you and Adam. I don't need Daisy Pitman's snooping to tell me, because I recognize the symptoms. I've had them myself. The coarsening of sensitivity, the disrespect for one another, the scorn, the indifference."

She watched the painful color rise in his face. He added: "Worse than everything—the indifference!"

Barto propped his elbows on his knees and fixed her with a steady gaze. "It was only when my own marriage was finished and done for that I began to think about it with any seriousness. In spite of Caroline we had our moments. Granted they were only moments, couldn't we have stretched them into hours, months, years? We just didn't bother. Marriage, we thought, was something that took care of itself, and if it didn't then it flopped."

408

Firelight glittered on the metal of his crutches and cast his eyes into shadow. "It was not until mine had flopped that I began to ask myself how it might have been saved. I began to see the union of two people as a possible creation of a third personality, so to speak—the personality of marriage itself. One would discover in oneself and in the other person not just a bedmate, a potential puppa and mumma, the other half of a joint bank account. Not romance necessarily. But to begin again, to discover or even try to contrive new attitudes toward existence, new excitements for the mind."

Patrice had never heard him talk in this vein, and she reflected sadly on the futility of it so late in the game. He and Caroline had passed the point of no return long before either of them could guess what was happening to them, and who was to say now that even had they guessed, either would have known or cared what to do about it?

Barto said abruptly: "I know what you're thinking: as far as Caroline and I are concerned it's all washed up. But what about you and Adam? After all, you have just about everything now. You've been published, made a success of yourself, made dough. You've won most of the big battles. Are you going to let this one go by default? No—hear me out! I've known for some time that things were going more and more sour between the two of you, which is why I finally decided to come down here and put it to you straight, Patrice—to you, not to Adam. Because it's going to be up to you just as everything has been up to you."

Patrice said after a pause: "Adam and I have weathered more than twenty years together. Isn't that something?"

He shook his head. "It's not enough. You could run out of weather —good weather, that is—before you know it. I know this sounds corny; most advice sounds corny, especially the gratuitous kind. But damn it, I feel strongly about this. I know you can begin again. You can recreate your marriage—or rewrite it, if you prefer the analogy."

Patrice recalled her remark to Hart Barrow on the afternoon of that first meeting with him at the Ritz in New York. Referring to divorce, she said: "Perhaps it's like tearing up an old manuscript."

She had never considered a divorce as the answer to the definitely souring relationship between herself and Adam. As she pointed out to Barto, they had weathered more than twenty years together. Why not carry on as they were doing? A far from ideal situation, true. No better than many others she knew of, but no worse, either. Financially they were now quite well off since she had sold the movie rights of two novels. They were no longer dependent on the Bannisters; Alice was as well taken care of as her own chronic nostalgia and discontent would ever make her.

To carry on indefinitely had seemed the best, in fact the only, response to what the versatile Jonas Brayne described as the State of Holy Deadlock.

Barto's uncharacteristic vehemence and his air of urgency brought Patrice back to face something she had tried hard to ignore: the knowledge of an inner corrosion, of falsity and hollowness in her life with Adam and of his with her. She had made up her mind that there was nothing to be done about it; she had her diversions, her work, the satisfactions of achievement, for what these were worth in comparison with all she very well knew she had missed. And now here was Barto telling her—commanding her, actually—that there was something she *could* do about it!

Watching the play of expression across her face, Barto returned to the charge. "Go back to the beginning, Patrice! Go back to India, where it all began. Not with the thought of repeating what has already happened. Not to wallow in the past. But to start afresh. Afresh!"

A fine spring rain pattered on the window and the dog at her feet stirred, lifting its head as though it heard a distant footfall. Barto had spoken with passion and now he sat back in his chair, looking exhausted. They heard a car approaching down the road. It slowed at the foot of the driveway, and with a bound the dog left them and started for the door.

Thinking of that last afternoon with Barto, recalling in every detail that attractive room with its mingled odors of birch smoke, tobacco, gun oil; the sound of spring rain and the sound of a dog's tail wagging expectantly against the door which would presently open to admit its master, Patrice went about the business of setting their stateroom on the *Cornelis* in order. "Here we are, Barto, old boy," she murmured as she clipped the stems of the pink tulips which Alice had telegraphed to the boat, and put them in a jar next to Barto's freesias. Here we are, my friend, going back to our beginnings . . . and let's hope that it works.

410

We've stayed together, she reminded herself busily. We've stayed together in spite of Damon, and after Damon in spite of Tom, Dick, and Harry—not that they counted for much in the long run, or even in the short. We've stayed together in spite of that long bout with the booze when Damon died and you embarked on the classic regimen of forgetfulness, which ended in self-disgust and a tough rehabilitation before the whiskey cooked your brains for keeps.

But sex had been more rewarding as an anodyne, especially when there was no danger of pregnancy. While the most frigid and unlikely women got themselves knocked up without apparent effort, you with your robust desires remained, as the books say, barren. And probably just as well. You would have made an overpowering mother, worse than Alice. And children would have interfered with your work. And as Barto need not have bothered to point out, you haven't done so badly with your work, at that. Five novels since that first manuscript you and Jonas Brayne lugged to new York in a big suitcase, and which Hart Barrow published the following spring.

Hart Barrow, that odd stick whom no one ever really understood but who understood people with such especial intensity. Hart had known that she *had it in her,* as Adam had not known and as Damon had refused to grant. Hart had known. He suggested, persuaded, guided. Conservative, puritan, shy, and shrewd, Hart Barrow was not really interested in his writers but in their work. So when Patrice had written him about the projected trip to India he had telephoned her from New York and in his gentle, hesitant voice suggested that he hoped she would find inspiration for another book, and had gone on to offer to obtain passage for her and Adam on a ship when passages were hard to get.

Bon voyage! She propped up the dreadful flashy roses he had sent and went back to unpacking her suitcase. Next she uncovered her portable typewriter and set it up on a card table under the porthole. This was a ritual performance, insurance against the ubiquitous, lurking sin of idleness. Their heavy luggage was in the hold, with an arsenal of firearms for Adam. There was no set plan, no itinerary. "Let's play it by ear," she had suggested to Adam. "It's such a huge country. Let's not go back to the old haunts." She suffered this sudden queer dread at the thought. Adam, ignorant of that conversation with Barto, had looked at her blankly. "Why not go back to the old haunts?

411

Be easier for us, wouldn't it, after this long time away?"

Easier for him, yes, perhaps, but for her? Patrice felt a warning knock at her heart, but she did not pursue the debate. Time enough . . .

Yet here in the *Cornelis*'s comfortable stateroom, as she unfolded the clothes which she had last seen when she packed them in the house at Garside, the immediate past crowded perversely upon her. She thought of the snow drifting over her doorstep at home, of shuttered windows, of rooms mysteriously silent, of an old wheelbarrow left outdoors. She thought of Alice, mutely reproachful: "I know I can't be expected to go with you, but if after all I had stayed out there where I really belong you would have found me waiting for you."

The sense of something fateful, of high purpose, had been difficult for Patrice to maintain even to herself, especially in the light of Jonas Brayne's parting admonition: "Maybe it's a good idea to go back and lay the ghost, little Patrice. Just take care that the ghost doesn't lay you!"

His levity could mask his own apprehensions. He was restless, uneasy; his marriage to Netta was in a parlous state and he counted on his friends to remain stable and within reach. But it was Netta's farewell remark which stayed longest in Patrice's memory: "I envy you your great decisions, Patrice," said poor Netta, worn out by the absence of her own—and Jonas's. "But can the finest decision stand up against the day-to-day triviality of life, I wonder?"

Adam returned excitedly to the stateroom. "Patrice! We're dropping the pilot. Come on up and watch."

It was a rough evening and the great river lay astern. They were in the Pacific now, and the masthead light picked out the slender shape of a cutter which rocked on the water, waiting for the pilot. Other passengers had gathered on deck to watch as the pilot, in yellow oilskins, clambered down the ship's ladder into a rowboat with two men at the oars. There was a heavy swell and the air spiked with ice. A storybook scene, Patrice thought, with Adam as excited as a boy. All his doubts and apprehensions seemed to have left him as he put his arm round her and she felt his happiness as something warm and simple, uniting them.

The entire ship glowed in a kind of incandescence which illumined the faces of the passengers and of the sailors who scurried along the

412

deck. Light streamed over the water and thrust upward above the cargo hatches into a tense pattern of masts and cranes. Every detail had meaning and purpòse: men's voices, an imperious clangor of bells, the heave and shudder of the ship, like a leashed behemoth longing to get to sea.

Then the rowboat pulled clear and the pilot's yellow oilskins glimmered briefly in the murk, in whose center the little cutter, crescent-shaped, rocked with gallant insouciance, a small dark sail like a fin steadying it in the swell. The figure in oilskins was aboard, the tender winched upon the cutter's deck, and an arm in yellow armor waved farewell. For Patrice there was something infinitely touching in that small human gesture against the waste of sea and sky. She felt a queer prickle of tears, then with a shock the engines panted into life and a blast from the siren returned the pilot's salute. This was what a ship was for. . . .

The cutter vanished, and they were nosing into a huge darkness of sea, a hiss of water white as snow churning against their bows. No triviality here, Netta. No triviality, but grandeur in the memory of everything one has ever read about such occasions, and an atavistic thrill in the decisive thrust of the engines under one's feet.

A man standing beside Adam turned from the rail and smiled at them. "May I introduce myself?" he asked. "Father O'Hara. I believe we sit at the same table with the first officer, Mr. de Koon. That is if I am addressing Mr. and Mrs. Bannister? The purser pointed you out to me a few minutes ago."

Father O'Hara's voice was Irish to the last syllable. He was dark-haired and, as Patrice had guessed, blue-eyed, and built like a rugger player. She had noticed him when he came aboard at Astoria, but since then he had changed his clerical garb for gray flannel trousers, a tieless shirt and black sweater. He looked anything but priestly, and quite absurdly young. They shook hands and he became instantly chatty, explaining that he was on his way from Ireland via Vancouver and Oregon to Burma, to rejoin his mission somewhere in the jungles north of Rangoon.

"My first trip back since the war. Japs chased us out in forty-two," he went on expansively as they lingered in the lee of a companion-way. "I thought I'd seen the last of the blasted country, and no tears shed as far as I was concerned. Lost the use of me feet sloggin' through those bloody awful jungles. Gangrene. Lucky to be alive, I am. The good Lard had me in His kapin'." Father O'Hara crossed himself modestly. "Me and me brave companions."

The story was evidently an indispensable gambit, and short of brushing him off there seemed nothing for it but to stay and hear him out.

"We fell in with some of Wingate's people and were three weeks in that jungle with the little yellow bastards sniffin' our trail. I saw some brave things done in those three weeks, I tell you."

Patrice thought she recognized the note of obsession. They were a new audience, perhaps offering yet another opportunity for exorcism. "Many a brave thing," Father O'Hara repeated solemnly. But his eyes seemed to dance in his face in a strange contradiction to this solemnity. He must, Patrice reflected, have been a cherubic infant. She had an irreverent vision of him with his mother, a pink-cheeked colleen with breasts like plum puddings. The thought made her smile faintly and Father O'Hara's alert glance picked it up at once. "Argh!" he growled, shaking his head. "It's healthy enough I may look now, but for months I lay at death's door. And there was many a brave man never came out of that hellish experience alive."

Adam resignedly lighted his pipe and Father O'Hara produced a package of cigarettes and struck a match for Patrice. They smoked, and several of their fellow passengers strolled past on the deck. The ship was well under way and there was already that sense of imperturbable continuity in the steady pulsing of the engines against the heavy, pacing sea.

Father O'Hara settled his broad shoulders against the companionway and smoked contentedly. He might have known his listeners all their lives. "Strange it is for me to be going back to Burma! I never believed this day would come. First the gangrene and the possibility of amputation. Then the malaria breakin' out when the doctors thought they had it licked. And the dysentery. Would you believe to look at me now that I was down to one hundred and five pounds in me bare feet? And lucky to have feet, at that. Sure there was many a time I believed I never would see the light of day again, let alone that cleaner greener land Mister Kipling loved so well." His laugh was boyish, infectious.

"I'd have settled for almost any other spot on earth, but it was not

414

for me to choose. The doctors fixed me up so they tell me I'm as good as new—almost. And now I hear the temple bells a-callin' where the flyin' fishes play and where the dawn comes up like thunder outer China crost the bay. And why Mr. Kipling never took the trouble to look at a map when he wrote that line I'll never know."

A figure sauntered past them, leaving a trace of perfume on the air, and Father O'Hara lowered his voice. "See the lady just went by? That would be Lady Mary Manchester. She's going to Singapore to meet her intended."

"How did you find that out so soon?" Adam asked, with a laugh. Patrice recognized the woman to whom he had waved earlier that afternoon.

"I make it a rule never to waste a moment," Father O'Hara explained gravely. "Part of me duty. I happen to be the only Catholic priest on the ship, and there are quite a few of the faith to whom I expect to minister during our voyage. As a matter of fact I came down to the ship early and arranged with the purser to post a notice to that effect. Those passengers interested in celebrating Mass are invited to leave their names with him and he will notify me. Lady Manchester is one who left her name." Father O'Hara smiled. "I take it yourselves are not?"

"Agnostics," Adam said. "Sorry."

"Guessed as much," Father O'Hara said cheerfully. "Not that it signifies. In my Father's house are many mansions." He broke off as Lady Mary Manchester approached on her return lap of the deck. Unhesitatingly he stepped forward and addressed her: "Milady! Would you care to join us in a cigarette before dinner?"

She stopped in stride and faced them. Again Patrice was struck by the likeness to Daisy Pitman. Even her voice had the same husky, feminine note: "Father O'Hara?" She peered at him through the gloom. "I saw you come aboard this afternoon, but without your dog collar . . ."

Father O'Hara laughed his boyish laugh. "Let's say I'm in mufti for the moment. It's allowed us of the cloth under certain informal circumstances. A cigarette, milady?"

"Thank you." She took a cigarette from the package he held out to her. "And let's drop the milady business, shall we?"

Adam struck a match for her cigarette and the flame illumined her shapely nose, her deep eyes, her brow. "Ta," she murmured as he flicked the match overboard. "The gay cavalier who waved at me from the rail, is it not?"

"It is, but you didn't wave back."

"They pulled that gangway in so fast I almost got left behind." She smiled upon them impartially. "I've been studying the passenger list and something tells me you must be Mr. and Mrs. Bannister. I'm Mary Manchester. I can't imagine where Father O'Hara gets the milady business."

"Well, now! It's on the passenger list plain as plain can be. The Honorable Mary Manchester, and if that doesn't make you a lady, what does?"

She ignored the obvious opening. "Nice," she murmured, "to meet civilized people. I rather dreaded this trip. Had to wait and wait for a boat going to Singapore or anywhere near it. The war raised the dickens with shipping, didn't it? As it is I have had to settle for Tanjom Priok. But that's not too far from Singapore, and my fiancé hopes to meet me. Luckily I was in Vancouver staying with friends when my travel agent heard about the *Cornelis*. The name almost put me off. Sounded Teutonic." She blew smoke delicately. "One can't help these little prejudices so soon after the war and everything. I find myself put off with little details like names. Our captain, for instance."

A bell clanged overhead, a deep voice speaking in Dutch reached them, and blew away on the wind. Mary Manchester went on: "I have met the captain. Apparently I'm to sit at his table."

"A very fine-appearing man, Captain Buberman," Father O'Hara declared heartily. "Nothing German about him. Dutch through and through."

"I had a letter of introduction to him from my friends in Vancouver. That probably explains the seating arrangements. It looks rather deadly, though. Besides the captain and me there's a dreary female and her child and a missionary couple from Idaho or some such place."

"Why not ask the purser to shift you to our table?" suggested Adam. "You could tell him that we are old long-lost friends."

Father O'Hara shook his head in disapproval. "I'd think twice about that if I were you, milady."

416

Mary Manchester trained a long, slow gaze on him. "Why?" she asked.

"Well, we wouldn't want to offend the captain. We shall be seeing him at Mass, you know."

Mary Manchester moved her slender shoulders in a slight shrug. Her coat and fur hat were mink, her throat was wrapped in a white silk scarf knotted like a hunting stock. As the ship lurched she seemed to rest lightly on one foot, inclining toward Adam, who put his hand quickly under her elbow.

Father O'Hara remarked that most people would consider it a bit of an honor to be placed at the captain's table.

"That's possible," Mary Manchester conceded listlessly. "I was thinking of the others."

"The Reverend Mr. and Mrs. Raudle, from Dodge City, Kansas." Father O'Hara ticked them off on his strong, thick fingers. "Baptist missionaries on their way to India. Far be it from me ..." His cigarette glowed cheerfully as he drew on it. "Then you'll be having young Mrs. Lambston and her little girl."

"They looked as green as cucumbers when I passed them on the stairs a minute ago," Mary Manchester murmured with distaste. "Sea-sick already. I must say it doesn't sound too promising."

"I am having Mrs. Lambston for confession tomorrow afternoon at four-thirty. She asked me herself first thing when she came aboard."

"Quick work," Adam observed with detachment. He glanced at Mary Manchester. "I understand that you are one of Father O'Hara's flock, too?"

She gave a faint, silvery laugh. "I am, but I wouldn't have anything to confess tomorrow at four-thirty. I won't have been on board long enough."

Adam laughed but Father O'Hara's expansiveness seemed to contract slightly. "Well, milady, please remember that I am at your service if you should change your mind. I've told the purser that I would like to say Mass every Sunday and he kindly agreed to put the dining room at my disposal first thing Sunday mornings, and for Benediction service Sunday afternoon. Confessions will be taken in my sitting room every Saturday afternoon."

"Thank you, Father."

There was a brief pause, then she made a small inclusive gesture of her hand. "So delightful to have found *some* congenial souls aboard! Voyages can be ghastly, especially on a small boat." She looked suddenly, directly at Patrice. "Would you three dear people be my guests at the bar in . . . shall we say half an hour? That should give us time for a tiddly before dinner."

She walked away with an elastic step, expertly countering the roll and pitch of the deck, and Father O'Hara flicked the last of his cigarette over the rail. "A tiddly," he murmured. "Now what would you suppose she meant by a tiddly?"

"A tiddly," Patrice explained, "is naughty English for a drink."

Father O'Hara lapsed into a wholesome laugh. "Naughty English for a drink, is it? Well, we'll meet at the bar, me friends. Better make it sharp. I have a feeling her ladyship is not one to appreciate being kept waiting."

Back in their stateroom Adam looked at Patrice. He was frowning. "Promise you won't overdo tonight, Patrice!"

She was busy picking out a dress to wear at dinner. "Overdo?"

"You know what I mean. Overdo on the liquor."

The habit of criticism, sometimes implied, sometimes direct, had grown on Adam since the success of her first book. She had given up trying to account for it as she had given up trying to account for his father's now open hostility toward her. While Adam concentrated his disapproval on her drinking habits and certain of her friends, Wilbur Bannister had confined himself to cryptic remarks concerning *bluestockings* and *female intellectuals,* italicizing the words in her hearing.

Well, Wilbur Bannister, like Daisy Pitman, was more than three thousand miles away at this moment, but as Patrice's glance came briefly to rest on Adam she thought she saw the father gazing at her from the son's eyes, just as a little while ago she fancied she had seen Daisy Pitman studying her through Mary Manchester's.

Patrice threw a raspberry-colored wool dress on her bed and eyed it speculatively. "Would you," she asked Adam pleasantly, "rather I didn't show up at the bar?"

"Now you're mad, and all I wanted was to protect you from yourself."

"What?" She stared at him in disbelief, then laughed.

Adam sat down on the edge of his bed, opposite hers, and unlaced

418

his shoes. "All right, so it sounds corny. But it just occurred to me that being on this ship, in a fresh situation, among strange people ... I just thought it was a good chance for you to take a round turn on yourself. That's all."

Patrice thought bitterly: So that's all. But we wouldn't be on the damn ship, in a fresh situation, among strange people, if I hadn't taken a round turn on myself a long time ago and made the cash. Barto's voice sounded in her ears: "It's going to be up to you ... You can recreate your marriage—or rewrite it, if you prefer the analogy." And Netta's: "Can the finest decision stand up against the day-to-day triviality of life?"

Adam, with a glance at Patrice's averted face, changed his tone: "Are you going to wear the red dress? I love it."

She said nothing, and as she slipped the dress over her head and her face appeared in the opening at the neck Adam rose suddenly from his berth and kissed her. "This is going to be a wonderful trip ... it's going to make all the difference."

Patrice managed a smile. "Put on the blue silk shirt," she said. "And the batik tie. We've got to make a good impression."

"You mean on her ladyship and the padre? Friendly types, aren't they?"

"I wonder," said Patrice, "who's going to convert whom on this voyage?"

"They're both Catholics. I wouldn't think there was any problem."

"I wasn't thinking of religion." She watched him dress. Time had dealt kindly with Adam. He had kept his figure, his fine carriage, his clear skin. Money, leisure, peace of mind—all became him. He was always honest about this. Though he had never been a spendthrift, this new access to funds provided him with all those little opportunities for refinement which came naturally to him. He chose his clothes with an eye to quiet elegance; he bought rare books on flora and fauna, and he enjoyed picking up small, precious objects: a carnelian carving of a bird from Japan, a Hokusai print, a piece of Chinese celadon. Patrice had been touched and amused by his pleasure in such things. All his life he must have longed for these unpremeditated little extravagances. Where his sister Caroline was motivated by the cash value of an object—she was forever having her belongings appraised by professionals—Adam's response was aesthetic. The feral being had made way for something very close to the English gentleman, and Patrice thought: I grudge him none of it, if only he wouldn't begrudge me. . . .

Adam, the batik tie knotted carefully under his chin, turned to look at her. He said abruptly: "I'm sorry I said that about the liquor. Forgive me, darling."

"I haven't overdone for months and months, and you know it."

"I do know it. It's just that I'm so damned proud of you, I'd hate to see a relapse."

"It's all right," Patrice said coolly. "I promise not to disgrace you."

"You didn't have to say that."

Just one of the countless things one didn't have to say. Leave it alone, part of her mind admonished her warningly. Leave it alone, leave it alone.

They found Mary Manchester and Father O'Hara in the bar. Mary was svelte in a coffee-colored silk which set off her hair and her eyes. Father O'Hara had shaved and changed his informal slacks and sweater for a clerical collar and a dark suit which added years to his age. As Adam and Patrice approached they heard him saying to Mary Manchester: "Many a brave thing happened in those jungles . . . many a brave thing that I will never forget for the rest of my life."

Patrice saw Mary Manchester's glance take Adam in from head to foot as she invited him to sit beside her. "Father's been telling me about how he escaped the Japs in Burma during the war."

"Wish I could forget it," Father O'Hara murmured, shaking his head. "But how can a man forget his friends' bravery? Better perhaps to have died with them . . . but the good Lard had other plans for his humble servant."

Patrice ordered a gin fizz and Adam a Scotch and soda; Father O'Hara confined himself to beer, and Mary Manchester to Dubonnet. "A schoolmarm's tipple, but I have no head for liquor."

Father O'Hara leaned back in his chair and clasped his hands on his clerical vest. He made a visible effort to shake off his gloomy memories of the war. "First night at sea! Means the officers won't be dining with the passengers." He lowered his voice. "The Opposition Shop just went by. My rivals, Mr. and Mrs. Raudle. They were preparing to come in when they saw the bottles. Milk drinkers, I'll make you any bet."

420

"Dreadful American habit," declared Marry Manchester with a shudder. "I never can get used to seeing grown men swill milk with their meals." She turned her slow smile on Adam. "Sorry! I forgot you're American."

"One hundred percent an unreconstructed Yankee," Adam told her gravely. "And you'll find that we have many less nauseating habits than swilling milk."

Her smile deepened, and Father O'Hara's dark-blue gaze rested on her with an indefinable expression. She said: "I don't really know many Americans, though I met quite a few during the war. Actually it was through an American friend in London, during the blitz, that I met my fiancé. Funny, isn't it, how these things happen?"

Patrice inquired politely whether her fiancé was an American, and Mary Manchester made a slight gesture of something like horror. "Nigel American? Goodness, no! He's the most English thing you can imagine."

"Nice," Patrice murmured, sipping her gin fizz. "Like Bubble-and-squeak. I have always thought that that was the most English thing I could imagine."

The ship lurched in a heavy swell and Adam gave it as his opinion that they were in for a spell of bad weather. "You ever seasick?" he asked Mary Manchester. She shook her head. "Never. Luck, I suppose. I've always thought that mal de mer must be the most unbecoming ailment that could afflict a female."

Patrice noticed a young, tired-looking woman pass the door. It must, she thought, be Mrs. Lambston, mother of the only child on the ship. Mary Manchester saw the figure pass and she said in a lowered voice: "I thought of asking that poor little thing to join us, but she seemed to be tied up with the child. Perhaps I'll ask her tomorrow night, if she can dispose of the infant somehow.

"She could throw it overboard, I suppose," Patrice suggested. She felt an unpleasant mood developing within her, and asked herself grimly: Can I be jealous of this dame just because she reminds me of Daisy Pitman? But how silly. It had been years since she had been jealous of Daisy Pitman—years, in fact, since she had been jealous of any woman. Her last remark had evoked a shocked laugh from Father O'Hara. "Argh, poor Mrs. Lambston. It's a trial for a parent on a long voyage, to have to mind a child, and a delicate one at that."

421

Mary Manchester turned diffidently to Patrice. "So wise of you not to bring your children. Or have you any?"

"Five," Patrice replied. "All grown up now, with moustaches."

Mary Manchester's eyes took on a faintly wary expression. "Children are darling, of course," she murmured. "Nigel insists that we have a large family. He's quite old-fashioned about such things. Now, can anyone tell me about life in Singapore?"

"I knew a boy from Singapore during the war," Father O'Hara began in the unmistakable tone of reminiscence. "He was stationed there with his regiment before the Japs moved in. Boy by the name of Harper. Came from India originally. Eurasian. Bravest of the brave." Father O'Hara raised his beer glass in a salute. "I've never been able to get him out of me mind. When we were fleein' the Nips through the Burmese jungles this boy was with us, and it was he that saved us. Strong as a horse he was, too. When me feet went bad he carried me on his back. Then when we knew the Nips were closin', in on us young Harper came to me one night and said: 'Father,' he said, 'I want to ask your blessing on a little project of mine.' He'd concocted it himself and had got our CO to agree, pointing out that it was our only chance. Whiles the rest of us—there must have been forty all told—were to concentrate on our escape, this Harper lad would fall back and let himself be captured by the Nips. He had it all worked out, down to the smallest detail. Under the Nips' interrogation—and we all knew what that would mean—he'd inveigle them into taking a different direction, giving the rest of us a bit of extra time."

Father O'Hara gazed into his beer glass, his face turned suddenly heavy. "Mine wasn't the only life at stake or I might have tried to dissuade him from his little project. Yes, I believe I would have tried to dissuade him. He was young, strong, and in far better condition than any of us. Could have turned out that he would have had a better chance if he'd just taken it along with the rest of us. But his mind was made up, and there was forty men to think of besides, and it was easy to see that he wasn't afraid, or if he was afraid he wasn't showing it, begor."

Father O'Hara took a swallow from his glass and made a face. "Bitther," he said. "Brings the bitterness to my lips whenever I think of him. But I gave young Harper me blessing and put me own rosary in his hands, and we pushed on into the jungles leaving him behind as a decoy, and we never saw nor did we ever hear of him again."

Harper. What's-His-Name Harper. Could it have been he? Patrice felt a renewal of an old superstitious dread, as though time had taken on substance, and the past, no longer innocent, waited for her with mysterious intent.

"All those days we were together in the jungles I had never asked him about his family in India. Did he have a wife and kids? Parents? Sisters and brothers? Of course, we were running for our lives, and talk wasn't encouraged for a number of reasons, chief of them being the Nips' proximity. But couldn't I have asked him a few questions that evening before he left us? I've tried and tried, ever since, to find out something about him, but me own illness and near dying disthracted me for a long time, and there was so many ... so many! Still and all ... couldn't I have done *something* for him? Couldn't I, after letting him lay his young life down for me, couldn't I have done *something?*"

A bell sounded somewhere and Adam said: "Feels as if we are picking up speed." He smiled at Mary Manchester. "Doesn't the thought make you happy?"

"Because I'll be seeing Nigel?" Her long, pale lashes quivered. "It will have been one whole year!"

Father O'Hara finished his beer and looked at her kindly. "Cheer up, milady. Tanjom Priok is no more than a hop, skip to Singapore, and you'll likely be setting up housekeeping while the rest of us poor sinners are still tied up to the dock discharging cargo."

Adam was gazing directly at Mary Manchester. "I hope," he said, "that when the time comes for you to leave us you'll remember to wave good-bye. Or will you be too preoccupied with Nigel to think of us?"

"You'll have to remind me, Mr. Bannister." She added after a brief pause: "There is just the barest chance that Nigel might not be able to get to Tanjom Priok to meet the boat, in which case he will have made arrangements for me to get across to Singapore somehow. But I'm not even going to let myself think of such a thing."

To Patrice's tuning-fork ear there seemed something off key in this exchange. Adam was not being himself, nor, she felt, was Mary Manchester, nor Father O'Hara. All three appeared self-conscious, as though trying to attain some unidentifiable goal.

Mary Manchester went on: "Nigel and I have waited so long . . . all the time he was a prisoner in Germany and I was doing war work in England. A few of my letters reached him, most of them didn't. Even now I sometimes find it hard to believe that we are going to be together at last." The last words were uttered on an almost despairing note, then she looked quickly at Adam: "Do you suppose we have time for another tiddly?"

Adam signaled the steward. Father O'Hara shook his head. "One's my limit for tonight, thanks."

Adam asked Mary Manchester whether she planned to live in Singapore indefinitely. "It all depends on Nigel," she replied, with a return to her earlier chattiness. "He's doing so awfully well in his firm. He says we are to have one of the nicest bungalows in Singapore. Out of town, you know. Far from the bazaars and all that. Four servants. A lovely garden." Her eyes glowed, "Nigel's letters made it all sound as if life for us was going to be like the old times, before the war ruined everything."

"When we were very young," Patrice murmured. "With Christopher Robin and Winnie the Pooh."

The steward brought the second round of drinks and handed Adam the chit to sign. Mary Manchester demurred: "The drinks are on me tonight. I invited you, remember?"

"Nonsense," said Adam. He glanced at his watch. "We'll have a third if there's time before the dinner bell."

Patrice eyed him with curiosity. He was definitely out of character and gave her the impression that he was trying to avoid her glance. Mrs. Lambston walked past the door and on an impulse Patrice hailed her: "Won't you join us?"

Mrs. Lambston hesitated in the door. Her dress was rumpled, her hair untidy. She looked young and friendless, but her smile was sudden and grateful. "Thank you, I can't. I've got to go back to my baby. I'm hoping she's asleep. I just went on deck for a breath of air."

She made an indecisive, apologetic gesture and went away. "The poor, sweet girl," Father O'Hara murmured compassionately. "Kind that needs a hubby to look after her, if I ever saw one that did!"

"Nigel," said Mary Manchester, sipping her second Dubonnet,

424

"Nigel adores tennis. I expect we shall play a lot. And there's riding, of course. And I'm told there's a lovely golf course. Little by little, Nigel says, things are getting back to normal."

"Do you believe they ever will get back to normal?" demanded Father O'Hara, with a momentary lapse into brooding.

"Why shouldn't they, Father?"

He shrugged his football player's shoulders. "Too much has happened. Too many have died. Too many souls have been betrayed."

Mary Manchester gave him a nervous smile. "Oh, come now, Father! People want to get back to normal. The whole world wants it. After all, we got over the first great war, didn't we?"

"Perhaps that's our trouble," Patrice suggested. "We tend to get back to normal rather too easily."

Father O'Hara nodded. "I agree. We don't want to remember our lessons."

Adam moved impatiently. "Aren't we getting a bit solemn? This is supposed to be a celebration—our first night at sea!" He raised his glass to Mary Manchester. "I drink to present company and future happiness."

Suddenly Patrice thought she got it. Adam was happy. He was happy now, at this very moment. Some lifelong restraint had dropped from him and at fifty there had emerged the man he had perhaps always yearned to be—resigned, content. Why had she not seen it before? Why had it taken the casual contact with two total strangers to bring it to her attention? Oh, Barto, she thought with a little spasm of internal laughter. Go back to the beginning, Barto had begged her. Go back where it all started. . . . But suppose one of us doesn't want to go back? Suppose one of us finds a beginning at some other, some quite different point in time and place? What then, Barto—what then?

Father O'Hara had raised his empty beer glass. "To the lad Harper," he said gravely, and Patrice too raised her glass and smiled at Mary Manchester. "To Nigel," she said. "To Nigel and Singapore and a new beginning."

The silvery notes of the dinner gong sounded in the passage, and Father O'Hara set his glass on the table. "It seems a long time ago that I had me tea," he said jovially. "This sea air brings on the appetite."

He stood a moment gazing down at Mary Manchester's shining

hair. "I'm asking the purser to set up a deck tennis net on the forward hatch, once we get into warmer weather. I can see your ladyship's the athletic type. So am I. And perhaps Mr. and Mrs. Bannister will join us in mixed doubles?" He turned to Adam. "Thanks for the refreshments. I'll be seeing you at table in a few minutes?"

When he had gone Mary Manchester made a slight grimace. "He's on my trail. I'm a Catholic, you see, and the dear man evidently feels responsible for my spiritual welfare."

"And Nigel's too?" Adam asked dryly.

"Oh, no. Nigel's a Protestant. It doesn't affect our getting married, though, as long as it is understood that our children will be brought up as Catholics."

She seemed disposed to talk indefinitely, but the dinner gong sounded again and, sighing, she put down her glass and smiled at Adam. "Thank you so much. But remember—next time it's on me!"

For several days they were in heavy weather and few of the passengers showed up for meals. Mary Manchester dined in splendor with the captain, and Adam and Patrice and Father O'Hara with the first officer, de Koon, a plump, melancholy Dutchman. Father O'-Hara, brisk and cheerful in spite of rough seas, did most of the talking. His appetite was impressive and he was loud in praise of Dutch cuisine. Clear-eyed, healthy, he tucked into second and third helpings while the ship lumbered along and they kept their seats with difficulty.

"Glad to see that you enjoy the weather as much as I do," Father O'Hara remarked approvingly to Patrice. "I'm told that the poor little Lambston woman is terribly sick, and the little girl, too. And the Opposition Shop—both of them." He fielded a careening glass and set it back in place. "But just give us a day of calm and sunshine and they'll all be out like violets in spring. Eh, Mr. de Koon!?"

"Nah vallets in Java," Mr. de Koon replied morosely. "Too bloody hot. Bloody country." He caught a cruet as it sidled toward the table's edge. "Bloody ungrateful people, the Javanese. We made their bloody country. Now watch them ruin it. Independence, ha ha!"

There was an exciting sound of falling crockery and Father O'Hara smiled. "Glad I had me second helping before that lot went on the floor. Did ye know, Mrs. Bannister, that the chef bakes his own bread on this ship, everyday?"

"Does he now?" Patrice exclaimed. "I was thinking it probably fell like manna from heaven."

"Get along with you!" He laughed. They had early established a lighthearted rapport, each fully aware of uncrossable Rubicons. But between Father O'Hara and Adam Patrice sensed a kind of tension. It was, she thought, a matter of chemistry, perhaps, of essential incompatibility, but as the days passed and the inescapable confinement of shipboard life threw them together, the strain between the two became marked. All three, with Mary Manchester, had fallen into the habit—initiated on their first night at sea—of meeting at the bar for a drink before dinner. Occasionally they were joined by one or another of the ship's officers, but more often than not it was just the four of them to sit round a corner table, Mary Manchester with her Dubonnet, Adam and Patrice with their Scotch and gin fizzes, Father O'Hara with a beer.

On every ocaasion the steward presented Adam with the chit, which he signed, smilingly ignoring Mary Manchester's insistence that it was her turn this time. It was during these meetings at the bar that Patrice became more and more aware of the tension between the two men, but if Mary Manchester noticed it she gave no sign, dividing her attention between them, with no more than a shade of emphasis on Adam.

On the fifth evening the weather showed signs of moderating, and when the foursome gathered at their corner table they were joined by the captain and the first officer. The captain was tall, lean, and good-looking in a zoological fashion; he made Patrice think of an elderly male lion and he was almost as uncommunicative as de Koon, though his English was more intelligible.

After one drink Captain Buberman came to life and became flirtatious in a heavy-handed, pawing sort of way. He made a pass or two at Patrice, first with one huge square foot planted on hers, then with an equally large square hand on her knee. When on each occasion she let hot cigarette ash fall on his wrist he turned his attention to Mary Manchester. Patrice noticed a glint come into Adam's eye and his jaw tighten, while Father O'Hara tilted back in his chair, his thumbs in his vest, his eyes watchful behind their genial smile.

The first officer downed his second drink in a silence which deepened with every swallow, and Captain Buberman announced with guttural heartiness that tomorrow was going to be a fine day. The worst was behind them and they could look forward to sunshine and calm seas probably for the rest of the voyage.

Mary Manchester turned glowingly to Adam. "Do let's celebrate the good news. Another round, and on me this time. I positively insist!"

"No!" roared Captain Buberman. "Who ever heard of a lady standing the drinks? Not in my country! Not in my presence!" He clapped his hands to summon the bar steward. Patrice had an occult conviction that he had corraled one of Mary Manchester's ankles between his own, as, a few minutes earlier, he had attempted to corral hers. Father O'Hara tilted forward suddenly and surprisingly opted for another beer. "As long as it is a celebration. And tomorrow being Saturday, I'll be taking confessions as usual and meting out the penalties."

Everyone laughed, with the exception of Adam and the first officer. Adam said in an even voice: "Of all religious aberrations I'd say that the ritual of confession was the silliest there is."

Father O'Hara's smile suddenly looked as if it might be glued on his face like a false moustache. He said softly: "And are you then an authority on aberration, Mr. Bannister?"

Mary Manchester with an abrupt movement upset an ashtray on the floor and stooped to retrieve it. "Allow me, allow me!" growled Captain Buberman, reaching sideways for the fallen ashtray as the ship, lurching suddenly, almost flung him on his head. The movement caused Adam to jerk his elbow unexpectedly, knocking another laden ashtray with its contents over Father O'Hara's knees.

"Sorry," Adam said urbanely. "Sea seems to be getting rougher."

"Would it be the sea, now?" remarked Father O'Hara, not attempting to retrieve the fallen ashtray. His face had flushed, his gaze lost something of its benignity.

The steward came forward and set fresh glasses and ashtrays on the table. The first officer seized his and raised it in what was apparently intended to be a salute. "Glah!" he exclaimed. "Glah glah glah!"

Patrice turned soberly to Father O'Hara. "It's probably Flemish," she said, "for 'Here's how.' What do you think?"

He replied with his eyes fixed on Adam. "Whatever it is, he means

428

well, which is more than I would say for some others."

The first officer looked from one to another with mournful eyes and pointed to his throat, clinched in its tight uniform collar. "Glah," he said. "Glah glah glah."

Light dawned on Patrice. "You've got a sore throat," she said. "You poor thing."

"Laryngitis," explained the captain, surfacing from under the table.

"Always at the beginning of a voyage de Koon comes down with laryngitis. I believe it is for leaving his wife. A very loving couple. But it will pass when we get into warm weather."

"To warm weather!" Mary Manchester raised her glass. "To warm weather, sunshine, calm seas!" She was lovely in a cream-colored silk shirt with pearls round her throat and in her ears. During the day she looked practical, svelte. At evening she bloomed. A night-blooming cereus, Patrice thought, watching Captain Buberman light Mary's cigarette, his great brown hands cupped round hers. She thanked him demurely, then asked: "Captain Buberman, what is your opinion of the situation in Java?"

"The situation is hell." He glowered. "They are kicking us out. After three hundred years of taking everything from us—railways, highways, bridges, ports, factories, plantations—everything we Dutch have built with our hands, our guts, our guilder. Now they kick us out and take it all for themselves." He gulped from his glass. "Schools, hospitals, tens of millions of guilder have we poured into the country. Civilization itself. If it had not been for us they would still be talking to their brothers the monkeys."

Father O'Hara shrugged. "We can thank the Japs," he said. "And for what is going to happen in Burma, and in India too, if you ask me."

"And Singapore?" Mary Manchester inquired nervously.

"And in Singapore, inevitably."

Captain Buberman shook his head. "I do not worry too greatly. All these backward people . . . drunk on their notion of independence. Yet they need *us*. You will see. They need our trade. They need our brains, our energy, our technology, no? They will fight us and murder us in our beds. But sooner or later it will begin again as it has always begun—by trade."

"First the padre," Adam suggested lightly, "then the bania!"

429

Captain Buberman took it seriously. "Correct. Christianity and trade—where would those black monkeys be without them?"

The dinner gong chimed and the steward brought the chit for drinks on a silver tray and unhesitatingly placed it before Adam. Captain Buberman was talking across the table, in Dutch, to the first officer, and Mary Manchester had taken her compact from her purse and was diligently powdering her nose. For a moment Adam seemed to hesitate, then he signed the chit and Mary Manchester gave him a reproving glance. "That was naughty of you, Mr. Bannister!" she told him. "Now *promise* me that next time . . ."

In their stateroom for a few minutes before going up to dinner, Patrice sat on her bed and began to sing softly: " 'Oh, promise me that someday you and I . . .' "

Adam interrupted angrily. "That little Bible-thumping bastard! Lapping up his beer, letting me sign for him night after night!"

"You signed for the others; why not for Father O'Hara?"

"The type of cheap European who thinks all Americans are well-heeled and should be made to foot the bills!"

Patrice went back to humming "Oh Promise Me," and Adam stared at her grimly. "All right, I know what's on your mind. I'm sailing under false colors. It's your dough that I sign with, not mine."

She looked at him without rancor. "What's become of your sense of humor?"

"I just don't find our priestly friend very amusing, that's all. Neither his wit nor his conscience about the poor boob who laid down his life for him in the Burmese jungles."

"Is that all you've got against him—that you don't find him amusing?"

"If you must know I don't care for his sneaking way with Mary, either."

"He's a priest, and she's one of his flock, don't forget."

"My eye! Keeps after her all the time about confession, communion, Mass—the rest of it."

"And what about our gallant skipper?" Patrice asked. "He had his legs coiled round hers like a boa constrictor most of the evening. You didn't cry foul at that, or didn't you know?"

Adam reddened. "He's such an obvious boob it doesn't mean anything. And Mary knows how to cope with men like that."

430

"I bet," said Patrice. Leave it alone, warned her mind. Leave it alone.

Next day the weather did not clear as the captain had assured them it would, but the sea was calmer. Late in the afternoon Patrice went to call on Mrs. Lambston. The invalid was sitting up in bed and gave her a wan smile. "Do come in. The Raudles have very kindly taken my little girl for an hour or two. Everyone is so kind."

"The captain has promised us good weather," Patrice told her. "That ought to make you feel better."

"It does. Won't you sit down for a minute?"

Patrice sat down on the vacant bunk and noticed a pile of books from the ship's library on the bureau beside Mrs. Lambston's bed. Her own face stared at her from the dust cover of one, and Mrs. Lambston, catching her eye, smiled, "I knew I had seen you somewhere before, then when I saw that photograph on the book I recognized you."

Patrice was never quite proof against the contradictory feelings of pleasure and dismay on being recognized. She lighted a cigarette and smoked nervously for a few moments, and Mrs. Lambston said: "Patrice Verrier. I suppose that's what they call a nom de plume?"

"It was my name before I married." Patrice hesitated. "Might I ask you a favor? Would you keep it under your hat? Of course, I realize that some of the other passengers might see the picture and put two and two together, but I'd like to stay anonymous as long as I can on this ship."

Mrs. Lambston nodded understandingly. "It must be a rather nice feeling to be anonymous. Perhaps we should all have a nom de plume when we feel like—you know—disappearing for a while."

Patrice warmed to her, a feeling which was deepened when Mrs. Lambston said shyly: "I've read your book but I won't try to talk about it because it might embarrass us both. Perhaps someday if we ever get to know each other better . . ."

She reached for a piece of candy from a highly ornamented box on the bedside table, then pushed the box toward Patrice. "Father O'Hara brought me these because he thinks it would give me more energy." She added thoughtfully: "He's the kindest man. Have you had a chance to see much of him?"

431

Patrice explained that they had drinks every evening with Father O'Hara. "And with Lady Mary Manchester," she added as an afterthought.

"Talking of nom de plumes," murmured Mrs. Lambston with a cryptic little smile. She helped herself to another piece of candy. "There's something I'd like to ask you, Mrs. Bannister. It's a little question of what I guess one might call ethics."

Patrice waited, and Mrs. Lambston continued: "It's been on my mind ever since I got on the ship and met Father O'Hara. I wouldn't have given it a thought but for him. He's so kind, so responsible. He takes his duty so much to heart. You can tell by how lovely he's been to my little girl and me—coming to see us several times a day, hearing Ellie say her prayers at night, telling her stories to put her to sleep, seeing that the steward takes good care of us."

Mrs. Lambston's eyes were a warm gray, and very young. "Father O'Hara and I have had many long talks together. He has sort of hinted that he's worried about someone on the ship, a Catholic person who he is afraid might be going—as he put it—astray."

Patrice smoked, watching her. "Anyway, Father's got it on his mind that this person is in some sort of trouble, and he would like to help. She was supposed to go to confession to him twice already, but she keeps putting it off, and though she has attended Mass she won't take Holy Communion as one would expect a good Catholic to do. Father takes this very much to heart."

"If you are talking about Mary Manchester," Patrice said after a moment, "I'd say she was well able to take care of herself."

Mrs. Lambston shook her head. "You see, he's a priest, and that's what makes all the difference." She raised her eyes to Patrice's. "There is something I could tell Father O'Hara, but I don't know that I should. It's not my business, and I'm not sure that it is his." She twisted over on her elbow among the pillows and propped her chin on her hand and spoke now without looking at Patrice. "Mary Manchester is no Lady Mary. She's plain Mary Manchester and she comes from someplace in Canada—I forget the name. How do I know this? Well, you remember the ship was delayed a few days getting off. So Ellie and I moved into a hotel in Portland to wait word from the agents before going down to Astoria. We had a room on the third floor, and Mary Manchester had the room right next to us. She was not alone. There was a man with her, a Colonel Riordan. I am not a very good sleeper and Ellie was restless so I was awake off and on a good part of the night. I didn't mean to eavesdrop, but the walls were so thin and they never made any attempt to lower their voices. In fact sometimes it seemed that they just didn't care who might hear them. Most of the time there was no more than a kind of mumble—you know how it sounds in hotels sometimes. And I'd hear a waiter bringing them up a tray. There was that sound of glasses and ice buckets and soda bottles being opened. Well, the night before we left the hotel to go down to Astoria and catch the ship there was some kind of a fight in the room next door. I tried not to listen—honest I did! But I guess he—the man—had gotten a bit high on liquor because it was his voice I heard mostly. Hers was quieter and she didn't sound high at all. Well, that night I heard the man—this Colonel Riordan— burst out in a real angry voice: 'Look, Mary, I've done all I can . . . every goddam thing in my power. How often do we have to go over the ground, for God's sake?' Then I heard her say something but I didn't get it. The man went on and he seemed to be getting madder and madder. 'It was different during the war. Everything was different during the war. I wasn't the only guy made promises he couldn't keep. And I love Sue. We've been married fifteen years and there are the kids to think of, too." At that point the man raised his voice so there was no mistake about what he said: 'All right, so I was a bastard and I am still a bastard. But I love my wife and children and I'm not running out on them. Look. I can give you your passage out to Singapore and a thousand bucks to tide you over. It's all I've got. I'd double and treble it if I could, you know damn well I would.' " Mrs. Lambston paused, picking at the coverlet with her fingers. "Then I heard *her* say something about someone called Nigel, and it sounded like she was crying a bit, softly. Then the man's voice again, not mad this time but still loud: 'Now don't hand me that stuff. You were crazy enough about him once. You just thought you had it made with me, that's what. You weren't sure of Nigel and you were of me, but you were mistaken. I never meant to run out on Sue and the kids—never. Now listen, goddammit! Go and find Nigel and marry him. Or why wait until you get to Singapore? Maybe you'll find someone on the ship just as you found me on that transport. . . .' " Mrs. Lambston broke off and stared at Patrice with round eyes like a kitten's.

433

"It was awful, Mrs. Bannister. I think she must have thrown something at him. Sounded like it. Then I heard a chair being pushed back and his voice again: 'I'm off. I wish you all the luck in the world, and I mean it. Just one bit of advice before I go. Don't start peddling your arse unless you really mean it, and don't go falling for some poor dope who can't marry you.'

"Then I heard the man's footsteps march past my door, and that was the end of it. Next morning I saw Mary Manchester in the hotel lobby, buying magazines at the newsstand, and you'd never have guessed looking at her what had gone on in her room next door to mine. Real elegant she was in her fur coat and hat and a handbag that must have cost a mint! She saw me and looked right through me as she had done every time we met and as she has done ever since on this ship. And that," said Mrs. Lambston, out of breath, "is the end of the story. Except . . ." She hesitated. "Except I'm wondering what her game might be. Is she truly a Catholic or just one for the duration of this trip; is she Lady Mary Manchester or just plain Mary Manchester from someplace in Canada . . . or what?"

Patrice said after a pause: "None of it is really our business, is it?"

"Isn't it?" Mrs. Lambston sounded anxious. "Don't you think I ought to tell Father O'Hara? I mean he's so concerned about her and he wants to help and I thought that maybe if he knew what I knew he'd quit worrying so much. As it is he's got it on his mind that she's in some sort of a religious tangle and it's his duty to straighten her out."

"Instead of which she may be in the same old worldly tangle of trying to land a husband before her dough gives out?"

Mrs. Lambston was insistent. "What would you do if you were me?"

"If I were you I'd leave well—or bad—strictly alone."

"Father O'Hara believes that there are too many people like that in the world . . . leaving things alone when they might help, or even save another soul. He's talked to me a great deal about it. He says we are too apt just to walk away from a problem and let someone else handle it . . . let someone else do the suffering, the dying perhaps."

Patrice stubbed out her cigarette and rose. "Does it ever occur to you," she asked slowly, "that some of us have a tendency to luxuriate in our guilty conscience?"

Mrs. Lambston gazed at her uncomprehendingly. "She could be a

434

complete phony and Father worrying himself to death over her!"

Patrice turned to the door. "Get well soon," she said over her shoulder. "And join us at the bar one of these evenings."

"I don't drink alcohol. Only beer sometimes. But thank you just the same, Mrs. Bannister."

On her way to the deck Patrice glanced into the lounge and saw Adam smoking and reading a book. She left him undisturbed and climbed a stairway into a blast of fresh blowing air. The sea was still leaden but there was a hint of pink in the western sky and the deck distinctly steadier underfoot. She paused in the lee of a ventilator shaft and leaned an elbow on the rail. There was a smell of steam, of hot oil, of salt-rimed canvas—the gray impersonal smell of the sea. And there was, suddenly, Mary Manchester's voice quite close by. It sounded sulky, childish, out of character: "But, Father, why should I?"

"Argh, the poor forlorn thing!" said Father O'Hara. A whiff of cigarette smoke sped past Patrice on the wind. "With only the stewards to tend out on her. Wouldn't it be a Christian act for you just to put your head in her stateroom door and ask did she need a bit of help or company?"

"I couldn't stand it. The steward told me that she and the child have been horribly sick. He's been in their room all the time, cleaning up after them. I'd die if I smelled that stateroom."

"I've been in it and I didn't die. And so grateful as she was for a word of kindness."

"I feel quite kindly, but I'm no Florence Nightingale and I don't pretend to be."

"I'm not asking that you be Florence Nightingale. But the poor girl's of our faith—it should count with ye."

"I'm afraid it doesn't. I just can't stand the smell of vomit and baby bottom and the rest of it. I wouldn't be of the slightest use to Mrs. Lambston."

"You could be charitable. As one woman to another."

"I don't particularly like women."

When Father O'Hara spoke again his voice had a hint of muscle. "It's not for me to be prying into your likes and dislikes, but as your confessor—"

"But you are not my confessor—yet!" She brought it out with a

435

laugh, and Father O'Hara joined in it with a return to breeziness. "That's up to you, too," he told her. "As you very well know, I am at your service. I like to think that every Catholic on this ship has come to me for confession in these few days since we left port. Even Mrs. Lambston, sick as she has been."

"I have told you I'd be coming to you, Father, one of these days."

"It's glad I am to hear you say it. Now to get back to poor little Mrs. Lambston."

"Father, for goodness' sake!"

"It's for goodness' sake I'm asking you, Mary . . . and you were named for the blessed mother of Our Lord, were you not?"

"If you must know, I was named for a rich aunt from whom I have expectations!" Mary Manchester sounded tart. The scent of their cigarettes blew past Patrice's face. Both, she conjectured, must be reclining in deck chairs in a sheltered angle made by the ventilator shaft and a stack of cargo battened down by chains.

"Well," said Father O'Hara at last in a tone of resignation, "if you won't you won't. I'll ask Mrs. Bannister if she would mind looking in on those two poor forlorn craytures."

"Why don't you ask Mrs. Bannister?" Mary Manchester took him up sharply. "You and she seem to get on very well."

"So you've got it in for her too, have ye?" Father O'Hara said softly. "And why would that be, I'm wondering."

She replied in an edged voice: "I can't imagine what you mean by such a remark."

"Argh! Ye sound like a silly spoiled child. All I asked was that you perform a slight act of compassion toward a fellow being, and you bite my head off."

"I admire your compassionate spirit," Mary Manchester told him sarcastically. "But after all, since you are a priest . . ." She broke off and Patrice wondered how she could sneak away without betraying her presence. Father O'Hara saved her the trouble. He appeared without warning from behind the ventilator shaft and stared at her without a trace of surprise. Then he took her arm and led her back along the deck as she had come, the wind at their backs. Patrice said after a moment: "Yes, I confess it. I was eavesdropping."

"And it's not sorry you are either, begor. I saw you the minute you arrived behind that ventilator thing. You shouldn't be wearing a red sweater when you intend to play Sherlock Holmes."

"I had no intention of playing Sherlock Holmes."

He stopped and turned so they faced each other. They were alone on the deck. He said slowly: "That girl's soul is in jeopardy and she doesn't know it."

Patrice suffered one of her attacks of ill-advised mirth. "Father," she said, "and did ye ever see a play by Somerset Maugham called *Rain?*"

The wind had blown his black hair over his eyes, whipped crimson into his cheeks. He looked again every inch the football player he must once have been. "Yes, I did see it. But you're wrong again."

He groped in his pockets for cigarettes. They took turns shielding each other from the wind while he struck matches and finally got their cigarettes going. "Mary is confused in mind and spirit," he muttered. "Her soul is in jeopardy because of it. And she happens to be one of the Faith, one of me own."

"Do you believe that her soul is in jeopardy because she contemplates marrying Nigel, a Protestant?" Patrice asked.

He laughed. "Nigel! No, not because of Nigel."

"You appear to have discovered a lot about the state of Mary Manchester's soul in the few days that we've all been together."

"Argh, the poor child!"

"I don't see—" Patrice began, when he interrupted: "Mrs. Bannister, would you be so good as to pop in on Mrs. Lambston and her baby and see if there is aught anyone can do for them?"

"I'm one up on you there, Father. I popped in on Mrs. Lambston a few minutes ago. She seems greatly improved in health and spirits."

He looked at her approvingly. "You're a good girl in spite of your facetiousness. And I'm just wondering why Mary Manchester . . ."

"Doesn't like me?" Patrice finished for him. "Perhaps she'll confide her reasons to you one of these days before the voyage is over. There is that little business of confession coming up, don't forget."

He frowned. "Now that's no matter for joking, Mrs. Bannister. We'll leave my sacred office out of the discussion, if you please."

They continued their leisurely pacing up and down the deck. It was getting dark and the sea had a sudden murderous appearance, with a towering swell. Patrice loved and hated the sea. She had a swift remembrance of Rosanna Burden's words: "I understand the land. You walk on it. Grass and flowers grow out of it."

Under their feet at this moment nightmare caverns yawned and the black sea roamed through its canyons. Over these waters Damon Edwards had voyaged for the first and last time, and somewhere in similar waters Rosanna's son, Monty, had been lowered overboard in his narrow basket with weights on his feet. The huge, indifferent, loutish sea . . . what was there to rhapsodize about? A killer sea. A suffocating, strangling sea, masquerading at its best as a summer dream of little white boats dancing in the sun, of boys' voices, and schools of shining smelt.

Father O'Hara glanced at her as they walked. "Mary Manchester was telling me you are an author, Mrs. Bannister."

"How did she know?"

"Your hubby told her. I've been racking my memory for something of yours I may have read."

The conversational turn made Patrice uncomfortable. Anonymity was a blessed shield and she and Adam had a pact to maintain it.

"Patrice Verrier," Father O'Hara murmured. "No, I must be honest, I haven't read anything by that name. But Mary Manchester said she had. She was most pleased and surprised to be told who you are."

Patrice frowned. She foresaw literary tête-à-têtes and the embarrassment of trying to dodge them. Mary Manchester would be neither as shrewd nor as tactful as little Mrs. Lambston. Patrice loathed talking about her work. Why in the world had Adam mentioned her writing to Mary Manchester, and why had he not told her—Patrice —that he had done so?

"They must have been hard up for conversation," she said dryly, and Father O'Hara nodded. He said: "It's sometimes difficult for strangers to find a subject for conversation, and your hubby had one all ready-made."

After a moment he added abruptly: "I have a feeling—strange as it may seem considering our short acquaintance—that your hubby has no very kindly sentiments toward me." He went on: "It sets one back, a bit. When I first saw the pair of you leaning on the rail back there in Astoria I said to myself: A nice-looking couple. Civilized. Friendly."

"Well?" Patrice challenged him. He walked for a moment, frown-

438

ing, then he said: "I take life seriously, Mrs. Bannister. I take people seriously. Even when they do not happen to be of my own faith. We are all God's craytures." He hesitated. "I set out liking your hubby. He has a kind quality one doesn't often meet . . . at least not in Americans, if you will pardon my saying so. I haven't got it myself. I was born in a one-room cottage in Kerry and I grew up without shoes." She felt that he was picking his words with care. "Elegance, I told myself, is what Adam Bannister has, and him being American, it would be different from the English brand, which is often no more than snobbery plain for the eye to see, if you get what I'm trying to say." He puffed on his cigarette. "Now I'm beginning to wonder. Little things. Little looks. Little silences. Little smiles. And little cracks at the Irish. At the faith, even." His voice hardened. "I have a hot temper, Mrs. Bannister. An Irish temper if you like, though I know that all temper is sinful. I try to control it. And I could overlook the little things, but there is something else. Perhaps I should not be mentioning it, but I feel it is me duty to do so. I cannot turn me back on danger . . . on any danger, but on spiritual danger in particular, especially when it threatens the innocent."

Patrice watched a gigantic swell roll past and fall in a vast serpentine coil astern the ship. She and Father O'Hara paused at the stern rail and stared into the flying murk.

"Mary Manchester," Father O'Hara said at last, "for all she'd like to appear the contrary—Mary Manchester is innocent at heart. Foolish, yes. Spoiled like too many of her class. But she is of the faith, and that I cannot ignore. It would be a serious matter if she—if your husband—if the two of them . . ." He finished in a rush: "And I like you, Mrs. Bannister. It would pain me to see you made unhappy."

Patrice turned to study his flushed, youthful face. His priestly role struck her suddenly as pathetic. She said gently: "Aren't you perhaps making a mountain out of a molehill?"

"I am not one to do that, Mrs. Bannister."

"Then let's put it this way: aren't you forgetting something, someone else in this situation, if it is a situation?"

"You mean Nigel? No, I'm not forgetting Nigel. And I wouldn't want Mary to be forgetting him, either."

"Even though he is not, apparently, one of the faith?"

"That he is not of the faith is of no account. He is unattached, free

439

to marry Mary Manchester. There is no sin in being a Protestant."

"Then what's worrying you?"

"Argh! You're a writer of books. It's part of your business to understand people—certainly to understand your own husband!" He laid
his hand on her arm. "Forgive me. You must think me presumptuous.
I don't intend to be, but I cannot ignore my duty, Mrs. Bannister.
That's a high-strung, emotional girl, and your husband, if I do say so
that doesn't like him any more than he likes me—your husband is still
a very attractive man."

Patrice said slowly: "You know, I'm just a bit confused as to which
one of them you are so bent on saving—Mary Manchester or my
husband."

Father O'Hara made an angry gesture. "Have ye no gravity at all,
then?"

Patrice shrugged. "It seems to me that you are interested only in
enlisting my help in saving Mary Manchester's immortal soul. Do you
call that cricket, Father O'Hara?"

He gave her a frustrated glare, then laughed. "Argh, I meant no
harm, Mrs. Bannister. You are not angry with me?"

She was not angry, and levity had always been one of her many
masks, though of course he could not have been expected to know
it. For a moment he gazed at her with eyes gone suddenly shy, then
he mumbled something about his prayers and left her, his head bent
into the wind. Beyond his retreating figure Patrice had a glimpse of
Mary Manchester and Adam strolling along the deck toward her,
then as if by unspoken consent they turned and walked in the opposite direction. A moment of vindictiveness, an impulse to disrupt, to
destroy whatever might be in the making between them passed as
swiftly as it came. You don't love him, she reminded herself. You
haven't loved him for a long time, so how dare you resent what after
all is no more than a reflection of your own experimentations in the
past?

Well, logic is one thing, emotion another. The sight of Adam leaning solicitously toward another woman brought her own loverless
state home to Patrice. It brought home, with a poignance she thought
she had long since outgrown, memories of her early struggles with
her work, her secret despairs, the recognition of her changed rela-

tions with Alice, with Adam himself. It brought home memories of Damon.

The war in the Pacific was a year old and one Thanksgiving Patrice and Adam were in Cambridge with his parents and an early snow was beginning to fall in the street. It had been a warm, sunny autumn and the lawns were still green. Snow built meringuelike blossoms among the last of autumn's scarlet leaves. Where the snow melted it left the grass a vivid green, and Patrice had been at a loss to account for a sudden, stupefying depression. It hit her like a sickness and she felt herself on the verge of tears. At that moment the telephone rang and Mrs. Bannister went into the next room to answer it. She was not gone long and when she returned to the parlor where Patrice was sitting with Wilbur Bannister and Adam they saw at once that something had happened. Her kindly, aging features looked as though they had been set in a stroke.

"That was Edith Edwards," she told them in a controlled voice. "They have just had a message. Damon has been killed."

In the silence which followed Patrice felt neither shock nor grief. The strange depression of a moment ago had left her. She felt nothing.

Mr. Bannister spoke slowly, with an intensity not usual to him: *"Damnation."*

Adam walked to the window, beyond which snow was still falling on the darkening grass. It was late afternoon and lights already shone cheerfully through the gloom, making a Christmas-card scene.

Mrs. Bannister said in the same controlled voice: "I'm going to get the car and drive over to Tom and Edith's. I feel I should. I won't stay long."

"Yes, do go, dear," Mr. Bannister urged, with unusual gentleness. "I couldn't face it."

"Nor could I," Adam said without turning round. "Later, perhaps."

Mrs. Bannister looked at Patrice. "Will you come with me, dear? Damon was so fond of you. I know his parents would love to see you."

They had been calm, those two people who had not expected nor wanted to outlive their son. They shook hands gently with Patrice and kissed Mrs. Bannister, and it was only by a slight waywardness in their voices that one could guess their world had fallen in, crushing them. As they sat side by side on a little velvet-covered sofa, holding each other's hand, Patrice remembered that room on Lexington Avenue, with a white flower in the window and a photograph in a silver frame of these two, somewhat younger then, but with the same vaguely homesick air they had now.

Patrice thought: If I had been his wife or his recognized and accepted girl I would be expected to weep or to be brave; I would have been entitled to my share of pitying love. As it is I was no more than a friend, older than he, married to another man, a woman for whom he'd had a boy's affection and admiration—no more.

She had not, thereafter, loved the men she slept with, but she had liked them, and she enjoyed the warmth, the gaiety, the charm of stolen fruit with its tinge of risk. The drinking was another matter. She had gone in for it deliberately, trying to knock herself out, never entirely succeeding. Alcohol inflamed her imagination to fever heat and achieved no more than a rousing of the sleeping mongrels of frustration and doubt. She could not honestly lay it to a continuing grief for Damon; she was too much of a realist for that. Nor, she felt sure, was it due to a subconscious discontent with her childless condition, nor to the emotional stalemate with her life in general. There was in her a core of vitality which denied morbid interpretations, yet she went on drinking, hating it, hating herself.

At last she decided that she must be suffering what, for want of a better diagnosis, could be called a nervous breakdown. It began with peculiar manifestations, when, without warning and while she seemed apparently in perfect health, she would suddenly find her vision darkening, a sense of something mysterious actually growing in her brain. When this passed, as it usually did after the first few moments of terror, she would be overcome by the blackest kind of despair, convinced that her friends despised and derided her behind her back, that Adam did likewise, and that people were spying on her.

She decided that her work was puerile and worthless and the individuals who assured her to the contrary hypocrites or fools. She and Clem no longer corresponded and no one had the least idea where he was. So he too had deserted her. It took every ounce of self-control to keep her temper with Alice, who, for the first time since Doey's death and thanks entirely to Patrice, now enjoyed a true measure of comfort and security, but whose perceptive gaze missed nothing of Patrice's deep malaise.

Outwardly Patrice was sure she gave no sign—or very little—of this malaise, but the solitude she had always loved had become unendurable, and society a jungle infested with prowling beasts. She could concentrate on nothing; reading no longer absorbed her, writing became an ordeal. Her mind crawled with fantasies. Out of the blue she created infamies directed against her by Adam and his family, by her own friends. She invented entire conversations, constructed entire tableaux whose sole purpose was somehow to destroy her. Then she proceeded to act them out, with Adam for audience and victim. There were frightful scenes, which she was careful to stage only when they were alone.

Could it be menopause? Hardly. Physically she had never felt fitter except for those terrible moments when she felt the Thing growing darkly in her brain. She was afraid to go to a doctor and ashamed to consult a psychiatrist. Yet during that entire period, which lasted a year, some part of herself seemed always to be standing aside and watching the strange ballet.

It left Adam confused, bitter, helpless. Naturally reticent, he shrank from seeking advice from his few intimate friends. Alice watched the bizarre farce in an agony of bewilderment and made one or two timid attempts to reason with Patrice, only to be met with such a freezing rebuff that she gave up.

One evening, after consuming almost half a bottle of Scotch, Patrice left the house and, backing out of the garage, narrowly missed running over one of the dogs. Adam, standing grim-faced on the porch, shouted in fury: "Kill yourself if you want, but watch out for my dog!"

Bringing the car to a shrieking halt, Patrice leaned out the window and replied in a taut, brittle voice: "It's always the dogs, isn't it? Or stuffed birds and dead things. You wouldn't know what to do with a live woman, would you? Unless she ran on all fours and slobbered over your boots."

She was shaking, hoarse, blind with rage. Then she stepped on the gas and the car shot down the driveway, across the road, and into an open field, where it lurched on its side, flinging her into the weeds. In their house down the road Rosanna and Ralph Burden heard the crash and came running. Rosanna dropped on her knees beside Patrice and cradled her head as she had done once a long time ago when Patrice was having a miscarriage. "Honey," Rosanna crooned. "Honey, honey."

Ralph walked up the driveway and met Adam. He put his arm round Adam's shoulders and said gently: "She's all right." Then he ran on into the house and telephoned a doctor, and the three of them waited in the darkening field with Patrice lying wide-eyed and silent in Rosanna's arms. She felt light, clean, clear, with a soft warm pain from her broken collarbone. Adam crouched beside her, holding her hand, tears slipping down his cheeks.

For months after that they were very close. Patrice gave up the bottle, and a fresh high dawn stood above them, softening them, illumining them. Patrice told herself that this, after all, was how it should be. Simple, like this. Forgiving, loving. How come it had passed them by until now? She brooded over Adam with a deep, passionless devotion. He was her child, her little one, her all.

And Adam, reassured, chose that interlude in which to go down to Northeast Harbor and spend a weekend alone with Daisy Pitman in her house. An anonymous letter apprised Patrice of this event, and she had a day or two to ponder it. Was he trying to prove something to himself after the taunt she had flung at him on the night of the accident? And Daisy was always in the offing, seldom farther than a day's drive away. Lately Adam had seemed to have gotten over his early aversion toward her. They had taken to exchanging notes on bird life, and they shared an obsession with dogs. Patrice had no reason to doubt the facts as they were detailed to her in the anonymous letter.

I ought to be angry, she told herself. I ought to be jealous, bitter, hurt. Yet she could muster up none of these reactions. She was not even curious as to the identity of the writer. A dirty commonplace trick perpetrated by some local yokel who had it in for Daisy, perhaps. It was easy enough to imagine Daisy stepping haughtily on touchy native toes.

Patrice burned the letter and said nothing about it to anyone. But the cure initiated by her accident seemed to have taken hold. She never again drank to excess, and a sort of calm descended on her life. The newly revived tenderness for Adam had run its brief course, but if he sensed this he gave no sign. He had the air now of a satisfied

444

man, happy with his wife, his house, his guns, and his dogs. He even put on a little weight, which, considering his height, became him.

It was at this juncture of their affairs that Barto Williams suddenly appeared at their door one spring afternoon and, sitting beside the fire, his crutches at his side, besought Patrice to go back to the beginning. "Not with the thought of repeating what has already happened. Not to wallow in the past. But to start afresh. Afresh!"

Father O'Hara had reappeared on deck. He had changed into his clerical collar with the dark vest and neat dark suit. He came and stood beside Patrice at the stern rail, where, earlier, he had left her; he smelled of toothpaste and carbolic soap, and Patrice wondered what he would have said if she had turned to him then: "Father, I am not a Catholic, but I would like to confess my sins and ask your blessing before I step into the unknown to make a fresh start."

Father O'Hara peered at her through the gloom. "You're smilin'. Could I be sharing in the joke?"

"It's not exactly a joke, Father, and it's too long a story before dinner."

He leaned on his elbows beside her and they faced the dark, receding sea.

"I've just had a word with Mrs. Lambston. She's received a radio message from her husband to say he would be meeting the boat at Tanjom Priok, and it's in the seventh heaven she is, the poor girl!"

29

Now, as many sperm whales had been captured off the western coast of Java, in the near vicinity of the Straits of Sunda; indeed, as most of the ground, round about, was generally recognized by the fishermen as an excellent spot for cruising; therefore, as the *Pequod* gained more and more upon Java Head, the lookouts were repeatedly hailed, and admonished to keep wide awake. But though the green palmy cliffs of the land soon loomed on the starboard bow, and with delighted nostrils the fresh cinnamon was snuffed in the air, yet not a single jet was descried ... when the customary cheering cry was heard from aloft, and ere long a spectacle of singular magnificence saluted us. . . .

Broad on both bows, at the distance of some two or three miles, and forming a great semicircle, embracing one-half of the level horizon, a continuous chain of whale jets were up-playing and sparkling in the noonday air. . . .

Patrice put down *Moby Dick* and gazed out to sea, where three whale jets were up-playing and sparkling in the noonday air. These descendants of the creatures Melville had seen a hundred or so years before lolloped against the same level horizon, and she fancied that her delighted nostrils snuffed the fragrance of fresh cinnamon in the air.

A vast humid light lay on the sea and bathed the deck where she

446

sat reading. She could barely feel the tremor of the ship's engines as it moved through the silky water, and she more than half expected to see Queequeg walking down the deck toward her.

Instead she saw the first officer, Mr. de Koon, and she had a moment to marvel at the wonders wrought by a snappy white uniform on an otherwise prosaic form. He spied her and came to a halt beside her deck chair. "All alone, Mrs. Bannister?" He gazed down at her with compassionate eyes. "Reading, reading, always reading. Vot is the book? *Mobby Dick.* I have not read it."

She was alone and lonely, his eyes seemed trying to tell her, but she deliberately misread them and informed him brightly that she had just seen whales in the offing. He nodded indifferently. "Yes. In Java waters lots of wells. You like wells?"

Patrice said she did indeed like whales. There was a pause and she wished he would go about his business. She suspected that he felt sorry for her because of Adam's open preference for other company, and that he would have been happy to console her. But she found him a bore, and not less so because she shrank from hurting his feelings.

"Tomorrow afternoon, I think, we dock at Tanjom Priok." He sighed. "Then our troubles begin. We have much cargo, but there is much dislocation because of the war. The Japanese left a mess. Equipment smashed or stolen. No transportation. And those bloody lazy coolies. God knows how long we shall be hung up at Tanjom. And the natives still fighting us in the back country. This cargo is for our soldiers. And that is another reason why the coolies will take their time unloading, the dirty ungrateful swine."

Patrice was by now familiar with the near hysteria of frustration among the Dutchmen on the ship. Mediocrities who all their lives had enjoyed extraordinary privilege now found their world gone or going, and the loss hard to take. "Whose bloody country is it?" Doey had demanded years ago. Well, whose bloody country was it? She stared at the whale jets in the distance, and Mr. de Koon stared at her.

"There will be much confusion," he said broodingly. "And I'm afraid it will be dull for the passengers. All day long the cranes and winches, and the coolies' voices: *'Ariya! Ariya!'* Nothing to do in Tanjom. A dirty little village. Ah, Gott."

"Couldn't you work the unloading by night as well as by day and get it over sooner?" Patrice asked him, for something to say. He shook his head lugubriously. "No. The bastards won't work properly even during the day. And at night there would be no peace for us. Too much s'outing and schwearing and hiding and schleeping."

Patrice murmured something commiserating and his gaze became ardent. "Can I help you, Mrs. Bannister? Is there anything I can do for you?"

"Thank you," she said. "You are very kind. No, there is nothing."

"I would much like to be kinder," he muttered. His big red hands clenched nervously at his sides. "I would much like."

Patrice repeated: "Thank you. There is nothing."

"A ship is a lonely place," de Koon said in a heavy voice. "A ship is the loneliest place in the world."

He went his way and Patrice returned to her contemplation of the whales. She had an impulse to go in search of Adam and tell him to bring his binoculars, but abandoned the idea at once. He would be with Mary Manchester, reading in the lounge, or in some nook on deck, sharing the binoculars with her, teaching her to recognize the dim outlines of the islands they were leaving astern, and the names of the few birds which strayed into view and vanished again in the still, warm air.

All through these long, uneventful days as the ship cruised through water smooth and glistening as silk, Adam remained close to Mary Manchester's side. They sat together in the lounge, sharing an electric fan, conversing in low voices. They strolled the decks or spent hours in their deck chairs side by side, apart from the other passengers. When the tennis court was set up on the forward hatch Adam invariably paired with Mary against Father O'Hara and Patrice or Mrs. Lambston—the latter fully restored to health and vigor with the coming of fair weather and quiet seas. The first officer and the purser occasionally joined in the game for doubles, but Adam made no pretense about his preference for Mary Manchester as partner.

He made no pretense about anything. To find oneself in love, observed Stendhal, is like having a tile drop on one's head. Was Adam in love with Mary Manchester? The spectacle of them constantly together had a peculiar fascination for Patrice. She felt that she was seeing him for the first time in their twenty-odd years of life together, seeing him as a man and a lover, seeing him as we see someone who has died and to whom we are no longer bound by the conventions of practice and habit. "Go back to the beginning," Barto had exhorted her. But wasn't that exactly what Adam was trying to do—go back to the beginning to find new freshness, new hope in an eternally recurring relationship?

Alone with her he was gentle, even diffident, but he made no move to discuss or even to hint at a situation which he must have known was as much on her mind as on his, and if once in a while he appeared to be on the brink of some confession or declaration, Patrice gave him no encouragement, for better than most people she appreciated the treachery of words, and her own faculty for equivocation when dealing with them. *Talking things over with Adam* would prove nothing.

Even in the early days of his love he had never paid court to her as he did at this late stage to this younger woman, and Patrice reflected that there must be some kind of snobbery in love, since we give so freely and grandly to those who neither need it nor want it. No neophyte, she found herself struggling with emotions saved from the banal only by her sense of comedy and the incorrigible curiosity of her trade.

Mrs. Lambston, who, ever since their conversation early in the voyage, had taken a liking to Patrice, sometimes gazed at her with troubled, questioning eyes, no doubt wondering why one astute enough to write about similar problems appeared to have so little command over her own. The missionaries from Kansas, Mr. and Mrs. Raudle, who from the start had kept themselves rigorously to themselves, observed the drama with distant disdain. Father O'Hara did not again venture an opinion in Patrice's hearing, though his attitude toward Adam hardened into open hostility.

People tried with varying degrees of clumsy goodwill to show sympathy to Patrice, who would rather have done without it. Captain Buberman made it a point gallantly to stroke her leg whenever opportunity offered; the first officer was unashamedly attentive and confided to her that she reminded him of his second "vife." "You haf her figure," he elucidated with nostalgia. "Up *here.*"

Mary Manchester, meeting Patrice in the lounge, spoke with an air of constraint and embarrassment: "I was so pleased . . . surprised . . . I know your writing quite well and I have always admired it. I never dreamed that I would have the pleasure . . ." Meeting

449

Patrice's blank stare she broke off, flushing. "Your husband has told me so much about you. He is very proud of you, as of course you must know."

Patrice had a macabre vision of the two of them discussing her "work" with the studied detachment of seasoned critics, while both secretly wondered how the hell they might manage to get into bed together. One of the many facets of the situation was the low comedy of her own role, hardly one she would have chosen. Then, as she suddenly met Mary Manchester's rather frightened gaze, the odd notion occurred to her that Mary was trying to tell her something.

They stood awkwardly in the middle of the room with its garish mirrors, banal furnishings, its smell of brass polish, but before Mary could find words for whatever was on her mind they were interrupted by the appearance of the missionary couple from Kansas, and thereafter both were careful to avoid anything approaching a tête-à-tête.

The whales had disappeared, but the scent of cinnamon lingered, and Patrice looked up to find Mrs. Lambston and her little girl standing beside her, the child munching a piece of toast. "Cinnamon toast," she said, and held it out to Patrice. "Would you like some?"

Patrice thanked her and declined. She added conversationally: "Did you know that cinnamon is the bark of a tree which grows in the country where we are going?"

The child looked at her impassively. "No it doesn't," she said. "It comes out of a little can with holes at the top."

Mrs. Lambston laughed. "That's what I used to get when I taught school," she said. "'It comes out of a wax wrapper marked Chiclet or out of a tin can, or out of a paper bag.'"

The little girl finished her toast and addressed herself with mild interest to Patrice. "Why," she inquired, "is your daddy always with that other lady?"

Mrs. Lambston turned to her. "Ellie, will you run down to our stateroom and find my pink scarf?"

When Ellie had gone Patrice shifted her legs on the wooden extension of the chair and said: "Won't you sit down a minute?"

Mrs. Lambston sat down. She turned a flushed face to Patrice. "I'm sorry. Kids seem to miss nothing these days, do they?"

450

"Did you?" Patrice asked lightly. "Did I? Don't let it get you down."

Mrs. Lambston was silent a moment, then she said explosively: "I don't see how you stand it!"

Patrice placed a marker between the pages of *Moby Dick* and closed the book. She said musingly: "There is something about life on an ocean liner—"

Mrs. Lambston interrupted in a trembling voice: "I know it's none of my business, but if it were my husband I'd tear her eyes out or push her overboard." She added violently: "Or jump overboard myself. I don't see how you . . . I mean . . ."

When Patrice remained silent she went on: "You know the type she is. I told you all about that business in the hotel in Portland. She's out to get a man—any man."

"And you think that my husband would do as well as any?"

Mrs. Lambston stared at her helplessly. "I've seen her kind before —you must have, too. An operator. With them love just doesn't come into the picture unless it's love of money."

"I wonder," murmured Patrice. She was thinking of that brief encounter with Mary Manchester in the lounge a few days before. Since then, whenever they met, it seemed to her that Mary was still trying to communicate with her in a confused and inarticulate fashion, through an insistent gaze, a timid, delaying gesture when they found themselves momentarily alone on a stairway or in a corridor, with the beginnings of sentences which were never completed. Patrice had an eye and an ear for such nuances, but she was determined not to follow them up.

"I wonder," she repeated, more to herself than to Mrs. Lambston, whose blue, innocent gaze seemed to match, for a moment, the shimmering sea behind her.

"You wonder? Well, if by that you mean to say she may have fallen in love with your husband, it only makes things worse, doesn't it?"

"It would certainly add to the complication," Patrice agreed absently. She was thinking: The cruelty of it, the irony! That Adam should possibly have achieved this psychological release and be bound still by the mundane. Without a cent of his own, since what they now had she had earned herself. He could offer Mary Manchester nothing and Mary was not one to settle for that. On the other

451

hand, if she were really in love with him, as he gave every indication of being in love with her . . .

Mrs. Lambston said abruptly: "Father O'Hara has given her up as a bad job. You know what? I think he hates her. I really believe he does."

"I have a feeling he hates my husband, too," Patrice said with a sigh. "That's an awful lot of emotion to be on the loose in such a short time and in such close quarters, isn't it?"

Both were silent, and Patrice reflected on the inanity of the past three weeks. The evening gatherings at the bar had been abandoned. Father O'Hara drank his glass of beer alone in a corner, or occasionally in company with Mrs. Lambston or Mr. de Koon. This left Patrice to sip her nightly gin fizz *à trois* with Mary Manchester and Adam. They managed nicely enough, with Adam as usual signing the chits, and Mary no longer quibbled about her end of it. Meals were a strain, Adam eating in stony silence, and Father O'Hara in ostentatiously Irish fettle. The first officer, baffled by the atmosphere, usually finished in a hurry and excused himself on some pretext of duty aloft.

Ellie Lambston returned, accompanied by Father O'Hara, more unpriestlike than ever in khaki shorts and a shirt open at the neck. Dressed thus he had a kind of rustic good looks accentuated by a tan acquired during the past week of sunshine.

Standing beside Mrs. Lambston, he returned Patrice's gaze with a tinge of suspicion in his own. "And what's the joke, if I might be asking?"

"I was thinking what a broth of a boy you look, Father."

"Get along with you!" He turned to Mrs. Lambston. "Tennis this afternoon? You and I taking on Mrs. Bannister and de Koon?"

Mrs. Lambston hesitated. "I don't know."

He said sharply: "There is no reason why others shouldn't be given first chance at the court once in a while. Whenever I feel like playing singles with de Koon or the purser, or with one of you ladies, there *they* are, hogging it." He reddened. "Well, this afternoon they can have the court when we have finished our game. Will that suit you, Mrs. Bannister?"

"I must ask to be excused," said Patrice. "Perhaps the purser would make up a fourth."

He gave her an angry glance, then shrugged. "I'll try and get him.

452

Four o'clock sharp, then, Mrs. Lambston. That'll give us an hour to play, and *they* can have the court for the rest of the evening as far as I am concerned."

He left, trailed by little Ellie, and Mrs. Lambston murmured: "I'll be glad when we get into port."

"Yes," said Patrice. "Your husband will be meeting you. I wonder whether Nigel will show up."

Mrs. Lambston said in a stifled voice: "I should be charitable, but women like that scare me. They are the natural enemy of other women." She added distractedly: "I had so looked forward to this trip. I've never been on a ship before. I've never been so far away from home. I was crazy at the thought of being at sea with Ellie, meeting new people, and then the tropics and everything, and at the end of it to find Johnny waiting for me."

"Well, you can still count on that last bit," Patrice told her gaily. She rose, tucking *Moby Dick* under her arm, and they stood for a moment gazing at the sea—sunlit, peaceable, everything the books had to say about it. Under that silken coverlet the great whales sported and made love; in the tranquil sky a single bird appeared, an eyelash in the immensity, then vanished. Patrice felt a tightening at her heart. To have someone waiting for you, or to be waiting for someone . . . a light in a darkened room, a step at the door, a dog raising its head in recognition. These are the clichés of love, the essential simplicities which poor Barto had hoped she and Adam might recapture on this voyage.

Tennis was in progress when she appeared on deck later that afternoon, but Father O'Hara and his friends were not the players. Before she arrived at the forward hatch Patrice heard Adam's voice calling the score, and Mary Manchester's clear laughter: "Oh, sorry!" Then Adam, jocular, reproving: "Butterfingers!"

Father O'Hara and Mrs. Lambston were standing together at the rail, watching the game. Father O'Hara wore a lowering expression, and Mrs. Lambston appeared distinctly nervous. She greeted Patrice with relief, while Father O'Hara nodded curtly.

"Mr. de Koon is too busy to play this afternoon," Mrs. Lambston explained. "And we can't find the purser."

Adam, changing from one side of the court to the other, waved at Patrice. "One game more and we'll have doubles," he said, addressing them impartially. Patrice, who had taken the precaution of arming herself with a sheaf of manuscript as an excuse for not playing, turned to Mrs. Lambston. "It looks like you and Father O'Hara against them," she said genially. "Meantime I'll get on with Chapter Twenty-one."

Father O'Hara gave her a sour glance, and Mrs. Lambston murmured: "We got here early, but they beat us to it."

Patrice wanted to laugh. "Do you realize," she said, "that if we were to tot up the ages of all four principals in this group the sum would amount to roughly one hundred and fifty-odd years?"

Mrs. Lambston dimpled. "I'd say," she murmured, "that you were off by a hundred!

The quoits were made of straw rope, clumsy and hard on the hands, and although Mary Manchester was agile enough—she must, Patrice thought, be good on a normal tennis court—she appeared clumsy with this makeshift equipment, and Adam beat her handily. "Forty love," he called, and mopped his face on his handkerchief.

"Love it is," Father O'Hara remarked in a loud voice as both players strolled across the hatch toward their audience. Adam jumped the two feet or so to the deck and turned as if to give his hand to Mary. Instead, he clasped her by the elbows and lifted her lightly down to the deck, holding her for a second before he let her go.

"Well, now," said Father O'Hara boisterously, "what are we going to do about doubles with just the three of us? Shall we make it singles, Mrs. Lambston, or will I be the ambitious one and take on you and Mrs. Bannister?"

Adam said calmly: "Mary's game for another round, aren't you, Mary? What do you say you and I take on Patrice and Mrs. Lambston?"

"No you don't!" declared Father O'Hara, dropping his false gaiety. "You've hogged the court every afternoon since it was set up. It's our turn now."

There was an instant's silence, then Adam suggested equably: "Let's toss for it."

He produced a coin from his pocket, flicked it in the air, caught it, and covered it with his free hand. Then he looked at Father O'Hara. "Heads or tails?"

"Heads," Father O'Hara replied, and his smile was nasty. Patrice

454

watched the color rise in Adam's face. He bared the coin on his palm.

"Tails it is," pronounced Father O'Hara with a laugh. "And not surprising, considering."

Adam turned wholly toward him. "Considering what?"

Patrice intervened. "It'll be dark before we know it," she warned. "Go ahead and play, Father O'Hara, and you, Mrs. Lambston. I just don't feel like it."

Mrs. Lambston took Father O'Hara by the arm. "Come on," she urged him in her practical, schoolgirl voice. "Let's beat the tar out of them."

He allowed himself to be persuaded, and all four climbed back on the hatch and took up their positions on the little court. Mrs. Lambston was first to serve and she sent the heavy quoit sailing neatly over the deck and into the sea. Everyone laughed and it eased the tension somewhat. She served again, and the second quoit followed the first. Father O'Hara patted her forgivingly on the back. "Now then, partner! Pull yourself together."

When it came Mary Manchester's turn to serve Father O'Hara caught the quoit nimbly in his left and and flung it back over the net in a powerful throw which caught Adam full in the chest. "Sorry!" said Father O'Hara, and turned smiling back to his corner of the court. His own service was fast and hard and this time the quoit struck Mary Manchester on her forehead, leaving a weal. She took it gamely, shaking her head at Adam, who looked ready for a fight.

Mrs. Lambston's next serve carried the quoit feebly over the net, but Adam caught it and tossed it in an upward stroke, forcing Father O'Hara to sprint across the court to field it. Mrs. Lambston gave him a seraphic smile. "Good work, partner." His answering smile was anything but seraphic. When next Adam served he launched the quoit with a vicious swipe from which Father O'Hara saved himself only by a lightning duck to one side. The quoit hit the deck and rolled to Patrice's feet. She picked it up and handed it back to Adam, who avoided her warning glance. Tense, furious, silent, he served again and Father O'Hara darted ahead of Mrs. Lambston, caught the quoit at the net and flung it into Mary Manchester's face. She put her hands to her cheeks, and Father O'Hara shouted a cheery "So sorry!" as he turned again, smiling, to his place.

Adam walked up to the net and said in a cold voice: "Is that how they play in Ireland, Father O'Hara?"

Father O'Hara grinned at him. "I said I was sorry."

"You goddam little mick," said Adam.

It was Mary Manchester who saved what was left of the situation. Gazing ruefully at her hands she said: "I don't think I can play any more. Those quoits are ruining my hands. You wouldn't take my place, would you, Patrice?"

Before Patrice could reply Mrs. Lambston said hurriedly: "I don't think I want to play any more either. I've never played deck tennis and those quoits are awful."

Patrice had observed Father O'Hara's fists clenching, and now she stepped between them, facing Adam. "Grow up," she said dispassionately. "Grow up, will you?"

An electric moment passed, then Father O'Hara turned and without a word jumped from the hatch and walked away from the deck, followed a little distance after by Mrs. Lambston. Adam turned anxiously to Mary Manchester. "Are you all right?"

"Perfectly, thank you. It's just these silly hands." She gave him a hesitant smile and walked away, and Adam and Patrice made their way silently down to their stateroom. Patrice closed the door and said: "I know he asked for it, but you didn't have to call him names."

Adam sat down heavily on the edge of his bed. "He was out for mischief from the start."

"And weren't you?"

He stared at the porthole, where the sunset glowed like a rose, Patrice sat down beside him and put an arm round his shoulder. "Adam," she said. "Adam."

He shook his head. "I'm interfering with your work and living off your dough. I'm no good to you or to anyone else."

She said: "I know it sounds stagy—literary—but I might as well say it: If you should want to try being good to someone else, I wouldn't try to stop you."

He gave her a strange look. "No," he said slowly, "no, you wouldn't, would you?"

"Well, what the hell would be the use?"

She started to get up but he suddenly held her still beside him.

"You've got to understand," he said hoarsely. "You've simply got to understand."

456

"Perhaps I do."

Perhaps she did, all too well.

Next day when she went on deck Patrice could smell the land. The breeze carried gusts of perfume which stirred a deep nostalgia for what she could not have named, as it had stirred Melville, as it had stirred Conrad, and thousands who smelled it for the first time. The breath of something eternally longed for become suddenly imminent, the foreknowledge of something forever lost.

The air was translucent after a fine rain and there was a great stir and bustle on the lower deck as the crew prepared for arrival at Tanjom Priok next afternoon. The ship had been delayed almost twenty-four hours due to some complication in the engine room and all night they had seemed scarcely to move. The unexpected delay induced impatience and tension among some of the passengers. Mary Manchester and Father O'Hara scarcely appeared and did not show up even for meals. The missionaries from Kansas were serenely indifferent. Experienced exiles as they were, with the comfortable assurance of a Big Rock Candy Mountain at home, they could not have cared less when they arrived at their destination. They ate regularly and with appetite, took their little constitutionals around the deck, and retired early to their stateroom; they slept soundly, and no doubt congratulated themselves on not being what others so patently and deplorably were.

Patrice and Adam had no further conversation after those few minutes together following the disastrous game of deck tennis. Oddly enough, he and Mary Manchester appeared to be intent on avoiding each other. Patrice had a glimpse of one or the other alone, reading in a deck chair or standing solitary at the rail staring at the shadowy mass of land which grew steadily thicker on the starboard bow. Whales loomed once or twice out of the pale-gray water; flying fish flew like leaves and landed on the deck—fragile creatures with staring jewel eyes—and little Ellie Lambston crouched over them in absorbed curiosity as their luminous bodies faded in the airless heat.

Mrs. Lambston alone seemed to glow now with some inward radiance. She created a small stir wherever she went, as though these loveless, jaded beings hoped, for a moment, that her happiness might rub off on them. As Patrice passed the open door of her room the

457

young woman called to her: "Mrs. Bannister, do come in a moment and tell me what you think I ought to wear tomorrow."

An assortment of finery was spread over both beds—airy summer dresses, all evidently new, absurd straw hats, improbable footwear. Mrs. Lambston stood before the mirror on her bureau, modeling a cotton dress of pale apple green which brought out the shining quality of her hair and the young freshness of her skin. She was so obviously a woman in love that Patrice, coming suddenly on the vision, caught her breath. She exclaimed: "You look like a young pear tree in spring!"

"How nice! And it's Johnny's favorite color on me. I guess I'll wear it."

The child Ellie sat on a corner of one of the beds, swinging her bare legs. She said in an important voice: "In a minute I have to go and talk to Father O'Hara. He said for me to come to his stateroom and knock and we'll go on deck and he'll tell me a story."

Mrs. Lambston said absently: "Father O'Hara is going to miss you, Ellie, when we leave the ship tomorrow."

"Yes," the child agreed. "But then I'll have my own father, and that will be much better."

She ran out of the room and Mrs. Lambston sighed. "Johnny wrote me he'd be bringing an amah—a native nurse—to take care of Ellie so he and I can have more time together. We shall be a few weeks in Batavia, where Johnny has business, then I expect we'll take another ship to Singapore." She turned to Patrice. "I'm going to miss you."

They sat down facing each other on the twin beds and lighted cigarettes. Mrs. Lambston said: "I wonder what Mary will do if Nigel isn't at the dock to meet her tomorrow." She went on: "It's a funny thing. I've hated her guts ever since we got on the boat together. Even if I had not overheard all that stuff at the hotel before we left Portland, I'd have mistrusted her." She gazed thoughtfully at Patrice. "She's made me wonder a bit whether it can be all that fun to be an operator!" Mrs. Lambston laughed, blushing. "I know Johnny loves me. I know in my bones that he would never be—you know—unfaithful to me. Still, with a woman like that, pulling no punches, on the make with any man she thinks she can get, I've been kind of thankful Johnny wasn't on this trip with me."

458

She sobered. "What still gets me is what happened between her and Father O'Hara. I mean before that awful tennis game. Because I'd be willing to bet something has happened. He was so concerned about her, making much of her, teasing her a little, but being—you know—like a priest should be, kind and responsible. Now he acts like *he* hates her guts. That wasn't any accident when he hit her with the quoit!" She went on after a moment: "He's so gentle and good inside. And when he's feeling gay, not a bit like a priest. Honest, if I didn't *know* he was a priest you couldn't have made me believe it. And so good-looking." She broke off, dimpling. "To see those two handsome men battling each other over *her!*" Then, apologetically: "Well, it will all be over tomorrow afternoon, I expect."

Yes, thought Patrice, it will all be over tomorrow afternoon, or perhaps it will be still another beginning. For you and your Johnny, for Father O'Hara and God, for Adam and me, for Mary Manchester and . . . who?

This voyage was to have been a bridge on which she and Adam would meet again. It was to have been the beginning of a beginning, all trivialities put aside. So we live by symbols, she thought, and how silly!

She left Mrs. Lambston and went down to her stateroom to write letters before the ship docked. She fitted the key in the lock, but the door would not open and she realized that it must be bolted inside. "Adam!" she called, puzzled, because it was not his habit to be downstairs at this hour. There was no response, and as an unpleasant possibility occurred to her she turned away, flushing. At that moment the stateroom door opened a crack and a voice murmured: "Mrs. Bannister!"

Father O'Hara's abashed gaze encountered hers as he stood aside for her to enter. Then he quickly closed the door and bolted it. They faced each other and the silence lasted some time because Patrice was determined to make him speak first. After a moment or two he walked to one of the beds and sat down, a small prayer book falling open on his knees.

"It's all right," he said at last. "Your hubby gave me the key. He knows I'm here."

Patrice felt herself on the verge of hysterical laughter. She sat down on the bed facing Father O'Hara. "Ye can laugh all you want," he told her sullenly. "It's funny, all right, if you're in the mood to see the humor of it."

"If I'm entitled to anything at this point," Patrice said, "I think it is to something like an explanation."

He came to the point with a rush. "Your hubby has given Mary Manchester the gate. She's been after me ever since with her wapin' and wailin'. And worse than that, begor." His face turned a rich crimson. "And no confession about it, I'll have you know! Just that if she couldn't have the one she was bound and determined to have the other. There is no Nigel. She's known it for a long time. He married years ago and she's not set eyes on him since. She's been living around with that colonel chap in America, and he's given her the gate, too. She's no Lady Manchester. She's not even a Catholic."

Dismally he offered her a cigarette and lighted it for her, and one for himself. "I've been a damned fool, Mrs. Bannister, and I admit it. I have apologized to your hubby for what happened at that deck tennis game. Argh, the poor man! We shook hands, and let bygones be bygones, I said, and he just nodded, proud like."

Patrice waited a moment. "And you asked him whether you might take refuge in our stateroom, is that it?"

"If I was to have stayed in me own room she'd have been there banging on the door. She's done it too often already, and every time, to make it appear respectable, I've let her in for a minute or two, leaving the door open, me in me clericals, as if she were there on some matter of spiritual importance." He glared at Patrice. "Go on then, laugh! But I knew damned well she wouldn't try to hunt me down was I in here. She would have if I'd tried to hide with Mrs. Lambston, whom she despises, the poor dear little woman. I had Ellie helping me for a while, keeping her beside me when I went on deck for a breath of air, reading to her, telling her stories. I thought it'd take a pretty hardened type to misbehave in front of a little innocent child. But a while ago when Ellie didn't show up I got dispirited, and your room seemed me only hope."

"I wonder," Patrice murmured, "why she didn't fasten on the skipper, or on de Koon?"

"The dear Lard alone knows the answer to that question." Father O'Hara smoked furiously, staring down at his square white tennis shoes. "Why didn't she fasten on the bar steward? There's enough

460

men on this tub to take care of fifty Mary Manchesters. Why did she have to pick on your hubby, a married man, and, when he came to his senses, pick on me, a priest? And all that talk about Nigel, and being a Catholic and all! Stage stuff, a disguise. And there I was fretting about her soul. Praying for her, trying to save her from her worst instincts. Holy Mother of God! She made her confession, all right, last week. She loves *me!*"

He stared at Patrice in horror. "Me, a priest in the house of the Lord!"

"Like a tile falling on one's head," Patrice murmured.

" 'You're crazy, Mary Manchester,' I tells her. 'You are clean out of your head. Don't you understand that it's a mortal sin even to think of such dirty matters? And furthermore, Mary Manchester,' I says to her, 'I don't give a good God damn for you, not one good God damn, and you can stuff that in your head or wherever else you think it might help.' "

"Heavens," murmured Patrice.

"Heavens, nothing," Father O'Hara said bitterly. "Trailing me down the corridors, sending me little notes by the steward, that grinning bastard, and even by that little innocent child, Ellie Lambston. And at first pretending it was the troubled spirit in her seeking a priest's guidance. It must have been right after that tennis game that your hubby . . . well, I mean, when the poor man came to his senses. Because first thing I knew there she was at me stateroom door, which I opened thinking it was the steward come to clean me shoes, or de Koon for a chat—there she was and before I could say Jack Robinson she was in the room with me and the door shut and she points to her cheek and says to me—in tears she was—'Look what you've done to me, Father!' And I says: 'I'm sorry, Mary. It was an accident.' And then I said would she be so good as to get the hell out of my stateroom, and she begins to weep in earnest, and me sweating in embarrassment. She says: 'I've known a lot of men, and I've loved a few, and I'm not saying that I've always been a good and honorable woman, Father.' As if I needed to be told *that.* Argh . . . 'And I never dreamed that such a thing would happen to me, Father, to fall in love with a priest.' 'And what about falling in love with another woman's husband?' I asks her, bitter like. And she looked at me with those big sad eyes and said: 'He was lonely too, and chivalrous, and only meant to be kind.' 'Bah,' I said, only it wasn't bah. 'Get along with you now, pull yourself together, Mary Manchester, and get the hell out of my room.' " Father O'Hara drew a deep breath.

"I thought she'd never come to the end of it, sniveling and managing to look the perfect lady at the same time. Oh, she bared her soul to me, all right, and it was tremblin' I was for fear she wouldn't stop at that, and the steward or de Koon come marching in on us."

He stopped and stared at the door with terrified eyes. Both were silent, listening, then the footsteps passed on up the corridor. Father O'Hara rounded it out in a low voice: "Well, anyway, I made my peace with your hubby, and thank God for it. I explained to him that I had been under a strain, and we didn't discuss his involvement at all. I didn't tell him what I've just been telling you, either, but I think he got the picture, all right." Father O'Hara looked at her steadily. "He's a gentleman, your hubby. He asked no questions of me, and when I asked him would it be expecting too much of him to permit me to come down here to this stateroom to read my prayers in a little peace and quiet, he just looked past me, handed me his key, and that was that."

Patrice said after a moment: "I take it Mrs. Lambston is not in your confidence in this business?"

He shook his head violently. "The fewer people know about it the better, for all our sakes." He dropped his histrionic manner. "She gets off the ship when we dock tomorrow—Mary Manchester, I mean."

"Nigel or no Nigel?"

"Nigel or no Nigel. I told her if she didn't get off the ship I would. It was cruel I was, and I know it. But what else was there for me to do? She took it well enough, considering. Every inch the lady."

Next afternoon the *Cornelis* docked in the haze of a steamy sun through which the green land shoved like some slumberous beast. The air suddenly thickened with the smell of life—the mixed odors of spice, of tropical fruit, of heavy-petaled flowers, the subtle tincture of woodsmoke.

The dock was a sleazy concrete expanse with a few nondescript buildings still pockmarked by the machine-gun fire which had raged here during the Japanese occupation. Small clots of human beings clustered near the buildings, staring at the handsome ship as she warped alongside. There were Javanese coolies in dirty rags, the look

462

of hunger unmistakable in their gaunt faces and scrawny limbs; a scattering of minor officials in shirts and sarongs, with the rakish *sangkok* headgear, and a group of Dutchmen, obviously shipping officials, their ruddy blond appearance almost shocking by contrast with the ragtag and bobtail surrounding them.

The ship's ladder was lowered and the Dutchmen ran up on deck, clutching briefcases, and were escorted out of sight by the purser and de Koon.

Patrice, standing at the rail with Adam, saw a thin young man in khaki slacks and a tieless shirt come striding down the dock, his face upturned to the deck where she stood. The missionary couple was sauntering to and fro, but there was no sign of Father O'Hara or Mary Manchester or the Lambstons. They were, Patrice decided, in the lounge with the health and immigration authorities, and she returned to her contemplation of the dock. Beyond the shoddy buildings she had a glimpse of red-tiled roofs, the sheen of banana fronds, a glitter of light on the palm trees. Beyond these lay an area of rich green which had survived the years of shooting and massacre, and as a faint warm breeze carried the fragrance of land to her nostrils Patrice felt herself thrilling to it, not now with nostalgia for the unknown, but with positive feelings of anticipation, affection, hope. Life was hard to beat.

At that instant Mrs. Lambston appeared on deck wearing the green cotton dress, her fair hair flowing on her shoulders, Ellie clinging to her hand. The young man on the dock had reached the foot of the gangway when Mrs. Lambston saw him. For a second she seemed transfixed, then with a cry like some wild bird she pulled her hand free of the child's and rushed to the gangway. A little more than halfway down she let go her hold of the rail and sprang, an extraordinary figure, slight, winged in green, in total ecstatic abandon, straight into her husband's outstretched arms. He caught her, held her for a moment on his breast, then, encircling her with one arm, held the other out to his child as she clambered, weeping, down the steps after her mother.

Patrice felt a stab of sweetness and envy, and instinctively she reached out her hand for Adam, to find that he had moved away and was standing near the head of the gangway.

Mary Manchester, dressed in cool white cotton with a small straw hat and carrying a white handbag and a white silk sun umbrella, made her way quickly past him, down the gangway onto the dock. She was followed by one of the ship's stewards carrying two neat linen-covered suitcases and a hatbox. Mary Manchester did not look back, nor did she appear to notice the Lambstons, who stood aside to let her pass. Followed by the steward and the purser, her elegant figure vanished among the buildings at the farther end of the dock.

Only then did Adam move. Turning, he walked back to Patrice, took her arm, and said in a composed voice: "It's too damned hot on deck. I think I'll go below and read awhile."

30

On the Calcutta maidan, brown and parched in the early March heat, the marble viceroys bestrode their marble steeds. Crows perched on the regal heads, anointing them with offerings compounded of garbage and funeral pyres, and local patriots had contributed graffiti in four of the world's major languages—Hindi, Bengali, English, and Urdu. But the marble horses curvetted with style and their riders sat them with distinguished disdain, as if to say: "Try as you may, you cannot draw blood from a stone, you kuchnais!"

The air was listless and in the pale sky brown kites wheeled and squealed in monotonous cadence. Patrice strolled on the maidan and studied the marble viceroys. Lord Curzon appeared to her the noblest of all as, half turning in his enormous saddle, he frowned sternly down at her with his marble brows. She could hear the drone of the huge, hideous city: the clatter of trams, squeaks of ramshackle taxis' horns, shrilling of bicycle bells, all sounding like some monstrous musical instrument—the tanpura perhaps—in the background of its clotted, teeming life.

She had left Adam at the hotel, unpacking and oiling his guns, fearful lest the long voyage by sea should have hurt them. He had

465

been entirely matter-of-fact about this return to the city where he had worked more than twenty years ago. The special pang of rediscovery, to which Patrice was always subject, was not for him. He could see little change in the city's superficiality, beyond which he characteristically had no inclination to probe.

He had wanted to leave immediately for that mountain spot in the north where they had first met, but Patrice begged that they linger somewhere else for a little while until, as she rather shamefacedly explained, she got her conflicting emotions under control. Adam was puzzled, but he fell in with her mood. He had been tractable, even humble toward her, ever since the disappearance of Mary Manchester on that dismal dockside in Tanjom Priok. Mary's name had not been mentioned between them since—she might never have existed —but Adam's new diffidence troubled Patrice and she felt that they must get back to a normal footing before she subjected herself to further emotional crises.

A strange fear had been growing in her ever since they had left the *Cornelis*. The voyage had been a kind of marking time, indecisive and, in the end, unimportant. The figures which had seemed to dominate those interminable days at sea and when tied up to the dock now shrank into insignificance. Father O'Hara had taken himself off to Burma, the missionary couple from Kansas had vanished, the ship's officers had become, in retrospect, make-believe figures on a make-believe stage.

But once in the heart of this monstrous city Patrice felt herself beset by realities unknown to her. Sounds and odors long forgotten, old discarded timidities, yearnings, gratifications, and deprivations hung about her like threadbare ghosts. She had never lived in an Indian city, but echoes of other places where she had lived were all here. Calcutta closed upon her like a humid fist, squeezing out memory and illusion to make room . . . for what? She was not yet prepared to find out.

They decided to spend the remainder of the spring and early summer at Khoos, a spot safely remote from the political upheaval which threatened the country, where there would be beautiful country walks, horseback riding, and trout fishing for Adam. The climate was cool at six thousand feet, and they would have leisure to plan for the winter. Patrice would have an opportunity to go back to her

466

writing, which had been in a state of suspension for the past six weeks. She felt the stir and itch to get back to work, to push all paradox and personal involvement aside and to breathe again the air of a world more of her own making.

Walking alone on the Calcutta maidan on this humid afternoon, she was glad of the solid ground under her feet and for the squealing kites overhead. It seemed as if she could have forgotten nothing. The pattern made by bare feet in the dust of the maidan, the flock of goats herded by a child in a dirty shirt which ended above his navel; strolling babus in voluminous dhotis which revealed chubby brown legs in socks and suspenders. There were slender schoolboys in shorts and open-neck shirts, big-eyed and noisy, who addressed her in impudent voices and burst into banshee laughter when she replied in her rusty Hindustani. Everywhere the sound of bicycle bells undermining the city's drone; everywhere the sense of life replenishing itself as it died.

India! The whole idea, the enormous physical fact, seemed about to engulf her. Nothing she had read, nothing she had written or felt about the country during these years of absence, had prepared her for the recurring, seismic shock of recognition and wonder which filled her. The featureless mass of Calcutta itself, its turmoil, its shameless vitality, was more Indian than anything she had known. She was mystified by her own response to it—by a kind of fierce, perverse affection in the face of its enormity, its banality, its noise and stink and its imperishability.

Stepping one evening into a movie house, she had been floored by artless mediocrity set in pure bedlam. The play was a direct steal from one of Rossellini's early films and every detail of the Bengali transformation was exaggerated to the saturation point. Love scenes dragged on and on; tears were larger, greasier, more glistening; sighs shook the walls; suffering and injustice sank through the floor like wet cement; humor hit you in the face like slops emptied from an upstairs balcony, and the incidental music shattered your eardrums.

And yet Patrice had experienced a kind of mad exhilaration. The whole production was dreadful, but it was not cynical. At the end of the performance when the lights were switched on in a stupefying blaze and she gazed round her at the almost wholly Indian audience, she felt a rush of emotion toward those dark, intense faces with their

467

essential simplicity, their ardor. And there was something else: from the moment of her arrival in the city she had been made aware of a directness of contact, of an immediate personal involvement which she never felt among her own people.

Now, sauntering among the bespattered viceroys and their absurd mounts, Patrice was not moved to feelings of irony. Alice would have been outraged by this neglect of precious symbols of the past. Clem would have philosophized. Adam was largely indifferent. Father O'-Hara, walking with her on the last afternoon of his brief stay in Calcutta before he left for Rangoon, had observed dryly: "I don't like the English, God knows, but they had a sense of order and fitness when they dealt with people not of their own color. Now just give this country five years and everything will come to a standstill—like these statues."

The prospect of impending immuration had a peculiar effect on Father O'Hara. He seemed savage, almost despairing. When Patrice shook hands with him, bidding him good-bye and good luck, he gave her a hard glance. "Luck has no part in a man's duty." And he added on that same note of savagery: "Might I presume to give you one word of advice, Mrs. Bannister? Don't let idealism carry you away; you may not be able to find your way back."

She said mildly: "Would you say that it was idealism that carried your young friend Harper away in the Burmese jungles?"

He stared out over the dusty maidan. "No," he said at last. "It was not idealism. It was duty."

Patrice had watched his short, powerful figure in its white robe and khaki topi disappear toward the crowded Indian street.

She thought about Father O'Hara, briefly, as she came to a halt before the Octerlony obelisk and, letting her gaze travel up its length, experienced the curious visual phenomenon of seeing the whole thing begin to topple toward her from the sky. "It is a shame," Father O'Hara had declared bitterly, "that the good work and good will of conscientious men should go for nothing!"

A young Bengali in black achkan and white dhoti standing nearby noticed her instinctive recoil, and smiled. His teeth were very white, his smile mocking. "Yes," he said in English. "It seems to be falling, isn't it? Symbolic of what is in store for you people."

Patrice turned to look at him. He was quite young, perhaps twenty.

468

His English was perfect, with a trace of the Bengali inflection, but his manner was hostile. Patrice replied calmly: "There is probably something in store for all of us, wouldn't you say?"

"But worse for you English."

"I happen to be an American."

The young man's manner changed somewhat. "An American, eh? A tourist, isn't it?"

"I was born in India. My husband and I are here on what I suppose one might call a sentimental journey."

He stared at her with intense, inquisitive eyes. "You have chosen a dangerous time for your sentimental journey, madam. We Indians are about to take over our country, by force if necessary."

"So it would appear from what I read in the newspapers."

"Tchah! English newspapers. They print nothing but lies, as they have always." He continued to stare at her unwinkingly. "You are in sympathy with our Indian aspirations, may I ask? With Gandhi, with Nehru?"

When she hesitated he said fiercely: "Then if you are not in sympathy there is no room for you in this country. We Indians have no time for sentimental journeys. The past is done, finished." He made a dramatic gesture with one slim brown hand. "The India you knew will be washed away in rivers of blood."

"I can't say that I care for rivers of blood," Patrice told him. "But then, I don't know as much about the situation as you do."

"Then you should inform yourself. It is necessary that strangers who come to our country inform themselves of our national aspirations."

Patrice assured him that she would endeavor to inform herself. For a moment they stood side by side, uncomfortably aware of one another. Crows flew noisily overhead, goats bleated under the listless trees, and somewhere in the distance a churchbell sounded, sweet, insistent, irrelevant.

The boy turned and as he walked away said over his shoulder: "*Gandhiji ke jai!*"

"*Gandhiji ke jai!*" Patrice echoed the slogan and he stopped in his tracks, turned, and gave her a long look. "Do you know what that means?" he demanded, still tough.

"I know what it means."

He said somberly: "I think perhaps many people are going to die for saying it."

"What makes you so sure that many people are going to die?"

"I have been educated to be sure. Next year I will obtain my B.A. from Calcutta University. We wish to be free of the British." He made a violent gesture of his thin boy's arms. "Look at all those statues! Every one of them a memorial to men who worked to crush us and keep us crushed. Look at that monument. Do you know who this Octerlony was? He was a British officer who crushed the brave, freedom-loving Gurkha people and stole their lands. But wait! Our turn is coming. By this time next year you will see."

After staring at her for another moment the boy turned and walked quickly away. Patrice watched him go. His had been a voice she had not heard before. She had read of it and had even coined it in her novels, but what she had just heard was the real thing. She remembered a letter from Clem, years ago, when he applauded the rebellious spirit of the young. The boy who had just spoken to her was involved in a passion she had never felt and probably never would feel. She had a moment of envy, a sense of loss. One had to be young to be so committed, to bare one's soul so forthrightly to a stranger.

As she turned away from the Octerlony monument the little goatherd, deserting his charges, ran toward her and murmured something. He could not have been more than five years old, and she saw his navel protruded from his bloated belly like a second penis, the result of a rupture in infancy.

"What do you want?" Patrice asked him in Hindustiani.

He held out a grubby hand. "I am hungry."

It was an inescapable fragment of the jigsaw. Father O'Hara had admonished her: "For heaven's sake don't go handing out baksheesh every time one of them comes whining for it. You Americans!"

You writers, you Americans, you bloody fools.

Patrice dropped a few coins into the child's palm. Then she started back to the hotel with a sense of restored tension as though some long dormant current had been switched on inside her.

After a week in Calcutta the train carried them north through a changing landscape. As she felt the rhythm of the wheels under her it set up a responsive chord and she found herself repeating the little ditty she had learned as a child and which she had not thought of

470

until now: "*Ek ek anna, doh doh paisa! Ek ek anna, doh doh paisa!*"

The lush rice fields and glittering palms of Bengal gave way to stretches of brown, eroded land where cattle moved sluggishly in their endless search for food and water. The March sky was already a burning glass in which vultures floated like cinders and descended with hideous voracity on some exhausted beast which had given up the fight. Patrice found herself thinking of The Game which she and Clem had played when they were children, and the old tremor of terror and fascination touched her nerves as she stared out of the carriage window and watched, fleetingly, the huddle of sprawling wings and trampling claws and beaks.

Great black-and-white storks posed beside a puddle, studying their own reflections, and one day out from Calcutta the silvery elephant grass brushed the carriage windows, and she felt the past swell and roll toward her in a vast prismatic wave. Her tongue was finding the savor of long-forgotten words; insentient objects hammered at her consciousness, demanding recognition, and as the train rushed onward she had moments of dizziness, of a lost balance. In the gamut of emotions she had experienced since her marriage to Adam there had been nothing as insidious as this.

She sat at the carriage window and stared at the unfolding scene. Clumsy country carts drawn by bullocks plodded along a dusty track; a scrawny jackal inured to the rush and clatter of trains glanced up from his disgusting meal; a wedding party all gauze and glitter and brand-new turbans camped to rest in the shade of an acacia by the roadbed. On one platform where the train paused a few minutes Patrice watched a group of solemn-faced gentlemen in white khadi and Gandhi caps exhorting a wildly applauding audience. At another stop, a procession of men carrying red banners and shouting an unintelligible slogan marched past her window and Patrice noticed the insignia of the hammer and sickle on one of the banners. A Eurasian guard wearing a pipe-clay helmet and many shiny buttons paused beside her window and gave her a sardonic smile: "Rum country, madam!" he said, and walked on.

Adam sat on the leather-covered bunk across from her, smoking his pipe and reading. It occurred to Patrice that he looked ten years younger and supremely content. He had forgotten Mary Manchester, or if not, her memory no longer troubled him. Patrice guessed that this journey was a surcease from the perpetual malaise which afflicted him at home. He was where he wanted to be, released from demands and responsibilities, back in a world whose complexities he was not bound to question, a world which afforded him the simple unspoiled pleasures beyond which he asked nothing.

Hour after hour as the train bore them along the enormous expanse, Patrice devoured the landscape which by day swam past in dun-colored haze and by night loomed like a moon crater pierced by an occasional pinprick of light from a pointsman's hut beside the track. Stations where the train paused became a thudding, resonant reminder of things she had never really forgotten: the restlessness of Indian crowds, the inextinguishable liveliness.

In Calcutta she had heard of the huge uncertainties which lay ahead for the country. The weary old English editor who had dined with her and Adam one evening at Firpo's had said resignedly: "It's all going. Everything we know, everything your father knew. Three hundred years!"

Adam had been sympathetic, but Patrice could summon nothing but pity and impatience. The vitality which she sensed everywhere and to which her own responded made it difficult for her to share in this hand wringing. And now as she watched the preoccupation of crowds on the railway platforms, the queer dizzy sense of imbalance left her. She felt instead a surge of elation and wondered whether she was recapturing, in maturity, something of the intense private emotions of a child.

One day the train stopped at a station whose name on a big white signboard struck her squarely between the eyes. This was where she had lived for a little while with Doey and Alice in the old thatched bungalow loaned to them by that distant cousin, the soi-disant Princess Sita Devi, otherwise Kitty Braithwaite. The house above the river where the avocets flew over the brown sand; the house where Doey had died.

Beyond a dusty straggle of trees and corrugated tin roofs and peeling yellow plaster of station buildings was the bazaar with its single narrow street, its thieving monkeys, its starving dogs, its smells. Beyond that would be the broken Mogul bridge leading to the European cantonment with its comfortable bungalows dating back to Warren Hastings' time. There had been an elaborate clock tower, its hands permanently stuck at half past three. She had forgotten nothing. Beyond the clock tower lay the artificial pool, the lawns, and the handsome white-pillared house where Hastings had lived. And everywhere, huge dusty trees under which herdboys grazed their insatiable goats. East of the town lay the river, opalescent at this hour, and above the river the ocher battlements of the Mogul fort where she had gone to meet the young man Roland, and whither Doey's servant Nizamat had come running to tell her that Doey was dead.

Within sight of that fort would be the little European cemetery where they had buried him, and Patrice guessed that the pomegranate trees would be in flower among the moldering graves. Or had the earthquake of 1928 spewed up that little coterie and returned their battered coffins and nameless bones to the glare of life?

The engine whistled and the train began to move with that almost imperceptible gliding of Indian trains. Patrice leaned against the window, her heart on fire, and then she saw him. A tall slight figure in white drill suit and topi, brown moustache carefully brushed, gray wide-apart eyes fixed upon her as she passed slowly, past his faintly quizzical gaze. "Doey," she said aloud. "Doey!"

But he was gone, and Adam put down his book and looked at her gently.

"What is it, Patrice?"

"Nothing," she said. The huddle of the old town disappeared in the haze, an arc of the river flashed in the distance, and the wheels took up their insistent refrain: *"Ek ek anna, doh doh paisa . . ."*

It was cold in the mountains, but in a few days the jacaranda trees clouded with their misty blue flowers, barbets called from the thickets, and strings of mules loaded with charcoal staggered down the mountain paths. This summer retreat from the gay old days of the past —Doey's and Alice's days—wore a rusty, dusty look, as though the ornamental benches along the Mall, the homesick English gardens, the very stones in the retaining walls, had a premonition that something was coming to an end.

The season, so called, had not yet got under way, and Adam and Patrice had no difficulty in finding a suite of rooms in the pleasant old hotel at the farthest end of town. Single-storied, red-tiled, it was built in the form of an arc, and had deep verandas hung with wisteria. The rooms opened on these verandas, with views of a garden thick

473

with ilex, dwarf oaks, and the cube-shaped flower beds in which roses grew primly under the fanatical eye of an ancient gardener, himself a relic of another, garden-loving age. Behind the hotel the hillsides rolled in blue-green vistas stopped at last by a snowy barrier toward which, in April, crimson rhododendrons would sweep like a rich carpet laid down for the gods to come tripping.

The rooms themselves were rather dark and musty, filled with cumbersome furniture and hinting at scorpions lurking in the woodwork. But there were open fireplaces and the chairs were covered in English chintz, somewhat faded like everything else. Adam made himself instantly at home, unpacking his books and his guns. "Aren't you," he asked Patrice, "going to unpack the typewriter? There's a nice desk to work at, under that window."

But Patrice was suffering from a curious revulsion against the thought of writing. She felt herself struggling to get command of something, some perspective that would stay put, and was prey to violently shifting moods of elation, delight, and sadness.

She had a dim recollection of Alice telling her that they—Alice, Doey, Clem, and Aunt Eve—had spent a summer in this same hotel before she, Patrice, was born, and she had not wanted to come back, just yet, to her own or to secondhand memories. But because of the political ferment that was rising in the country, Khoos had, in the end, turned out to be the wisest choice for Adam and herself. She would know soon enough, when letters from Alice began to reach her, whether Alice and Doey had lived here. In the meantime she wandered about the rambling old building and through the gardens rather like a somnambulist, unable quite to awaken or quite to dream.

She sometimes surprised Adam's questioning gaze upon her, and on one occasion he said abruptly: "We are here together, you and I, and it is all I ask."

Was it all she asked, too? These musty old walls had no answer to her question, nor, for the moment, had Patrice. To distract herself from these aimless broodings she turned to a contemplation of their fellow guests, a few English and a scattering of Americans, all early arrivals for the summer season, or on leave of absence from their jobs on the rapidly heating plains. But the scene was dominated by several towering bearded Sikh gentlemen and their wives; by sleek individuals in the schizophrenic costume of the day—part Indian,

474

part English—and by a handful of khadi-clad parliamentarians from Delhi, snatching a respite from the furnace of the capital and the storm signals of impending holocaust.

Patrice and Adam had quickly struck up an acquaintance with their next-door neighbor, a handsome, serious-faced Muslim magistrate, Nasrullah Khan, and his seventeen-year-old son, Kasim. Patrice fell into the habit of sharing her tea tray with them on afternoons when Adam left her for one of his exploratory walks. Often the boy Kasim would betake himself to the tennis court, and Nasrullah Khan would hover uncertainly behind the bamboo screen of his door, joining Patrice at the tea tray only when she invited him to.

He seemed more at ease with her alone than when his son or Adam was present; with them conversation was superficial, centering on sport, and, lightly, on politics. Alone with Patrice, Nasrullah liked to talk of books, and of his career as assistant magistrate under the British in the district of Agra, where he had his ancestral home.

But that, he informed Patrice one afternoon as they sat drinking tea together, "that is all up now, or about to be so." He shrugged. "My family has owned land near Agra for centuries before the British came. My son and I are the last of our line. The Hindus are taking over our property, and if this notion of Pakistan comes into effect we shall have to migrate to Sind, where I shall have to find a job under Muslim government."

He gazed at her with the slightly yellowed eyes of one who has suffered bouts of jaundice. "For the past year my Hindu tenants have found one excuse after another not to pay their rents and taxes. My revenues have fallen and I can no longer afford to make the improvements and innovations which they keep demanding of me as their landlord. They boast of what they intend to do when the British leave." He sighed. "Independence! The magic of a word. But the truth—as you Americans would express it—is that the English are selling us Muslims down the river."

This in one form or another was the prevalent theme among most of the guests, every one of whom seemed to have a stake in what was happening in the country, or if not a stake, an almost irrational anxiety and fear.

Besides Nasrullah Khan and his son, Patrice had made friends with other Indians at the hotel. One day a large, ornamental Sikh lady seated with her family at a neighboring table during breakfast had abruptly risen from her chair and, carrying her plate, bore down on Patrice and Adam, who were finishing their meal. "Please to look at this!" she invited them in tones of outrage. "Three cigarette butts in my scrambled eggs! The cooks here are Muslim, and this is deliberate insult to me because I am a Sikh."

"Why don't you have it out with the manager?" Adam suggested. "Complain. Tell him you'll leave."

Mrs. Singh gave him a dull stare. "Complain! Yes, and then what? Next time it will be arsenic."

There was in addition to these Indians a young English couple, Jack and Noreen Bullock, he an officer in the Royal Air Force, and an ardent walker. Adam and he spent days tramping the hillsides, often coming home after dark. The young wife, tied down with a two-year-old child, hung around Patrice, who, when not drinking tea with Nasrullah or Mrs. Singh, was happy to share her *cha* and buttered scones with Noreen Bullock on the veranda overlooking the garden. Like her husband, Noreen Bullock was unaffected and communicative. She was also lonely, and inclined to be nervous. "This country is going to hell," she murmured to Patrice one afternoon over the tea tray. "They all hate each other, and I for one don't want to be caught in the middle."

She was also, on occasion, inclined to bitterness on another score. "See that chappie over there in the air force blazer?" With her knitting needle she indicated a figure strolling among the roses. "Major Humphries. He's Jack's superior officer. Holds a desk job in New Delhi. Never saw action in the war—he had the right connections!" She laughed. "Jack rose from the ranks. He was badly wounded, and won the Military Cross. But he's still only a captain, and that chappie is a major, and he never lets us forget it." She knitted busily for a moment. "We all believed that when the war was over this rank business would be forgotten so far as ordinary life was concerned. Everyone had had it. Everyone was going to be as good as everyone else now that we'd licked the Nazis. Ha ha. But that fat-arse won't speak to me when we meet and he barely bothers to nod at Jack. Why? Because the major is *county*. Do you know what that means? It means that he is our social superior. Jack and I are from Glasgow,

476

where Jack's father works in a brewery and my parents own a sweet-shop." She gazed speculatively at Patrice. "It's worse out here in India than it is at home. I suppose that being in a position to yell at your servants may have something to do with it."

Patrice said after a pause: "I thought that that was all old hat."

"Far from it. It's the same old hat and it always will be."

They drank their tea and watched Major Humphries chatting affably to a spectacular Sikh gentleman with whiskers like a water buffalo.

"That's Major Krishen Singh," Noreen explained. "The rank makes it all right, you see." She giggled, then turned her clear eyes once more on Patrice. "You were English to begin with, but you don't seem to have this bloody class feeling. I suppose it comes from having lived so long in America."

"I don't know. Perhaps it's just one of those things some of us escape, like certain diseases."

Noreen Bullock bore a vague resemblance to Patrice's late traveling companion Mrs. Lambston, but where Mrs. Lambston had a soft, pampered prettiness, the Englishwoman had a plain, strong face. Patrice could see her standing up to life, steady-eyed, long after she had become old. Noreen said after a moment: "I think one has to be very sure of oneself not to turn into a snob just in self-defense. I mean, one has to be self-reliant, like. Jack's like that. He laughs at me for minding, but I can't help minding. It hurts."

Patrice said gently: "Jack is right. Snobbism is a cult of fools, really." She changed the subject. "What's your and Jack's reaction to the Indians? And to what's happening out here?"

Noreen Bullock put the ends of her knitting needles between her teeth and stared into the sunshine, where yellow butterflies hovered among the roses. "I like the Indians well enough, though I don't see why they should want to be rid of us. We've been here a long time and we've done a lot for them."

The old refrain. Catching Patrice's satiric glance, she added quickly: "Now you think I'm being a snob, but I'm not. It's not that we don't like them or don't get along with them, because we do. Of course, we're limited to those who can speak English, and to our servants. We never really get a chance to know the hundreds and thousands who go on living their lives as though we didn't exist." She smiled ruefully. "Still, I'm blessed if I can see what they think they're after."

Patrice experienced one of those blurred, double-negative images of a big bearded man in a blue turban spinning a silver rupeee in the air, and of a youth gazing at the Octerlony monument with liquid, hate-filled eyes, and she heard herself say to Mrs. Bullock: "Whose bloody country is it, anyhow?"

"Oh, you're sympathetic to them, I realize that," Noreen Bullock said after a moment. "You seem to be just as much at home with them as you are with Jack and me."

It was brought out with such artlessness that Patrice's quick temper died at once. She said calmly: "I can only tell you this, that once you have sorted it out for yourself it's like being able to draw a deep clean breath knowing you are not sucking in a lot of garbage-laden air."

Noreen Bullock gazed at her with luminous eyes. "I don't think I have to ask you that bitchy little question: would you go to bed with an Indian, or even let him kiss you? It doesn't really matter, does it? You've made me feel—for the first time—that it doesn't really matter."

Well, of course it did matter; it mattered as much to a man like Nasrullah Khan as it did to Jack Bullock or Major Humphries. You can't laugh off sex; if you could the world would have split its sides a long time ago. The important thing, Patrice thought, was that it mattered only in part. And as she saw in Noreen's young, strong English face the bemused expression of one who has made a discovery, Patrice felt a sudden blitheness of spirit. She poured herself another cup of tea and said in a practical tone of voice: "One can't stop trying."

A group of children—English, Eurasian, and a little Sikh boy in a top-heavy turban—were playing hopscotch on the veranda. Mrs. Singh, the lady who had complained about cigarette butts in her eggs, was strolling in the garden with another portly Sikh lady, both industriously knitting, their long black pigtails swinging against their broad backs. Nasrullah's son, Kasim, in a blue shirt and white shorts, was on his way to the tennis court, and Major Humphries was still engaged in conversation with the orchidaceous Sikh major. Their English accents rose upon the air like bubbles of whipped cream. Behind this pleasant charade the pines sighed in a faint breeze,and

478

a family of big gray monkeys sported in the branches.

Noreen Bullock excused herself and went indoors to attend to her child, and Nasrullah Khan materialized from behind his bamboo screen, where he must have been waiting in hope of finding Patrice alone. He had read her novels and short stories, and had expressed a naïve admiration which she would have found irritating from anyone else. Patrice realized that he was drawn to her with a mingling of loneliness, curiosity, and sex, and she found herself liking him without the spur of any of these ingredients of friendship. His attitude toward Adam was courteous, if slightly puzzled. "He leaves you so much alone!" Nasrullah had exclaimed on one occasion when they had got to know one another better. "I do not understand. If you were my wife I would not leave you so much alone."

Patrice had turned it aside lightly: "Adam and I understand each other. That is the main thing."

For a moment it had looked as if Nasrullah would question the remark, but he said nothing, his smile only faintly skeptical. He was a shy man, long widowed, wrapped up in his only son and obsessed, now, with the terrible uncertainties which he believed lay ahead for himself and the boy. He talked freely of his troubles, taking Patrice into his confidence as she felt sure he was not in the habit of doing with other Occidentals. "Faced with the unbelievable, what does a man do?" he had asked her once and, unable to find an adequate answer, moved to compassion for him, Patrice had laid her hand on his arm. Slowly, he had brought his gaze down to rest on her hand but he had made no attempt to touch it himself.

On this afternoon when Noreen Bullock had left the veranda to attend to her child, Nasrullah Khan pushed aside the bamboo screen before his own door and stepped out. "May I join you?" he asked, and without waiting for her answering smile he dropped into Noreen's empty chair. "I am afraid I eavesdropped, a little, while you were talking with Mrs. Bullock. You are not angry?"

"I said nothing to Mrs. Bullock that I would not say to you," Patrice replied, conscious, suddenly, of a stir of nervousness behind his polite manner. "How about some tea? I'll send for another cup."

"Thank you, I have already had tea." He clasped his long, firm hands between his knees and stared at the floor. "I am an Indian. You can understand that it would mean much to me, what I heard you say

479

to Mrs. Bullock." He raised his eyes to her face. "You are sincere, I think, Mrs. Bannister."

"I think I am, Nasrullah."

"Sincerity is a quality in short supply these days." The nervousness became more apparent and Patrice cast about her for something to say that might put him at his ease. "Look, Nasrullah. Sincerity is a habit of thought, isn't it? We shouldn't be self-conscious about it."

Nasrullah shook his head. "You are a clever lady and you write books and you have this sincerity which is more than a habit of thought. It is rather, I believe, that deep clean breath of air of which you spoke, just now, to your friend." Before she could speak he finished in a kind of desperation: "To be with you, to talk to you, to look at you is the nearest I will ever come to drawing that deep clean breath."

Patrice realized with dismay that he was on the verge of falling in love with her, a complication she had not bargained for. She liked him greatly and it would have been simple enough for her to have embarked on an affair with him, and thus, perhaps, exorcised the demons of unrest and suspense which had been gaining on her since her arrival in India. Her relations with Adam had reached an impasse which neither he nor she knew how to break. They slept together with affection but without passion and often without desire. Propinquity and a latent fear of total alienation kept them together, but where, oh, where, was the least vestige of that third personality which Barto Williams had insisted that she might create—the personality of marriage itself, sprung anew from some fresh and limpid source?

Nasrullah Khan was leaning toward her. For a troubled moment he seemed on the brink of giving himself away, but both were saved by the reappearance of Noreen Bullock, and he rose quickly from his chair. "You will excuse me, ladies?" He gave them a polite, impartial little bow. "I must go and find my son."

As late March passed into April and day succeeded beautiful day on the mountains, Patrice's uneasiness increased. She was unable to write or to concentrate on reading. The beauty of Khoos at this season seemed, itself, an anachronism beside her personal distress and the malaise that was creeping upon the country. Visitors from the plains brought stories of murder, massacre, revolt, and the Indians at the

480

hotel wore grim and anxious faces.

"Serve 'em right!" Major Humphries was heard to say to an American on leave from the embassy in New Delhi. "They asked for it and they're going to get it."

"I'll be glad when they send us home," Noreen Bullock confided to Patrice. "No joke when the fur begins to fly."

"Couldn't be in a safer spot than this," her husband reassured her. "These mountain people ... all grins and salaams. Sahib this and sahib that. They don't need to be told the meaning of independence, damn it!"

And one day there came a strange letter from Alice: "You write from the Tivoli Hotel in Khoos. Patrice, darling, I must tell you something ... it was in that hotel you were *conceived*, the summer Doey and I were there with Clem and Aunt Eve."

In this room, with its windows giving on the icy peaks of Tibet and the summer wind drifting through the pines. Coincidence—no more than coincidence. But for Patrice that long past moment of love came full circle as she stood with Alice's letter in her hand. She glanced up at last to see Nasrullah Khan in the door. "I am returning *Death in Venice*," he said, and as she took the novel from him: "You look strange, Mrs. Bannister. Bad news?"

Should she tell him? But it was not important. It was finished, finished. Yet here she stood in this simple room with the sun beating against the windows, the unfinished past lodged in her flesh.

She said abruptly: "Let's go for a walk. I'll leave a note for Adam in case he gets home before I do."

The prosaic words, the prosaic act of writing a note to Adam, restored her balance. With Alice's letter in her skirt pocket she turned lightly to Nasrullah. "Tell me what you think of Thomas Mann."

They chose the mountain path below the hotel where the stored heat and perfume of the day rose about them and the seething sound of tree croakers filled their ears. Nasrullah launched enthusiastically upon his subject: "Only a European could have written *Death in Venice*. How wonderful to experience so many levels of thought and feeling, to be so aware of one's own past, so free from romantic hope!"

In his well-cut English jacket and riding breeches, the silk shirt open at the neck, and with his distinctive head and pale, sensitive

481

face, Nasrullah might have passed for a European himself. He carried a little leather-covered riding crop, with which he snapped off the top of a small plant growing beside the path. "Mann's is the European mind . . . a distillation of history and consciousness."

He often talked to her in this vein, with a touch of pedantry, artificiality, trying to impress her, perhaps.

"Don't you find that distillation in your Arabic poets?" Patrice asked him. She felt Alice's letter in her pocket, and a stir of that strange emotion which had overwhelmed her back there in the hotel. *Finished,* declared her mind, fiercely. *Finished.*

Nasrullah snapped off another blossom with his riding crop. "No. Our Arabic writers are obsessed with universality. It makes them mystical, flowery. And that is true of the East generally. It is perhaps an attempt to escape from the tyrannical closed society in which we live. But to my mind there is no escape except to turn wholly to the West, with its rationality, its endless *scope.*"

Finished, Patrice exhorted herself. Tears burned behind her eyes. She walked on beside Nasrullah under the cascading song of the tree croakers. Nasrullah said: "In Mann's novel . . . the beginning so quiet, so ordered, so ordinary—a man of letters worn out and jaded by art and labor. The arrival in Venice. After that every detail—the villainous gondolier, the atmosphere of that hotel, and then the first glimpse of the beautiful boy."

Nasrullah was silent a moment. Three dusty mules crowded past them along the path, and the driver greeted them cheerily and turned once in a bend of the path to stare back at them with curiosity and mischief in his face. The sound of the mule bells died in the distance and Nasrullah said: "It is more than study of sexual perversion, of course. I didn't grasp it at first, then I understood. The loss of youth, the passing of a man's creative powers, the pitiless clarity of the intellectual mind!" He turned his head to smile at Patrice. "For two whole days I have thought more about Thomas Mann than I have of you. Imagine!"

Finished. The word beat in her mind like a refrain. Though you walk on this fragrant path with this stranger and feel the stones under your feet, though your heart beats strongly and you taste the wind, it is *finished.*

A troop of gray monkeys swung away into the treetops beside the path. Suddenly Nasrullah stopped and pointed with his crop. Patrice stood beside him, their sleeves touching. "Nanga Parbat," Nasrullah said softly. The faint golden haze had lifted slightly and the peak appeared, airy, insubstantial in the slowly sinking light. At the same moment the trees and bare shoulders of the nearer hills swam into greater clarity as though magnified by some element between observer and observed, and from far away the sound of the mule bells returned with a fragile sweetness which hung in the air long after the sound had ceased once more.

Nasrullah said in a strained voice: "Ten years ago I brought my wife on this same walk, at this same time of day, at this same time of year. She was already ill then and she had a month to live. I did not know it at the time, but afterward I realized that she must have known, though she said nothing of it to me." His voice was somber. "She loved this place and we came often to stay at the hotel. Since her death I have always arranged that my son and I should occupy the same rooms."

Patrice stared into the distance, where the lovely cone was already dissolving in the prismatic stupor of the hour. "The last time my wife and I came here she drew me to a stop, like this." Lightly, Nasrullah took Patrice's hand. "She said: 'Look, Nasu!' and pointed, and there was Nanga Parbat, as you see it now."

He kept Patrice's wrist between his slim, strong fingers as though taking her pulse. "My wife said to me: 'Nasu, when you walk here with another woman, think of me!' I did not, at the time, understand what she was trying to tell me, and I was annoyed with her. I loved her, but because she had seemed cold and withdrawn and sickly for the past year, and because the doctors had told me that she would give me no more children, I had been thinking of taking another wife. I was therefore additionally angry because I thought she must have learned of my intention and was rebuking me."

Gently he released Patrice's hand. Without looking at her he said: "This is the first time since her death that I have walked here with another woman."

"You married again?" Patrice asked after a moment's hesitation.

"Yes. But my second wife died two years ago. She was a good, sweet girl, but I never brought her to walk here and look at Nanga Parbat."

483

Abruptly, flushing a little, he faced Patrice. "You and your husband," he said. "You are good friends, yes. But you do not love each other."

"We have been married a long time," Patrice countered. "And to be good friends is important."

"You told me you had no children."

"That is not always as important with us as it is with you," she explained, and before he could say more she added: "Adam and I love each other in our own way." She tried to keep it light. "In the somewhat complicated Western fashion, shall I say?"

Nasrullah gazed at her, unsmiling. "You can say what you like, Patrice, but it does not convince me."

She turned away and they fell into step. A pair of pheasants which had been feeding on the fresh mule droppings rose before them on a rush of wings and scaled out of sight down the hillside. Nasrullah said: "You have made me see many things to which I used to be blind. I have not known many English or American women. I have never in my life talked to any woman as I have talked to you."

Once more he drew her to a stop beside the low retaining wall. "See," he said, pointing with the crop. "There she is again, Nanga Parbat." The peak had reappeared, clearer now, seeming nearer as a wash of fading sunlight blazed upon it. "Nanga Parbat," Nasrullah repeated. "You know what it means?"

"The Naked Goddess?"

"A typically Hindu appellation," he said with contempt. "It is not naked, and it is not a goddess, nor a woman. A mountain, merely."

"Nasrullah," Patrice said suddenly. "Will you do something for me?"

He turned swiftly. "Anything!"

"Then speak to your wife now, this minute."

"*What?*"

"Yes, say something to your wife—your wife whom you loved and who walked here with you."

His face had darkened. "What do you want me to say?"

"Tell her you miss her. Tell her you wish she were here with you."

For a moment he was silent, then he said harshly: "It would not be true."

Dropping the riding crop, he suddenly took Patrice in his arms and

484

kissed her on the lips. And at that moment Noreen Bullock and the Sikh lady who had found cigarette ends in her scrambled eggs turned a corner of the path, and Patrice had an uninterrupted view, over Nasrullah's shoulder, of their two thunderstruck faces.

Nasrullah released her, picked up his riding crop, and they continued on their way, hearing the sound of the two women's voices talking in agitated trivialities behind them until another bend in the path cut off the sound. Patrice began to laugh.

Nasrullah said stiffly: "I am most sorry. I most humbly apologize. If I have made any trouble for you I will willingly take all the blame."

"It's all right," Patrice assured him. "Don't take it so much to heart."

But he was deeply agitated. "If they should go to your husband with the story! I am utterly ashamed, utterly."

"They won't go to my husband with any story. I would be willing to bet that Noreen Bullock won't mention the incident even to her own husband."

"You may be right about Mrs. Bullock, but Mrs. Krishen Singh will spread the story far and wide." He kicked a pebble ahead of him. "Already she will barely trouble to be polite to me, although she has been coming to the hotel almost as long as I have."

Patrice stared at him. "You mean that our silly little episode will add fuel to her suspicions of Muslims in general? Come, Nasrullah!"

"Ha! You are amused. You have confidence in yourself, in your husband, in your friends. Cannot you appreciate my position?"

When she was silent he added on a note of desperation: "Yes, you can laugh, but it is no laughing matter. Everything we do, every move we make, every word we utter, is taken down, examined, turned inside out, and the worst possible construction put on it."

"What possible construction could be put on that—that little indiscretion, except that we were most decidedly and inopportunely indiscreet?"

Quite suddenly she was filled with an irrepressible excitement. "Nasrullah! For goodness' sake, don't you see?"

"See what?" He glanced worriedly over his shoulder at the sunlit path along which they had come. But it was empty. There were no voices, no mule bells, no footfalls. "See what?" He was sweating. He removed his hat, and mopped his face with a silk handkerchief.

"Did you ever read *A Passage to India?*" Patrice asked him.

"Yes. What about it?"

"You're acting like Doctor Aziz. And it's absurd. All those moth-eaten attitudes about a white woman's honor and the rest of it."

Nasrullah shrugged. "It is not absurd. You think that everything can be explained and decided on the rational level, but nothing can —not in India. In the absence of true communication between people—and in a fragmented society like ours how can there be such a thing as true communication?—we have rumor, gossip, innuendo."

He was beside himself, all because of that kiss! "Here in the hotel there are people—yes, even my fellow Muslims—who delight in misconstruing everything. There is no innocence in our country. Our country!" His voice rose in bitterness. "Whose country? Nehru's country, Gandhi's country? The Muslims' country? The Sikhs'? Mine or my son's? Nobody's country. Today it still belongs to the British, tomorrow it will belong to the street sweepers. Meantime, every maker of mischief will have his day. Every minor incident will be magnified into a hundred sinister meanings. I am a Muslim, you an American woman, and married. We have been observed in an indiscreet moment on a lonely mountain road. Shall I tell you what will be made of that incident which you dismiss as having no importance? It will be given about that, aside from the purely moral aspect, that you, a well-known writer, a citizen of a great and powerful country, did not hesitate to make a display of your preference for Muslims as against Hindus and Sikhs. Yes, yes, you are amused, I can see. But let me tell you it is not so funny. I agree with you that the era of Doctor Aziz and Mrs. Moore is done with, finished. No one is going to write a book about an obscure Indian daring to embrace a white woman. There are in this country already too many white women who are willing enough." He laughed without humor. "But prejudice remains, a different and more terrible kind of prejudice than you can guess. Sikh and Muslim prejudice, Hindu prejudice, caste prejudice against untouchables! Let Gandhiji rant. He has his own prejudice against the British, and the British theirs against the lot of us. Even if you were not a respectable American woman no longer in her first youth —excuse me, I am being frank!—even if you were not married to another man, your being seen in my arms makes it impossible that

486

either of us can escape the beastliness, the horrible vulgarity of *gossip*."

She said slowly: "I should take all this seriously, Nasrullah, but I cannot."

He went on, headlong: "The era of Forster's Doctor Aziz, of Miss Quested and Fielding—that era is finished, you say. E. M. Forster would not today have the incentive to write *A Passage to India*. The resplendent British Raj with its middle-class standards is about to pass away forever. You and I are emancipated people, free to be friends, to converse on any subject under the sun, to take walks together, like this, as we would not have dreamed of doing a generation ago and, as I understand, you Americans think twice about doing with a black man in your own country today. Isn't it?

"Well, let me tell you something. Today we Indians—Muslim, Hindu, Sikh—all of us except perhaps the wretched sweeper caste, are as middle class as the British ever were. Every day Gandhi preaches love, brotherhood, self-sacrifice, and Nehru echoes him. It is all bosh. Legalistic bosh. But you are idealistic, Patrice; you are sincere. You meant what you said to your friend Mrs. Bullock up there on the veranda this afternoon, that to cast off prejudice is to draw a deep breath of clean air." His voice quivered. "You did not repulse me a little while ago when I kissed you. You did not respond either, no. But then, I did not really expect that you would respond. I have not been deceived by your warmth and friendliness. I am a man and I would have known at once if you had been drawn to me as I have been drawn to you, by sex. Yes, and by love."

They were walking slowly and now by mutual consent they came to a halt under an arch of branches where the shade was heavy and the air suddenly cold, scented by some nameless weed growing nearby. Patrice took Alice's letter from her pocket and put it in Nasrullah's hand. He read it slowly, then replaced it in its envelope and handed it back to her. He said in a changed voice: "Your mother?"

"Yes." Patrice looked at him. "It had a strange effect on me, that vision of love out of which I was born. I wanted you to kiss me, Nasrullah."

"Just because I was a man and happened to be there?"

"I can't tell you why, because I don't know myself."

487

They finished their walk in silence and parted at the entrance to the hotel gardens, where he turned in the direction of the tennis court and Patrice returned to her room.

The following day she came on Noreen Bullock alone, seated on the veranda with her knitting. Adam was gone as usual on one of his mountain-climbing expeditions with Jack Bullock, and, obeying an impulse, Patrice stopped by Noreen Bullock's chair and watched a tide of color sweep her neck and brow. She raised troubled eyes to Patrice. 'Won't you sit down?"

Patrice found a chair and Noreen resumed her knitting. She said in a stifled voice: "I feel awful about yesterday."

"I really don't see why you should."

"Well, I do. I'm not stuck up, or a prude, or anything. But how could you?"

"Because I wanted to."

Noreen Bullock burst out fiercely: "I don't believe it. He took advantage of you, and God knows why you should feel that you have to shield him."

She laid her knitting in her lap and stared into the garden. "I did my best to make light of the whole thing with Mrs. Singh, but she kept going back to it, first laughing as if she agree with me, then telling me that most Muslims were like that. She said she knows as a fact that Nasrullah Khan has a bad reputation with women. I'm afraid she doesn't seem to like you much, either."

"Whatever have I done to Mrs. Krishen Singh?" Patrice asked, really surprised.

"You hurt her feelings by laughing at her when she went to your table one morning to show you the cigarette butts in her scrambled eggs."

"But I didn't laugh!"

"She insists you did, that you seemed to consider it a huge joke." Noreen Bullock went on with a rush: "Yesterday, by the time we had got back here after our walk, Mrs. Singh had told me a great deal. Even allowing for exaggeration, she made me see the picture a little more clearly, from her point of view. She feels that we—the English, I mean, and also many Americans—tend to favor the Muslim side of this godawful political mess. She's got it all mixed up with the religious angle, too. That we consider the Muslims nearer us in their faith

488

and their democratic principles and all that. I can't remember everything she said, but the gist of it was that one can't trust a Muslim round the corner and that Nasrullah Khan in particular is a lecherous bastard of the first water."

Patrice said slowly: "I'm afraid it's my word against Mrs. Singh's, then."

Noreen Bullock sighed unhappily. "After all, we saw you with our own eyes!"

"Yes," said Patrice, "you did."

"If only there were some—some other explanation."

"If only there were," said Patrice. She asked after a pause: "What about your husband? Does he know this story?"

"No. Jack is very broad-minded, but he likes your husband and I'm afraid he'd think it was a bit thick."

"Thicker than if Nasrullah should have been—let us say—a white man?"

"Well," Noreen Bullock replied defiantly, "what do you expect?"

"I don't know," said Patrice thoughtfully. "I just don't know."

Major Humphries appeared, coming from the direction of the tennis court. He wore the sleeves of a white sweater knotted round his neck and swung a tennis racket, and as he stepped jauntily on the veranda he found himself face to face with the two women. He gave Patrice a long, hard stare, then walked quickly away down the veranda and out of sight.

Patrice shrugged. "Word seems to have reached the outlying tribes," she said lightly, but Noreen's brown eyes were blazing. "The dirty sod!" she exclaimed. "Who does he think he is?"

It became obvious to Patrice in the days that followed that Mrs. Singh was determined to avoid her, and she herself did nothing to force a confrontation. What, after all, would be the point? Better to ignore the whole affair. It was not especially difficult. She had an established routine of remaining in her room most of the morning while Adam took walks alone or with Jack Bullock. In the afternoon she and Adam explored the bazaar, or spent some time in the moldy old English library on the Mall, or read or wrote letters. Accustomed as he was to her moods, Adam asked no questions and seemed content just to be with her. He evidently had heard nothing of the incident with Nasrullah, for he gave no hint of curiosity and concern except to inquire, once or twice, why they saw so little of him all of a sudden.

It was true that Nasrullah was no longer so much in evidence. He kept to his rooms, or rode horseback alone or with his son, or sat beside the tennis court watching Kasim play tennis with his friends. He rarely appeared on the veranda at teatime, and when he encountered Patrice and Adam he had a harassed, preoccupied air which made it plausible enough for Adam to suggest that the poor guy was probably consumed with anxiety about his future and his son's.

One day a week after the contretemps on the mountain path something occurred to shake Patrice somewhat out of her boredom with the whole affair. The hotel servant who had charge of their rooms was a young Hindu whose manner had always been irreproachable. He was well-trained, quick, efficient, and unfailingly polite. He made the beds, tidied the rooms, dusted, took care of Adam's clothes, and polished their shoes. He was paid by the hotel, but Patrice gave him baksheesh at the end of every week in return for numerous small services such as mailing letters and carrying messages. The boy's name was Budhu; besides her rooms he took care of the Bullocks', of Nasrullah's, and of Mrs. Krishen Singh's.

On this afternoon when Patrice was alone, writing letters at her typewriter, the servant entered the room without knocking and passed into the bedroom at her back. The fact that he had neglected to knock struck her only fleetingly, and she said nothing. It was part of his duty to take their shoes on the veranda and polish them, and she barely noticed his reappearance in the sitting room as he carried a pair of Adam's shoes to the door. But something indefinable in his manner, and the recollection of his having neglected to knock on the door before entering the room, stuck in her consciousness like a burr. It also occurred to her that he had not given her the customary polite salutation, obligatory from servants.

One of the readjustments which Patrice had had to make since her return to the country was to this master-servant relationship. She disliked it. She hated the way in which Major Humphries yelled at his servants, at the tone Nasrullah and his son used toward Budhu— the minatory tone of master to man of which even the genial young Bullocks were not always guiltless. She had even found it necessary to chide Adam when he showed a propensity in the same direction,

490

and had tended, herself, to lean over backward in consideration of this boy who fetched and carried for them, and who, until this moment, had seemed a model of decorum.

She said nothing, continuing with her letter, but when Budhu returned from the veranda carrying Adam's newly polished shoes, she said: "My shoes need cleaning, too. The brown laced pair in the next room."

He stood in the bedroom door, his duster flung across one shoulder, and stared boldly into her eyes. "Your shoes do not need cleaning," he told her, and omitted the "memsahib" or "huzoor" indispensable to such an exchange between them.

Patrice thought swiftly: Better skip it. But she guessed that there might be something serious behind this show of impertinence and that she could not afford to let it pass. Slipping a fresh sheet of paper under the platen of her machine, she said casually, in Hindustani: "My walking shoes need to be cleaned. You will clean them."

He hesitated, then turned back to the bedroom and reappeared carrying her shoes. Without speaking he went out to the veranda, and came back almost at once, the shoes in his hands. She saw at a glance that they had not been cleaned. Patrice experienced a quite unexpected emotion, a kind of brilliance of anger which brought the blood to her cheeks, though she kept her voice under control. "Those shoes are not clean, Budhu. You will take them out and clean them, now, at once."

He faced her, insolence in his smile. "The shoes are clean. I have cleaned them."

"Very well," she said quietly. "Leave the shoes and go. You are dismissed."

The nerve went out of him and he cringed. "Memsahib . . ."

"Go."

He clasped his hands. "I meant no offense, Protector of the Poor! I have a wife and old parents to support. I am a poor man."

"Go."

He whimpered: "The manager sahib will kick me out. He will not give me a reference, and where will I find work? I shall starve. My wife and my parents will starve."

"You should have thought of that earlier. Now go and do not come back."

He went and she heard his bare feet shuffling up the veranda. She had a moment's savage satisfaction in the thought of him making a beeline for Mrs. Singh's room with his tale of woe, and of Mrs. Singh's unerring interpretation of its cause.

Yet Patrice felt shaken by the little scene. That she had done the right thing to send him packing she had no doubt. Not to have done so in the face of his studied insolence would have invited more of the same and would have set the tone for the other servants in the hotel. No, she could not have done otherwise, yet it left a bad taste. Unable to settle down to finish her letter, she left the room and started up the veranda toward Noreen Bullock's door. Major Humphries was coming in the opposite direction, and Patrice, her blood still humming, looked through him as she passed, her cold, apparently unseeing eye registering his shock at the cut. Only slightly mollified by this small triumph, she arrived at Noreen Bullock's door to find no one at home.

Still borne along on the unfamiliar impetus of rage, Patrice made her way past Mrs. Singh's rooms. The door was open, the screen down, but she had a fairly distinct impression of two figures standing in the gloom beyond—Mrs. Singh and Budhu. Patrice marched on without turning her head. The manager was not at his desk, but she found his assistant, a chubby young Parsi from Bombay. She came directly to the point: "I must ask you to appoint another servant to take care of our rooms—Mr. and Mrs. Bannister, number twenty-three."

The young man had a most winning smile. "Of course, Mrs. Bannister. Might I inquire what is the complaint, if you please?"

"I don't like Budhu's manners. I suspect he's been hobnobbing with the wrong kind of people, and I would prefer a politer servant."

"Quite. But you see, madam, Budhu is a member of the hotel servants' union, and if the rest of the staff . . . ?"

"Quite," Patrice agreed indifferently. "But if you cannot arrange to appoint another servant to take care of our rooms, Mr. Bannister and I will leave the hotel immediately."

The young man suddenly became natural and direct. "I understand, madam. I shall see that you get another servant to take care of your rooms."

"Thank you," said Patrice.

On her way back to her room Patrice met Mrs. Krishen Singh on the veranda and looked through her as she had looked through Major Humphries a few minutes before. Back in her little sitting room, she opened the window wide and leaned on the sill, staring across the quiet, sunny distance at Nanga Parbat, shining like a ghost.

A few days later, Nasrullah Khan knocked on the door while she and Adam were drinking afternoon tea. It had turned out a cold, dreary day and their new servant had lighted a fire in the smoky little grate and ostentatiously carried out every pair of shoes he could find to polish on the veranda outside.

Nasrullah entered. He wore a gray turtleneck sweater under his jacket, and his face had a worn, pinched look. Adam greeted him warmly. "Where have you been hiding yourself, Nasrullah? We've missed you."

For a moment Nasrullah looked as though he might burst into tears. He grasped Adam's hand and held it. "I have been preoccupied with my affairs and have not felt like seeing my friends. You must forgive me. Things are going from bad to worse on my property in Agra. The whole country is going to hell."

"Tea?" Patrice lifted the teapot. "Sit down, Nasrullah. Take the weight off your feet."

He released Adam's hand and gave her a melancholy smile. "That is one of your Americanisms, I think? It is not the weight on my feet that tires me. It is the weight on my mind, on my heart. Thank you, I would like a cup of tea."

He sat down next to the fire and she handed him a cup. "Thank you. It is such a beastly afternoon. I had a fire in my room but the wood is wet so it will do nothing but smoke." He coughed. "I think I may have caught a chill."

What, Patrice wondered, had become of the debonair man she had known only a few days ago? Now he seemed to have aged, with the querulous tone of the old. "I see," he said, "your fire does not smoke. You must have special wood."

"Perhaps it's because we have a new slave," Adam suggested. "And by the way, how come, Patrice?"

"I sacked Budhu," Patrice replied. "He was cheeky, so I asked the management to send us someone else."

Adam looked at her with amusement. "Quite the little memsahib!"

Nasrullah said: "One has to be, one has to be! The poison is spreading even to the servants. That Budhu cheeked me, too. I should have complained to the management."

"Why didn't you?" Adam asked him.

Nasrullah stared into the fire. "Budhu is a Hindu. He could have put something in my food."

"Cigarette butts?" Patrice suggested, but Nasrullah did not smile. "You do not know this country," he said heavily. "You have idyllic memories about it. But something new is happening here that you cannot understand."

"Another scone, Nasrullah?" She offered him the plate.

"Thank you." He munched disconsolately. "Servants are always the first to show signs of a change in the wind. They take their cue from their masters, but often they know more than their masters know. There is little that servants don't hear." He coughed again, looking sick. "By today's post I received word that two of my servants, both Hindus, men who have served me for twenty years, are leaving my service. They did not think it necessary, or even polite, to give me their reasons for this."

Tea, warmth, companionship, revived him by degrees. His voice took on spirit. "How can I blame them, when the same thing is happening on the other side?"

They were silent. The fire sparkled gaily and rain beat on the gravel outside. Nasrullah sighed and passed his empty cup to Patrice. "I have come this afternoon to bid you good-bye. Tomorrow morning, early, Kasim and I leave for Agra."

Adam asked: "Why this sudden departure? I thought you always stayed in Khoos until after the rains."

"This year it is different. This year everything is different. I must go home and make arrangements for my old relatives and dependents to go to Sind. Perhaps I shall send Kasim also. It might be safer."

Patrice stared at him. "Is it really as serious as that?"

"It is serious." He drew a sharp breath. "It will be a terrible uprooting."

There seemed nothing to say. The servant knocked on the door and entered carrying the newly polished shoes. Even with his hands full he managed to salaam Nasrullah before passing into the bedroom. Nasrullah glanced at Patrice. "You see?" he said. "One has to descend to their level in order to get results!" Then, abruptly: "I shall miss you and Adam."

Adam said slyly: "Have you forgotten that you invited us to shoot on your property later this year?"

"You will come?" Nasrullah leaned forward, suddenly all eagerness. "If all goes well and I find I can stay a little longer in my home, you will come?"

"Wild horses won't stop us," Patrice told him. "Will they, Adam?"

Adam spoke with, for him, unusual warmth: "We do not intend to let you slip out of our lives if we can help it, Nasrullah."

Nasrullah's eyes filled with tears as he stirred his tea. "Friendship," he murmured. "Friendship, kindness, understanding . . ."

Next morning he departed with Kasim. They rode away from the hotel on two hired ponies, a brace of coolies carrying their luggage. Adam and Patrice bade them good-bye on the hotel steps. Patrice was quite aware of the hovering presence of Mrs. Krishen Singh and Major Humphries, and of the Bullocks' rather pointed absence from the scene.

"We are going to miss you both," Patrice said as they shook hands. "But we shall meet in Agra."

"Fatten up that leopard for me," Adam exhorted them, and Nasrullah, casting aside self-consciousness, put an arm around Adam's shoulders and said gaily: "You shall have the fattest, largest leopard in the district, I promise you!"

Turning to Patrice, he took both her hands in his. "This is not good-bye. This is—what do the French say?—au revoir."

When they had gone it seemed to Patrice that the ugly strain of the past few weeks dissolved and vanished, and she found it quite easy to smile at Mrs. Singh when they met in the garden, and to make a simple and unaffected response to her conciliatory remark that it was, after all, going to be a nice day. Mrs. Singh seemed suddenly to overflow. "You will come for tea in my room this afternoon perhaps? Mrs. Bullock is coming and I have invited a few other ladies."

Patrice accepted the invitation with thanks, then added: "We are going to miss Nasrullah Khan and Kasim. With all this feeling of doom and gloom in the air I think it is very important that people try to understand each other."

Mrs. Singh's handsome dark eyes rested on her fleetingly, and she smiled. "It is not always easy to understand," she murmured after a moment. "But I agree with you—we should try."

Early in June the monsoon broke with a mighty impact on these Himalayan slopes. Standing in the door of her room Patrice watched the downpour and saw the red-turbaned postman with his heavy satchel and huge black umbrella plodding across the garden toward her. Letters. She thrilled to the sight of the tricolored airmail envelopes and their familiar stamps. A letter from Alice, from Rosanna Burden, from Hart Barrow and Jonas Brayne. A thick, elegant envelope with Daisy Pitman's name and address expensively embossed on the back flap. It was addressed, as all Daisy's letters had been, exclusively to Adam. Patrice propped it on the mantel, and opened one from Adam's mother. Barto Williams was dead.

"A merciful release," wrote Mrs. Bannister. "He was *riddled* with it. I can't help feeling sad that he should have been alone at the last. Timmy and his wife in California, and naturally it is not always convenient to leave one's job . . . and I understand that lately Barto had become very withdrawn, refusing to see people . . . not that he had many friends left . . . difficult and cranky . . . poor Barto."

Patrice pulled a chair to the door and sat with the other letters unread in her lap. Adam, indifferent to the weather, was away on a two-day walking trip with Jack Bullock. Now, in the special luxury of solitude, Patrice concentrated on thoughts of Barto. A merciful release . . . possibly. But quite without warning she felt a surge of tears and spoke his name aloud in these alien surroundings which he would not even have been able to visualize. Just as she had once begged Nasrullah Khan to speak to his dead wife, to tell her that she was missed, so now, alone in this room where she herself had been conceived, and with the monsoon thrashing the gravel outdoors and thunder cannonading in the distance, Patrice spoke to Barto: "I miss you, Barto. I wish you were here."

Alice wrote in characteristic agitation: "The newspapers and radio are full of the dreadful things that are going to happen in India. I cannot bear to think of you and Adam out there. With the English leaving the country . . . the army . . . the police . . . there is bound to be a complete breakdown of administration, if not worse. You could find yourselves isolated, without help or protection. It is no longer the country Doey and I knew. . . . Please, darling, come home."

496

Rosanna wrote about the health of Adam's dogs and of the summer drought. The garden had not amounted to much this year and vandals had stolen the wreath of artificial flowers from Aunt Jinny's grave up on the hill.

Hart Barrow wrote of the continuing sales of her last book. He was eager to hear news of what she might be working on now. She must not be discouraged if the impulse to work seemed to falter at times. Patrice could hear the hesitant voice, sparing of words, with a wry touch of humor at the end: He had always believed that Roosevelt was the worst thing that had ever happened to the country, but he had to take it back. Truman promised to be even worse.

Jonas Brayne wrote that he and Netta were getting a divorce. "Goddammit, little Patrice! She complains that she's exhausted, living with me. I use up all the oxygen . . . she can't breathe! Doesn't believe she has the stamina to have another child—I could have told her that a long time ago. She hasn't the stamina to produce a white mouse. But I don't intend to pine away for lack of feminine companionship either. . . ."

A crash of thunder directly overhead made her jump and the letters slide to the floor. As she stooped to retrieve them she found one from Clem. It had been two years since she and Alice had had any news of him. Now he wrote that he had left Melissa and the children and was living on a Caribbean island with another woman. They had a child, a girl not yet a year old. He was defiantly happy, painting well, actually selling some of his work. Patrice and Alice were not to worry about him. Perhaps one of these days when he had achieved success they would meet again . . . who could say?

Patrice put Clem's letter aside and stared at the splash and glitter of the rain. Thunder thumped and echoed among the hills. In the room next door Noreen Bullock's little girl whimpered and Noreen comforted her: "It's only the rain, darling. It's only the thunder . . . clouds bumping into one another up there in the sky!"

"They sound like lions, they sound like tigers!"

"It is only the rain, only the clouds. . . ."

Farther down the veranda a servant squatted on his heels polishing Major Krishen Singh's boots, and from the Singhs' room came the sound of a radio giving out the latest musical hit from an Indian movie. Wind shook the pines, and Patrice wondered what had hap-

497

pened to the gray monkeys. Where did they go in such weather, sorting out their wet fur, scratching their armpits for fleas, dreaming of acorns when the sun would shine again?

When Adam returned from his trip he carried Daisy Pitman's letter into the bedroom to read, then tore it up and dropped the pieces in the grate without comment. He was grieved to learn of Barto's death, casual in his reaction to the Braynes' divorce and to the letter from Clem. The uncommitted man, Patrice reminded herself. Something vindictive flared in her, then died. She seemed incapable of sustaining any emotion for more than a few minutes, and as the days passed and the rain beat on the tin roof she found herself obsessed by inconsequential things: the dance of the rain on the gravel, children sailing paper boats in the gutters, the excruciating noises from the Singhs' radio two rooms down from hers.

She became aware of Adam's growing concern, and one day he came out with it unexpectedly: "Anything wrong, darling?"

"Why should there be anything wrong?"

"Well, you don't seem to be working, for one thing."

His putting it into words made her suddenly furious. "I don't feel like working!"

They were sitting at the open door of the room, a fire sputtering in the grate behind them, and before their eyes the relentless downpour. Adam reached out a hand. "Patrice."

"Let's skip it, shall we?"

"But we've been here almost four months and you've written nothing except a few letters."

Patrice stared at the paper boats which the children were sailing in the gutter. A little Sikh boy, minus his turban and with his long wet hair fastened with small iron combs, pranced in excitement. "My boat is best! See how fast it goes! Much faster than the others."

"If you're upset about Daisy's letters," Adam began, and Patrice said without turning her head: "Why should I be upset about Daisy's letters?"

"No reason at all. She always writes the same kind of stuff which I know doesn't interest you particularly. All about their doings in Cambridge and Northeast, her boys, her garden, her dogs. They expect my sister Caroline and Hal to join them on a cruise later this year. That's about it."

498

She said nothing, and after a moment he asked in a low voice: "Is it Nasrullah?"

"No, it is not Nasrullah."

"Darling, forgive me. He's an attractive guy, and I just wondered. . . ."

Mrs. Singh, her knitting of bright green wool streaming like a banner, surged down the veranda toward them. "That son of mine! Head soaked, feet soaked . . . pneumonia . . . *Dulip!*

"My boat is the best! See how fast it goes!"

Adam knocked out his pipe, hesitated a moment, looking down at Patrice's averted head, then left her for a chat with Jack Bullock next door.

In September the monsoon came to an end with pomp and circumstance. Thunder rolled like kettledrums, sunset dyed the treetops, flushed the children's faces gold, and a new world unfolded like some gigantic complex flower from whose center Nanga Parbat rose in perfection, and on the lovely plains of the Punjab, a day's journey distant, a sticky red tide crept among the green blades of growing wheat.

Nasrullah wrote from Agra. He had sent his elderly relatives to Sind, but Kasim refused to go. They were together in the family homestead, which Nasrullah was trying to sell before he and the boy left it forever. "I shall be needing the money, but I am being offered one-quarter the value, if that. Buyers pretend indifference, knowing that in the end I shall have to let the place go for what I can get, or leave it to be quietly appropriated when the time comes. What can I do? Nothing."

The monstrous exodus had begun, Hindus and Sikhs flooding eastward, Muslims to the west. When the lines of demarcation were finally laid down, wrote Nasrullah, when Pakistan became a reality and the British were gone, the holocaust would strike. "It will be brother against brother, friend against friend. The undreamed-of will be here. Thousands alive today will next year be no more. The world I know will have vanished and my son will reach manhood among strangers. But now Kasim and I long to see you just once more before we have to part, perhaps forever. My house waits for you, the last guests I shall be able to entertain under my own roof."

By the middle of September the hotel was empty. The Bullocks had returned to Delhi preparatory to their departure for England. Major Humphries followed them. The Sikh families departed in noisy droves, and the tempo of holiday life in the old hill station settled to a diminuendo. As she listened to the news broadcasts on the hotel radio Patrice tried to reconcile the precise diction of English and Indian voices to the sinister overtones which reached upward from the plains. The Bullocks had advised Adam and Patrice to leave the country while the going was good.

"Anything can happen," Jack Bullock warned them, his early optimism daunted by the news. "I don't mean to say that these chappies would single you out, necessarily—they are going to be far too busy slitting one another's throats to bother about people like us. But there is sure to be the most awful disruption. Things like postal services, trains, communications generally. Don't forget that all the subordinate posts in government are held by Indians. They'll all be running in different directions and you can imagine the confusion." He finished on a gloomy note: "And I wouldn't bet on the steadiness of the police, or for that matter of the Indian army itself."

Adam looked uncertainly at Patrice. "What do you think, darling? Had we better beat it before all hell breaks loose?"

Patrice felt a powerful aversion to the thought of leaving the country. To her troubled spirit flight now would have spelled defeat, an admission of total failure, which she was not prepared to face. She shook her head at Adam's question. "Let's see it through."

They bade good-bye to the Bullocks, who invited them to come and visit in Glasgow, and when Patrice had watched their young, strong, honest backs disappear down the hillside she returned to the radio to hear—faint, far away, and with an aching poignance—a Mozart duo for violin and viola, stunning the heart with its irrelevance.

31

*N*asrullah's house stood in a grove of trees several miles outside the city of Agra. In a corner of the grove was a small Hindu temple with the silver trident of the god Vishnu over the arched entrance, and pomegranate trees clustered against the walls. East of the grove but within sight of the temple stood the Muslim mosque, with minarets and finials painted brilliant blue. Pomegranates grew against these walls also, and all day flights of green parrots flew vociferously overhead and hoopoes dropped down from the branches to feed in the dust. It was a peaceful, pleasant spot, blessed with shade and with sound of flowing water, for Nasrullah had long ago built a small marble fountain in his garden, and here, at evening, the birds came to drink. The Persians and the Arabs, with their interminable desert history, had this feeling for water and had passed it on to other generations who had never set eyes on the desert.

Nasrullah loved his fountain and liked to sit on the veranda of his house and watch the light dancing on the water, and the flicker of birds' wings. One of the many things which hurt him at the thought of leaving his home was the question of what would become of his fountain. Water was scarce in this area, even after the monsoon, and

501

his Hindu neighbors had spoken disapprovingly of his prodigality, even in happier days.

The house was two-storied, with a balcony above and verandas below. It was painted white, with decorations of the same blue which adorned the little mosque. Nasrullah's grandfather had built the house and the mosque and both had always been painted in these two colors, cool and refreshing to the eye, and always very neat, with a cared-for lawn and stiff flowerbeds planted to cannas in winter, and marigolds and nasturtiums in spring.

Behind the house was a courtyard, its high walls topped with broken glass and its single massive door studded with iron bosses, a relic of the days when the women of the house kept strict purdah, using the courtyard for their evening promenades, and elephants would have had to be used to force the door—hence the iron bosses, set at the level of an elephant's powerful, battering brow.

There were stables where Nasrullah's cross-bred Arab horses stamped and shifted in their stalls; beside the stable was a carriage house with its nostalgic reminders of vanished elegance—a dusty phaeton and a governess cart shaped like a large basket, in which Nasrullah and his brothers used to drive when they were children. Side by side with these antiques stood another, a Wolseley-Siddeley touring car with lumpy leather cushions, highly polished brasswork, and Nasrullah's monogram in blue on its yellow-enameled doors.

Kasim had long wanted to turn this gem in for something a little more up to date, but Nasrullah would not hear of it. His father had bought the Siddeley in 1918. It had then been the only motor vehicle in the area and a source of reverential wonder for miles around, and of bitter envy in not a few neighborly hearts. What was more, it still *went.* Noisy, smelly, back-breaking, it still *went.* When the day came for Nasrullah and his son to pull up stakes and leave the place, they would, Nasrullah had resolved, travel in the Siddeley with their luggage, two greyhounds, and one old servant, now almost blind, who had been his father's valet since both were boys.

Long afterward Patrice was to hear of what happened to that brave and glittering chariot. Leaving it parked near a friend's house on their journey westward, Nasrullah and Kasim had found it next day a charred and tangled ruin, and the old servant shot to death beside it.

502

But that day was still a little distant. Today the Siddeley stood proudly in its stall beside the phaeton and the governess cart, and Patrice and Adam admired it without stint. For Patrice this visit to Nasrullah's home stirred a long dormant happiness. It evoked memories she could not quite place, and a sense of continuity and timelessness she deeply craved. Walking with Nasrullah one afternoon, they paused beside the fountain and she said suddenly: "Let's pretend that you are not going away, that you and Kasim will go on living here, and that you will bring your grandchildren to play in the fountain!"

He looked at her somberly and started to speak, then shrugged and said nothing. Myna birds chattered as they drank at the fountain, and the hoopoes stepped in the shade of the trees, raising and lowering their golden crests.

At daybreak peacocks called from the surrounding fields, and Patrice saw them from her bedroom window as they scurried along the narrow paths or posed regally in the slanting light. In the courtyard below, veiled figures of women glided between house and kitchen—these were the wives of the cook and his helpers—and the old blind servant squatted on the kitchen steps with his grandchild on his knees.

At odd moments of the day or night Patrice was stirred into full awareness by the sound of a drum throbbing in some dim corner of the grove or by the notes of a flute which sifted all other sounds with its unbearable sweetness. Home, she thought. Home. A place where the same people have lived all their lives, and their fathers before them—undisturbed, industrious, secure. And now it was about to end. Sometimes, waking at night to a scent of woodsmoke drifting in at the window, she felt tears rising in her like a tide, yet she could not weep.

She played tennis and badminton with Kasim and his young friends; she went riding, sometimes alone, sometimes with Nasrullah and his son, the greyhounds loping behind them. They chased rabbits and jackals, and one day, coming on a herd of black buck, Kasim gave an exultant shout and spurred his horse in pursuit, followed by Patrice. They thundered along the verge of growing arrah, the buck always well ahead. She caught up with Kasim and, horses and dogs winded by the chase, turned homeward at a walk with the scent of approaching winter cool on their faces.

Kasim said: "I shall miss this when we leave."

"When all the nonsense is over you will come back, Kasim."

He shook his head. "No. We shall have lost everything. The horses will have to be shot. We raised them from foals, and Father will not give them away even to friends."

They rode in silence, and the greyhounds, tongues lolling, trotted patiently alongside. Patrice said: "You are young. You have a lot to look forward to."

He smiled. "Yes. Revenge!"

She glanced at his young, resolute profile. He did not resemble his father, but he was graceful and elegant and she found it difficult to picture him in the role of an avenger. A year from this day Kasim would be dead, cut to pieces in a fracas he could as well have avoided. But now he was the personification of youth, vigor, health.

They rode on in the falling light and it was difficult to believe that any corner of the world could be any more peaceful. On either side the standing arrah swayed in the breeze, a partridge called, a peacock answered it, and from a distant village came the cool minor notes of a flute. It had always been like this. Centuries of light had shone upon this scene, generations of children like Kasim had gazed upon it with no fear of their future. Unthinkingly, she caught and whistled the air played by the distant flute and Kasim glanced at her curiously. "It is the exact sound! You know, for an American you sometimes seem to me to be very Indian."

There was no sign of Nasrullah, whom they had left far behind in their chase of the black buck, and now they left the fields and rode out on a rolling meadow dotted with mimosa trees and threaded by a little stream of water which emerged from a hillock of ocher-colored rock on their left. Cattle were grazing under the trees, white paddy birds strutted among them, and a plover flew low along the ground with plaintive cries. Kasim said: "From the top of that little rise you can sometimes just see the Taj Mahal, ten miles away."

He reined in abruptly and gestured with his riding crop. "See, see! The leopard!"

Patrice turned in time to see the beast as it bounded up the slope and disappeared toward the summit. A big animal, its mottled hide gleaming in the sun.

"Adam's leopard," Kasim said excitedly. "Father has had it

watched for months. He has forbidden anyone to shoot it or disturb it, even though it has killed several cows from these herds."

The following morning they set out after the leopard. Nasrullah wheeled the Wolseley-Siddeley out of the carriage shed and parked it ceremoniously by the front steps of the house, where it stood quivering like a thing of nerves because he would not turn off the motor for fear it might not start again. The cook had packed a hamper for lunch—roast wild duck, chapatties, apples from Kashmir, and jelabies, the sticky native sweet which Patrice remembered of old.

Kasim insisted that they take the greyhounds in case it should be necessary to track a wounded animal or pursue it on horseback. The horses had already been sent ahead to the hunting ground, and Nasrullah had marshaled a dozen villagers to act as beaters. Adam had shown little sympathy with this Persian style of pageantry evidently indispensable to their hosts, although there was certainly nothing very Persian about Kasim's costume—an American cowboy hat and chaps and a big German Luger strapped to his thigh, in which he obviously took the greatest pride.

Adam glanced at Patrice. "You look better," he told her. "This is what you need—fun and exercise. I've thought so all along."

It was a delicious morning with a strong scent of dew lying on the dust, the air cool enough for jackets. Kasim climbed into the back seat with the picnic hamper and the dogs, while Patrice sat in the front seat between Adam and Nasrullah. Nasrullah fiddled importantly with an array of gears and switches, the Siddeley gave out a sudden roar, backfired, balked, smelled vilely, and crept out between the gateposts in a succession of jerks and stops. Kasim giggled. "Do be careful, Father. Don't break the speed laws."

"You are very funny, isn't it?" Nasrullah retorted crossly. "Wait until we get on the main road. She'll do forty with ease."

It was agreed that in order not to disturb the leopard they should leave the car at a distance and walk to the hillock, at the foot of which the beaters were waiting, squatting on their heels and passing a chelum full of smoking tobacco from hand to hand. They reported to Nasrullah that the leopard had been seen twice since the previous afternoon, and that early this morning a herdboy had spied it lying among the rocks halfway up the slope, evidently watching the cows on the meadow below.

505

"Good," said Nasrullah. "He will be hungry, therefore perhaps less shy about showing himself."

Nasrullah gave the beaters their instructions. They were to proceed to the southern end of the ridge, form a rough line, and at a given signal to make their way slowly toward the northern end of the ridge, talking, beating sticks together, and throwing pebbles to scare the leopard into showing himself and offering the hunters a good shot as he broke cover. Adam was to have the first shot.

The beaters departed and Nasrullah lighted a cigarette. He had a relaxed, happy air. This was like old times, he was lord of his own domain, in company with his cherished son and his good friends. The horses, which had been waiting with their attendants nearby, were sent away, making noises calculated to deceive the lurking leopard into the belief that he had nothing more to worry about than the string of intruders on the ridge.

Adam and Patrice, with Nasrullah and his son and the dogs, crouched in the shadow of a mimosa, and Patrice listened to the orchestration around her: the leisurely tinkle of cattle bells, the melancholy crying of a plover, and, from the hillock, the voices of the advancing beaters and the tapping of their sticks. She felt an old, familiar thrill, a mindless physical delight. Adam had assumed the half-kneeling stance of a trained rifleman, his face under its khaki cloth hat tense with anticipation. On her left the boy Kasim crouched with the dogs beside him, their dun-colored slender bodies shivering with pent excitement. Nasrullah knelt beside Kasim, and the fragrance of his cigarette drifted toward Patrice and brought back, fleetingly, a memory of their walk on the mountain path at Khoos, when he had kissed her.

Kasim stirred and whispered: "There he is!"

Patrice saw the leopard at the same instant. Disturbed by the approaching beaters, he had crept out from his lair among the rocks and was making his sinuous way under the ridge toward the northern end. At this distance he had an elongated appearance, and only his movements made it possible to pick him out against the tawny background, flushed now from the full beam of the sun.

Adam saw him. Swiftly, with the peculiar grace of the natural hunter, he settled his weight on his right heel, planted his left elbow on one outthrust knee, and brought his cheek down to sight along the

506

rifle barrel. It was all done in one smooth, lightning movement, and the shattering crash of the shot seemed no more than part of that sequence.

Patrice saw the leopard rear up on his hind legs, claw the air, and fall backward.

"Good shot!" Kasim cried, as the beaters made prudent haste down the hillock toward the meadow. Next moment Patrice saw the leopard again, evidently wounded, for he moved differently. He was rushing up the slope toward the ridge and she tried frantically to point him out to Adam, but it was too late. The beast disappeared over the thin serrated line of the ridge, and Adam said: "Damn."

They rose to their feet. "It is no matter, we'll get him," said Nasrullah, the perfect host. "You wounded him seriously, I think. Possibly in the shoulder, but too far forward."

"I aimed for his neck," Adam said. He looked angry, mortified. It had been a fair enough shot and he should have killed the animal clean.

The beaters came up, panting, and Nasrullah ordered them to stay away from the hillock. He turned to Adam. "You and I will follow up. He can't have gone far."

Kasim turned imploringly to his father. "Let me! I'll take the dogs. Adam will cover me with his rifle, while you and Patrice stay down here and watch in case the leopard breaks cover in another direction."

Nasrullah hesitated. Following a wounded animal on foot even when the hunter is armed is highly dangerous, but Kasim was staring hard at his father, and said in English: "These villagers are of the other persuasion. Would you have me appear a poltroon in their eyes?"

"Go, then," Nasrullah told him. "Keep the dogs on a tight leash, and be sure you give Adam plenty of room to shoot."

Kasim proudly unlimbered the monstrous pistol strapped to his thigh. "Just in case," he said, and he and Adam made off across the strip of meadow, the dogs straining at their leads. Nasrullah stood beside Patrice, his face a mask of anxiety. "I do not like it. Unless that brute is really badly wounded, he could make trouble."

Patrice said reassuringly: "Adam's a fine shot and he's not likely to miss it this time."

The beaters squatted on the ground and Nasrullah tossed them a package of cigarettes. They were obviously glad to be off the hillock, and began to chatter until Nasrullah ordered them to be quiet. His gaze was riveted on the slope where the figures of Adam and Kasim and the dogs moved cautiously among the rocks. Suddenly to Patrice's eye the sky seemed boundless, the hillock a detail artificially imposed on the flat green plain, and the morning light a semaphore blinding her gaze. She expected in every nerve to see the leopard come charging from some crevice and to hear the crashing report of Adam's shot, but nothing happened.

"He has gone," Nasrullah murmured, with visible relief. "He was not badly hit. We will not find him now."

The two men and the dogs reached the ridge and in a few minutes Adam's voice floated down to the watchers on the meadow: "We've found blood up to this point, but now we've lost it."

"Better come down," Nasrullah called. "We'll have another try tomorrow."

After a pause Adam shouted again: "There's a wonderful view from up here. Clear as a bell. I can see the Taj Mahal!"

Patrice turned to Nasrullah. "I'm going up. I want to see the Taj." Nasrullah put his hand on her arm. "I do not think you should go. The leopard may be anywhere."

"If the dogs have lost the scent, then he's off," Patrice said. "I'll load the shotgun with buckshot. Don't worry."

He stared at her. "Please, Patrice."

"Nonsense. I've crossed Central Park alone at night, and that's a lot more dangerous than this."

She gave him a quick smile and walked across the meadow to the foot of the hillock with her gun under her arm. It was not difficult to find the thread of path which Adam and Kasim had taken and she was soon climbing, the gunstock under her right arm, the fore end resting in her right palm while she used her free hand to fend against the sharp rocks. A few hardy weeds grew among them; there were rabbit droppings, the occasional imprint of a jackal or a goat. She reveled in the moment with its hint of danger, the strain of effort in her muscles. Adam was right, this was what she had needed all these months, and she felt the burden of her strange depression begin to slide from her shoulders.

508

In a few minutes she arrived at the spot where the leopard had been hit by Adam's bullet. A splash of blood on the dusty path and a splatter on the nearest rock. The blood was still wet and glistened in the sunshine, and suddenly Patrice experienced an extraordinary sensation, one which had occurred to her a long time ago; one which she recalled, later, having read in Jim Corbett's hunting stories of India. It was no freak of imagination, but a distinct physical shock like contact with an electric current. The hair rose at the nape of her neck as she brought the gun partway to her shoulder and slid her thumb up to the safety catch.

At that moment she saw the leopard. He rose from between two large rocks which almost exactly matched his hide, and she had a second to stare into his blazing golden eyes before he charged. She heard the report of her gun, saw a flash of blood like a great scarlet feather float in the air, then the leopard was upon her and she fell on the harsh stones. She hid her face in her arm as she felt his teeth in her shoulder. He lay on top of her, heavy, pulsing, sensuous; he smelled of blood, of fur, of weeds, and then she felt his hind claws ripping down her legs and thighs. There was a brief moment of wonder that it didn't hurt. What hurt was the rasp of stones against her bare right arm and her cheek. Then she fainted.

Adam, unable to shoot for fear of hitting Patrice, stood for a moment immobilized on the ridge. Nasrullah and the coolies were sprinting across the meadow toward the slope, but it was Kasim who thought and acted faster than anyone. The instant that he saw the leopard charge upon Patrice he unleashed the greyhounds, which bounded down the slope and flung themselves on the leopard's hind-quarters. Kasim raced after them and as the leopard raised its head to snarl at him he put a bullet from the Luger through its skull.

When they dragged the dead beast off her body Patrice stared up at Adam's contorted face and murmured: "Where is Rosanna?"

She was back in that weedy field below the road at home in Garside where she had crashed in the car after a quarrel with Adam, and now as he knelt beside her with Nasrullah and Kasim she stared from one to the other and repeated: "Where is Rosanna?"

The hospital room at Agra was small and square with a single window behind a neat bamboo screen. The air smelled pleasantly of antiseptic and she lay a long time, staring at the white ceiling where an electric fan hung motionless, and heard some small unidentifiable bird twitter in the roses beyond the window. Could it be the hoopoe? "Hoopoes can't sing," Clem told her as he walked into the room, his face pale and narrow under his big sun hat. "What's the first thing you remember?"

"I remember Alice's white dress with yellow roses and a blue sash."

"That was long ago and you weren't even born."

"I remember it from the time I was dead."

She walked in a grove of mango trees and there was the semicircle of white tents, and the horses and elephants tethered at the farthest edge of the grove, and beyond the grove the plain rolled toward the jungle. But whatever became of Mr. Onions' tame panther, and did the sound of Alice's laughter still hang in the silence, somewhere? Where was Bipper the governess with her teeth like bad cheese and her smell of whiskey and cigarettes? Where was the little grandmother who had lain in her charming little bed, quite still, her childlike hand clasped in Alice's, as though the touch might bring life back to those faintly smiling eyes which for some reason would not stay closed?

And where was Nizamat, Doey's young servant, and old Mohommed Ali the tailor with his immaculate turban and his knowledgeable brown hands making clothes for Alice and Aunt Eve? And where was Aunt Eve and her embroidery frame? And who had written that poem which she had not thought of for years:

I fled Him, down the nights and down the days;
I fled Him, down the arches of the years;
I fled Him, down the labyrinthine ways
Of my own mind; and in the midst of tears
I hid from Him, and under running laughter. . . .

But it was Clem who had done the fleeing. Clem, who desperately needed Him in any shape—in art, in thought, in women's bodies.

It is not the leopard's teeth which make the real trouble; it is the claws, filled with the dried blood of previous kills. Strange that when that great soft vibrant body had fallen upon her up there on the hillock she should have felt no pain. The pain had come later. Worse than having a baby, or the miscarriages. It had come in steady streamers, like summer lightning, from her feet to the top of her head. Pain

510

had become her identity, beyond tears or outcry. And she stood on the darkened veranda of that house, somewhere, and watched the moon come out of the earth and soar without a sound, leaving a great wound in the darkness into which it would sink again. It was into that wound that she was being drawn and submerged as the poison sifted her blood, and death became a person, herself.

And then one day it passed and she lay studying a muted light move on the ceiling fan in that clean little room, and heard the bird outside her window. She felt hard and clean, like a piece of silver. Someone bent over her pillow and said softly: "Better?"

Patrice stared into a pair of dark hazel eyes. "Edna Meadows," she murmured, quite unsurprised. The young nurse smiled. "I'm Edna Meadows' daughter. We read about your accident in the paper, and Mummee sent me up from Bombay to help nurse you. They are short of nurses here because of the trouble, everyone running off."

"And Edna, where is she?"

"Mummee is living in Bombay. She is very well, but rather fat. Granny died last year."

"There was a frog," Patrice murmured. "A big frog in your mother's garden. The frog's name was Barley. Someone ran over Barley with a bicycle. What's-His-Name Harper."

The young nurse took a thermometer from its little jar of alcohol, held it to the light, shook it. She was brisk and businesslike in her starched white uniform, and the image of her mother. "I remember Mummee and Granny used to talk about the Harpers who lived near them once. Also about you and your brother and your parents. It was a long time ago and things were different then."

She placed the thermometer under Patrice's tongue and held Patrice's wrist in her slender fingers. Sounds reached them from the passage beyond the door—English voices, Indian voices. The bird sang its single note outside the window, a bicycle bell pealed. The nurse removed the thermometer, read it, and smiled at Patrice. "Normal," she said. "At last. You are on the mend."

Patrice asked: "What became of young Harper?"

"No one knows for certain, but we heard that he had been killed in Burma during the war. He did something very brave. I forget what it was." She gazed at Patrice. "You mustn't tire yourself talking. Rest now, and your husband will be coming to see you this afternoon."

From a distance came a sound of voices chanting, and a rattle of drums. The chant was rhythmic, and as it passed the hospital Patrice caught the words: *"Gandhiji ke jai! Gandhiji ke jai!"*

The nurse gave Patrice a reassuring smile. "It's all right. Just the usual." She left the room, closing the door softly behind her. The chanting voices drifted away. Doey said: "Whose bloody country do you think this is, anyhow?" And Alice said: "Please, Doey, not politics!"

"Three hundred years," said Nasrullah. "Now I must go."

"Yes," said Kasim, proud in his cowboy hat. "Revenge!"

Old Mrs. Meadows was dead and Edna married to a Gujarati merchant in Bombay, and grown tubby with years. "That must be the Verriers' daughter who married an American. . . . Mauled by a leopard near Agra! Fancy after all these years and coming back and everything. I'll send Monica with a letter to Doctor Macdonald. With this shortage of nurses it should be a help, and Monica has had the very best training."

So Monica Meadows—for her mother had insisted on keeping the English name—Monica Meadows had come to Agra, a pretty gentle girl who went about her duties singing "All the world is waiting for the sunshine," and who in a matter of months would suffer rape and abduction when this hospital was burned to the ground. A hundred years before, Jat villagers had sacked Akbar's tomb a few miles away and had scattered the imperial dust to the four winds. But what was to be done with all those marble viceroys and their prancing chargers on the Calcutta maidan? Tons of the best marble, all dead weight.

In the Pacific jungle where Damon Edwards had died, a glossy vine encircled his rusted helmet, and back in his little mission north of Rangoon Father O'Hara, sweating in his white cassock, led his almond-eyed flock in prayer: "Our Father Which art in heaven, hallowed be Thy name, Thy kingdom come, Thy will be done!"

In Singapore Mary Manchester, soignée in white linen, sipped a Dubonnet with a middle-aged Australian who had just broken it to her that unfortunately he had a wife and four kiddies back in Brisbane, and in their tidy little apartment near the Botanical Gardens young Mr. and Mrs. Lambston made affectionate love through the languorous afternoon.

The day before she was to leave the hospital Patrice sat on the

512

veranda outside her room, Adam beside her. The winter air on these plains has a desert freshness, and she breathed it with a sense of having never really breathed until this moment.

Adam held her hand. The ordeal of the past weeks had left him spent. They had told him at the hospital that Patrice could not possibly recover from the mauling, and that if she did she would carry the scars for the rest of her life, walk with a limp, and perhaps later suffer unpredictable miseries of the flesh. It might, the old Scots doctor suggested bleakly to Adam, be better that she die. But he had labored night and day to save her.

Dr. Macdonald had lived in India sixty years, and this hospital was the joy and pride of his life. He had delivered untold numbers of women of their babies—Englishwomen, Frenchwomen, Indians, Germans. He had succored the helpless, sustained the hopeless, brought the dying back to life. He had buried his wife and three daughters, and his son, who had fought throughout the last war and had survived, implored the old man to chuck India and come home to Scotland. But Dr. Macdonald had buried something more than his wife and girls in this parched soil. He had buried his heart. When, eight months after he had saved Patrice, the mob appeared at the hospital gate, the old man went out to meet it, wearing his doctor's smock, his stethoscope dangling round his neck. He argued with the crowd in its own idiom, and when they shouted him down he called them violators of their own sisters and despoilers of their own hearth. There were Hindu and Muslim women and children in the hospital; there were young nurses, all under his protection. If this rabble forced their way into the building it would, Dr. Macdonald promised them, be over his dead body, and that was what they did.

But at this moment Dr. Macdonald was gravely incising a boil in a quaking brown bottom; the afternoon sun fell in benign warmth on the roses growing against the wall, and the scene had that settled, domestic air of eternal things: of people coming home from work; young men in white shirts and dhotis riding bicycles; country women in bright saris plodding barefoot with bundles on their heads and babies on their hips; an occasional lordly automobile throwing up the dust. A little file of schoolchildren passed, carrying banners. Spying Adam and Patrice on the hospital veranda, they raised their voices in the familiar chant: *"Gandhiji ke jai!"* and burst into giggles when

513

Patrice waved to them from her chair and cried in response: *"Gand-hiji ke jai!"*

Adam said: "Nasrullah and Kasim have gone. I think we ought to be going, too."

"Going where?" Patrice listened to the children's voices in the distance.

"Home."

"No."

"Darling, things are getting hot out here, and I don't mean the weather."

"I don't want to leave the country yet."

"But we shall have to go sometime!"

Patrice was silent. Something strange was happening to her. From the moment when she recovered consciousness for the first time in that small white-painted room to find Edna Meadows' daughter bending over her, she had become aware of a change in herself, an alteration of being which matched the alteration of her body. Yet it was not a laming of the spirit, not a distortion of it, rather it seemed an accentuation of both. She was puzzled by the recollection that she should have felt no terror when the leopard attacked her, that in a curious way she seemed to have expected the attack and had gone to meet it.

When they removed her dressings Dr. Macdonald and Monica Meadows were hesitant about letting her see the scars, but she had insisted, and sensed their surprise in her interest in the new, shining, discolored flesh. "Luckily, they are where they won't show," Monica Meadows had said comfortingly, and Dr. Macdonald added with his broad Scots laugh: "And after twenty-so years of marriage you don't have to worry about your husband's continuing devotion!"

How explain, *why* try to explain to these two kindly souls, or for that matter to herself, that she had known the attack was coming, that the death of feeling in her demanded no less than the death of life? But the boy Kasim had seen to it that she should live. Flapping down the slope in his cowboy hat and leather chaps, brandishing the enormous pistol, he had thwarted her by his sanity, his cool young nerve.

Well, she was not prepared to read anything psychic into her present state of mind, and as if Dr. Macdonald suspected that she might entertain such notions, he had said dryly: "I have taken care of too many people who have been bitten by rabid dogs, and I have seen too many rabid dogs. I'm sure that if one could read the mind of a mad dog one might make invaluable discoveries, but then, so one might if one could read the mind of a sane person. What one cannot read is the collective mind of the crowd." He had stared at her absentmindedly for a moment. "Against the collective sanity or the collective madness of the crowd, my dear Mrs. Bannister, you and I haven't got the ghost of a chance."

Adam was staring at her now with an expression of anxiety. "I'll do anything you say, Patrice. I just want to see you quite well again. I want to see you happy."

He had been told, but he did not want to believe, that she would never walk again without a cane, that she would never again ride a horse, or lift her left arm higher than her shoulder. That the alteration went deeper than that he could not guess.

Patrice said after a pause: "I am going to be all right. I would like just a little more time to—to make sure, that's all."

"Make sure of what?" He pressed her hand in his. "Make sure of what, Patrice?"

"I don't quite know. But I have this feeling that I'm going to find out, and soon."

Adam shied away from further questioning. He said gently: "We have another month before the cold weather really sets in. Would you like to go back to the hills?"

Dr. Macdonald had said to him in private: "If she insists on sticking it out in this country, why don't you both go back to the hills for a month or six weeks? The weather should be beautiful up there now, like Scotland. And it will be safer in the hills."

"Safer?" Adam echoed.

"The country could go up in smoke tomorrow. It's a tinderbox. Jinnah gave us a taste of direction once before. He'll stop at nothing this time. Nor will the other side."

Patrice was thinking: We could go back to the old place, to the old house which belonged to Kitty Braithwaite, the house where Adam and I first met, where it all began, where it could, just possibly, begin again.

Adam held her hand closely in his. He had suddenly a desperate air of resolve. "I love you, Patrice. You must believe me. I love you."

We could go back to that house, Patrice thought. That house in the lower hills, the house above the lake. We could walk in the garden where I walked with Alice after Doey died. Go back to loving Alice again, accept her as she is and as she has always been—changeless in her devotion. We could go back to feel the past well up round us, the past with its promise, its fun, its green assurance. Why not? Perhaps Barto was right. Perhaps the third personality of marriage is waiting for us in that place where we first thought we had discovered it.

Adam gripped her hand. "Patrice, there is something I've got to tell you. All the time that you were lying in that room, sick, and I thought I might be going to lose you, I faced up to a lot of things for the first time in my life."

A second file of schoolchildren marched up the street chanting: *"Gandhiji ke jai!"* Behind her she heard Monica Meadows singing: "All the world is waiting for the sunshine!"

Adam said: "Just to prove to you how I feel about you, have always felt, even when I've known what you never intended that I should know . . ." He flushed. "At home, years ago, just before the war . . . Damon Edwards. Oh, hell, I knew. And I knew why. He could give you something you had to have that I couldn't give you. And I don't mean sex. There was that other need, and I found out what it was that morning when Nasrullah and Kasim and I carried you down the hill to the car. I realized then what the need in you must have been, because I felt it myself."

He released her hand and lighted his pipe. His fingers trembled so he dropped the match and struck another. He said: "I suspected something was going on between you and Damon, and Daisy Pitman fed my suspicions. I felt more useless than ever, envious, jealous. But still I wasn't sure, and I let Daisy persuade me to do something. . . . She said that it would help my peace of mind if I could *know* one way or another. So I bribed Monty Burden to spy on you."

"Gandhiji ke jai!" chanted the schoolchildren. *"Gandhiji ke jai!"*

Patrice said slowly: "It was all a long time ago and Damon is dead. So is Monty Burden. Why go into it now?"

"Because I want to get it off my chest. I want to have everything clear between us from now on. No more deception, no more lies. Even when I knew that you and Damon were lovers I couldn't stop

516

loving you, needing you. And then afterward, that afternoon in Cambridge when the Edwardses telephoned Ma to tell us that Damon had been killed . . . I couldn't look at you. When I did you showed nothing. Absolutely nothing. I thought for a wild moment that perhaps I had been mistaken, that Monty Burden had been lying to me, because how could a woman put on the act you did—conventionally pitying, no more than a friend who had lost a friend?"

Patrice said: "It's all that it amounts to now, after all."

"All right. But there's more. I've tried to get you out of my system —my love for you, my need for you. So I used the time-honored methods. I screwed Mary Manchester on the ship coming out here. She was attractive, she flattered my bruised vanity. I even fell in love with her after a fashion." He stared broodingly at the arching light. "What a farce! Then when I came to my senses and told her it was no soap she turned to Father O'Hara and tried to make *him*. And back I went to feeling like the fool I've always been. Until a month ago when that damned leopard mauled you and you lay in my arms and I thought I had lost you."

Patrice thought: He has told me nothing that I have not, in one way or another, always known. She reached out and took his hand. "Let's not talk about it. Let's go back to the hills."

"To Khoos?"

"Not to Khoos. To the old house."

In that place where they had first met everything was the same yet changed. Distances were shorter or longer. The bazaar seemed busier, the little shops newer, and radio loudspeakers had taken over from the little earthenware drums and the reed flutes. Wild honeysuckle tangled the old iron gate of the house above the lake, but Patrice's hand remembered the latch and the gate swung open with its faint protesting cry and she waited for Alice's voice from the upper veranda: "Who is it?"

But there was no voice to greet Adam and herself as they walked up the weedy gravel to the terrace before the house. It had stood empty for several years and now wore that disheveled, indifferent air one sometimes finds in old people who have passed beyond vanity. A few flowerpots lay broken on the steps, others still contained the dried and blackened corpses of an anonymous generation of plants.

The doors were locked and there was no sign of the caretaker they had been told lived on the premises. There were neither curtains nor shutters on the windows downstairs, and as Patrice pressed her face to the dusty panes she felt that some boneless, gigantic hand had struck her on the breast. Nothing was changed. There were the same faded blue durries on the floors, the same down-at-heel furniture, and above a smoky fireplace hung the reproduction of the idyllic wedded pair, embalmed in time until death should them part, and it never would.

Adam left her and walked away to explore the garden and she went from one window to another. Then, finding a broken pane in a rear door, she put in her hand, found the bolt, and swung the door open. The light was like egg white, the air like a sigh coming up from the floor at her feet. A large spider ambled across the concrete, and a bat, disturbed by her entrance, flew madly down the narrow passage and disappeared into one of the rooms which opened upon it. Patrice held her breath. Then she called softly: "Alice? Clem?"

"Here, darling!" cried Alice, and then Clem said crossly: "Where on earth have you been? We've been waiting and waiting."

Patrice heard the bat squeak, saw it come flying back toward its eyrie. The spider, as large as her hand, bony-legged, huddled in a corner and seemed to be eyeing her malevolently out of its pinpoint eyes. Patrice turned and stumbled blindly through the open door.

A glaze of sunlight lay everywhere and the lake shone like a moonstone below the hill. She heard voices from the little bazaar below the stony path which led between the monkey puzzle trees to the gate. A Pahari voice sang lustily, then fell silent. There was no sign of Adam. In her moment of desolation Patrice called to him, and then she saw him crossing the lower terrace. He stopped to look up at her and laughed on the most carefree note she had ever heard from him. "Patrice! Isn't it the damnedest? Nothing is changed—nothing! I even heard the black partridge down there near the gate. What is it you once told me it said?"

She leaned on her cane and stared down at his glowing face. " 'Shir dharam ke shakrak!' " I have milk and honey!"

In January she and Adam went back to Calcutta to await passage on a ship that would take them home. Nasrullah had been right; so

518

had Dr. Macdonald and young Jack Bullock: the country was falling apart. It celebrated its metamorphosis by murder on a grand scale, with lovely villages burning like pyres, and serpentine processions of humanity moving hopeless across the rich Punjab plains in diametrically opposite directions. The winter sunlight glittered on the hieratic faces of great, snowy bullocks dragging carts heaped with the small, indispensable data of domesticity—polished brass pots and pans, braziers, quilts and blankets gay as banners under which frightened children lay hidden, and young men strode beside them along the fearful miles.

With all their preparations complete, there was little for Adam and Patrice to do except wait for the shipping company to let them know when they might board their ship. Adam was in a frenzy to be off. An Indian friend of Dr. Macdonald's had rented them a small house in the suburb of Alipur for the duration of their stay, and they took walks in the park nearby, taxied into the city or to the zoo, and listened to the radio. The sense of something impending, of some irremediable decision in the making, haunted Patrice almost unbearably. It was a relief to escape into the garden with its well-watered lawn and flowering hedges where, in the morning and at dusk, a bulbul sang its trite little song. There was a hoopoe which fed regularly on the grass, and striped tree rats, which Patrice tried unsuccessfully to tame with bribes of peanuts. She craved these innocent little distractions as an antidote to chaos; she enjoyed going to the zoo with Adam, and watching small boys flying their paper kites in the park.

Late one afternoon when she and Adam were driving back to the house from the city their Sikh taxi driver brought them by an unfamiliar route, explaining that there had been *trouble,* and people were fighting on the main thoroughfare. He wore a grim look and had laid his kirpan, the traditional dagger, on the seat beside him. Patrice felt Adam's uneasiness as they drove along a deserted side street lined with trees, and she took his hand. As they turned a corner and came abreast of the little park where, earlier, she had seen the boys flying their pink, blue, and yellow paper kites, the driver drew a deep breath and spoke jovially in English: "All well now. Almost home." Adam relaxed and took out his pipe, and Patrice, glancing out of the window on her side, saw a boy of about ten years standing with his back against a tree, his kite string in his hand, the blue triangle of the

519

paper kite moving aimlessly in the air above him. There was something strange in his stance, and then she saw that he was headless, the crimson bundle of his turban lying at his feet. Patrice screamed at the driver to stop, but the man had seen what she saw, and he stepped on the gas, sending the car careening up the street. "No stop," he flung at them over the shoulder. "Never stop! Dangerous . . . dangerous . . ."

That night the servants, employees of their landlord, begged to be allowed to sleep in the house instead of returning to their own homes as they customarily did. They informed Patrice that they had sent their families out of town for safety, and that they themselves were afraid to be on the street after dark. Patrice, almost hysterical herself after what she had seen in the park, told them that they might sleep in the guest room. Adam put his arm around her. "I wish the hell that ship would make up her mind when she's going to sail."

One afternoon a telegraph messenger in a neat blue-and-scarlet uniform wheeled his bicycle between the ornamental gateposts and handed Patrice a telegram. Adam had gone to the shipping company's offices, and she was alone with the servants. The message was a cablegram from Jamaica and it told her briefly that Clem had been killed in an automobile accident the day before.

When Adam returned he took her in his arms and said bleakly: "It has been such a long time since you last saw him, Patrice."

It had been a long time, and her grief should have been brief accordingly. Now she found it impossible to weep, but the memory of him met her at every door and walked beside her in the soft Indian winter of that little garden, and she heard his stuttering voice:

> K-K-K-Katy, beautiful Katy,
> You're the only g-g-g-girl that I adore,
> When the m-m-m-moon shines over the c-c-c-cow-shed
> I'll be waiting at the k-k-k-kitchen door!

Clem had become a bundle of old letters, no more. And at Garside, in Maine, Alice would be waiting and her grief would be for the child she would have had live forever. And there would be Adam's and her own house, and the dogs, and the hydrangea bush which Rosanna Burden had given them, and the order and procession of days and months and years, and nothing would be changed.

Adam came into the garden and put his arms round her. "The shipping people have just phoned. We should be able to go aboard the *Omar* day after tomorrow."

Words rose to Patrice's lips but she could not speak. He gave her a worried look, then went away to pack, and that evening while they were at dinner Patrice glanced up to see one of the servants standing at the door. It was his duty to wait at table, but now his appearance struck her as odd. He was quite rigid, his face ashen, staring at her.

"What is it?" she asked him in Hindustani.

The man replied in a low voice: "Gandhiji is dead. He has been shot."

Patrice translated the words to Adam, then turned back to the servant. "How do you know this?"

"It is coming over the radio from New Delhi now. Listen."

From the radio in the pantry, in measured, monotonous cadence, came the announcement from New Delhi: *"Kisi shaitan-ne Gandhiji ko goli dediya!"* Some fiend has killed Gandhiji.

The servant was weeping. "We Muslims, too, loved him. It was not one of us who killed him."

Patrice was unable to finish dinner. Her mouth felt dry, the palms of her hands were sweating, her brain seemed incised by the memory of that child standing under a tree with his paper kite still flying from his hand and his head lying at his feet.

She left the table, followed by Adam, and they mounted the narrow staircase to the roof, a flat space where, in hot weather, the householders had their beds carried for the night, to make the most of the cool hours.

It was cool now, with a faint rustle of breeze through the branches and a scent of growing things from the garden below. An owl hooted in the darkness. From the neighboring houses they could hear the muffled sound of radios, and occasionally catch the grim refrain: *"Kisi shaitan-ne Gandhiji ko goli dediya!"*

Adam said passionately: "I can't wait for us to get the hell away from here!"

The faint notes of the new Indian national anthem crept toward them from a shuttered window, then a broken voice, Nehru's: "The light has gone out of our lives."

Patrice said: "I am not going home with you, Adam."

He stared at her through the gloom, and she repeated the words, steadily: "I am not going home with you. I am staying in India."

"Then I'll stay with you," said Adam.

She shook her head. "No. I want you to go without me. I'm through."

She had not intended to put it in those words. She had wanted to explain, to make clear to him what was now irrevocably clear to herself: that she had made that journey with him once before, and that she could not bring herself to make it a second time. She had no plan for the future nor scarcely any thought of it. Someday perhaps she would go back to Garside; she would see Alice again, and his parents, and him also if he should still care to see her. She would walk the familiar streets of that pleasant New England town, but if she did it would be as the stranger which she had now become.

Adam was silent. The owl hooted in some distant tree, a police car with its loudspeaker at full blast cruised down the street, exhorting listeners to stay in their houses, to keep calm, as Gandhiji would have them do. When the noise had died away Adam said slowly: "You mean you're through . . . with us?"

"Yes."

"And you intend to stay on here, lame as you are, not well?"

"Yes."

"But in God's name why?"

"Perhaps because here . . . now . . . everything is real."

He gave a short, hard laugh and knocked his unsmoked pipe on the parapet. He said in a cold voice: "So it will be a single passage home this time?"

"Yes."

He hesitated for another moment, then: "I'll move into another room tonight, then."

"Perhaps it would be as well."

"Good night, Patrice."

"Good night, Adam, dear."

It was what she had been waiting for. It was the object in the dark stream, toward which she had been carried relentlessly for the past twenty-five years. Something wistful and tender stirred within her and she held out her hand to Adam, but he had turned away. She heard him descending the staircase into the house, then a loudspeaker broke upon the heavy night and Nehru's voice fell somberly on her ears: "The light has gone out of our lives."

Patrice leaned against the cool, rough brickwork of the parapet and stared toward the great city whose opaque glare beat upward to a starlit sky. She thought she heard the humming of its myriad voices, the rhythm of its myriad beating hearts. Life came bounding into her veins, into her brain. Life drowned out death, life drummed down the rhetoric of despair. And cooled by the surging night she watched the fan-shaped glow of the city fade as people, at last, went to their beds, and one by one the radios fell silent, and some small nameless creature moved among the roses, making the rounds of its tiny world.

About the Author

CHRISTINE WESTON, long familiar to readers of *The New Yorker*, is the author of several books, among them, *The World Is a Bridge, The Wise Children, The Dark Wood, Bhimsa the Dancing Bear* (a children's story), and *Indigo* are most memorable. Miss Weston was born in India and spent most of her childhood there. She has also lived in the United States for many years, and this country is now her home.

Format by Gloria Adelson
Set in Video Gael
Composed, printed and bound by The Haddon Craftsmen, Inc.
HARPER & ROW, PUBLISHERS, INCORPORATED

70 71 72 73 10 9 8 7 6 5 4 3 2 1

47

Weston   c/
The hoopoe